W9-CFQ-698

The Glass Lake

G·K
Hall
&Co.

Also published in Large Print
from G.K. Hall by Maeve Binchy:

The Copper Beech
The Lilac Bus
Circle of Friends
Firefly Summer
Echoes
Light a Penny Candle

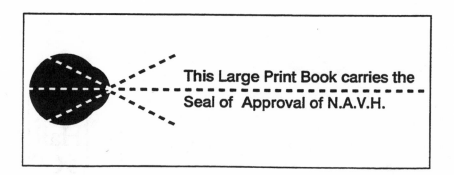

This Large Print Book carries the
Seal of Approval of N.A.V.H.

The Glass Lake

Maeve Binchy

G.K. Hall & Co.
Thorndike, Maine

Published in 1995 by arrangement with
Delacorte Press, an imprint of Dell Publishing, a division of
Bantam Doubleday Dell Publishing Group, Inc.

G.K. Hall Large Print Core Collection.

The text of this Large Print edition is unabridged.
Other aspects of the book may vary from the original edition.

Set in 16 pt. Plantin by Minnie B. Raven.

Printed in the United States on permanent paper.

Library of Congress Cataloging in Publication Data

Binchy, Maeve.
    The glass lake / Maeve Binchy.
      p.   cm.
    ISBN 0-7838-1118-7 (lg. print : hc)
    ISBN 0-7838-1119-5 (lg. print : sc)
    1. Large type books. I. Title.
  [PR6052.I7728G57   1995b]
  823'.914—dc20   94-38990

*For my dearest Gordon,
with the greatest gratitude for everything
and with all my love*

CHAPTER ONE

Kit always thought that the Pope had been *at* her mother and father's wedding. There was this picture of him in their house — a different pope, a dead one — and the writing underneath said that Martin McMahon and Mary Helena Healy had prostrated themselves at his feet. It had never occurred to her to look for him in the wedding picture. Anyway, it was such an awful photograph. All those people in embarrassing coats and hats standing in a line. If she'd thought about it at all Kit might have assumed that the Pope had left before the picture was taken, got on the mail boat in Dun Laoghaire and gone back to Rome.

That's why it was such a shock when Mother Bernard explained that the Pope could never ever leave the Holy See; not even a war would make him leave the Vatican.

"But he went to weddings, didn't he?" Kit said.

"Only if they were in Rome." Mother Bernard knew it all.

"He was at my parents' wedding," Kit insisted.

Mother Bernard looked at the little McMahon girl, a mop of black curly hair and bright blue eyes. A great wall-climber, an organizer of much of the devilment that went on in the schoolyard, but not until now a fantasist.

"I don't think so, Katherine," the nun said,

hoping to stop it there.

"But he *was*." Kit was stung. "They have a framed picture of him on the wall saying that he was there."

"That's the papal blessing, you eejit," said Clio. "Everyone has them . . . they're ten-a-penny."

"I'll thank you not to speak of the Holy Father in those terms, Cliona Kelly." Mother Bernard was most disapproving.

Neither Kit nor Clio listened to the details of the concordat that made the Pope an independent ruler of his own tiny state.

With her face down on the desk and hidden by the upright atlas Kit hissed abuse toward her best friend. "Don't you ever call me an eejit again, or you'll be sorry."

Clio was unrepentant. "Well, you are an eejit. The Pope coming to your parents' wedding, *your* parents of all people!"

"And why shouldn't he be at their wedding if he were let out?"

"Oh, I don't know."

Kit sensed something was not being said. "What would be wrong with their wedding, for example?"

Clio was avoiding the matter. "Shush, she's looking." She was right.

"What did I just say, Cliona Kelly?"

"You said that the Holy Father's name was Pacelli, Mother. That he was called that before he was called Pius the Twelfth."

Mother Bernard reluctantly agreed that this was what she had been saying.

8

"How did you know that?" Kit was full of admiration.

"Always listen with half your mind to something else," Clio said.

Clio was very blonde and tall. She was great at games, she was very quick in class. She had lovely long fair hair. Clio was Kit's best friend, and sometimes she hated her.

Clio's younger sister Anna often wanted to walk home with them but this was greatly discouraged.

"Go away, Anna. You're a pain in the bottom," Clio said.

"I'll tell Mam you said 'bottom' out loud on the road," Anna said.

"Mam has better things to do than to listen to stupid tall tales. Go *away*."

"You just want to be fooling around and laughing with Kit . . ." Anna was stung by the harshness of her dismissal. "That's all you do all the time. I heard Mam say . . . I don't know what Clio and Kit are always skitting and laughing about."

That made them laugh even more. Arm in arm they ran off and left Anna, who had the bad luck to be seven and have no friends of her own.

There were so many things they could do on the way home from school.

That was the great thing about living in a place like Lough Glass. A small town on the edge of a big lake. It wasn't *the* biggest lake in Ireland but it was a very large one by any standards. You couldn't see across to the other side except on a clear day and it was full of little creeks and inlets. Parts of it were clogged up with reeds and rushes. They called it the Glass Lake, which wasn't a real translation. Lough Glass really meant the green lake, of course, all the children knew that. But sometimes it did look like a mirror.

They said that if you went out on Saint Agnes' Eve and looked in the lake at sunset you could see your future. Kit and Clio didn't go in for that kind of thing. The future? The future was tomorrow or the next day, and anyway there were always too many half-cracked girls and fellows, old ones nearly twenty, pushing each other out of the way to try to see. As if they could see anything except reflections of themselves and each other!

Sometimes on the way home from school Clio and Kit would call to McMahon's pharmacy to see Kit's father, with the hope of being offered a barley sugar from the jar. Or they would go to the wooden pier that jutted out into the lake to see the fishermen coming in with their catch. They might go up to the golf course and see could they find any lost balls which they could sell to golfers.

They rarely went to each other's house. There was a danger attached to going home; it was a danger of being asked to do their homework. In order to keep this option as far away as possible the girls dallied on their way back from school.

There was never much to look at in the post office . . . the same things had been in the window for years, pictures of stamps, notices about post office savings stamps and books, the rates on letters going to America. They wouldn't delay long there. Mrs. Hanley's, the drapery shop, sometimes had nice Fair Isle sweaters and the occasional pair of shoes you might like. But Mrs. Hanley didn't like schoolgirls gathering around the window in case it put other people off. She would come out and shoo them away like hens.

"That's right. Off with you. Off with you," she would say, sweeping them ahead of her.

Then they would creep past Foley's bar with the sour smell of porter coming out, and on past Sullivan's garage where old Mr. Sullivan might be drunk and shout at them, calling attention to their presence. This would be dangerous because McMahon's pharmacy was right across the road and someone would surely be alerted by the shouting. They could look in Wall's hardware in case there was anything exciting like a new sharp shears, or across the road in the Central Hotel where you might see visitors coming out. That was if you were lucky. Usually you just saw Philip O'Brien's awful father glowering at everyone. There was the meat shop, which made them feel a bit sick. They could go into Dillon's and look at birthday cards and pretend they were going to buy, but the Dillons never let them read the comics or magazines.

Kit's mother would have found them a million things to do if they went home to McMahon's. She could show them how to make shortbread, and Rita the maid would watch too. She might get them to plant a window box, or show them how to take cuttings that would grow. The McMahons didn't have a proper garden like the

11

Kellys did, only a yard at the back. But it was full of plants climbing out of barrels and up walls. Kit's mother showed them how to do calligraphy and write *happy feast day* for Mother Bernard. It was in lovely writing that looked as if a monk had done it. Mother Bernard still kept it in her prayer book. Or sometimes she would show them her collection of cigarette cards and the gifts she was going to get when she had a book filled with them.

But Clio often asked things like "What does your mother *do* all day that she has so much time to spend with us?" It seemed like a criticism.

As if Mother should be doing something more important like going out to tea with people the way Mrs. Kelly did. Kit didn't want to give Clio the chance to find fault, so she didn't often invite her home.

Where they liked to go best was to see Sister Madeleine, the hermit who lived in a very small cottage by the lake. Sister Madeleine had great fun being a hermit, because everyone worried about her and brought her food and firewood. No one could remember when she came to live in the old abandoned cottage at the water's edge. People were vague about what community Sister Madeleine had belonged to at one time, and why she had left.

But nobody doubted her saintliness.

Sister Madeleine saw only good in people and animals. Her bent figure was to be seen scattering crumbs for the birds, or stroking the most snarling and bad-tempered dog. She had a tame fox which came to lap up a saucer of bread and milk in the evenings, and she was rarely without splints

12

to mend a broken wing of a bird she had found on her travels.

Father Baily and Mother Bernard, together with Brother Healy from the boys' school, had decided to make Sister Madeleine welcome rather than regard her with suspicion. As far as could be worked out she believed in the one true God, and did not object to the way any of them interpreted his will. She attended Mass quietly at the back of the church on Sundays, setting herself up as no rival pulpit.

Even Dr. Kelly, Clio's father, said that Sister Madeleine knew as much as he did about some things: childbirth, and how to console the dying. Kit's father, who ran the chemist's, said that in olden days she might have been thought a wise-woman or even a witch. She certainly knew how to make poultices and use the roots and berries that grew in abundance around her little home. She never spoke about other people so everyone knew that their secrets were safe.

"What will we bring her?" Kit asked. Nobody ever went to Sister Madeleine empty-handed.

"She always says not to be bringing her things." Clio was practical.

"Yes, she *says* that." Kit still thought they should bring something.

"If we went to your dad's chemist's he'd give us something."

"No, he might say we should go straight home," Kit said. That was a possibility they wouldn't risk. "We could pick some flowers."

Clio was doubtful. "Yeah, but isn't her place full of flowers?"

"I know!" Kit got a sudden inspiration. "Rita's making jam, we'll take a pot of it."

That would of course mean going home; Rita was the McMahons' maid. But the jam was cooling on the back window, they could just lift a pot of it. This seemed by far the safest way of getting a gift for Sister Madeleine the Hermit without having to run the gauntlet of a home interrogation.

The McMahons lived over the chemist's shop in the main street of Lough Glass. You could get in up the front stairs beside the shop, or else go around the back. There was nobody about when Kit slipped into the backyard and climbed the back steps — clothes were hanging on the line in the yard, but Rita wasn't in sight. Kit tiptoed to the window where the jams sat. They were in containers of every sort and shape. She took one of the more common jars, less likely to be missed.

With a shock she saw a figure through the window. Her mother was sitting at the table perfectly still. There was a faraway look on her face. She hadn't heard Kit, nor did she seem even aware of her surroundings. To Kit's dismay she saw that tears were falling down her mother's face and she wasn't even bothering to wipe them.

She moved quietly away.

Clio was waiting at the back. "Were you spotted?" she asked.

"No." Kit was short.

"What's wrong?"

"Nothing's wrong. You always think something's wrong when nothing ever is."

"Do you know, Kit, you're becoming as bad a pain in the bottom as awful Anna is. God, you're lucky you haven't any sisters," Clio said with feeling.

"I have Emmet."

But they both knew Emmet was no problem. Emmet was a boy, and boys didn't hang around wanting to be part of your secrets. Emmet wouldn't be seen dead with girls. He went his own way, fought his own battles, which were many because he had a speech impediment, and the other boys mimicked his stutter. "Emm-Emm-Emmemm-Emmet," they called him. Emmet always answered back. "At least I'm not the school dunce," he would say, or "At least I don't have the smell of pigs on my boots." The trouble was it took him a long time to say these telling things and his tormentors had often gone away.

"What's annoying you?" Clio persisted as they walked down the lane toward the lake.

"I suppose someone will marry you eventually, Clio. But it'll have to be someone very patient, maybe stone-deaf even." There was no way that Kit McMahon was going to let her best friend Clio worm out of her the fact that it had been very shocking to see her mother sitting crying like that.

Sister Madeleine was pleased to see them.

Her face was lined from walking in all weathers, her hair was hidden under a short dark veil. It was a cross between a veil and a head scarf really, you could see some gray hair at the front. Not like the nuns at school, who had no hair at all.

15

It was all cut off and sold for wigs.

Sister Madeleine was very old. Kit and Clio didn't know exactly how old, but very old. She was older than their parents, they thought. Older than Mother Bernard. Fifty, or sixty or seventy, you wouldn't know. Clio had once asked her — they couldn't remember exactly what Sister Madeleine had said, but she certainly hadn't answered the question. She had a way of saying something else entirely, a little bit connected with what you had asked so that you didn't feel you had been rude, but it wasn't anywhere near telling you.

"A pot of jam," said Sister Madeleine with excitement, as if she were a child getting a bicycle as a surprise. "Isn't that the nicest thing we could have . . . will we all have tea?"

It was exciting having tea here, not boring like at home. There was an open fire and a kettle hanging on a hook. People had given Sister Madeleine little stoves and cookers in the past, but she had always passed them on to someone less fortunate. She managed to insult nobody by this recycling of gifts, but you knew that if you gave her anything for her own comfort like a rug or some cushions it would end up in the caravan of a traveling family or someone who needed it more.

The people of Lough Glass had got used to giving the hermit only what she could use in her own daily life.

The place was so simple and spare it was almost as if nobody lived there. No possessions, no pictures on the walls, only a cross made out of some simply carved wood. There were mugs, and a jug of milk that someone must have brought her

16

during the day. There was a loaf of bread that had been baked by another friend. She cut slices and spread the jam as if it were a feast that she was preparing.

Clio and Kit had never enjoyed bread and jam like it before. Little ducks walked in the door in the sunlight; Sister Madeleine put down her plate so that they could pick at her crumbs. It was always peaceful there; even restless Clio didn't need to be jumping up and moving about.

"Tell me something you learned at school today. I love facts for my mind," Sister Madeleine said.

"We learned that Kit McMahon thought the Pope came to her mother and father's wedding," Clio said. Sister Madeleine never corrected anyone or told them that they were being harsh or cruel, but often people seemed to realize it themselves. Clio felt she had said the wrong thing. "Of course, it's a mistake anyone could make," she said grudgingly.

"Maybe one day the Pope will come to Ireland," Sister Madeleine said.

They assured her this could never happen. It was all to do with a treaty; the Pope had to promise to stay inside the Vatican and not to go out conquering Italy like popes used to do years ago. Sister Madeleine listened with every sign of believing them.

They told Sister Madeleine news about Lough Glass, about old Mr. Sullivan up at the garage coming out in the middle of the night in his pajamas chasing angels; he said he had to catch as many as he could before the dawn, and he

17

kept knocking on people's doors asking were there any angels hiding there.

Sister Madeleine was interested in that; she wondered what he could have dreamed that was so convincing.

"He's as mad as a hatter," Clio explained.

"Well, we are all a bit mad, I expect. It's that stops us being too much alike, you know, like peas in a pod."

They helped her wash and tidy away the remains of tea. As Kit opened the cupboard she saw another pot of jam exactly the same as the one she had brought. Perhaps her mother had been here today. If so, Sister Madeleine had not told them. Any more than she told anyone about the visits from Clio and Kit.

"You have some jam already," Kit said.

Sister Madeleine just smiled.

Supper in the McMahon household had been at a quarter past six for as long as Kit could remember. Dad closed the pharmacy at six, but never on the dot. There was always someone who had come for a cough bottle, or a farmer in for marking fluids for cattle or sheep. It would never do to rush people out the door. A chemist's after all was a place you came when you were contemplating some of the greater mysteries of life, like your health or the welfare of someone in the family. It was not a visit that was taken lightly.

Kit had often heard her mother asking why she couldn't work in the chemist's shop. It would be sensible, she had pleaded, people would like to deal with a woman when they were buying sanitary napkins, or aids for breast-feeding, and then there was the cosmetics side of things . . . Travelers from the various cosmetic companies were paying more and more visits to country pharmacies to sell their wonders. There wasn't a week that a visit from Pond's, Coty Dawn, or Max Factor didn't happen.

Martin McMahon had very little interest in such things. "Give me what you think," he'd say, and take an order of expensive bath soaps and assorted lipsticks.

They were badly displayed, often fading in the window and never sold. Kit's mother had said that the women of Lough Glass were like women everywhere, they would like to look their best. These cosmetics companies would give little training courses, tell the chemists' assistants how best to display the products, how the women customers should use them for best advantage. But Kit's father was adamant. They didn't want to be pushing paints and powders on people who couldn't afford them, selling magic potions promising eternal youth . . .

"I wouldn't do that," Helen McMahon had argued often. "I'd only learn how to make the best of them and give them advice."

"They don't want advice," her husband said. "They don't want temptation either, don't they look fine the way they are. And anyway would I want people to think that I had to have my wife out working for me, that I can't earn a living for her and my children?" Father would always laugh when he said this and make a funny face.

He loved a joke and he could do card tricks

19

and make coins disappear. Mother didn't laugh as much, but she smiled at Father and she usually agreed with him. She didn't complain like Clio's mother did when he worked late, or when he went with Dr. Kelly to Paddles' bar.

Kit thought that Mother would have liked to work in the pharmacy but she realized that for people such as they were it would have been unsuitable for Father to have let her work there. Only people like Mrs. Hanley who was a widow and ran the drapery or Mona Fitz who was the postmistress because she wasn't married, or Mrs. Dillon whose husband was a drunk . . . worked in businesses. It was the way things were in Lough Glass, and everywhere.

Kit didn't usually think about it much, but she couldn't get the vision of her mother's tears out of her mind as they went home from Sister Madeleine's. She walked up the stairs slowly, almost unwilling to go in and discover what was wrong. Perhaps there was some very bad news. But what could it be?

Dad was fine, he was there closing up the chemist's. Emmet was home safely from rolling around in the dirt or whatever he did after school. So there couldn't be anything wrong with the family. With a sense of walking on eggshells Kit went into the kitchen where they all ate their meals. Everything was normal. Mother's eyes might have been a bit bright, but that's only if you were looking for something. She wore a different dress, she must have changed.

Mother always looked so gorgeous, like a Spanish person even. Someone had sent them a postcard from Spain of a dancer, where the dress was of real material, not just a photograph. Kit always thought it looked just like Mother, with her long hair swept up in a roll, and her big dark eyes.

Dad was in great form so there couldn't have been a row or anything. He was laughing and telling them about old Billy Sullivan coming in for some tonic wine. He had been barred from every other establishment that sold alcohol, and suddenly he had discovered his salvation in the shape of tonic wine. Dad did a great imitation of Mr. Sullivan trying to appear sober.

"I suppose that's why he saw the angels, due to the drink," Kit said.

"God knows what he'll see after the Emu Burgundy," her father said ruefully. "I've had to tell him that's the last of the stock, that you can't get it anymore."

"That's a lie," said Emmet.

"I know it is, Son, but it's tell a lie or have the poor fellow lying on the road, roaring up to the skies."

"Sister Madeleine says that we're all a bit mad; it's what makes us different to other people," Kit said.

"Sister Madeleine is a saint," Mother said. "Did you go to see her yet, Rita, about the other thing?"

"I will, Mrs. McMahon, I will," Rita said, and put the big dish of macaroni cheese on the table.

Even though they ate in the kitchen Mother always insisted that everything was elegantly served. They had colored place mats instead of a tablecloth, and there was a big raffia mat for the casserole dish. It was decorated with sprigs of parsley, one of Mother's touches for making food look nice.

"Wouldn't it all taste the same no matter the way it looked, Mam?" Rita used to say at one time.

"Let's have it looking nice anyway," Mother would say gently, and now it was second nature for Rita to cut tomatoes into triangles and slice hard-boiled eggs thinly. Even though the Kellys ate in a separate dining room Kit knew that their meals were not served as graciously as they were in *her* home. It was another thing that made her feel her mother was special.

Rita was made part of the family, unlike the Kellys' maid. Emmet loved Rita, he was always very curious about her comings and goings. "What other thing?" Emmet asked.

"Helping me with reading." Rita spoke out clearly before Emmet could be asked not to be nosy. "I never learned it properly at school, you see. I wasn't there often enough."

"Where were you?" Emmet was envious. It was so wonderful to be able to say casually that you skipped school.

"Usually looking after a baby, or saving the hay, or making the turf." Rita spoke in a matter-of-fact way. She didn't sound bitter about the book learning missed, the years of child-minding, growing old before her time, culminating in going out to mind other people's children and clean their houses for them.

Not long after tea Mr. Sullivan saw devils

everywhere. In the fading light he noticed them creeping with pitchforks into the houses along the street. Including the chemist's. Maybe they had gone in through the floorboards and through cracks in the wall. Kit and Emmet listened giggling from the top of the stairs to their father remonstrating with Mr. Sullivan, while issuing orders out of the corner of his mouth.

"You're all right, Billy, there isn't a devil here except yourself and myself.

"Helen, ring Peter will you.

"Now sit down, Billy, here, and we'll talk the thing out, man to man.

"Helen, let him know how bad it is.

"Billy, listen to me. Am I a man who'd let fellows with pitchforks into my house?

"As quick as he bloody well can, with any kind of tranquilizer he can get into a syringe."

They sat on the stair top and waited until Clio's father arrived. The cries, and shouts of panic, and the hunt for devils stopped.

They heard Dr. Kelly saying to their father that it was the County Home now. Billy was a danger to himself and everyone else.

"What'll happen to the business?" Dad asked.

"One of those fine sons he threw out will come back and learn to run it for him. At least the uncle sent the boys to school. They may be able to turn it into something rather than the doss-house it is."

Emmet was sitting with his chin in his hands. His stutter always came back when he was frightened. "Are they going to lock him up?" he said, his eyes big and round. It took him ten attempts

23

to get his tongue around the word "lock."

Kit thought suddenly that if she had been given a wish now at this very moment it would have been that Emmet's stutter would go. Sometimes it would be that she had long blond hair like Clio, or that her mother and father might be friends with each other like Dr. Kelly and Mrs. Kelly were. But tonight it would have been Emmet's speech.

When Mr. Sullivan had been taken away Dad and Clio's father went for a drink. Mother went back inside without a word. Kit saw her mother moving around the sitting room, picking up objects and putting them down, then she went to the bedroom and closed the door.

Kit knocked.

"Come in, sweetheart." Mother was sitting at the dressing table, brushing her hair. She looked like a princess when her hair was down.

"Are you all right, Mam? You seem a bit sad."

Mother put her arm around Kit and drew her toward her. "I am fine, just fine. What makes you think I'm sad?"

Kit didn't want to tell about the sighting through the kitchen window. "Your face."

"Well, I suppose I am sad about some things, like that poor fool being tied up and taken off to a mental home for the rest of his life because he couldn't drink in moderation. And about Rita's selfish, greedy parents who had fourteen children and let the older ones rear the younger ones until they could send them out as skivvies and then take half their wages from them . . . otherwise I'm fine." Kit looked at her mother's

24

reflection in the mirror doubtfully. "And are you fine, my little Kit?"

"Not really. Not completely fine."

"What would you like that you haven't got?"

"I'd like to be quicker," Kit said. "I'd like to understand things immediately the way Clio does, and to have fair hair, and to be able to listen to one thing while saying another. And be taller."

"I don't suppose you'd believe me if I told you that you were twenty times more beautiful than Clio, and much more intelligent."

"Oh Mam, I'm not."

"You are, Kit. I swear it. What Clio has is style. I don't know where she got it, but she knows how to make the most of everything she has. Even at twelve she knows what looks well on her and how to smile. That's all it is, it's not beauty, not like you have, and you have my cheekbones, remember. Clio only has Lilian's."

They laughed together, grown-ups in a conspiracy of mockery. Mrs. Kelly had a plump face and no cheekbones at all.

א א א

Rita went to Sister Madeleine on Thursdays, her half day. If anyone else called Sister Madeleine would say, "Rita and I are reading a bit of poetry, we often do that on a Thursday." It was such a tactful way of telling them that this was Rita's time people began to recognize it as such.

Rita would bake some scones, or bring half

an apple tart. They would have tea together and bend over the books. As the weeks went on and the summer came, Rita began to have new confidence. She could read without putting her finger under the words, she could guess the harder words from the sense of the sentence. It was time for the writing lessons. Sister Madeleine gave Rita a fountain pen.

"I couldn't take that, Sister. It was given to you as a gift."

"Well, if it's mine, can't I do what I like with it?" Sister Madeleine rarely kept anything that she had been given for more than twenty-four hours.

"Well, could I have a loan of it then, a long loan?"

"I'll lend it to you for the rest of your life," Sister Madeleine said.

There were no boring copy books, instead Rita and Sister Madeleine wrote about Lough Glass and the lake and changing seasons.

"You could write to your sister in America soon," Sister Madeleine said.

"Not a real letter, not to a person."

"Why not? That's as good as any letter she'll get from these parts, I tell you."

"Would she want to hear all this about home?"

"She'd be so full of happiness to hear about home you'd nearly hear her thanking you across the Atlantic Ocean."

"I never got a letter. I wouldn't want them to be thinking above in McMahon's that I was in the class of having people writing to me."

"She could write to you here."

26

"Would the postman bring letters to you, Sister Madeleine?"

"Ah, Tommy Bennet is the most decent man in the world. He delivers letters to me three times a week. Comes down here on his bicycle whatever the weather, and he has a cup of tea."

Sister Madeleine didn't add that Tommy never came without some contribution to the store cupboard. Nor that she had been instrumental in getting his daughter quickly and quietly into a home for unmarried mothers and keeping the secret safe from the interested eyes and ears of Lough Glass.

"And you'd get enough post for that?" Rita said in wonder.

"People are very kind. They often write to me," Sister Madeleine said with the same sense of wonder.

א א א

Clio and Kit had learned to swim when they were very young. Dr. Kelly had stood waist-deep in the water to teach them. As a young medical student he had once pulled three dead children from the Glass Lake, children who had drowned in a couple of feet of water because nobody had taught them how to swim. It had made him very angry. There was something accepting and dumb about people who lived on the edge of a hazard and yet did nothing to cope with it.

Like those fishermen over in the West of Ireland who went out in frail boats to fish in the roaring Atlantic, and they all wore different kinds of

27

jumpers so they would know whose family it was when a body was found. Each family had its own stitch. Complicated and perverse, Dr. Kelly thought. Why hadn't they taught the young fishermen to swim?

As soon as the young Kellys and McMahons could walk they were taken to the lakeshore. Other families followed suit; the doctor was a figure of great authority. Young Philip O'Brien from the hotel learned and the Hanley girls. Of course, Old Sullivan from the garage told him to keep his hands off other people's children so Stevie and Michael probably couldn't swim to this day.

Peter Kelly had been in other countries where lakes like this one had been tourist attractions. Scotland, for example. People came to visit places just because there was a lake there. And in Switzerland, where he and Lilian had spent their honeymoon, lakes were all-important. But in Ireland in the early fifties nobody seemed to see their potential.

People thought he was mad when he bought a small rowing boat jointly with his friend Martin McMahon. Together they rowed out and fished for perch, bream, and pike. Big ugly fish all of them, but waiting for them on the ever-changing waters of their lake was a restful pastime.

The men had been friends since they were boys. They knew the beds of reeds and rushes where the moorhens sheltered and sometimes even the swans hid from view. They occasionally had company on the lake as they went out to fish, a few local people shared their enthusiasm, but normally the only boats you saw on Lough Glass were those carrying animal foodstuff or machinery from one side to the other.

Farms had been divided up so peculiarly that often a farmer had bits of land so widely separated by great distances, the journey across the water could well be the shortest route. Yet another strange thing about Ireland, Peter Kelly often said, those inconvenient things that weren't laid on us by a colonial power we managed to do for ourselves by incessant family feuds and differences. Martin was of a sunnier disposition. He believed the best of people, his patience was never-ending. There was no situation that couldn't be sorted out by a good laugh. The only thing Martin McMahon ever feared was the lake itself.

He used to warn people, even casual people who came into his chemist's shop, to be careful as they went along the paths by the lakeshore. Clio and Kit were old enough to take a boat out alone now. They had proved it a dozen times, but Martin still felt nervous. He admitted it to Peter over a pint in Paddles' bar. "Jesus, Martin! You're turning into an old woman."

Martin didn't take it as an insult. "I suppose I am, let me look for any secondary signs, I haven't developed breasts or anything, but I don't need to shave as often . . . you could be right, you know."

Peter looked affectionately at his friend, Martin's bluster was hiding a real concern. "I've watched them, Martin. I'm as anxious as you are that they don't run into trouble . . . but they aren't such fools when they're out on the water as they seem to be on dry land, we've drilled that into them. Watch them yourself and you'll see."

"I will, they're going out tomorrow. Helen says we have to let them go and not wrap them in cotton wool."

"Helen's right," Peter said sagely, and they debated whether or not to have another pint. As always on these occasions they made a huge compromise by ordering a half pint. So predictable that Paddles had it ready for them when they got around to ordering it.

א   א   א

"Mr. McMahon, will you please tell Anna to go home," Clio begged Kit's father. "If I tell her it only starts a row."

"Would you like to go for a walk with me," Kit's father suggested.

"I'd like to go in the boat."

"I know you would, but they're big grown-up girls now, and they want to be having their own chats. Why don't you and I go and see if we could find a squirrel?" He looked at the girls in the boat. "I know I'm a fusser. I just came down to be sure you were all right."

"Of course we're all right."

"And you'll take no chances? This is a dangerous lake."

"Daddy, please!"

He went off, and they saw Anna grumbling and following him.

"He's very nice, your father," said Clio, fitting

30

the oars properly into the oarlocks.

"Yes, when you think of the fathers we might have got," Kit agreed.

"Mr. Sullivan up in the home." Clio gave an example.

"Tommy Bennet, the bad-tempered postman."

"Or Paddles Burns, the barman with the big feet . . ."

They laughed at their lucky escapes.

"People often wonder why your father married your mother though," Clio said.

Kit felt a bile of defense rise in her throat. "No they don't wonder that. *You* might wonder it, *people* don't wonder it at all."

"Keep your hair on, I'm only saying what I heard."

"Who said what? Where did you hear it?" Kit's face was hot and angry. She could have pushed her friend Clio into the dark lake and held her head down when she surfaced. Kit was almost alarmed at the strength of her feeling.

"Oh, people say things . . ." Clio was lofty.

"Like what?"

"Like, your mother was a different sort of person, not a local person from here . . . you know."

"No, I don't know. Your mother isn't from here either, she's from Limerick."

"But she used to come here on holidays, that made her sort of from here."

"My mother came here when she met Dad, and that makes her from here too." There were tears in Kit's eyes.

"I'm sorry," Clio said. She really did sound repentant.

31

"What are you sorry about?"

"For saying your mother wasn't from here."

Kit felt she was sorry for more, for hinting at a marriage that was less than satisfactory. "Oh, don't be stupid, Clio. No one cares what you say about where my mother is from, you're so boring. My mother's from Dublin and that's twenty times more interesting than being from old Limerick."

"Sure," said Clio.

The sunlight went out of the day. Kit didn't enjoy the first summer outing on the lake. She felt Clio didn't either, there was a sense of relief when they each went home.

א א א

Rita got two weeks holidays every July.

"I'll miss going to Sister Madeleine," she told Kit.

"Imagine missing lessons," Kit said.

"Ah, it's what you didn't have, you see. Everyone wants what they don't have."

"What would you really like to do in the holidays?" Kit asked.

"I suppose not to have to go home. It's not a home like this one. My mother'd hardly notice whether I was there or not, except to ask me for money."

"Well, don't go."

"What else would I do?"

"Could you stay here and not work?" Kit suggested. "I'd bring you a cup of tea in the mornings."

32

Rita laughed. "No, that wouldn't work. But you're right, I don't have to go home." Rita said she would discuss it with Sister Madeleine; the hermit might have an idea.

The hermit had a great idea. She thought that Mother Bernard above in the convent would simply love someone to come and help her spring-clean the parlor for a few hours a day, maybe even give it a lick of paint. And in return Rita could stay in the school and some of the nuns would give her a hand with the lessons.

Rita had a great holiday, she said, the best in her life.

"You mean it was nice staying with the nuns?"

"It was lovely, you don't know the peace of the place and the lovely singing in the chapel, and I had a key and could go to the town to dances or to the pictures. And I got all my food and hours of help at my books."

"You won't leave us, will you, Rita?" Kit felt a shadow of change fall over them.

Rita was honest. "Not while you're young and the way you are. Not till Emmet's grown up a bit."

"Mam would die if you left, Rita. You're part of the family."

"Your mother understands, honestly she does. She and I often talk about trying to take your chance in life, she encourages me to better myself. She knows it means I hope to be doing better than scrubbing floors."

Kit's eyes felt full of tears suddenly. "It's not safe when you talk like that. I want things always to be the same, not to change."

Rita said, "That's not going to be the way it is. Look at the way Farouk stopped being a kitten and is a cat now, we wanted him to be a kitten forever. And look at the way those little ducklings in Sister Madeleine's grew up and sailed away. And your mother wants you and Emmet to be young and nice like you are, but you'll grow up and leave them. It's the way of things."

Kit wished it wasn't the way of things, but she feared that Rita was right.

"Will you come out in the boat with me, Mam?" Kit asked.

"Lord no, my love. I'd not have time for that. Go on yourself with Clio."

"I'm sick of Clio. I'd like you to come, I want to show you places you haven't been."

"No, Kit, it's not possible."

"But what do you do in the afternoons, Mam? What do you do that's more important than coming out in the boat?"

It was only in the school holidays that Kit was aware of how her mother's pattern of living differed from other people's. Clio's mother was always getting a bus or a lift to the big town to look at curtain material or to try on clothes, or to have coffee in one of the smart shops with friends. Mrs. Hanley and Mrs. Dillon were working in their shops, Philip O'Brien's mother went up to the church and cleaned the brasses or arranged the flowers for Father Baily. There were mothers who went to Mother Bernard and helped in making things for the various sales of work, bazaars and functions that occurred regularly to aid the Order's work on the missions.

Mother did none of these things. She spent time in the kitchen with Rita, helping, experimenting, improving the cooking, much more than other people's mothers spent with maids. Mother arranged leaves and branches as decoration in their sitting room and framed pictures of the lake so that one whole wall had two dozen different views of Lough Glass. If people came in they were amazed to see the collection.

But people didn't often come in.

And Mother's work was swift and efficient. She had a lot of time on her own . . . all the time in the world to come out with Kit in the boat. "Tell me," Kit asked again, "what do you like doing if you won't come out with me?"

"I live my life the best I can," her mother said. And Kit felt a shock at the faraway look that came over Helen McMahon's face as she said it.

"Dad, why do you and Mam sleep in different rooms?" Kit asked.

She picked a time when the chemist's was empty, when they would not be disturbed. Her father stood in his white coat behind the counter, his glasses pushed back on his head, his round, freckled face full of concentration. Kit was only tolerated to sit on the high stool if she didn't distract him.

"What?" he said absently.

She began again, but he interrupted. "I heard you, but why do you ask?"

"I was just asking, Dad."

"Did you ask your mother?"

"Yes."

"And?"

"And she said it was because you snored."

"So now you know."

"Yes."

"Any more questions, Kit, or can I get on with earning my living and making up compounds."

"Why did you and Mam get married?"

"Because we loved each other, and still love each other."

"How did you know?"

"You know, Kit, that's it. I'm afraid it's not very satisfactory, but that's the only way I can explain it. I saw your mother at a friend's house in Dublin, and I thought, isn't she lovely and nice and fun and wouldn't it be great if she'd go out with me. And she did, over and over, and then I asked her to marry me and she said yes." He seemed to be telling it from the heart.

But Kit wasn't convinced. "And did Mam feel the same?"

"Well, darling child. She must have felt the same. I mean, there was nobody with a great big stick saying you must marry this young chemist from Lough Glass who loves you to distraction. Her parents were dead, she didn't do it to please anyone, because I was a safe bet or anything."

"Were you a safe bet, Daddy?"

"I was a man with a steady job. In 1939 with the world on the edge of the war and everyone very confused by everything a man with a good job was always a safe bet. Still is."

"And were you surprised that she said yes?"

"No, darling, I wasn't surprised, not at that stage . . . we loved each other, you see. I know it's not like the pictures or the things you youngsters giggle about, but that's what it was for us." Kit was silent. "What is it, Kit? Why are you asking all this?"

"Nothing, Daddy. You know the way you get to wondering, that's all."

"I know the way you get to wondering," he said.

And he left it there so Kit didn't even have to think anymore about what Clio had said. Clio had told her that she overheard a conversation in her home where someone had said that Martin McMahon had a job keeping that wife of his tied to Lough Glass and the miracle of the whole thing being why she had ever come here in the first place.

"I'm only telling you," Clio had said, "because you and I are best friends and I think you ought to know."

"Sister Madeleine?"

"Yes, Kit."

"Do you know the way people tell you everything?"

"Well, they tell me things, Kit, because I haven't much to tell them, you see. What with gathering sticks and picking flowers and saying my prayers there isn't much to tell."

"Do people tell you their secrets, like, their sins even?"

Sister Madeleine was shocked. "No, Kit McMahon. Don't you know as well as I do that

37

the only one we'd tell our sins to is an anointed priest of God, who has the power to act between God and man."

"Secrets then?"

"What are you saying to me at all? Chook, chook, chook . . . will you look at the little bantams. Brother Healy was so kind. He gave me a clutch of eggs and they all hatched out beside the fire . . . it was like a miracle." She knelt on the floor to direct the little chickens away from some perilous journey they were about to undertake and back into the box of straw she had prepared for them.

Kit would not be put off. "I came by myself today because . . ."

"Yes, I missed Clio. She's a grand friend for you, isn't she?"

"She is and she isn't, Sister Madeleine. She told me that people were talking about my father and mother . . . and I wondered, I wanted to know maybe if you . . ."

Sister Madeleine straightened up, her lined, weatherbeaten face was in a broad smile; it was as if she was willing the anxiety away from Kit. "Aren't you the grown-up woman of twelve years of age, and don't you know that everyone talks about everyone else. That's what people do in a village . . . you're not going to get all upset over that, are you?"

"No, but . . ."

Sister Madeleine seized the word "no." "There. I knew you weren't. You see, it's a funny thing when people go miles and miles away to big cities where they know nobody and nobody knows them, the whole thing is turned around. It's then they want people to be all interested in them and their doings.

"We are a funny sort of people, the human race."

"It's just that . . ." Kit began desperately. She didn't want to discuss the human race, she wanted Sister Madeleine to tell her that everything was all right, that her mother wasn't unhappy or wild or bad or whatever it was that Clio was suggesting.

But she didn't get far.

Sister Madeleine was in full flight. "I knew you'd agree with me, and one of the funniest things — animals are much more simple. I don't know why the Lord thought that we were so special. We're not nearly as loving and good as the animal kingdom."

The old dog, Whiskers, that Sister Madeleine had rescued when someone had tried to drown him in a bag, looked up when she said this. Whiskers seemed to understand when she was saying something good about animals, it was as if the tone of her voice changed. He gave a sort of gurgle to show he approved. "Whiskers agrees with me, and how's Farouk? That fine noble cat of yours."

"He's fine, Sister Madeleine. Why don't you come and see him?"

"Sure you know me, I'm not one to be visiting people's houses. All I want to know is that he's well and happy, and stalking around Lough Glass as if he owned it."

There they were, talking about Farouk and

Whiskers and the human race, and it would be rude now to go back to the reason why Kit had walked down the leafy lane to see Sister Madeleine on her own.

"How are things, Kit?"

"Fine, Mrs. Kelly."

Lilian Kelly stood back to look more attentively at her daughter Clio's friend, Kit. The child was very handsome, with that great head of dark curly hair and those unexpected blue eyes. She would probably be a beauty like her mother.

"And tell me, have you and Clio had a falling-out?"

"A falling-out?" Kit's blue eyes were too innocent. She repeated the phrase with wonder, as if she hadn't a clue what the words meant.

"Well, it's just that up to now you've been like Siamese twins joined at the hip. But in the last few weeks you don't seem to be going within a donkey's roar of each other, and that seems a pity seeing that it's the summer holidays." She paused, waiting.

But she was getting nothing from Kit. "We didn't have a row, honestly, Mrs. Kelly."

"I know. That's what Clio said." Kit was anxious to be away. "Nobody listens to their own mother, so maybe you might listen to me instead. You and Clio need each other. This is a small place, you'll always be glad to have a friend here. Whatever silliness this is it doesn't matter, it'll soon be over. Now you know where we live. Come on up to the house this evening, will you?"

"Clio knows where *I* live too, Mrs. Kelly."

40

"God protect me from two such stubborn women. I don't know what's going to happen to the next generation . . ." Mrs. Kelly sighed and went off good-naturedly. Kit watched her go. Clio's mother was large and square, she wore sensible clothes, today she had a cotton dress with white cuffs and collar, and a small daisy print. She was carrying a shopping basket. She was like the picture of a mother in a storybook.

Not like Kit's own mother, who was very thin, and wore bright greens or crimson or royal blue, and her clothes were sort of floaty-looking. She looked much more like a dancer than a mother.

Kit sat on the wooden pier.

Their boat was tied up beside her, but there was an iron-hard rule that no one took the boat out alone. Someone had been drowned in the lake because she went out alone. It was ages ago but people still talked about it. Her body wasn't found for a year, and during that year her soul used to haunt the lake calling out "Look in the reeds, look in the reeds." Everyone knew this. It was enough to frighten the most foolhardy, even the boys, from going out on their own.

Kit watched enviously as she saw some of the older boys from the Brothers' school untying a boat, but she would not go back up and pretend to Clio that everything was all right.

Because it wasn't.

The days seemed very long. There was nobody to talk to. It didn't seem fair to go down to Sister Madeleine on her own. It had been the place that she and Clio always went to, and that one time she had gone to try and find out things Sister Madeleine must have known what she was after. Rita was working always, or else she had her head in a book. Emmet was too young for any conversation. Daddy was busy and Mother . . . Mother. Mother expected Kit to be less clingy, less worried. It had been very easy when Clio was around. Perhaps Mrs. Kelly was right and they did need each other.

But she was not going to go up to that house.

She heard footsteps behind her and felt the spring of the wooden pier as someone walked along. It was Clio. She had two milk chocolate biscuits, their favorites.

"I wouldn't go to your house, and you wouldn't come to mine. This is neutral ground, all right?" she said.

Kit paused. "Sure." She shrugged.

"We can just go on as we were before the fight." Clio wanted it defined.

"There wasn't a fight," Kit reminded her.

"Yeah, I know. But I said something stupid about your mother." There was a silence. Clio went on to fill it. "The truth is, Kit, that I was jealous. I'd love to have a mother who looks like a film star."

Kit reached out and took one of the Club Milk biscuits. "Now you're here we can take out the boat," she said.

The row that had never been was over.

During the holidays Brother Healy came up to the convent for his annual discussion with Mother Bernard.

They had many things to discuss, and they got on well together when discussing them. There was the school curriculum for the year, the difficulty of getting lay teachers who would have the same sense of dedication, the terrible problem they shared about children being wild and undisciplined, preferring the goings-on on the cinema screen to real life as it should be lived in Ireland. They coordinated their timetables so that the girls should be released from school at one time and the boys at another, leaving less chances for the two sexes to meet each other and get involved in unnecessary familiarity.

Brother Healy and Mother Bernard were such old friends now that they could even indulge in the odd little grumble, about the length of Father Baily's sermons, for example. The man was inclined to be hypnotized by the sound of his own voice, they thought.

Or the excessive love the children had for that difficult Sister Madeleine. It was somehow highly irritating that this odd woman, who came from a deeply confused and ill-explained background, should have taken such an unexpected place in the hearts and minds of Lough Glass's children, who would do anything for her. They were eager to save stamps, collect silver paper, and gather sticks for her fire. The boys had been outraged when Brother Healy had stamped on a spider. There had been a near mutiny in the classroom. And these were the same lads who would have pulled the wings off flies for sport a few years ago.

Mother Bernard said that Sister Madeleine was

altogether too tolerant for this world, she seemed to have a good word to say for everyone, including the enemies of the Church. She had told some of the impressionable girls that Communists might have their own very reasonable belief in dividing wealth equally. That had been a headache, Mother Bernard said . . . and one that she could have done without.

And it wasn't only the children who were under her spell, Brother Healy said in an aggrieved tone. Oh no, no. A man who should know better, like Martin McMahon the chemist.

Brother Healy had heard with his own ears the man suggesting to Mrs. Sullivan, whose poor Billy had been carried off screaming, that she should go to Sister Madeleine for some advice about a nice soothing drink to make her sleep.

"Next stop will be black magic altogether," said Mother Bernard, nodding feverishly in agreement.

And, of course, if Martin minded his business and paid a bit of attention to that fancy wife of his, he'd be better off. Brother Healy might have gone too far now in uncharitable gossip. He knew it and so did Mother Bernard. They both began to shuffle their papers together and end the meeting.

It would remain unsaid that Helen McMahon, with her disturbing good looks, walked too much alone, beating at the hedges with a blackthorn stick, her eyes and mind far, far away from Lough Glass and the people who lived there.

It was a Wednesday, and Martin McMahon

closed his shop with a sigh of relief. The flypaper was thick with dead bluebottles. He must remove it quickly before Kit or Emmet came in with a lecture about their being God's creatures and how unfair of him to lure them to their death.

He was relieved that Kit and Clio Kelly seemed to have gotten over whatever childish squabble it had been that kept them apart for a few weeks. Girls were so intense at that age, it was impossible to know their minds. He had asked Helen if they should interfere, try to bring the children together, but Helen had said to let it run its course. And she had been right about everything.

When Helen said something it was always likely to happen. She had said that Emmet would be able to cope with his stutter, that he would laugh away the mimicry and criticism. That had come to pass. She had said Rita was a bright girl when everyone else had thought the child mentally deficient. Helen had known that Billy Sullivan was drinking behind his garage doors when no one else knew. And Helen had told him all those years ago that she could never love him totally but she would love him as much as she was able to.

Which wasn't nearly enough. But he knew it was that or nothing.

He had first met her when she was pining for someone else, and she had been open with him. It would not be fair to encourage his attentions, she had said, when her mind was so committed elsewhere. He had agreed to wait around. He had made more and more excuses to be in Dublin, to invite her out. Gradually they became close. She never spoke of the man who had left her to marry some girl with money.

And little by little the color returned to her cheeks. He invited her down here to see his place — his lake, his people — and she came and walked with him around the shores.

"It might not be the greatest love the world has ever known for you . . . but it will for me," he said.

She said it was the most beautiful proposal that a man could make. She would accept, she said. She sighed as she said it.

Helen had told him that she would stay with him, and if she ever left she would tell him why, and it would have to be for a very good reason. She said that it was dangerous to try to know somebody too well. People should have their own reserves, she said, the places they went in their minds, where no one else should follow.

He had agreed with her, of course. It was the price he paid for getting her as his wife. But he wished she didn't go off so often and so far in her mind and he dearly wished she wouldn't wander around the lake in all kinds of weather. She assured him that she loved to do this, it brought her peace to see the lake in its changing seasons. She knew all kinds of things about its nesting creatures. She felt at home there, at peace, she knew all the people around.

Once she had told him that it would be lovely to have a little cottage like Sister Madeleine's and have the lake water lap up to your door.

He had laughed at that. "Isn't it hard enough to squash the whole family in here into this place . . . how would we fit in the hermit's cottage?" he had asked.

"I didn't mean the whole family, I was thinking of going there by myself." Her eyes had been far away that day. He hadn't followed her train of thought; it had been too unsettling.

Martin let himself in his own front door beside the chemist's shop. It led straight upstairs to what they called their house. Even though Kit had complained that they were the only people she knew who had a house without a downstairs.

Rita was setting the table. "The mistress won't be here, sir. She said to say she'll see you after your game of golf."

He was disappointed and it showed.

"Women have to have their time off, too," Kit said defensively.

"Of course they do," he said, over-jovially. "And it's a Wednesday so everyone except Rita has an afternoon off. I'm going to play a round of golf with Clio's father. I'm feeling in powerful form, I'm going to beat him into the ground today. I can see a few pars coming up, and a birdie and an eagle and . . . maybe an albatross."

"Why are they all called after birds?" Emmet wanted to know.

"I suppose because the ball soars like a bird or it should anyway. . . . Come on, I'll be Mother," he said, and began to ladle out the lamb stew.

He realized that he had been saying this more and more recently. He wondered why on earth had Helen not said she was going out. Where on earth could she be?

47

From the golf course you got fine views of the lake. People said it was one of the most attractive courses in Ireland. Not as rugged as the great championship courses on the coast, but very varied with rolling parkland and many clusters of trees. And always the lake, dark blue today with hardly any shadows on it.

Peter Kelly and Martin McMahon stopped to rest and look down from the eighth green upon the high ground. Unlike at busier golf courses, they were holding nobody up. There was always time to stand and look down on Lough Glass and its lake.

"The tinkers are back, I see." Peter pointed out the colored roofs of caravans on the far shore of the lake.

"They're like the seasons, aren't they? Always coming back the same way and at the same time."

"Desperate life to inflict on the children, though. Some of them come up to get bits of machinery out of them or with dog bites . . . you'd pity them," said the doctor.

"They come in to me, too, only the very odd time. Often I tell them they know more than I do," Martin laughed. He had indeed said that between the travelers and old Madeleine there was a very good second line of defense as regards medicine in Lough Glass.

"Some of them are very fine-looking people." Peter peered into the distance, where two women walked by the water's edge. Martin looked too, and then they both moved at the same time to go back to line up their shots. It was as if they

48

both thought one of the women looked very like Helen McMahon but neither of them wanted to say it.

Clio told Kit that there was a woman among the travelers who told fortunes. And that she knew everything that was going to happen. But that Mother Bernard would kill you stone-dead if you went anywhere near her.

"What would Sister Madeleine say?" Kit wondered.

This was a good idea. Sister Madeleine wasn't black and white about things. Happily they scampered off down the lane to consult her. She thought it might well be possible, some people did have a gift.

"How much silver do you think she'd need to cross her palm, would a threepence do?" Kit wondered.

"I'd say she'd want more, what would you say, Sister Madeleine?" Clio was excited. It was her birthday next week, maybe they might get enough money before the caravans left. How marvelous to know the future.

But to their disappointment Sister Madeleine didn't seem at all in favor of it. She never told anyone not to do anything, she didn't use words like "foolish" or "unwise," Sister Madeleine never spoke of sin or things being wrong. She just looked at them with her eyes burning from her brown lined face and her look said everything. "It's not safe to know the future," she said.

And in the silence that followed both Clio and Kit felt themselves shiver. They were glad when

49

Whiskers stood up and gave a long, unexplained yowl at nothing in particular.

Rita made her quiet way down the narrow road to Sister Madeleine's cottage. She carried her poetry book and the warm shortbread that was just out of the oven. To her surprise she heard voices. Usually the hermit was alone when she called for her lessons.

She was about to move away but Sister Madeleine called out. "Come on in, Rita. We'll have a cup of tea together."

It was the tinker woman who told fortunes. Rita knew her immediately, because she had been to her last year. She had given her half a crown and had heard that her life would change, she would have seven times by seven times the land that her father had owned. That would mean she was to have nearly fifty acres. The woman had seen that she would have a life with book learning, and she would marry a man who was at this moment across the sea. She also saw that the children of the marriage would be difficult, it wasn't clear whether in their health or their disposition. She said that Rita would be buried when she died in a big cemetery, not in the churchyard in Lough Glass.

It had been very exciting to go to the woman, who told fortunes only by the lakeshore. She had said she didn't like doing it near the camps, near her own people. They didn't approve of her doing it. She said it was because she was too good. Listening to her, Rita had believed that this might be true. Everything had been said with a great, calm certainty. And the bits about the book learning had begun to come true.

Rita had been struck then and now how like the mistress she was. If you saw them in a poor light you'd swear that the tinker woman and Mrs. McMahon were sisters. She wondered what she was doing here with Sister Madeleine, but she would never know.

"Rita and I read poetry together." Sister Madeleine made the only gesture she would ever make toward an introduction. The woman nodded as if she only expected as much; she was sure that everything else she had seen in the future was true also.

And suddenly, with a slight sense of alarm, so was Rita. There was a man across the sea who would marry her, she would have fifty acres of land, and money in her own right. She would have children and they would not be easy. She thought about her tombstone, far away in a city with lots of other crosses nearby.

The woman slipped silently away.

"My dark Rosaleen," said Sister Madeleine. "Read it nice and slowly to me. I'll close my eyes and make pictures of it all."

Rita stood in the sunlight by the little window where people had brought pots of geraniums for the hermit, and with the bantam chicks around her feet she read . . .

"My dark Rosaleen,
My own Rosaleen,
Shall glad your heart and give you hope
Shall give you health and help and hope
My dark Rosaleen."

"Wasn't that beautiful!" Sister Madeleine spoke of the poem. Rita laughed aloud with pleasure, sheer pleasure that she had read without stumbling. "That was beautiful, Rita. Don't ever tell me you couldn't read a poem," she said.

"Do you know what I was thinking, Sister?"

"No. What were you thinking? Your mind was far away; poetry does that to you."

"I was just thinking that if young Emmet were to come to you . . . ?"

"Emmet McMahon?"

"Yes. Maybe you could cure his stutter, getting him to read sonnets and everything."

"I can't cure a stutter."

"You could make him read, he's too shy to read at school. He's fine with his friends but he hates when Brother Healy comes to him in class. He was the same when he was in Babies, he got red in the face with fright."

"He'd have to want to come. Otherwise, it'd only be a torture to him."

"I'll tell him the kind of magic you do."

"I think we should talk less about magic, you know people might take you seriously."

Rita understood at once. There were people in Lough Glass who were suspicious of Sister Madeleine, the hermit. And thought she might not come in a direct line from God. It had been whispered that people who believed in herbs and cures from the olden times might be getting their power from the very opposite of God.

The Devil hadn't been mentioned, but the word had stood hovering in the air over such conversations.

Dan O'Brien stood at his door looking up and down the street. Business in the Central Hotel was never so pressing that he couldn't find several opportunities during the day to come out and survey the main thoroughfare. Like many towns in Ireland, Lough Glass consisted of one long street, the church in the middle, the Brothers at one end and the convent strategically placed far at the other, giving the children as little chance of accidental meetings as possible. In between, there were the shops, houses, and businesses of his neighbors, fronting onto the same street as he did himself.

You could learn a lot by standing at your own door. Dan O'Brien knew that Billy Sullivan's two boys had come back from their uncle's once their father had been locked away. The fiction was that they had been visiting, helping the uncle out with the farm. Everyone knew, of course, that Kathleen had sent them there to avoid the drunken rages and the unsettled atmosphere in the family home.

It was hard on children like that.

The lads were not to blame for the life they were born into. Handsome little fellows too, the very image of Billy himself before his face had turned fleshy from the drink and he had coarsened beyond recognition. They would be company for poor Kathleen. Stevie must be about sixteen, and Michael was the same age as his own lad, Philip.

Philip didn't like him, he said that Michael Sullivan was tough, and he was always ready for a fight.

"So would you if you had been brought up with an old man like his," Dan O'Brien said. "Not everyone is as lucky as you are, Philip." Philip had looked at him doubtfully. But then the young were never satisfied with what they got.

Dan watched as the summer afternoon took its leisurely course. There was never much of a sense of urgency in Lough Glass, even a Fair Day had a relaxed air about it. But when the weather was warm like this people seemed to move at half speed.

He saw young Clio and Kit McMahon arm in arm practicing the steps of some dance along the footpath, oblivious to anyone else. It only seemed a few months since those two had been skipping ropes, and here they were getting ready for the ballroom. They were the same age as his Philip, twelve, an unsettled age.

And as he watched he saw Mother Bernard from the convent walking in a stately manner accompanied by one of the younger nuns. Her face was one line of disapproval. Even in the holidays her charges should not behave like that. Treating the public road as a place for silly dancing.

They sensed her coming, and changed their antics rapidly.

Dan smiled to himself at the contrite appearance of the two rascals. He would like to have had a daughter. But his wife was not well enough to face another pregnancy after Philip was born.

"Haven't we the son? Isn't that enough for you?" Mildred had said. As there were going to be no more children there was no more love-making. That was obvious, Mildred had said.

Dan O'Brien sighed, as he often did. Imagine being a man with a normal married life, like . . . well, like anyone really. His eye fell on Martin McMahon crossing the road to Sullivan Motors. A man with a spring in his step and a very attractive wife. Imagine being able to take a woman like Helen McMahon upstairs and draw the curtains and . . .

Dan decided not to think about it anymore. It was too frustrating.

Mother Bernard and Brother Healy were discussing the autumn retreat. Sometimes the priests who came to do the Mission weren't at all suitable to face the children in a school. But this year they heard that there was a very famous priest coming to Lough Glass, a Father John who gave sermons that were attended by hundreds of people at a time. They traveled to hear him, or that's what Father Baily had told them.

"I wonder can he keep order with a crowd of hooligans." Brother Healy had his doubts. Famous preachers could be a bit ethereal for his liking.

"Or realize when those girls are making a fool of him." Mother Bernard had an eagle eye for mischief makers.

"I don't know why we're even debating it, Mother Bernard. These decisions are never left to us, the people who know about how things should be done."

They often asked each other why they bothered

55

discussing things, but in their hearts they knew that they loved discussing things. As educators of Lough Glass's young they were united in facing the problems of the uncaring world.

Secretly Mother Bernard thought that Brother Healy had life easy. Boys were so simple and straightforward. They weren't devious like girls. Brother Healy thought that it must be a very easy number just to have little girls in uniform. They didn't write terrible words in the bicycle shed and beat each other black and blue in the yard. But neither of them had much faith that Father John, preacher extraordinary, would keep the minds and attention of the children of this lakeland town.

א א א

The day before schools reopened the children were all down by the lake, enjoying the last hours of freedom, and even though they groaned about the awfulness of going back to the dreaded classroom the next day quite a few of them were relieved that the long summer was over.

Philip O'Brien from the hotel was particularly pleased. It had been very hard to fill the hours. If he stayed in the hotel his father was inclined to say that he should wash the glasses or empty the ashtrays.

Emmet McMahon was looking forward to showing off his new confidence. A few weeks with Sister Madeleine had done wonders. He had even asked her if she could do the poems in his schoolbook, in case they might make sense like the ones

56

in her book. As if you read them with your heart.

"Why doesn't Brother Healy teach them like that?" he asked Sister Madeleine.

But she had no explanation. She seemed insistent that Brother Healy did teach them like that. It was very unsatisfactory.

Clio Kelly didn't want to go back to school. She was fed up with school. She knew enough now, she wanted to go to a stage school in London and learn to dance and sing, and be discovered by a kind old man who owned a theatre.

Anna, her younger sister, would be quite happy when lessons started. Anna was in disgrace at home. She claimed she had seen the ghost. She said she saw the woman crying, she couldn't exactly hear what the words were but she thought it was "Look in the reeds, look in the reeds." Her father had been unexpectedly cross with her and accused her of looking for notice.

"But I *did* see her," Anna had wept.

"No, you did not see her. And you are not to go around saying you did. This is a hysterical enough place already without you adding to it. It's dangerous and foolish to let simple people think that an educated girl like you should give in to such foolishness."

Even her mother had been unsympathetic. And Clio had a horrible smirk of superiority, as if she were saying to her family "Now wasn't I right about how awful Anna is."

Kit McMahon was pleased to be going back to school. She had made a promise that this year she would work very hard. It had been a promise made during the only good conversation she had had with her mother for as long as she could remember.

It was the day she got her first period. Mother had been marvelous, and said all the right things, like wasn't it great she was a woman now, and that this was a fine time to be a woman in Ireland. There was so much freedom and so many choices.

Kit expressed some doubt about this. Lough Glass wasn't a place that inspired you with a notion of wild and free, and she wondered how very unlimited were the options that lay ahead of her. But Mother had been serious. When the next decade came, when they got to the 1960s, there'd be nothing a woman couldn't do. Even this year people were beginning to accept that a woman could run things.

Look at poor Kathleen Sullivan over there across the road, filling tractors with fuel, supervising the man from the oil company when he came to restock. A few years ago they wouldn't have taken an order from a woman, preferring to deal with any man, even one as obviously incapable as Billy Sullivan.

"But it all depends on being ready for it, Kit. Will you promise me, whatever happens, that you'll work hard at school?"

"Yes, yes of course." Kit was impatient. Why did it have to come back to this in the end. But there was something in Mother's face that made this sound different.

"Sit here beside me and hold my hand, and promise me that you'll remember this day. It's

an important day for you, let's mark it by something else. Let's make it the day you promised
your mother that you'd prepare yourself for the
world properly." Kit had looked at her blankly.
"I know it sounds like the old refrain . . . but
if only I were your age again . . . if only . . .
I would work so hard. Oh Kit, if I'd known
. . ." Her mother's face was anguished.

Kit was very alarmed. "Known what? What
is it, Mam? What didn't you know?"

"That being educated makes you free. Having
a career, a place, a position, you can do what
you want."

"But you did what you wanted, didn't you?
You married Dad, and you had us?" Kit knew
her own face must be white because she saw her
mother's expression change.

Her mother stroked her cheek. "Yes, yes of
course I did." She was soothing, like she was
when she told Emmet there were no demons in
the dark, when she encouraged Farouk the cat
to come out from a hidey place behind the sofa.

"So why did you wish . . . ?"

"I don't wish it for myself, I wish it for you
. . . so that you'll always be able to choose, you
won't have to do things because there's nothing
else to do."

Mother was holding her hand. "Will you tell
me something truly?" Kit had asked.

"Of course I will."

"Are you happy? I often see you looking sad.
Is this where you want to be?"

"I love you, Kit, I love Emmet, and I love your
father with all my heart. He is the kindest and

best man in the whole world. That is the truth. I would never lie to him and I don't lie to you either." Mother was looking at her, she wasn't half looking out the window with her mind abstracted as she often did.

Kit felt a wave of relief flood over her. "So you're not sad and worried then?"

"I said I wouldn't lie to you and I won't. Sometimes I do get sad and a bit lonely in this little town. I don't love it as much as your father does; he was brought up here and knows every stone of it. I sometimes feel I might go mad if I have to see Lilian Kelly every day, and listen to Kathleen Sullivan whinging about how hard life is in the garage, or Mildred O'Brien saying that the dust in the air is making her feel sick . . . but then, you know that . . . you get annoyed with Clio and with school." Mother had treated her as an equal. Mother had told her the truth. "So do you believe me now, Kit?"

"Yes, I do," Kit said. And she did.

"And will you remember, whatever happens, that your passport to the world is to have your own career and that's the only way you are free to choose what you want to do."

It had been a great conversation, she felt much better about everything now. At the back of her mind she had one nagging worry. Why had Mother said twice, not once, "whatever happens"? It was as if Mother could see the future. Like Sister Madeleine seemed to do. Like the gypsy woman down by the lake.

But Kit had put it out of her mind. There was too much to think of, and wasn't it great that

60

she had got her periods before Clio. That was a real triumph.

א א א

Dr. Kelly called as Martin was closing the shop. "I am the living embodiment of temptation. Will you come down to Paddles' with me and have a pint?"

In another town the local doctor and chemist might be expected to drink at the hotel, which would have a better-class bar, but O'Brien's was so dismal and gloomy that Martin and Peter much preferred to bypass it in favor of Paddles' earthier but more cheerful atmosphere. They settled into a snug.

"My advice?" Martin held his head on one side quizzically. He didn't think there was any real excuse other than a need for a companion.

"It's young Anna, she has me worried. She keeps saying that everyone has a down on her, and that she really did see a woman down at the lake crying . . ."

"At that age they're so full of drama." Martin was consoling.

"I know, God don't I know. But you know the way you sense when someone's telling the truth."

"Well, you don't think she saw a ghost?"

"No, but I think she saw something." Martin was nonplussed. He didn't know what he was expected to say. "Do you remember her?"

"Remember who?"

"Bridie Daly, or Brigid Daly, or whatever her name was? The one who drowned."

61

"How would I remember her, weren't we only kids?"

"What did she look like?"

"I haven't a clue, when was it? It was way back."

"It was in 1920."

"Peter, we were only eight."

"Was she dark with long hair? It's just that Anna is so positive."

"And what are you thinking?"

"I was wondering was there someone dressing up to frighten the kids."

"Well, if there was they've succeeded, and the kid's father, it seems too."

Peter laughed. "Yes, you're right. I suppose it's nonsense. I just didn't like to think of someone deliberately setting out to upset them. Anna has many faults God knows, but I think she did see something that worried her."

"And what did she say the woman looked like?"

"You know children . . . they have to relate it to someone they know. She said she looked like your Helen."

א   א   א

The senior girls in the convent were going to have a special session of their own with Father John. That meant that the twelve- to fifteen-year-olds would hear something the younger ones would not.

Anna Kelly was very curious. "Is it about babies?" she asked.

"Probably," Clio said loftily.

62

"I know about babies," Anna said defiantly.

"I wish I'd known enough about them to suffocate you while you still were one." Clio spoke from the heart.

"You and Kit think you're terrific. You're just stupid," Anna said.

"Yeah, I know, we can't see ghosts and we don't get nightmares . . . it's desperate."

They shook her off eventually and went to sit on the low wall of Sullivan's Motor Works. It was a good vantage point to survey Lough Glass and no one could say they were causing trouble if they just sat still.

"Isn't is a wonder that Emmet is so normal, I mean for a boy and everything," Clio said in admiration. Privately Kit thought that Anna Kelly might not be so irritating if Clio had ever spoken to her younger sister with anything other than disdain.

"Emmet's just born that way," Kit said. "I never remember him getting into trouble or anything. I suppose they didn't roar at him much because of his stammer. That must have been it."

"They didn't roar at Anna enough," Clio said darkly. "Listen, what do you think he'll really talk to us about, do you think it might be about doing *it?*"

"I'd die if he did."

"I'll die if he doesn't," Clio said, and they pealed with enough laughter to bring Philip O'Brien's father to his usual position at the door of his hotel to view them with disapproval.

Whatever Father John, the Missioner, had intended to talk about to the senior girls in Lough Glass convent was never known, because it happened that his visit coincided with a huge argument that raged through the senior school, about whether Judas was or was not in hell. Mother Bernard was not considered a satisfactory arbiter on the matter. The girls were persistent that the visiting Missioner give a ruling.

There was a very strong view that Judas must be in hell. "Hadn't Our Lord said that it were better for that man if he hadn't ever been born."

"Now that *must* mean he was in hell."

"It could mean that for thousands of years his name would be connected with 'traitor' and 'betrayer' and that was his punishment for betraying Our Lord. Couldn't it?"

"No, it couldn't, because that would only be name-calling. Sticks and stones could break your bones but words would never hurt you."

Father John looked at their young faces, heated and red with excitement. He hadn't come across such fervor in a long time. "But Our Lord couldn't have chosen him as a friend, knowing that he was going to betray him and that he'd be sent to hell. That would mean Our Lord was setting a trap for Judas."

"He didn't have to betray him, he just did it for the money."

"But what would they want with money, they just went around as a gang."

"But it was over. Judas knew it was coming to an end, that's why he did it."

Father John was used to girls shuffling with embarrassment and asking was French-kissing a

64

venial or a mortal sin, and accepting whichever he said it was. He was not normally faced with such cosmic questions and debates on the nature of free will and predestination.

He tried to answer as best he could, with what was, after all, fairly inconclusive evidence. He said he thought that, as in all things, the benefit of the doubt must be extended, and that perhaps in his infinite mercy Our Lord had seen fit . . . and to remember that one never knew the heart of a sinner, and the words that passed between man and his maker at the moment of death.

Loosening his collar a little, he asked Mother Bernard afterward about their extraordinary preoccupation. "Was there any case of anyone local who perhaps ended their own life?"

"No, no. Nothing like that. You know the way girls get something into their heads." Mother Bernard sounded wise and certain.

"Yes, but this is very intense. Are you sure . . . ?"

"Years and years ago, long before any of them were born, there was an unfortunate woman who found herself in a certain condition, Father, and is believed to have taken her own life. I think the ignorant people had a story about her ghost or some such nonsense. Maybe they are thinking of that." Mother Bernard's lips were pursed with disapproval for having to mention a suicide and an out-of-wedlock pregnancy to a visiting priest.

"That could be it all right. There are two little girls, two of the younger ones in the front row, a very fair girl and a very dark one, who seem most het up about it, and whether or not people

65

who take their own lives should be buried in Holy Ground."

Mother Bernard sighed. "That will be Cliona Kelly and Katherine McMahon. Those two would argue with you that blackbirds were white, I'm afraid."

"Well, it's good to be forewarned," said Father John, as he went back into the convent chapel and told the girls very firmly that since taking your own life was taking away a gift that God had given you, it was a sin against Hope — one of the two great sins against Hope — despair. And that anyone who did so was not fit to be buried in a Christian burial ground.

"Not even if her poor mind . . ." began the blond girl in the front pew.

"Not even if her poor mind," Father John said firmly.

He was worn out from it, and he had the boys' school to do still. Serious warnings on the evils of drink and self-abuse.

Father John sometimes wondered did any of it do any good at all. But he reminded himself that thinking along those lines was almost a sin against Hope. He must be careful of it.

CHAPTER TWO

Y ou don't have proper cousins," Clio said to Kit as they lay on the two divan beds in Clio's room.

"Oh God, what are you picking on me for now?" Kit groaned. She was reading a magazine article telling you how to soften your hands.

"You never have families of cousins coming to stay."

"Why would they come to stay? Don't all the other McMahons live just a few miles away?" Kit sighed. Clio could be very tiresome sometimes.

"We have cousins coming from Dublin always, and aunts and things."

"And you're always saying you hate it."

"I like Aunt Maura."

"That's only because she gives you a shilling every time she comes to stay."

"You've no aunts." Clio was persistent.

"Oh Clio, will you shut up. Of course I've aunts, what is Aunty Mary and what's Aunty Margaret . . . ?"

"They're just married to your father's brothers."

"Well, there's Daddy's sister in the convent in Australia. She's an aunt. You can't expect her to be coming and staying and giving us a shilling, can you?"

"Your mother has no people." Clio lowered her

voice. "She's a person with no people of her own at all." There was something in the way she said it which made it obvious that she was repeating it like a parrot from something she had heard.

"What do you mean?" Kit was angry now.

"Just what I said."

"Of course she has people, she has us, a family, here."

"It's peculiar, that's all."

"It's not peculiar, it's just you are always picking on my mother for some reason. I thought you said you were giving that up."

"Keep your shirt on."

"No, I won't. And I'm going home." Kit flounced off the bed.

Clio was alarmed. "I didn't mean it."

"Then why did you say it? What kind of booby goes round saying things she doesn't mean?"

"I was only saying . . ."

"What *were* you saying?" Kit's eyes flashed.

"I don't know what I was saying."

"Neither do I." Kit ran lightly out of the room and down the stairs.

"Are you off so soon?" Clio's mother was in the hall. Mrs. Kelly always knew when there had been a row. "I was going to offer you some short-bread," she said. Many a skirmish had been avoided by the timely appearance of food.

But not today.

"I'm sure Clio would love it, but I have to go back home," Kit said.

"Surely not yet!"

"My mother might be a bit lonely. You see, she is a person who has no people of her own."

68

Kit was as near to insolent as she could get away with. A dark red flush around Mrs. Kelly's cheeks and neck showed her she had been right. She left, pulling the door gently behind her. With a smile she realized that there would be little short-bread for Clio. Good, Kit thought in satisfaction. I hope her mother eats the face off her.

Mother wasn't at home. She had gone to Dublin on the day excursion, Rita said.

"What did she want to do that for?" Kit grumbled.

"Wouldn't we all love to go to Dublin on a day excursion," Rita said.

"I wouldn't . . . we have no people there," Kit said.

"There's millions of people in Dublin," Emmet said.

"Thousands," Kit corrected him absently.

"Well then?" Emmet said.

"Right." Kit let it go. "What did you read with Sister Madeleine?"

"It's all William Blake now. Somebody gave her a book of his poems and she loves them."

"I don't know anything he wrote except 'Tyger, Tyger.' "

"Oh he wrote lots. That's the only one in the schoolbook, but he wrote thousands and thousands."

"Maybe dozens and dozens," Kit corrected, "maybe. Say me one."

"I don't remember them."

"Oh go on. You say them over and over."

"I know the one about the piper . . ." Emmet

69

went to the window and stood, as he had stood in Sister Madeleine's cottage, looking out the window.

> *"Pipe a song about a lamb*
> *As piped with merry cheer*
> *Piper, pipe that song again,*
> *So I piped, he wept to hear."*

He looked so proud of himself. It was a difficult word to say, "piper," at the best of times, and coming so often in the one sentence. Sister Madeleine must be a genius to have cured his stutter like that.

Kit didn't notice that her father had come in as Emmet was speaking, but the boy hadn't faltered; his confidence was extraordinary. And as they sat there in the September evening, she felt a shiver come over her. It was as if Mother didn't belong to this family at all. As if all there was was Emmet, and Dad, and Rita, and herself.

And that Mother wouldn't come back.

Mother came back, cold and tired; the heating had broken down on the train; the train itself had broken down twice.

"How was Dublin?"

"It was noisy, and crowded and everyone seemed to be rushing."

"That's why we all live here." Father was delighted.

"That's why we all live here," Mother said flatly.

Kit watched the flames in the fire. "I think I'll be a hermit when I grow up," she said suddenly.

"You wouldn't want this lonely kind of a life. It's only for odd people like myself."

"Are you odd, Sister Madeleine?"

"I'm very peculiar. Isn't that a funny word, 'peculiar'? I was saying it with Emmet the other day; we were wondering where it came from."

It reminded Kit that Clio said it was peculiar her mother had no family. "Did you get hurt when people spoke badly about your family when you were young?"

"No, child, not ever."

"How did you make yourself not worry?"

"I suppose I thought if anyone would try to pull down my family they would just be wrong." Kit was silent. "As they would be if they said anything about your family."

"I know," but the little voice was doubtful.

"Your father is the most respected man in three counties; he's so kind to the poor and he's like a second doctor in the town. Your mother is as gentle and loving a soul as it was ever my good fortune to meet. She has a poet's heart and she loves beauty . . ." The silence lay between them, so Sister Madeleine spoke again; her face was hard to read, you wouldn't know what she was thinking. She spoke slowly, deliberately. "Of course, people often say things out of jealousy, because they're not secure in themselves. Because they worry they lash out, like a man with a stick might hit a hedge and take all the lovely heads off the flowers not knowing why he did it . . ."

71

Sister Madeleine's voice was hypnotic. It was as if she knew all about Clio. Maybe Clio had been here and told her. Who could know? "And often a fellow who beat the heads off the flowers with a stick would be sorry he did it but he wouldn't know how to say that."

"I know," Kit said. She was pleased to know that Sister Madeleine thought her mother had a poet's heart and was a good and gentle soul. And she'd forgive Clio in her own good time.

Provided, of course, Clio apologized properly.

"I'm very sorry," Clio said.
"That's all right," Kit said.
"No, it's not. I don't know why I did it, why I keep doing it. I suppose I just want to be one better than you or something. I don't like myself, that's the truth."

"And I don't like myself sulking," said Kit.

Their families were relieved. It was always unsettling when Kit and Clio had a falling-out. Like thunder in the air, and the hint of a bad storm ahead.

א א א

Sometimes it was harder to break the news of a death that was meaningless than one which would cause huge grief. Peter Kelly paused for breath before he went to tell Kathleen Sullivan that her husband had finally succumbed to the liver disease that had been threatening him as seriously as the brain deterioration which had given him his place in the County Home. He knew there would be no conventional words of grief or consolation. But it was never simple.

Kathleen Sullivan took the information with a stony face. Her elder son, Stevie, a dark, good-looking boy who had felt his father's fist once too often, and left of his own volition for the uncle's farm, just shrugged. "He died a long time ago, Doctor," he said.

The younger boy, Michael, looked confused. "Will there be a funeral?" he asked.

"Yes, of course," the doctor said.

"We'll have no funeral," Stevie said unexpectedly. "No mourning or making a mockery of the whole thing."

His mother looked startled. "There'll have to be a funeral," she began.

They all seemed to be looking at the doctor for the solution. As he so often felt, Peter Kelly wondered what kind of social structure had made him the fount of all wisdom in such matters.

Stevie, a boy of sixteen maybe, looked him in the eye. "You're not a hypocrite, Dr. Kelly, you wouldn't want a charade." There was something strong about the boy's face, and determined. Maybe six or seven years of his childhood robbed from him had been a good training for life as well as a high price to pay. The lad should not have to take part in a sham ceremony.

"I think the whole thing can be arranged very quietly at the Home. That is often done in such cases, and just the family attend a Mass there. Father Baily will arrange it, I know."

Kathleen Sullivan looked at him gratefully.

73

"You're very good, Doctor. I just wish it had all been different." Her face was set and hard as she spoke. "I can't go to anyone for sympathy or anything because they'll all say it was for the best, and we're all well rid of him."

"I know what you mean, Kathleen." Peter Kelly did, only too well, and if he didn't have any suitable words of comfort, no one else in Lough Glass would be able to find them. "You could always call on Sister Madeleine," he said. "She'll be the very one to comfort you at a time like this."

He sat in his car after he left the house, and watched while Kathleen Sullivan, now wearing her coat and head scarf, followed his advice. He saw her heading down toward the path that led to the lake. As he drove home he passed Helen McMahon walking with her hair blowing in the wind. The wind was cold and she wore a woolen dress but had no coat. She looked flushed and excited.

He stopped the car. "Will I drive you back, take the weight off your legs?" he asked.

She smiled at him, and he realized again how very beautiful she was. Sometimes he forgot, and didn't really see the beauty that had broken all their hearts in Dublin. The girl with the perfect face, who had chosen Martin McMahon, of all people, to be her consort.

"No, Peter, I love to walk on an evening like this . . . it's so free. Do you see the birds over the lake? Aren't they magnificent?"

She looked magnificent. Her eyes were bright, her skin was glowing. He had forgotten that for a slight woman she had such a voluptuous figure, her breasts seemed to strain at the blue wool dress. With a shock he realized that Helen McMahon was pregnant.

"Peter, what is it?"

"You keep asking me that." He was irritated with Lilian. "What is what?"

"You haven't said a word all evening. You just keep staring into the fire."

"I have things on my mind."

"Obviously you have. I was just asking what things."

"Are you some kind of Grand Inquisitor? Can I not even think now without your permission?" he snapped.

He saw the tears jump into Lilian's eyes and her plump face pucker. It was very unjust of him. They had the kind of relationship where each would ask the other how they felt and what they were thinking. It was monstrous of him to behave like this.

He admitted it.

"I only asked because you looked worried." Lilian was almost mollified.

"I'm wondering did I do the right thing over Kathleen Sullivan, telling her to have the funeral above in the Home," said Peter Kelly, and listened with part of his mind to some of his wife's views on the subject while he tried to work out the implications of Helen McMahon's pregnancy. In the pit of his stomach was the feeling that all was not as it should be.

There was no reason why Martin and Helen

should not try for a late baby. Helen must be thirty-seven or thirty-eight, an age when most women around here would think nothing of having children. But Peter Kelly was uneasy. Just scraps of conversation floating around in the air coming back to disturb him: Clio saying that Kit McMahon's parents slept in different rooms, something Martin said one night down in Paddles' place about the old days, some reference to making love as if it were all in the past, something Helen had said when Emmet was a toddler, about there being no younger brothers and sisters for him. It all made a crazy jigsaw in his head. And he realized that it had to be crazy because just suppose, suppose for the sake of argument, that all these jumbled ideas spelled out the truth.

Who on earth could be the father of Helen McMahon's child if it were not her husband?

Martin heard footsteps on the stairs. He got up and came to the sitting room door. "Helen?"

"Yes, love."

"I was looking for you, did you hear about poor Billy Sullivan?"

"Yes, Dan told me. I suppose it's a blessing in a way, he was never going to get better."

"Should we go in, do you think?" Martin was always a good neighbor.

"No, Kathleen's not there, only the two lads. I called on my way back."

"You were out late . . ."

"I was just walking, it's a lovely night. They say their mother went down to Sister Madeleine.

76

That was a good idea, she always knows what to say."

"Were you in the hotel then?"

Helen looked surprised. "Lord, no. What would I go in there for?"

"You said Dan told you about Billy Sullivan."

"Doesn't Dan stand there at the door, telling the dogs in the street bits of information. . . . No, I told you, I was walking. Down by the lake."

"Why do you want to walk by yourself — why won't you let me walk with you?"

"You know why. I want to think."

"But what is there to think about?" He looked blank, bewildered.

"There's so much to think about that my mind is overflowing . . ."

"And are they good, the things you think about?" He sounded almost fearful of the answer, as if he regretted asking.

"We must talk . . . we have to talk . . ." Helen looked to the door as if to see were they out of earshot.

Martin was alarmed. "There's nothing to talk about — I just wanted to know were you happy, that's all."

Helen sighed. A heavy sigh. "Oh Martin, how many times have I told you. I was neither happy nor unhappy, there was nothing you could have done — it would have been like asking you to change the weather. . . ."

He looked at her, crestfallen. His face showed that he knew he should not have asked.

"But it's all different now, it's all changed. And

we have always been honest with each other — that's more than many other couples." She spoke as if giving him crumbs of comfort.

"More than that, surely?" His voice was full of hope.

"Of course more than that — but because I never lied to you, I would always tell you if there was something important."

Martin moved away, putting up his hands as if to ward off any explanation that she was about to begin. Her face was agonized. He was unable to bear it.

"No, my love, I was wrong — haven't you every right to walk by yourself. By the lake, or anywhere. What am I doing cross-questioning you? I'm turning into an old Mother Bernard before my time, that's what I'm doing."

"I want to tell you everything. . . ." Her face was empty.

"Now, hasn't enough happened tonight with that poor man across the road going to meet his maker —"

"*Martin* . . ." she interrupted.

But he wasn't going to talk. He took her hands and drew her across the room toward him. When she was right beside him he put his arms around her very tight. "I love you, Helen," he said over and over into her hair.

And she murmured, "I know. I know, Martin, I know."

Neither of them saw Kit in the shadow pass the door, wait for a moment, and then go on to her own room. She lay in bed without sleeping for a long time that night. She couldn't decide whether what she had seen was very good or very bad.

At least it didn't look as if her mother was wild and fancy free, or whatever Clio was constantly hinting at.

Halloween was a Friday, Kit wondered could they have a party.

Mother seemed against it. "We don't know what we'll be doing," she said in a fussed sort of way.

"But of course we know what we'll be doing." Kit was stung by the unfairness of this. "It's a Friday, we'll be having scrambled eggs and potatoes like every Friday, and I only asked for a few friends to come in . . ."

Mother looked quite different when she spoke. She seemed to underline every word as if she were giving a message or reading a notice, rather than having a normal conversation. "Believe me, I do know what I'm saying. We do not know what we will be doing on Halloween. This is not the time to be thinking of Halloween parties. There will be parties again, but not now."

It was very final. It was also very frightening.

"Are there really ghosts about on Halloween?" Clio asked Sister Madeleine.

"You know there aren't ghosts," Sister Madeleine said.

"Well, spirits."

"There are spirits around us all the time." Sister Madeleine was being remarkably cheerful about it, as if she wouldn't indulge Clio Kelly's

79

wish to be dramatic.

"Are you afraid of spirits?" Clio persisted. She wanted to get a bit of terror into the conversation somehow.

"No, child, I'm not. How could you be afraid of someone's spirit? A spirit is a friendly thing. It's the life that was in them once — the memory of it — that stays around a place."

This was more promising. "Are there spirits round here, round the lake?"

"Of course there are, the people who loved the place and who lived here."

"And died here?"

"And died here, of course."

"Would Bridie Daly's spirit be here?"

"Bridie Daly?"

"The woman who said 'Look in the reeds.' The woman who was going to have a baby without being married." Clio sounded too eager, too gossipy, for Sister Madeleine.

She looked at them thoughtfully. "And are you girls having a party for Halloween?" she asked.

Kit said nothing.

Clio grumbled, "Kit was going to have one and then it was all canceled."

"I only said I might." Kit was mutinous.

"Well, it's stupid to say you might and then give no explanation," Clio said.

Sister Madeleine looked at Kit sympathetically. The child was distressed about something. The Halloween party was not the right distraction to have made. "Have you ever seen a tame fox?" she asked them, with the air of a conspirator.

"You can't have a tame fox, can you?" Clio knew everything.

"Well, you can't have one that you'd trust with the ducklings and the chickens," Sister Madeleine agreed. "But I have a lovely little fellow I could show you. He's in a box in my bedroom. I can't let him out but you can come in with me and see."

Her bedroom! The girls looked at each other in delight. No one knew what was behind the closed door. Forgotten now were bodies in the lake, spirits of the dead, and the intransigence of canceling a Halloween party. In they went and Sister Madeleine closed the door behind them.

There was a simple bed with a small iron headboard, and a smaller bed-end made the same way. It was covered in a snow-white bedspread. On the wall was a cross, not a crucifix, just a plain cross. There was a small chest of drawers which had no mirror, just a comb and a pair of rosary beads.

There was a chair, and a prie-dieu facing the cross. This is where Sister Madeleine must say her prayers.

"You have it very tidy," Clio said eventually, trying to think of some compliment and finding this the only thing she could say in honesty about a place which had the comfort of a prison cell.

"Here he is," cried Sister Madeleine, and pulled out a cardboard box with straw in it. Sitting in the middle was a tiny fox cub with his head on one side.

"Isn't he gorgeous!" Clio and Kit spoke in one

voice. They reached out awkwardly as if to stroke him.

"Will he bite?" Clio asked.

"He might nip a little, but he's so small his little teeth wouldn't hurt you." Any other grown-up in the world would have said not to touch him.

"Will he live here forever?" Kit wanted to know.

"He broke his leg, you see. I was mending it . . . it's not the kind of thing you can take to the vet. Mr. Kenny wouldn't thank you for bringing up a fox to him." Sister Madeleine knew that even the warm feelings of Lough Glass she enjoyed would not extend toward her harboring a fox. Foxes were rodents; they killed people's chickens and geese, and little turkeys. If a baby fox was to be cured then you wouldn't get any branch of the medical profession or establishment to help you. They looked admiringly at the little piece of wood tied to the tiny leg. "He'll soon be able to walk and run, and then we'll send him off to whatever life awaits him." Sister Madeleine looked at the little pointed face that stared trustingly up at her and stroked his small soft head.

"How can you let him go?" Kit breathed. "I'd keep him forever."

"His place is out there. You can't keep anything that wants to go; it's in his nature to be free."

"But you could make him into a pet . . ."

"No, that wouldn't work. Anything or anyone who is meant to be free will go."

Kit shivered. It was as if Sister Madeleine was looking into the future.

Helen went slowly down the stairs and into the pharmacy. She gave a wan little smile.

"It's like the shoemaker's children being never shod . . . I can't find an aspirin up in the bathroom," she said.

He ran to get a glass of water and put out two little tablets for her. His hand lay over hers for a moment. She smiled the same feeble attempt to respond to him.

"You look washed out, love . . . did you not sleep?" Martin McMahon spoke very fondly.

"I didn't actually. I kept walking around. I hope I didn't wake the house."

"You should have come in to me. I'd have fixed you something to make you sleep."

"Ah, I don't like calling you in the middle of the night. It's bad enough not wanting you in my bedroom, I don't want to be raising your hopes."

"The hopes are always there, Helen. Maybe someday?" His face looked eager. She was silent. "Or some night?" he smiled.

"I have to talk to you, Martin."

He looked concerned; immediately he felt her forehead.

"What is it, love? A fever?"

"No, no, it's not that."

His eyes were wide with distress. "Well, tell me about it, and don't be putting the heart across me . . ."

"Not here — it's all too long and confused and . . . I have to get out of here . . ." She was flushed now, her earlier pallor gone.

83

"Will we get Peter?"

"No we will not get Peter," she snapped. "I want to talk to you by yourself. Will you come out for a walk with me?"

"Now? But aren't we going upstairs to have the meal that's on the table for us?" He was utterly bewildered by her.

"I told Rita that you and I would not be having our meal today, I made you a few sandwiches." She had a neat packet wrapped in greaseproof paper. "I have to talk to you." Her voice was not menacing, but yet Martin seemed to fear her words.

"Listen, love, I'm a working man, I can't go off wandering where the fancy takes me," he said.

"It's early closing today."

"But I have . . . I have a hundred things to do — will we bring those sandwiches upstairs and have them with Rita? Wouldn't that be grand?"

"I don't want to talk in front of Rita . . ."

"You know, I don't think you should be talking at all — come on now, and I'll settle you into your bed, and we'll have no more of this nonsense." His voice was the same as when he was taking a splinter out of a child's finger, or painting iodine onto a cut knee. He was soothing and full of encouragement.

Helen's eyes filled with tears.

"Oh, Martin, what am I going to do with you?" she asked.

He patted her hand. "You're going to smile at me. There is nothing on this earth that is not made better by a good smile."

She forced a smile and he dusted away the tear-drops.

"What did I tell you?" he said triumphantly. He was still holding her hand, and they looked like a happy couple sharing a secret, a life together and maybe a loving moment, when the door opened and Lilian Kelly came in followed by her sister Maura, who had come on a visit as she did every year around this time.

"Well, isn't this the way to live, like a courting couple in the middle of all the potions and the bottles," Lilian laughed.

"Hallo Helen, and there isn't a pick on you this year as well." Maura was a plump woman like her sister, bustling and enthusiastic, a great golfer. She worked for a horse trainer and it had been said that she had hopes of him. The hopes had not materialized. Maura must be forty now, but always cheerful and full of activity.

They pulled up the two tall chairs that Martin McMahon kept for customers to use, and an ash-tray was produced as both Lilian and Maura smoked the Gold Flakes, waving them around as they gestured or exclaimed at whatever was being said.

Martin noticed Helen back away a little from the smoke. "Will I open the door a bit?" he suggested.

She gave him a grateful look.

"You'll freeze us all to death, Martin."

"It's just that Helen's a bit . . ." He was protective.

"Aren't you well?" Lilian was sympathetic.

85

"I'm fine, just a bit nauseous today, I don't know why."

"Would it be the oldest reason in the book, do you think?" Lilian was arch.

Helen looked at her levelly. "I don't think so," she said with a faint smile.

She stood in the street, gulping the cold air. It was chilly even for the end of October, and there was a mist coming up from the lake. Still, it brought more color to her cheeks.

"Listen, we called because we're going to treat ourselves to lunch in the Central. Ah come on, Helen. It's early-closing day — Peter'll come down too, to make an occasion out of it. You will come, won't you?"

Helen looked at her husband. A few moments ago he had been pleading that he had hundreds of things to do. He couldn't take the time off on early-closing day to be alone with her. And yet now there was the chance of an outing with a group, he was obviously dying to go.

"Well, I don't know, I really don't know . . ." he said.

Helen said not a word to help him decide.

"We don't do this kind of thing very often." Lilian Kelly was trying to be persuasive.

"Martin, I insist." Maura seemed eager too. "Come on now, it'd be my treat, all of you. Let me do this — I'd love it." She beamed at them all.

"Helen, what do you think?" He was as eager as a boy. "Will we be devils?"

Lilian and Maura almost clapped their hands with enthusiasm.

"You go, Martin, please. I can't, I'm afraid. I have to go . . ." Helen waved her hand vaguely in a direction that could have meant anywhere.

Nobody questioned why she wouldn't come, or where she was going.

The Brothers had a half day on Wednesday, the convent did not. Emmet McMahon went to Sister Madeleine and read the *Lays of Ancient Rome* with her; over and over he told the story about how Horatius kept the bridge. She closed her eyes and said she could see it all, those brave young men fighting off the enemy hordes, just three of them and then being flung into the Tiber. Emmet began to see it too, and he spoke it with great confidence.

" 'O Tiber, Father Tiber / To whom the Romans pray —' " He interrupted himself. "Why did the Romans pray to a river?"

"They thought it was a god."

"They must have been mad."

"I don't know," Sister Madeleine speculated. "It was a very powerful river, rushing and foaming, and it was their livelihood in many ways . . . a bit like God to them, I suppose." Sister Madeleine found nothing surprising.

"Can you show me the little fox you showed Kit?" he asked.

"Certainly, but tell me more about those brave Romans first, I love to hear about them."

And Emmet McMahon, who had not been able to say his own name in public with any hope of finishing it, stood and declaimed the verses of Lord Macaulay as if it were his mission in life.

"Aunt Maura'll be at home when I get back," Clio said.

"That's nice for you," Kit said.

"Yes, she said she'd teach us golf. Would we learn?"

Kit considered it. It would be a very grown-up thing to do, certainly. It would put them in a different class to those who just collected golf balls. But Kit felt a resistance. She wondered why. Possibly because her mother didn't play, Mother had never shown any interest in the game at all. It seemed a bit disloyal somehow for Kit to learn, as if she didn't agree with her mother's choice.

"I'll think about it," she said eventually.

"With you that means no," Clio said.

"Why do you say that?"

"Because I know you very well." Clio spoke menacingly.

Kit resolved to discuss the golf with her mother that evening; if Mam encouraged her to go ahead, she would. That would show Clio Kelly that she wasn't always right.

"Don't give me very much, Rita. I had a meal that you wouldn't give to a condemned man there was so much on the plate," Martin McMahon said ruefully.

"Why did you eat all that, Daddy?" Emmet asked.

"We went on an outing to the hotel as a treat."

"How much did it cost?" Emmet wondered.

"I don't know, to tell you the truth, Clio's auntie Maura paid for all of us."

"Did Mother enjoy it?" Kit was pleased there had been an outing.

"Ah. Your mother wasn't able to come with us."

"Where is Mother now?"

"She'll be back later," Dad said.

Kit wished she was there now, she wanted to talk about the golf to her. Why did everyone think it was so normal for Mother not to be around anymore?

Clio came around after tea. "Well, what did you decide?"

"Decide?"

"About golf. Aunt Maura wants to know."

"No she doesn't. *You* want to know." Kit knew that and said it very definitely.

"Well, she *would* want to know."

"I haven't decided yet."

"What'll we do then?" Clio looked around Kit's bedroom, waiting for inspiration, or an invitation to look at the dance steps of the cha-cha-cha, which they had nearly mastered. The pattern of where the feet should go was worse than geometry with Mother Bernard.

"I don't know," Kit said. She wanted to hear Mother's light step on the stair.

There was a silence. "Are we having a fight?" Clio asked.

Kit was full of remorse. She nearly told her best friend that she was just worried because Mother wasn't home. Nearly, but she didn't.

"Clio didn't stay long." Kit's father was drawing the curtains in the sitting room.

"No, she didn't."

"Another fight?"

"No, she asked that too," Kit said.

"Good, that's a relief."

"Daddy? Where's Mother?"

"She'll be back, love, she likes people not to be policing her."

"But where is she?"

"I don't know, love. Come on now, and stop pacing the room like a caged animal."

Kit sat down and looked at the patterns in the fire. She saw houses and castles, and big fiery mountains. The same pattern never appeared twice. She looked at her father from time to time.

He sat with a book on his lap, but never turned a page.

In the kitchen Rita sat beside the range. The Aga was a comfort on a windy night like this. She thought of people who had no home, like the Old Woman of the Roads in the poem. They had a framed print from the Cuala Press of the poem by Padraic Colum up on the wall. It was a great thing to have a bit of comfort.

She wondered about the tinker women traveling on and on in those damp caravans, about Sister Madeleine, who didn't know where the next crust was going to come from but it never worried her. Someone would bring her wood for the fire, or potatoes to cook.

And Rita thought about the Mistress.

What would have her, a fine young woman with a family that adored her, wandering about down by the lake on a cold, windy night like this, instead of sitting by the fire in her own room with the thick velvet curtains drawn.

"People are funny, Farouk," Rita said to the cat.

Farouk leaped up on the windowsill and looked out over the backyards of Lough Glass, as if he too might have been out wandering had he the mind.

Emmet was in bed, Father was straining, listening for the sound of the door. Kit felt the ticktock of the clock going through her, almost shaking her body. Why did they have a clock with such a loud sound, or maybe it had just got louder. Kit hadn't remembered it like this before, dominating the whole house.

Wouldn't it have been wonderful if Mother was there teaching her some game. Mother said you could learn any game from a book, there was no such thing as having a head for that sort of thing or having a good card sense, you did it for yourself.

Soon they would hear the door opening and Mother's light step running up the stair. Father would never ask her what kept her out so late . . . even though this was surely later than she had ever been out before.

Perhaps he should ask her, Kit thought with a surge of impatience. It wasn't normal, it wasn't what Clio would call normal.

And then they heard the sound at the door downstairs. Kit felt the color return to her face. She and her father exchanged conspiratorial glances of relief, the relief that would not be mentioned when Mother came in. But the door didn't open. It wasn't Mother, it was somebody rattling the door trying to turn the handle and then resorting to knocking. Kit's father ran down to answer it.

It was Dan O'Brien from the hotel, and his son, Philip. They were wet and moving very slowly.

Kit watched them from the top of the stairs. It felt as if everything were moving very slowly.

"Martin, I'm sure everything's all right," Dan began.

"What is it, man? Tell me. Speak, God damn you." Father was in a panic, wanting the words which Mr. O'Brien didn't seem able to say.

"I'm sure it's all fine, the children are home, aren't they . . . ?"

"What is it, Dan?"

"It's the boat, your boat . . . your boat, Martin. It's cut loose and it's upside down drifting, there's fellows pulling it in. I said I'd run up and see . . . make sure the children were at home." Dan O'Brien seemed relieved to see the two faces peering down at him. Emmet had come from his bed in his pajamas and sat huddled on the top of the stairs.

"Well, sure, it's only a boat . . . and there's maybe not much damage." He stopped.

Martin McMahon was holding him by the lapels of his jacket. "Was there anyone in the boat . . . ?"

"Martin, now, aren't the children there behind you . . ."

"Helen?" Martin almost sobbed out the word.

"Helen? Sure what would Helen be doing down there at that time of night? Martin, it's a quarter to ten, have you taken leave of your senses?"

"Helen . . ." Father cried, and ran out in the rain, leaving the door open.

"Helen . . ." they heard him cry as he ran down the one street of Lough Glass toward the lake.

That was the bit that was all very slow, the bit that Kit heard with the words taking ages to come out of Father's mouth and Mr. O'Brien's, even though they looked as if they were shouting . . . and even when Father ran . . . his legs seemed to be going up and down the way they showed the slow-motion bits in athletics at Pathé News when you saw people doing the high jump or the long jump.

Then things returned to normal speed and Kit saw Emmet's frightened face looking up at her.

"What's happened?" he began, but he couldn't get the word out, his lips kept circling the start of "happened" and he seemed as if he would choke before he said it.

And at the same time, Rita had run to close the hall door, which was banging in and out, while Philip O'Brien stood looking foolish, unable to help.

"Either come in or go out," Rita snapped at the boy.

He came in and followed her up the stairs.

"There was nobody there," he said to Kit. "I mean your mother wasn't in it or anything. They all thought that it was you kids tricking and trick-acting with the boat."

"Well, it wasn't me," Kit said in a voice that felt as if it were coming from somewhere else.

"Where's Daddy?" Emmet couldn't get that word out either; Emmet, who could read every

93

poem in the Primary Certificate Primer.

"He's gone to bring Mother home," Kit said. And she listened to the words to see what they meant. They sounded safe. She said them again. "That's where he's gone, to bring Mother home."

They had flashlights down at the lake.

Sergeant O'Connor was there, and Peter Kelly, and the two Sullivan boys from the garage.

They were bending over the boat when they heard the sound of running feet and noises in Martin McMahon's throat. "It's not Helen. Tell me you haven't found Helen in the lake." His eyes went from one to another, the semicircle of men he had known all his life. Young Stevie Sullivan looked away; the tears pouring down a man's face were too naked to look at.

"Please, tell me?" Martin said again.

Peter Kelly pulled himself together. With his arm around the shaking man he moved him away from the group. "Now, Martin, will you catch ahold of yourself. What brought you running down here anyway?"

"Dan came to the house, he said the boat —"

"God blast that great interfering Dan O'Brien into the pit of hell, what did he have to go upsetting you for . . ."

"Is she . . . ?"

"Martin, there's nothing here, man. Nothing except a boat that wasn't tied up. It was blown out into the lake . . . that's all there is."

Martin stood trembling beside his old friend. "She didn't come home, Peter. I sat there saying she's never been as late as this. I wanted to come looking for her. If only I'd come. But she wanted to be left alone; she said she felt like a prisoner unless she could walk on her own."

"I know, I know." Dr. Kelly was listening and patting the man's shaking shoulders, but he was looking around him too.

In the trees the oil lamps shone through the windows of the caravans. The travelers might have a fire built in a sheltered spot. He could make out their shapes; they stood watchful, silent, observing the confusion and drama on the lake's edge.

"I'll bring you up there out of the wind," Peter Kelly said. "They'll give you somewhere to shelter, till we make sure that everything . . ." His voice trailed away as if he sensed the uselessness of his words.

Peter Kelly had always been in two minds about the traveling people. He knew for a fact that they took poultry from nearby farms, there weren't enough rabbits in those trees to keep them in food. He knew that some of the boys could be troublesome if they came into Paddles' bar. But to be fair, they were often provoked into anger by locals.

Peter wished they could see that the traveling life didn't offer much opportunity to the children of their group. The youngsters could barely read and write. They never stayed long enough anywhere for any education to sink in if they were welcomed in the school, which wasn't always the case. They had little need of his services. They coped with birth, illness, and death in their way. And their way often had more fortitude and dig-

95

nity than the other way. He had never approached them for a favor before.

"Could you give this man something to throw around his shoulders?" he asked a group of unsmiling men.

The men parted and from behind came a woman with a big rug and a cup of something that had steam coming from it. They sat Martin McMahon on a fallen tree nearby. "Do you want any help?" said one of the dark men.

"I'd be grateful if you could bring more light down to the shore," Peter said simply. And he knew that for the rest of his life he would not be able to remove the image of his friend sitting on a log wrapped in a rug while the whole encampment lit up with the blazing torches made from dipping tar-covered sticks into the fire.

And then there was the procession down to the edge of the lake.

Martin hugged himself in the rug and moaned. Over and over he said, "She's not in the lake, she'd have let me know. Helen never told me a lie. She said she wouldn't do anything without letting me know."

The clock was ticking and there was a little whir between each tick. Kit had never noticed that before. But then she had never sat at the foot of the grandfather clock before, leaning against it, holding her brother in her arms, while Philip O'Brien sat on the bit of stairs that went up farther still, up to the attic where Rita slept.

Rita sat on a chair in the doorway of the kitchen. Once or twice or maybe more often she

96

got up and said, "I'll throw another log on the fire, they'll need that when they get back."

Someone had sent for Clio. She came through the door and up the stairs. They had left the key in the door. She saw the little tableau. "My mother said I should come down to you straight away," she said. They waited for Kit to reply. Kit said nothing. "She said this was where I should be."

Something exploded in Kit's mind.

How dare Clio talk about herself, it was always I, I, I. It was the place she should be, she came straight down. She knew she must not speak, not until this huge wave of rage passed over. If she opened her mouth now she would hurl abuse at Clio Kelly, order her out of the house.

"Kit, say something." Clio stood awkward on the stairs.

"Thanks, Clio," she gulped. Please may she not say something terrible, something for which she would be apologizing for the rest of her life.

Emmet sensed the odd silence. "Mummy . . ." he began, but he couldn't get beyond the first "M."

Clio looked at him sympathetically. "Oh Emmet, your stammer has come back," she said.

Philip stood up. "There's probably enough people here, Clio. Could you go home now," he said.

Clio snapped at him.

"He's right, Clio." Kit found her voice very calm and clear. "Thank you very, very much for coming, but Philip was asked to keep the place sort of clear, for when everyone's coming back."

97

"I want to be here when everyone comes back." Clio seemed like a spoiled child.

There was the "I" again, Kit noticed. "You're a wonderful friend. I knew you'd understand," Kit said. And Clio went down the stairs.

The clock ticked on with its new whir, and none of them said anything at all.

"There's not going to be anything until the light of day," said Sergeant O'Connor, shaking his head.

"We can't just leave it and go home." Peter Kelly's face ran with sweat, or tears or rain, it was impossible to tell.

"Be sensible, man. You'll have half the people here as your patients and the other half up in the graveyard if they go on. There's nothing to be found, I tell you. Go on, tell the tinkers to go home, will you."

"Don't call them tinkers, Sean." But Peter Kelly knew it was neither the time nor the place to try and impose some sensitivity onto Sergeant Sean O'Connor.

"What'll I call them, Household Cavalry? Apache Indians?"

"Come on, they've been a great help . . . they've no reason to be friends to any of us . . . they're doing their best."

"They look like savages with those torches. They make my flesh creep."

"If it helped to find her . . ." Peter began.

"Oh she'll be found all right, but it won't make any difference to anyone whether it's tonight or next Tuesday week."

"You're very sure?" Peter said.

Sean O'Connor had a simple direct way of getting to the truth of things, and tonight it left no area for doubt or hope. "Sure wasn't the poor woman out of her wits?" the sergeant said. "Didn't you see her night and day, wandering around here, half talking to herself. It's only a mystery that she didn't do it sooner."

A tall dark woman brought Martin McMahon a cup from her caravan.

"Drink this," she said. It was like an order.

He sipped it and made a face. "What is it? I thought it was tea," he said.

"I wouldn't give you anything to harm you," she said. Her voice was low; he barely heard it above the wind, and the calling all around the lake's edge.

"Thank you indeed," he said, and drank what tasted like Bovril with something sharp in it. It could have been anything; he didn't care.

"Be calm," the woman said to him. "Try not to shake and tremble, it may well be all right."

"They think my wife . . ." he said.

"I know, but she wouldn't. She wouldn't go anywhere without telling you," said the woman in her low voice that he had to strain to hear.

He turned to thank her, to tell her that he knew this was true, but she had slipped back into the shadows.

He heard Sergeant O'Connor calling off the search for the night. He saw his friend Peter coming to take him home. Martin McMahon knew

99

he must be strong for their children.

Helen would have wanted that.

א א א

Rita heard them coming.

She knew by the shufflings and low voices down at the hall door there was no good news to tell. She ran into the kitchen to put on the kettle.

Philip O'Brien stood up. It wasn't often he was in charge, but he knew he was in charge now. "Your father will be all wet from the rain," he said. Kit was wordless. "Is there an electric fire in their bedroom? He might want to change."

"In whose bedroom?" She spoke from far away.

"In your parents' room."

"They have different rooms."

"Well, in his room then."

She flashed Philip a grateful look. Clio would always use an opportunity like this to comment on how strange it was that Kit's mother and father did not sleep in the same bed. Philip was being a great help. "I'll go and plug it in," she said. It took her away from the top of the stairs, she didn't have to see her father's face when he came up. She didn't want to have to look at it.

Emmet wouldn't know how bad things were. He wouldn't know that Mother and Father were unhappy, and that Mother might not be coming back. Might be gone.

She wanted the moment on her own.

The room was cold as she found the one-bar electric fire and plugged it in the socket in the wall just above the yellow skirting boards. Everything seemed very clear somehow. She could see the pattern on the carpet and the way the fringe of the bedspread hung unevenly, more to one side than the other.

Maybe if Daddy was very wet he might put on his dressing gown. He wouldn't if there were other people there, and Kit had heard Clio's father's voice, and people like Father Baily and Philip's father were outside. No, he would wear a jacket. She walked past the top of the bed toward the big chair where her father's tweed sport coat hung as it always had.

It was then she saw the letter on the pillow. A big white envelope with the word *Martin* on it.

Over Daddy's bed hung the picture of the Pope, the Pope that Kit had always believed was a guest at their wedding. Time seemed to stand still as she looked at it. The Pope had small round glasses, they looked like a little boy's spectacles that were much too small for him. He had a white fur trim around his garment, a bit like the frill Santa Claus wore when they went up to Clery's in Dublin for a Christmas treat. He had his hand raised as if to give a blessing.

She read the words very slowly: *Martin McMahon and Mary Helena Healy humbly prostrate at the feet of Your Holiness, beg the apostolic blessing on the occasion of their marriage, 20th June 1939.* And there was a kind of raised seal beneath.

She looked at it as if she had never seen it before. It was as if by memorizing every single detail she could somehow control what was about to happen now.

And for some reason she never understood she bent down and unplugged the electric fire. It was as if she wanted it to be thought she had never entered the room.

Kit stood with the letter in her hand. Her mother had left a message. She had explained why she had done what she did. The words of the priest who had come to give their retreat came back. She could almost hear his voice speaking as he had that day in the chapel. Life wasn't yours to take, it was a gift from God and those who threw it back in God's face had no place being mourned by the faithful. And had no place in the burial grounds of God's family on earth. She could see his face. And she acted as an automaton. She slipped the envelope deep in the pocket of her blue tunic and went to the stairs to greet the party that was coming up and to face her father's terrible smile.

"Now there's no sign of an accident. We're not to worry about a thing. Your mother could walk in that door as right as rain. Any minute now." Nobody spoke. "Any minute at all," said Kit's father, with hope written all over his face.

Rita built up the fire in the sitting room, and hunted Farouk from his important-looking place in front of the grate. People stood about, awkward, embarrassed, not sure what to say next.

Except Clio's father. Dr. Kelly always knew what to say. Kit looked at him with gratitude; he was being the host. "Do you know everyone's frozen solid from standing in the coldest spot in Ireland. Now I hear that Rita has the kettle on.

Philip, will you run round to your father's hotel like a good lad, and ask the barman for a bottle of Paddy and we'll have a hot whiskey for ourselves, everyone."

"There's going to be no money changing hands at a time like this." Philip's father, Mr. O'Brien, had a funeral face on him.

Dr. Kelly hastened to make things more cheerful. "Well, that's very good of you, Dan. And we have a lemon and some cloves, and that'll put the heat into all of us. I'm prescribing it as a doctor now, mind you, so you all have to take heed." Sergeant O'Connor kept saying he wouldn't have a drink, but he waited as they were poured out. "Sean, it's for your own good. Drink it," Dr. Kelly said.

"I don't want to drink this man's whiskey, I have to ask was there a note . . . ?"

"What?" Dr. Kelly looked at the sergeant in horror.

"You know what I mean. I have to ask it sometime, this is the time."

"This is not the time," Clio's father whispered.

But not quietly enough for Kit. She turned away as if she hadn't been listening.

She heard the sergeant speak in a lower tone. "Jesus God, Peter. If there is a note, isn't it as well we know?"

"Don't you ask him, I'll do it."

"It's important. Don't let him . . ."

"Don't tell me what's important or not, don't tell me what I'm to do or not do . . ."

"We're all on edge . . . don't take offense."

"I'll take as much offense as will suit me. Drink

that whiskey, for God's sake, and try not to open your mouth until you've something to say."

Kit saw Sergeant O'Connor redden, and she felt sorry for him. It was like getting a telling-off at school. Then she saw Clio's father move through the people to get to her father. Surreptitiously she moved nearer to them.

"Martin . . . Martin, my old friend . . ."

"What is it, Peter? What is it? You don't know anything you're not saying?"

"I don't know anything I wouldn't say." Peter Kelly looked wretched. "But listen to me, would there be a question at all that Helen went off somewhere on her own? Like . . . Dublin, to see anyone . . . you know . . ."

"She'd tell me, she's never gone anywhere without telling me. That's the way it is between us."

"Where would she leave a note if you weren't here to tell?"

"A note . . . a message . . ." Martin McMahon finally understood what his friend was struggling to say. "No, no," he said.

"I know. Jesus Christ, don't I know. But that ignorant bosthoon Sean O'Connor says he can't go on looking until he's made sure."

"How dare he even suggest . . ."

"Where, Martin? Let's just rule it out for him."

"I suppose in the bedroom . . ." Kit saw them walk into her father's bedroom, the cold room with the picture of the Pope over the bed. She stood with her hand at her throat, and realized that they were both watching her. "Kit love, will you go back inside out of the cold, and sit by

104

the fire with Emmet."

"Yes," she said. She watched as they went into her father's bedroom, and then she slipped into the kitchen.

Rita was busy pouring the whiskey into glasses that had cloves and lemon juice and sugar. "It's too like a party for my taste," she grumbled.

"Yes." Kit stood beside the range. "I know."

"Should we put Emmet to bed, do you think? Would your mother like that if she come home?"

"I think she would." Neither of them noticed the "if."

"Will you get him or will I?"

"Could you go, Rita, then I'll go and sit with him?"

Rita carried the tray of whiskies out of the kitchen, and with a quick move Kit lifted the handle and opened the mouth of the range. The flames inside licked up at her as she threw in the envelope that said *Martin*, the letter that would mean her mother could not be buried in consecrated ground.

ℵ ℵ ℵ

For a whole week every day was like the day before. Peter Kelly got a friend to come and work in the pharmacy, with instructions to bother Mr. McMahon only when really necessary. It seemed that Lough Glass put off having problems that only the chemist could cure.

Clio's mother and her aunt were in and out of the McMahon house all the time. They were

105

very polite to Rita. They kept saying that they didn't want to interfere but they happened to have a pound of ham, or an apple tart, or an excuse to take the children up to their house. And the days seemed to fit into a sort of mad pattern.

They all slept with their doors open. Only Mother's door was closed. Every night Kit dreamed that her mother had come back and said, "I was in my room all the time, you never looked."

But they did look. Everyone had looked in Mother's room. Including Sergeant O'Connor in case there were any clues that she had gone away.

There had been all kinds of questions. How many suitcases were there? Were any of them missing? What had Mother been wearing? Only a jacket, not an overcoat, not a raincoat. And the drawers were opened as well as the wardrobe. Were any clothes missing?

Kit felt very proud that everything was so tidy, so neat.

She felt that maybe Sergeant O'Connor would tell his wife that Mrs. McMahon had beautiful sprigs of lavender in the drawers of nightdresses and slips. That her shoes were all polished and neat in a line under her dresses in the old wardrobe. That the brushes on the dressing table had silver handles matching the mirror. And most of all she was pleased that she had done what her mother would have wanted.

Yes, surely it was what Mother would have wanted.

There was hardly any time to think, but from

time to time Kit stole into her own room to try and work it out. Was it possible that Mother, who always knew what she was doing, wanted that letter found? Should she have read it? Suppose there had been a last wish in it. But then it had not been addressed to her and if there was something for Daddy . . .

Kit felt young and frightened. But she knew she must have done the right thing. She had burned the note. Now when they found Mother's body it could be buried in the right place, and they could all go and put flowers on the grave.

There were divers in the lake, men who wore suits of rubber. Kit had not been allowed to go down and watch, but Clio told her. Clio was being very nice. Kit couldn't remember why she ever got annoyed with her.

"They want you to come up and stay with me," Clio said over and over.

"I know and it's nice of you all, but . . . Daddy, you know. I don't like to leave Daddy alone."

Clio understood. "Would it help or be worse if I were to stay here?" she asked.

"It would be different, and we're trying to make things feel a bit the same, I think."

Clio nodded in agreement. "Can I do anything? I'd do anything to help."

"I know you would." And Kit did know.

"Well, think then."

"Tell me what people say, tell me if there are things they wouldn't say in front of us."

"Anything, even if it's not what you want to hear?"

"Yes."

So Clio brought her all the gossip of Lough Glass, and Kit got a picture of the investigation. People had been asked if they had seen Mrs. McMahon on the bus or at the train station, in the nearby town, out in the road looking for a lift, or in anyone else's car. The guards were ruling out the possibility of her having left town alive and well.

"Wouldn't it be great if she had just lost her memory?" Clio said. "If she were found in Dublin and didn't know who she was."

"Yes," Kit said flatly. She knew that this would not happen. She knew that Mother had not left Lough Glass that night. Because Mother had written a note to say why she was taking her own life.

"It could have been an accident," Clio said, trying to put the minority view.

All Lough Glass was saying it had been coming for a long time. The poor woman was unbalanced, there was no way she would have taken the boat out on a night like that except to end her life.

"Of course it was an accident," Kit said, eyes blazing.

When Mother's body was found it would be buried properly, thanks to the good work Kit had done in thinking so fast. It must always be considered an accident. Mother must never become a name like Bridie Daly, a ghost to frighten children, a voice calling in the reeds.

"If she's in heaven she could see us now," Clio said, looking at the ceiling.

"Of course she's in heaven," Kit said, putting

aside the fear that sometimes bubbled up to the surface that Mother might be in hell suffering the tortures of the damned for all eternity.

The callers to the house were legion.

Everyone in Lough Glass had something to offer, a word of comfort or hope, a special prayer or a story of someone who was missing for three weeks and had been found.

Sister Madeleine didn't call. But she never went visiting people. After a week Kit went down the lane to the hermit's cottage. For the first time she went with no gift.

"You knew her, Sister Madeleine . . . why did she do it?"

"I suppose she thought she knew how to manage a boat." To the hermit it was simple.

"But we never take the boat out alone, she never did before . . ."

"She must have wanted to that night. It was a very beautiful night, the clouds kept racing across the moon like smoke from a fire. I stood at the window and watched it for a long time . . ."

"You didn't see Mother?"

"No, child, I saw nobody."

"She wouldn't be in hell, Sister Madeleine, would she?"

The nun put down the toasting fork and looked at Kit in amazement. "You can't mean that you seriously think that for a moment?" she said.

"Well, it's a sin against Hope, isn't it? It's despair, the one sin that can't be forgiven."

"Where did you hear that?"

"At school, I suppose. And at Mass, and at the retreat." Kit was trying to draw up some kind of reinforcement.

"You heard nothing of the sort. But what makes you think that your poor mother took her own life?"

"She must have, Sister, she must have. She was so unhappy."

"We're all unhappy, everyone's a bit unhappy."

"No, but she really was, you don't know. . . ."

Now Sister Madeleine was firm. "I do know. I know a lot. Your mother would not have done such a thing."

"But . . ."

"No buts, Kit. Please believe me, I know people. And suppose, just suppose, your mother did feel that there was no point in going on, I know as sure as we are both sitting here that she would have left a note to tell your father and you and your brother what had happened to make her feel this way, and to ask your forgiveness . . ." There was a silence. "And there was no note," Sister Madeleine said.

The silence between them was stifling. Kit was tempted to speak. Sister Madeleine would not tell, she would advise what to do. But it would be the end of everything if she told.

Kit said nothing. Sister Madeleine said it again. "Since there was no note then there was no way that your mother took her own life. Believe me, Kit, and sleep peacefully in your bed tonight."

"Yes, Sister Madeleine," said Kit, with a pain in her chest that she felt would be there forever.

The sergeant was at their house that evening. He was talking to Rita in the kitchen. The con-

110

versation ended when Kit came in.

She looked from one to the other. "Is there any news?"

"Nothing. Nothing new." Rita spoke.

"I was just asking Rita here if she was sure that you had all looked everywhere . . ."

"I assure you that if the mistress had left any account of her plans, whatever they might have been . . . it would have been a great relief to this family, and there is no way anyone would have kept it to themselves."

The child looked pale to the point of fainting.

His voice softened. "I'm sure that's right, Rita. We've all got our job to do, you have to swill out the pots, I have to ask hard questions in places where there's grief." His tread was heavy as he went down the stairs to the street.

"Swilling pots, huh," Rita said.

Her indignation made Kit smile. "He has a great way of putting things," she said.

"As if we didn't hunt the house high and low for a letter from the poor mistress."

"And suppose we had found one . . . ?"

"Wouldn't it have stopped them all asking bosthoons at the bus office and the railway station did they see the mistress all dolled up in a head scarf . . . ? If there had been a letter wouldn't the poor master be at rest instead of wandering like a lost soul?"

Kit sat very still. Rita didn't know everything. Rita was wrong. If the letter had been shown Mother would be buried outside the walls of the cemetery. Like Bridie Daly.

Now when they found Mother's body it could

111

be buried with honor. When they found it.

Brother Healy told the boys that young Emmet was coming back to class. "If there's one mention or murmur out of any one of you about Mem Mem Memmet, or the lad's stutter I'll knock your heads sideways off of your necks in a way that no one will ever fix them straight again." He had a ferocious look about him.

"Would you think it's definite, Brother, that she's drowned?" asked Philip O'Brien, the young lad from the hotel.

"I think we can assume that, O'Brien, and we'll go on saying the three Hail Marys that her body will be found."

"It's nine days now, Brother," Philip said.

"Yes, but bodies have been found after a longer time than that. . . . It's a deep lake, our lake, that's why you're all being warned about it night and day."

"Brother, what would happen if . . . ?" said Michael Sullivan, son of the garage. The boy was about to ask what condition the body would be in. Would it have begun to deteriorate? The kind of thing boys of that age would love to discuss.

"Kindly open your Carty's *Irish History*, page fourteen," he roared. Not for the first time he wished he taught the gentle girls up in Mother Bernard's school. The nun had told him they were organizing a daily rosary in the school chapel for Kit McMahon's mother. Girls were a pleasure to teach, he had said it over and over. There was no comparison with what he had in front of him day in and day out.

Martin McMahon ate hardly anything. He said he got a scalding feeling once the food was swallowed. It was like a lump in his chest all day. But he was adamant that the children had their proper meals.

"I don't feel like a whole dinner," Emmet had said.

"You need to keep your strength up, boy. Eat it up. Rita's made a grand spread for us."

"And don't you need your strength, Daddy?" Emmet asked.

There was no answer.

Kit brought a cup of Bovril into the sitting room later on, and two fingers of soft buttered toast. She and Rita had decided that he might be able to manage this.

"Please, Father," she urged. "Please, what'll I do if you get sick, then we'll have no one at all to be able to tell us what to do." Her father obediently tried to swallow the spoonfuls. "Would it be better . . ." she began. His eyes lifted slowly to know what she was going to say. Her father was moving like a man with a heavy weight attached to him. "Would it have been better if Mother had left a note, do you think . . . ?"

"Oh, a million times better," he said. "Then we'd know why . . . and what . . . she did."

"It could have been an accident, something she didn't know was going to happen?"

"Yes, yes it could . . ."

"But even if it wasn't . . . it would be better to know?"

"Anything on earth would be better than this,

Kit. Than wondering and worrying and wishing I had done something different. Even if they found Mother's body and we could bury her in a grave and go and pray there . . . then surely that would be better than this?"

She knelt beside him, her small hand on his. "They'll have to find her body, won't they, if she is in the lake?"

"It's a deep lake, it's a treacherous lake. They might not find it for a very long time."

"But the people who are looking every day . . ."

"They'll be looking no more. The sergeant told me that they're going to have to call off the search." His face was desolate.

"Father, you couldn't do any more. I know there was nothing you should have done. Mother told me, she told me she loved you and that she'd never hurt you."

"Your mother was a saint, she was an angel. You'll always remember that, won't you, Kit?"

"I'll always remember it," Kit promised him.

She went through another night of broken sleep, of waking with a start to hear her mother say, "It wasn't your letter . . . you should have left it the way it was. . . ." Then she would see as clearly as if it were really in the room a picture of a grave with a simple wooden cross outside the churchyard walls. And the goats and sheep would walk over the grave of the woman who had not been allowed to have a Christian burial.

"They've called off the dragging of the lake."

114

Philip O'Brien's mother rarely left the hotel but she knew all the business of the town.

"Does that mean that Kit's mother mightn't be drowned?" he asked with some hope. Kit had been white-faced for so long and there were big black lines under her eyes.

"No, it just means that she's very deep," Mildred O'Brien spoke with no great emotion. She had not been close to Helen McMahon, she had found the woman a bit distant and hard to fathom.

"What will they do for a funeral then?" Philip asked. He didn't like the way his parents looked at each other.

"There might not be a funeral anyway," his father said.

"Why not, if they found her body?"

"Ah, well. It doesn't do to be speaking ill of the dead," said Dan O'Brien, in his most pious voice. "But of course, if there was a sort of shadow over how she got into the lake, then the Church has to be very careful . . ." He could sense that Philip was about to speak again, so he headed him off. "No need at all to be talking along those lines to the unfortunate McMahon children. It was none of their doing."

The matter was closed.

Clio was being a good friend. She wasn't asking questions that couldn't be answered as she so often had in the past. She was coming up with no far-fetched solutions. She was just there. And sometimes didn't talk at all. It was very comforting. In the old days it had often been Clio who came up with ideas of what they might do, or where their outings might take them. But nowadays she waited until Kit gave her the lead.

"I'd like to go for a walk down by the lake," Kit said.

"Would you like me to come with you?" Clio was gentle. A while back she'd have tossed her head and given all the reasons why it might be a bad idea.

"If you've got the time."

"I have the time," Clio said.

They walked the main street together. Kit wanted to drop off her schoolbag and tell Rita that she would be late. Since the day of the disappearance neither she nor Emmet had ever been half a minute later than their expected time of arrival. They knew too well the agony of waiting.

"Where will I say you are?" Rita asked.

"Say I'm with Clio, that's all."

"Above in her house, is it?"

"Yes, with Clio." Kit was impatient to be gone.

At the garage they saw Michael Sullivan with his friend Kevin Wall. They were two of the tougher pupils at the Brothers'. Normally they would have shouted and jeered at Clio and Kit, but these weren't normal times. Kit saw Michael begin to form some comment and then choke it back; the McMahons were not fair game for shouts and taunts. Not after what had happened to them.

"Hallo," he said lamely.

His elder brother, Stevie, looked up from under the hood of a car. "Get into the house and leave those girls alone," he shouted.

He was good-looking in a way, hard to see because he had such filthy overalls on, and his hair was all grease from either the car or Brylcreem. Clio had once said that if somebody dressed Stevie Sullivan up properly he could pass as anybody.

He had a nice smile.

"It's okay," Kit called. "He only said hello."

"That must be the first civil word he said to anybody." Stevie was back into the car again.

Kit and Clio looked at each other and shrugged. It was nice to be defended and protected by a great grown-up sixteen-year-old, but not when there wasn't any need. Michael Sullivan could be such a pain, and very rude, like asking what color their knickers were. But to be honest, all he had said was a simple hello.

They walked past the hotel, nodding to Philip's father, who stood at his doorway.

"It's dark for you girls to be heading down to the lake," he said as he saw them turn down the small road.

"It's just for some fresh air, everyone knows where we are," Clio called back to him.

They walked companionably along the road that Kit's mother must have walked every day or night of her life.

"Going round the block" was what she called the walk. She either turned down at the hotel and came back up by the Garda station, or else she did it the other way around. On finer days and on longer evenings she walked all the way around to the woods and the travelers' camp at one end of the lake or else she might go in the

117

other direction to Sister Madeleine's cottage and farther beyond. It was as if she had been looking for something. Something she couldn't find in the house over the pharmacy or in Lough Glass.

And it wasn't as if it was trying to get away from work. Helen McMahon had worked with Rita at the sewing machine, putting new linings on the curtains, turning the sheets so that the same bits didn't get all the wear. Rita and Helen McMahon made jam and marmalade, they bottled fruit and they made pickles. The McMahons' kitchen shelves looked as if people were working at them day and night.

When she walked by the lake it was not to escape work, it must have been so that she never had to sit down and think. What had she seen in those dark waters that was better to look at than touring the length of the street like other women did?

Clio's mother would know every item to wear in the one clothes shop, P. Hanley, Drapery. Mrs. Kelly often called in even if she wasn't buying anything to admire new soft cardigans, or blouses with embroidery on the collar. Other mothers would go into Joseph Wall and Son Hardware Merchants and look at new kitchen beaters, and baking tins.

But Kit's mother had no interest in these things. The paths and lanes and woods of the lake were the only places that seemed to gladden her heart.

"I wonder what took her down here all the time," Kit said eventually as they came to the wooden pier where the boats were moored.

"She was happy here, you said that yourself," Clio replied. Kit gave her a grateful glance. Clio was being so unexpectedly nice, saying the right thing always instead of the wrong thing. It was as if somebody had told her how to behave. Clio began to speak hesitantly. "Kit, you know my aunt Maura . . . ?"

"Yes?" Kit was watchful again. Was this some of Clio's old style coming to the surface again? Was she going to boast of her nice settled normal family, her plump cheerful aunt who had wanted them all to play golf, something Kit had been going to discuss with her mother four long weeks ago?

"Well, she's gone back to Dublin, you know . . ."

"Yes, I know."

"And before she went she gave me some money. She said I was to get you a treat, that I'd know what treat to get."

"Yes, well . . ." Kit was at a loss.

"But I don't know, Kit. I don't know."

"It was kind of her . . ."

"She said it wouldn't cure anything but it might distract us. Sweets, new socks, or a record . . . whatever I thought you'd like."

"I'd like a record," Kit said suddenly.

"Well, that's great . . . we could go to the town on Saturday and get one."

"Is there enough money for that?" Kit was taking the bus fare into account, and the lemonade and biscuits they would have afterward.

"Yes, there's plenty . . . she gave me three pounds."

"Three pounds!" They both stood in the wind, awed by the huge amount of money. Kit's eyes filled with tears. Clio's aunt Maura must have thought that things were very bad indeed if she gave that much money to distract them.

"Stevie?"

"What is it?"

"Stevie, I want you to tell me something."

"I'm busy."

"You're always busy, you never have time for anything except the cars."

"Well, isn't that what I have to give my time to, not let everyone go on thinking that if you give your money into Sullivan's it'll be spent on drink instead of on spare parts, like the way it used to be."

"Promise not to bite the head off of me."

"No, I won't promise that. It might well be a thing that your head has to be bitten off for."

"Then I won't tell you." Michael was definite now.

"Thanks be to God," said Stevie Sullivan. He had enough on his mind. He had to get cleaned up and dressed; he had a date to meet a girl for the first time. Deirdre Hanley had agreed to go to the pictures with him. She was seventeen, a whole year older, and she would expect him to make advances. Stevie Sullivan was anxious to do it right. It was a relief not to have to waste time biting his brother's head off over some misdemeanor that would undoubtedly come to light with a stormy visit from Brother Healy to his mam.

"What time will you be home?" Mrs. Hanley, the draper, felt there was something that didn't sit right on this outing.

"Aw, Mam. How many times do I have to tell you? Won't I be back on the bus."

"Yes, and I'll be looking out to see you getting off it," her mother said in a heavy warning tone.

Deirdre nodded meekly. There would be no problem about that. Stevie would drive her in his car for a bit of a court, she imagined, and then pick up the bus a mile out of Lough Glass. Her mother could be as suspicious as she liked, there was no way she could be caught. Deirdre wiped off the lipstick she had been rehearsing; she wouldn't let them see her leave the house too dolled up. That would definitely make them think she was on a different kind of outing than the one she had said.

Meeting a group of girls in the cinema in the town.

"Come with me to Paddles'."

"No, Peter."

"Martin, she's not going to come back, she's not going to come in that door, you know. I know it."

"No, I must stay here."

"Forever, Martin? Forever and ever? Is that what Helen would have wanted for you?"

"You didn't know her." Martin was flustered.

"I knew her well enough to know that she would want you to try and behave as normal, not turn yourself into a hermit." There was a silence. "We have one hermit in the place already.

121

Lough Glass wouldn't be able to afford two." Peter Kelly was rewarded with a watery smile.

"I was wrong, Peter. You did know her. Did she ever . . . was there ever . . . ?"

"She never told me anything, she never asked me anything that you should know about . . . I swear it. Like I have sworn it for twenty-eight days to you. You ask me every single day and every single day I say the same thing."

"Do I ask you every day? Every day?" Martin McMahon looked pitiful.

"No, I exaggerate. You may have missed out a few."

"I'll not come for a pint until they find her body, Peter."

"Then I will be drinking alone for some considerable time, won't I?" The doctor looked resigned.

"Why do you say that?" The words seemed bleak and full of horror.

Peter Kelly wiped his brow. "Jesus, Martin, it's only her body. Her soul, her spirit, had gone long ago, soared way up over us all. You know that, man, you know it. Won't you admit it?"

Martin wept, his shoulders shook.

Peter stood beside him, unwilling to reach out. Theirs had not been a friendship where a man held another man through a storm of tears. Eventually the shaking stopped.

Martin looked up, his face tear-stained and red. "I suppose I won't admit it because I keep hoping . . . Let's go to Paddles'."

Emmet told Sister Madeleine that he couldn't

concentrate on poetry. It all seemed to remind him of . . . of . . . well, what had happened.

"Well, that's all right, isn't it?" Sister Madeleine said. "You wouldn't want to forget your mother."

"But I don't seem to be able to say it, feel it, the way I used to. . . ." His stutter was as bad as it had ever been. Sister Madeleine never gave any sign that he was taking any extra time.

"Well, don't say it at all." To Sister Madeleine everything was simple.

"Don't I have to? Isn't this a lesson?"

"Not a real lesson. More a chat. It's you reading to me because my old eyes can't see to read all that well by the candle and firelight."

"Are you very old, Sister Madeleine?"

"No, not very old. Much older than you, much older than your mother." Sister Madeleine was the only person who ever mentioned Mother, everyone else avoided the subject.

"Do you know what happened to Mummy?" he said hesitantly.

"No, child, I don't."

"But you sit here all the time and look out at the lake . . . you might have seen her falling out of the boat . . . maybe?"

"No, Emmet, I didn't. Nobody saw her, it was dark, remember."

"Would it have been terrible . . . like choking?" He couldn't ask this to anyone else. They would have hushed him up or soothed him down.

Sister Madeleine appeared to give the matter some thought. "No, I think it would have been very peaceful, you know, a lot of dark water just lapping over, like silk or velvet, sweeping you

123

away. I don't think it would have been very frightening . . ."

"And would she have been sad?"

"I don't think so. She might have been worried about you and about Kit . . . mothers always worry, you know, about silly things like people wearing warm, dry socks and doing their homework and having enough to eat . . . all mothers I have known worried about those kinds of things . . . but not, not when she was drowning." If Sister Madeleine noticed that Emmet's stutter had gone she gave no sign. "No, no of course not, but just hoping that you'd all be all right, that you'd carry on . . . that kind of thing, I'd imagine."

"Imagine her thinking of that . . ." His voice was shaking.

Sister Madeleine looked at him expectantly, as if she were waiting for him to say something else, something positive. And right on cue Emmet McMahon said: "Well, she needn't have been worrying, of course we can carry on."

Father Baily gritted his teeth when he saw the McMahons at Mass on Sunday. He was fast running out of words of consolation for the family. There were just so many times a priest could explain about things being God's will to a bereaved family.

And the more he heard, the less he could accept it as the will of God. It was much more the will of that poor disturbed woman, Helen McMahon, who had come to Confession to him and knelt in the dark, telling him that her heart was heavy.

124

What kind of way was that to confess sins? Father Baily felt that he had often given the woman absolution when she had not really sought it, when there was no contrition, no firm purpose of amendment.

He couldn't recall now what she had to tell.

If only people knew how similar and unremarkable their sins were to a confessor. But what did stand out was that she seemed to think she was not in control of her life. She accused herself of feeling distant, detached, of being an outsider instead of a participator. But she had not followed his suggestions of joining the sodality, getting herself on the flower-arranging committee, or cooking for the Sales of Work.

After Mass he greeted his parishioners by name.

"There you are, Dan. Cold day, isn't it?"

"It is, Father. Perhaps you'll come and have something to warm you up in the hotel?"

"Well, I'd love to, but I have a few sick calls to make after my breakfast."

Father Baily would have liked nothing better than to sit in the obscurity of the back room of the Central Hotel and have three brandies to keep out the cold. But a breakfast table had been set by his housekeeper, and then he had to go up to Mother Bernard's convent to see an elderly nun, out to a farm in the back of beyond to bring the Blessed Sacrament to a farmer who had not thought to cross the door of a church until he had got a diagnosis of terminal cancer and now wanted the Church to come to him.

And everywhere he went people asked him

what would happen when Helen McMahon's body was found. Always he had been vague and hopeful, committing himself to nothing, saying that the poor woman must always be in everyone's prayers.

He made a great point of shaking the hand of Martin McMahon warmly. "Good man, Martin, a tower of strength, that's what you are. I pray every day that you'll get the grace you need. . . ." The man looked pale and wretched. Father Baily wondered what good his prayers were doing.

"Thank you, Father."

"And Kit and Emmet. Good, good." The words were meaningless, he knew it. But what could he give in the way of comfort? The only merciful thing was the woman had left no note. When they found the body, the coroner would surely be discreet enough to talk of accidents and misadventure. They could bury Helen McMahon in the churchyard where she belonged.

Sister Madeleine was at Mass too, quietly in the back of the church, a gray cloak wrapped around her thin shoulders.

"Will you come back and have your Sunday dinner with us?" Kit said to her suddenly.

"Thank you, child, but no. I'm not much good at going to people's houses."

"We need you," Kit said simply.

"You have each other."

"Yes, but it's not enough these days, it's gone on too long. We just sit and look at each other."

"Wouldn't you ask one of your friends, Clio . . . young Philip O'Brien from the hotel . . ."

"You're my friend. Please come."

"Thank you. That would be very nice," said Sister Madeleine.

Rita carved the meat, a big piece of beef from Hickey's.

"I never saw so much meat in my life." Sister Madeleine was full of wonder.

"It's not extravagant. It's for today, then cold tomorrow, and mince on Tuesday, and there's often enough for rissoles on a Wednesday." Rita was proud of the way she ran the house.

Sister Madeleine looked around the kitchen where they sat at the table, a home with a tragedy hanging over it so heavily that you could almost see it there in the air.

"The travelers are still looking, you know," she said. They all seemed to sit up startled, shocked that a visitor was mentioning what everyone else wanted to avoid. "They go all around the lake. If there's anything to be seen they'll see it."

There was a total silence. The McMahons were not able to respond when someone spoke about the subject uppermost in their minds. Sister Madeleine waited. She never minded silences, she didn't rush to fill them with words.

"That's good of them . . . to take such an interest," Martin said eventually.

Sister Madeleine appeared not to notice his unease. "Helen was always very courteous to them on her walks, she knew their names and the names of their children. She often asked them about their ways, the language they spoke." Kit looked at her, amazed. She had never known this about her mother. And yet Sister Madeleine

127

spoke with total sincerity. She wasn't making up a story to console them, to wrap the dead up in soothing phrases. "They know the need for a funeral," Sister Madeleine said. "They have wonderful funerals of their own people. They travel all over the country to be there, it's a way of saying good-bye, of finding a resting place up in the churchyard."

"That's if —" Kit began.

Sister Madeleine interrupted: "That's if they find her. But they will, either the travelers or someone else, and then you'll be able to pray at her grave. . . ." Sister Madeleine's tone was firm.

She was having no dealings with the idea that Helen McMahon would be buried outside the walls of a churchyard. A grave without a tombstone. Marking her as someone who had taken her own life.

That night Kit sat with her father.

"It's so long now . . . it's over a month. Would there be any of Mother left to bury?"

"I asked Peter Kelly that, Kit, the other night in Paddles' bar. He said we mustn't think of that, we must think your mother's spirit and soul left her that night, and what's left of the body doesn't matter."

"I suppose he's right."

"I suppose he is, Kit, I suppose he is."

Mother Bernard was called out of class.

The conversation in the classroom rose to a high level. There was great excitement anyway because Deirdre Hanley, a senior girl, had been

128

seen in a hedge with Stevie Sullivan, sort of wrapped around him, not just kissing, mind, but more, much more. They were so anxious for more details that they didn't notice Mother Bernard coming back and were startled by the crack of her voice, like a whip across the classroom.

"I expected big grown-up girls of your age to be able to continue with your work. But I was wrong. Very, very wrong." They had crept shamefacedly back to their places. Mother Bernard's face was white. She must be very angry indeed. "This time however I shall put you on your honor. Each girl is to take out her composition book and write one full page about Advent. The season of waiting, the preparation for Christmas." They looked at each other in despair. A whole page about Advent. What was there to say about it except that it went on forever and was nearly as bad as Lent? "And there shall be no blots, and no big spaces between words. This will be a work of which we will all be proud." Mother Bernard spoke with menace in her tones.

They picked up their pens, knowing that this time she meant it. There would be no more news about Deirdre Hanley at this time.

"Katherine McMahon, could you come with me for a moment," Mother Bernard said to Kit.

Brother Healy had told Kevin Wall that he would be a very fortunate lad if he were to see the day out without feeling the weight of a stick on both his hands. The boy looked fearful, but not fearful enough. He busied himself making pellets out of blotting paper soaked in ink.

Brother Healy was called to the door.

"I'll be back in five minutes. Is that clear?" he roared at his class. And then went to find young Emmet McMahon and tell him what he had to tell him.

No training could prepare you for this kind of job. Brother Healy sighed to himself as his cassock swished down the corridors to the room where second class were sitting with Brother Doyle, not knowing what lay ahead.

By nightfall everyone in Lough Glass knew.

A body had been found in the reeds. It was already badly decomposed. There wasn't any way that anyone would have to identity it.

Dr. Kelly had gone to his friend Martin McMahon. Everyone heard and said that there was no way he should look on something that bore no relation to what his wife had been. The state pathologist had come from Dublin; he had agreed. It would take some days, they were told.

A section of the lake had been cordoned off. People told each other how they had heard the ambulance coming. As if an ambulance would be any use after a month, but still, what other way could the poor woman's body have been brought to the morgue in the hospital.

Everyone had a story to tell about the McMahon family.

Kathleen Sullivan from the garage said that the lights were on in that house all night. None of them must have gone to bed. Clio Kelly said that things were much different there now, more normal. They had all stopped speaking in funny tight

130

voices. Mrs. Hanley from the draper's said she had gone to pay her condolences and that very pushy maid of theirs hadn't let her in, she said the family were suffering from nervous exhaustion.

Mrs. Dillon in the newsagent's said that she had a great demand for Mass cards, because now that there was a body and there was going to be a funeral, everyone wanted to show their respect by having a Mass said for the repose of the soul of Helen McMahon.

Sergeant Sean O'Connor had to say that the men who came down from Dublin from Garda headquarters were as nice a pair of fellows as he had ever come across.

They told him that he had completed all the paperwork very well, and that he wasn't to worry himself over the length of time it took to find the body. This was wild country around here. "Indian country," one of them suggested. They didn't know how a man could live in such a place, with nothing going on. Sean O'Connor didn't like this, he felt it was a bit disparaging, but they told him that Dublin was full of drawbacks too.

And they stayed with him in Paddles' bar until an unconscionable time in the morning, nodding to the rest of Lough Glass who were drinking late.

"You know everyone in the place," one of the guards had said to him.

"Indeed I do, and all about them."

"Did you know the deceased?"

"Of course I did."

"Why did she do it, do you think?"

131

"Well, we don't know if she did." Sean O'Connor had a caution that no number of pints could dislodge.

"No, we don't know she did, but we think she did. What drove her to it, do you think?"

"She wasn't right for here. She didn't settle, she sort of floated along the surface. Maybe she was too good-looking for the place."

"Had she a fellow at all?"

"God, you couldn't have a fellow in Lough Glass if you were a married woman. If you're a single woman it's hard enough with every eye in the place watching you . . ."

"So she wasn't crossed in love, no hint of a baba or anything . . ."

"No." Sergeant O'Connor was suddenly alert. "They didn't find anything like that, did they?"

"No." The young Dublin guard was cheerful. "No, I'd say it was all far too late to discover anything like that, even if it had existed. Will we have another, do you think?"

Philip O'Brien called to the McMahon house to know if Kit would like him to sit with her for a bit. "You know, like the night she got lost," he said.

Kit's eyes filled with tears. That was such a nice way of putting it. Mother had got lost.

"Thanks very much, Philip," she said, and reached out and stroked his cheek. "You're very kind and good. But I think we'd —"

He interrupted her. "I know. I just wanted you to know I was always here down the road, like." He went down the stairs again, and felt the spot on his face where Kit McMahon had stroked him.

It was oddly peaceful in the house, better than it had been for a month. They knew the formalities would take some days, but the funeral would be next weekend. They had something they could do for Mother now. They could give her a good farewell.

"Are you sorry they found her, Father? Did you hope she might have been alive somewhere, kidnapped even?" Kit asked.

"No, no. I knew that wasn't going to be the case."

"So it's better that she's found?"

"Yes, it's much better. It's bad enough to have Mother dead, without leaving her forever in the lake. This way we can go to her grave." There was a long silence. "It was a terrible accident, Kit, you know that," her father said.

"I know," said Kit. And she looked into the flames, big red and gold flames licking upward.

They were right in thinking that the formalities would not be long drawn out. Since Dr. Kelly who was the local doctor had identified the body, there had been only brief consultations with the pathologist. There was no question of foul play or of anyone else being involved.

Nor was there any mention of taking a life while of unsound mind. If there was doubt about the advanced state of decomposition of the body it was never aired publicly. Helen McMahon had only been in the lake a month, but it was wintertime, the fish in that part of the lake . . . well, there was no need for details.

And who else could it have been? Nobody from

these parts had disappeared. The coroner spoke of the great need to clear the inland waterways of Ireland, too many tragic accidents had happened among the reeds and overgrown parts of lakes.

And then the body of Helen McMahon was released for burial.

On the day of the funeral Clio arrived at their house. "I brought you a mantilla," she said.

"What's that?"

"It's like a black lace veil, a bit like a handkerchief. It's what Spanish people and posh Catholics everywhere wear on their heads when they don't want hats and when head scarfs aren't right."

"Is it for me to wear at the church?"

"If you'd like to. It's a present from Auntie Maura."

"She's very nice, isn't she?" Usually Kit found something to criticize about Clio's aunt.

Clio seemed pleased. "She is, and she always knows what to do."

Kit nodded. It was true. Rita had told her last night that Mrs. Kelly's sister had come to advise her about the food to serve. She had suggested a big ham, and to ask Mr. Hickey at the butcher's to cook it for them. Rita had said they'd never do that, but Clio's aunt had been firm. Theirs was good custom, always at the shop. The Hickeys would be happy to do something to help. Let them bring it up on Sunday afternoon, when it was needed, before the people came back from the churchyard.

Rita said it was a great help, she didn't want to be mounting guard on a huge pot and smelling the whole house with it. She could concentrate now on asking people to bake homemade bread, and asking Mr. O'Brien from the hotel to lend them three dozen glasses.

And yet Kit felt somehow that it was disloyal to Mother to say that Clio's aunt Maura was being a great help. Mother hadn't liked her; she had never said so, but Kit was sure of it. But it was idiotic to think that Mother would want her to carry on a distance that was never even spoken of.

Would Mother like Kit to wear the mantilla? Kit stood still, wondering if Mother had thought about her funeral at all, before she had gone and done what she did. When she was writing the letter, had she paused to think about how Lough Glass would bury her.

A surge of anger passed across Kit.

"Are you okay?" Clio looked worried.

"Yes, I'm fine."

"Aunt Maura said I wasn't to hang around you in case you wanted to be by yourself." Clio looked uncertain, her big blue eyes full of concern.

Kit was covered in guilt. This was her best friend, who couldn't do more for her. Why was she always being so prickly and defensive toward her? "I'd love you to stay," she said. "I need you. It would be great to have you there." Clio's smile lit up the room. "Do you have a mantilla too?"

"No, Aunt Maura said it was just for you." Kit put it on. "It looks terrific. Your mother would have been proud of you."

And then for the first time in front of her friend

Kit let herself go and wept.

The hymns at a funeral were always sad. But on this wet winter afternoon, when the wind whipped up the lake and the church was cold and drafty, Father Baily thought that they never seemed sadder.

Perhaps it was the round simple face of Martin McMahon, bewildered and unbelieving. Maybe the two children, the girl in a Spanish-type veil, the boy who had a speech difficulty which was cured and had got as bad as ever again.

Father Baily looked around the church.

The cast was assembled as usual. The choir sang "I'll Sing a Hymn to Mary." They sang the first verse and the whole congregation joined in for the second.

> *"O lily of the valley,*
> *O mystic flower what tree*
> *What flower in the fairest*
> *Is half as fair as thee . . ."*

Between the coughs and splutters they sang, eyes misted with tears for the woman who had died out on their lake.

When he had been saying his Office the previous night Father Baily had thought about Helen McMahon's death. Suppose she had taken her own life. But he had told himself firmly that God did not expect him to act as judge, jury, and executioner. He was merely the priest to say the funeral Mass and to commit her body to its resting place.

It was 1952. It wasn't the Middle Ages. Let her rest in peace.

The Sullivans stood together, Kathleen and her two sons. Stevie was busy catching the eye of Deirdre Hanley from the drapery shop. Kathleen glared at him. A church was not the place to make eyes at a girl. A funeral was not the time. Michael was kicking the front of his shoe trying to get some of the loose bits off. She gave him a sharp jab to get him to stop.

Michael had been a worry to her for a while. He kept moping about and asking her strange questions to which there were no answers. Like, if you knew something that other people didn't know, what should you say? Or, suppose everybody else thought one thing and you knew another thing, were you meant to tell them the other thing? Kathleen Sullivan had scant patience with such imponderables. Last weekend she had told her son Michael that she hadn't a notion of what he was talking about, and would he please consult his older brother. She was certain it must be about sex in some shape or form, and Stevie would give him the basic information he needed. At any rate, he seemed to be less agitated now. She hoped that Stevie had spoken with some kind of authority. She didn't at all like the glances he was giving that big bold strap of a Hanley girl, who was far too old for him, and a forward madam if ever there was one.

Kevin Wall thought that it must be desperate to have your mother all eaten up by fish. That's what had happened to Emmet McMahon's mother. And all on the night that he and Michael

137

Sullivan had gone out on the lake. They might have been near to it happening. Michael had been very worried. He said they should tell people that it was they who had taken the boat out that night. Kevin had been against it, they'd get the arses beaten off them, he said. Michael, who didn't have a father to beat the arse off him, said maybe they shouldn't have guards and everyone looking for Emmet McMahon's mother when she hadn't gone near the boat. They had been playing in it and rowing up and down by the pier when it slipped away from them and they couldn't reach it. It had been blown out into the middle of the lake and then the waves had overturned it. Kevin said it didn't matter one way or the other, but Michael had been all frightened.

He said with guards involved they could all end in jail. Anyway it had all turned out fine. Kevin had been right after all to say nothing. Michael Sullivan was half mad. Of course, his father had died in an asylum. Not that Kevin would mention that.

Maura Hayes and her sister Lilian stood in good dark coats and their sober velour hats. Peter blew his nose loudly many times during the Requiem Mass. Young Clio and Anna stood beside them for the final hymn.

"Kit is holding up very well," Lilian said approvingly to her daughter. "Isn't she very composed that she doesn't cry?"

"She's cried a lot. Maybe all her tears are gone," Clio said.

Lilian looked at her in surprise. Clio was not always so sensitive. Perhaps the child was more feeling than Lilian had realized.

As the crowds came out into the biting cold wind Stevie Sullivan managed to be near Deirdre Hanley. "Will you come to my house . . . you know, after this?"

"Your house? You must be mad!" she said.

"My mother's going to be across the road in McMahon's."

"Yes, so's mine."

"So, we'll see from the window when they're all leaving and you can slip home."

"See from where?" She ran her tongue across her lips.

"My bedroom . . ."

"You're joking?"

"A bed's just like a sofa, isn't it?" he said.

"And better than a car seat," said Deirdre.

At the grave Kit spoke to Sister Madeleine. "Will her soul be at peace now?" she asked.

"Her soul has always been at peace," said Sister Madeleine. "It's the rest of us will be at peace because we are seeing her laid to rest." In her mind Kit saw the white envelope with the word *Martin* on it. Sister Madeleine took her arm and held it tight. "I beg you think only of what your mother would want of you, to be a strong young woman looking to the future and not to the past." Kit stared at Sister Madeleine in amazement. Her mother had indeed wanted that for her, said it in almost those words. "That's what you must think of now. That's how you make her feel at peace, knowing that you did what she wanted you to do."

Kit looked around and saw all the people of Lough Glass preparing to say a decade of the Rosary for Helen McMahon. Kit had made this possible. She burned the letter that would have meant her mother being put in an unmarked grave outside the place where Christians were fit to lie.

She held her shoulders back.

"I'm doing the best I can, Mother," she said, and reached for her father's big cold hand and Emmet's small trembling one, as they stood at the grave in the rain.

CHAPTER THREE

Helen McMahon reached for another cigarette. She needed to calm herself, she needed to think.

She did not believe that Martin could have reacted this way. She had fulfilled every promise that she had ever made him, telling him that she could not love him fully, as she knew there would be no forgetting Louis Gray. She had said that she would be faithful to Martin and live with him and be as good a wife as she could possibly be, if he allowed her freedom to walk and think and escape from the stifling boredom of a small town.

She had sworn she would not leave him without telling him exactly why. She had written it all out, painstakingly, in a letter. And left it on his bed before she left. She had told him about the child. About how she had met Louis again, how he had said it had been a mistake ever to have left her. They must try for their chance of happiness.

She would take nothing. Nothing that Martin had given her.

It had taken her a week to write that letter, the week before she left. She said he could say whatever he liked, and she would go along with it. That she had gone away with Louis. That she was visiting relatives. That she was ill and needed treatment. It was all she could give him, the

141

choice to cover her departure with whatever story he wanted.

It wasn't much to give him in terms of dignity or face-saving when you considered how much she was taking.

She had given him the address and phone number of an organization that rescued Irish girls in trouble in London. There was a grim irony about it. That's what she was, in many ways, an Irish girl in trouble. She had said she would be there every day from four to six. She had said she would wait to hear what he wanted to say.

They had arrived on the afternoon of October 30th, tired and wet, she still nauseous with her pregnancy. She had sat by the phone as she had promised for four days. There had been no call.

She had said that she would not get in touch with him, she would wait until he had decided what to do. Her letter had been very firm on that point. She would give him time, all the time he wanted to digest the news and to respond as he saw fit. Twenty times she had tried to tell him and on every occasion he had smiled his foolish loving smile, or made a silly child's comic joke.

The only way she could let him know the totally serious nature of her decision was to write it to him. And now, in spite of her impatience to know his reaction and what he planned to tell the children, she was sitting here in agony. But fairness meant that she must keep her word. Now she couldn't telephone . . . she could not write again.

The days of her new life, the life she had run to with Louis Gray, the man she had always loved, were nightmare days.

She had steeled her heart for the tearful call from Martin begging her to return.

She had prepared explanations for the accusations that she was a monster to leave her children. She was having another child now, her responsibility was to the future. She knew he would not lower himself to get the children to beseech her to come back. He would not use them as pawns. If he was reasonable and calm she might be able to give him advice. She had rehearsed how she would tell him that people would forget in time. The way they had forgotten about so many people who had left Lough Glass for this reason or that. There would be questions for a few weeks, then the interest would die down. He would not be a figure of scandal or of pity and scorn.

And she owed him this . . . she would cooperate with anything he wanted to do.

And she waited for four days and four nights without hearing anything at all.

"Ring him," Louis had urged.

"No." She was adamant.

"Jesus, Helena, it's Monday night. You've been gone since Wednesday. He'll have us both in a madhouse with these tactics."

"They're not tactics, Louis. Martin isn't like that."

She looked at him, his thick dark hair, his handsome face white with worry. He wore a slate-blue jacket exactly the color of his eyes. He was the most handsome man she had ever met in her life.

After she had seen him nobody else counted.

She still could not believe that he had come back for her. She believed him utterly when he said it had all been a mistake, his own greedy mistake to run away with a rich woman. Helen knew that was true.

His face had lines on it now. They made him more handsome than ever, but they were lines of sadness. And what was so wonderful was that he was so grateful she had forgiven him. That she had put behind her his desertion and betrayal.

"I don't deserve you," he had said a thousand times since he had come back to find her. "I wouldn't blame you if you sent me away," he had said.

Send him away?

Louis Gray, the man she had wanted since she was twenty-three. The man she had still wanted on the day she married Martin McMahon when she was twenty-five. The man she had thought of with her eyes tightly closed every time that Martin made love to her.

Send him away?

She would have wandered the world looking for him had she thought that there was a chance to get him back.

But he had come to look for her. He had come secretly to Lough Glass, to beg her to believe that his eyes were open now. There was just one love in the world for everyone, Louis had said. He had been so wrong to think that he could create the same thing with another woman.

It appeared that Helen might have been wrong to try and create it with Martin McMahon, kindly, honorable, and dull chemist in Lough Glass. Then it was clear to both of them that they had to seize it and run. The stolen hours in the spring and summer around the woods of Lough Glass had been proof that the magic was there. The discovery that Helen was pregnant had been the spur they needed.

They were like teenage lovers in their excitement about the adventure ahead. Irresponsible, uncaring about the world around them as they hid from the inquisitive eyes of the small town. Would they disguise themselves when they went to London? It would be just their luck to meet someone from Lough Glass — Lilian over on a secret expedition to have her facial hair dealt with, Mrs. Hanley to look at exotic lingerie for her drapery shop. They giggled with each other at the madness of it all, yet when they did arrive Helen had gone immediately to a hairdresser to have her hair cut. It was more than an effort to disguise herself, it was also the start of a new life.

Helen watched her long, dark curls fall to the ground and she felt the wasted years slipping away. She looked younger, stronger now. And Louis loved it. That was the important thing. Not that anyone would find them in this part of London. Irish visitors would go to Piccadilly or Oxford Street, or Camden Town to see their relations. They wouldn't come to this street in Earl's Court.

They had been so lucky to find the flat, or room really. It was in a tall house which the landlady was in the process of doing up. But so far she had only got around to doing up one floor. She certainly hadn't got around to this room, and by the time she would manage to include that in her plans for making the place more elegant Helen and Louis would be far away, in a house more suitable for a family.

They would be living with their child. But in the meantime this was their home. A room in Earl's Court, London SW 5. Helen had to keep saying it over and over to herself. A city so big that you had to tell people whether you were north or south or east or west in it. You had to give your area a number as well as a name.

After thirteen long years in Lough Glass, a place with one street that had little laneways off down to the lake . . .

This was heady excitement.

It was a small room certainly, with a sofa that turned into a bed. There were few adornments, just a couple of pictures of Alice Springs left by the previous tenants, who had been Australian. A small table and two wooden chairs. The carpet was threadbare, and the paper that lined the chest of drawers was grimy and smelled of must. The sink had a rust mark where the tap had dripped, and the little shelf beside it which did as dressing table and draining board had a torn piece of oil-cloth.

But it was their home, the home she had always wanted to live in with Louis Gray.

Four days away from their previous life Helen had forgotten the carved furniture in her bed-room. The mahogany wardrobes that had belonged to Martin's parents, the graceful dressing table with its ball-and-claw legs. They were part of something that was far behind. Or that should have been far behind if Martin had played his part in the bargain.

Louis was very certain what was happening. "I don't blame the man, truly I don't. We made him suffer, now he's making us sweat. It's what I'd do if someone stole you away from me." He hunkered on the floor beside her and looked up at her.

Helen didn't want to argue it any further. She had lived for thirteen years with Martin Mc-Mahon. It was not in his character to let people sweat, to make them suffer. What she had most feared was that he would telephone her and cry. That he would promise to be better, different, kinder, stronger . . . whatever she wanted him to be. "I suppose he got the letter?" she said suddenly.

"You said you left it where he couldn't miss it."

"I know I did . . ."

"And no one else would have taken it . . . it *was* addressed to him?"

"No one else would have taken it." Helen had been over this ground before. It wasn't helping her and it was beginning to irritate Louis. She forced it out of her mind. "I love you, Louis," she said.

"And I love you, Helena."

He had always called her that. It was special between them. She remembered helping Kit with her history homework — the island where Napoleon spent his exile. Saint Helena. Like my

147

name, she had said.

"You're Helen." Kit had corrected her sharply as if there was something dangerous about Mother's having a different name. It was as if the child had known.

"Will you take me out on the town?" She smiled at him. She hoped her eyes didn't look as old and tired as they felt from inside.

"Now you're talking," he said. He got their coats and he handed her the red square she wore to cover her hair. She tied it like the gypsy woman had tied hers. Jaunty, cheerful. "You are so beautiful," he said.

She bit her lip. She had dreamed so often that he would come back for her. It was impossible to take it in now that he had.

They went down the stairs, past the bathroom they shared with three other flats. There were rules on the wall, in a plastic frame so that the writing could not fade with the steam. Hot water from the geyser had to be paid for. The place was to be left as you would like to find it. Sponge bags were not to be left in the bathroom.

Helen's thoughts never went back to the big comfortable bathroom over McMahon's pharmacy, where the thick towels were warmed by a radiator, where there was a woolly mat to keep chilly feet warm.

"This is great fun," Helen said as she ran down the stairs lightly. She saw from his smile that she was doing the right thing. Louis Gray loved life to be easy, to be free from furrowed brows.

Ivy looked out from her flat near the door. She

was a small wiry woman with short pepper-and-salt hair. She had a lined face but a bright smile. It was hard to know whether she was nearer forty or fifty. She wore cotton coveralls with tiny pink and purple flowers on them. She had the look of someone who had always worked very hard and who could take on any task. Certainly she found the business of being a landlord to many varied tenants no strain. She had a glass-fronted door with a thick curtain so that she could observe the comings and goings of her tenants.

"Off out to enjoy yourselves?" she said.

Helen didn't resent Ivy Brown's questions.

They weren't like the inquiries back in Lough Glass. "Going for a walk by the lake, Mrs. McMahon?" "Off on your own again, Helen?" "And where have you been this afternoon?" She hated every greeting from Mrs. Hanley of the draper's, from Dan O'Brien of the Central Hotel, from Lilian Kelly the doctor's wife, with the eyes that knew too much.

Ivy Brown was different. She only checked the stairs so that Australian youngsters wouldn't bring in a dozen more tenants to sleep on the floor, or that no one sublet so that some could use the room by day and some by night depending on the shifts they worked.

"He's taking me out to see a bit of London, Mrs. Brown." She flung her head back and laughed at the pleasure of it all.

"Call me Ivy, dear. Otherwise we're all Mrs. Gray and Mrs. Brown, a bit gloomy," Ivy laughed.

Louis stepped forward to shake her hand, to

make the change from acquaintance to friend. "Louis and Helena Gray," he said.

Helen felt a thrill as he said it. Like a sixteen-year-old, not a middle-aged runaway wife, expecting someone else's child.

"Lena Gray," said Ivy Brown thoughtfully. "That's a lovely name. Sounds like a film star. You could be a film star, love, and all."

They walked hand in hand down to Earl's Court Road, and on the Old Brompton Road. Everywhere seemed to be commemorating somewhere or something important. Baron's Court . . . and the places named after battles, Waterloo, and Trafalgar. The places sounded noble and dignified somehow, especially if you had lived for years in a place where people talked about Paddles' Lane, meaning the narrow path down to the lake behind a bar run by a man who had great big feet.

"I'll be very happy here," she said, smiling at Louis and squeezing his arm.

"I know we will," he said. A shopkeeper was bringing in the unsold fruit and vegetables that he had on display outside on the pavement. A flower fell on the ground. Louis picked it up. "Is this any use to you?" he asked the shopkeeper. "Or shall I give it to my beautiful wife?" His smile was infectious.

"That's not your wife, mate," the man said, his tired face breaking into a smile.

"Oh yes she is, this is Lena Gray, my wife." Louis seemed outraged.

"Nah, never. Give her the carnation, but she's

150

not your wife. You're having too good a time."

They laughed like children as they ran from him up the street and found an Italian restaurant.

At the table Louis took her hand. "Promise me something?"

"Anything on earth, you know that."

"Promise we won't become like couples that have nothing left to say to each other. Promise?" His eyes were troubled.

"I'll always have something to say to you, but you may not always want to listen." He had tired of listening before and gone away, leaving her weeping for him alone in Dublin. It was in her eyes.

"You are *my* Lena . . . like Ivy said, Lena Gray. It's a film star's name. You are full of glamour and beauty, my love. Think of yourself now as Lena, as exciting as living a new life." His eyes burned and she knew that if she was to keep him, there must be no more talk of one-horse towns, or of being provincial. She would indeed become Lena Gray, woman enough to hold a man like Louis with no fear of becoming dull and old.

For this whole week they said they would give themselves a honeymoon. No looking for work, no harsh realities of the living they would have to earn. They'd start that next Monday, November 10.

There would be plenty of time for that.

Louis was a salesman. There was nothing he could not sell. He would not have references, of course. Well, he had worked for this company in Ireland, and been highly regarded. Highly regarded until he had run off with the daughter of the family. That was that. They had gone to Spain. The details were never clear, and they had never been asked for. There had been years of movement since then, vaguely accounted for, never probed.

And Lena Gray would not probe for them now.

Louis had been paid some money to leave the girl, the only child of that family, alone. Naturally he had refused it. And then when the fire had run out of the relationship, when he had seen what a mistake he had made, he took it to give himself a start in life. The start was never discussed too much either.

It had involved going to America and working there, but without a visa, and then there was a time in Greece.

He would have come back for Helen, the girl he truly loved, but he had thought it would not have been fair. Her children were babies, she was trying to make a new life for herself. He would not come for her until he could prove he loved her and wanted her for the rest of his life.

He had known she was in Lough Glass, of course. And apparently he had come once or twice just to look at her from afar. He would not have spoken to her this year had he not seen her look so unhappy. He saw her on a winter's day last January walking by the lake, tears or rain on her face, hitting away the nettles and bramble.

And he had spoken to her.

She had looked at him wildly as if he had come straight out of a dream, and then thrown herself into his arms. He had been mad to have waited so long, he accused himself. But Lena had said no, it was perfect. If he had come for her earlier she would never have been able to leave.

But now the children would be old enough . . . if not to understand, at least to make their own lives without her. They would be better without her if the truth was told. There was no life living with a mother who had no joy in her heart, no hope, and no wish to see the next day dawn. Kit was able to fend for herself . . . she had been trained over the months that her mother was planning to leave. And Emmet, she had done as much as she could for the boy, helped his stutter by taking him to Sister Madeleine, the old hermit woman whose clear eyes seemed to see everything and know what was going on in every heart.

And she had even done what she could for the maid, Rita, encouraged her to work toward an education so that she could be a better companion for the children when . . . after . . . well, when it all happened.

Martin would survive. She had always known that. He had married her knowing that she loved another man. She had given him her promise that she would not leave him without a full explanation. Yes of course it should have been face-to-face. But he was so emotional. He would have cried, he would have done something entirely inappropriate, like kneeling and begging her to stay, like threatening to kill himself maybe? Hadn't she tried to talk to him . . . but each time he turned away?

No, he was too levelheaded for that. But he would accept it. He was realist enough to know that it had always been in the cards. It was just so odd, so strange that he hadn't responded.

Louis was telling her where they would go the next day. He would take her on a train to the seaside. There was nothing as wonderful as to walk on a beach in winter where there was no one but themselves. They might go to Brighton, and see the two great piers jutting out into the sea. They would go to the Pavilion, and walk in the little lanes looking at the tiny shops, each with its own magic.

His face was alive with the excitement of showing her all these places.

"You will never forget it," he said.

"I never forget anything I do with you," she said simply, and she saw his eyes water because what she said was so obviously true.

Lena Gray never forgot Brighton. That was where she began to lose her child. The feeling was a dragging one, a downward pain, a bit like a period. But she decided to ignore it. They had walked hand in hand as had been promised, and laughed at the gray clouds and run from the white-flecked dark waters.

They said that when their child was four they would take him, or her, back here and they would all play on the sands in the summer. They would stay in the same hotel. They would be rich and happy, their child would want for nothing.

Lena ignored that dragging cramp in her stomach.

At Brighton railway station on the way back she felt a dampness but decided not to go to the ladies' to investigate. Some superstition made her feel that if she didn't acknowledge it here in Brighton where they had been so happy it would go away.

By the time they got to Victoria she was in no doubt.

"Something's wrong," she said to Louis.

"Can you make it home?" He had fear in his eyes.

"I don't know."

"It's only whatever number of stops on the District Line," he said.

It passed in a nightmare haze. She remembered being put on the bed and Ivy's face very near her.

"You're all right, love. Hang on. Hang on. Stay as still as you can." Louis was over by the window, biting his hand. "The doctor's coming, he won't be a minute now . . . hold my hand."

"I was going to tell you . . ." Lena wept. They had been told very specifically that this was a house where no children would be allowed.

The pain was sharp. The journey up and down to the bathroom intolerable. There seemed to be blood everywhere, even on Ivy's flowered coverall.

Then a doctor's face, a kind man, old, tired. Lena mixed him up with the greengrocer who had given them the flower last week, some week. Maybe everyone in England looked the same.

Questions about the number of weeks pregnant, about any complications earlier on in the pregnancy. What had her doctor said then?

"There was no doctor," Lena said.

155

"She's from Ireland, you see," Ivy explained.

"They have doctors there too," said the man with the tired face.

"Don't tell Peter," she said. "Don't tell Peter and Lilian, whatever you do." She gripped the doctor's hand. Her eyes were wild.

"No, no," he soothed. And to Louis standing by the window, "Who are Peter and Lilian . . . ?"

"I don't know. People back in . . . back in the place she came from."

"Your wife has lost a lot of blood . . ." the doctor began.

"Will she be all right?"

"Yes, she will. She doesn't need to be taken into hospital, we've done everything. I'll give her a sedative. You have children already?"

"No," Louis said.

"Yes," said Lena.

There was a silence.

"From a previous marriage, she had," Louis said.

"Poor lamb," Ivy said.

"I'll send a nurse in the morning. I'll come again tomorrow on my way home from the surgery."

"Thank you, Doctor." Lena's voice was weak.

The doctor supported her head as she drank the sedative. "The worst is over, Mrs. Gray," he said kindly. "The best is ahead."

"What did you call me?" She was drowsy.

"You'll sleep now." He spoke in a low voice to Ivy, technical matters, towels, buckets, water, keeping the room warm.

When they had gone Louis came and held her

hand. There were tears running down his face. "I'm so sorry, Lena . . . Oh Lena, I'm so sorry this should happen."

"Do you still want me, do you want me to stay with you, even though there is no baby now, no family for us?" Her face was white and anxious.

"Oh my love. Of course I do . . . more than ever, my love. Now that there are the two of us we need each other more than ever. Nothing will separate us. Nothing."

Lines seemed to fall from Lena's face and she slept holding his hand under her cheek. He sat there for a long time stroking her hair. All he could hear was her even breathing. Not the hiss of the oil heater that Ivy had brought in. Not the traffic out in the London streets below.

She found it a funny world for a couple of days. She kept expecting Rita to come in with tea and scones, but it turned out to be Ivy with Bovril and biscuits. She found herself waiting for the children to come home from school. And then Louis would come in the door again beaming with yet another treat. A little glass of tonic wine on a tray with two chocolates wrapped up in silver paper. Or a magazine for her to read with a card pinned inside saying "I love you." Or a dish of chopped-up chicken he had got from the restaurant on the corner when he told them his wife was sick in bed.

"You've got a good one there," Ivy said sagely about Louis when he had gone running off on yet another errand.

"Don't I know it." The color was coming back to Lena's cheeks.

"Other fellow a sod, was he?" Ivy asked sympathetically.

"Other fellow?" Lena was bewildered.

"Your first husband . . . you know you said, he said the night the doctor was here . . ."

"Oh no. No, Ivy. He wasn't a sod. No, not at all."

Ivy felt she had put her foot in it. "Well, you never know. Takes all sorts . . ." she said vaguely. Then, as if to show comradeship she said, "My first husband was no loss. I don't care who knows it."

"I'm glad." Lena was glad. Ivy was so kind to her.

"You and your first husband been split up long then?"

"Not long." Lena drew down the shutters on the conversation.

How could she tell this woman that she had left Martin McMahon just nine days ago. How would Ivy, or anyone, understand that two weeks ago Lena Gray had gone to Mass in Lough Glass with her husband Martin and her children, and people had thought that she was Helen McMahon.

By Sunday Lena had color in her cheeks.

"How long have I been in bed?" she asked Ivy.

"It happened on Thursday, love. You're not ready to get up yet."

"But I have to. We're meant to be looking for jobs tomorrow."

"Not a chance of it. Not for another week at least."

158

"You don't understand . . ."

"No. *You* don't understand. I told the doctor I'd keep an eye on you. Letting you go down to the Employment Exchange isn't keeping an eye on you."

"I have to, Ivy. Truly. Louis may not get a job at once, I can do anything . . ."

"I'm sure you can, but not this week. Believe me."

"I need to." Lena spoke the words she didn't want to. "I need to, for the rent. You must have the rent." She was thinking of the treats Louis had bought, the reckless disregard for money that had to be paid to Ivy. He would probably say that she was a good old soul, she'd not push them for it, not for a week . . .

But Lena had her pride. She would not let this kind woman think that they were the type of people who would skip a week's payment. Even if she had to drag herself out.

Ivy bit her lip. "One week's not going to come between us," she said.

"No." Lena was adamant.

"Well then, let Louis earn it, love. I'm not taking any money you get out of your bed to make, and that's a promise."

They heard his foot on the stair. Lena looked up alarmed. "Not a word please, Ivy."

"As long as you know my word is law." Her frown was terrifying but they laughed together.

"What are you two conspiring about?" Louis came in with his arms full of newspapers.

"Louis, did you buy the whole shop?" Lena looked in dismay at the selection.

"Have to, my darling. This isn't for pleasure, this is my research. I've got to find a job tomorrow, or had you forgotten? I have to take care of my beautiful sick wife, and pay my wicked landlady . . ." He looked mischievously from one to another.

Ivy spoke first. "The circumstances have changed. I wouldn't mind letting you have a couple of weeks credit."

Louis leaned over and patted Ivy on the hand. "You're a good true friend to us, even though you've only known us a week. I don't want you to think that we're just unreliable Paddies who come in and take advantage of your hospitality. We'll pay, Ivy. We want to be here a long time."

Ivy stood up from the chair beside the bed. "I'll leave you to it then. You're a lucky girl, Lena. You got yourself a real man."

"Don't I know it." She smiled up at him.

"And any references or anything . . . I'd be happy . . ." Ivy said.

"That's so good of you." His eyes were warm with gratitude. "People are very good," he said as he spread the papers across the bed.

Lena stroked his dark hair. "Isn't she so kind, it would break your heart . . . Imagine poor Ivy thinking she could give you a reference."

"I'll be very glad to take her up on it," he said. He was utterly serious.

"Ivy! A landlady running a rooming house?" Lena was astonished.

"Well, who else will say I'm reliable?"

"But Louis . . . in business, in a company

. . . you can't say you have a reference from Ivy . . ."

Louis sighed. "It won't be business, darling. It won't be a matter of talking to sales directors, or marketing managers. You know that. It'll be whatever I can get. Ivy will be very useful if I want a job as a hotel porter, or in a bar. She can say she's known me for five years, not ten days."

Lena looked at him aghast. "You can't take a job like that, Louis. I won't have it. It was never meant to be this way."

"It was always meant to be this way," he said, holding both her hands. "It's just that I was the fool who didn't see it. And you gave me the second chance."

She cried for a long time.

She cried over the lost baby. And the dreams of Louis having a fine living, dreams which were based on nothing. She cried because she heard church bells ring somewhere in West London and she thought of her children going to Mass and she had absolutely no idea what Martin had told them about her. She cried because she knew she was a bad mother, the worst kind of mother. One who could leave her own children.

No wonder God had taken this much-wanted child away from her.

"I'll make it all right, believe me." His eyes had tears in them too.

"Louis, tell me something . . . ?"

"Anything, my love. Anything."

"Is God very angry with us . . . is that why

this happened?" She touched her stomach as she spoke. "Is it a punishment, a warning?"

"Of course it isn't." He was utterly certain.

"But you're not all that well up in God, you've not gone to Mass all the time." She was doubtful.

"No. But I know he's there, and he's the God of Love. He said that himself, didn't he. He said that was the greatest of the commandments, that you should have love for each other and for God."

"Yes, but I think he meant that we should . . ."

"You think he meant . . . you think he meant . . . now, now, now. What way is this to go on? When you're happy you think he meant great things for us. When you are low you think he meant punishments and all this doom and gloom." He held his head on one side and smiled at her. "What kind of faith have you at all, that you start giving everyone bad motives? This was an accident. The doctor said it. Brought on by stress maybe . . . and he hadn't an idea how much stress. Listen, love, you can't start thinking that God is lined up against us. He was one of the things meant to be on our side."

"I know." She felt better, he was very reassuring.

"So?"

"So, I'll stop attacking him and laying it all at his door."

"Excellent. Now a great big blow, then help me find a job."

She blew her nose, wiped her eyes, and looked through the Situations Vacant advertisements with a heart that was much less heavy.

"I'll go to Mass myself next Sunday," she said

in a half mutter. "That way God will know I haven't given up on him."

"God knows that," Louis said. "If you didn't give up on me, who treated you really badly, you won't give up on God."

It was a strangely endless week.

On Monday, Louis came home despondent. There were any number of building jobs, he said. Half of Ireland seemed to be over in London signing on with subcontractors, using a different name for each job. But he hadn't the build, the experience, or the liking to swing a pick or carry a hod. It had been a wasted day.

He was determined to be cheerful. "Now, stop looking upset. Don't get out of that bed, listen to me. This is just day one. Day two will be fine. If you're going to look so mournful then it makes it worse for me. I can't come home and tell you the truth; I'll only have to be making up lies."

She saw the reason in what he said. She lay awake Monday night while he slept beside her, but she didn't let him know how anxious she was.

Day two was fine. Louis came home elated. He had got a job and would start tomorrow. As a hall porter in a big hotel, not far away on the Underground. He would begin at eight A.M. and work days for the first two weeks, but there was the possibility of nights after that. Which was great.

"Why is it great?" Lena wanted to know.

Because then, of course, he could use some of the days for going for interviews for other jobs, the ones for which they felt he was more suited.

Meanwhile wasn't that great. The rent was secure. It had only taken him twenty-four hours
to find honorable employment.

Lena couldn't smile. She forced her face but
it wouldn't go into the right position. "I can't
bear you having to do this," she said.

"Jesus Christ, won't it be hard enough to do
the bloody thing without having to listen to you
being so negative," he burst out. Lena looked
at him, stricken. But he was quick to apologize.
"Forgive me, forgive me. I didn't mean to lash
out at you. It was a long day. I'm nearly forty.
They sort of implied I might be too old for a
job like this. It was hard, darling; I didn't mean
to take it out on you."

The reconciliation was as sweet as ever.

They had always known there would be things
like this to trip them up along the way. The main
thing was to recognize them, admit them. They
were both so sorry.

On Wednesday night Louis had funny stories
about the hotel. The head porter was a crook,
the manager was hopelessly ineffectual, the receptionist had a moustache and she was a woman,
the guests he had talked to were mainly American
(GIs) serving in the various bases in Britain, nice
fellows, kids a lot of them. The day had seemed
long, but it was interesting.

Lena took a huge interest and learned all their
names. On Thursday night Louis told her how
the head porter had tried to take a tip that should
have belonged to Louis, but the Scots lady had
insisted.

"It's for the nice wee man with the blue eyes," she had said.

The head porter had smiled good-naturedly in front of the Scottish lady, but out of the corner of his mouth he had hissed to Louis, "I have my eye on you."

"What did you say?" Lena showed great enthusiasm.

"I said that I had my eye on his job. That silenced him."

Lena pealed with laughter.

Louis would be out of there, gone to something worthy of him in days, or weeks at the very worst.

On Friday, Louis was tired but he had a pay packet. They got paid every Friday, and his three days work paid the rent. They handed it to Ivy in an envelope.

"I think you're well enough to go out and celebrate," she said. "My treat. A couple of pints in a place that a friend of mine runs."

They went on a red bus, Lena's legs felt weak still, but she was buoyed up by the outing. Ivy pointed out places to her as the bus went through the London traffic, and Louis pointed out other places. She felt like a child on a birthday treat.

Ivy showed her a big office where she had worked during the war, and areas that had been bombed. She said that this was a great eel shop and that was a very honorable pawnbroker, in case they fell on a really bad time, and to be sure to say that Ivy had recommended him. Louis showed her restaurants and hotels and theatres. He knew all the names, but he didn't have a little story to go with each one like Ivy did. This was part of Louis's past, places she didn't inquire about but was grateful to be shown. They got to a big noisy pub where Ivy knew a lot of the clientele.

"Very far from home for a local," Louis said.

"Ah love, I used to work here, but we won't go into all that now."

"Certainly." Louis squeezed Lena's hand. This was more like it. Going out on a raffish adventure where things mustn't be said . . . this was the kind of thing they liked.

They sat at a table the three of them. A lot of people came over and were introduced as Doris and Henry and Nobby and Steve and the landlord was called Ernest. A small man with a lot of tattoos up his arm. He made it his business to come to the table several times.

Lena and Louis noticed this because unlike in the pubs at home there wasn't table service, you had to go up to the bar to get your pint refilled.

But not Ivy.

Their glasses of bitter and Louis's pint were refilled by the guvnor, as people called him. Lena saw no money change hands. They had just enough to buy a drink themselves and offered, but the offer was waved away.

"Ernest will look after us," Ivy said firmly. "He likes to do that."

During the evening Lena saw Ivy's eyes follow the small wizened man as he moved behind the bar and greeted customers. From time to time his eyes sought out Ivy's and he smiled.

Some of the customers asked, "How's Charlotte then?" and Ernest always said, "Gone to

166

her mother's like every Friday."

Lena knew why Ivy visited on Fridays only. She wondered how long it had been going on. Ivy might tell her sometime. But then again, she might not. This was not Lough Glass where everyone's life was discussed inside out until it had no meaning anymore.

Tonight in Paddles' bar they would be saying . . .

Suddenly she realized with a start that she didn't know *what* they would be saying. Had Martin said she had gone on a visit? Had he said she was sick? No, surely Peter Kelly would need to have been involved in that.

But what had he told the children? She felt her face redden with rage that he hadn't told her what story he was going to give Kit and Emmet. She had urged him to tell them the truth if he could bear it, and to let them write to her. But that had obviously not been done.

Ivy was talking to Ernest, the two of them sitting together like a long-married couple while she picked pieces of fluff from the sleeve of his jacket.

Lena felt Louis's eyes on her. She smiled, shaking away memories of Lough Glass. "What are you thinking about?" he asked her.

"I was thinking how I'm well enough to get a job now . . . and next week I'll take us all out for a celebration," she said.

"I don't want you to have to work."

"I don't want you to either . . . but it's only for a while . . . then we'll have careers and a home like real people . . ." She smiled brightly.

It was one of the many lies she told him.

On Saturday, Lena dressed herself up and went to Millar's Employment Agency. She stood outside and took three very deep breaths. She drew in the cold London air right down to her toes. This could be the start of many fruitless interviews. What would they want with her? A woman with no shorthand. No typing skills to speak of. No references. She was too old to be an office junior. She was too ill-equipped to be an office senior.

At the desk sat a woman in a cardigan, sucking a pencil. She had a pleasant smile and a vague expression on her face. She was a gentlewoman, not at all the sort of person you might have expected to come across in an employment agency.

She pushed a form across the desk and Lena filled it in with a shaking hand. At almost every category she felt she sounded like a loser. *Be confident,* she told herself. So she didn't have any real experience or any written reference, but she had more than some of the school dropouts had, she had the ability to think on her own, to take the initiative. She smiled encouragingly at the woman in the cardigan, with hair like a bird's nest, in order to hide her own feelings of dread. At least this wasn't the kind of woman who would laugh at her and order her out of the office, implying that she had been wasting valuable time.

"There, I think that's everything," she said with a bright smile. Lena dug her nails into her palms as she watched the woman read slowly through the completed form. She willed herself not to explain, not to apologize.

"It's rather hard to see . . . well, to know what exactly you could . . . where we might . . ."

Lena put on her most confident face. "Oh, I know I'm not the run-of-the-mill clerical or secretarial appointment," she said, hardly believing the sound of her own voice. "But I *was* hoping that there might be something where my particular skills, more mature qualities might be useful."

"Like what, exactly?" The woman at the other side of the desk was more embarrassed than she was, Lena realized.

"Excuse me, what is your name?" Lena asked.

"Miss Park, Jessica Park."

"Well, Miss Park, you know maybe the kind of firm that wants someone who can try anything, not a young woman on her way up through some kind of ladder. Somewhere that I could turn my hand to anything, to answering the phone, doing the filing, making the tea, keeping the place nice, thinking up new ideas . . ." Lena looked around the dingy office of Millar's Employment Agency, waving her hands to illustrate her point.

"I know what you mean, every office wants someone like you," said Miss Park wistfully. At that point the phone rang and immediately after, two girls came in saying they just wanted leaflets, and the phone rang again.

Lena sat there biting her lip. Nothing in her life as wife of the pharmacist in Lough Glass had prepared her for the action she was about to take.

She must forget that she was an insignificant housewife from a small Irish village. She must remember that she was a career woman in a huge capital city. She watched the other woman speaking ineffectually and breathlessly on the telephone.

It had given Lena time to think. When Jessica Park was free again she decided to speak her thoughts. "For example, here in this office," she said, hoping the shake in her voice was not obvious. "I can see you're very busy. Perhaps this is just the kind of place I might be useful."

Jessica Park was not a decision maker; she seemed alarmed. "Oh no, I don't think so . . ." she began.

"Well, why not? You seem very overworked. I could do some of the more routine stuff, you know, keep the files . . ."

"But I don't know anything about you . . ."

"You know everything about me." She indicated the form.

"I don't run the place . . . Mr. Millar will need . . ."

"Why don't I start now. . . . You can see whether I'm any good or not, and then you can ask Mr. Millar."

"I don't know, I'm sure . . ."

Lena paused. It was hard to tell what age Jessica Park was. She might have been forty or forty-five. But she could equally have been thirty-five, a woman who had taken no care of herself and aged beyond her years.

Lena decided to choose this option. "Well, Jessica. I'll call you that because I can see you're younger than I am . . . why don't we give it a try? Nothing to lose, nothing to pay if it doesn't work out."

"Jessie, actually, and I'm a little older than you," Jessie admitted. "But all right. Just so long as we don't get into any trouble."

"What trouble can we get into? Look, I'll find a chair and sit beside you."

Before Jessie could change her mind Lena was installed. She sharpened pencils, tidied up the desk, and rearranged the enrollment forms so that there was a carbon paper attached to each one and a second sheet below.

"I never thought of that," Jessie said in wonder.

"Of course you did," said Lena. "It's just you're too busy to have time for it." Lena answered the phone with a cheerful "Millar's Employment Agency, how can we help you?" which was a vast improvement on Jessie's tentative "Hello."

She said that she would really like to become familiar with the filing system, that way she could be of the greatest assistance. Jessie gave her vague outlines and left her to it. Lena's eyes raked through the lists until she found what she wanted. It wasn't long before she tracked down the section that she was really interested in.

The situations vacant in sales and marketing.

The kinds of jobs that Louis Gray might be able to apply for, once they knew what was wanted and where to go.

"You mean you just walked in and said they needed you?" Louis was amazed.

"More or less," Lena laughed, hardly daring to believe it had worked. There was no need to tell him how frightened she had been.

Mr. Millar had said that Miss Park was intelligent to have picked a mature woman from the many people she saw, and to suggest her. Jessie had been delighted with the unexpected praise. Lena would start on Monday.

She said nothing to Louis about her real reason for taking the job. And the possible gold mine it might turn out to be for them. She wanted to call these firms herself in her role as employment agency and arm herself with the information.

Then Louis could apply on his own behalf.

It was all working out for the best. Lena thought she would be able to talk to God without bitterness at Mass next day.

Ivy was so sorry but she didn't know where there were Roman Catholic churches. She was always seeing them. She'd ask. She said there was a great big one in Kilburn, Quex Road it was. Always huge crowds going in and out of it on a Sunday. That might be the place.

"Kilburn . . . would it be a bit Irish for us? Would people know us?" she asked Louis.

"No," he said. "There's hardly anyone from Lough Glass emigrated since you've left."

"No, no of course not. But you . . . would people know *you?*"

"It doesn't matter if they know me, love. It's you who's on the run. Anyway, am I coming?"

"I'd like you to, if you wouldn't hate it. Just to give thanks."

"Well, I've a lot to give thanks for. Of course I'll come."

It was such an adventure going to Mass in London.

Finding the right bus, remembering which direction to take it. Crossing Kilburn High Road and following the crowd with head scarves and collars turned up against the cold. There were a few Polish people, and Italians too.

They knew nobody.

Lena compared it to the Sunday journey to Mass in Lough Glass. Good morning Mrs. Hanley, Mr. Foley, Dan, Mildred, Mr. Hickey, Mother Bernard, Mrs. Dillon, Hallo Lilian, Hallo Peter. How nice to see you again, Maura. How are you, Kathleen? Stevie? You were exhausted before you got up to the church. And then when you got there you recognized everyone's cough and splutter. And you knew what Father Baily would say before he said it.

The familiar Latin words washed over her. It must be terrible being a Protestant. You couldn't have the same service all over the world. You wouldn't understand Protestants in Africa or Germany. Being a Catholic was so safe. And indeed if you were like Louis, so simple. It was a God of Love up there looking down.

Lena felt peaceful and happy as they came out into the cold wind. Just by the church was a kiosk that sold newspapers.

"They're all the Irish provincial ones, or religious ones," Louis said. "I'll get a real paper from the man over here and we'll go and have a Sunday drink . . . Okay?"

Lena nodded her encouragement, but she

looked at the headlines all the same. There were all the papers from home, *The Kerryman*, the *Cork Examiner*, the *Wexford Echo*, the *Connaught Tribune*. And among them the paper that was delivered to the pharmacy each Friday. They looked at it for the times of the cinema, the property for sale, for news of fellow county men and women who had done well in civil service examinations, postings overseas, who had married or celebrated a golden wedding.

She was about to look away when she saw there on the front page a picture of the lake in Lough Glass and some of the boats. Underneath it was the heading SEARCH CALLED OFF FOR MISSING LOUGH GLASS WOMAN.

With her eyes widening in disbelief she read that Helen McMahon, wife of noted Lough Glass pharmacist, Martin McMahon, had last been seen walking by the treacherous lake waters on Wednesday, October 29th. Divers and volunteers had searched the reed-infested water of the lake that gave Lough Glass its name, but nothing had been found. A boat had been seen upside down and it was assumed that Mrs. McMahon must have taken it out and failed to cope with the sudden squalls that blow up in that region.

"Are you going to buy it?" asked the man who sold the papers. Helen handed him half a crown and began to walk away, still clutching the paper. "Hey, they're dear, but not that dear . . ." he called after her with her change.

But she didn't hear. "Louis . . ." she called, her voice roaring in her own ears. "Louis, oh my God . . ."

174

They lifted her to her feet, everyone suggesting something different, air, brandy, whiskey, water, tea, walk her around, sit her down.

The man trying to give her change kept insisting that it be put into her handbag.

Eventually his arms supported her along the road. Half walking, half being carried, she knew they were hastening to somewhere they could be alone. He kept saying that they should get a doctor.

"Believe me, there is nothing more to lose. Just get me somewhere away from people."

"Please, darling, please." There were mainly Irish accents in the bar, but they were far away. They were all concentrated on their own business. They had no interest in the man and woman who sat with the untouched brandy between them while they read unbelievingly the account of the search for Helen McMahon.

"He can't have got the whole town out, guards, detectives from Dublin Castle." Louis was shaking his head.

"He mustn't have got the note," Helen said. "He must have thought I was really in the lake. . . . Oh my God. Oh my God, what have I done?"

"But we've been over this a hundred times already. Where did you put the note?"

"In his room."

"And how could he not see it? How, tell me?"

"Suppose he didn't go in there?"

"Lena, have sense. He must have gone in there. They got the guards, for God's sake. The guards would have gone in there even if he didn't."

"He couldn't do all this, bring all this horror

on the children, let them think I was lying dead in the bottom of the lake like poor Bridie Daly."

"Who was she?"

"It doesn't matter. Martin wouldn't have done this, not to the children."

"Well then, how could he not have got the note?" Louis's face was anguished and he kept looking back at the account in case the article might go away.

"The maid, you say she wouldn't have kept it . . . ?"

"No, not a chance."

"To blackmail you, or anything?"

"We're talking about Rita. No, that's not possible."

"The children then. Suppose one of them opened it . . . suppose they didn't want to believe you'd gone. You know how strange children can be. Hid the note and pretended none of it was true."

"No." She spoke simply.

"How can you be so sure?"

"I know them, Louis. They're my children. First . . . they wouldn't open it if it was addressed to Martin . . . but if they did . . . if they did . . ."

"Suppose they did. Just suppose it."

"If Emmet opened it he would show it to his father. If Kit opened it she would have phoned me at Ivy's. She would have telephoned the moment we arrived. She would have demanded that I come home."

There was a silence.

A silence that seemed to have gone on forever

176

when Louis spoke. "Will you accept that he read it?"

"I find it very hard to think he could have unleashed all this . . ." She waved at the newspaper.

"It might have been his only way of coping, you know."

There was another silence.

"I'll have to know, Louis."

"What do you mean?"

"I must telephone him." She almost went as if to stand up now. He looked at her in alarm.

"And say what? What would you say . . . ?"

"Tell them to stop looking in the lake, tell my children I'm alive . . ."

"But you're not going back to them. You're not, are you?"

The longing in his eyes was almost too much to bear. "You know I'm not going back, Louis."

"Then think. Think for a moment."

"What is there to think about? You read it yourself, all that stuff about what I was wearing when I left. I'm a missing person . . . like you hear about on the news. They think I'm in the lake . . ." Her voice became almost hysterical. "They might even have a funeral, for God's sake."

"Not without a body, they can't."

"But they'll have me presumed dead. I can't be presumed dead. Not for my children. They must know their mother is alive and well and happy . . . not in the mud and reeds at the bottom of the lake in Lough Glass."

"It's not your fault they think that."

"What do you mean it's not my fault? I left them."

177

"It's his fault," Louis said slowly.

"How do you say that?"

"That's what he told them. You gave him a choice of what he could say. This is what he said."

"But he can't say that. It's preposterous. He can't tell them their mother is dead. I want to see them. I want to meet them, watch them grow up."

Louis looked at her sadly. "Did you ever think he would let you do that?"

"Of course I did."

"That he would forgive you and say 'There there, you have a nice life with Louis in London, and from time to time come home to Lough Glass and we'll all kill the fatted calf.' "

"No, not like that."

"But like what then? Think, Lena. Think. This is Martin's way. It might be the best way."

She leaped to her feet. "To tell two innocent children that I'm dead, because he can't face telling them I left him!"

"Maybe he thinks that it'd be better for them. You're always saying it's a mass of whispers in that place, maybe the sympathy over a dead mother is better than the gossip over one that ran away."

"I don't believe any of this. I'm going to ring him, Louis. I have to."

"That's so unfair of you. You told the poor bastard that the one thing you'd do for him was let him sort it out whatever way he wanted. You'd give him that dignity, wasn't that what you wrote . . ."

"I don't know the exact words."

"'Was it or wasn't it?'"

"I didn't have a carbon paper," she snapped.

"But we went over it often enough."

"That's what I told him," she agreed. "But I must know. I must know do they really . . ." All the fight had gone out of her.

"Suppose they do think you're dead, Lena. Think, I beg you. Might not that be the best for the little girl and the little boy. If you phone now you'll have to go home and explain everything. Martin will be in deep trouble. You'll make it so much worse for him . . . think all the harm you might do."

"I must know," she said, tears falling down her face.

"Right. We'll ring them."

"What?"

"I'll ring," he said. "I'll say I want to speak to you, find out what I'm told."

"You can't."

"I'll get change," he said. His mouth was in a grim line as he went to the bar.

Lena drank the entire brandy in one gulp. It felt like swallowing nettles.

They didn't phone from the bar, there was too much noise. But just along the road they came to a public box.

"What will you say?" Lena asked for the tenth time.

Louis had said little, but now as they heard the phone ringing he held her face in one hand and said, "I'll say what's right, trust me. I'll wait to see what he says first."

She gripped his hand tight and leaned very

close so that she could hear.

"Lough Glass three double nine." It was Kit's voice.

Lena raised the hand that held Louis's hand to her lips to bite back the words. Then the operator came on the line. "A call from London for you . . . go ahead, caller."

"Hello." Louis spoke in a slightly altered voice. "Is that McMahons'?"

"Yes, this is McMahons' in Lough Glass."

"Is Mr. McMahon there please?"

"No, I'm sorry. He's out at the moment . . ." Lena's eyes widened. Martin should be well back from Mass by now. They should have started their lunch. The house had gone to pieces since she left. Then she remembered this was a house in mourning, a house where everyone professed to think that she was drowned.

"When will he return?"

"May I ask who is calling please?" Lena smiled proudly. Only twelve and already practical and efficient. Don't give information until you get information.

"My name's Smith. I'm a commercial representative. I've been to your parents' chemist's in the nature of business calls."

"This is our home, not the chemist's," Kit explained.

"I know, and I'm sorry to intrude on you. Might I have a word with your mother?" Lena squeezed his hand so hard it hurt him. Her eyes were enormous. What was the child going to say?

It seemed an age before she answered.

What did she want Kit to say? Something like

180

"There's been a lot of confusion over where my mother is, but it will all be sorted out before Christmas."

"You're ringing from London?" Kit said.

"That's right, yes."

"Then you won't have heard. There's been a terrible accident. My mother was drowned." There was a pause as she struggled to get her breath again.

Louis said nothing. His face was white. Then in a choked voice he said, "I'm very sorry."

"Yes, I know you would be." The voice was very small.

Lena had often fantasized about her children talking to Louis. She knew they would like each other. Somehow she had felt it would turn out to be all right. But that was before this. Before this terrible turn in events.

"So where is your father now?" he asked.

"He's having lunch with friends of ours. They're trying to take his mind off things a bit."

That would be the Kellys, thought Lena.

"And why did you not go?" Louis sounded genuinely caring. The lump in Lena's throat was enormous.

"I thought someone should be here in case there was any news, you know . . ."

"What kind of news?"

"Well, they haven't found . . . in case they found Mummy's body," said Kit. Louis's face was working but he couldn't speak. "Are you still there?" she asked.

"Yes . . . yes."

"Will I ask my father to ring you?"

181

"No, no. It was just a call, in case I was going to be passing that way. Please don't tell him and disturb him. I'm so sorry to have intruded . . . at such a time . . ."

"It was an accident," Kit said. "They had prayers for the repose of her soul at Mass today."

"Yes, I'm sure. I'm sure."

"So that she'd be at peace," Kit explained. "So I won't say you rang?"

"No. No. And is your little brother managing all right?"

"How did you know I had a brother?"

"I think your father and mother said it when I was in the shop."

"I bet she did, she was always talking about us." Kit's voice was near tears. "It was only the winds, you know. It would have been all right but for the winds." There was a silence. The silences had eaten up a lot of the three minutes.

"Do you want further time, caller?" asked the operator.

"No, thank you. We have finished," Louis said.

And across the distance on that wet November Sunday they heard Kit's voice saying "Good-bye" and again, hesitantly, in case she hadn't signed off properly, "Good-bye now."

They hung up and held each other tight in the phone box as the rain lashed against the window. And anyone who came hoping to make a call saw the anguish between them and went away. Nobody could ask a couple who had obviously had such bad news to leave a phone box and go out into the real world.

"I could kill him," Louis said, when they were at home sitting in this half world of disbelief.

"If he did it on purpose."

"Let's go through it again."

Louis would ask "How could he *not* know?" and always it was unanswerable.

They couldn't sleep even though they needed to. They both had jobs to go to in the morning.

Once Louis asked in a wide-awake voice, "Did he think people wouldn't buy his bloody cough bottles if they thought his wife had run away, but they would if she had drowned?"

"Don't ask me. I don't know him at all."

"You lived with him for thirteen years of your life."

She was silent. Then an hour later she asked, "What did Kit mean about the winds . . . what winds?"

"I suppose the night we left."

"I don't remember any winds."

"Neither do I, but then . . ."

He didn't need to say any more. They would have noticed neither thunderstorm nor snow on the night they began their new life.

She had crossed to the far side of the lake before the gypsy camp where Louis was waiting with his car, well, his friend's car. His friend had known nothing of the plan, only that Louis needed transport for the day. They had driven to Dublin and taken the tram to Dun Laoghaire. They were the first people on the boat. And they had talked all night from Holyhead to Euston, and laughed over their breakfast in a Lyons Corner House.

And all this time, every day and night since then, people in Lough Glass had assumed that Helen McMahon was at the bottom of their lake.

Louis was right. Martin's bitterness must have been greater than any of them could ever have realized.

Jessie had a mother who was poorly. She had been poorly for a long time. Nothing that you could put your finger on. Lena learned this in a lot of detail on her first full day at work, on that first Monday.

"Why don't you pop back and see her at lunchtime?" Lena suggested.

"Ooh, I couldn't do that." Jessie was very timid.

"Why ever not? I'm here, aren't I. I can hold the fort."

"No. I wouldn't like to."

"Jessie, I'm not going to take your job. I'm your assistant. I'm not going to go out and leave the place wide open to the public. If anything comes in that I can't handle I'll ask them to see Miss Park later on. What's the sense of us both sitting here when you're worried about your mother . . . ?"

"But suppose Mr. Millar comes in?"

"I could say that you have gone to investigate better stationery. You could, too, on your way. There's a big place on the corner. Why don't you see if they have any discounts for bulk buy? We do get a lot of envelopes at a time. They should give us a reduction."

"Yes . . . I could do that." Jessie was riddled with doubt.

"Please go," Lena insisted. "Isn't this why I was hired, to be a nice sensible mature woman who can keep things ticking over. Let me earn my wages."

"Will you be all right?"

"I'll be fine, I've lots to do." Lena felt her smile was nailed onto her face. If only Jessie Park knew how much she did have to do, how many decisions she had to make if she could just get a little peace to make them.

While she was pretending to keep down a real job Lena Gray was going to have to decide today whether or not to telephone Lough Glass and say that Helen McMahon was alive and well. Hours of conversation with Louis had not convinced her. She couldn't write her own obituary and move out of the lives of Kit and Emmet.

Even if the baby she had been carrying had continued to live within her she would still have had to face the fact that she had somehow allowed her son and daughter to believe she was dead. It was no use railing against Martin and his weakness of character. She wanted some time to think. Time on her own, where she had access to a telephone.

That's why it was so important to get poor Jessie out of the office.

Lena delayed looking up the job opportunities for Louis. After all, a lot depended on what she did now. If she were to telephone home and tell the news that she was alive and well, then it might change everything. It might mean that she and Louis would not be starting their life as planned here, in London. It might mean that she would have to return home and face the consequences of everything she had done.

So it would be folly to try to set up interviews for him when she did not even know whether they would be still here. She tried to imagine the scene of Louis escorting her back to Lough Glass.

Her imagination let her down. She could not begin to run the conversation that would take place among the three of them, Martin, Louis, and herself, in the sitting room. There were no words, no explanations. She thought of the children holding her, clutching her. Of Kit saying "I knew you weren't dead. I just knew it." Of Emmet with his stutter getting worse until every word seemed to choke him.

She thought of Rita being discreet in the background and baffled. She thought of the false conversation with Peter and Lilian. Of Maura, Lilian's sister, being determinedly cheerful and saying that life was short and they should all rejoice in the good fortune that had resulted from all this instead of dwelling on the bad side.

All the time she tried to imagine a role for Louis and couldn't find one. His smile, his charm, his love for her would all be so inappropriate.

She knew she would have to go alone. And she supposed she would have to go. You couldn't tell two innocent children the news that their mother was not dead without telling it to their faces. She didn't even think about talking to Martin. The years of respect for him had just vanished away. She could not believe that anyone could have behaved in such a way over a blow to his pride.

She must really not have known Martin at all.

Jessie left, and took her incessant chatter with her. Lena hoped for some time on her own. But the lunch hour was one of the busiest times in Millar's Employment Agency. All those already in jobs which they hoped to change used their lunch break to seek details and to register for other posts.

Lena was rushed off her feet. Perhaps it was all for the best, she thought, as the wire trays filled up with application forms and personal details. Perhaps she would not have been able to work anything out even if she did have the free time. Twice she had lifted a telephone receiver and twice she had replaced it. If she had spoken to Martin in the pharmacy she would not have been able to control her anger with him. Maybe she should wait until the children were home from school.

Or should she go through someone else? But who?

Not the Kellys. Never the Kellys. Now, if Sister Madeleine had had a telephone. Lena smiled at the notion of a modern instrument like a telephone in the hermit's little cottage.

"You're smiling, that's good," Jessie said to her.

"Do you mean I don't always smile?" Lena pulled herself together.

"You look a different woman today than the one that was here on Saturday. I thought you had something bad happen to you over the week-end." Jessie looked eager to hear.

But Lena was well able for her. "No, divil a bit of it . . . now how was your mum? Glad to see you?"

"Well, it was a good thing I did go back." Jessie began another lengthy tale of her mother's difficulty in digesting her food.

Up to this Lena had thought that Mrs. Hanley in the drapery at Lough Glass was the only woman in the world whose food passed through a hundred different stages, all of them fascinating to herself, before it was digested. Now she realized that Mrs. Hanley had a sister figure in West London.

Lena had thirteen years' experience in molding her face into an expression of interest in awful Mrs. Hanley's gullet. It was no problem to assume acceptable interest in the digestive tract of Jessie Park's mother.

Her hands were busy putting new and clearer labels on the files, her mind was hundreds of miles away by a winter lake in Ireland.

She knew when she saw Louis's face that there would be no conversation about it tonight. This was not a man who would sit down to work out yet again the best way to tell her children that she was still alive.

He was tired and drawn from his long day. His hands were chapped and his shoulders ached. "Do we have the money for a hot bath, or is it madness?" he asked.

His eyes were like huge dark smudges in his

face, his smile as lopsided and heartbreaking as she had ever known. She felt such a rush of love and protection for him that it nearly took her breath away. She would work from dusk to dawn and then to dusk again to look after him, to take away this tiredness.

And she knew that he would do that for her too.

Remember how he had nearly died of anguish over her miscarriage, how he had sat holding her hand and stroking her brow, leaving only to get some treat. Her eyes filled with tears. This was her man, her great love.

She was so lucky. So few people really had the love of their lives with them. Most people yearned for lost chances. For opportunities missed. It would be a stupid woman who would give away one moment of this time by fretting and agonizing and trying to redefine the past.

She would think about it herself . . . she would waste not one precious minute of her time with Louis in what he would think was regoing over old ground.

"I think this company can run to a hot bath for one of the workers," she said, eyes bright and dancing. "But on one condition."

"What's that?"

"That I get to come into the bathroom and rub your back."

"Ivy'll be shocked . . . goings-on in the bathroom."

"Back rubbings isn't goings-on . . . ."

"It might lead to it, though. Mightn't it?" He looked at her eagerly.

"Oh, I'd say it most certainly will," she said, her way of telling him that she felt able to make love again. And not just able . . . eager, to a degree that startled her.

"We'll splash out on a bath then," said Louis happily, taking up his towel and sponge bag and reaching for a sixpence from the saucer of coins they called Spending Money.

There was no mention of the crisis in Lough Glass that night.

Lena woke at five in the morning and couldn't get back to sleep. Perhaps we'll talk about it, perhaps the time will be right, she told herself. But as she thought, she knew she was deceiving herself. As far as Louis Gray was concerned, her life in Lough Glass was over. In some ways the way it was seen to be over seemed the best solution. He was busy planning their new life. He did not want to be dragged back to her old life.

The faces of Kit and Emmet were as clear as if they were thrown by projection onto the wall opposite the bed. Kit pushing her hair out of her eyes, face wet from rain and tears at the lake, her expression grim and set. Emmet, his eyes bewildered, raising his hand to his throat as he often did when he stammered, in an effort to force the words out.

She couldn't let them believe she was dead. She would find a way to tell them.

She didn't find a way on Tuesday.

Mr. Millar stopped by the agency.

His visits always made Jessie very nervous. "I don't know what he thinks he's at, coming spy-

190

ing," she hissed to Lena.

"It *is* his own business," Lena said mildly. "He just wants to make sure it's going well, see if there's anything we need . . . that sort of thing . . ."

Jessie was doubtful. "If he thought it was all going well and we were running it properly then he wouldn't need to come in at all," she said, biting her lip.

Lena forced herself to laugh even though her mind was far from the subject. "Come on now, Jessie. Let's look on the bright side, because it is going well he likes to be here and to be part of it. Did you ever think of it that way?"

Jessie never had. "I suppose it's being married and all that makes you so confident, Lena," she said.

Lena swallowed. Imagine, they thought she was confident. She was as weak as a kitten if they only knew. "Let's make him very welcome when he comes in today, and get him involved in it rather than waiting until he's gone to make our plans."

"I wonder . . ." Jessie didn't want to rock the boat.

"Let's try anyway," Lena said.

"I was wondering, Mr. Millar, do you think that we might have some chairs and a little table so that clients could sit down while they're waiting?"

"I don't know about that," he said. He was a tall bald man with an egglike head and face, and an expression of permanent surprise.

"You know, if we made them feel that this was a place where they could drop in . . . almost a social occasion rather than standing in a line queuing like they might at a post office or a bank?"

"But what would be the advantage to us . . . ?"

Jessie began to cringe, but Lena knew that the man just wanted to know . . . he wasn't dismissing the suggestion.

"Miss Park was pointing out to me . . . you know she's being marvelous at showing me the ropes . . . well, she was saying that so much of our business is actually repeat business. Someone will come again if they have got a good placing the first time . . ."

"Yes, but armchairs . . ."

"Oh I don't mean anything very grand, Mr. Millar. I think what Miss Park had in mind was the feeling that Millar's was a sort of place they could trust, a place they felt at home in." Her smile was bright and confident.

And he was nodding. "It's a good idea, Miss Park. Yes it is. I wonder where we'd get that kind of furniture."

"You wouldn't need to spend too much, Mr. Millar . . . you'd need to look around a bit." He looked at a loss. "The real person to do this of course is Miss Park . . . she's wonderful at finding exactly the right thing." Jessie looked up, she gave the impression of someone who had never been able to find the right thing, the right cardigan, hairstyle, expression on her face. But Lena sailed past that. "You know these second-hand places. I bet with a bit of hunting there'd

192

be great bargains there. Suppose after her lunch hour . . . that is, I mean if . . . what do you think . . ."

Even Jessie's slow uptake got the message this time. Lena was trying to get her time off so that she could spend it with her mother. "If I were to have a little extra time . . . ?" she began, like a dog begging to be whipped.

"It would pay for itself over and over," Lena finished for her.

"Well, if you wouldn't mind, Miss Park?" He was doubtful about everything. Fortunately, Jessie's naturally apologetic manner stood her in good stead, she didn't sound too eager for the whole endeavor.

"I suppose I could . . ." she began.

Then Mr. Millar became eager. "We could have a couple of ashtrays," he ventured. "An old umbrella stand even, for weather like this . . ."

"A table with all our information on it . . . rather than having them read it at the counter, taking up time." Lena remembered to curb the enthusiasm before they might get carried away and abandon the whole project as being unrealistic.

"Yes, and as Miss Park said, it wouldn't have to cost a lot."

Mr. Millar went away happy. Delighted, in fact, with his visit.

Jessie looked at Lena as if she had braved a lion in a den. "I don't know how you think of things, I really don't . . . and you always make me look so good." She was like a spaniel in her gratitude.

"You are good," Lena said. "You were very good to find me and let me work here."

"It was the best thing I ever did in my life," Jessie said happily.

Lena patted her on the hand. "Right. Now don't find the furniture too quickly. Not for a couple of weeks anyway. Gives you more time to get home without it all being a huge rush."

Lena realized she had been acting all day.

Acting since she got up and told Louis that she had slept so well and happily in his arms. When she told Ivy she was just sweeping the office and making the tea because she didn't want to seem to have a better job than Louis had. She had been acting a whole series of little charades to clients who phoned, to job seekers who came in, promising everyone that huge opportunities existed.

Was this what it was going to be like from now on?

There had been so many years of acting already in Lough Glass. Assuming an interest in the new lumber jackets that Mrs. Hanley had got in, individually boxed, in the drapery. Forcing her face to smile at Lilian Kelly's stream of consciousness about people she didn't know who lived in big houses out the country. Telling the Hickeys that the round steak was good and the rib steak was inclined to be a bit tough, but that naturally if you didn't pay for sirloin then you didn't get sirloin.

Acting in the shop as she felt Martin's eyes on her. Knowing that he would ask as he so often did, "Are you happy?" "Are things all right?" and trying not to give him her answer in a scream.

The only time she hadn't acted was with her children. And yet she had been able to put on her coat and leave them. Leave them to follow Louis Gray.

She had thought it would turn out so differently. A new life, the life she had always wanted. A new baby, hers and Louis's. And look what had happened. She had lost the baby, her family back home thought that she was dead, and she was still acting.

She longed to be in the small spare cabin where Sister Madeleine lived. To be able to talk as she had talked there, where there was no advice, critical or otherwise, but the very talking helped. Somehow if she could talk this over in front of the old hermit things would become clearer.

But this was dangerous fantasy.

Imagining telling a nun that you were tempted to please your fancy man by putting off the moment you told your children that you were not dead. It would be beyond anyone's belief.

Lena sighed and settled her face into a position that might be acceptable to a young woman called Dawn, who wanted a job as a hotel receptionist.

"I've gone for lots of interviews, but they take one look at me and say I wouldn't do," she said in an aggrieved tone.

Dawn looked like a tart, her blond hair was dark at the roots, her nails were dirty, and her lipstick was a big red gash across her face.

"You're too glamorous," Lena told her. "You give the wrong impression. They want something safe-looking in a hotel. Why don't you change

195

your appearance a bit . . . come on, it's worth it . . ."

The girl listened, fascinated. No one had ever taken such an interest in her before. "Like what way change myself, Mrs. Gray?" Her eyes were bright and eager.

Lena looked at her thoughtfully and gave her considered advice. Nothing appeared as criticism. Everything sounded positive. "Getting a job is like auditioning for a part . . . it's like being an actress. Now, Dawn, we'll see if we can get you the role you want."

Dawn gave her a look of gratitude bordering on love as she left to see to nails, hair, and outfit, before coming in tomorrow for a dress rehearsal. "This is a terrific agency," she said from the door. "It's more than an agency really, it's a place you'd want to come back to."

Lena, Jessie, and Mr. Millar looked at each other, delighted.

They were on their way.

Louis ran up the stairs excitedly. "They want me to do the desk tonight," he said.

"The desk?"

"Yes. Someone called in sick, they have nobody. . . . So I'm promoted from porter to night manager."

"Will you have to work all night?"

"Yup. That's what we night managers do. Now, that's not too bad in terms of climbing the ladder, is it?" He was like a glowing handsome puppy dog looking for praise.

Lena looked at him as dispassionately as she

could. No wonder the hotel saw him as a person who could stand behind a desk welcoming late guests, coping with any problems that might arise. It was amazing that they had let him wear a porter's uniform at all. He was obviously a man who should have had a higher status.

"You'll be exhausted."

"Ah, but I'll have tomorrow off," he said. "And I thought maybe you might have a diplomatic flu and stay here to keep me company."

"You'll need to sleep."

"I'll sleep better if my arms were around you."

"I'll see." She smiled at him.

It was not the time to tell him she was devastated that he would not be here tonight to discuss with her finally what she must do. And how to give the children the good news. She knew that it was not the time to tell him that she had no intention of taking a day off from her job.

Instead she smiled as they found him a shirt that would be up to his new position.

"Will you miss me? Will you be lonely?"

"Yes to the first, no to the second. I'll put my feet up, maybe go out and explore the neighborhood."

"And you won't do anything . . . you know, you won't make any sudden decisions . . . ?"

He was asking her not to ring home. She knew that. "Not a decision in the world," Lena said. "Not until you and I talk about them, and make them together."

He seemed relieved. And then he was off, his quick light step running down the stairs so soon after he had come up them.

Lena lit a cigarette and inhaled deeply. Now, for the first time since she had woken this morning, she was on her own. With time to think and no other calls on her time. But it didn't seem right somehow. The walls of the room, with their pink and orange paper, seemed to be closing in on her. She remembered the Count of Monte Cristo and how the walls of his cell moved a little every day. This must be happening in her room. There was definitely less distance between the table and the window than there had been before. By the time she had finished her cigarette she knew she could not stay there a minute longer.

She would go down to Ivy.

"I don't want you to think I'm going to be a dropper-in."

"No, love. Don't say that. I can always do with the company." Ivy had been doing the football pools. She gave it a great deal of time every week. When she won it was going to change her life. She would buy a big hotel by the seaside, install a full-time manager, and she would live like a lady in a flat of her own on the top floor. "Isn't that right, Hearthrug?" she asked the old cat. The cat purred happily in anticipation.

Lena stroked his old grizzled head. "They're a great comfort, cats. I was very fond of Farouk at home, though he was truly the cat that walked by itself." Her eyes seemed far away.

"Was that when you were a little girl?"

"No, no. Just back home," Lena said. It was the first time she had let down her guard. She realized that Ivy had noticed.

198

Ivy said nothing but busied herself making the tea. There was no need to explain. Lena felt the same ease that she felt in Sister Madeleine's cottage.

Though two places more different it would be hard to find.

Sister Madeleine on this winter night would be sitting by her fire, speaking with some one of Lough Glass's citizens. It might be Rita planning her future, it might be Paddles, the man who had run a bar for thirty-seven years without ever having a drink in it. Perhaps it was Kathleen Sullivan, the mournful widow who ran the garage and seemed to despair over every aspect of it, including her two strapping sons. And there would be some animal sitting on a sack, a fox, a dog, a turkey that had been saved from becoming a Christmas dinner because it had the good luck to wander to the hermit's house.

And there would be no questioning, no trying to defend the indefensible.

As it was here in Earl's Court in the busy room where there was hardly a square inch of the wallpaper showing. The wall was covered with shelves of knickknacks and there were pictures of outings long ago. A big mirror was almost useless as a looking glass since so many letters and postcards had been wedged into its frame. There were vases of colored glass, gnomes, little egg cups, and souvenir ashtrays. And yet the place had the same feel. A place where you could be yourself.

And where no one would demand any explanation that you might not be ready to give.

And very simply, as if it had all been intended,

Lena Gray began to tell Ivy Brown the story. The tea was poured, the packet of biscuits opened. And when it got to the bit about last Sunday, the discovery of the newspaper, the phone call home, Ivy stood up and without a word produced two small glasses and a bottle of brandy. Lena opened her handbag and showed the cutting. At no stage did Ivy's small quizzical face look anything except sympathetic. It registered no shock, no disbelief, not even as they smoothed out the newspaper page and read of the death that had distressed everyone so much. Ivy seemed to take it all in, and to realize the enormity without resorting to panic.

Sister Madeleine never reached out and touched you. She gave warmth and support without the clasp or the embrace. Ivy Brown was the same. She stood across at the far side of her sitting room and leaned against the chest of drawers that held all her records.

Her arms were crossed. She looked like the kind of picture you would see in a newspaper to illustrate the British housewife. All that was needed was to have her hair in curlers. Her floral apron was tied tightly around her small frame, her mouth set in a grim line as she listened to the tale unfolding. The waves of solidarity and support were almost tangible. If she had held a weeping Lena close to her breast she couldn't have radiated more concern.

"Well, love," she said after a long pause. "You've made up your mind, haven't you?"

"No." Lena was surprised. She had never been so much at sea.

"You have, Lena." Ivy was very sure.

"Why do you say that? What have I decided to do?"

"You're not going to phone them, love. That's it, isn't it? You're not going to do a thing. You're going to let them think you're dead."

They talked for what must have been hours.

Lena told of how Louis had loved her and left her. How he had come back. How this was the life she had dreamed of. She painted a picture of Martin McMahon that she hoped was fair. Until yesterday she would have spoken with admiration and deep affection. There would have been guilt, even though she had kept her part of the bargain to the letter.

But the letter was it.

His reaction had killed any feeling that she ever had for him. The man was a monster, a victim of small-town respectability. They went through it bit by bit, as she had done with Louis. The possibility of the letter not getting to him. The eventual knowledge that this must not be a reasonable thing to suppose.

But with Ivy it was not tense to talk. She didn't have to fear upsetting her at every turn. And in the end Ivy was as unshaken as she had been at the outset.

Louis Gray was the love of Lena's life. She had waited for him for thirteen years, and now they were together. Ivy and Lena both knew that nothing would be done that would jeopardize this.

"But my children?" Lena's voice was shaky. It was as if she knew that tears were not far away.

"What can you give them by going back?" Ivy

201

asked. The silence between them was not a hostile one. Lena tried to think. She could hold them, and stroke them. But that would be taking, not giving. She might shame them. And then she would leave them again anyway. "Why do you have to leave them twice?" Ivy asked. "Wasn't once hard enough?"

"If they drag the lake and don't find a body, they'll know I'm not dead . . . they'll start looking . . ." As she spoke Lena knew she had begun to make up her mind. She was in fact only hunting for flaws or danger areas in the plan.

"You said it was a deep lake."

"Yes, yes."

"So there may well have been people who drowned there and were never found."

"Yes, that's true . . ."

"You love him, Lena . . . let him know you're not going back to your other life. Let him be very sure. He doesn't want you wavering or dithering."

"He left me to waver and dither for half a lifetime."

"Yes. But you forgave him, you ran off with him. Don't end up losing them all."

"Maybe I only ran after a dream." Lena did not sound convinced. She only said it so that Ivy would contradict her.

"It seems substantial enough. Don't lose him, Lena. There'll be too many waiting to catch him if you let him fall from your grasp." She seemed to speak with great authority.

"Do you know all this because you did it?"

"No, love. I know it because I didn't do it."

Lena looked at her blankly. "Ernest, in the pub. He may not be a looker like your Louis is . . . but he's the man I loved . . . and still do."

"Ernest? That we met on Friday?"

"Ernest that I've met every Friday for years now."

"Why do you meet him on Fridays?"

"Because it's what makes the week have a bit of purpose for me and because his cow of a wife goes to her mother on Fridays."

"And what happened?"

"I hadn't the guts. I wasn't brave enough." Again the silence was an easy one. Ivy refilled their brandy glasses. "I worked in the pub with him. I'd just started when the war broke out. Ron, that's my husband, he was called up. Anyway, it was a good time then. It sounds silly to say we all enjoyed the war, but you know what I mean. Folk were very friendly. You didn't know whether anyone would be here next week. It made for a lot of shortcuts. I might never have got to know Ernest if it hadn't been for the time. . . . You see, there were air-raid warnings, and we went down to shelters, and we all listened to the radio in the pub. It was very close, like people being wrecked together after a ship goes down."

Ivy smiled at the memory of it all. "He had two children and Charlotte was all eyes of course, suspecting things before they even began. And there was lots of chat about our brave boys fighting at the front and the tarts of wives having a great time running around. Everyone got the drift of it, it made things very unpleasant."

"And did you love Ron at all?"

"No. Not like I knew love was when I met Ernest. You see, girls just got married then. And I wasn't a raving beauty as you can see. I didn't get many offers. I was glad to take Ron. I was twenty-nine, nearly thirty, when we married. He was ten years older. He wanted everything just so. He liked a nice clean house, a good meal on the table. He didn't ever want to go out. When we didn't have children he didn't seem all that put out. I think he thought they'd mess up the house. I went and got myself tested and all, but he wouldn't. I said we might adopt and he said he wouldn't raise another man's son."

"Oh Ivy, I'm so sorry."

"Yes. Well, it was no worse than a lot of people had. And from what you say people in your Lough Glass put up with whatever hand they were dealt too."

"Absolutely. All of them except me."

"Well, I had your chance and didn't take it. That's why I know what I'm talking about. . . ."

"Ernest?" Lena asked.

"Yes. He said we should go off together. But I was guilty. I was dead guilty. There I was, my husband out fighting for his country. Ernest with a wife and family. I was afraid. Afraid he'd regret it, that I wouldn't be woman enough for him. Afraid that Ron would have a breakdown. . . . I didn't go, you see."

"And what happened in the pub?"

"The pub. Yes. There was more action there than there was out at the front, I tell you. Charlotte seemed to know all about it by radar. She knew when he had asked me to go with him,

204

and when I had said no. She picked her time perfectly. She said that she'd like me to leave and not darken the door again while she was on the premises. I left that day."

"What did you do?"

"I went back to our flat and I cleaned it until it shone. When Ron came home from the war he had less to say than before he went. He was very discontented . . . the country didn't appreciate the soldiers, he said. There was no pleasing him. And then the lovely Charlotte wrote to him and told him that she thought he ought to know. It drove him over the top. He said I was filth and I was disgusting and he didn't want to know. There's a nice depressing story for you, isn't it, love?"

"What are you telling me?"

"I'm telling you I have my Friday nights."

"And Ron?"

"He left. It was strange really. He just said he wanted to hear no more about it. He moved out that very week, the week he heard from Charlotte."

"And did you want him to stay?"

"At the time I suppose I did. I was frightened. I had no one, I had nothing to show for my life. But of course he had to go, he hated me, and I didn't even know him. I moved here to this flat . . . it was as different to the place we had together as you could imagine. I cleaned the house, and I did cleaning in other houses. I got the money together and when the house went on the market I got a mortgage and bought it."

"Wasn't that wonderful?" Lena's eyes shone with admiration.

"Cold comfort as they say. Believe me, Lena, very cold. When I think of what I could have had."

"And did you think . . . will she . . . suppose she . . ."

"It's too late, love, I made my decision. I let go of my chance."

There was a silence.

"I know what you're telling me," Lena said eventually.

"You have him, you love him, you've always loved him. If you ring them at home you'll have lost everything."

"So I have to fake being dead?"

"You never pretended to be dead. You left a letter telling what you did. You can't be blamed for what they think."

"Kit and Emmet?" Lena's face was white.

"This way they'll remember you with love, not hate."

"I don't think I can do it."

"I've seen you look at him. You'll do it," said Ivy.

Louis was back in high good humor at seven-thirty in the morning. "So you're going to take the day off and spoil me?" he asked, head on one side, looking at her with the half smile she loved so much.

"Better than that," Lena said to him. "I'm going to drag you into bed with me now, and love you to death, then let you sleep peacefully for the day."

He was about to complain. But she had already taken off her blouse slowly in the way he liked to see her undress. "You're a very bossy lady," he said. She had started to unbutton his shirt.

He was asleep before she left the flat.

"You always look so bright and cheerful, Mrs. Gray," said Mr. Millar approvingly. She looked up at him from her desk, pleased.

She had crept from her bed so as not to wake Louis, she had dressed in the bathroom, she had run along through the rush hour crowds on wet streets. Her mind was racing at the enormity of allowing her children to think of her evermore as having drowned in the lake beside their home. She had miscarried a child.

And yet this man thought she looked bright and cheerful.

Back in Lough Glass people always thought she looked tired. "Have you had the flu, Mrs. McMahon?" they might ask in Hickey's, the butchers. "Do you need a tonic at all?" Peter Kelly had boomed so often. "You look pale, Helen my love," Martin must have said a hundred times a year.

But here in the midst of terrible confusion but with the man she loved they all told her she looked blooming and happy. It must prove something.

"It's a very nice place to work, Mr. Millar, and it's great to be in at the start of such new changes with you and Miss Park."

Lena Gray had brightened up their office and their lives. She could see this in their faces and it made her feel better than ever.

The days passed. Sometimes they flew by, and Lena wondered how it could be time to close, she could hardly remember having reached lunchtime. Other days time went so slowly, she wondered was the world coming to an end and had everything slowed down. She roamed the secondhand shops and auction rooms of London and found wonderful wall hangings and Indian bedspreads to drape the shabby furniture in the flat. She bought a briefcase, a leather one with brass locks, for Louis. She polished it until it shone.

"Not really essential for a hall porter," he said ruefully.

"Come on out of that. How many times have they asked you to do night manager? Your portering days are drawing to a close."

And indeed they did.

Soon Louis was working on the night desk three times a week. And it didn't seem fitting for the guests to meet someone they had known in the administration to appear carrying their bags.

One evening Lena went with him to see where he worked.

"I can imagine you much better if I see it," she said.

He hadn't wanted it at first. "It's very hard to explain why . . ." he said. "I sort of play a role at work, you know, I'm not my real self."

"Neither am I," Lena agreed.

And he had let her come.

208

Mr. Williams, the manager, had been impressed with the handsome dark-haired woman the Irishman had produced. "No wonder he had been keeping you hidden," Mr. Williams said.

Lena knew just how to reply. "Ah, that's very flattering of you, Mr. Williams, but it's all my fault. I'm still so unfamiliar with London . . ." She was throwing herself on his mercy, saying she was a country person who didn't understand the big city.

Not flirting, that would have been crass.

It was exactly the right course to have taken. Mr. Williams, a large bluff man, became protective and gallant. "I hope you have both taken to the place. Louis is a very valued employee."

"Oh, we intend to make a good life here, I assure you. London has so much to offer."

"I'm surprised you can leave this attractive wife and work here at night . . ."

Lena spoke quickly. "It wouldn't be my choice, Mr. Williams. But I know that if Louis wants to work his way to working on the desk in the daytime he has to put in his hours at the more antisocial end of things as well." They all smiled. This was not a couple who groaned or complained. But it was a couple who intended to move upward.

It was not long before Louis Gray was offered a position on the desk as an assistant manager. He was unfailingly courteous to those who had worked with him as porters. Particularly the head porter, who had been so difficult when he came first.

The Christmas lights were going up in London.

Lena forced her mind away from the trains of thought that brought her down the road to Hickey's to order the turkey. There would be no decorations above McMahon's pharmacy this year.

As she had guessed, Ivy did not refer to the conversation they had had together on the wet Tuesday night when Lena had decided against ringing Lough Glass. If Ivy understood how strange and hard the decision had been she gave no sign, instead just little gestures of friendship. A pot of homemade jam that someone had given her, a couple of records that she didn't play anymore. Lena knew that these were a gift because she had heard Louis say how much he loved *Singing in the Rain*.

Ivy made no mention of Christmas. She must have known that it would be a time of tension and drama for the young couple on the second floor. Sometimes Lena wondered about the kind of Christmases Louis had spent during the long years of their separation. But part of the promise and the plan had been that they would not talk about the past.

He would not ask about sleeping with her husband. She would not ask him about the times and the people and the places she knew nothing of.

It worked very well. They had their own little world. Sometimes he came to Sunday Mass with her, sometimes not. It was easier when he didn't go with her, then she could buy the paper and read about what was happening in Lough Glass and the places for fifty miles around it. She read of land bought and sold — of children born, of people buried.

And on Sunday, December 21st, when she went to the big church in Quex Road, Kilburn, to pray that God would help her sort out how to make Christmas a good Christmas for Louis and herself, Lena made a deal with God. She said to him that he had always loved sinners, and shown them mercy and that if her only sin had been to run away with Louis, then God might see it with a more forgiving eye.

"So," Lena said, "I don't cheat, I don't steal, I don't lie, apart from the one big one that we are husband and wife. I don't say bad things about people, I don't blaspheme, I don't miss Mass." She had no way of knowing if God went along with the deal. But then, even if you weren't living in mortal sin you often didn't know whether God was going along with the deal either. You had to try and interpret his answers in your heart. It was hard to interpret sometimes. Especially in a big strange church with a lot of coughing and sneezing. It was a cold December day.

Lena went to the kiosk and bought the paper that told her of home. She read that her body had been found in the lake. That a verdict of death by misadventure had been returned. And that a large crowd had attended her funeral at the parish church in Lough Glass. Through her tears she saw that the chief mourners had been the late woman's husband, Martin McMahon of the Lough Glass pharmacy, her daughter, Mary Katherine, and her son, Emmet

211

John. Their mother was dead and buried now in the churchyard. Someone else's bones had been found. And identified as hers.

Lena thought suddenly, and knew somehow, God had acted for her. Perhaps he had answered her prayers. Lena had no decision to make now.

Now she could never go home.

CHAPTER FOUR

Lilian Kelly brought up the subject again. "Peter, I wish you'd put it more clearly to Martin. Tell him to bring the lot of them here for their Christmas dinner."

"I suggested it . . ."

"Ah, you only suggested it. Tell them it would be the right thing to do. And that girl of theirs in the kitchen too if he's worried about her. She can help Lizzie here, Lizzie'd be glad of it. They don't want to be sitting looking at each other in that house after all that happened there."

"Nothing happened there, Lilian," Peter Kelly said. He was reading a medical journal as always, and seemed to give little attention to his wife.

Lilian appealed to her sister Maura, who had come to join them for the Christmas holiday. "Come on, Maura. Tell him they can't sit there looking at each other. . . ."

"But they're going to have to sometime," Maura said. "Maybe they should get used to it rather than running away."

Peter looked up, surprised. "That's what Martin said himself."

"Well then." Maura seemed pleased.

In the hotel Dan O'Brien asked Mildred did she think they should ask the McMahons in for their Christmas dinner.

"We don't want to be imposing on them."

"It wouldn't be imposing, it would be a kindness." Dan didn't relish the thought of yet another empty celebration with his wife and son, and little conversation. At least the presence of the McMahons might force some talk around his dinner table.

"I think they're going to have their own kind of a meal, you know, to make things seem normal," Philip suggested. He too would have loved Kit sitting at his table and to have stood to serve her, but he knew it wouldn't happen.

"Well, there you are then," said Mildred O'Brien. She had never liked that arty Helen McMahon, and everyone knew that there was something suspicious about her death. Note or no note, there were a lot of people in Lough Glass who thought she had ended her own life.

Mrs. Hanley in the drapery was having severe trouble with her daughter Deirdre. "You want to go where on Christmas Day?" she asked.

"Out for a walk, visiting graves, you know."

"No, I don't know. Whose graves?"

"People who died, Mam. That's what's done on Christmas Day, they go and say prayers for the dear departed."

"You have no dear departed at the moment. Except yourself might be heading that way if you're not careful."

"You're a very selfish, unfeeling person."

"Tell me, who would you pray for if you went out on Christmas Day . . . just one."

"Well, I could pray up at the graveyard for Stevie Sullivan's father."

"He's not buried there, he's buried in a madhouse thirty miles away!" Deirdre Hanley's mother was triumphant.

"Well, for Kit McMahon's mother."

"She's barely buried. Come on out of that, Deirdre, you want to go out to get up to no good with someone, and when I find out who it is there'll be trouble, I tell you."

"Who could get up to no good in this town?" Deirdre asked with a sigh.

"You could. And I have my eye on you. Is it that young fellow, Dan O'Brien's son?"

"Philip O'Brien!" There was genuine horror and revulsion in Deirdre Hanley's voice. "Philip. He's a child, an awful child."

Mrs. Hanley knew she had to look elsewhere for the suspect.

Sister Madeleine refused invitations for Christmas Day, but it was said that she had more on her table than most of the people in Lough Glass. They tactfully found out what others were bringing so that items would not be duplicated.

Rita said she'd just take her a loaf of bread. "At least I know you'll eat that. You'll be giving the plum pudding to the gypsies and the slices of turkey to the little fox or whatever you have nowadays."

"I have a big lame goose," said Sister Madeleine. "And it would be very undiplomatic of me to feed her something as nearly related as a turkey. But you're right, I love the bread."

215

"It'll be very hard above in the house there on Thursday," Rita said.

"No harder than any other day." Sister Madeleine was surprisingly unsympathetic.

"But you know, thinking back on other Christmas Days . . ."

"It's better that she's safely buried. It does give people a sort of peace, you know."

"Would you mind where you were buried yourself, Sister Madeleine?"

"No, not at all. But then, I'm as odd as two left shoes. You know that."

"Is there anything I should do, do you think?"

"No, I don't believe in putting on an act. Whatever's going to happen will happen."

"I wish they'd talk about her."

"They might at Christmas."

א א א

"Brother Healy! Always good to see you. They tell me that the Christmas Crib down at St. John's has to be seen to be believed." Mother Bernard was loftily gracious.

"All the work of that young criminal Kevin Wall. Apparently the hermit gave him greenery and hay and all kinds of things. The Lord moves in mysterious ways, Mother Bernard."

"And isn't it a good thing that the Lord directed them where to land the body of poor Helen McMahon in time to have her buried in holy ground before Christmas." The nun spoke as if it were another tiresome problem that God had conveniently tidied up and got out of the way

216

before the Christmas season.

But Brother Healy knew what she meant. "Lord have mercy on her. It was indeed," he said. Teachers hear more than they are meant to, and he had heard a lot of speculation, mainly in the schoolyard.

There was some complicated story that young Wall had taken out the McMahons' boat and that this meant that Emmet's mother had not drowned from it. And then there were rumors that she might have been having a romance with one of the gypsies. Maybe she had run away with him. Or they were hiding her in their caravans.

Nothing you'd want to burden Sean O'Connor with up at the Garda station, but all the same, it was great when that body had been found. Mother Bernard was right, it had been good of the Lord to direct them to land Helen McMahon and finish her troubled life off as every life should be finished, with hymns being sung and Father Baily accompanying the coffin to the churchyard.

"What does Emmet think about Santa Claus?" Clio asked on Christmas Eve.

"He thinks like we all think."

"No, I mean would he be expecting something . . . your father mightn't remember."

"It was always Mam that did it." Kit was defensive in the recall of her mother's good deeds.

"Oh!" Clio was surprised.

"It's all right. He knows, but I'll do it for him anyway. Something beside the chimney."

"And who'll do it for you?"

"Dad might leave me some soap from the

chemist's." She sounded doubtful.

There were so many things that Mother used to do, things that everyone took for granted. At Christmastime she used to fill the house with holly boughs; Father used to laugh and say it was like living in a forest. He would never say that again. Mother used to go to town and buy presents ages before Christmas and there was never a trace of them around the house. Kit still didn't know how she had got the bicycles home with her the year of the bikes, or how she had hidden the record player last year. Was it only last year when everything had been all right?

And Mother knew the right kind of clothes to get Rita, always something brand-new in a box from the big town. Kit and Father wouldn't even know what size Rita was and couldn't go looking or measuring or anything. Mother always had boxes of crackers stored somewhere, and long paper chains that crisscrossed the kitchen. Kit wondered should they look for them. They weren't in the kitchen cupboards; perhaps they were in Mother's room, her little secret surprise.

But they were in mourning, maybe they wouldn't have a Christmas tree even. They would have to have a crib, with the straw in it. That hadn't to do with celebrating, that had to do with welcoming baby Jesus. Kit sighed with the weary burden of it all.

Clio thought it was still about the Christmas stockings. "We could do them for you, you know, my mother and father could. They'd be glad to do something," Clio said, her eyes full of tears.

Kit shook her head. "No, I'll manage it, thanks

very much all the same. The Santa Claus bit isn't the worst bit, let me tell you."

"What is the worst bit?"

"She won't know how I turn out. She'll never know."

"She'll know from heaven."

"Yes," Kit said. The silence lay between them. Despite the comforting words that Father Baily had intoned over the coffin, Kit knew that her mother had not been met by the angels and led into Paradise. She had committed the great sin against Hope, for which there is no forgiveness.

Kit's mother was in hell.

"Christmas Eve can be hell on earth," Ivy said to Lena. "Everyone running round doing their last-minute shopping. It's as if Christmas comes on people by surprise, as if they hadn't known for weeks it was on its way."

"We work until lunchtime . . . though I don't know why. Nobody wants to come to look for a job on Christmas Eve."

"Probably Mr. Millar and Jessie Park have nowhere to go," Ivy said shrewdly.

"I'm sure you're right." Lena realized that this was indeed true.

Some people's lives just revolved around their work. In the hotel where Louis worked they stayed open for Christmas mainly because the staff had nowhere else to go. Mr. Williams had told them there would be a big staff meal at four o'clock. He would be honored if Lena would join them. It had indeed been an answer to all her problems. There would be no false re-creating of a Christmas scene for the two of them. The flat had been nicely decorated but it would make things much easier for her if they had a duty dinner to attend.

"And what will you do for the day?" Lena looked into Ivy's face as she spoke and she knew the other woman was lying.

"Oh, don't let me begin. I have to go here, there, and everywhere. I'm like a doctor on Christmas Day . . . too many obligations from the past."

Lena nodded sympathetically. It was better that way.

א א א

"Isn't this a barbarous country that they don't open the pubs on Christmas Day?" Peter Kelly said to Kit's father as they all walked home from Mass.

"Aren't you the one who's always saying it's the number of pubs that has us in the state we're in, as a nation."

"Ah yes, but that's a different argument entirely."

"Would you like to come in then and have something sociable?" Kit thought her father looked wretched. A morning of having people sympathize all over again had taken its toll.

Dr. Kelly seemed to sense this too. "Not at all. You've enough of chat, go back to the family."

"Yes." The word hung there, empty and sad.

They took off their coats and blew on their fingers.

"That smells very nice, Rita."

"Thank you, sir."

They sat down together the four of them, as they had done since Helen had left that day two months before. Martin sat in the seat that Helen had used, and Kit had moved to her father's place. Emmet had moved up one, and Rita sat in the place that Emmet used to have.

When Helen McMahon had been alive they still ate in the kitchen, but Rita had taken her meal at the end of the table, or sometimes she had just served and eaten her own meal later. It might appear that the departure of the mistress had somehow equalized things more, had done away with the class distinctions, but this was not Mother's fault, and Kit wanted that known, defined in some way.

"You could always have had your Christmas dinner with us, Rita, do you know that? I mean, it was just that you'd be standing up, making gravy and everything . . ."

"Of course I know that," Rita said.

"Rita doesn't need to be told such a thing." Her father sounded sharp.

"But Daddy, in a way people have to say things. Sister Madeleine says that we don't often say the most important things, we say little silly ones."

"True for her, true for her," Father nodded. He looked very old, Kit thought. He nodded like an old man would nod and repeat things. They were silent for a while after that, as if none of them knew what to say.

Rita spoke eventually. "Will I serve it, sir, dish it up for you . . . for us all?"

"Yes, please, Rita. That would be fine." Father's face looked wretched, he had great dark hollows under his eyes. He must not have slept at all last night, remembering, the way they had all remembered all the Christmas Eves before . . . when there was so much to do. This one had seemed unbearably long.

"Well, we have grapefruit first," Rita said. "The mistress taught me to cut it with a jagged edge, you see, so that it looks a bit like an ornament or something . . . and to put a glacé cherry on top of each one divided into four like a flower, and a bit of angelica pretending to be the stem of the flower. . . . The mistress said it didn't hurt to make things look nice . . . presentation was what she called it."

They all studied the grapefruit, trying to think of something to say about it.

There was a lump in Kit's throat. "No one else in Lough Glass or anywhere else would be having anything as nice as this," she said in a voice that sounded unnatural in her own ears. It was as if she were reading lines from a play.

"Oh, that's right, that's right," her father said. "Nobody else would have a dinner like this, we always said so . . ." He didn't quite finish the sentence because it was obvious that he realized that nobody else was having a dinner under such circumstances. Everywhere else behind the closed curtains of Lough Glass people were eating and drinking . . . they were planning an afternoon laughing or arguing or sleeping in front of the fire. They weren't sitting bolt-upright, trying to swallow sections of a grapefruit so bitter it stuck on their tongues and made their eyes water again.

And when the turkey came to the table they all looked away from Father's face. Mother used to say that it was well he had chosen to be a chemist and not a surgeon or the population here would have been wiped out. Mother had taught herself to carve, and did it deftly. Rita had not liked to usurp her position.

"Isn't this grand?" Father said with a death's-head grin on his face, trying to cheer them up. "This is the grandest turkey we ever had." They said that every year too, and talked about the Hickey family going to the turkey market five miles away and picking the best, the plumpest and younger birds. There was a silence. "Isn't it grand, Emmet?" Poor Father was waving the carving knife, trying to smile and spread cheer. He didn't realize he looked like a butcherous murderer in a film, or in one of the mobile theatres that came to the town every two years.

Emmet looked at him mutely.

"Say something, lad, your mother wouldn't want you to be moping there and all of you sitting in silence, she'd like there to be a bit of chat. It's Christmas Day, and we're all here and you have the memory of a great mother to keep with you for the rest of your lives. Isn't that grand?"

Emmet looked at his father's red face. "It's not grand at all, Daddy," he said. "It's t-t-t-t-errible." His stutter was as bad as it had ever been before.

"We have to pretend that things are all right, Emmet son," he said. "Don't we, Kit? Don't we, Rita?"

They looked at him wordlessly.

Then Kit said, "Mother wouldn't pretend. I don't think she'd have said things were grand if they weren't."

They could hear the clock on the landing ticking. In other houses people would barely hear a word anyone else was saying, but in this house they could hear the purring of the old cat, the ticking of a clock, and the gurgling sounds of saucepans still simmering on the Aga cooker beside them.

Father's face was grim, gray and grim. Kit looked at him in anguish. Father must still be turning in his bed at night wondering why Mother had left that night and got drowned.

For the hundredth time she wondered if she had done the right thing in burning that letter. And yet again she told herself that she had. Think of what would have happened when Mother's body had been found if her daughter had not acted in the way she had. And Father must have heard too the story that fool Kevin Wall had told about how he took the McMahon boat out on the night that Mother had drowned. As if anyone would believe Kevin Wall even if he told you today was Christmas Day.

Father was speaking again. "I'm going to start by telling the truth just like your mother did . . ." His voice broke. "And the truth is that it's *not* all right," he said through his tears. "It's terrible. I miss her so much I can't be comforted by the thought of seeing her in heaven later on. I'm so lonely for her . . ." His shoulders heaved. The mood changed. Kit and Emmet left their places to go and put their arms around him. They crowded together for what seemed a long time. Rita sat at her place. She was like the background. Like the kitchen curtains, like old Farouk asleep on the stool beside the Aga. Like the gray wet rain outside.

And then they stopped, and it was as if a thunderstorm had cleared the air. They spoke with lighter voices; the tightrope of pretense had been taken away. Wasn't it extraordinary that Sister Madeleine had more or less foretold to her that this would happen?

Into the midst of this came a sharp shrill sound. It was the telephone ringing. On Christmas Day, a day when nobody made any calls except for an emergency.

א   א   א

In the Dryden Hotel they made a great effort to have a cheerful Christmas for the staff. A lot of them had been there a long time, most had weathered the war years with loyalty, and as James Williams knew there were many who had no real homes to go to.

A Christmas tree that had been set up in the hall to establish a festive mood for guests was now in the dining room, and everyone had a role, including spouses. Lena's job was to do place cards.

Louis gave her the list. "They want artistic writ-

225

ing," he explained. "It's a mad idea, but you did volunteer."

"No, I think it's a good idea. It'll be a souvenir of the day," she said. She asked him to bring her a sheaf of Dryden Hotel notepaper, so that she could stick the name on top of each card. "It's more like an invitation then," she said, and painstakingly wrote out the names. Barry Jones, Antonio Bari, Michael Kelly, Gladys Wood . . . Each one with great attention and little holly leaves and berries drawn as a border.

At the start they were shy, awkward to be allowed sit down at the tables instead of serving at them or sweeping up under them. But James Williams kept circulating with the bowl of punch and soon the inhibitions went. By the time they were carving the turkey some of them had already pulled the Christmas crackers which were meant for the plum pudding stage. There was a roar of conversation from the twenty-nine strangely assorted people sitting around the table.

Lena slipped away to the ladies' room and just beside the door she saw the little booth for the telephone. It was five-thirty in the afternoon. This time last year she had been down by the lake with the children, walking off the effects of the dinner. That's what she would have called it, but escaping the stifling walls of the house is what it would have been. Martin had looked at her eagerly, but she had advised him to have a little sleep by the fire. At the time she had felt guilty denying her husband the simple pleasure of a walk with his own wife on Christmas Day.

Now she felt no pity, only rage with the man

226

she had begged to play fair. If it had not been for Martin she could have spoken to Kit and to Emmet this Christmas, sent them presents, told them that she loved them, planned for them to come and see her at Easter.

Anger rose in her throat. She could feel it. Before she realized what she was doing she was in the phone box and dialing the operator. She gave the number and waited.

The operator came back. "It appears that Lough Glass is a small place, caller, with a manual exchange. Unless the call is in the nature of an emergency it cannot be put through on Christmas Day."

"It is an emergency," she said in a tight voice.

She heard the clicks and the sounds as the phone rang in the post office on the corner of Lakeview Road and the main street. It seemed to ring endlessly. Lena wondered that Mrs. Hanley next door hadn't come in and answered it. She was as nosy as anyone in the town, surely she wondered who could be ringing for what emergency.

But eventually the slow feet of Mona Fitz must have moved themselves to the phone. Lena heard her halting voice and the sense of outrage that she had been woken from her sleep.

The number of the house was given.

"It's only emergency calls on Christmas Day," Mona said.

Lena clenched her fists with impatience. What trouble was it to the stupid woman just to plug the bloody piece of equipment into one of the row of holes in front of her. She could have it done and finished with by the time she went into all this tiresome explanation and cross-questioning.

"That's what the caller says; it is an emergency."

"Very well, so."

Lena could imagine her putting on her glasses to direct the call a few yards down the street.

A few rings and she heard Martin reply. "Hallo," he said, his voice hesitant and doubtful. Did he know that she would ring on Christmas Day? That he couldn't keep her from her children forever just by pretending she was dead. Was he frightened now, and in an agony wondering how he was going to explain the whole terrible mess that he had created? "Hallo," Martin said again. "Who's that?"

The whole terrible mess. It could be undone in a moment. But so would Lena's life. The life that had only just begun. She said nothing and clicked the bar in the cradle that held the receiver. She could hear the operator in London saying, "Are you there, caller? Your number has been reached . . ."

She could hear Mona Fitz saying, "What kind of an emergency call is this if there's no one on the line?"

She heard Martin saying, "Hallo. Hallo. Who is it?"

Then Mona spoke to Martin. "I wouldn't have had this happen for the world, Martin, but it's a man from England, from London. They said it was an emergency."

"A man . . . ?" Martin sounded startled, but

not guilty. He didn't sound like a man who was trying to hush everything up. But then she didn't know him at all.

"No, Martin. I think I was only speaking to the operator . . . hold on till I see is he still there . . ."

Lena listened, she heard Martin and Mona and the operator discuss the fact that someone had definitely phoned that number. "It's all right, I have the number the caller was phoning from. I'll get them back," he said.

She hung up, shaking from head to toe. Why had she done anything so stupid? Now they would call the hotel, and ask who had phoned Lough Glass in Ireland. Louis would be furious. The coins in her hand were hot and sweaty.

Then, as she knew it would, the phone rang. She lifted the receiver at the first sound. "Are you trying to call Lough Glass in the Irish Republic?"

"No," Lena said, she tried to put a Cockney accent into her voice.

"But someone from that number was calling Lough Glass . . ."

"No, I said I was calling *Loughrea* . . ." she said.

The operator got back to the others. "It was the wrong place," he said.

"I don't know how you mixed up Lough Glass and Loughrea," Mona grumbled.

"That's all right then," said Martin.

"Caller, do you want to give me the Loughrea number then . . . ?" The operator was a man who had to work on Christmas Day and did not

229

seem to be enjoying it.

Lena said nothing. In the background she heard the voice of her daughter asking who was on the phone.

"It's nothing, Kit. It's someone trying to phone Loughrea." She couldn't hear what Kit said, but whatever it was Martin laughed. Had she said "That's a roundabout way to do it?"

"Caller?" The operator was impatient now.

"Listen, I've changed my mind, it's too late," she said.

"Thanks a million," said the young man.

"So I'll hang up now." Lena was anxious that there should be no further checking on the number.

"Yes, madam."

"And you are not going to call back?" She wanted to make sure it was safe to leave the booth.

"No, madam. Good-bye, madam." She stood in the box feeling dizzy. She hadn't been buried a month and her daughter was still able to laugh about things. She took deep breaths until she had the strength to walk back to the festivities.

"Are you all right?" It was James Williams who asked the question. "You've been gone a long time."

"I'm fine. Did I miss anything?" she asked.

Louis was the center of a laughing group. Gladys Wood, whose name she had carefully written out, had a paper hat at a rakish angle, had her arm around Louis's neck.

"Read my fortune to me again," she shouted happily.

"It says you will meet a dark handsome man," Louis read obediently from the little piece of paper that Gladys had found in her Christmas cracker.

"I've met him," screamed Gladys.

"Oh dear," whispered James Williams. His benevolent smile of the owner glad to see the staff enjoying themselves was a little strained.

"A little overexcited." Lena was amazed at her own power of speech. She had thought that after the incident on the telephone she might not be able to talk at all.

"For three hundred and sixty-four days a year that woman works in the still room, quiet as a mouse. Christmas, regular as clockwork, she gets drunk. And spends the rest of the year apologizing for it."

"Will she get sick, do you think?" Lena asked, in a detached professional way, as if she were asking the time of a train.

"Very probably, I fear."

"Do you think someone should take her out . . . just in case?" Lena was looking at Louis's jacket. It had been her Christmas present to him, and cost a lot of money. She didn't want to see it ruined.

"Yes, I wonder could I prevail on you . . ."

"Well, I don't think I am exactly the person who should approach her . . . after all, it is my husband she is manhandling. Perhaps it might be thought I had a special interest in seeing her escorted from the room."

"You are truly wonderful, Mrs. Gray," he said, flicking his fingers for Eric, the head porter.

"Lena," she corrected him.

"Lena," he smiled, and ordered Eric to get one of the girls to march Miss Wood out to the ladies' room and to stay with her. Right now.

Louis ran his finger around his collar and smiled at them ruefully.

He could have escaped earlier, Lena thought with a flash of annoyance. But then, women always went for Louis, he was used to it. It made him smile, and she had to remember to smile about it too.

א א א

"What are you going to make as a New Year resolution?" Clio was eager to know.

"I haven't thought, what with everything."

Clio had thought. "I'm going to get good-looking, really good-looking, mind."

"But you are good-looking, aren't you?"

"No I'm not. I'm going to read books and look at what beautiful people get themselves up like."

"Do you mean clothes? We haven't any money for clothes."

"No. Just their faces, their way of going on."

"We're not allowed to wear makeup."

"Well, we could put Vaseline on our eyelashes. It makes them grow. And I think we should suck in our cheeks a bit to give us interesting shapes in our faces," said Clio.

They puckered their faces in and laughed at the results.

"There must be more to it than that," Kit said. "It looks as if we're going to kiss someone."

"You could kiss Philip O'Brien; he's always ogling you . . ."

"And who could you kiss?"

"Stevie Sullivan maybe." Clio smiled archly.

"But isn't he always kissing Deirdre Hanley?" Kit was surprised that Clio should choose someone so busy.

"She's old. She'll go off in looks, men often turn to younger women."

"She's only seventeen."

"Yes, well. In 1953 she'll be eighteen and she'll go on and on, just getting older."

"Do you like Stevie . . . ?"

"No. But he's good-looking."

"And is Philip O'Brien good-looking?"

"No, but he's keen on you." Clio had the world sorted out.

There was snow in January. Anna Kelly threw a snowball at Emmet McMahon. In the time-honored ritual he scooped a handful of snow and pushed it down her neck as she screamed with excitement. He laughed too.

"Are you over it now?" Anna asked.

"Over it?"

"Your mammy being dead?"

"No, I'm not over it. I've sort of got used to it, I suppose."

"Can I play with you and Kevin Wall?" she asked.

"No, Anna. I'm sorry, but you're a girl."

"But that's not fair."

"It's the way it is." Emmet was philosophical.

"Kit and Clio won't let me play with them, they're girls."

"But they're old girls."

"Are they horrible to you like they are to me?" Anna hoped Emmet was a victim too.

"No, they're not horrible at all."

"I wish I was really really old. Like twenty. Then I'd know what to do."

"What would you do?" Emmet was interested.

Anna was a funny little thing in her scarlet coat and pixie hood and red excited face. "I'd come back here and take Clio and Kit out on the lake and hold them both under the water and drown them," she said triumphantly. Then she remembered. "Oh Emmet," she said. Emmet said nothing. "Emmet, I'm so sorry."

He was walking away. Anna ran after him. "I'm so stupid. That's why nobody will play with me. I just want you to know I forgot. That's all. I just forgot."

Emmet turned. "Yes, well. It was my mother and I didn't forget." He began to stammer at the words "forget" and "mother." Anna had tears running down her face.

At that moment Stevie Sullivan came out of his garage. "Hey, leave her alone, Emmet. She's only a baby. Don't make her cry."

Emmet turned on his heel and went into his house.

Anna turned her tear-stained face to Stevie. "I have no friends," she said.

"Yeah, that's a problem," said Stevie, looking idly down the road toward Hanley's Drapery in case he might catch sight of his enthusiastic friend Deirdre taking a little stroll down the snow-covered street of Lough Glass with plans for another meeting.

א א א

James Williams took a personal interest in training Louis Gray to be the person that most customers met first when they arrived at the Dryden. He made sure that the handsome Irishman was well dressed and smartly turned out.

"I can get my shirts done in the hotel laundry," Louis told Lena proudly. "That'll save you washing and ironing."

It certainly saved time and space. But in a way she had enjoyed doing it for him. It was part of playing husband and wife. Back in Lough Glass she had never done the ironing. Rita had done it as a matter of course. Sometimes now she wondered how had she spent her days in a home where she had no role.

And Louis told of more and more successes.

This was a place and a time where people just wanted proof that you could do a job and had the ability to get on with others. The war had changed everything. There was no need for written certificates and coming up through some traditional profession.

Lena knew that Louis was not exaggerating when he said that being on that desk was being at the heart of the whole hotel. Everyone in the Dryden had to consult him about some aspect of the way the place ran. The housekeeper and the chambermaids checked about the times that the different rooms should be made up. He would talk to the chef about the possibility of placing a copy of the menu on a stand in the hall. This way when visitors were going out they might be persuaded to come back again for their lunch.

It was Louis who suggested that the porters wear name badges.

"I know who I am, thank you," said Eric, the head porter, who had always regretted having allowed Louis to be taken on and to rise so far above him.

Louis never acknowledged any resentment. Perhaps he didn't even see it. "Of course you do, Eric. And so do the regulars. But what about the Americans? They'll want to know the name of the good guy who welcomed them to the Dryden."

Eric saw the reason for it, but did not notice any increase in his tips. In fact, most of the dollars that changed hands went toward Louis Gray. Americans did appreciate the personal service, the way he remembered their names, how he could give them good suggestions of where to go and how to spend their holidays.

Nobody ever called Louis a manager, he was Mr. Gray-on-the-desk. People were urged to consult him on everything and Louis never let them down.

"I'd never get another job nearly as good as this. I must make myself as indispensable as I can possibly be here," he said, and Lena knew he was right. Not even the most glowing reference would give Louis an entree to any similar position at another hotel. He had no written qualifications, but he would always get by on charm once installed.

Her mind went sometimes to his previous lives in Spain, in Greece. Even back in his early days in Dublin as a traveling salesman, which was how she had met him first, he was never impatient with people or seeming anxious to be out of their company but always restless to do more or get more out of whatever was going. That was an extraordinary mixture in one man. He looked so alive with the lopsided small-boy smile.

Month by month his wages increased and so did his perks, a lot of this due to Lena. She had seen that there was a small storeroom behind the front desk. Little by little the place was transformed. All the old boxes, broken bicycles, and legless chairs were moved out. In their place came old tables beginning to show too much wear in bedrooms or reception rooms. Louis found an old umbrella stand and a row of brass coat hooks on a mahogany stand. No longer did he have to put his coat in the crowded area where staff garments were pushed. And yet no one could question it. He was giving himself no lordly airs. He was only taking over a disused room. Making the place tidier in fact.

Louis noted with pleasure that people who were senior to him in status in the hotel took him very seriously, but he moved cautiously.

"I can't just go in there to that room and close the door, when I'm meant to be on the desk," he said to Lena.

"Have you any friend in maintenance, some-one who could put a pane of glass in the top of it? Like Ivy's door. You could even have a curtain, a net curtain. Then you could see when you were wanted outside. It would give you the option of being in or out."

And it worked.

James Williams, if he noticed the expansionist tendencies of the new clerk on the desk, must have approved of them because nothing was said. And no one entered Louis Gray's territory with-out knocking.

The months passed. Their love grew stronger. Lena was sure of that. There was nothing they could not talk about. They spoke of her children and how she had done the best thing for them. He praised her for her courage. "You're like a heroine, a real-life heroine," he would tell her. And he meant it, as he stroked her hair and took her face in his hands he said that she was like a lioness, that there was nothing she could not do.

Sometimes Lena wondered whether there might be other people in London living new lives like she was. Perhaps there were hundreds and thousands of them, people who left one way of living and took up another. It wasn't as hard as it sounded. After all here she was with a new husband . . . in the eyes of the world anyway . . . a new home, a new job, a new look. Few people from Lough Glass would recognize the tailored trim figure hastening through the streets of London as Helen McMahon, wife of Martin the cheerful local chemist. If they saw her bending over files and encouraging young applicants for jobs in large companies they would be amazed. Mrs. McMahon, so private a person, someone who didn't engage in long chats yet here she was urging these girls to make the best of themselves, telling them the sky was the limit, begging them to take more night classes, increase their speeds, improve their image. How would Mrs. McMahon of Lough Glass know such things and get people to believe her?

When she looked back on her life there, thirteen years of living in the small community by the lake, Lena realized that there was so much she *could* have done. She could have suggested that she work with Mrs. Hanley and brighten up her dowdy shop, get in the kinds of clothes that the women of Lough Glass would have enjoyed wearing, colorful garments for the children . . . she would have suggested training one of the Hanley daughters as a dressmaker so that alterations could be done on the premises.

Or Mildred O'Brien in the hotel? Look at all the things she could have done to help the Central Hotel out of the last century, things that she was doing now with Louis for the Dryden.

If she had persuaded Martin to let her work in the pharmacy she could have done the kinds of windows and displays she was doing here in an employment agency where there was so little scope. Think what she might have done if she had all those soaps and cosmetics to work on. She could have lined the windows with greenery and draped them with fancy materials and papers so that no one could resist coming in.

But Martin wouldn't hear of it. No wife of mine is going to have to go out to work. He used to say it with his face bursting with pride, as if by standing alone hour after hour in that dreary poky place he was somehow making her into a queen, someone who wouldn't have to raise a hand.

A lot of the time she had felt grateful to him, Martin the undemanding husband who had taken her to a peaceful place by a big beautiful lake when her heart was broken and yearning for Louis who had left her. Martin who had asked her no questions and promised her escape from anxiety and a restful life.

But now she felt totally differently about him. No longer could she see his jokes as kindly meant and his funny faces as loving attempts to entertain her. Now she saw everything about him as a deep and destructive insecurity, a wish to trap her, keep her like a caged bird. A man who could not face up to the fact that his wife had left him for another man, but who had carried on a charade . . . even to the point of getting his friend Peter to identify a totally different body as hers.

What kind of people were these? They were barbarians. She had given birth to two children in a land of barbarians.

Lena ached for her children. Although she talked a little about them to Louis it was only skimming the surface. She could not let him know how large a part of her mind they occupied. Louis was in many ways a child himself . . . he would not want to share this part of her with Kit and Emmet. She loved and needed him so much, it would be an act of folly to weep and cling to him and tell him how much she missed her children. It would be to tell him that he was not enough for her, that the decision to go with him had involved too much sacrifice. And that was not true.

Old Sister Madeleine had once said to her that in the end people do what they want to do. Even not doing something is a decision. So she had decided to leave her children. She must remember that and face it, even though she could not have foreseen that Martin would go through this grotesque charade she had made the choice to leave them. She must have wanted to be with Louis more than with them.

It was a harsh fact to face but Lena felt stronger for admitting it to herself. She must plunge herself into her new life and live it without regret. Live it in as full a way as possible, do all the things that she always had the power to do but never the chance. Sometimes she wondered would they be surprised back in Lough Glass to know just how very much she was doing. And to know that there were not enough hours in the day for all she had to do.

That she was nearly running Millar's Employment Agency on her own. Neither Mr. Millar nor Jessie Park had contributed one single idea to her entire reorganization program. But they were easy to lead and quick to agree that business had doubled. Bigger and more known bureaus had come to have a look at them. There had even been a feature about their new-look offices in a local paper. Lena had kept very much in the background.

"Please, Mrs. Gray, you would be an adornment to the picture," Mr. Millar begged.

Lena had prepared for this. She had given Jessie a voucher to a hairdresser and the loan of a smart jacket to replace the old fuzzy cardigan.

"No, no truly. You are the ones who run it," Lena said, refusing to pose for the press picture.

After all, she was meant to be dead. There was no use having her photograph in a newspaper. Who knew who might see it?

"You're looking pale," Ivy said to her one day.

"I don't know what it is, but I don't feel great certainly," Lena agreed.

"Are you pregnant?" Ivy asked.

"No, not that." Lena spoke sharply.

She saw Ivy look at her thoughtfully. Those small buttons of eyes understood everything. They probably understood that Louis and Lena would not have a child. The matter had been brought up and discussed. But both their careers were starting out so well here. Perhaps they should not think of it for the moment. Lena smiled wryly at the idea of putting things off for the moment. She was thirty-nine years of age. Next year she would be forty. The moment had probably passed already. The child that she had begun to lose in Brighton was her last. The two she had in Ireland were lost to her.

She was a woman with no children.

A career woman, as they were beginning to call themselves in the London of 1953.

"Suppose I were to send you a lot of business, could we come to a deal?" Lena asked Grace at the hairdresser's.

Grace had once come to Millar's, looking for a secretarial job. She was so elegant-looking and had such a way with customers that Lena realized she would be lost in an office. Her sympathetic personality was much more suited to a post where she would meet the public. Grace West, a tall, handsome young woman whose mother was from Trinidad, had been anxious to get what they called an office job. It would be such a step up. She had been doubtful at first about hairdressing. A lot of West Indian girls did that. It wouldn't be seen as a great success.

"Yes, but when you're running the place, then you'll be a success," Lena had said.

Grace did not do people's hair, she made the appointments, she kept the till, she strolled around in her elegant suits, advising and admiring.

"A little more conditioner on Mrs. Jones, I think," she would say. "Why not give Miss Nixon an extra rinse with a little squeeze of fresh lemon?" Customers thought they were getting special attention. They loved it.

"What's the deal?" Grace pretended to be resigned. She was standing behind the chair as Lena got her usual Friday shampoo and set. Only the best hairdresser in the salon was allowed to touch Mrs. Gray's wavy dark hair.

The others didn't see that no money changed hands. Grace knew how to pay her debts. Lena Gray had got her this position by advising her every step of the way. They had almost rehearsed the interview line by line.

"A lot of the girls who come in to us . . . they haven't an idea how to present themselves."

"Who are you telling?" Grace remembered how self-deprecating and humble she had been until Lena taught her how to make her height, her color, and her startling stylish good looks into an asset.

"You were always a looker," Lena said. "No, they come in with frightened faces and no makeup, or else looking like something from a music hall. Suppose I sent you at least ten a week, would you throw in a free makeup lesson as well?"

"Ten a week? You'd never get that." Grace's eyes were wide in disbelief.

"That would be the deal . . . If I get fewer you don't have to give the discount."

"What kind of makeup lesson? In a classroom?"

"No. Just telling them what would suit them. You don't sell them anything, just tell them how to put it on so it doesn't look as if it was laid on with a garden trowel."

Grace laughed. "You have such funny ways of putting things."

"What do you think? Is it worth your while?"

"Of course it is . . . someday when you're famous I'll say that I helped you on in your career, like you did for me."

"Famous. I doubt it."

"I don't. I see that Mr. Millar handing over to you. I see big interviews in the papers . . ." Grace was excited.

"No. I don't see that at all." Lena spoke quietly.

Whatever happened there would be no interviews with her in any paper. Not now.

א א א

Clio was a month older than Kit, so for the whole month of May she was thirteen. "There's many a country I could get married in," she said loftily.

"Ah, wouldn't that be a very foolish thing to do all the same," Sister Madeleine said. They were arranging the blossoms that the girls had brought in a series of jars along the window-sill.

"Isn't it good to get married early?" Clio asked. It seemed to be her one superiority, having reached an age where technically in some faroff land she might be able to be a bride.

"No, not good at all." Sister Madeleine was adamant.

"But if that's what you're going to do eventually, why not do it soon?" Clio asked.

"Because you might marry the wrong person, you eejit," Kit said.

"You could do that anytime," Clio said.

They looked at Sister Madeleine for another view. "It's all a matter of luck anyway," she said, poking.

"Well, of course it was different for you, since you had a vocation. There was no luck about that. You had the call from God," Clio said.

There was a silence.

"Would you like to have been married at all, Sister Madeleine, do you think?" Kit asked.

"Oh I was," Sister Madeleine looked at them with her clear blue eyes, smiling as if they should have known this.

They looked at her openmouthed.

"Married?" said Kit.

"To a man?" asked Clio.

"It was a long time ago," Sister Madeleine said, as if that explained everything. The goose came in the door at that moment, waddling and looking from side to side foolishly. "Well, would you look at Bernadette." Sister Madeleine's face creased into a smile, as if a friend had come in for tea. "You're welcome in, Bernadette. The girls here will get you a bit of cornmeal in a nice dish now."

Clio and Kit would hear no more about Sister Madeleine's marriage.

"She did say married?"

"Yes, I heard her."

"To a man. Not just to Christ or anything."

"No. She agreed with that. She said it was long ago."

They sat down on mossy stone by the lakeside.

"She couldn't have been married. Not sleeping with a man and all."

"Well, she said it, didn't she?"

"I wonder does anyone else know," Clio said.

"I'm not going to tell anyone, are you?" Kit said suddenly.

Clio seemed disappointed. It would have been a great thing to tell.

"She didn't say to keep it a secret."

"No, Clio, but she sort of trusted us, didn't she?"

Clio thought about it. This way there was

some importance attached to the momentous piece of information they had just been given. If they were guardians of a huge and privileged piece of information that no one else knew, then Clio Kelly could just about keep it to herself. "I suppose so."

"Imagine her telling us. You and me," Kit said in wonder.

Clio liked that. "She knows we wouldn't let each other down," she said.

They walked home companionably and came up from the lake by Paddles' bar. Paddles was standing at his door. "When will you ladies be old enough to frequent my premises?" he asked.

They giggled. "Ah, it'll be a few years yet, Paddles," Clio said.

"Well, the place will be honored, Miss Kelly, when you're ready for us."

They clutched each other with laughter the whole way home. Imagine, whatever age you were, wanting to go into Paddles' bar!

"Maybe you could have your thirteenth birthday there. We could send out invitations. Miss Kit McMahon will be launched into society at Paddles' bar on June second 1953."

They laughed so much they had to hold on to the wall of the Central Hotel to stop themselves falling.

"You're having great fun." Philip was very envious.

"We're planning Kit's birthday party," Clio said.

"Are you having a party?" Philip brightened up.

"Of course not. She's in mourning," Clio snapped. "But that's no reason why we couldn't have a laugh over it."

א א א

Everyone in London was getting ready for the Coronation. There would be bunting on the houses in the street. Ivy was getting hers ready. She had had some since the end of the war, kept as a sort of souvenir from the really memorable days down in the King's Head.

"It'll be a great day," she told Lena.

"I suppose so."

"Sorry, I keep forgetting you're not all that interested, being Irish and all."

"No, it's not that. Of course I'm interested. I keep forgetting it . . . I'm working so hard these days."

"Don't I see it. You're home later every night."

"Well, so's Louis . . ."

"Don't work too hard, love." Ivy's face was full of concern.

And she was right, of course. Lena did stay later and later at the agency, writing letters to large companies explaining the kind of screening techniques they used, how Millar's did not just send any applicant for any job. She also had a mailing list of schools and secretarial colleges. A Millar's girl would get much more than a list of job opportunities. She would get career advice and more intelligent women would assess her potential, giving young applicants the necessary confidence to prepare them for interviews and for their early working careers.

Mention was made of the low-price hairdressing and makeup services and of the fashion suggestions. Business was increasing at a great rate. Mr. Millar had doubled her salary in six months. Lena had insisted on a similar rise for Jessie Park.

"We're a team, Mr. Millar. I couldn't work without Jessie," she had said.

Mr. Millar's eyes were sharp. He saw the changed image and new confidence of Miss Park, who had been the most mouselike of employees. If Lena Gray could do this for the woman that she had outstripped a hundredfold and still remain loyal and supportive, then she was indeed a treasure and must be humored. Anyway, profits were looking very good. He could afford to pay Jessie as well.

He had met Mrs. Gray's husband once, a strikingly handsome Irishman. A hotel manager, it appeared. She was very quiet and uninformative about her private life. Which made a refreshing change to the daily detail they got from Jessie Park.

"Mr. Millar," Lena said. "Miss Park and I were wondering should we do a special window display for the Coronation?"

"But what would we say in our window?"

Jessie looked at them eagerly. Jessie didn't look so hopeless these days, she had a smartly fastened blouse with the modern cameo brooch. Instead of a picture it said "Millar's" in the blue and gold which had become the company colors.

The cushions on the new chairs were blue and

gold, as was the decoration on their stationery, the fresh paint on the exterior, the frames for the pictures on the walls. Jessie used to wear floppy open-necked blouses until Lena had thought up this smart new uniform for them . . . a white blouse, a blue skirt, and a gold-looking scarf. Jessie's new hairstyle and the occasional application of makeup had transformed her.

Lena had even suggested that with an increased wage packet Jessie might pay someone to look after her mother on an occasional evening, and she could get accustomed to having some free time. It was such a relief to hear Jessie talking about how much she had enjoyed *Singing in the Rain*. Lena and Mr. Millar would have listened to every song and every line of the dialogue over and over rather than revert to Mrs. Park's eating difficulties.

The old Jessie would have agreed with Mr. Millar that she didn't know she was sure, but today Jessie spoke up. "In a way, Mr. Millar, our very colors are royal, you know. A nice blue and gold display in the window, with a picture of the new Queen . . ."

"Yes, that's a great idea," Lena said. "We could put something like 'Welcome to a New Elizabethan Age . . . from Millar's, who look to a great future for all of us.' "

They loved it. They were so excited. A lump came to Lena's throat at their eagerness. Are the English much more simple and less critical than the Irish? Or was it that she had never been able to play any part in the town where she had withered away for thirteen years?

"Do you think they should get a television in the hotel for the Coronation?" Louis asked.

"You mean they haven't got one? Not one in the whole place?"

"No. It sort of prides itself on being quiet."

"It'll pride itself on being empty before long." He looked at her in surprise. This wasn't the usual way Lena spoke. It was too sharp.

"Very well. I'll know not to ask in future," Louis said. He had a funny tight look around his lips.

"Louis!" she cried in alarm. "Oh Louis, please don't sulk."

"Sulk? Me! I'm not sulking. You're the one who bit the head off me." He was really hurt.

"I'm sorry. It's all my fault." There was a silence. "Louis, I had a rotten day."

"Mine wasn't great either."

She reached for him, but he pulled away. "Louis, please talk to me about the television set. I'm very interested, honestly. Truly, truly I am." She was beseeching him now.

"No, Helena. It's all right. This time the Dryden Hotel will have to manage without your advice."

She pleaded with him again. "I spoke quickly. I'm sorry. You often do too when you're tired. It doesn't mean anything, not between us. Does it?"

"No. Of course not." He was frosty.

She bit her lip. She would do whatever it took to get him back to the way he had been before she had so stupidly snapped at him. Did it need

251

more apology or was it better to change the subject? She decided to move on. "We've been having all kinds of debates about how to celebrate the day, too," she began cheerfully.

"How interesting." Louis spoke with a deliberate sneer. She had never seen his face curl up like that.

"Love?" She felt her face redden.

"No, go on. Tell me more tales of Mr. Millar and Jessie Park. I mean, these are really interesting people now. Not just dross like the poor fools that try to earn a living in the Dryden Hotel."

"I must have sounded sharper than I meant to. I can't tell you how sorry I am." Lena hung her head.

She hoped he would come over and put his arms around her, say that it didn't matter, that they were both overtired. Maybe he might say they would go out to the little Italian restaurant and they would be closer because of it. But he was a long time coming over to her and she began to doubt that this would happen.

She heard his hand on the door handle and looked up. "Where are you going, Louis?" she asked.

"Out."

"But where out?"

"You told me, Helena, that the thing that drove you mad all those years in Lough Glass was when people kept asking you where you were going. Just out. Isn't that enough?"

"No, it's not enough. We love each other . . . don't go."

"We don't want to stifle each other."

"I won't stifle you. Please." She was begging now.

Had Martin begged her this way? Louis came toward her and took both her hands in his. "Listen, my love. We're annoyed with each other. Let's cool off."

"Let me go out too if you want to. That's what grown-ups do. We're grown-ups, remember."

His smile was so loving, so much part of him . . . it almost hurt her to see it. She felt almost paralyzed. Did she want to flounce out before him? Could she plead with him once more? She said nothing. Not a word. He released her hands, and she heard the door close behind him. She would not cry. She would not go down to Ivy for consolation. But she would go out.

She bought an apple and a piece of cheese at the corner shop, and walked on toward Millar's Employment Agency. She let herself in, and looked around her with pleasure. This at least had been an achievement, something to show for her months in London. The little glass-covered notice board with carefully edited letters from satisfied customers, the blue and gold motif everywhere . . . the cushions covered by Jessie's mother who had now found a role in life, the gold-painted tray with the blue mugs where coffee was served to all who came in.

Lena sat down at her desk and took out her files. Exactly what she needed. A few hours on her own to sort things through. This was the time she hardly ever had to herself, so anxious was she to run home and have everything ready for Louis.

Louis. She would not think about him because it made her shake with rage at the injustice of it all.

The time flew past. She could hardly believe that it was eleven. She felt her heart jump. This was later than she had intended to stay. He would be long home by now, and there might be more words if she were to say she had gone in to the agency. But she couldn't pretend to have been wandering around London on her own all this time.

As she ran up the stairs she rehearsed what she would say, but first she would see what mood he was in. That was the secret. Respond to him, react, don't fire off herself. She opened the door and the flat was empty. Louis had not come back yet. When he'd said he was going out, he'd meant it.

Her eyes were closed when he came in, but she was wide-awake. It was twenty past three. He slipped quietly into the bed beside her. He did not reach for her, which was his automatic gesture whenever he got into bed.

Where could he have been until this time in the morning? He was too proud to go back to his place of work, he wouldn't have gone back to catch up on things like Lena had done. Which meant that he must have been in someone's house. Someone he knew well enough to entertain him until all hours in the morning. She made her breathing sound even, as if she were asleep.

Lena Gray could swear that she slept not a wink that night.

Her head was full of pictures, but none of them were dreams. She pictured her daughter Kit. It would be her birthday on June 2nd, the day of the Coronation. She would be thirteen years of age, a girl whose mother was dead. If only she had been able to write to her even. Suppose Martin had let them think that she was far away and never coming back, but that she could still write them letters.

And as the light came up on London, and the yellow blinds on their window started to turn a pale color rather than seeming black like the night, Lena knew that was what she would do. She would write a letter to her daughter. Pretending to be someone else. The thought of it made her feel exhilarated. Nobody seeing her get up and dress would have thought that this was a woman who had not slept all night. Louis was surprised, she could see that.

"Less angry with the world today?" he asked, head on one side, waiting for her to apologize yet again. But he got no apology.

"Weren't we like a pair of Kilkenny cats last night?" she said, marveling at it.

Louis paused. This wasn't what he had expected. "What made us like that do you think?"

"As you said, crowding each other out." She was anxious to be gone, it was written all over her.

So now naturally he wanted her to stay. "I didn't mean that it was bad crowding out," he

255

began. It was as near to a climb-down as she would get.

"No, no. Of course not. See you this evening . . ."

"I didn't wake you when I came back."

"Lord no. I was asleep. Out like a light." She kissed him quickly on the forehead, and he pulled her back to his lap.

"We don't kiss like that. That's for old people."

"True, true," she laughed, and responded to him, but she pulled away firmly. "Let's not start anything we can't continue . . . see you tonight, hey? hey?" She laughed at him suggestively.

"You're a terrible tease," he said.

They were happy again. But it wasn't at the forefront of her mind. Her brain was racing with ways she could write to her daughter.

Mr. Millar was at work before her.

"You remind me of a story about the Little People," he said to Lena.

"What Little People?"

"I don't know . . . they used to come and do the work at night for some fairy prince, spin and weave or something and . . . do you know it?"

"I think I've heard of it all right, but why do I remind you of it?"

"I think someone must have come in at night and done all your work. The basket is full of letters written and notes made . . ."

"I came in for an hour or two last night."

"I don't know what lucky good fairy brought

you here." He took off his glasses and polished them. "My brother used to laugh at me, and say I had no business sense. Now, in a few short months he wants to buy in to the business. What do you think of that?"

"What do you think of it, Mr. Millar?" Lena knew that there was little love lost between the brothers.

"I'm happier doing it without his help really, Mrs. Gray. That is, if you're going to stay."

During the morning her thoughts went back to the conversations she had had with Kit about her life before she'd come to Lough Glass. They had of their nature been sparse. You didn't tell a daughter that you only married because you were on the rebound and that your every waking thought was so filled with the memory of Louis Gray it didn't really matter what you did. Had she spoken of the girls she was in digs with when she was at secretarial college? Possibly. It was so hard to remember. But if she couldn't remember then maybe Kit didn't either.

She would write the letter and see how it looked.

Dear Kit,

You will find it strange to get a letter from someone you do not know. But a while back I read in an Irish newspaper of the death of your mother and I wanted to write and offer sympathy. I do not know your father because your mother and I were friends long long ago *when we were very young, well before she met him. Sometimes she used to write to me about you all, and the life you lived in Lough Glass, I even remember the date you were born, and know that you will be thirteen very shortly.*

Your mother was so pleased with her little girl, she wrote and told me about all the dark hair you had as a baby, and determined little fists. I don't want to write to you at home in case it makes your father sad. Your mother told me that there was a sort of second postal system in Lough Glass and that people often write care of this nun.

If you would like to write to me, and to know more things about your mother as a girl when we were all only about four or five years older than you are now, then let me know.

I hope I might hear from you, but if not I will understand. At your age you will have more important things to do than writing to strangers in London.

Warm wishes for a happy birthday from your mother's old friend,

Lena Gray.

When she put the letter into the red pillar box on the corner of the street, Lena left her hand for a long time on the mouth where the letters drop in. It was like reaching out and touching her daughter.

Tommy Bennet helped to sort the letters in the post office. Mona Fitz was very interested in the origin of a lot of them. She could comment when the Hanleys got a few dollars in a fat letter from America. Sometimes she examined the mail that arrived for Sister Madeleine. For a woman who said she had retreated from the world, she was still using quite a lot of the world's services. Like the postal system.

Tommy Bennet deflected any comment. Sister Madeleine was a saint as far as he was concerned. She had done the impossible and made things all right when Tommy's fifteen-year-old daughter came home with the most feared news in any Irish village, the news of an unexpected pregnancy. He had wept at Sister Madeleine's fireplace. And somehow the hermit had made it all all right. A friend had been found and his daughter went to live with her. Another friend had been found somewhere else who adopted the baby. And Sister Madeleine had found a third friend who gave the girl a job. Nobody in Lough Glass knew the secret. Nor even suspected there was anything unusual about the girl's long absence.

Tommy delivered three letters to the hermit's cottage on a warm sunny morning in late May. One contained a five-pound note, to be put to good causes. She gave the note to Tommy.

"Give it where it should be given."

"I don't like you trusting me to dole out all that money. I mightn't give it away right."

"What would I be doing with it? You know where it is needed," she insisted.

Tommy always felt a hundred feet tall; Sister Madeleine thought he was a man of responsibility. Nobody else much did. His wife thought he was lazy, Mona Fitz the postmistress thought he was soft. His own daughter, whose life he had saved, thought him old-fashioned and strict, and knew nothing of her father's role in all her good fortune.

"I'll leave you in peace to read your other letters, Sister."

"Put on a pot of tea for us both, it's a thirsty walk up and down that lane." Sister Madeleine shooed the collection of animals in front of her and sat on the little three-legged stool to read the letter addressed to her.

Dear Sister,

I am a friend of the late Helen McMahon, and would like to correspond with her daughter Kit.

For a variety of reasons I do not wish to write to her at her house. I have said to the child that I do not wish to make Martin McMahon sad to see reminders of his dead wife coming to his home, but the truth is that I was part of Helen's earlier life when she loved another man. This would make it inappropriate for me to resurrect such memories for him.

I shall write nothing disturbing to the girl, and you are at liberty to read my letters in case you think that the effect will be unsettling. I am sending what I hope will be the first of many letters to you. I am marking the corner of the envelope KM so that you will know they are for her. And perhaps you might send some mes-

sage to say whether this is acceptable to you.

> *Yours sincerely,*
> *Lena Gray.*

It was neatly typed. There was an address in West London. And it said in capital letters PLEASE ENSURE THAT YOU WRITE C/O MRS. IVY BROWN. Sister Madeleine looked out over the lake for a long time. When Tommy made the tea and brought it out to her he stood for quite a while looking at the small woman entirely lost in thought.

"Clio, you're great with the dogs. Will you go and see if you can find Ambrose for me," Sister Madeleine said later that day.

"Where's he gone, Sister?"

"I couldn't say truthfully, but he's lying low somewhere and you've always been able to make dogs come to you."

Clio headed off, pleased to be singled out.

Kit looked after her jealously. "I'm better with cats myself," she said.

"Don't I know it," Sister Madeleine agreed. "The cats nearly talk to you, Kit McMahon. Even half-wild cats." She gave Kit the letter.

There were very few words, but Kit knew it was something to be opened at home alone. And probably not something to be shared with Clio. Nor, since it had been addressed to Sister Madeleine's home, something to be shared with her father.

She must have read the letter forty times. She

knew every line of it by heart. Mother had told this woman all about her, about her little fists, her dark hair. She might have told her more. The letter was typed, which made it easy to read. But it looked like a business letter that would come to the pharmacy.

She sounded nice, but a bit standoffish too. Was it Mrs. Gray or Miss Gray? Did she want to know more? Kit felt reassured because Sister Madeleine had said that Mother had in the past mentioned this woman as a friend.

"I didn't know Mother had any friends," Kit had said.

"Your mother was a friend to everyone," Sister Madeleine had said.

"She was, I know she was." Kit's eyes were shining. "People liked her a lot, didn't they?"

"Very much so." The old nun nodded in agreement.

"But you didn't know her well, she didn't come here all that often, did she?" Kit was eager to hear more good about her mother. "But you don't have to meet people often to know them." That was true. You sort of knew immediately who you liked and who you didn't. "What did you and Mother talk about when she came here?"

"Oh, this and that." There was a seal of confession on anyone's conversations with Sister Madeleine.

"But did she talk about this Lena Gray?" Kit's face was troubled.

"She mainly talked about you, about you and Emmet." Helen McMahon on her infrequent visits spoke with such love about her children that

262

it was inconceivable she could have drowned herself and left them behind.

Sister Madeleine had always believed that.

It took Kit two weeks to think of something to write back. She began once or twice. But it always seemed wrong, it seemed like a school essay, or else too friendly for someone she hardly knew. She wondered what Mother would have done. Mother would have thought about it for a bit, not rushed in.

That's what Kit would do too.

א א א

"I've given your address, Ivy, in case I get any post," Lena said.

"Well, it's your address too, isn't it?" Ivy was mystified.

"No, I mean your flat."

"I see."

"No you don't."

"Are you going to tell me then?"

"It's just that I want to get a letter from Ireland now and then that I'd prefer Louis didn't know about."

"Be very careful, Lena."

"No. It's nothing like love letters . . ."

There was a silence between them.

"But it's from Ireland?"

"Yes. It's a kind of lifeline to my daughter . . ."

"Who thinks you're dead?"

"Yes. I'm not pretending to be me, I'm pretending to be someone else. Another me."

"I wouldn't, love. I really wouldn't."

"I've done it now."

"You're not still sulking about the television in the hotel?" Louis asked.

"Of course not. I was never sulking in fact, I was being bad tempered. You were the one who was sulking. Let's get the memory of the row right." Her eyes laughed and there was nothing but ease and pleasure between them.

"Right, so you'll come and watch it down there . . ."

"Certainly not. If I'm going to be in London for a big historic occasion like this, I'm going to watch it on the street."

"You'll have to queue all night with rugs and a flask?"

"No, of course I won't. Ivy and Jessie have found a corner."

"And what about me? What about Mr. Millar and Jessie's mother, and the rest of the cast?"

"You have to work, you've told me a dozen times. Ivy doesn't want to go to Ernest's pub because the horrible Charlotte will be there. Mrs. Park will be parked on a potty at a neighbor's, looking at their television. Mr. Millar will be with his brother whom he hates . . . now does that answer the interrogation?" she asked jokily.

"I love you," Louis said suddenly.

"I should hope so. Didn't I run away with you?" she said.

"And didn't I run away with you too?"
But it wasn't an equal running away.

"Of course you did," Lena said gently. "We ran like silver fish across the sea."

"Did Mother have a best friend like I have Clio?" Kit asked.

"Well, she had Clio's mum, of course." But they both knew that wasn't true. Mother hadn't liked Lilian Kelly.

"I mean before. Before she met you."

"She had girls in the digs. She spoke of them a bit."

"What were they called, Daddy?"

"It's so long ago, love, I can't remember. There was Dorothy, I think, and a Kathleen maybe . . ."

"Would she have been called Lena?"

"I don't know. Why?"

"I just wondered what people shorten their names to. Might the short name for Kathleen be Lena?" She looked flushed and eager.

McMahon gave it some thought. She seemed to want it to be that way. "I think it might have been all right. It certainly is a way of shortening the name," he said. Kit nodded, satisfied. As he did so often, Martin McMahon wished he knew what was going on in his daughter's mind.

Boys were so much simpler. He went fishing with Emmet many evenings on the lake. At first Emmet had been unwilling to touch the boat, but Martin had persevered. "We have no idea what happened that night, but we know one thing. Your mother would want you to grow up as part of this lake that she loved so much. She wouldn't want you to stay away from it."

"But the boat, Daddy . . ."

"The boat is part of the lake, son. We won't

ever know what happened in that boat and how your poor mother got dragged away. She'd surely want yourself and myself to go out in it and love the place as she did."

It had been the right thing to say. His son went with him happily on the lake. And it seemed that Emmet enjoyed his fishing trips catching perch and pike.

The boy never noticed that his father's eyes were dead as he rowed.

א א א

"No letters for you to my flat, Lena."

"No? Well, there you go."

"You're getting lots of London expressions," Ivy said.

"If I'm going to live in London then I'd better learn to talk like Londoners," Lena said.

"I thought you might be thinking of going back across the sea."

"No, there's not any chance of that."

"But the lifelines . . . ?" Ivy persisted.

"Probably just as you said, very dangerous, very foolish."

"Take that hard look off your face, Lena Gray. I'm your friend . . . I never said it was dangerous or foolish, I just told you to take care."

"You're a great friend, Ivy."

"When I get a chance to be, but that's not at the moment, so let it lie." Ivy went back into her room on the ground floor. She didn't ask Lena in. She knew the time for intimacy was not now.

Jessie Park was worried whether her mother might be able to make the bathroom in her neighbor's house during the Coronation.

"She gets very excited, you know, when things are emotional." Lena listened patiently. "Oh Lena. I know I'm wittering on a bit and I'm always telling you my woes, but I just don't know where to turn and you're always so calm, so practical."

Lena looked at her kindly. It was a huge compliment to be called calm and practical, a woman like she was, on the run, living a life with a man who might leave her again as he had done before.

Here she was in this great strange city, heartbroken that she had heard nothing from Kit and fearing that the letter had frightened the child. Yet Jessie thought she was as strong as an oak tree. "Let's see," she said. "Didn't you tell me that flat was all on one level? There won't be any stairs."

"I know, Lena, but she moves so very slowly . . . suppose she had a little accident?" Jessie bit her lip.

"I saw some pads in a chemist's last week. She could wear those and then there'd be no problem." Lena was bright and positive.

Jessie thanked her so profusely that it almost brought tears to Lena's eyes. It was so easy to solve a little problem for someone else when they asked, and so hard to sort out your own.

In the Dryden Hotel all the preparations had gone ahead for Coronation Day. The chairs had been arranged in a semicircle in the drawing room just as Lena had suggested to Louis, and he had advised the hotel.

"Your lovely wife will not be with us for the day?" James Williams said with disappointment. He thought that Lena would have added a touch of class to the proceedings.

"Sadly no. She is needed in her own work."

"I'm not surprised. I'm sure she is excellent in that employment agency. Perhaps she might be able to fill places for us as they become vacant."

"Ah, yes. Of course she's always looking for the perfect position for her husband," Louis joked.

"I'd be so sorry to lose you, Louis. You'd never take anything without letting us discuss a salary and conditions."

"Mr. Williams, I wouldn't even want you to think I was speaking seriously."

"And although I have asked you a dozen times to call me James you never will."

"I am very happy here."

"And is your wife happy in London? She doesn't yearn for somewhere else?"

"What makes you ask that, Mr. Williams?" Louis's eyes had narrowed.

"I don't know, something she said at Christmas, about everyone on earth should be forced to work in London for a time. I thought there was a message in those words."

"She's my wife, and I never heard a message like that." The words were perfectly polite but James Williams decided not to pursue it any further.

"Wouldn't it be great to go to England for the Coronation?" Clio said.

"Where would we stay?"

"Aunt Maura has friends there, she's going to go."

"Would she take us if we asked her?" Kit wondered.

"No, probably not. It's still term-time and they'd say we're too young."

"I'd love to go anywhere," Kit said.

"I know. So would I. By the time they let us we'll be too old." Clio was glum and resigned about it.

"Philip O'Brien's going to Belfast with his mother," Kit revealed.

"Yeah, but imagine going anywhere with Philip's mother."

"He's all right though, I like him."

"You're going to marry him. I can see it." Clio was definite.

"You're always saying that. I haven't a notion of it. Why do you keep saying it?"

"Because he fancies you."

"Well?"

"It doesn't matter that you don't fancy him, people always end up marrying people that fancy them."

"That couldn't work out." Kit fought it.

"No, I mean women do, girls do."

"Why? I thought we were the ones meant to do the choosing and refusing and all that."

"No, that's only in books and films. In real

life we marry people who want to marry us."

"All women do that?"

"Yes. Honestly."

Kit thought about it. "Your mother? My mother?"

"Yes. Yes definitely."

"And nobody fancied your aunt Maura?"

"That's different. She told me that she wasted time on a man who didn't fancy her. That was her mistake."

"But was it a mistake?" Kit wanted to know. "You always said she was very happy, happier than anyone we know."

"Yes, I know I did say that, but that's the way we see it. Maybe inside she's desperately unhappy."

"What about Sister Madeleine who says she was married and is a nun?"

"I'll never understand that," said Clio. "Not till the day I die."

א א א

"What are you thinking about?" Lena asked.

Louis smiled at her lazily. "I was thinking how beautiful you are," he said.

"No you weren't."

"Then why ask me?"

"I don't know. I suppose I sometimes want to know what goes on in your handsome head. We had a cat at home called Farouk. I used to look at him and wonder what could be going on in his head."

"And am I like Farouk the cat?"

270

"Not nearly as handsome I'm afraid."

"I don't like you saying 'at home.' Lough Glass is not your home, your home is with me. It has always in some way been with me."

She looked at him for a moment or two. A few weeks back she would have rushed in, begged, pleaded, said that she had been using only a form of words. But the night that he had left in the petty sulk, the night she knew she needed to write to her daughter, everything had changed. She didn't wish to tie him to her with humble words of apology, it could be no love if it was bought at such a price.

"Well, tell me, do you agree?" He was challenging her.

"No, my love, I don't. It wasn't where I wanted to be but I was there for thirteen damn years and other people called it my home and it was where I lived. So if I mention in passing that a cat who lived there with me, a fine handsome cat called Farouk lived at home with me . . . . I don't think it's a slip of the tongue that is going to make or break us."

He looked at her with admiration.

With a sudden flash of regret, she realized that if she had behaved like this years ago he might never have left her in the first place. But if he had stayed . . . what about Kit and Emmet? Would they have been the same people? Or different people? Or not existed at all?

No price was worth paying for them not to have existed at all.

"I'm going to have a perm for the Coronation," Jessie Park said.

"Great idea," Lena said.

"Mr. Millar has invited us both around to his brother's house in the evening." Jessie spoke with reverence.

"Yes. I hope you'll go and tell me about it. I have to meet Louis, I think he's a bit let down that I won't be with him all day . . ." She saw Jessie's face crumple.

"Oh Lena, do you have to? Please come to Mr. Millar's, you can be with Louis any night . . . this is special."

Lena looked at her fondly. Although she still called him Mr. Millar, Jessie had very fond thoughts about her employer. Lena had seen her looking at him in a way that had nothing to do with the employment agency. "No, honestly. I would if I could, but this is something I have to do. Anyway, you'll have more fun without me. I'd only be a gooseberry."

"He doesn't see me in that way at all." Jessie's face was long and sad.

"How do we know what way men see things? You'd need a fleet of interpreters to work out what they're thinking . . . but it's better you go on your own. You'll get to know him more than if I were there."

"Do you think so? Do you think it will be all right?"

"Certainly it will, it's not as if he were a stranger, a man you only met at a party or somewhere. You and he have so much in common, shared so much already . . ." Lena was full of encouragement.

"But I never know what to say when you're not there." Jessie looked flustered.

"Maybe this is the time to begin."

"I hope I'll look all right. Do you think it's worth having a perm . . . ?"

"Oh indeed I do, and anyway it will cost half nothing. Grace owes us. We've been sending so much business her way, she practically runs the salon on the people we refer."

Jessie left for the salon cheerfully full of plans. Lena picked up the phone. "Grace, do me a favor. When Jessie makes a booking give her everything, I mean every single thing. I'll sort it out with you later. Nails, facial, color . . . anything you think."

"She's never going to look for a new job?"

"Better than that," Lena said, "she's looking for romance."

א א א

Deirdre Hanley dropped by the pharmacy. "I came to know if you'd be needing an assistant or anything, Mr. McMahon," she said.

"Are you going to study pharmacy, Deirdre?" Martin McMahon was surprised.

"No, but I wouldn't need to for working here, would I?"

"Well, to be any help to me you would really." He spoke mildly.

She was a restless girl, Mrs. Hanley's daughter. A child who had always been loud in her impatience for the day when she could leave Lough Glass. Sometimes she had even said it to Helen and found, Martin feared, only too sympathetic an audience.

"But isn't it all a matter of trying to get people to buy makeup and all?" she asked.

"I think there's a bit more to it than that, Deirdre. But were you going to train as a beautician? Is that it?"

"You wouldn't need much training, Mr. McMahon. All you'd need is to talk one of the cosmetics companies into giving you a bit of a course, then you push their stuff, tell people it's great. You know the sort of thing."

"And you'd like to do that in Lough Glass?"

"Yeah, why not?"

"But do you think . . . suppose we were able to find a place for you here, which I don't think is possible . . . do you think you'd be happy doing that?"

"Mr. McMahon, you have to do something from dawn to dusk to justify your existence. That's what it's all about," Deirdre Hanley said.

"And you'd like your existence here in Lough Glass?" He'd had nothing but despair from this child about her hometown, what had changed her? Deirdre looked across the road at Sullivan's garage. It was only a glance, but Martin McMahon remembered having seen her with Stevie Sullivan on a few occasions. Usually down by the lake or away from the public eye. "What would your mother like you to do?" he asked suddenly.

"She'd like to get me out of here. She says she doesn't know why but she thinks it would be the best thing for me."

"Go, Deirdre. You'd be much more exciting to him if you were an out-of-town girl."

"Mr. McMahon, imagine you knowing all about women and life and everything," said Deirdre in amazement.

"I know," Martin McMahon said good-naturedly. "Isn't it extraordinary all right!"

"Will the pair of you come into the chemist's with me, do you think?" he asked the children that night.

"Now?" Emmet asked in surprise. Once the door had been locked their father hardly ever opened it again, unless it was an emergency for someone.

"No, I meant in the future," he said.

"Would you like us to?" Kit asked.

"Only if you want to, or one of you wants to. It's long hours and you'd need to enjoy the work."

"I thought I might be an actress," Kit said.

"And I thought I'd be a priest out on the Missions," Emmet said.

"Oh well then, it's all settled." He looked from one to the other. "Father Emmet . . . out in Nigeria with his long white soutane, saving souls, and then back to catch the first night of Katherina McMahon in the Abbey Theatre. It'll be a busy life for me. I suppose I'd better take Deirdre Hanley in to help me."

"Deirdre Hanley?" Emmet and Kit said in a voice of disbelief.

"She came looking for a job today, to help out."

"You wouldn't want her, Daddy," Kit said.

"I don't have to be a priest, it was just an idea." Emmet rushed in.

"And I mightn't get accepted as an actress, to be honest . . ."

"So you might fall back on the chemist's; like if all else failed."

"Exactly," said Kit.

"Children are marvelous," Martin McMahon said to the air around him. "Who'd be without them."

א א א

On the morning of June 2nd, Lena woke eagerly. Her daughter was thirteen today, she hoped Martin would mark the day for her, make it special, cheerful.

She got an urge to ring him and whisper encouragement down the phone. She longed to cry, and tell him that it was very hard to live without her children, but she knew this was a fanciful thing to indulge herself. She had a life to live. A life of her own. And here she was in London on the day of the Coronation.

Everyone was listening to the wireless from the moment they got up. It was as if they feared the whole thing might be canceled. They wanted to know every detail. The newspapers were full of the splendor of the day and a minute-by-minute itinerary of how the procession would go to Westminster Abbey, and a step-by-step guide to the ceremony.

Lena looked around her with delight at the crowds who were determined to enjoy the great day. Less than ten years ago they had been in the middle of a terrible war. Thirteen years ago, the day her child was born, the day that Martin had wept for joy at her bedside to say they had a beautiful daughter, there had been fear and panic in these streets in London.

In a way, Lena thought, the English don't have enough celebrations . . . they don't have Saint Patrick's Days, and Corpus Christi processions, and the Blessings of the Boats, and pilgrimages to Croagh Patrick, and all the things that give people a chance to take a day off and think about something else. It was heartening to see them all smile and talk to strangers. She made her way to the corner that Ivy had managed to secure by knowing the family who owned a small shop there. The children had been out since long before dawn guarding the places for them. There were little wooden stools and picnic baskets, and flags and bunting.

For a moment Lena felt as if she were outside herself looking at it all from somewhere else. She didn't feel part of the great excitement and anticipation. The knowledge that the young Queen was going to pass feet away didn't fill her with awe. But neither was it foreign to her. These were as much her people as were those who lived in the main street of Lough Glass.

She was as much at home here as she would be anywhere in the world.

They settled into their vantage point and heard the news about Everest. Britain had conquered the highest mountain in the world; the excitement knew no bounds. The roar became louder as the carriages came into view, the horses gleaming and decorated, the magnificent brocades and livery. And then the smiling but slightly anxious face of Princess Elizabeth, as they still referred to her, waving her gloved hand, eagerly responding to all the love and welcome from the pavements.

She seemed to look straight at them, they all said it, Ivy, Jessie, everyone all around. And Lena thought it too. She looked back and waved at the woman who was going to be crowned. A woman who still had her little boy and girl. She felt tears spring into her eyes.

A man beside her clutched her arm. "It's a great day, love, isn't it. You'll be able to tell your children about this."

Lena squeezed his arm back. "Great day, great day," she stumbled.

אא א א

"Do you always know what to do, Sister Madeleine?"

"No, Kit, I hardly ever know what to do."

"But you don't worry about it."

"No, that's true. I don't."

"Is that why you weren't good at being married?"

"I never said I wasn't good at being married."

"No, but you can't have been, otherwise you'd still be married, wouldn't you, not a nun?"

"Oh, you think I left a marriage and went into a convent, is that it?"

"But isn't that what you told us, Clio and myself?" Poor Kit was wishing she hadn't brought it up. The nun's blue eyes were interested and alive, but giving nothing away. "I mean we didn't just imagine it, did we?"

"I did have a husband once, but he left me. He went away far across the world."

"Did you have a fight?" Kit was sympathetic.

"No, not at all. I thought everything was fine. He wasn't happy, he said." She looked out over the lake as she remembered it.

"And did the nuns take you then because he wasn't coming back anymore?"

"Oh no. Not for a long time. I sat in the house polishing it and cleaning it and growing the flowers in the garden and telling everyone he was coming back soon . . ."

"Where was all this, Sister Madeleine?"

"Oh, far away from here. But anyway, the weeks passed and the months and one day I asked myself what I was doing, and God made a little voice in me say that all I was doing really was minding possessions, keeping silver clean and polishing glass . . . I surely should be doing something else."

"So what did you do?"

"I sold it all, and I put the money in the bank for my husband, and I wrote a letter to a friend of his and said I was going to join a convent, and that if ever he came back everything was there for him."

"And did he come back, Sister Madeleine?"

"I don't know, Kit. I don't think so." She was very calm. Not sad or confused.

"So you were a nun?"

"For a while. Then one day I asked myself in the convent what was I doing. Polishing tables in the parlor, and polishing pews in the church and the marble around the base of the altar. And I heard the little voice from God again."

"What did it say this time?" Kit scarcely dared to believe that Sister Madeleine was telling her all this.

"It said the same thing. It said that I was spending my time polishing and cleaning possessions. They weren't mine admittedly, they belonged to the convent, but still it didn't seem a good thing to be doing."

"So you left and came here?"

"Yes. That was it, more or less."

"And you couldn't hear a voice from God saying that you're wrapped up in possessions here because you haven't any." Kit looked around the spare house and marveled at how it had all turned out.

"Yes, I think it was the right thing to do. I hope so."

"But it was God talking, wasn't it?"

"Of course it was, but God is always talking to us. The thing is to be sure and hear the bit that he wants us to hear."

"Like when making up your mind you think one thing is right and then you think the other is." Kit seemed to know the problem of indecision.

"Exactly, Kit. You have to listen carefully and work out what is actually being said, what God wants you to do."

"And is it an actual voice, like you and me talking?"

"No. It's more a feeling."

"So if I wasn't sure whether to do something

or not . . . I'd just wait and see which feeling was the stronger."

"It usually works." Kit closed her eyes. "But you can't force it, Kit. It's not like a fairy granting you three wishes or anything." Kit stared out over the lake. It was so calm, not a ripple. A perfect June day. "Write to her, Kit," Sister Madeleine said.

"What?" Kit started in alarm.

"You're wondering whether to write to your mother's friend or not. It can't do any harm. Write to her."

א א א

"Lena?"

"Ivy!"

Ivy hadn't seen Louis was there too. "Did you think of coming down to the pub on Friday? Ernest was asking about you both the other day."

"Hey, that would be good," Louis said. "But can we never buy a drink there? That's the only thing that turns me up about it. Tell Ernest, he'd understand."

"The only thing Ernest can do for me, Louis, is to buy my friends a few beers. He loves to do it, give him the chance."

"Oh, I'm easily turned into a kept man," Louis said, continuing up the stairs.

Ivy called up after them, "I have that leaflet you wanted, Lena . . . you know, about those evening classes . . ."

Louis groaned. "She's not taking up more activities, is she? Don't encourage her, Ivy. Please, if you love me don't encourage her."

"They're not for me, silly. They're for the clients. Right, Ivy, I'll come down later and have a look at them with you." Her voice was calm, she looked as if nothing had happened. But inside she was churning.

A letter from her daughter.

Ivy was waiting, the letter in her hand. "It's a child's writing, Lena. You wrote to the children."

"You knew that."

"I didn't know they'd write back. I'm frightened for you, I really am."

"I'm frightened too." They looked at each other for a long moment.

Then Ivy pulled out a chair. "Sit down and read it. I'll get us both a drink."

Lena began to read.

Dear Miss Gray,

Or maybe it's Mrs. Gray, you didn't say. I took a long time to answer because I was thinking. I almost felt afraid. I don't know what I was afraid of. I think I am worried that you'll tell me something sad about my mother, like that she wrote to you and said she didn't love us or she was unhappy in Lough Glass.

So I wanted you to know she had a great time here, a really good time. We have a terrific home, and Daddy is so good to everyone, and was best of all to Mother because he didn't fuss her. He knew she liked to walk by herself, and even if he was lonely he let her go. Sometimes he would stand at the kitchen window at the back of the house where it looks down over the lake and he'd say, "Look, there's your mother walking by the lake, she loves the lake in Lough Glass." And she had a lot of friends here, the Kellys were great friends of all ours, and my mother knew everyone in the town, and they all still talk about her. So I thought I'd tell you that, in case you were going to tell Emmet and myself that mother didn't have a good time or had any complaints. So that you would know what it was like.

I haven't told Emmet about your letter because he's very young and doesn't really understand anything at all. It's not much of a letter but I wanted to explain.

> *Yours faithfully,*
> *Kit McMahon*

Lena looked at Ivy. Her face was empty, as if someone had reached in and taken all the life and feeling out of it. Ivy wondered if Lena was going to faint, she had never seen such a deathly white.

"Oh my God, Ivy," she said. "My God. What have I done? Oh Ivy, what on God's earth have I done?"

"It's all right, it's all right," Ivy soothed.

"I have destroyed so many lives. Oh, I wish I were at the bottom of the lake like they all think. That's where I deserve to be."

"Stop it!" Ivy spoke in a voice that Lena had never heard her use. "Stop it this minute. I can't abide that kind of self-pity. Think. You have a man upstairs who loves you and who is the love of your life. And now you have a chance to set the record straight, to make amends to this child."

"How can I make amends? How can I ever undo all this . . . ?"

"Tell her Helen McMahon was as happy as a sandboy. Tell her a pack of lies, let her have some good thoughts about her mother. You can do that."

"It would all be a lie. I can't write my daughter lies."

"Well you sure as hell can't write her the truth, can you?" Ivy said, refilling the glasses.

א   א   א

Clio's aunt Maura brought them both Coronation mugs. She had a great time in London, she said. It was very exciting. Everyone was in such a good mood.

She was always very kind to Kit, and managed to say the right thing much more often than Mrs. Kelly did. "You look lovely, Kit, you're so tall and strong-looking too. Your mother would be proud of you." Mrs. Kelly always said "your poor mother," as if Mother was someone to be pitied. "She had a great love for this place, she knew every fern and reed that grew by the lake," Clio's aunt Maura said, and Kit agreed. Mrs. Kelly would have steered clear of any mention of the lake, a difficult thing to do in Lough Glass.

And it was true that Mother knew all the plants. Kit had heard that from Lena Gray, Mother's friend in London. Kit had been asked to call her Lena, not Miss or Mrs. The woman typed such long, interesting letters about Mother that Kit would love to have shown them to Dad. Surely it would cheer up his sad heart to read about how much Mother loved the place, sunset over the lake in the evenings, and the little clumps of primroses and cowslips in the spring. But she knew that Lena Gray was right, these were thoughts that somehow didn't concern anyone else.

And Kit's heart was full to think that her mother had loved her so much she had written all these things about her to a woman in England. It was so strange that Mother had never mentioned her. How private Mother must have been to have kept this great friendship all to herself.

א א א

Lena kept all her letters from Kit in Ivy's flat. "It's not that I don't trust Louis," she told Ivy.

"I know, love." Ivy did know.

"It's such a comfort to me," Lena said.

"I know, love, I know."

"But you're warning me again about something, aren't you?"

"Don't tell her too much. Don't get too close to her."

"Sister Madeleine?"

"Yes, Kit."

"Do I ask too many questions?"

"Not at all. It's good to ask questions, people don't have to answer them any more fully than they want to."

"So, I was wondering . . ." She paused. It was as if she didn't want to know the answer. "I was wondering did my mother use you as a letter box too?"

"Why do you ask that, child?"

"Well, you see her friend, Lena . . . she sort of said that she and mother were writing to each other all the time, and I never saw any letters coming from England up at home. We'd have noticed the stamp, you see."

"I know, I know." Sister Madeleine was thoughtful. But she had not said yes or no.

"So did she, do you think?"

"Did she what, Kit?"

"Did she get letters addressed to her through you . . . ?"

"Well, of course, there could be lots of ways . . . everyone does things differently." Sister Madeleine was sliding away without refusing to answer.

"How do you mean?" Kit was trying her best.

"About people being different? It's a thing that could keep you thinking every day of your life how different we all are. And how different the animals are from each other. Like how do the little ducks know they can swim, and the little sparrows know they can fly. And people have such different ways of looking at things.

"Take your mother now. She knew every name of every child over there in the gypsy camp, and they all knew her yet they lived such different lives. They would have done anything for your mother."

"So, you mean she could have had letters addressed there . . ."

"Neither you nor I would ask them, would we, Kit? It's like what we've always said, people are special . . . they have their own lives in their souls to live. And I wouldn't tell anyone about our conversations or who writes letters to whom. And you wouldn't tell Clio about what I told you, all about my cleaning those possessions, because we know that it doesn't have to come up. Not that we're making secrets or anything — there's just no need to know."

"I know." Kit knew that she would never know whether this was the letter box for Lena Gray and Mother. But she was sure it was. Now only one problem. If Lena was so nice and such a close friend, why couldn't Father have known about it?

Mother Bernard welcomed Rita to the convent with pleasure. "Are you sure that you want to do this, Rita? We love your excellent work here, of course, but I wonder are we taking advantage of you?"

"No, Mother. It is a pleasure. I love to clean your beautiful things. I get lodgings like the Queen of England wouldn't have . . ."

"I can't see her coming to a convent in Lough Glass on her travels, mind you." Mother Bernard, of course, disapproved of the new Queen of England thinking herself the head of a church. Any church.

"Well, it's her loss, Mother, I tell you that. And I don't want to go back to my family, they don't need me and they only upset me. Also . . ." She paused.

"Do you have a young man in Lough Glass possibly?" Mother Bernard was coy.

"No, not a fear of it, Mother. No, what I was going to say, I don't like to be too far from Emmet and Kit. My heart goes out to them."

"Kit seems to be managing very well, better than I would have thought."

"Yes, of the three of them she does seem to have found some kind of peace. It's as if she had a secret. Maybe she prays to her mother, do you think?"

Mother Bernard didn't want to go as far as this.

Although it would be a sin against charity to go around repeating it, Mother Bernard was one of the very sizable number who believed that Helen McMahon might well have ended her own life, and would therefore not be in a place where anyone might pray to her with any hope of an answer.

CHAPTER FIVE

Maura was very reassuring to her sister Lilian Kelly. "They're all terrible between thirteen and sixteen. It's their glands . . . it's to do with nature."

"Nobody has a nature like Clio. I'll swing for her before it's over, I really will."

"No, no. I see it everywhere. It's their bodies, you see. They're all ready to breed and raise families, but society won't let them, and so it's a very confused time . . ."

"All we need is for them to be breeding all round us. That's the only thing she hasn't done yet." Lilian Kelly's mouth was grim.

Clio was a handful. The odd thing was that Kit, the motherless girl who had been restless and wild herself, seemed to have settled down. Clio's blond good looks had caught the attention of many a young man, but her parents had been strict. There would be no outings of that sort until the summer she left school. Lessons were important. Fun could come later.

Maura came down almost every weekend. She said it was no distance from Dublin. She loved seeing them all. And as the months and indeed years went by the weekends had fallen into a pattern. There would be a supper up at Kellys' on a Friday night. And the next day spent playing golf. Martin McMahon had been assured by his friend the doctor that exercise was essential for a man in his forties. They would have dinner at the golf club on a Saturday night.

Martin had to be persuaded that it was a good thing to leave his children to their own devices some of the time. "I'm sure Helen would want you to encourage them to be independent," Maura had said. And that had settled it. Martin McMahon liked the easy way that she mentioned his dead wife. So many people dropped their voices when they mentioned her. If they mentioned her at all.

But while every other girl fought with a mother, Kit McMahon developed a friendship that became closer and closer with her mother's friend, Lena. Lena's typed letters arrived at Sister Madeleine's cottage week after week, pages and pages of conversation and memory and reaction to things that Kit wrote to her.

Sister Madeleine mentioned the letters once. And only once. "She writes long letters, your mother's friend?"

Kit had paused for a moment. "I'd show them to you, Sister Madeleine, but it's hard to say . . . it's kind of . . . not exactly a secret but you'd get the feeling she's only writing to me."

"Oh, child. Don't think for a moment that I'd want to read what she says. She tells you good things about your mother . . ."

"Marvelous things, they must have known every single thing about each other. But then, they wrote to each other a lot. You know that because they must have written through here." Sister Madeleine looked into the fire and said nothing. "I feel so much better about Mother. I know her properly, what she was like as a child and everything. It's like finding her diary or something . . ."

"That's a great blessing for you," Sister Madeleine said, and she watched the little flame catch the wood.

א א א

Lena had a ritual about reading the letters.

It was in Ivy's flat at the kitchen table, surrounded by the cluttered shelves and the walls on which there wasn't an inch of free space, so great was the festooning of postcards, scarves, ornaments, and posters.

She would sip her small brandy and be transported to a world of breezes on the lake, end-of-term exams, Father Baily's being an hour late because he had forgotten that the clocks went on.

She read about her own son's getting his tonsils out, and eating only jelly and ice cream, and how Rita had done her secretarial course but fortunately hadn't left to go to Dublin and get a good job, she was working in the office of Sullivan's garage across the road.

Lena read of people she had disliked for thirteen years that she now found fascinating.

The Hickeys weren't speaking to each other, it appeared. If anyone went into the butcher's and asked for three lamb chops Mrs. Hickey would repeat the phrase in the tones of a Christian martyr and then Mr. Hickey would go and chop them. The days when she would talk to the customers and shout in to her husband were gone. Kit wrote that it was better than going to a play just to go in and watch them. Sometimes she begged Rita to let her go and do the shopping just for the sheer fun of it.

She read about Philip O'Brien's being so nice, and his mother's being so awful. How Clio was fighting with her mother too, and how Deirdre Hanley wasn't in the door of Hanley's Drapery before she and her mother had a row.

"I sometimes think that if my mother had lived we would have had a fight too. Otherwise it wouldn't be natural."

Lena's hands shook as she read this. She wrote page after page about it. *Your mother always spoke of you so lovingly, you were so strong, so full of courage. You would never have fought, you would have seen her for all she was, her weaknesses as well . . .*

Then she stopped and tore the pages up. She mustn't give herself away. She had been so careful for these years she must not throw it all away now.

א א א

Rita kept the accounts for Stevie Sullivan.

His mother, a mournful woman, felt that there was something not entirely appropriate about this. There was that maid of the McMahons' coming across the road and putting on airs as she did so. She decided she would set the relationship off on a correct footing.

292

"I'm glad you're going to be with us in the mornings, Rita."

"Thank you, Mrs. Sullivan."

"And I thought maybe I'd leave a little ironing a couple of days a week . . ." Rita looked at her politely. But said nothing. "To do in your own time, of course."

"What was that you said, Mrs. Sullivan?"

Kathleen knew when she was beaten. She began to retreat. "If there's time, of course . . ."

"That's always the problem, isn't it. Your son is paying me to work three hours a morning. I hope we'll be able to get all his books and correspondence dealt with in that time. It's certainly going to be a challenge, isn't it?"

"And then you'll go back to domestic work across the road?" It was a barb.

But Rita didn't pretend to see it. "I've always felt McMahons' was my home in many ways. I wouldn't dream of leaving Mr. McMahon until his children are reared."

In Paddles' bar Peter Kelly asked Martin about Rita's job.

"She seems to be doing very well." Martin was proud of Rita. "She's cleaned it up for a start."

"I know, didn't I see it. Fresh paint, shelves, filing cabinets, in old Sullivan's! Could you believe it?"

"I'd say she has a hard time with Kathleen."

"Everyone has a hard time with Kathleen," said Peter Kelly. "But on the other hand, she wasn't dealt much of a hand herself, and she's got a handful in those two boys."

"Stevie's a bit of a lad, isn't he?"

"We'll have to lock up our daughters, Martin. Stevie Sullivan knows a lot more than you and I knew when we were nineteen."

"And the young lad, Michael, a hooligan. Himself and young Wall were found drinking the dregs of empty bottles behind Shea's the other night. Little pups."

But Peter Kelly was not as outraged as he might have sounded. He was very tolerant of what other people in Lough Glass regarded as the criminal side of young people. He couldn't see that it was all that very bad for Clio to have gone out in her mother's black satin slip to the pictures on a summer night, but Lilian still hadn't recovered from the outrage.

"It's a great blessing that Maura comes down so regularly," he confided to Martin. "Lilian would be at Clio's throat a lot of the time if we didn't have company to be pleasant in front of, so to speak . . ."

Martin's face brightened up. "She's great company Maura. I'm surprised that she's able to find so much time to visit, but it's grand to see her."

Peter Kelly sipped his pint thoughtfully. He knew very well why Maura found so much time to come and visit. He wondered would Martin McMahon ever realize that he was the main attraction.

Rita realized it, however. She spoke about it to Sister Madeleine.

"I thought that might be the way the land was laying all right."

"How on earth would you know, Sister? You don't go visiting . . . how do you know things?"

"I just feel them."

Sister Madeleine knew that Kit mentioned how her father laughed when Clio's aunt was around, and that the golf had become a regular feature of the weekends. When Emmet came to read his poetry with her, he sometimes mentioned Anna Kelly's aunt. She liked poetry too, apparently, and had often asked him to read for her because she had forgotten her glasses.

"And is she a kind woman?" Sister Madeleine asked.

"Very, I'd say."

"Well, maybe he should ask her to supper, don't you think?"

"I was wondering about that, with the Kellys would you say?"

"Oh, I'd say so, the first time anyway."

. . . and next week we've asked the Kellys and Clio's aunt Maura to supper. It's a mad idea really, but Rita said that Dad was getting too many meals up in their house, and not giving any in return. I said that Dad paid for meals in O'Brien's Hotel or up at the golf club, but Rita said hadn't he got his own home to entertain them in. So that's it. Not us, mind you, not Emmet and me, or Clio and Anna or anything . . . just grown-ups. There'll be soup and roast lamb and trifle. And wine. Dad's delighted. I'm in two minds. You might think this is very silly but I feel it's a bit disloyal. You see, when Mother was here she could have cooked a meal for the Kellys and their aunt Maura anytime she wanted to. Mother was such

a terrific cook. It seems silly all of us struggling to make a dinner when she could have done it so easily. But she didn't. Perhaps she didn't like the Kellys. It's so hard to know. I have this feeling that if she had liked them then she would have had this dinner . . .

Lena felt her eyes mist over. How little escaped the quick mind of a child. She had neither liked nor disliked the Kellys; they represented all that was safe and dull about Lough Glass. She had deliberately held herself from confiding in them from a wish to stay separate and free, as if she knew Louis would come back one day and take her away.

And now she had left the legacy of that in-difference with this innocent girl who thought so well of her that even after her death she didn't want to do anything to compromise her memory.

Lena wrote immediately.

I don't know if you're right about the Kelly family. Helen always spoke of them in her letters as people she liked. She said you and Clio had such a stormy friendship — sometimes it was till death do us part, other times worst enemies. I know she didn't want to play golf with them, but she sometimes felt guilty about depriving your father of it. She used to urge him appar-ently, but he'd say no, not without her.

So it's good now that he does play. I hope the dinner party goes well. I'd love to be a fly on the wall.

"What'll happen if he marries again?" Ivy asked one day.

"Who?"

"Your ex. Martin."

"Oh, he won't marry again." Lena was surprised at the question.

"From all you tell me I know these characters better than *Mrs. Dale's Diary* . . . there's this Maura appearing a lot."

"He wouldn't marry Maura." Lena smiled at the thought.

"Well, why not? He thinks you're dead, he thinks he's free to marry. Wouldn't it be sensible?"

"Martin wasn't sensible when it came to love. If he had been sensible he'd have married Maura in the first place and none of this mess would have happened."

"And Kit and Emmet would never have existed."

"It might have been better. They're only existing for me in a limbo."

"What's wrong, love?"

"I don't know, Ivy. I don't know."

But Lena did know what was wrong.

Louis had been restless. He had been nearly five years in one place. He felt it was time to move on. He said they should go somewhere warm, like the south of Spain.

A lot more British people were going there these days. They could get a partnership there. There wasn't much he didn't know about the business. They could make a killing. Live in a proper climate.

"What about my job?" Lena had asked.

"It's only a job, darling. You went in there the first day and stayed . . ."

"So did you," she countered. "But we both stayed because we got on, made something of the jobs."

"Lena, there are millions of jobs . . ."

"They're our jobs, they're our careers. You practically run the Dryden, I practically run Millar's."

"So? We're not married to them," Louis had said.

"Nor to each other," she had replied.

It was a bit of a problem, the marriage business. Technically, Helen McMahon was dead. If she went to get a birth certificate, then a corresponding death certificate might be produced. Better not to risk it and unearth the Lord knew how many problems.

That's what they had said. But there was a part of Lena that thought Louis had taken the whole thing very calmly. If he had really loved her with the deep love he claimed, he would have made some more determined attempts to marry her.

Jessie Park and Mr. Millar had a long romance. It was assisted throughout by the best efforts of Lena Gray. Often on a Saturday, Mr. Millar, Jessie, and Lena had lunch together. Then Lena would excuse herself early and leave them to chat.

They made the big decisions about the business at these meetings. Lena would take notes and type them up on Mondays. Business at the agency was booming, they needed to take on someone

298

else. Probably someone young, they thought. Young and glamorous-looking.

"What about Dawn Jones?" Lena had suggested. "She's between jobs. We couldn't get much more glamorous than her."

"Would Dawn find us lively enough?" Jessie wondered. "She usually likes places with lots going on."

"Lots going on with us," Mr. Millar said, missing the point.

"I think Dawn's a bit tired of getting pawed by people," Lena said. "She might well be glad of a spell in a more responsible setting . . ."

Dawn Jones had been one of their earliest success stories. She had arrived for an interview looking like a tart about to set out for Soho, heavy makeup, low-cut sweater, and nicotine-stained fingers. "None of my sisters ever had an office job, I'd love to say I worked in an office," Dawn had begged.

Her innocence and enthusiasm had appealed to Jessie and Lena. Tactfully they had advised her about dressing differently and she had been given a new hairdo in Grace West's salon. Her typing speeds were adequate, it had not proved difficult to place the lovely Dawn in any office. The problem was that it had proved difficult to persuade many of her employers and colleagues to keep their hands off her. There was something about Dawn even in a neat navy twin set and pale blue skirt that suggested excitement and adventure.

She had done a spell in the Dryden, in Mr. Williams's office. Louis had said she was sweet but silly. Nothing you could put a finger on, but just not someone you'd trust to take a message or type up a report. Dawn had left the Dryden after three months, James Williams had got a pleasant middle-aged woman, motherly, efficient, much more what was needed. An excellent reference had been provided for Dawn, but everywhere it was the same story. She was too sexy to be taken seriously.

Lena wondered if this might be to their advantage. Young girls loved someone to follow, a role model they could identify with. She and Jessie were too old and settled, if they saw Dawn in Millar's they might think that secretarial work was much more glittering than they had believed.

Jim Millar said yes, he saw the point, and Jessie said she thought Jim was absolutely right. So Dawn was approached.

"I'm not sure, Mrs. Gray, really. I don't know. Would I be right here, do you think?" Dawn looked doubtfully around the office.

"We're doing a face-lift, Dawn. And having journalists and photographers come in and everything."

Lena knew she had won the battle. She sent a press release to the local newspapers and to the trade magazines. And with it she sent a description of Dawn Jones who had left her job in a model agency to join Millar's. The model agency had been a very brief interlude and one on which Dawn had not wanted to dwell. There were many definitions of modeling, it appeared. Still it gave her the necessary glamour to attract the interest of the press.

And if they came and took pictures of Dawn then they had to mention Millar's also, the agency where there was emphasis on grooming and presentation as well as on typing and shorthand speeds. It was just the right approach and resulted in a great many inquiries for the agency.

Jessie and Jim were delighted.

"It's going so well I can hardly believe it." Jessie was breathless.

"What would I do without my two girls?" said Jim Millar, looking at them both with pride.

"Do you think he's fond of me, Lena?" Jessie asked in a whisper when Mr. Millar had left.

"Of course he is, of course he is." Lena was reassuring.

"I wish I knew what to do, I'm so inexperienced at all this sort of thing . . . you'd know, Lena?"

"No, I'm pretty hopeless too," Lena said. She felt she spoke the truth, until recently she had no idea how to produce the kind of passion that Louis had for her. She would have given anything on earth to know.

"But you're so . . . well, so terrific-looking and you've got such a gorgeous husband. I was wondering had you any hints or anything . . . ?" Jessie's big pale eyes were full of innocence and hope.

"I think he's a man who takes his time over things but makes the right decision in the end," Lena said.

"Suppose someone else comes along?" Jessica was biting her lower lip.

"No, not for Mr. Millar, believe me."

And Jessie did because Lena looked so authoritative. If only she knew, Lena thought, if only she knew where she was asking advice about love and marriage.

Dawn was delighted with all the publicity. "You've really done me a good turn, Mrs. Gray," she said, "and I like working here with women actually. I didn't think I would. They're sort of more reasonable than men, aren't they?"

"Some of them are, I suppose." Lena tried to hide her smile. Dawn was proving a wise choice. They had even included her name in the brochure they sent out, just in order to use her picture.

Lena was proud of all they had achieved, she couldn't help talking about it to Louis. He was still in poor form but at least he had stopped mentioning Spain.

"You're putting a lot of effort into that place," Louis said to her.

"So are you, in the Dryden . . . it's the kind of people we are." She sat on the floor with her head in his lap. She loved the evenings they had together, the shabby flat was in no way small and shabby to her.

"What's the point?" Louis said, waving around him. "Working our guts out to keep four walls in a kip like this?"

"It isn't a kip." Lena was indignant.

"Well it's hardly the Camino Real," he said, his mouth turned down. He was playing with her hair as she spoke, idly twisting the strands around.

Louis touched a lot, he wasn't a man to sit in his own space and make statements across a table, he always had a hand on her arm or neck, or was stroking her cheek.

"What's the Camino Real?" she asked.

"It's just a phrase, like the kind of names hotels would have, but in Spain . . . where we could easily work . . ." She was silent. "Easily," he said again, his big dark eyes pleading at her.

She felt a rising panic in her throat. She must keep the conversation away from Spain. Lena would have given up so much else, so much that was far more important. She could arrange for Kit to write to her anywhere, that wasn't the problem. The problem was that if Louis went to Spain he would go alone. She could not get a passport. Lena Gray did not exist.

א א א

"Do you think we should get drunk?" Clio asked Kit.

"Now?" They were walking up to school for the last frantic weeks of revision before the exams.

"Well, not this minute but soonish . . . it's an experience we haven't yet had."

"How soonish? Should we turn round and go back to Paddles' or maybe ask Mr. and Mrs. O'Brien to make us a few cocktails before class?"

"You make a jeer out of everything," Clio complained.

"I do not." Kit was indignant. "I'm prepared to do anything, you know I am. But I think it might be poor timing to get plastered just coming up to the exams. Suppose it took ahold of us like those old fellows with runny eyes and red noses waiting for Foley's to open . . ."

303

Clio giggled. Sometimes Kit could be very funny. But then sometimes for no reason she flared up and took offense. There were certain subjects that made her very touchy. Clio was dying to ask her whether she thought that Aunt Maura might be going to get engaged to Kit's father, and if she would like the idea of having a step-mother and of their being cousins. But this was territory she mustn't venture into.

She would love to know whether Aunt Maura and Mr. McMahon . . . well . . . courted a bit. And if they got married would they do it properly in bed? Normally these were things you could talk about with a best friend, but with Kit McMahon there were so many areas that were off limits.

"Have you ever been drunk, properly out-of-your-mind drunk?" Kit asked Stevie Sullivan.

"Why do you ask?" he said. He was handsome even when covered in grease and wearing filthy overalls. But unreliable of course. Everyone knew that.

"It's just that you've done most things . . . Clio and I are thinking of getting drunk when we finish our exams and I was looking for sug-gestions. Like what's cheap and quick and wouldn't make us too sick?"

"You're asking the wrong one, I don't know."

"I bet you do," Kit insisted.

"No, truly, we had too much of that in this house when I was young."

Kit had forgotten. She felt ashamed that she hadn't remembered the alcoholic father who saw animals and all kinds of things emerging from walls when he was in the horrors. But she decided against apologizing, she hated people saying thoughtless things about drownings or people gone missing and then being covered with confusion. She disliked the embarrassment and the apologies more than the original mistake.

"Yes, I suppose that makes sense," she said in a matter-of-fact way.

"It does to me, but not to Michael. He'd drink it off a sore foot as they say."

"God, who are they, the people who say that?" Kit recoiled at the thought.

"The low kind of people I mix with, Kit McMahon," he said, and left her.

There was always a keen rivalry between Mother Bernard and Brother Healy about the Leaving Certificate results. They were published in the local newspaper so that all could see and compare. Brother Healy always said that the odds were weighted in favor of Mother Bernard. Girls did all those easy subjects like art and domestic science. It was not so difficult for Mother Bernard to build up a frightening total of passes and honors among her pupils.

But the nuns were adamant that she had a harder route to go. Many of the small farmers were anxious for their daughters only to learn the basic skills that would turn them into acceptable farmers' wives. When the time came they were suspicious of girls learning French and Latin. They would have preferred classes in butter making and poultry raising and in many ways they had a point. Why raise the expectations of a girl

305

who was going to leave her father's house and move into one fairly similar a parish away?

"And have you a very bright crop this year, Brother Healy?" Mother Bernard asked courteously, but disguising her deep interest to know the lay of the land and assess her own chances in this year's contest.

"Dunderheads, Mother Bernard. Dunces and idle blocks of wood. And you . . . you have the crème de la crème this time, I expect?"

"Empty vessels, I'm afraid, Brother. Empty vessels with nothing tinkling inside except jazz music."

"This jazz is a great distraction to them all right," agreed Brother Healy.

Wise though they were about the ways of the youth of Lough Glass they were not sound on its musical taste. Jazz was not the enemy within that it had been for a previous generation. The noise tinkling in the hearts of the young people of Lough Glass was the sound of early rock and roll.

"Peter, will you speak to Clio?"

"No, Lilian. To be frank I won't."

"Well, that's a nice thing to say, you won't speak to your own daughter."

"She's only my daughter, my own daughter, and I'm only asked to speak to her when some dreadful thing has happened for which some terrible punishment is to be metred out. As it happens . . . as it happens, Lilian, I've had a very bad day, a horrible day. And I'm not going to speak to either of my own daughters or even my own wife, I'm going down to Paddles' for a pint with my friend Martin. Right?"

"Well, sorry for existing, and running your house and minding your children, both of whom are turning into juvenile delinquents."

"Let them turn, they'll turn back again when they see there's no future in it." Peter Kelly was out the door. He knew Anna's offense had something to do with cosmetics and perfume. He suspected that Clio's had something to do with getting her ears pierced like a gypsy without asking permission. It was too trivial. He banged out of the house and down the road toward the privacy and peace of Paddles'.

There wasn't much peace in Paddles' as it happened. Mr. Hickey was singing away in a corner.

"If I've told you once, John, I've told you a dozen times. This is not a singing house," Paddles remonstrated with him.

"Oh bollocks, Paddles. You wouldn't know a singing house if you saw one."

"Well, I see *this* one and what's more I run it, and you're getting no more drink in it unless you cut out that caterwauling this instant," Paddles said.

"Are you barring me . . . ? Do my ears deceive me or do I hear you barring me — John J. Hickey High Class Victualler barred from your pathetic premises?"

"You heard me, John," Paddles said.

"Well, I'd deem it an *honor* to be barred from such a dump. An honor I will wear proudly." He staggered to the door. "And an honor not to have to drink with the scum who frequent it."

Mr. Hickey smiled pleasantly around at all his neighbors, friends, and clients before stepping out briefly into the fresh air that he would encounter on the way to Foley's bar.

Martin and Peter exchanged glances.

"That was a good day's work, Paddles," Peter said approvingly.

"Can't you frighten him, Dr. Kelly? Tell him his liver's packing up? It probably is," Paddles added.

"No I can't, Paddles. I'm in a poor position to be telling him that, seeing as I've seen him across this bar every night since time began. And you're in an equally poor position, Paddles, seeing that you sell him drink. It's a strange world where no one takes any responsibility."

Paddles had moved away grumbling to serve the other end of the bar when the door flew open and Mrs. Hickey stood there carrying something very alarming on a tray.

"What's that, Mrs. Hickey?" Paddles' voice sounded less than confident.

"Ah, Paddles, this is a sheep's head. I thought you'd like to see it, and maybe the rest of the clientele might like to have a look at it too . . ."

There was an uneasy murmuring around the premises, a low dark pub very basic in its design and decor, and not a place where ladies came at all, not to mention carrying a large sheep's head on a white butcher's tray.

"Yes, well, thank you, Mrs. Hickey. Thank you indeed."

"I'll just take it round so everyone can see it properly," she said. She had a very mad glint in her eye and no one wished to upset her or even enter into conversation with her. They nodded and muttered vague sounds of approval as the object was carried around for their inspection. "This is the way John looks when he comes home from here each evening, he has the features and color of a sheep's head. I thought you should not be denied the pleasure of seeing this for yourself."

"Well, John isn't actually here himself at the moment . . ." Paddles began uneasily. "But when we see him . . . well . . ." His voice trailed away.

"No need to mention it at all," Mrs. Hickey said airily. "Just wanted you all to be aware of everything that's going on."

"Thank you, Mrs. Hickey," said Paddles gravely, in the tone of voice that implied the show was over.

"Would you live anywhere else?" Martin asked Peter Kelly when Mrs. Hickey and her tray were safely off the premises.

Peter Kelly had come in about to inveigh against the kind of society they lived in, people who had told him that a baby's death was all for the best, all for the best because you see she hadn't got a father. It had upset him greatly that a pious morality should be so inverted that it could think a bastard child better dead than surviving to be a child raised with love in a small mountain cottage. But there was Martin, peaceable, easygoing, and finding everything about Lough Glass comic and delightful. He couldn't impose his misery on his friend.

"You're right, Martin," he said after an effort. "It's got everything here except a three-ring circus. Maura says there's more life here than in the whole of Dublin."

Kit came home and found Rita whitewashing the walls of the yard. "Will I help you, is there another brush?"

"Aren't you meant to be studying?" Rita said.

"Oh God, Rita, not you too . . . Here, I'll go from this end."

"Take off your school uniform first anyway." Kit did that immediately, standing in her bra and knickers. "I didn't mean that," Rita laughed. "I meant get some old clothes."

"No, what's the point? By the time I'm upstairs and changed and downstairs you'll have finished. And who'll see me anyway except Farouk?"

The old cat looked at them sleepily and indifferently. It was hard to get Farouk interested in anything.

The gray-streaked walls transformed before their very eyes, the yard was soon the bright gleaming color it had been before the damp and spatters changed it to its messy state every year.

"I don't know why we bother sometimes," Kit said. "It just gets mucky again and no one sees it but us."

"Your mother always said that made it even more important that it was kept nice," Rita said.

"Did she?" Kit laid down her brush for a moment.

"Yes, she said you had to have pride in a place for its own sake, not for what the neighbors saw or didn't see."

"She liked nice surroundings, didn't she?"

"Yes, she did."

"Wasn't it sad she didn't have a garden like the Kellys do? It must have been hard stuck in the side of the street here with only a yard."

"She said the lake was her garden," Rita said. She was unselfconscious, she didn't stop and put her hand over her mouth as if suddenly remembering that Helen McMahon had died in the lake. "She said no one could have a better garden on their doorstep."

"I didn't inherit that from her, I couldn't care less about my surroundings," Kit said.

"You will when you have a place of your own," Rita promised. "Now, get some clothes on before Sergeant O'Connor comes over the wall and arrests you for indecent exposure."

א א א

Lena looked around her little home and tried to be objective. Why did Louis say it was a kip? Why did he say they hadn't much to show for their years of hard work?

Ivy's house had improved considerably since they had gone to live there. The outside was painted and the railings had been repaired. So many of London's railings had disappeared during the war, wrenched up to form part of the war effort. Lena had never known that before. The hall was carpeted now and the banisters had

311

been replaced. In fact the only flat that had not been given an overhaul was the one that she and Louis lived in.

And they had beautified it themselves, done it up with pictures and rugs and wall hangings. To Lena it was a haven, the place where she made passionate love to the man who was the center of her life, where she cooked him little meals and talked to him and looked out at the sky of London . . . she felt the freedom of the place everywhere she looked. True, it was small. But they didn't entertain people, they didn't want to. Louis was out so late, his hours were getting worse and worse. It was the same everywhere, once you got some responsibility you found your life was no longer your own.

But Lena loved it here, she loved the undemanding friendship of Ivy Brown, she would never find anyone to share her post secrets with such glee. She loved the road being around the corner from the agency. She could even dash home at lunchtime and put a flower and a love letter and maybe a sticky almond bun for him to find if he came home early on a split shift.

And Louis loved this place too. He had shopped with her in markets for outlandishly colored bedspreads, and for the mirror with a cherub on the side of it that looked as decadent as you could get. Why had he said it was a dump, a kip, and that they had nothing to show for their time here? He liked Ivy and it was near the tube station. Perhaps it just wasn't smart enough for his image of how they should live.

A flat without a bathroom. But suppose, suppose one of the other flats in the house came free . . . suppose.

But it was silly to think that. Most of the people in the house were settled. She must not start chasing rainbows.

But there was a God or a fate or something, Lena told herself. Three days later Ivy told her that the New Zealanders on the second floor were leaving.

"Homesick, they say." Ivy shook her head doubtfully. "You couldn't be homesick for out there surely." Anyway, they'd given her a month's rent and they were moving out now. "You can help me choose the tenants," Ivy offered. "After all, they'll be your neighbors, you want to have people you'll get along with."

"How did they leave it?" Lena asked.

"Come and have a look." Ivy picked the key off her rack and they went upstairs.

It had high ceilings and big windows. This was never a place that Louis Gray could dismiss and run down. Not if they furnished it properly. "How much does it cost?" Lena asked.

"I never offered it to you . . . I thought you were saving for a place of your own to buy," Ivy said.

"No, no, nothing like that." Lena would not let Ivy know that the savings were very little. They spent what they had. She would have to make economies to rent this place but it would be worth it.

"Does he know?" Ivy asked.

"Of course not, I only knew myself ten seconds ago."

"Let me get it spruced up a bit before you show it."

"What will you do?"

"What do you think . . . ?" They stood looking at it, minds full of ideas. "Ernest can send me a few chaps over from the pub, you know, meant to be doing a day's work for the brewery but out on six other jobs at the same time."

"A big cupboard in the bedroom maybe."

"To hang all Louis Gray's jackets in and lay out his nice shoes." Ivy was teasing her.

"Don't say a word against him."

"I wouldn't dare," Ivy said. "Listen, give me a week, then I'll show it to the pair of you and see what you think. If you change your mind that's no problem I'll let it anyway."

"I'd say he'll love it," Lena said, her heart full of hope again. This might chase the notion of Spain out of his mind. For a while anyway.

And he did love it. He was so excited by the proportion of the rooms, better than the Dryden, he told Ivy. He waltzed Lena around the big empty rooms and said that at last they'd have space for a proper life in London. He bought a bottle of champagne and three of them drank the health of the new home.

"I can't wait to move in," Louis said. He was eager and excited like a child, he moved around the room touching the walls, the door handles . . . stroking them almost. "Now we're making something of ourselves," he said, as pleased as punch.

314

There was a hoteliers conference in Scarborough.

"That's a place I've always wanted to go," said Lena.

"I'll tell you about it."

"Will I not see it with you?" Lena had been about to take a few days off from the agency.

"No spouses, I'm afraid."

"Tell me about it then," she said with a great smile.

She was choosing fabric for the curtains of the new flat when she ran into James Williams in Selfridges.

"More blue and gold for your agency?" he asked. He had remembered.

"No, just browsing."

"You're looking fit and well." He always eyed her rather overappreciatively she thought.

"Thank you, James." She smiled her routine smile, acknowledging the compliment.

"Enjoy Scarborough," he said.

"Will you be there too?" she said, her voice coming somehow through the icy feeling in her throat.

"No, I have no excuse, unfortunately. They do some work, but mainly it's a thank-you to a lot of these guys who work so hard and such highly unsocial hours. Gives them a chance to entertain their wives properly without having to count the pennies."

"And do all wives go?"

"Yes. They're not going to pass on a trip like that. Enjoy it anyway."

315

"I will," she said. And held the counter to steady herself.

It's probably all in my mind, Kit wrote, *but I have this feeling that Dad and Clio's aunt Maura are walking out. I know that's a very old-fashioned expression, but I can't think what else to call it. And there's nobody I could say it to. They've had a couple of meals in O'Brien's Hotel. Philip told me their heads were very close, but Philip is always talking about people's heads being close. It's sort of on his mind.*

But would you think at their age they might really and truly be thinking of getting married? I know it wouldn't come to anything like that without Dad discussing it with us, but I was very keen to know what you thought.

This time the answer came to Kit very quickly. It must have been by return of post. It was a very short letter.

Kit, write and tell me. Do you think Maura would make your father happy? He has had a hard life. He deserves happiness. Then tell me would you and Emmet like it or would it make you upset to see another woman walking around where your mother did, in her room. When you tell me these things I'll write and tell you what I think.

Kit wrote:

How did you know Mother had a separate

room? I never told you that. I can't believe she would have told you. Please let me know.

Lena paced her office.

She must never write quickly again, that's how mistakes happened. But it was all right. It could be covered.

How observant you are, Kit, Lena wrote.
Your mother did indeed tell me that she had a separate room. She said she didn't sleep well at night with anyone else in the room. She didn't need to ask me to tell it to nobody, since I spoke to nobody about her. Our correspondence was a sort of secret life, in a way like yours and mine is. Other people might think it sad, pathetic even. But I don't. And I hope you don't. Your mother never did. You have no idea how lonely I felt when her letters ceased. Tell me you under-stand.

I understand, Kit wrote. *But I don't know why you said you read in a paper that Mother died. You must have known at once when she stopped writing to you.*

I only said that in the first letter, Lena ex-plained, *so that I could get on to introduce my-self to you. Perhaps you might not have wanted to write, to stay in touch, out of loyalty to your mother. I didn't want to tell about our letter writing.*

It's all so confusing, Kit wrote. *You're such*

317

a mystery woman, I know nothing about you, nothing at all. And yet you know everything about me. Did you tell mother about yourself? Did she destroy your letters? There was nothing found when she left. Nothing at all that would make us know of you.

I'll tell you anything you like, Lena wrote. *Just make a list of questions and I'll try to answer them.*

She knew it was risky, she was getting in too deep. She would have to invent a persona for Lena, a past that had never existed. She feared what questions would be asked.

But in fact there were no searching questions. It was as if Kit had decided it would be impolite. Instead there was something much more heartbreaking . . . something Lena could never have foreseen. And yet, of course, it was the normal response of a friend. Kit wanted her to come to Ireland.

Can you come and see us? You have plenty of money. And if you want it all to be a secret still you could just stay in O'Brien's Hotel.

There were ways in which Kit hoped she wouldn't come. Maybe she would be a disappointment to meet. Perhaps she would have a funny Cockney accent from living in England. Perhaps she wouldn't be nearly as nice to talk to as to write to.

But it was getting to be silly now . . . and if

Lena was mother's age she must be in her middle forties, too old really for having a life writing to a teenage girl in Ireland about events long ago. Lena sounded very normal, and she had a husband who was a hotelier. And she worked in a big employment agency somewhere. And she lived in the house of some woman called Mrs. Brown.

And maybe she was mad like Miss Havisham. Anyway, if she came Kit would know.

Dear Sister Madeleine,

You have been acting as a postbox for me for nearly five years. I want to thank you for your discretion and lack of curiosity. Kit McMahon speaks of you with such admiration and devotion I wonder if I could ask you a great favor. Kit has suggested that I come to Lough Glass. For a great variety of reasons I do not want to do so. It would not be good for her or for anyone. But I am not thinking about myself first in this instance, I am thinking of others. From what Kit tells me you can always come up with some solution to a seemingly impossible situation. If there was any way you could help Kit to see that it would be a good thing for us not to meet in Lough Glass or at all, I would be forever in your debt.

I don't want to invent a string of lies, I just know you will believe me when I say it would not be for the best.

Yours in despair, dear Sister Madeleine,
Lena Gray.

My dear child,

I have always believed that there is a life of the imagination which suffers when it is mixed with reality. Two worlds can be kept separate. Lives can live in parallels and never meet. I wish you peace and happiness and the knowledge that you have friends, and have always had them, here.

Sister Madeleine,
Lough Glass.

"She knows, doesn't she?" Lena handed the letter to Ivy.

"I expect so," Ivy said. "What now?"

"She won't tell," Lena said. "That much I know for certain."

א א א

"Are you doing a line with Philip O'Brien?" Clio demanded to know.

"God, Clio. I wish I had a different friend. I've been saying it forever, of course I'm not doing a line with Philip. Whatever that means."

"He's always here. Hanging around. Or else you're in there," Clio grumbled.

"Well, we do live beside each other."

"Has he kissed you?"

"Shut up."

"So he *did* kiss you, but because you and he are in love you can't tell me, is that it?"

Kit couldn't stop giggling. "That's not it, okay?

320

He sort of kissed me, but he missed because I didn't know it was happening, and I looked the other way and he got my chin. And he said sorry, and I said sorry and we tried again, and it seemed a bit awkward. So you know every single thing. Now, will you leave me alone."

"You never told me."

"I'll tell you what I will tell you. Stevie Sullivan's got a new girl."

"No!" Now this did seem a matter of interest and some disappointment to Clio.

"Yes. An American girl staying at O'Brien's Hotel. Her parents came here to look for their roots. They're up in the graveyard most of the time, and she went across the road and got talking to Stevie."

"I bet she did."

"She's gorgeous-looking according to Philip. And anyway, Stevie came over to the hotel and she said to her mom and pop that he was taking her to meet a gang of kids across the lake, and they said fine. And there was no gang of kids at all, of course. It was just Stevie putting on the act."

"Well, she'll be gone soon," Clio said grimly. "Once the parents have found their roots they'll be out of here like bats from hell. And it'll be bye-bye from Mr. Stevie Sullivan's little new pal."

"It's another careers talk this afternoon," Kit groaned.

"Yeah, hopeless," Clio said. "I suppose they have to tell us what's available."

"Nothing's available except nursing and teaching, and that's only if you get called."

"And I'd hate both of those," Clio said.

"Mother Bernard's mad keen for you to be a doctor," Kit said.

"That's because she wants to say that a doctor came out of the convent here, and because she'd like me to have my head down studying for seven years."

"So what *are* you going to do?"

"I'm going to do a B.A. Aunt Maura says it's a great stepping-stone."

"Where will it make you step?"

"Into the arms of a rich husband, I hope."

"You don't want that."

"No, I want him sexy as well, and experienced. I don't want him missing my mouth and hitting me on the chin with his nose."

"Is it a wonder that nobody'd tell you anything, Clio?"

"But you're getting very secretive altogether," Clio said, with narrowing eyes.

"What about now?"

"You go down to Sister Madeleine's when I'm not with you, for one thing."

"Yes."

"And then there's this face-bashing with Philip. And you're going off mysteriously to study."

"Well, I do study. We are doing our Leaving exams in three months time, if you haven't forgotten."

"And are you studying now?"

"Yes."

"You haven't any books, you only have paper . . ."

"I'm making notes."

"Let's see." Clio snatched the writing case and unzipped it. Inside she saw a stamped envelope and a half-written letter. "No you're not studying, you're writing letters . . . love letters."

"Give it to me." Kit's face was white with anger.

"Let me read . . ."

"Give it to me, Clio."

Clio was reading " 'Dearest' . . . Dearest what? I can't read his name."

With a cry Kit lunged at her. "You are such a selfish, greedy person. You have no manners, you have no decency."

"No manners, no decency," Clio mocked, holding the letter high.

But Kit gave her a totally unexpected punch in the stomach that winded her, then Kit grabbed the letter and ran out of the classroom.

She met Mother Bernard in the corridor. "Ladies are rarely seen running, Katherine."

"I know. Sorry, Mother. I was running to the library to do more revision."

"Right. But just walk briskly. Do you feel all right? You look flushed."

"I'm fine, Mother." Kit escaped before the groaning lie should be discovered and further explanations sought.

"Emmet, will you deliver a note up to Kellys' for me."

"No."

"I'll pay you."

"How much, threepence?"

"I was going to say a penny."

"I won't do it for a penny."

"You're a horrible, horrible person."

"Okay. I won't do it at all."

"When I think of all I do for you." Kit was stung.

"What exactly do you do for me?"

"I protect you."

"Who do you protect me from?"

"From people shouting at you."

"Oh, don't be silly, Kit. You don't protect me. People shout at everyone."

"I always speak nicely about you. I even think nicely about you."

"Well, why shouldn't you? I'm not that bad. Why should you be giving out about me?"

"Everyone else gives out about their sisters and brothers. I don't."

"Who gives out?"

"Clio does. Stevie does. Patsy Hanley gives out about Deirdre."

"Well," Emmet shrugged, as if these were people with crosses to bear.

"Oh all right. Be as rotten as everyone else. I used to think you were special."

"What did you want delivered?"

"A note to Clio."

"Why couldn't you walk up with it yourself? You and Clio have a path worn to each other's house . . ."

"I'm not talking to her."

"So it's a note making it all up?"

"No it's not. It's a note saying how bad she is, and how she pokes her horrible nose everywhere it isn't wanted."

"That'll only make things worse." Emmet was philosophical.

"Yes, but I don't care. They couldn't be bad enough between us as far as I'm concerned."

"But then you'll go and apologize or she will, and it will all be back where it was." Emmet had seen these fights ebb and flow over the years.

"I don't think so this time."

"That's what you always say," Emmet said. "You'll forgive her or she'll forgive you, and things will be the same for a while."

Kit thought about it. He was quite right, that was the way the pattern always had been. But not this time. No, Clio had almost snatched her secret from her.

Out of nothing but sheer pique she had nearly found out that Mother's friend Lena was writing these letters. And if Clio discovered that, then it would all have been over. In some way Kit knew that it had to be secret to continue. She wished that Lena had been able to say something sensible about why she couldn't come to Lough Glass. It sounded like a load of excuses.

"So what happens now?" Emmet asked. He was wondering whether to bring his price down.

But life was full of surprises. "I'll tell you what happens next," Kit said cheerfully, tucking her arm into his. "I am going to buy you an ice cream, how about that."

"What do I have to do for it?" Emmet asked.

"Nothing, nothing at all. Just admit that you have the best sister in these parts for miles."

"I suppose I do really," Emmet said thoughtfully. And together they ran up toward the shop before Kit might change her mind.

א א א

"Sweetheart?" Louis rang Lena at the agency.

"The very person," she said, and the smile came into her voice.

"You know this conference?"

"Oh, yes." Did it sound casual enough, she wondered? Did it give any telltale hint that she had been thinking about nothing else for weeks?

"The rules have changed."

"In what way . . . ?"

"We are allowed to take spouses, partners, whatevers." A great silence. "So . . ."

"So, Louis?"

"So, isn't that great? Pack your glad rags and we'll have a ball."

"I can't."

"You what?"

"I can't, love. You know that. I've arranged to baby-sit Mrs. Park, and to keep the office open. No, there are too many people. I can't back out."

"We'll never have anything like this again . . . you can't turn it down."

"If I'd known earlier I wouldn't have set all this up."

"Well, I didn't bloody know earlier."

Oh, how she would love to have gone on a train journey, all expenses paid, to Yorkshire. She would have taken out a map and wondered were they passing places like the Wash and the Humber.

They would have stayed, for the first time since

the time of the miscarriage, that terrible visit to Brighton, in a hotel together. They would have had free time . . . time to talk and relax together. She could have looked well for him, and been happy. She could have sparkled in front of other people and made him proud of her. The tight knot in her stomach would have gone because he would have wanted her.

She had allowed a silence to fall between them. She heard him grumble. "Are you making your mind up or is that it?"

"Why didn't you tell me earlier?" she asked.

"Because I didn't know earlier," he said, as if explaining to an idiot or a child.

"James Williams knew earlier," Lena said.

"What do you mean?"

"I met him. And he asked me was I going. I said there were no spouses, he said he thought there were."

"And he was right," Louis cried triumphantly. "He was the one who said from the start that this was the way it should be."

Lena felt very, very tired. What would someone else have done in her shoes? A cleverer woman? Would she have dropped everything and gone, gone with him, stormed her way back to his heart again? Or would she have allowed herself to be persuaded slowly, played hard to get?

"I can't go, Louis," she said. Because she had thought she would be alone for the weekend Lena had set up so many activities to distract her that she was going to be busy every second of the time. Now she realized with bitter irony it would be impossible to unpick them. There were too many people depending on her. Louis believed she was sulking and trying to make a point about staying behind. She decided it would be best not to apologize or explain too much. Just to let him know that she would have loved the trip. "Let me take you to lunch on the Friday," she suggested.

"I don't know. If you've time to go gallivanting off to lunch with men like me, why haven't you time to come to Scarborough?"

"Because, you idiot, I thought you couldn't take me. Come on, let's have a lunch like people do in the movies." She had persuaded him.

But as Lena sat in her office and studied her face in the mirror of her compact she saw with alarm that she must look many, many years older than she was. There was a tight drawn look, a near permanent frown. Her hair seemed dull and her eyes lifeless. No wonder he had asked someone else to Scarborough. Someone who had let him down at the last moment. No, no. She would not allow herself to think that way. But what a dreary wife she would look.

"Jessie," she said, suddenly standing up. "I have to go out on business. See you after lunch."

She knew her voice sounded raspy and tinny. She saw Dawn and the two other assistants look up in surprise. Mrs. Gray always spoke gently and moved smoothly from place to place. She didn't grab up a handbag and scamper out the way she had today.

Dawn looked after her in amazement. "What's happened to her?" she asked.

Jessica didn't like office gossip, and especially

not about Lena. "Carry on, Dawn," she said briskly.

But inside in the inner sanctum she confessed to Jim Millar that she thought Lena Gray was working too hard. "She's looking after my mum while you and I go out, she's coming in to deal with workmen here . . . carpenters she found herself. She's got the girls doing overtime so that we'll have the whole new filing system set up by Monday . . . I don't know."

"What's that handsome husband of hers going to think if she's working in here all hours of the day and night?"

"I think he's going away on some conference or other."

"Maybe that's what has her on edge," said Jim Millar.

"Grace, can you squeeze me in?"

"Sure thing. Come to the end cubicle." Grace started to take out the shampoo.

"Not you yourself . . . you're the manager . . . I meant one of the girls."

"They're all busy . . . I'm glad to say." Grace's singsong voice never sounded anything other than cheerful, yet Lena knew she had a hard life. The man Grace loved had two children by other women. They were not spoken of.

"I feel so awful, I look old and sad and no use to anyone."

"Tired maybe?" Grace suggested.

"We know what 'tired' means." They laughed. It was a polite way of saying that age was showing.

"Work is it?" Grace asked as her firm fingers

massaged Lena's scalp.

"No," Lena muttered into the towel as she leaned over the basin. "No, work runs itself."

"Me too," Grace said. "Funny, isn't it? Men had such a big deal about work. To women like you and me it's nothing. Nothing at all."

"He has someone else," Lena said as she sat and looked at herself turbaned with a towel.

"No, I'm sure that's not so," Grace said.

"I'm sure it is."

"I'll give you a hot oil treatment, make your hair shinier, and I'll find some nice makeup for you."

"It won't get him back."

"Perhaps he has not gone."

"I think he has . . . you know the way you know these things."

Grace had massaged in the warm olive oil and replaced the towel with another one. "Has he said he has someone else?"

"No, of course not."

"Well then . . ."

"I didn't ask him," Lena confessed.

"No, of course you didn't." Grace grinned.

"But I can't stop thinking about it . . . all the time everywhere, at home, at work, in bed, even here. And I'm going to find out . . . I really am. I can't sleep until I know."

"Not much sign of sleep recently." Grace gently touched the dark shadows under Lena's eyes. Lena wanted to cry and hold the woman close to her. But it was a public place, and she had years and years experience at hiding her feelings.

"Think of something nice, think of something you really know is constant and true . . ."

"My daughter," Lena said.

Grace looked up startled. In all the time they had known each other the previous life had not been discussed. Only Ivy knew the whole story.

"How old is she?" Grace asked gently.

"Soon to be seventeen."

"That's a great age, they're lovely at seventeen. And can you talk to her?"

"No, not directly."

"Why?"

"She thinks I'm dead," Lena said. And wondered had anyone in the world ever felt so lonely before.

"Well well, don't you look a treat," he said in the restaurant.

And indeed she did, Grace had worked miracles.

"Have to send you off with a good memory of me," she said, smiling at him.

"I wish it wasn't only the memory."

"So do I, but honestly it's only a weekend . . . there'll be others." She was determined to make a virtue out of it now that it had to be done this way.

His eyes were on her, she could feel them without looking up. "You look so alive . . ." he said.

"Thank you, Louis."

"Let's have a glass of wine and go home, hey . . . ?"

"What! We've only just arrived."

"We can be home in a few minutes . . . I can't

go away to the wilds and leave unfinished business behind me." He wanted her now. She could still arouse him, make him desire her.

Lena smiled. "Well, I said let's have lunch like people do in the movies . . . but this is even better," she said, and went ahead of him out of the restaurant.

They ran like youngsters down the road, and if Ivy heard them come in she didn't come out to make conversation.

When they got into the flat he held her very tight. "There's no other woman in the world for me except you, Lena," he said. "Oh God, I need you so much. I can't tell you how much I need you."

Afterward she helped Louis pack his case.

"I'm a very understanding man," he said as she folded his shirts.

"And tell me, Louis Gray, how is that?" She was determined to laugh and be happy with him. No letting away with the memory of a grousing, sulking woman at home.

"My wife doesn't do her duty, her conjugal duty, and accompany me on a works outing." His smile across the case was heartbreaking.

"Aha, but I'm *not* your wife, Louis."

"Well, whose fault is that? I must be the only man in the world teamed up with a woman who is officially dead. I'd marry you tomorrow if I could. You know that."

"Do I?" She couldn't help the question.

"Well, if you don't know you'll never know." He reached into the shelf of the cupboard where they kept his underwear. As he took out his folded underpants, vests, and socks two packets of condoms remained deliberately on the shelf.

"Not much point in taking those if I can't take you," he said.

"None at all," Lena laughed.

But her laugh was hollow. There were many chemists where such things could be bought between here and Scarborough.

I suppose it's because I'm so involved in an employment agency that I wonder about what you'll do when you leave school, Lena wrote to Kit. *You see, girls get such a poor start because nobody gives them any proper career advice at all. You don't talk much about the future, and I am very interested in what you are going to decide to do.*

You never say whether you'd like to be taken on in the pharmacy or not, or whether you want to go to university.

She didn't expect a reply so soon.

It's funny you should ask that question just then, but I've been thinking I'd love to do hotel management. Now there are things for this and against. The main thing against is this Philip O'Brien. I've told you all about him. He's very nice, but he sort of likes me more than I like him. I'm not the kind of girl people fancy much, so it's quite nice . . . but I wouldn't want him to get the notion that I was going to enroll in Cathal Brugha Street, the hotel school, just to follow him, or be with him.

Lots of times he has talked about us running the hotel together in Lough Glass, and honestly, Lena, if you saw it you'd prefer to be in partnership with the Draculas running their castle.

I do know it, Lena thought grimly, and I never heard a better description. The letter went on.

Your husband is in a hotel, maybe I could come and work in that for summer experience . . . if you could put in a word for me.

Lena sat for a while with the letter in her hand. It was a grotesque thought that Louis might all unknowingly start a relationship with her daughter. A beautiful dark-haired girl with dancing eyes. Almost seventeen years old, a prize for any man who might think he was growing old. What a cruel fate to allow a situation where mother and daughter would be seduced by the same man. Where daughter and mother would share Louis Gray as a first lover. It was of course entirely impossible as a scene even to fantasize about.

Kit could never come to London. Kit could never meet her. She only had Ivy's address, with Ivy's name. There were no names on bells that would identify their flat, suppose Kit were to come. Kit didn't know the name of Millar's Employment Agency. She didn't know the name of the hotel where Louis worked. The name Dryden had not been allowed to appear in any letter.

She knew Louis's name, of course, but that was all.

Lena wrote:

The problem is, Kit, that everything has changed here. The hotel industry has changed. Louis never had any real written qualifications, so he's moving. He's going into marketing, everyone seems to think that's where the future lies. He is in Scarborough at the moment trying to sort out his future . . . so he'd be no use to you at all. I miss him a lot I can tell you. The weekend seems very long . . .

Kit read the letter. She read it over and over. It was obvious that Lena and Louis had had a row. They might even be going to separate, divorce possibly. It was England after all, where such things could happen.

She wished she had a phone number, she could ring her and say something helpful. But what could she say, Kit McMahon, almost seventeen and studying for her Leaving Certificate. Kit who knew nothing about men except that she really didn't want Philip O'Brien to go on kissing her. Imagine her being able to say something helpful to Lena Gray, who was so confident and ran a huge agency and had a handsome husband.

Many times in her letters she had said things that made Kit know Louis was handsome. Like he had a new jacket, or how well he had looked in the car they had been lent that time, or the night he had worn the dinner jacket for the formal function. Kit knew that Lena Gray must be beautiful too. It was clear to see that Louis Gray would want to have a beautiful wife.

On Saturday Lena played gin rummy with Mrs. Park.

"I wish I had more people to play cards with . . . the days are very long," she said.

"Why don't you move to the little close I was telling you about before . . . they have a dining room where everyone has their lunch, then you all go back to your own flats in the evening . . . that way there are plenty of people to play cards with all afternoon."

Was she imagining it, or did Mrs. Park look wistful? "Oh well, we'll wait and see," she said.

"Oh, that's not like you, Mrs. Park. A fine decisive woman like yourself . . . surely you must make up your own mind."

"Lena, you don't understand. You don't have children of your own. Jessie is very dependent on me, she loves to come home and make my lunch. Her day is built around it. She might think I didn't need her . . ."

"Oh, I don't know, Mrs. Park," she said. "From what Jessie tells me I know she'd love to think you had more of a life of your own."

"But what about her life?"

"I could involve her in more social outings if I thought you were able to take care of yourself more. I don't like to ask her to socialize when I think she feels she should go home to you."

"I'm not sure that you're right." Mrs. Park was doubtful.

"I think I am, but then I may not be. Why

don't you test it out, suggest it to Jessie when she comes home."

"And you'd be able to get her to go out a bit and meet people."

"I would, Mrs. Park, truly I would."

"You're very kind, Lena Gray, but you don't understand how it is between a mother and daughter. You want the very best for your girl, it's like that from the moment they're born. Nothing can ever get in the way of it . . . ."

"I'm sure you're right, Mrs. Park," said Lena Gray, with a forced smile on her face.

Ivy moved her curtain. Lena stopped at the door.

"All right, Florence Nightingale? Are you going to come in and have a chat?"

"You don't need to cheer me up," Lena said.

"No, selfish, I don't. But maybe I want to be cheered up myself," Ivy said.

"You!" Lena raised her eyes to heaven.

"Yes, me." Ivy's mouth was in a tight line. Perhaps for once she was in low spirits. Lena went in and sat down. "It's Charlotte," Ivy said.

"Charlotte? What's she done now?" Lena had scant patience with the dog-in-the-manger wife. Charlotte did not appear to want Ernest for herself, and yet she would let no one else have him.

"She's gone and got cancer, that's what," Ivy said.

"No!"

"Yes. That's what he said. He left an hour ago. On the way back to the hospital. She won't come out, Lena."

Lena looked at her blankly. It was one of those very rare times when she didn't know what to say. Part of her wanted to be glad, glad that the unknown woman who had stood between Ivy and happiness would no longer be there. But she couldn't rejoice in another woman's cancer. "Where had she got it, Ivy?"

"Everywhere."

"And an operation?"

"No use."

"How is Ernest taking it?"

"Hard to know. He was very quiet. He just said he wanted to sit here. We hardly said anything." Ivy looked up at her pitifully, her eyes were red from crying. "Do you know, Lena. I've been sitting here thinking, it may be that there's nothing to say." Lena looked bewildered. She didn't follow what Ivy meant. "We left it too long, too late."

"But you're always so close, every Friday of the year . . . nearly."

"Fooling ourselves probably. When Charlotte's gone it will all be gone. Mark my words."

"No, I won't mark your words. What a silly expression. It's like 'wait and see.' What do these things mean?"

"It's only a saying," Ivy said. "You say lots of things that mean half nothing too, Irish things."

"Well, what were you trying to say?" Lena's voice was more gentle.

"I suppose I'm saying that it only lasted because it was impossible. Now that this bloody illness might make it possible he's off like a bat out of hell."

Lena saw the pain in her friend's face. "Listen, of course he's upset. He's guilty too, and relieved, and guilty about being relieved. He's a mass of feeling, why pick out the worst one to dwell on . . . ?"

"If you've loved someone for as long as I have you can read them like a book."

"You can read them wrong sometimes," Lena said.

She might have been wrong herself about Louis. She might have imagined this whole thing about him being interested in someone else, asking some other woman to go on the trip with him and then being left suddenly in the lurch. It was possible after all.

And look at how he had been so loving yesterday afternoon before he went on the train. And remember how excited he was about the new apartment. And how he said he'd miss her and find it hard to sleep without her in the bed where she was meant to be. It was possible, wasn't it, that she might have been working too hard and seeing dangers where there were none.

Maybe somebody outside could see better. Like Grace, for example.

"Had you thought he might have been telling the truth?" Grace had asked. "That he really didn't know spouses were invited."

"No, I hadn't thought that," Lena had replied. "Which shows how very deeply I mistrust him." And Grace had tried to give her a hope that she was brushing aside.

Just as she was doing now to Ivy. Trying to convince her that the love of a lifetime had not been wasted. "Do you know, Ivy, women are wonderful. I wish the world was run by women."

"It is," said Ivy, with a trace of her former self returning.

Lena woke with a headache on Sunday morning. She would so love to have been waking in Scarborough in Louis's arms. What was it that James Williams had said when he was describing it to her . . . just a little holiday to thank the employees for putting in such antisocial hours . . . a chance for them to be with their wives in nice surroundings.

She must have been insane to have arranged all these million things to do. Minding Mrs. Park, supervising carpenters that she had hijacked from Ernest's pub to do finishing touches to the new flat in Ivy's house and to the office. She must have been crazy to offer those girls extra money to come in on Sunday and set the place up properly.

The day seemed very long. She kept thinking of other things. Like what they were doing on a sunny Sunday in Lough Glass. She knew so much more about the place now than when she lived there. She could write a book about the people of the small lakeside community just based on Kit's letters. She wondered about Jessie and Jim Millar. Maybe this weekend would be the one where they would make up their minds. Or rather Jim would. Jessie's mind was already made up. She thought about Ivy and her love for the strange dour Ernest. She thought of the woman Charlotte whom she had never met, lying in a hospital bed which she would never leave. Did this woman believe in God and that he was going to take her to heaven?

But then did anyone believe in God, Lena wondered.

How could Martin McMahon, a man she could have sworn had a firm personal faith in a God who was all-powerful, possibly contemplate a bigamous marriage with Maura Hayes?

He knew she was alive, Martin knew that he had a living wife.

Lena shook her head in disbelief at the thought of him standing in the church in Lough Glass while Father Baily pronounced him and Maura man and wife, having asked anyone to say if they knew any reason why they shouldn't be joined together.

Possibly Kit was imagining it all. The child might be lonely, well she must be lonely otherwise she wouldn't pour her heart and soul out like that in letters. Maybe she hoped for a pleasant, placid, unchallenging stepmother to replace the mother she had loved so much. The mother who was taken from her by her father's arrogance and vanity.

As these thoughts went through her head Lena worked on, organizing the new shelf space, encouraging the girls to fill it in the correct manner. Never again would they be confused about application forms, leaflets, documentation. This was a very professional setup.

She had even thought of a picnic for them, and as they all sat down to eat at three-thirty Lena said that she thought they had done brilliantly.

"But you're paying us until six, we'd better eat up quickly," Dawn said.

Beautiful Dawn, who could have been a cover girl with her flawless skin and her shining hair. She looked years younger than she must be.

"No, you've worked like slaves, you all get paid until six, but relax, let's enjoy the feeling that we set up a great office." Lena raised her cup of coffee from the blue and gold mugs, the mugs that were used to give clients coffee when they came to call and discuss work.

They tidied up and finished the sandwiches she had brought for them, and the shortbread biscuits. And she gave them each an envelope. "Go out and enjoy what little there is of the weekend," she said.

They ran like children released from school. They were hardly more than that, the two younger ones. Dawn hung back for a moment. "That was fun, Mrs. Gray, I did enjoy it . . . nobody could ever have told me that a while back . . . that I'd enjoy working on a Sunday, but I did."

"Don't run yourself down, Dawn . . . you could be a business tycoon if you wanted," Lena laughed at her.

"No, I'm not cut out for it. Finding me a nice rich husband, that's what I'll start to doing soon."

"Marriage isn't the only goal."

"How can you say that, Mrs. Gray . . . you've got a gorgeous husband?"

"What . . . ?" Lena had forgotten for a moment that of course Dawn had worked in the Dryden some time back. She would have known Louis then. "That's true, Dawn, I've been very lucky."

"He's lucky too," Dawn said. She looked as if she were going to say more but changed her mind. Lena waited. "Very lucky too," Dawn said. Then she went out into the warm London air.

Lena sat at her desk and wondered whether Louis could possibly have had any kind of fling with Dawn Jones. Maybe he had even asked her to go to this conference with him and that she had changed her mind.

Dawn Jones, born in 1932, would have been a golden-haired moppet when Lena went up the aisle to her loveless marriage. It wasn't possible. Then she took a deep breath. No, it wasn't possible. This was the way to go mad. The surefire way to end up in a mental hospital.

Louis loved her, he told her that, he would be home to her tonight. Dawn was a brainless child. Louis probably hardly met her when she was in the Dryden, she had worked for James Williams. It was only because she was so tired and had so much on her mind. The phone rang shrilly beside her as she sat in the empty office. It was Jessie.

"Oh Jessie . . . well, it all went very well. Tell Jim that the place is fantastic, and the carpenters took all the rubbish away with them so you'd never know there had been any work done at all." She was eager to give the good news.

"Lena, Lena, we're getting married," Jessie cried. "Jim asked me to do him the honor of becoming his wife. Those were his words, Lena. Isn't it wonderful?"

Unaccountably two tears came down Lena's face. "It's wonderful news, Jessie. I'm so happy for you," she said as the tears splashed into one of the blue and gold ashtrays.

"We're going round to tell Mother tonight, but I wanted you to be the very first to know."

Lena said that she thought it was the most marvelous thing she had ever heard. She sat quite still for a long time after the call. She had an almost uncontrollable urge to ring her daughter.

But fortunately she just managed to control it.

After an age she stood up from her chair, cleaned the ashtray, packed the picnic things in her basket, and locked up the offices. She walked very slowly down the road with its Sunday evening crowds beginning to gather for whatever festivities they had in mind. She went home and lay on her bed to wait for Louis.

At eleven o'clock he burst into the flat. "Oh God, I missed you, Lena. Lena, I love you," he said, and he launched himself at her like an over-affectionate puppy dog. "I brought you a rose," he said.

It was all done up with a fern and a safety pin as if it were a corsage. It didn't matter where he got it, he might have found it, or bought it, or stood for ages while it was being made up. Someone could have left it on the train.

He had brought it for her. He smelled of the sea and she loved him. Nothing else mattered at all.

א   א   א

"Kit, you know that friend of yours and Clio's, this Mother Madeleine?" Clio's aunt Maura spoke hesitantly.

"Yes, she's Sister Madeleine, Miss Hayes."

"I was wondering, would you mind if I went to see her?"

"About us, do you mean?" Kit and Clio had not been speaking for twenty days. It was the longest silence ever between them. Most of the town seemed to be aware of it.

But Clio's aunt laughed. "No, not at all about you . . . about me. I gather she's a very fine person at sorting things out."

'Yes, but some things can't be sorted out." Kit was very adamant about that. And Sister Madeleine was about the only person in the place who hadn't urged her to make it up with Clio.

"It's just that I didn't want to be moving in on her if you thought it was your territory . . ."

Kit looked at the woman with new respect. "No, no. Everyone sort of talks to her, and she tells nothing on, it's like the seal of confession."

"So, if I went to see her it would just be considered like a passerby dropping in?"

"That's very nice of you, Miss Hayes, to ask I mean."

"I wouldn't want to tread on your toes. And do you think you might ever feel like calling me Maura?"

"I'd be happy to," said Kit. And indeed she was, more than happy. It would be great.

Imagine saying it in front of Mrs. Kelly. Better still, imagine saying it in front of Clio.

"Sister Madeleine, I'm Maura Hayes."

"Of course you are. Haven't I often seen you at Mass on a Sunday with Dr. Kelly."

"I hear nothing but good about you, Sister."

"I'm blessed to live in such a warm place, Maura. Would you join me in a cup of tea and some nice scones? Rita up in McMahon's is a gifted cook and she often leaves me a batch of these in case someone drops by."

"A fine girl indeed, Sister. Maybe she should better herself."

"I know, I know. It's a problem."

They both knew the problems. Rita would not leave the McMahons until the place was settled. The question was now which of them would mention that a solution might be in sight.

The hermit decided to make it easy for Maura Hayes. "Of course you're a regular visitor here to these parts yourself," she said.

"I do come down often. My sister has such a happy home here herself."

"And one day you might make a happy home yourself."

"There are many who might say I was far too old to be considering any such thing."

"I wouldn't say that, Maura. I've never been a great advocate of young marriages myself. They don't seem to work somehow. The danger, of course, in leaving it late is that you mightn't be able to replace what had gone before. That would only be a danger if you were trying to replace it with the same thing. I wouldn't imagine you'd be trying to do that."

"No indeed. If it were to happen I'm sure it would be a very different variety."

"Well then . . . I feel very sure it would work very well." The kettle that had been moved to the center of the fire began to hiss and splutter. The old nun lifted it away deftly.

By the time they had finished their tea a lot had been straightened out. Without confidences being broken or anyone named by name Maura understood that if Martin McMahon was to be enthusiastic about a union there would be no opposition in his house. The daughter Kit would be going to Dublin to study hotel management. The son Emmet was like all boys, hardly aware of his surroundings. The maid Rita was only looking for an excuse to leave the family in good hands so that she could go to live in Dublin. There was a chance of a position in a car-hire company. Warmly recommended by Sullivan's of Lough Glass she would be sure to get the position and start a fuller life.

"I wouldn't ever be anything like as special as Helen," Maura said in a small voice.

"No, of course not."

Maura ached to ask what she was really like, what had she talked about, had she ever said what made her soul so tormented and so far away as she paced the length and breadth of Lough Glass. But there would be no point. The nun would just look away across the lake, the lake where Helen had met her death, and would speak distantly. It's hard to know what anyone's like, she might say. Maura would not ask. Instead she said: "If it does work out . . . and Martin and I do make a life together, do you think that Helen McMahon would have been pleased rather than upset about it?"

The nun's eyes seemed very far away as if she

was thinking of something much farther away than the lake. There was a long silence. Then she spoke. "I think she would be very pleased," she said slowly. "Very pleased indeed."

א א א

They moved into the new flat two weeks after Scarborough. Louis was loving and enthusiastic about it all. He didn't mention Spain anymore. He said no more about England being finished and men of vision getting out while the going was good. He was so much the old Louis that the days and nights of bleak despair almost disappeared.

Almost, but not quite. He was still out very late. And he resented it terribly if Lena asked him why.

"Sweetheart, is it clocking in and clocking out at home as well as at work?" he said impatiently.

And of course she had been wrong about that weekend. Lots of people had said to her it was a pity she wasn't there, the whole thing had been an innocent mix-up. And she must have been mad to think there was anything between him and Dawn Jones. Dawn worked beside her day in and day out, putting in extra hours coming up to the official opening of the new premises. If Louis telephoned Dawn would say, "Oh hello, Mr. Gray, I'll get her for you now." Unless she was trained in the Royal Shakespeare Company she wouldn't have been able to do that and hide a liaison. Lena felt she had been foolishly suspicious, yet she knew that this was not the same

Louis who had run with her to London so eagerly and without a care.

This was a man who did not feel caught up with her to the exclusion of all others as he had once been, as she still was. Sometimes he stayed on a bit in the Dryden because a few of them were having a drink in the pub around the corner. It didn't do to be seen imbibing on your own premises.

"You were having a drink rather than coming home?" Lena had said. But she had only said it once in that hurt tone.

"Jesus Christ, Lena. If I tell you where I am you get offended, and if I don't tell you where I am you get offended. Shall we go down to some ironmonger now and get a ball and chain welded on and it would save us a lot of trouble."

"Don't be an idiot," she said in a voice disguising her terror. She had seen real annoyance and impatience in his eyes.

The new premises were opened in May, and there was the expected publicity. Yet again Dawn was photographed and Lena managed to stay out of the limelight, but this time there was something she could offer in return.

"Mr. Millar, our managing director, and Miss Park, our senior executive, are going to be married later this year," she told the reporters who attended the opening ceremony for Millar's new-look agency.

Nobody except her own colleagues would notice that she wasn't properly acknowledged. Some of the clients maybe. Louis would know why, so would Ivy.

Grace did ask. "Are you on the run, by any chance?" she asked, when the papers were published telling everyone's life story except Lena's, and showing every face except that of the woman who made the agency what it was.

"Sort of," Lena said. "Not the law, we're all right there, I think."

"A man then."

"Well, yes. I more ran to one than from one."

"But there was one, and a daughter?"

"Yes, and a handsome boy."

"I hope he's worth it . . . your Louis."

"Grace, you know he isn't. Stop having silly hopes like that." They collapsed in giggles.

I miss the laughing more than anything else, Clio wrote.

I don't miss the secrets and the plans. Those are separate, and different anyway. I should never have looked at your letter and the truth is that I didn't see who it was to. But I shouldn't have looked. I was trying to see if it was Philip and if you were holding out on me. If ever we do get to be friends again I swear I will always regard letters as sacred. Also, I don't want to spend any more time persuading you to come to university with me. I know you won't, and it's your life. I'm not much of a friend I know, a bit bossy, and I'm very ashamed about that letter. But I'm lonely and I miss you, and I can't study properly and I was wondering whether you thought it might be worth patching it up.

Love Clio.

Dear Clio,

Okay. But remember something. We don't have to be friends. There's no law saying that we must walk forever two by two in this town or anywhere. I'm glad you got in touch. I'm sick to death of Lonny Donegan. Have you anything better to play?

Love Kit.

Emmet delivered the letter to the Kellys' house.

"They're mad, aren't they," Anna Kelly said to him.

"Stone mad," Emmet agreed.

"They go to the same school, sit in the same classroom, and they use us as postmen."

"It must have been a big row," Emmet said in wonder.

"Don't you know what it was?"

"No, Kit never said."

"Clio's never talked of anything else. Apparently Kit dropped some letter and Clio picked it up and gave it back to her and accidentally looked to see who she was writing to. And Kit lost her head altogether."

"And who was she writing to that was so secret?" Emmet asked.

"A fellow called Len," said Anna, proud to be the bearer of such important news.

"Thanks Emmet, you're a pal."

"No," said Emmet. "I'm an eejit."

"Why do you say that?"

351

"I felt such a fool. I didn't know you have a fellow called Len. Anna Kelly had to tell me."

"What fellow called Len?" Kit was mystified.

"The one you wrote the letter to, the one that you let fall."

Kit looked at him levelly. "Was Clio at home when you went there?"

"No, just Anna."

"I'll give you anything if you go and get it back."

"No, Kit. This is silly, you're going mad."

"I may be, but I'll give you sixpence."

"You haven't got sixpence."

"I'll give you the sixpence out of the bottom of the Infant of Prague statue and then I'll put it back when I get my pocket money."

"Why do you want it back?"

"Please, Emmet. Please."

"You're old. You're not meant to be like this."

"I know, but it's the way I am. I'll do anything for you. Anytime you want something for the rest of your life . . . I'll do it."

"Will you?" He seemed doubtful.

"Remember this day, remember this act you did for me."

"And you'll do anything at all?" Emmet weighed it up.

"Yes. Hurry."

"If she's back?"

"Then it doesn't count, so go off as quick as you can."

"Are you a bit of a doormat?" Anna Kelly asked Emmet.

"No, I did a great deal," Emmet said.

"What was it?"

"She's going to do me any favor I want ever in life."

"That's soft. She won't." Anna laughed.

"She will. Kit's as straight as a die," Emmet said, pocketing the letter and going home.

At school next day Mother Bernard told the Sixth Years that she had now counted exactly twenty-three working days for intensive revision, prayer to the Holy Spirit, and little else. The Leaving Certificate would soon be upon them with all its attendant anxieties. She wanted to hear nothing of silliness or divilment until the examination was over.

At break Clio said, "I hear you sent a letter up and then thought better of it."

"Your information service is as good as ever," Kit said.

"Why, Kit? Why did you change your mind?"

"You don't know what I said."

"Yes I do. Anna read it, she steamed it open and told me. I've brought you 'Che Sarà, Sarà' as a peace offering."

"You're such a liar, Clio. You lie about everything."

Clio's face reddened. "No I don't. I have it in my schoolbag."

"You said you didn't see who it was to, but you did."

"Only the name . . ."

"You said I dropped it on the floor. You didn't say you snatched it."

"Bloody Anna."

And for the first time Kit smiled. "All right, you dishonest old fraud, give me the record and come round this evening and we'll go for a walk."

"We're meant to be studying!" Clio could hardly believe the long row was over.

"Well, study then. I'm going for a walk."

"And you'll tell me everything," Clio said.

"I'll tell you nothing," Kit promised.

Martin had not asked Maura Hayes to marry him. He just couldn't say the words. They were like lines from a play. He knew that every woman deserved to be proposed to, but he was afraid it would come out wrong. He was afraid that the echo of years ago would sound through what he said without his intending it to.

He was hoping that somehow it could all be agreed to and organized without having to ask. She was so understanding and undemanding. She cheered him up and made him laugh. She loved to go walking with him, but she didn't choose the routes that Helen had walked so ceaselessly by the lake. Instead she found new places to go, a sheltered glen where you saw the mountains in the far distance, and just a shimmering line of the lake on one side. Sometimes she packed a flask of coffee and a slice of Fullers cake that she had brought down from Dublin. It was companionable and close, something Martin had never known in a marriage.

He had spoken to both his children separately, told them that his friendship with Maura Hayes was special. Both had said they were enthusiastic.

Kit in particular. "Dad, you don't have to explain to us that she's not Mother, we know that. And she's very nice, I always liked her much more than Clio's mother."

Peter Kelly drank a pint each night with Martin in Paddles' bar. The solidarity was huge, but the subject was never broached. Both men knew that when there was something to be said, then it would be said.

And yet something in his heart, some unfinished business, prevented Martin McMahon from doing what he knew was the honorable and right thing to do. It depressed him that he seemed to be a weak man, unsure and dithering. There were so many areas of his life where he was sure and confident: in the pharmacy where he gave advice and consolation as well as compound medicines; as a father for the past years his children had been able to trust him and talk to him. Even possibly as a friend.

But not as a suitor to this good woman who deserved more from him. "I wonder are you wasting your time with me, Maura," he said to her.

"I wouldn't say any time spent with you was wasted." She was calm, unflustered.

"I am not what you hoped."

"You are what you are."

He looked at her fondly. It was the night before the Leaving Certificate started. She had been so helpful to Kit, explained to her that examinations were all about showing what you did know rather than fearing you would be caught out in what you didn't know.

Kit had found it not only useful but a revelation. "I never knew that," she said truthfully.

"Well, that's the system," Maura had said, going over an old examination paper. "Look here when it says as an essay title *The place I love most in Ireland* or here it says *My earliest memory* . . . now you were telling me that you know all about Glendalough and you were hoping to get a subject like *A place of historic interest.* You could always turn either of those titles to your advantage."

Maura suggested that Kit have tea and a chocolate biscuit to take with her to bed.

Martin and Maura sat in the large sofa, side by side. He had never sat there with Helen. She had perched on the window seat, or gone to read in a narrow high-backed chair that had been gradually moved to a position of less importance over the years. Helen's bedroom had now become a storeroom. The signs of her presence had lessened but her spirit was still there.

Martin reached for Maura's hand. "It's not fair to you, Maura. I'm not ready, you see."

"Did I ask you to be ready . . . for anything?"

She leaned over and kissed him, the kind of kisses they had, gentle and lingering. This was not an area where he compared her to Helen. Helen had never reached to kiss him in her whole life. Helen had just accepted his love. He never knew whether it pleased her or not. There had been no sign of great delight, and certainly none of revulsion. But it had been a passive thing. Never had she raised her hand to stroke his cheek even.

He clung to Maura. "Is it fair to ask you to give me some more time?" he murmured into her neck. She smelled of Elizabeth Arden Blue Grass soap and talcum powder. He felt himself aroused to hold her longer and to know her body more. But this would be the final betrayal. If he were to have Maura Hayes it must be as a wife and a life companion. Not as a quick coupling on their sofa.

She seemed to know this, and pulled gently away. "Have all the time you want, Martin," she said. "What else am I doing that you're keeping me from?"

Just then they heard a foot on the stair, and Kit knocked at the door. "I just wanted to tell you I can't sleep. The tea didn't work."

"Would you like to come in and talk?" Maura was courteous, not directive.

"Well, what I'd really like to do is to walk up to Sister Madeleine's for a half hour or so." Kit always said where she was going. The history of going out for a walk and not returning was too heavy in this house for anyone to make unexplained journeys.

"I don't know. Isn't it a bit late?" Martin sounded worried.

"Sister Madeleine is probably the best place on earth to go," Maura said. "That woman is able to make everything seem reasonable."

Kit flashed her a grateful look and ran down the stairs.

"I wish I could find the same kind of consolation in Sister Madeleine that everyone else does . . ." Martin had never been able to confide in the old lined woman whom most of Lough Glass seemed to hold in such respect.

"That's probably because Helen used to go there so much . . . you are afraid that she knows too much and might think you were coming to find out something for yourself."

"That's quite true." Martin was surprised.

"Well, I wouldn't worry about that side of it. Whatever she has been told or not told seems to be totally secret." Maura gathered her cardigan and handbag. "I'll be off now, Martin. I don't want Lilian and Peter thinking I'm up to no good." She had a brave smile on her face. If Maura Hayes was hurt to the heart that Martin could make no commitment she was not going to show it. She waved to him as he stood at the door, then watched Kathleen Sullivan's curtains twitch. At least she would be able to report the doctor's foolish sister-in-law had left the widower's home at a reasonably respectable time.

"Tell me now why the exam is so important to you," Sister Madeleine asked.

"Oh, Sister Madeleine, you must be the only person in Ireland who doesn't know that the Leaving is the making or breaking of you. My whole life depends on it."

"I'd hardly say that."

"Well, it does. If I get it, I get into Cathal Brugha Street training college and do hotel management for two whole years and then I have a career. Otherwise I'm finished, my life is over."

"I suppose you could always go back to school for another year." The suggestion was a mild one.

"Another year at school with Mother Bernard, with all those horrible girls in Fifth Year laughing and mocking you, with Clio gone off to Dublin to university. I'd die, Sister Madeleine, die . . . and anyway I want to be something, be someone. Not just for myself."

"Who for?"

"Well, for Daddy, so he wouldn't look foolish down in Paddles' bar with Dr. Kelly. And . . . well, for my mother really."

"I know." Sister Madeleine did know.

"I told her I'd amount to something. You know . . . long ago."

"And you have and will."

"But these are kind of milestones, markers along the way, these exams."

"Your mother told you that?"

"No. Lena her friend, you know . . . who writes here. She told me."

"You pay a lot of heed to this friend?"

"Yes. You see, she knew Mother very well . . . it's almost like . . ."

"It must be."

"I wish she'd come over here . . . I did suggest it," Kit said.

"Maybe she prefers to live in her own world."

"I'll have to wait until I go over to see her then."

"Yes, but that may be a while. In the meantime you can stay friends with her by writing."

"It mightn't be all that time, Sister Madeleine. After the Leaving I think I'm going to London."

"You are?" The nun seemed startled.

"Yes. Daddy said I could have a holiday . . ."

"But London! On your own?"

"It wouldn't be on my own, it would be with Clio and others from our class. Mother Bernard's arranging that we can stay in a convent in London . . . then none of our parents will get frightened and think we're going to join the white slave traffic."

"My goodness. And what will you do?"

"Well, I'm going to see Lena."

"And will you tell her that you're coming to visit?"

"No. I think I'll turn up and surprise her."

Sister Madeleine's eyes seemed farther away than usual as she looked across the calm lake. Eventually she spoke. "Well, we'll have to make sure that you get your Leaving Certificate then. I'll say special prayers for you tonight."

"Will you kneel down and say a Rosary?" Kit was eager to know how much support she could count on.

"Now, Kit. You're a grown-up woman of seventeen. You know God just wants to listen to a request and hear the reasons why it should be granted. He doesn't want a great numerical totting-up of Hail Marys. That's not how the system works."

Kit knew that Sister Madeleine was absolutely right, but she was sure that this was the kind of talk that made Father Baily, Brother Healy, and Mother Bernard suspicious of the hermit. It was the kind of talk that at another time might have her burned at the stake.

As Kit went off home by the lake Sister Madeleine took out her writing paper.

Dear Lena Gray,

I am writing to let you know that Kit McMahon is hoping to go to London when the Leaving Certificate examination is over . . . she wants to surprise you with a visit. I feel that surprises lose their excitement after a certain age, and thought that perhaps you might like to be prepared for such an eventuality.

If there is anything I can do for you please let me know. I have tried to suggest a relationship based entirely on letters but I am afraid she is too drawn to you and your memories of her mother, as well as your insights about her own future, to let matters rest there.

She is a very determined young woman . . . just like her mother.

> *Yours sincerely in Jesus Christ,*
> *Madeleine.*

"She doesn't know which flat I live in," Lena said to Ivy.

"No, but all she has to do is ask anyone on the stairs," Ivy said.

"She'll ask *you*. You'll say we're away."

"Yes, but she'll come back when she thinks you'll be back."

"I'll write and say we're going away for the summer."

"You can't keep running away from her."

"I can't meet her, we know that."

"Could you dye your hair, wear sunglasses?" Ivy was serious.

"I'm her mother, for God's sake."

"I'm trying to help." Ivy was aggrieved. Things were hard for her. Ernest spent every evening at the hospital where Charlotte was sinking fast. He called at Ivy's flat for a drink on the way home each night. A drink and a long recounting of the guilt he felt in his life at how poorly he had treated his wife. It was increasingly hard to bear.

Lena was full of shame at having spoken so harshly. "I'm terrified, that's why I'm snapping at you. You're the only friend I have in the world."

"I'm *not* your only friend . . . you have dozens of friends. You have Louis, and all those people at work who dote on you and depend on you. You have a daughter who loves you even if she doesn't know who you are . . . don't tell me about having few friends."

"Oh, Ivy. Do you now what I'd love to do for you? I'd love to take you to Ireland for a holiday."

"So, take me," Ivy challenged.

"I can't, you know that. They'd see me, they'd find out."

"Yes. I imagine they have armed guards posted at the airport and the ferries, waiting for you," Ivy scoffed. "After all, they do that when anyone drowns in a lake is found and buried." Ivy sounded bitter.

"We could go someday. I'm too frail these days. Everything's coming apart," Lena said.

"Don't crack up on me, Lena. Charlotte only has another week at the most."

ℵ ℵ ℵ

"Can I come to London?" Anna Kelly asked.

"Daddy, don't even let her think of talking like that," Clio protested.

"Shush, Clio. Anna, when you get your Leaving Certificate of course you can go to London."

"But Daddy . . . wouldn't this be a heaven-sent opportunity? My big sister could look after me and my mind would get broader by travel, and I'd be in no danger."

"Don't waste your breath, Anna," Clio warned.

"None of the others would mind. I asked Kit McMahon and Jane Wall and Eileen Hickey who are going and they said they didn't care."

"Of course they don't care. You aren't their rotten sister." Clio was incensed.

Aunt Maura spoke unexpectedly. "I hope you won't go, Anna," she said.

"Why is that?" Anna was suspicious.

"Well, you see, I'll be coming down for the golf tournament and we need to have caddies, but everyone in the club is taken up and Martin McMahon and I were wondering whether you and Emmet might do it for us."

"No, I don't think . . ."

"It's awfully well paid," said Aunt Maura. "And much more fun in a way than trailing around London in the heat with a lot of people who aren't your real friends. I know I'm only trying to persuade you because Martin and I would like our own families to be there to support us, but there'll be lots of parties . . . and a dance with a lot of young people."

"I was never allowed to a dance when I was her age." Clio was stung.

"The world is changing since you were young, Clio," Anna said.

For a fraction of a second Clio's eyes met those of her aunt Maura. There was a hint of a smile. Clio knew that her aunt had succeeded where no one else could have in putting an end to Anna's bleating. Anna Kelly was showing alarming tendencies of getting her own way in everything she suggested.

"Do you think they're ever going to do anything about it or are they going to go on mooning about forever?" Lilian asked her husband.

"I don't know," Peter Kelly said mildly.

"Well, you must know. He's your friend."

"She's your sister," he countered.

"There are things you can't say to sisters if they are old and still spinsters," Lilian explained.

"Yes, and there are things you can't say to friends if they are old and have been through a lot," Dr. Peter Kelly said.

"It's nice to see you down here so regularly, Maura," Sister Madeleine said.

"Well, Sister, I'll come for as long as I think he likes me to be here."

"He likes you to be here."

"But would you know? I'm not being rude to you, but would you?"

"I think I would, Maura. From what people say."

Maura realized that people did say a lot and

Sister Madeleine listened a lot. She probably did know.

"You're such a kind person I wish there was something I could do for you."

Sister Madeleine looked at her thoughtfully. "There is something I would like done, but it's very, very complicated, and I could never tell you why."

"I wouldn't need to know why."

"No, God bless you, I don't think you would. Well, I'll ask you and it may not be possible, but if you could . . ."

"Please ask, Sister. It would be a great pleasure to do anything for you, anything at all."

"You know there's talk of Clio and Kit and a few of the girls in Sixth Year going to London after the Leaving Cert . . ."

"Don't I know it. They talk of so little else."

"Yes well, what I was wondering was could you persuade Kit and Clio not to go?"

"But why on earth? I'm sorry, I forgot . . ." Maura paused. After a while she said, "I think it would be very, very difficult."

"I was afraid of that."

"And is there a good reason?"

"A very good reason."

"I can't think what I could do. I can't tell them London is full of typhoid fever. I can't offer to take them to France or anything, I've just managed to prevent Anna from trying to go with them by offering her a job as my caddy in the golf tournament." There was a silence. "Is there no one else?" Maura asked.

"No one I could ask," the hermit said.

Maura felt a surge of pride that she was among the very few who could be approached. "I believe Mother Bernard up in the convent is organizing it, maybe if she told . . ."

"No. Sadly she'd need every detail and these are impossible to give."

There was another silence.

"I'm really trying but I can't think of any single thing that would distract them, not at this stage."

"Thank you for trying anyway. I know you are."

"What will you do now?"

"I suppose I'll pray that the Lord will sort things out, and that you won't puzzle too much about what may seem like a very odd request."

"I will put it right out of my mind and forget it was ever mentioned." Maura Hayes smiled.

And Sister Madeleine reached over and took her hand. This was a truly kind woman who would make an excellent wife and companion for poor Martin McMahon if . . . if . . . well, if things were different.

א   א   א

Charlotte died in hospital on a Thursday morning.

Ivy wanted to come to the hospital to be with Ernest but he said no.

"I'll just stay in the waiting room away from everyone in case you need me," Ivy had pleaded.

"No, love. Honest. Don't cause a fuss, don't let's make trouble at this stage for everyone. Stay at home. I'll come to you later in the day."

Thursday passed and Ernest never came. Ivy

rang the pub around closing time. She spoke to a barman she knew. "He's with his family in the front snug, Ivy. It's probably best I don't tell him you rang."

"Absolutely," Ivy said. She sat in her little room awake all night. She was sure he would come at some stage, when everyone else had gone home.

At three o'clock she heard a taxi drawing up at the door. She moved the curtain and looked out, but the taxi was not Ernest, it was a woman in a white sweater, with very blond hair, very red lips, and very high heels. She had got out of the taxi to kiss Louis Gray good-bye properly with a great deal of squeaking and lifting one leg at a time as she embraced him. She was oblivious to his shushing sounds as he paid the taxi and urged the driver to take her away as quickly as possible.

"Will I go to the funeral with you?" Lena asked.

"What?"

"You'll need someone to go with, you can hardly be up there in mourning with the family. I thought you'd need a friend as a sort of disguise."

"Lord, Lena, you're great."

"So I'll go with you then. When is it?"

"Love, we're not going whenever it is. It would not be, as Ernest has put it, appropriate. Can you imagine Ernest knowing a big word like 'appropriate'?"

"But of course we can go, anyone can go to a funeral."

"In Ireland maybe, not here."

"They don't sell tickets, do they? We'll go."

"He doesn't want us, why push?"

"All right, all right. Maybe she has relatives, maybe it will be small. Maybe he's right not to want you there."

"He doesn't want me anywhere. That's what I'm mourning, not bloody Charlotte," Ivy said.

א א א

"Are you definite about doing hotel management?" Philip O'Brien asked.

"Sure I am, Philip. You know that."

"So we'll be together in Dublin."

"At classes, yes, but not exactly together. I'm staying in the hostel in Mountjoy Square. It's just around the corner, I'd say it's a bit grim."

"I'm staying with my aunt and uncle and I *know* that will be grim." Philip was glum these days. He had agreed unwillingly when Kit had said she didn't want to get into kissing and groping and all that because of exams.

"It might distract me," she had lied to him.

The day the Leaving Certificate finished Philip came back. "It won't distract you now," he had said, eager as the two Jack Russell terriers that terrorized people in the Central Hotel.

So Kit had to give him a different excuse. "It's an odd time for a girl being seventeen. Please be understanding. I promise I don't fancy anyone else, but I really and truly don't want to get involved at the moment."

368

"But aren't you fond of me . . . ?" Philip would ask.

"Very fond of you."

"So then?" He was eternally hopeful.

"So then you'll understand."

"And are you waiting for me and am I waiting for you? Just tell me," Philip had begged.

"Let's say we're not hunting for anyone else, but if someone else turned up for you it wouldn't be a betrayal or anything. I'd quite understand," she had said.

"And for you, Kit?"

"I won't have time for anyone else to turn up. I'm so busy."

"No you're not. You're on holiday."

"I'm going to London. Who could turn up in London?"

"You're only going to London for ten days."

"Then I'll be back. Philip, please."

And because he didn't want to be tiresome, he stopped. And they went to the pictures just on their own, and sometimes with Emmet, sometimes with Anna. Because, as Clio said, Anna was so awful and such a troublemaker the only thing to do was to let her come to places where she couldn't do much harm, like at the cinema, a place where nobody had to talk to her.

א   א   א

Dear Kit,

I am so eager to hear the result of your exams. It will be so exciting to plan your course in hotel management. Do tell me more about it. And what are you going to do for the holidays? I'll be away a lot traveling, but your letters may be forwarded to me, so I can reply from wherever I am. It's a pity I won't be in London during the summer because, unlike everyone else, I actually enjoy the city when all the visitors come. If you have Sister Madeleine praying for you, and your father's nice friend, Maura Hayes, rooting for you, and if you've done all the work you say you did, I'm sure you don't need me on the case as well. But I do keep my fingers crossed for you.

> *Love as always,*
> *Lena*

"London could be very crowded during the summer," Maura Hayes said to Kit the day after she got this letter from Lena.

"I'd say it's nice when it's full of tourists, holiday-like," Kit said.

"Not the best time to see it, in a way."

"Oh, don't join all the others who say not to go, please, Maura."

"I'm not saying not to go . . ."

"What are you saying?" Kit asked.

"I don't know," Maura answered truthfully, and for some reason it made both of them laugh helplessly. Martin McMahon came into the kitchen and asked what the joke was. "If I were to go through the whole conversation there wouldn't be a laugh in it," said Maura, wiping her eyes.

"They'd lock us up," Kit agreed.

Rita was finishing the ironing. She had heard the whole exchange and all she could understand was that it was really time Mr. McMahon made a move. Miss Hayes was a very nice person. He would never find anyone who got on so well with his children.

Mother Bernard got a phone call in the school. It was from a lady in London. She wanted to know when the results of the Leaving Certificate were expected.

"They arrived today." Mother Bernard sounded pleased. It had been a very good result as far as she was concerned. The lady wanted to inquire about the successes and failures.

"And to whom am I speaking?" Mother Bernard wouldn't reveal that the Wall girl and young Hickey had done so badly, not to any stranger on the phone.

"I am a distant relation of Cliona Kelly."

If Mother Bernard thought it odd that this woman had not called the Kelly family she said nothing, instead she listed with pride the number of honors Cliona Kelly had got in her examination.

"And her friend, Kit McMahon?"

"Mary Katherine McMahon did very well also. The whole standard was very high."

"And I believe the girls are coming on a visit to London, to your sister house?"

"That is so, but . . ."

"I was going to write a letter there to whoever you would suggest . . . perhaps arranging to meet

371

Cliona. Can you tell me what date they are arriving?"

"Mother Lucy is in charge of the London house and our girls for the duration of their stay. They will be arriving on August ninth for nine full days . . . and you are . . . ?"

"Thank you so much, Mother Bernard." The connection was broken. Mother Bernard looked at the receiver. How did this woman know she was Mother Bernard?

At Mass on Sunday, Mother Bernard was talking to the Kellys. "Your relation rang up from England to inquire about Cliona's Leaving results," she said.

"England?" said Peter Kelly.

"Relation?" said Lilian.

"That's what she said." Mother Bernard sounded defensive.

What could she mean? they asked each other on the way home. "Getting a bit dozy maybe," Lilian suggested.

"She seems sharp enough." Peter was thoughtful.

"Let's hope she lasts out for Anna's time anyway." Lilian was always practical.

. . . and so I am off on a tour leaving August 8th. I told you I'd be out of London for about two weeks. Still, it's a great opportunity for me. Hope your summer plans are going well, and that you have everything ready for your new life in Dublin.

Again, I want to say how great it was to

hear from you so quickly. Thank you so much for writing on the day you got your results. I kept crossing my fingers and got on with my work. I drank your health last night with my friend Ivy Brown.

It's so exciting to be on your way at last.

"What will I do if Louis comes in?" Ivy asked.

"He won't." Lena was grim. "As you very well know. He hasn't been in much."

"He never stays out all night." Ivy was aghast.

"No, but if Kit comes to look for me, it won't be at night. They won't clash."

"And what about you, suppose she sees you on the street?"

"There's eight million people in this city."

"Not in this road, there aren't."

"She doesn't think I'm hiding on her, she doesn't know I'm me. Relax, Ivy."

"You're not relaxed."

"Well, that's because my daughter's going to be in the same city and I want to see her."

"I have an awful feeling about it, I really do."

"Nonsense, Ivy. Just let me spend the evenings in your back kitchen, that's all."

"How do you know she'll come looking for you?"

"I know."

א א א

The boat journey was marvelous fun. They met a great crowd of Irish builders who had been back home for their summer holidays. It was some relief that they were making the return journey to England and freedom.

"Why are they all singing about how wonderful Ireland is if they're leaving it?" Kit asked.

"That's the point of Irish songs. They're only good if you sing them while you're abroad." Clio was very knowledgeable.

"Imagine! We're abroad," Kit said.

"Nearly." Clio was being lofty.

"We're in the middle of the Irish Sea, that's abroad. We're beyond the three-mile limit."

The men asked them to come and listen while they sang "The Rose of Tralee." It was always good to have beautiful girls listening when you sang that song.

"We really are going to London," whispered Clio. "We'll see real teddy boys, real coffee bars, everything."

"I know," said Kit. "I know." She was thinking about how she would find her mother's friend, Lena; the woman who knew much more about her mother than anyone. She would go to her house and ask Mrs. Brown where she was. Then she would go and surprise her.

If ever they had thought Mother Bernard was bad they soon realized that compared to Mother Lucy she was a wild and free soul. Mother Lucy assumed that they would all want to see cultural sights only, and that evenings would be spent playing table tennis and making cocoa once the Rosary had been said in the convent chapel.

Although they enjoyed the visits to Westminster Abbey and the Tower of London, the Planetarium and Madame Tussaud's, the girls were bleakly disappointed with their escorted tour. It was tantalizing being so near and yet so far.

"We could always escape," Jane Wall said.

"Is it worth the bloody trouble?" Clio asked. "It will be painted as black as sin, they'll think at home we did the divil and all, and all just for a cup of coffee in Soho."

"Your aunt rang again, Cliona," Mother Lucy said on the third night.

"My aunt?" Clio was alarmed. "There isn't anything wrong, is there?"

"No, she just wanted to know your movements, if you had any free time on your own."

Clio shrugged at Kit. "Why on earth did she want to know that?" she said.

"I don't know. I think she may have wanted to take you out somewhere, she was very anxious to be filled in on your timetable."

It was a mystery. Aunt Maura, in London.

"Is she going to ring again?" Clio wanted to know.

"I'm not sure. But if she does want to take you out then I assume it will be in order."

Clio's eyes met Kit's and began to dance. "If she does ring again, then it would be nice to see her," Clio said in her fawning voice.

"Yes, well, of course."

"Maura's not in London, she's back in Lough Glass playing golf," Kit whispered later.

"I know, but it must be some glorious mistake sent by God and Saint Patrick and Saint Jude, the patron saint of hopeless cases. Go out and ring and leave a message for me."

"Where?"

"Anywhere, phone box in the street. They'll think you're in the bathroom."

Kit found a red phone box and put the money in. "May I speak to Cliona Kelly, it's her aunt?" she asked the little sister who minded the door.

In a moment Kit was put through to Cliona in the recreation room. "Hallo," she whispered, terrified that it was all going to be unmasked.

"Oh, Aunt Maura, how nice of you to call. Mother and Father were so much hoping you would get in touch."

Kit listened wordlessly to the easy flow of Clio's lies. They would so much love to meet Aunt Maura at five o'clock tomorrow. No, no, Mother Lucy would be happy to let Kit and herself out for just a few hours.

"Aren't you lucky," said Jane Wall. "Imagine your aunt being in London."

"I know," said Clio. "Makes you believe in fate."

"What will we do?" Clio asked. "Where will we go?"

"You go where you like. I'm going off on my own."

"Oh, Kit, you can't. We can go on our own, but together."

"You're the one who said it was ludicrous, grown-up women like us being tied up in a convent."

"Well, it is, of course, but it doesn't mean you're going to get into some kind of mood and go off and leave me. I got you this free time after all, it was my aunt who was in London."

"You know as well as I there was no aunt in London. It was some kind of mistake that poor sister at the door made."

"It's still me that got it."

"No it isn't. I was the one who went out to a phone box."

"Where are you going?" Clio demanded.

"I'm not telling you. I'm going nowhere, I'm just trying to be free."

"We can be free together, and have a bit of fun."

"No we can't. Stop whining, Clio. Do what you like, we'll meet at ten and then you can tell me everything."

"I hate you at times."

"I know, I hate you at times too, but a lot of the time we get on quite well," Kit said.

"I can't imagine why," Clio grumbled.

Kit had the map and she knew where to catch the Underground to Earl's Court. But first she had to shake Clio. "You've been talking about Soho since we were fifteen. You just get on a bus and get out at Piccadilly Circus."

"You're meeting someone, I know that's what you're doing," Clio said.

"Clio, already you're eating into the bit of free time we have. Will you get the bus or will you not?"

When she was sure that the bus had gone out of view carrying Clio aboard, Kit ran down the steps of the station and took the Circle Line. At least she would see the house where Lena and Louis Gray lived. She would leave a note and maybe talk to this Mrs. Brown. Once or twice she had asked in letters who Mrs. Brown was, but there had never been a real explanation. Kit felt a surge of excitement well up in her throat. In twenty minutes she would be there.

Kit had thought it would be a more fashionable street. Somehow she had always seen it as a place with big houses that had drives leading up to them. She thought that Mrs. Brown might be an aunt, or a relative anyway. A rich woman whom they partly looked after. But this was definitely the road. And number 27 was definitely the place she had been writing letters for almost four years.

Lena had never said the place was elegant, but neither had she said it was so ordinary. The paint was peeling on several of the doors and nearby the railings were rusty. There were dustbins in the street and in basements. It wasn't the kind of place that this friend of Mother's should be living in.

Kit looked at her own reflection in a window. She had dressed carefully, in her best tartan skirt, and a yellow blouse. She wore a tartan scarf around her neck, a present from Maura. She had put on lipstick, of course, as soon as she left the convent gate. Over her shoulder she wore a black shoulder bag. Her long dark curly hair was tied up with a smart black ribbon. She thought Lena would think she had made an effort, that is, if Lena was there. Anyway this Mrs. Brown would tell her that Kit was a smart girl.

With a feeling of anxiety that was near dread, something she couldn't understand, Kit Mc-

Mahon knocked on the door of number 27.

Louis had come into Millar's at lunchtime. "Quick half pint?" he asked Lena.

Jessie Park always liked to see Louis Gray, he had such distinction and good looks. She wagged her finger at him. "You don't come to see us nearly often enough," she said with mock severity. Jessie had certainly improved over the years. Her hair was no longer the wild bird's nest of hair. She wore a smart gray dress with a blue and gold scarf, her nails were painted. She looked a perfectly acceptable London businesswoman.

"You look very lovely today, Jessie," he said.

Her blush and smile were predictable, Lena had seen the same response on the faces of so many women since she had been with Louis. A response to flattery. An innocent pleasure at being appreciated and admired.

Lena excused herself from the clients. This was important. Louis never came to see her at work. A sudden fear came to her. Had Kit arrived? Had she met Louis? Then she told herself this was impossible. She had checked in the convent where the girls were staying. There would be no chance of Kit being released during the daytime, the educational program was too intense.

They walked side by side to the pub nearby, and she sat at the table while he bought them a drink.

"Remember you tried to make me get this week off," he said.

"Yes." She had begged him, beseeched, offered to take them to any hotel . . . offered to go where he'd choose. But he had said it was impossible, he was needed at the hotel. He had become annoyed about it also, claiming that Lena never accepted that he too had responsibilities at work. She had dropped it.

"You go alone if you need a holiday so badly," he had said.

But Lena couldn't leave number 27 knowing that Kit McMahon was on her way there to give her a surprise. She couldn't risk that Kit might meet Louis and learn everything.

His smile was as warm as ever. "My love . . . wasn't it well that you didn't let me weaken and take a little holiday?"

"Why was that?" She forced her voice to be up and bright.

"They're sending me to Paris," he said triumphantly.

"To Paris?" Her heart was like a stone.

"Not forever . . . just for ten days. To see how this French hotel is run. It's an exchange. A Frenchman is coming here. Won't that set their pulses racing at the Dryden?"

"Not as much as you do." It was an automatic response, but oddly it came out wrong. It sounded bitter, it sounded like an accusation.

"So, I'm off."

"You're off?"

"Well, you can hardly come with me, can you?" he asked.

"I suppose I could get some time . . ."

"You don't have a passport," Louis said. His glance was very level. Of course Lena didn't have a passport. How could a dead woman apply to get a passport? He could go abroad forever without her.

"When do you go?" she asked.

"I thought today," he said.

Lena's head felt very heavy, as if it was a great weight to lift up and look him in the eye. "Do you love me at all, Louis?" she asked.

"I love you very much," he said. There was a silence. "You believe me?" he asked.

"I don't know." Her voice was bleak. She saw the impatience in his face. This was what he hated, but she was too tired, too weary to care. And he was going anyway, whether she was light and cheerful, or heavy and gloom-laden.

"Well, you should know," he said. "Why would I stay if I didn't love you. I'm here, aren't I?"

"That's right." She was resigned.

"Lena, don't make me go with this big draggy feeling of guilt about it. It's an opportunity, it's a chance, it's what we want. You are making squeaks just like a wife now. It's not like you."

"No, you're right. It's much more like me to be jolly and full of smiles and turn a blind eye to what's happening."

"And what is happening?" His voice was very cold.

"What's happening is that you are treating me like dirt. You are coming in all hours of the night . . ."

"Oh God, no. Not a scene in a public place." He put his head in his hands.

"What's happening is that you know you can do anything you bloody well like. You don't have to marry me because I'm dead. You don't have to take me abroad because I'm dead. When I die you won't even have to bury me because I'm dead and buried already. Did you think of that, did you?" Her laugh had a hysterical tinge.

"Jesus, Lena, get ahold of yourself." He looked around him, alarmed.

"I've got ahold of myself all right, but I have no hold on you, none at all."

Now he was angry. "Nor should you have. We don't believe in all that business of tying each other down, we've been through this. Love isn't about making rules — thou shalt not do this or do that . . ."

"And love certainly isn't about going off to France with whatever bit of stuff you're sleeping with nowadays."

"Lena, you're disgusting. Ring the Dryden, ask them am I doing an exchange, ask them."

"Give me credit for something, for some bloody bit of dignity. Do you think I'd lower myself to make a call like that to check on you?"

"See, you have it every way now. You want proof, I give you proof, you won't take it."

"Go to Paris. I'm sick of you, Louis, go there and stay there."

"I just might," he said. "And if I do . . . you sent me."

The afternoon was stifling. Jessie looked at her several times, but always Lena waved away any question or sympathy.

"Not bad news, was it?" Dawn asked.

"Absolutely not. Louis is going to France, I may join him there at the weekend."

"Aren't you a lucky couple," Dawn said in genuine admiration.

At six o'clock with a great sense of relief, she put her cover on her typewriter, locked her files into her drawer, and left the office. Louis would be out of the flat by now. He would have gone straight home and packed his things. The only problem was how much he had packed. Enough for ten days in France, or enough for a longer time away from her. And as he had said, it was she who sent him.

She put off the evil moment of arriving home, and went to a pub.

"You're too good-looking to drink alone," the barman said as Lena bought her gin and tonic.

"Chat me up at your peril," she said to him.

He laughed but he moved away smartly. There was something about her eyes that made him know she wasn't joking.

Ivy made tea for the strikingly attractive Irish girl in her fresh yellow blouse and tartan skirt. She was a younger version of Lena, with the same shiny curly hair, and big dark eyes.

"I thought you'd be different, Mrs. Brown. I've been sending you letters for years, I didn't know you'd be . . ." She paused.

"I'd be what?" Ivy had a mock threatening look.

"Well, young and kind of fun. I got the impression you were old and sort of making people be quiet in front of you."

"Is that what Lena wrote about me?"

"No. She wrote nothing about you, she wrote

always about me. I know so little of her life here, but all about her time with my mother. And she's so interested in everything I do it makes me a bit selfish in my letters, I'm afraid . . ."

"She loves to hear from you, I do know that."

"What a pity she isn't here."

Kit sounded so bereft, Ivy found herself swallowing. "Yes . . . well, you can't have let her know you were coming. I'm sure she'd have stayed."

"I wanted it to be a surprise."

"And didn't you know she was going away? She didn't tell you?"

"Yes, she did. But you know this is very odd, I got the feeling that she might not be going, that it wasn't really definite. I thought she might still be here."

"And now you've had a wasted journey."

"No it's not, I've met you. I know where she lives. She's the only person who ever made sense of anything about my mother to me, they were great friends. And I can see why. Lena's such a letter writer, she makes it like a conversation."

"Yes, I'm sure," Ivy said.

"I don't suppose you could show me their flat. You know, I bet she wouldn't mind."

"No love, I'd better not. People rent from me and they have absolute privacy. It wouldn't be right."

"But you have all the keys hanging on the wall here."

"Yes, but that's only for an emergency."

"Am I not an emergency?"

"No darling. You're just someone she'll be heartbroken to miss, and she'll say . . ." Ivy's voice broke off. Behind Kit there was a hammering on the door.

"Sorry love, just a moment." Ivy leaped to the door with a speed Kit wouldn't have suspected her capable of. Just before Ivy pulled the door behind her Kit saw a very handsome man in an open-necked white shirt and gray flannels standing there. He looked like a film star.

"Ivy . . ." he began.

"I'll talk to you farther down the corridor if that's all right."

"Hey, where's the fire . . . ?" Kit saw him being dragged out of view.

She looked around Ivy's amazing room. Every inch of wall was covered with pictures and posters, programs, beer mats, and little clippings from magazines. You could never get bored in this room, Kit thought, it would be a comforting place to stay. But she must not wear out her welcome. She would have to leave when she finished the tea. She could write a letter to Lena, and leave it.

The voices outside seemed to be raised. The handsome man, whoever he was, did not seem to meet with Ivy's approval. "Listen here, let me leave the box in here out of the way. You don't want people falling over it, breaking their necks and suing you, do you?"

"I'll take it in later, I said it's all right."

But he would hear nothing of it. A big wooden chest was pushed in the door and then the man looked up and saw Kit. "Well, for heaven's sake," he said.

"Hallo," she smiled.

Ivy seemed very anxious to get him out. "So if that's everything," she said.

"I'll give you my key, Ivy, hang it up there with the others. The box will be collected later."

"Fine, fine," Ivy cut across him. "Yes, I understand everything. Safe journey."

"And who's this?" His smile was so warm.

"That's a friend of mine, her name is Mary Katherine."

Kit opened her mouth amazed.

"Lovely to meet you, Mary . . ." he said.

"And you?" She had an upward lift on the words as if asking him to give his name.

There was a hoot from the street. "Your taxi won't wait forever," Ivy said.

And he was gone. They spoke in the hall and through the glass door. Kit could see the man was trying to kiss Ivy on the cheek and noticed she recoiled from him.

"Who was he? He's gorgeous."

"He was trouble, Kit. A lot of trouble."

"Why did you call me Mary Katherine?"

"Your mother . . ." Ivy began, and managed to change the sentence by going on ". . . your mother's friend always said that this was your baptismal name and that this was how you were known at school."

"Imagine you all knowing about me over in London." Kit clasped her hands with pleasure.

Ivy hadn't the heart to shoo her out. The girl had nowhere else to go. And if Lena wasn't home by now she probably would be late. They had an agreement anyway that Lena would not pause at her door.

"Kit sweetheart, will you hold on a moment. I have to leave something upstairs, I'll be right back." Ivy ran up the stairs with a pencil and paper. *She's here,* she wrote, and slipped it under the door. Then she came down the stairs two at a time. Kit hadn't moved. She hadn't read the label on the box that Louis had left, the label saying that it was to be collected, the label giving his own name.

"We'll have another cup of tea," Ivy said.

"If you're sure I'm not keeping you."

"No my love, I'm happy with the company." And since Lena was going to come home to a life without Louis it would be good if at least there were details for her about the visit from her child.

The hall door opened. Ivy looked up. There was something about her glance that made Kit look too, the sense of anxiety, the frown. All she could see was the outline of a dark-haired woman through the glass door. The curtain obscured a better view.

"It's all right," Ivy called in a high, unnatural voice. "I've left a note in your room, no need to come in." She couldn't hear what was being said outside. It sounded a bit strangled. "I'll go up and talk to you later. I have a visitor just now." It was said like the lines from a very bad actress.

Kit never knew afterward what made her do it, but she went to the door. She had a feeling it was Lena, home unexpectedly. The woman who was about to go up the stairs turned as the door opened.

There she stood. A woman in a cream dress

387

with a cream jacket, loose over her shoulders, a long blue and gold scarf around her neck. Her dark curly hair was like a frame around her face.

Kit gave a cry, it sounded strangled in her throat. The moment lasted forever. The woman on the stairs, Ivy Brown in the doorway behind, and Kit with her hand to her throat.

"Mother!" she cried. "Mother!"

Nobody said anything.

"Mother," Kit said again.

Lena stretched out her hand — but Kit backed away.

"You didn't die — you ran away. You're not drowned — you just left us — you left us."

She was white as she looked at the figure on the stairs.

"You let us think you were dead," she cried in horror, and with her eyes full of tears made for the front door out into the street.

CHAPTER SIX

Ivy reached her as she got to the traffic lights. "Please," she begged. "Please come back."

Kit's face was ashen, all the life and vitality had gone from her. This was not the bright girl who had sat chatting in Ivy's room a few minutes before. But then she was a girl who had seen a ghost.

"I beg you to come back." Ivy reached out but Kit shrank back. "It's been a terrible shock. Don't stay here in the street."

"I must go . . . I must go." Kit looked around her wildly at the traffic swirling in every direction, the big red buses so unfamiliar, people who looked different to the people back home. The thud and pound of a London evening.

Ivy didn't touch, didn't grab her wrist, she was afraid that Kit would break free and run headlong into the traffic.

"Your mother loves you so much," Ivy said, hoping it was the right thing.

"My mother is dead," Kit flared.

"No, no."

"She's *dead,* she drowned in the lake . . . she drowned herself. I know that, I'm the only one who knows it. She can't be here, she drowned herself . . ." Kit's voice had the high tinge of hysteria.

Ivy realized it was time to take control. She

put a small wiry arm around Kit's shoulders. "I don't care *what* you say, you can't be allowed to be alone. I'm taking you back with me now." And she half led, half supported the girl back to number 27 and in the door of her own flat.

Lena wasn't there. It was as the place had been not ten minutes ago, the walls covered in their idiotic decorations. Kit sat on the same chair where she had been sitting when she had heard the woman on the stairs and gone out to investigate.

What had drawn her there? Suppose she had not gone? Her head felt very strange as if the top of it had turned into paper. Then she heard a roaring in her ears and felt the floor rise up toward her. Everywhere it seemed there were voices shouting, shouting from a distance.

Then she felt something jabbing at her face and a strange terrible smell that nearly choked her. Ivy's face came into focus, big now and anxious, very near her. She had a small bottle in her hand.

"Don't speak, just sniff it."

"What? What?"

"It's smelling salts, sal volatile they call it . . . you fainted."

"I never faint," Kit said indignantly.

"You're fine now. Here, let me help you onto the sofa . . ."

"Where is she?" Kit asked. The whole thing had come back to her with all its enormity.

"She's upstairs, she won't come down until I tell her."

"I don't want to see her."

"Shush, shush . . . all right. Put your head between your knees for a bit to get the blood back."

"I don't want . . ."

"Did you hear me, I said I won't get her until you're ready."

"I won't be ready . . ."

"Right. Now for a cup of very sweet tea."

"I don't take sugar . . ." Kit began.

"You do today," Ivy said in a voice that was not going to be argued with.

The strong sweet tea began to bring back some of the color.

Eventually Kit spoke. "Was she here from the start . . . ? From the very beginning when we thought she was dead?"

"She'll tell you herself."

"No."

"More tea . . . another biscuit . . . *please,* Kit, it's what we did in the war when people had a shock. It worked then, it will work now." The woman was trying so hard.

She had a lined lace, and bright eyes like buttons. She looked a little like a friendly inquisitive monkey that Kit had seen in the zoo. Was that the time they had gone with Mother or was it the next year when Father had brought Emmet and herself as a treat, as something to take their minds off the tragedy that had happened to them all?

She had been about to refuse the second cup but suddenly she realized that it was the only thing this woman had to give; so she took it.

"How did she know to come to you?" Kit asked.

"What do you mean?"

"Were you friends already?"

"I rent flats, rooms. That's all."

"But you're friends now."

"Yes, we're friends now."

"Why?" Kit asked, her face was full of misery and incomprehension.

"Why? Because she's such a great person, who wouldn't be friends with her?" Ivy was brisk and cheerful and deliberately misunderstanding the question. She wasn't going to attempt to answer that one.

They could hear the clock ticking on Ivy's wall, and outside the muffled sound of traffic. There were footsteps on the stairs but it was not Lena. It was the couple from the third floor going out. Kit and Ivy strained to see through the net curtain.

When they heard the hall door click Ivy said almost triumphantly, "I told you she said she wouldn't come down until you wanted to see her here."

A silence.

"Or to go up to her even?"

"I can't."

"Take your time."

"No, not anytime."

There was another silence then Ivy asked, "Do you mind if I go up and tell her that you're all right . . . No, I promise I won't fetch her downstairs. It's just that she'll want to know."

"What does she care whether we're all right or not . . . ?" Kit said.

"Please, Kit, don't let me leave her sitting there

not knowing. I won't be a minute." Kit said nothing. "Don't run away."

"I'm not the one that ran away," Kit said.

"She'll tell you."

"No."

"When you want to hear," Ivy said, and was gone.

Kit went to the door after she heard Ivy's footsteps go upstairs.

This was the room where her letters had arrived for all those years, letters to Lena Gray, saying private secret things about her mother, talking about the grave and the flowers they had planted around it. She had told this Lena secrets she had told no one, and all the time she had been deceived. A wave of anger and shame rose in her. She would not leave it like this, slip quietly away from this house and pretend that it hadn't happened. Mother was alive, Father must be told, and Emmet and everyone.

It was almost too huge to grapple with. She felt dizzy once more as if she was about to faint again. But she steeled herself. She would go up the stairs and speak to her mother. She would find out what had happened and why. Why her mother had left them all like that to come here and live in this place in London, letting them hunt for her in the lake.

Kit went out and climbed the stairs. She would knock at doors until she found them. But she didn't need to.

She heard Ivy's voice on the first floor. "I'll go back down to her, Lena. The child has had such a shock, she shouldn't be on her own . . ."

Then Ivy saw Kit on the stairs. She stood aside silently to let the girl walk into the room.

"Kit?" Her mother was sitting in a chair with a small rug around her shoulders. She was shivering, Ivy had obviously put it around her. She had a glass of water in her hand.

Ivy closed the door softly behind her and they were alone.

Mother and daughter.

"Why did you do it?" Kit said. Her eyes were hard and her voice was cold. "Why did you let us think you were dead?"

"I had to." Lena's voice was flat.

"You didn't have to. If you wanted to go away from us, from Daddy and Emmet and me, you could have gone . . . you could have told us you were going, not have us hunting for you, praying for you and thinking you were in hell." Kit's voice was breaking up with the emotion of what she was saying.

Lena said nothing. Her eyes were wide in horror. Everything had turned out in the worst possible way. Her daughter had found her. She was filled with loathing and contempt. Must Lena speak now? Tell the girl that it was her father who had done the real betrayal? Or should she protect him? Let Kit think that she had at least one trustworthy parent instead of being saddled with two who had let her down?

The girl was so fiery and strong. And Lena knew the secrets of her heart from her letters. Now she would never hear any more. It was as bad a pain as the open cupboard which had once held Louis Gray's suits.

Lena indicated a chair but the girl would not sit down. Instead she looked around the room, her face working, trying to get control of herself possibly. Lena's eyes followed her, wondering how she saw the place, wishing she could read the thoughts that were darting around inside Kit's head.

She took a breath as if to speak and then changed her mind. She went over to one of the windows and pulled back the heavy curtain to look at the street beneath. Again it was as if she was struggling to work something out before she trusted herself to speak.

Lena sat there, eyes enormous, hand shaking as she laid down her glass of water. Everything seemed to have gone into slow motion. "Say something," Lena said.

Kit's voice was steady. "Why should I say *anything*? What have *I* got to say? You're the one who should say something."

"Will you listen?"

"Yes."

"I made a decision. I loved another man . . . it was such a powerful love I left you and Emmet and my life with you."

"And where is he, the man you loved so much?" There was a sneer in Kit's voice.

"He's not here," Lena said.

"But *why* did you pretend to be dead?" The voice had a false calm, as if she were holding on by a thread.

"I didn't pretend to be dead, that's something that came about by mistake."

"Oh, listen to me," the temper broke, "now

listen to me. Since I've been twelve I thought you were dead. My brother and I go up to your grave, you are prayed for every year on your anniversary. Daddy's face is so sad when he speaks about you it would make a stone statue cry . . . and here you are in this, this place . . . because you loved some other man . . . a man who doesn't love you . . . and you say it's only a mistake that people think you're dead . . . you must be mad, mad."

Kit's anger somehow galvanized Lena. She flung the rug from her shoulder and stood up to face her daughter. "I was no part of this conspiracy to pretend I was dead. I told your father that I was leaving him. I said that he must choose how to explain it to his neighbors and friends, that this was the least I could give him, some dignity . . .

"I didn't make any demands. I wasn't in a position to do so. I just said I hoped he'd let me see you over the years."

"You did not tell Daddy you were leaving. You didn't tell him. I don't care what kind of lies you tell yourself, you're not going to lie to me. I'm the one who heard him crying night after night in his room. I'm the one who walked with him by the lake all the time they were still looking for you.

"I was there when the body came back and he was so pleased and he said that you'd rest easy in your grave. Don't tell me that Daddy knows about all this . . . this setup. He doesn't." They were standing a few feet from each other, faces angry and upset.

"He must be a much better actor than I gave him credit for if he fooled you as well." Lena had a great bitterness in her voice. "And I will never forgive myself for what I have done to you and Emmet, but he has his share in the blame. I told him. He knows. I left him a letter."

"What?"

"I left him a long letter telling him everything, asking for nothing, not even understanding."

Kit backed away. "A letter. Oh my God!" She held her hand to her throat. Her face had gone white. Kit McMahon had never fainted before this day, and now she thought she was about to do so again. She staggered as the floor started its climb toward her, but she forced back the dizziness and nausea.

"I know that you're not going to believe me," Lena said.

"Yes, I do believe you." Kit's voice was strangled.

"You knew?" Lena said.

"I found it . . . and put it in the Aga."

"You *what?*"

"I burned it."

"You burned it? A letter addressed to someone else? In the name of God, why did you do that? Jesus Christ, why did you do that?"

"I wanted you to be buried in the churchyard," Kit said simply. "If they knew you'd committed suicide they wouldn't let you."

"But I didn't commit suicide. Oh God, why did you have to interfere?"

"I thought you had . . ."

"What made you think that . . . what right had you to decide what to do? I can't believe this, I really can't believe it."

"Everyone was looking for you. There were people out with lights and Sergeant O'Connor . . . and the boat turned upside down . . ."

"But for Christ's sake, if you had *given* your father the letter . . ."

"But you had been so strange . . . so wild, don't you remember . . . that's what we thought."

"That's what *you* thought, what you took it on yourself to think."

"Quite a lot of people thought it, as it happens."

"How do you know?"

"You hear whispers."

"And what about the inquest . . . the put-up job between your father and Peter Kelly identifying some other unfortunate as me?"

"They thought it was you, that's what we all thought."

"But who *was* it? Whose body is in my grave?"

Kit looked at her, stricken. "I don't know. It could have been someone who drowned a long time ago."

Lena dismissed this. "Imagine. He would have done anything to hide the fact that I'd left him."

Kit was very quiet. "Father doesn't know you left him. Thanks to me, Father thinks you're dead."

Lena looked at her and let the horror of this sink in. For years and years Martin really had thought she had drowned herself in the lake on his doorstep. How could this grotesque thing have happened?

"And does he know why . . . or did he suspect that I was about to leave him and that's why I took my life?"

"No, he doesn't think you took your life, he thinks that you drowned accidentally. He may be one of the few, but he thinks that. He told Emmet and me over and over."

Lena reached for a packet of cigarettes. Automatically she stretched the pack toward Kit. Kit shook her head. The room that had heard such shouting was now so silent that the striking of the match sounded like a whip cracking.

After an eternity Kit said, "I'm sorry for burning the letter. It seemed like the only thing to do at the time."

Another long silence and Lena said: "You don't know how sorry I am to have left you, but at the time . . . at the time . . ." Lena sat down, but Kit still stood.

"You could have come back to us, told us you were alive, that it had been a mistake." Lena said nothing. "I mean, I couldn't have unburned the letter, and anyway I didn't know I should have. But you didn't want to, did you? You didn't mind leaving us there thinking . . . thinking . . ."

"I was trapped," Lena said. "I promised your father . . ."

"You made the trap," Kit said. "And don't talk of what you promised Daddy. Presumably you promised you'd love, honor, and obey him when you got married. You didn't think much of that promise."

"Sit down, please, Kit."

"No I won't sit down. I don't feel like sitting down."

"You look very pale . . . you look ill."

"People at home don't say ill, we say 'sick.' You're forgetting words even . . ."

"Kit, sit down. You and I may not have much time to talk . . . this may be our only chance."

"I don't want a cozy chat."

"I don't want a cozy chat either." But Kit sank into a chair gratefully, her legs were feeling very wobbly. "What's the very worst part of it?" Lena asked eventually.

"What you did to Daddy."

There was a silence. And then Lena said very gently: "Or what you did to him?"

"No, that is not fair. I'm not going to take the blame for this."

"I'm not asking you to take the blame I'm just asking you to talk to me . . . tell me what we should do now . . ."

"How can I talk to you? I haven't seen you since I was a child of twelve. I don't know who you are. I don't know anything about you." Kit seemed to shrink away from her.

Lena hardly dared to speak. Anything she said seemed to upset the child further. She sat there waiting. Eventually she could bear it no longer. "You do know about me . . . we have been writing to each other for years . . ."

Kit's eyes were cold. "No, you're wrong . . . you know all about me. You know things no-body else on earth knows. I told them all to you in good faith. I know nothing about you.

Nothing but lies."

"I wrote the truth," Lena cried. "I wrote that your mother loved you and was so proud of you . . . didn't I tell you that . . . all the time?"

"It was lies, you didn't say my mother had left . . . ran away and left us there to think she was dead."

Lena's eyes flashed. "And you certainly didn't write saying that you had burned the letter of explanation."

"I didn't do that because I wanted to protect her reputation."

Lena noted with pain that she spoke of her mother in the third person. As if in any real sense her mother was dead.

And would always remain so.

"You seemed fond of me in your letters," Lena tried. "And I am that person who wrote. All the things I told you were true, I work in the employment agency, Louis works in the hotel . . ."

"I don't care about any of that . . . you can't think that any of that has any interest for me. I want to go now."

"Don't go, I beg you. You can't go out there in London all alone with this terrible news."

"I've had terrible news before. I survived." The girl's voice was bitter.

"Just sit for a while. I won't talk if it annoys you. But I don't want you to be alone after this shock."

"You didn't care about the shock before . . . when you went away." Kit had her hand against her mouth, fist clenched as if she were willing back the tears.

Lena knew she must make no gesture to hold her, to touch her. Kit was poised to leave, the only thing keeping her in this room was her attempt to gather the strength and courage to leave it. She was fighting back the tears. Her face was working and she was almost biting her knuckles in her efforts not to give way.

Lena sat very still. She didn't stare at Kit, she rested her head on her hand and looked out the window to the outside world where people were living ordinary lives.

Kit raised her head and looked at her.

Mother had always been like this. Able to sit still for ages on end. When they sat by the lake and everyone else was running here and there and pointing things out, Mother would sit there composed and peaceful, not needing to speak or to move. And at night when they sat at the fire, Father would do card tricks or teach them tongue twisters and riddles, or he would play Ludo with them. And Mother just sat there looking at the flames, sometimes her hand on Farouk's neck, stroking him, saying nothing but being peaceful.

It had all seemed so safe then. Why had this man come in and taken Mother away from them? The anger against the man who had broken up their lives took over from the tears. Kit was able to speak.

"Does he know about us?" she asked eventually.

"Does who know?" Lena seemed genuinely startled.

"The man . . . Louis, whatever his name is?"

"Yes, his name is Louis. Yes, he knows about

you, of course he does."

"And he still took you away?" Kit's voice was full of distaste.

"I went willingly. I wanted to go. You must realize how much I must have wanted to go . . . how else could I have left you?"

Kit put her hands over her ears. "I don't want to hear what you wanted. I don't want to think about you wanting. It makes me sick to think about it." Her face was red and upset. It was hard enough for a girl to think about her mother mating with her father, let alone think about wanting anyone else.

Lena realized this. "I only said it because I wanted to take the blame," she said.

"Blame!" The word from Kit sounded like a snort.

Lena feared that Kit might leave, that suddenly she might get up and go out that door without turning her head. "What are we going to do?" she asked again.

"I don't know what you mean."

"Are you going to tell Emmet and . . . well, your father that . . . that things are not the way they thought."

"You've always known things weren't the way we thought."

"Kit, please . . . you know this was not my intention. It's what you did that brought this about."

"So what are you asking me?" Kit's voice was cold.

There was a long pause. Then Lena raised her head and looked her daughter in the eye. "I suppose I'm asking you whether you want me alive or dead."

There was another pause, then Kit said slowly: "I think since you've wanted to be dead as far as we're concerned for the last five years . . . you should stay dead." She stood up to leave the room and for Lena it was like the lid closing on her coffin.

Ivy saw the girl go down the stairs and walk toward the hall door. Her face looked more composed now. She didn't look as if she needed anyone to support her, help her through the traffic. She looked as if she could manage by herself. But her face was very dead. There was something empty and cold about her expression which had not been there before.

Ivy longed to go up to Lena. She wanted more than anything to comfort the woman who had lost her lover and her daughter in one day. But she knew better than to approach. Lena knew where she lived. When she was ready she would come downstairs. Not before.

Kit found a cafe. It had a jukebox and a group of girls her own age played record after record. How wonderful to be like that. To live in ordinary homes. Their mothers hadn't run away . . . and pretended to be dead. None of these girls had ever come across a ghost. They had enough money to have play after play.

They talked of the fellows they were going out with. Two of them were black girls with London accents. Imagine, this whole kind of life went on, people of different colors and dozens of cafes in the same street, and nobody knowing everyone on the street like at home.

And this is where Mother had been living since the day she drowned.

Mother alive. What would Emmet say . . . ? He'd be so delighted. Daddy. What would Father say when he heard? And then the black heavy weight again. But they couldn't hear. They couldn't hear now. It would be too much hurt and unhappiness after all these years.

And it was all Kit's fault.

So often over the past years she had wondered guiltily if she had done the right thing by burning the letter. But she had always told herself that God would know she had done it for the best of motives. She wanted Mother to have a burial place with everyone else. Not like a criminal outside the walls. She had done it for love of Mother. But who would care or understand that she had meant it for the best? She had created the most terrible situation for everyone.

Kit felt the coffee scald her throat.

The best thing was that no one should ever know. That was the way that . . . she . . . wanted it. Kit didn't think of her as Mother, not this thin woman who sat in the elegant apartment and talked about wanting Louis . . . and needing him or whatever it was she said. Why should Emmet be put through everything Kit had been through? And Father. What would it do to Father to think his beloved Helen whom he had cried over so much had left him because she wanted this man called Louis?

And where *was* this Louis anyway? If she was so crazy about him, why wasn't he there or any sign of him? Kit remembered that man who had come into Ivy's. The handsome dark-haired man like an actor. But that couldn't have been Louis, he was going away somewhere. He was leaving a big crate of his belongings to be collected. That wasn't Mother's Louis. Anyway he was far too young. Too young to be Mother's fancy man.

Someone touched her arm. She looked up startled. Surely Mother or Mrs. Brown couldn't have followed her here.

But it was a boy of about eighteen. "Are you on your own?" he asked.

"Yes." Kit looked at him cautiously.

"Would you like to join us?" He waved over at a table where the group was sitting. They smiled encouragingly.

"No thank you . . . thank you very much . . ."

"Come on, can't have you sitting on your own when there's music playing," the boy said.

Kit looked at him doubtfully. They were just singing and clapping to the music. As she and Clio would have done with them had things been different. She couldn't sit with them laughing, pretending that nothing was wrong. But neither could she sit with her thoughts going around and around like a red-hot circle in the groove with no solution.

"Thank you." She smiled at him.

He looked pleased to have brought such a pretty, well-dressed girl to their table. She smiled brightly and nodded at their names. She must have told them she was Kit, because that's what they called her when she said she had to go, and ran from the cafe to catch a bus back to the convent.

Clio was walking up and down, grumbling. "You're late," she said.

"No, you're early." It was the way they had always been. Yet the last time Kit had seen Clio she hadn't known this awful fact. The fact that Mother had never died, she had run away. And that Kit had helped her to continue the deception by burning the letter.

"What did you do?" Clio was still sulking that they hadn't gone to do the town together.

"Mainly a coffee bar," Kit shrugged.

"That all? I saw lots of places."

"Good for you."

"Did you get talking to people?" Clio's eyes were piggy for information.

"Yeah, a whole group. They played the jukebox."

"And were there fellows?"

"Mainly fellows." Kit's mind was miles away. Miles from Clio and from the coffee bar.

"What were they like?"

"They were okay . . . What about you?" Kit knew she must make things seem normal.

But Clio obviously had found no satisfying adventures in London on her own. "I just looked here and there. What were their names?"

"Who?"

"The fellows you met."

"I can't remember." Kit obviously couldn't.

Clio looked alarmed as they walked up the steps to the convent door. "Kit, you didn't have

sexual intercourse with any of them, did you?"
Clio asked suddenly.

"Jesus, why would you say that?" Clio never
failed to surprise her.

"Well, you look different," Clio said. "And you
know you can always tell someone who's done
it from someone who hasn't."

"Sorry to disappoint you, but I didn't. We
didn't get around to it in the coffee bar. Maybe
too many people there or something."

"Oh shut up, Kit. It's just that you've changed.
I don't know what it is, but I know you so well
and something happened."

"It wasn't the loss of my virginity on a coffee
table, I can tell you that."

"What was it?"

"It was nothing, it was being in a strange city
and not really a part of it, I suppose."

That was the right thing to say. Clio bought
it. She had felt her outing a miserable failure.
It was consoling to think that Kit McMahon had
found nothing to do either. But odd that she
looked as if something had happened, as if she
had been in an accident or something.

Kit hardly slept all night. She sat and looked
out the window as the dawn came up over London. She wondered if her mother was worrying
the same way. No, she was probably with this
Louis she had wanted so much. Again, Kit wondered was it possible that Louis might have been
the handsome man who was leaving his belongings to collect later.

Then a thought came from nowhere, with the

408

force and pain of a sharp cold wind. Suppose Louis had gone, and Mother knew that she was now proven to be alive, then Mother might come home after all. She might come back to Lough Glass after all those years and try to take up life again. Come back as a ghost to poor Father, who thought she was a dead saint. And to Emmet who had been so young when she had drowned. And to stop Maura Hayes from getting married to Father. Of course Maura Hayes could never marry Father now.

And no one would ever forgive Mother.

Alternately Kit's face burned with a feverish heat and felt ice-cold. By morning light she was far too unwell to join them on the excursion which that day was a walking tour of Dickens's London.

Mother Lucy was worried. "Do you often get such a reaction?" she asked. The girl had a high temperature certainly.

"I'll be fine if I can lie in bed for a while. In a nice dark room," Kit had said.

"I'll call in on you every hour or so," Mother Lucy said.

"That'll put a stop to your gallop," Clio said.

"I've no gallop. You are such a pain, Clio. Such an awful one-track pain."

"If I find your coffee shop will I tell them you'll be back for more?" Clio was annoyed that Kit wasn't coming with them. Things were much funnier when Kit was there, but she really did look as if she had caught some illness or disease.

Kit lay in the small narrow bed in the dormitory that held eight girls. Eight English girls slept here during term time. The girls from Lough Glass slept here this week. All of them could go to sleep on these pillows without having barbed-wire coils of fear around their heart.

Kit lay with her eyes open in the dark room, and every time the nun put her head around the door she pretended to be asleep. This way there was no need for more speculation about what might have caused her fever.

Lena had not slept. By six o'clock she knew there wasn't a chance of closing her eyes. She got up and dressed and went downstairs. She pushed a note under Ivy's door. *I'll talk to you tonight,* she wrote. There was no need to say anything else. Ivy would know how grateful she was to be left alone last night. Ivy knew she wasn't closing her out, excluding her from a life which she had once invited her to join.

At Millar's, Lena began to write a letter to her daughter. She wrote and wrote, tearing up the pages, ripping them from her typewriter. She tried to write by hand but that didn't work either. When the door rattled and Dawn Jones came in Lena had given up. There were no words to say any of the million things that should be said. She had torn the rejected letters into tiny fragments. Therapeutic almost, reducing them to confetti-size pieces from which no clue could be read.

No one would ever know that the calm Mrs. Gray had spent a night in anguish. That in one day she had found her daughter, lost her again, and been abandoned by the man with whom she had lived as man and wife for five years. She had nothing to live for, yet she was going to live through this day. The thoughts that had chased around in her head all through the wakeful hours had convinced her that her daughter was right. She must remain dead. She had caused enough harm and hurt already.

But what had come to her in a sudden and unwelcome flash had been the fear that perhaps Kit would change her mind. When the initial horror and revulsion had passed by, when her own guilt at the part she had played — the tragic and well-meaning gesture of burning a letter to avoid the disgrace of a public suicide — then she might change her view. She might think that her duty lay in revealing that she had found Lena, that it was her duty to tell Emmet his mother was alive, and then to tell Martin.

Lena's guilt at what had happened to Martin knew no bounds. She had misjudged him utterly. For years the man had lived in the shadow of her death, her possible suicide. Kit had said the town was full of whispers. He had survived it, brought them up to revere her memory. He could not be exposed now as what he was, a man whose wife had run off with another man, and had allowed the explanation of her death by drowning to be accepted.

Martin deserved more dignity. He deserved some happiness. Kit must be warned never to relent.

During the night Lena had thought that she would find the words if she were at her desk, the desk where she had so often written long letters to her daughter of a supposedly dead friend.

411

Letters that would never be written or answered again.

But it had not been possible to write the words.

And there was Dawn, fresh as a daisy. "Well, I thought I was an early bird . . . but no, you're here before me again." Dawn's voice was like the chirrup of a bird. She looked like a little canary or a budgie in her blue and gold outfit, her shining hair and her perfect makeup.

Lena felt old and tired. "Dawn, I may have to take some time off today. I wonder could you get your pad and come in to me until I list some of my work that you and Jessie may have to divide between you."

"Certainly Mrs. Gray." Dawn listened attentively.

Lucky Dawn, thought Lena. Dawn who had slept a full night's sleep and had a dozen admirers. Her only decisions after work today would be whom to go out with.

Lena went back to number 27. She knocked on Ivy's door. "Ivy, when you have a minute can you come upstairs with me?"

She was so frail-looking, Ivy was alarmed. "Shall I take you to the doctor?" she asked.

"No. Just a helping hand up the stairs would be nice."

Ivy took Lena's clothes as she undressed and got into her bed, the big bed that she and Louis had shared but which was far too wide and empty for her now. She folded the clothes and laid them on a chair, then handed her a nightdress as if she were a lady's maid. Lena slipped it over her head. Her face was lined deep with pain and tiredness.

Neither of them had spoken.

Then Ivy said, "She's a very beautiful girl, Lena. She's a lovely daughter for you to have . . ."

She couldn't have said anything guaranteed to open the barrier that was holding back the tears. Lena had not cried since it all began, but hearing Ivy Brown praise the beauty and warmth of the daughter she had lost forever let it all out. She cried like a baby for what seemed like an age. And only after a very long time was she persuaded to blow her nose and tell Ivy the depth of the tragedy . . . the wrong that in all innocence her daughter had done by ensuring that Helen McMahon could never go back and see her family again.

ℵ ℵ ℵ

"You didn't enjoy it all that much, did you?" Martin McMahon said.

"Oh, I did, Daddy, and it was a lot of money and everything . . ."

"That doesn't matter. We sometimes spend a lot on things that don't work out. Was it a bit schoolish, is that it?"

"No, it was fine, I told you. I sent you cards, we saw everything."

"Where did you like best?" Emmet asked.

Kit looked at him suddenly. He reminded her of her mother saying "What was the worst thing?" She swallowed and tried to find something to say

413

that would satisfy him. "I think I liked the Tower of London best," she said.

"And this fever you got . . . ?" Her father was still anxious.

"It was only a temperature for a day or two . . . you know the way nuns fuss."

"Clio was telling Peter about it, she said you were in bed two days."

"Clio is worse than the nuns, Daddy."

"Don't let poor Mother Bernard hear you say that, after all the effort she put into educating the pair of you." Her father had been satisfactorily sidetracked.

Trust Clio to make it into a big, big deal.

"There you are, Kit McMahon." That was Father Baily's normal greeting to people. He more or less gave them permission to exist by saying it.

"Here I am, Father," said Kit mischievously.

He looked at her sharply to see if she was making fun of him, but couldn't prove it. "And tell me, what did you all make of London?"

"It was interesting, Father. We were lucky to have been given such an opportunity." She spoke primly as if she were a little girl reciting what she had been told to say.

Clio giggled.

"A fine place in its own way," Father Baily said. "If you look at it for what it is there isn't a thing you could criticize about it."

Kit wondered how you could look at London as if it were something other than it was. But decided this was not the time to argue it with

414

the elderly priest. "Were you ever there yourself, Father?" she asked.

"I passed through it twice on the way to the Holy City," he said.

"Were there coffee shops at that time?" Clio asked.

"We hadn't much time to spend in coffee shops," Father Baily said.

"Just as well," Clio hissed as they left. "Think what he might have seen if he had been given the time to visit them."

"Wasn't it a great coincidence, you being in London at the same time as our school trip?" Mother Bernard said to Maura Hayes.

"What's that, Mother?"

"You know, Clio and Kit going out to meet you from the convent . . . Mother Lucy was telling me about it."

"Ah, Mother Lucy . . ." She was at a loss but didn't want to let the nun realize.

"What a coincidence!" Mother Bernard said again.

"Wasn't it," Maura said, her brow darkening.

"Oh Clio, a word, please."

"Yes, Aunt Maura?"

"Was there some confusion in Mother Bernard's mind or did anyone tell her I was in London when you were?"

"I swear I didn't. I swear it," Clio said.

"Well, who did, Clio?"

"I haven't a clue. But some daft nun over there said our aunt phoned so we kind of used the heaven-sent opportunity . . ." Clio giggled. "You couldn't turn your back on a heaven-sent chance like that, could you?"

"And where did you and Kit go on the heaven-sent opportunity?"

"I don't know where Kit went, she was most mysterious. I had a dull time actually, looked in shop windows and went in and out of cafes and bars pretending I was looking for someone."

"And did you not inquire about this sudden aunt who was asking for you?"

Clio shrugged. "Nope, I just thought it was a bit of rare good luck. But I was wrong."

Orla Reilly was in her mother's shop. "Why can't I help you, Mammy? You used to always complain that I didn't help."

"That was when you were living here, now you live with your husband and I'd like you to go back to him."

"God, Mammy. You'd need to get out of that house from time to time. I told him you needed a bit of a hand in the shop."

"Well, you told him wrong. And who is minding the baby?"

"Old Ma Reilly. Give her something to do, the old rip."

"I've said it once and I won't say it again, there's no work for you here, Orla."

"Mammy, please."

"You should have thought of this before all the other business." Her mother's face was hard. Orla's shotgun wedding had not been a matter of pleasure to her family.

Clio and Kit were reading the magazines. They usually managed to read about five for every one they bought. Clio had been following the whole conversation between Orla and her mother. "Marriage isn't all it's cracked up to be," she whispered to Kit.

"What?" Kit said.

"You're miles away," Clio said. It was like talking to the side of a wall, talking to Kit McMahon these days. She just had no interest in anything.

The prospectus from St. Mary's College of Catering in Cathal Brugha Street arrived. It lay unopened on the hall table for three days.

"Aren't you going to open it, Kit?" Rita asked. "It will have all the details about your uniforms and everything."

"I will, of course," Kit said.

But she didn't.

"Catering?" Mrs. Hanley in the drapery said. "Catering, well, I'm sure that's very nice. You're not going to university then like Clio?"

"No, Mrs. Hanley. I'd love to learn the hotel business. It's meant to be a very good course, you learn to cook and do accounts and all kinds of things."

"Is your father disappointed you're not going to university? I know he had his heart set on it."

Kit looked at Mrs. Hanley. "Had he? You know he never said. He never said a word about that. Maybe I should go home and ask him. I never knew that till you said it this minute."

"Well now, I may be mistaken, and you wouldn't want to go round upsetting people."

Mrs. Hanley looked alarmed.

Kit's eyes were blazing with annoyance. She didn't know that Mrs. Hanley was so ashamed that her daughter Deirdre was working in a low-class kind of cafe in Dublin — not even waiting tables properly, just clearing up after people with a broom and a cloth — she did everything she could to belittle the opportunities and futures of other girls from Lough Glass.

Mrs. Hanley didn't know that the red-faced angry girl in front of her had hardly heeded her words and their meaning. It was just the trigger of mentioning her father that had set off the storm.

Kit slept badly at night and concentrated not at all during the days. What if her mother was to write from England or, worse still, arrive? Suppose that the nice safe future her father seemed about to embark on was going to blow away in front of his eyes?

"Emmet, you smell of drink," Kit said.

"Oh, do I? I thought it would have gone by now."

"You thought what?"

"You won't tell?"

"Did I ever tell?"

"Well, Michael Sullivan and Kevin Wall and I . . . we had a cocktail."

"I don't believe this."

"Yes, we made it from all the bottles outside Foley's. We poured it into a jug and shook it."

"You are mad, Emmet. Quite mad."

"Actually it was awful. And it was mainly watery stout, there was hardly anything left in the whiskey and brandy bottles."

"What a shame," Kit said.

"But anyway, thanks for telling me, I'll wash my teeth."

"Why on earth did you do it?" Kit asked.

"It was something to do. Sometimes it's kind of lonely here. Wouldn't you say that's true?"

Kit looked at Emmet and bit her lip. Should she tell him?

"How are you, Kit?" Stevie Sullivan called.

"Not well," Kit said.

"I hate to hear of a good-looking girl not being in good form." Stevie smiled a crooked attractive smile.

It cut no ice with Kit McMahon. "I'd be a lot better if you could stop your brother arranging cocktail parties in the backyard of Foley's and Paddles'," she said.

"What are you all of a sudden, Pioneer Total Abstinence Society? Father Matthew, Apostle of Temperance?" Stevie asked.

"I'm someone who'd prefer my own brother not to come home smelling of booze," she said.

"Okay." Stevie nodded.

"What do you mean okay."

"I mean okay, I'll stop it."

"Thanks," she said, and let herself in the door. As she climbed the stairs Kit asked herself why she had reacted so strongly to something that was only a kid's game. They hadn't been really drunk. It was pretending to be grown up.

But she told herself that it was for her father. Daddy had enough behind him. And enough

419

ahead of him when he realized his wife hadn't died in the lake. Because Kit now thought this was too big a secret to keep. She wouldn't be able to hide it as she had hidden the burning of the letter. It would all come out now, everything, and their lives would all be ruined.

She dreamed that Mother was home, and that they were all having tea in the kitchen. "Don't be too hard on Kit," Mother was saying, and they all sat grouped together with Rita standing behind them. Kit seemed to be the outcast far away across the table. And in her dream she heard Maura crying noisy sobs.

א א א

"I have a lovely present for you to start your new career, Kit." Mrs. Hanley handed Kit a flat box.

"That's very nice of you, Mrs. Hanley."

"Open it and see do you like it."

It was a lemon-colored short-sleeved sweater, something Kit would never have worn. But under a jacket it might look all right.

"It's beautiful, Mrs. Hanley, that's very very kind of you."

"I spoke a bit out of turn the other day, you were a good girl not to take any notice of me."

Kit looked at her blankly, she hadn't an idea what the woman was talking about. Everything was so odd these days, and she could hardly remember anything she had done since she came back from London. It all seemed suspended somehow, unreal.

420

The days and nights were endless in London for Lena. She slept or tried to sleep curled up in a little corner of the great bed that they had shared so happily.

In the office she worked on like a machine . . . there was no purpose to the working day for her anymore. No plans for an evening meal with Louis, no running home at lunchtime to catch him on his split shifts so that they could have an hour together.

Impossible to believe that her birthday would come and go, and nobody would know. Louis in France would have forgotten. Kit in Ireland would not remember. Everyone else in Ireland thought she was dead. Maybe Ivy knew but she would be tactful enough to realize that this year there was nothing to celebrate.

Sometimes on Saturday lunchtimes when they closed the agency doors Lena congratulated herself that she had survived another week. Perhaps this was what the rest of her life would be like, unless of course her daughter could bear the strain no longer. Unless she was unmasked as living, alive if not well, in London. Living in the empty bed of a man who had left her just as she had left her own husband.

Some days were harder than others. There was a widow who came in looking for part-time work, saying she had to be home at four o'clock in the afternoon when her son got back from school.

"He's thirteen, you see, and they really need their mothers at that age," she confided to Lena.

To her surprise Mrs. Gray's eyes filled with

tears. "Yes, I expect they do," she said earnestly. "Let's try everything until we get you something suitable." And Lena threw herself into the task. It was as if she could somehow reach out to Emmet by helping this woman to see her son.

She thought about Emmet a lot. Perhaps he might be less hard of heart, less quick to condemn than Kit had been. After all, he was blameless in every way. He had burned no note of explanation. Was there a way she could write to him, tell him she was alive? Or was this the way madness lay?

And then there was Martin. Martin whom she had so sorely misjudged. Was it better, as Kit had said, that she remain dead? But suppose that Kit was not constant in her intentions? Might she not give in and admit everything? Would it be fairer to Martin to tell him now, tell him herself, rather than let him hear it secondhand?

She had given him her promise that she would never leave him without explanation, but he had not known. Was she only telling him because Louis had gone? Or would he think that this was the case?

Like mice the thoughts scurried around in her head while she was awake. And when she slept she dreamed often that Louis had come back. She would wake cold and cramped and realize it was not true. One night she dreamed she went back to Lough Glass, that she got off a bus outside the Mercy Convent and walked through the town, past the Lakeview Road which led up to the Kellys' house, past the post office where Mona Fitz closed the door in her face. Tommy the postman tried to come out and talk to her but Mona called him back, and the curtains in the Garda station across the road twitched as they saw her but nobody came out to greet her. Mrs. Hanley had EARLY CLOSING written on the shop so as to avoid meeting her.

And a sullen crowd stood in the doorways of Foley's bar. Sullivan's garage was deserted, Wall's Hardware people turned the other way, Father Bailey hastened up Church Road so as not to have to see her, so she tried to come back up the street on the other side in case there would be someone to meet her but at Paddles' the doors were closed and Mrs. Dillon didn't speak. Dan and Mildred O'Brien in the Central Hotel avoided her eye.

And then she was at the pharmacy. "I'm home," she called up the stairs. But there was no reply. Rita dressed in black came to the top of the stairs. "I'm afraid you can't come in, ma'am, the mistress is dead," Rita said solemnly. "I am the mistress," Lena cried in her dream. "I know, ma'am, but you can't come in."

At that she woke up sweating. It was true. There was no life of any sort ahead for her. She might as well be dead.

Lena missed the letters terribly. There was no point in looking in to Ivy hopefully. There would never be a letter from Kit again. Never a letter overflowing with news to her mother's friend.

Kit missed the letters. There was nobody to sound off to, no one to tell about all the things that lay ahead, the catering college, the doglike

423

devotion of Philip O'Brien, the increasing boss-iness of Clio. The Lena Gray she had written to would have been able to come up with some course of action about everything, everything, of course, except what was really wrong.

It was a great lacking, the letters. Not having Sister Madeleine slip her the envelope with the English stamp which she would take home and read in her room. Now the knowledge that these letters were all lies made them worthless. She could hardly bear to think of what they had said. She didn't believe Lena Gray anymore. About anything.

There was a postcard from Philip. He was in Killarney.

Dear Kit,

I have a holiday job here in this hotel that you see on the front of the card. Imagine having a picture of your hotel on the card. How boastful.

I can't wait to start the course, can you? We'll be so much ahead of the others, after all we're going out together. They'll all have to find new friends.

Love,
Philip.

Dear Kit,

Your father tells me that you will be in the Mountjoy Square Hostel, which I am sure will be excellent for you while you are studying

424

in catering college.

I also realize that some of the greatest joys of coming to Dublin center around the sense of freedom you have from home, and everything connected with your own place. I would like you to know that I have a very comfortable flat in Rathmines. If ever you would like to come and see me I would be delighted. But most of all I want you to know that I shall not be sitting at home waiting for you. I leave work at five-thirty and very often when the weather is good I go on the golf course an hour after that time. Often I go to the cinema, or to the houses of friends. Sometimes people come to my flat for supper.

I tell you this so that you will know I am not trying to seek for company, nor am I trying to keep an eye on you while you are in Dublin. But this is my phone number just in case you'd like to come for a meal sometime.

> *Yours affectionately,*
> *Maura.*

Dear Michael Sullivan,

This is from a well-wisher. You have been observed drinking the dregs from bottles outside various public houses in Lough Glass.

This must now cease.

Immediately.

Otherwise Sergeant O'Connor will be informed.

And Father Baily.

And most important your brother who will beat the shit out of you.
You have been warned.

Dear Philip,

Whatever else we are doing when we get to Dublin we are not going out together. I want you to know this from the very start so that there will be no misunderstanding.

Love (but only if you take it in the right spirit), Kit.

"They want me to start soon in Dublin, Stevie," Rita said.

"Oh Jesus! You run everything here like a dream."

"It's nearly time."

"But your woman hasn't moved in with Martin yet."

"If you are speaking of Miss Hayes, they are very close friends. But you are right, there is no engagement . . . as yet."

"I thought you'd stay with me and keep the garage afloat."

"Your mother doesn't approve of me, Stevie."

"Don't mind her. I don't."

"It's not pleasant to be asked to empty the rubbish, scrub the pots, take in the washing . . ."

"But come off it, Rita, you don't *do* any of those things. She just asks you, you refuse. It's a game."

"Not to me it isn't."

"I don't believe this. There's another reason

". . . you've been offered a better job?"

"No, not really."

"What do you mean?"

"I've come from nothing, I've made myself acceptable. I want to be somewhere that I *am* accepted."

"I pay you well."

"If I went on the streets I'd be paid even better. Money isn't everything."

"Okay, I've been working my arse off here. I agree I don't have time to be polite to people."

"You're quite polite to customers, Stevie. And to the people who might get you a Ford agency."

He looked stricken. "That's true."

"And to girls who catch your eye, and to people you want credit from, or those you think might be in the way of buying a new car."

"You've had your eyes open."

"Yes, and I don't particularly like everything that I see."

"Jesus, Rita, I'm ashamed. That's all I can say."

"Funny, I think you mean it," Rita said.

"So will everything be all right now? I've learned my lesson, and I'll be as good as gold." He smiled his heartbreaking smile.

"You're only a kid, Stevie. That won't work with me," Rita laughed at him.

"So what do I have to do?"

"Nothing really. Just a nice reference and I'll be off tonight. Everything's in apple pie order."

"You're never walking out on me."

"More on your mother."

"She's nothing to do with this."

"Then she has no business in your office."

"Who taught you to be so tough?"

"Mrs. McMahon, the Lord have mercy on her."

"I doubt if he will, she drowned herself."

"You've a big mouth, Stevie Sullivan."

"I'll give you a lot more money. Stay, Rita. Please."

"No, thanks all the same."

"Who will I get?"

"An older woman, even older than me."

"How old are you, Rita? You're only a girl."

"I'm a good five years older than you."

"That's nothing these days."

"Get someone older. And someone who'll frighten the bejaysus out of your mother."

"What'll I say in the reference you want from me?"

"I have it written here." Rita smiled at him.

"I can't believe this, Rita. I really can't," Martin McMahon said to her.

"It's time for me to go, sir."

"Is there anything I can say to make you stay?"

"Everything you did here was always for my good, but I could find you someone, sir. Someone to work in my place."

"There's no one that could equal you, Rita."

"What I was going to suggest was a young cousin of mine. She might just work mornings, do the cleaning, ironing and wash the vegetables . . . you'll probably be able to make your own arrangements and maybe want the house run in a different way." It was as near as she could come to telling him that it was time he married Maura.

Maura Hayes opened the letter. It was typed and postmarked Lough Glass.

You may think this an extraordinary letter, Miss Hayes, and if you are offended by it then my judgment has been wrong.

Maura hastened to see who it was from. The signature *Rita Moore* meant nothing. Then she understood. The girl who had worked in Martin's house was telling her that she was leaving. That there were two vacancies. Housekeeper, and in the office across the road.

"Is there an understanding between you and young Kit McMahon?" Dan O'Brien asked his son that night before the course began in Cathal Brugha Street catering college.

"What do you mean?"

"You know what I mean."

"No I don't, actually," Philip said.

"Well, actually for your information, I meant do you and she intend to be boyfriend and girlfriend?"

"And suppose we did?"

"Suppose you did I want to warn you that she could be a bit flighty like her mother, and I wouldn't want to think that you'd have your name up with someone like that."

"Thank you, Father."

"Don't take that tone with me."

"What tone?"

"Mildred, speak to him."

"There isn't any point, is there? He's determined to be like all the modern youth today."

"Sister Madeleine," said Kit. "There was a thing I was going to say about the letters from London."

"What's that now?"

"I think my mother's friend will write to me in Dublin now, at the hostel."

"Yes, of course . . ."

"I just didn't want you to think I took things for granted, or was keeping things secret on you."

"No, of course not . . . and often things that sound complicated are quite simple." Sister Madeleine was lighthearted about her alternative postal service. "Anyway, Kit, when you're as old as I am and half talking to the birds and the foxes and the butterflies that come in at the end of the summer, you're not sure what you know and what you only dream . . ."

"Does everyone have a secret, do you think?"

"Certainly. Some are more important than others, of course."

Kit looked at her. There was one more thing she wanted to ask. It was hard to know how to put it. "Suppose you knew something . . . something that should actually stop something . . ." The nun's eyes were very blue and gave nothing away. "I was wondering if that were to happen to someone . . . should that someone try to change what was going to happen, you know, by saying everything, or would it be better to let things go ahead?"

"A very hard question all right." Sister Madeleine was sympathetic.

"But you'd need to know more before you

could answer it . . . is that it?"

"No no. Not at all. I couldn't answer a question like that for anyone else. They'd have to find the solution all on their own. They'd know it in their hearts anyway."

"They might know what they want but that needn't be the right thing."

"If it was the right thing that helped people and made them happy . . ." Sister Madeleine paused.

Not for the first time the thought crossed Kit's mind that the hermit had an easy, simplistic view of the laws of God that might not be found totally acceptable to the more official wings of the Church.

א א א

Lena bought the paper every week. She read it from cover to cover, wishing there was more about Lough Glass and less about the surrounding countryside and villages in the area.

She read it first in fear. Fear that news of a great local scandal might be revealed. And then as the weeks went on she realized that Kit had not broken down under the strain of the knowledge she had come by. There were not going to be stories unmasking the great mistake that had been made in identifying a body all those years ago.

Lena read how two Lough Glass students had been accepted in St. Mary's College of Catering. Kit was described as daughter of Martin McMahon, the well-known pharmacist, and his late wife, Mrs. Helen McMahon.

She read of the new drainage scheme, the improved roads, and the campaign for street lighting. She saw a picture of a bus shelter and read the outraged correspondence when it had been defaced.

And one day most unexpectedly she read that Martin McMahon, pharmacist of Lough Glass, and Miss Maura Hayes were to marry. She sat still for a very long time. Then she read it again.

Kit McMahon must be a strong girl to be able to take that in her stride. At her age she could allow her father to make a bigamous marriage. She knew that her mother was alive and she would have the courage to stand in a church and watch a wedding ceremony that she knew was a sham. She must be very courageous indeed to face the wrath of the Church or the State if it ever came to light.

Either that or she must hate her mother and have forced herself to believe that she was really dead.

Kit knew it was the right thing to do. She had no doubts at all. Sister Madeleine was right, you followed your conscience.

But she did have one worry. Suppose Lena found out. Suppose Lena wanted to spoil things. She might come at the last moment. It would be unforgivable if Kit was to let her father's day be ruined, and have him and Maura made into a laughingstock. But she couldn't write and ask a favor now.

She had left that day knowing she was doing

the right thing. Her mother didn't exist for them anymore in the way she once had. She couldn't go crawling now, begging, pleading, asking her not to come back and haunt the happiness that had been so slow to come to this family. She would have to hope and pray that Lena would never hear about the wedding. How could she hear? She didn't know anyone who lived in Lough Glass. It wasn't going to be on the news or anything.

It was hard to pray in conventional terms about this. Kit said big swooping prayers which skirted the issue of God's law on marriage.

God was out for the best too, wasn't he?

Lena thought about it for a long time.

Martin holding the hand of Maura Hayes and saying the words that couples said all over the world. Martin taking Maura home to his bed. Maura presiding at the table in the kitchen, going to Kit's graduation, buying Emmet's clothes.

She smoked late into the night. But what was another sleepless night? She had had so many of them.

By morning she had made up her mind. At lunchtime she took a bus to one of the smarter shopping streets and spent two hours choosing a dress. She had it wrapped for postage and took it to a post office. She addressed it to Kit Mc-Mahon, First Year Hotel Management Student, St. Mary's College of Catering, Cathal Brugha Street, Dublin. And before she had time to change her mind she put in a note.

I thought you might like this to wear at the wedding.
L.

And she left the parcel into their hands so that she could have no second thoughts.

She didn't tell Ivy, not about the dress, nor even about the wedding. Somehow it was better if it wasn't spoken about. It made her own position less vulnerable, less lonely.

She dreamed about the children every night. Emmet looking for her everywhere — behind rocks on a beach, behind trees in a wood, calling always "I know you're there, please come out, come back, come back." And of Kit wearing the dress, and standing stonily at the church gate. "You can't come in, you must not come to the wedding, you're buried over there. Remember this and go away."

א א א

Maura Hayes gave a lot of thought to the wedding.

It would be small but not hole-in-the-corner. It should be held in Dublin, far from the eyes of a too interested Lough Glass. Lilian would be her matron of honor, and Peter the best man. Or was that the wrong way? After all Peter had been best man at Martin's first wedding, when he had married Helen with all the hope that had been involved there. But if it wasn't Peter who else would it be? Martin had no other close friend in Lough Glass or anywhere. It would be deliberate and wrong to exclude Peter.

Maura would wear a cream-colored suit and a blue hat with a cream ribbon.

Maura's wedding plans came as a surprise to

her Dublin friends, who hadn't somehow thought of sensible golfing Maura as a likely bride. They heard of this kind widower, a pharmacist in a small country town, with two children whom Maura liked very much and who as far as she could tell seemed to be pleased that she was marrying their father. They learned with amazement that Maura had already found herself a job in this town. There was a position as a bookkeeper/administrator in a fast-growing motor business. It was two steps from her front door.

And her sister was married to the local doctor, and there was great golf. Her colleagues and friends were grudgingly pleased on her behalf. Father Baily from Lough Glass would attend as a guest, but the couple would be married by a priest that Maura knew in her own parish in Dublin. There would be about twenty people to lunch in a restaurant.

Maura had studied the earlier wedding pictures, the ones taken in 1939. On that occasion there had been sixty people. Maura recognized the brother and sisters of Martin, a dispersed silent family who met only at funerals and weddings.

They would not be included in the guest list. It would look like asking for a present a second time around. She saw her sister Lilian, young and innocent-looking and Peter, stern as the best man. She saw the bridesmaid, a girl called Dorothy, and her eyes stayed long on the beautiful face of Helen Healy, the woman that Martin McMahon had loved with a wild and unreasonable love.

He had told her all about it one day by the lake. He had been truthful and fair, to everyone, to Helen, to himself, and to Maura. He said she was something that filled his mind like a sandstorm.

Maura's eyes searched the face. What had she been thinking that day while she stood for the photographs? Had she hoped that the years with a kind, good man like Martin would smooth out the hurt of a man who had left her, a man she had loved and hoped to marry? The face was oval, the eyes were big and dark, the smile was sweet. But surely even someone who didn't know the whole story could see that this was not the normal expression of a bride on her wedding day? This was someone looking out way beyond the camera to something no one else could see.

Maura put aside her reflections, and went back to her list. The O'Briens from the hotel were invited, mainly to get over their sense of grievance at the wedding not being held in their premises. Young Philip who was at the catering college with Kit might come too, Maura would ask Kit. It was foolish to assume that all young people liked each other just because they grew up next door.

א   א   א

Ivy called Millar's Agency.

"I'm afraid she's with a client, Mrs. Brown," Dawn said. "Can any of the rest of us help you?"

"No darling, tell her it's Ivy. It'll only take thirty seconds."

"But Mrs. Brown, I know you're a friend and

everything, but she is with a very senior business-man, someone who might be able to put a lot of business her way. I don't know whether she'd thank me or indeed thank you for being interrupted."

"She'll thank us," Ivy said.

"Mrs. Gray, Mrs. Ivy Brown is most persistent. May I put her through for a short moment?"

"Thank you, yes, Dawn." Lena's voice was unruffled.

Ivy knew that Dawn would be listening. "Oh, Lena, sorry to interrupt you, but Mr. Tyrone turned up looking for his key. I told him I had given it to you."

"And so you did." Lena's voice was bright.

"So I suppose I should mention to Mr. Tyrone when you might be back."

"Tonight. Eight o'clock at the very earliest, and thank you so much for calling, Ivy." Lena hung up.

But Ivy remained on the line until she heard the click showing that Dawn had hung up also. She smiled to herself grimly. They had never had to use a code before. How quick Lena was on the uptake. Together they had giggled about how handsome Louis was, that he really did look like a film star. Tyrone Power possibly.

Ivy would not give young Dawn the satisfaction of knowing that Mrs. Gray's erring husband was back. And particularly Ivy did not want to let Dawn or anyone know how eagerly and willingly Lena would take him back.

Eight o'clock. That meant she must be going to the hairdresser.

Grace was philosophical. "Of course I don't think you're silly. I think you're right. Look as well as you can . . . that way if he stays you'll be glad you made the effort. If he doesn't you'll think you look so damn good anyway you'll have no trouble getting any other man."

"I don't want any other man, of course," said Lena.

"Of course," Grace agreed. "That's the problem. That's the meaning of the universe, isn't it?"

Ivy had been upstairs and tidied around. She had polished the table by the window and put a glass bowl of gold roses in the center of it. She had ironed some of Lena's blouses and put fresh sheets on the bed. She had thrown out the remains of old, hastily grabbed meals, the packets of slightly stale biscuits, and installed instead some fresh bread, ham, and tomatoes. And a bottle of wine. Something that would not look as if she had been expecting Louis, but which gave no appearance of desperation either.

Ivy hadn't prayed much in recent years, but she found herself offering up a little wish all day that Louis's return would be glorious. That this time he would find something that would make him stay.

There was a cafe across the street, a place where workmen had heavy-duty sandwiches and big cups of tea. Louis Gray sat there, out of it because of his clothes and his suntan, but still acceptable because of his easy way with people, his need to know about the chances of a horse in the following day's races. Out of the corner of his eye he watched number 27.

He had been there for an hour. Ivy said that Lena would be back at eight. Lena would not know he was coming home. When he saw her coming he excused himself from a conversation on form, and slipped across the road. He wanted to catch her as she went up the stairs.

He saw her legs disappearing around the corner. "Lena," he called softly.

She looked around, glowing and confident. A woman that any man would stop to look at. Her hair, which never ceased to amaze him, was shining, her makeup perfect. No other woman returning home after a long working day looked like this. He went up and stood close to her. She smelled as fresh as a daisy, her eyes were big and dancing with interest and surprise. "Well, well, well," Lena said slowly.

"You didn't call in to Ivy."

"I don't every night, no." They were speaking like old friends.

"Can I come in?" He pointed upward at their flat.

"Well, Louis, it's your home. Of course you can come in." How had she learned to be such an actress! She marveled at her own skills.

"I gave my key back to Ivy, she said you had it."

"As indeed I have." Lena knew that Ivy would have returned the key in her absence. And as she went in to the newly cleaned flat her heart filled with love for the good woman downstairs. Everything was perfect for the reconciliation, for the promises, the assurances, the night of love. And there on the mantelpiece where no one could miss it in a small glass dish was Louis's key. Lena went straight over to it, picked it up and handed it to him.

"I brought some champagne," Louis said.

"That's nice." Lena had steeled herself, drilled herself all day, to be calm.

"I thought if you'd let me come home it would be a celebration, and if you wouldn't then I could drink it to console myself." He smiled his boyish smile.

Lena smiled back. In a way it was no different to her going to the hairdresser's and having a facial. As Grace had said, if Louis stayed then it would be a celebration, if not a consolation. Very much the same thing.

"Let's celebrate then," she said, and she turned her face a little to one side as he came to take her in his arms. She didn't want him to see how much she hungered to hold him so tight that she would squeeze the breath from him. She wanted to kiss his lips, his eyes, his neck, to take his clothes off slowly and walk with him into the bedroom. But this way she would seem too eager.

He moved her face to kiss her lips. "I'm a fool, Lena," he said.

"No more than most of us," she said.

"This is my home, I knew that five minutes after I left it."

"And now you're back," she said.

"Don't you want to know . . . to hear . . . ?"

"Oh no, I do most certainly *not* want to know . . . Now, are you going to pour me a glass of

440

champagne or is this all just an empty promise?"

"There'll be no more empty promises, Lena,"
he said. "I'll love you forever and I'll never leave
again."

א א א

Kit had been helpful. "What would you like
me to wear?" she had asked Maura.

"Oh, Kit, whatever you like. Whatever you
think would be nice for later."

"No, it's your day, you should have a say in
it," Kit had said. Maura's eyes had filled with
tears. She tried to say something but the words
wouldn't come. "And Daddy's," Kit had added.
"But men don't really notice things of importance. Tell me if there's anything I can do that
would help to make it nice for you."

"The fact that you are happy your father is
marrying me makes it very nice for me," Maura
said, having found her voice at last.

"And Emmet too, Maura. It's just that he's
hopeless at saying it."

"A boy remembers a mother in a different way,
I suppose."

"No, that's not so, he was only nine when it
happened. And anyway I was always the one who
was closer to her. I understood her more, he was
still a baby in many ways. He just saw her as
'there's my mummy' . . . he didn't know her
as a person, as I did."

"I hope she'd be pleased that Martin's marrying again. You see, I'm such a different person,

441

it would be no question of trying to be a second Helen . . ."

"I'm sure she would," Kit said.

Kit asked herself how was it that she was allowing a marriage to go ahead that was sinful. There was a bit in the service which asked if anyone knew any impediment to this couple's being joined together. And when the priest asked this, Kit, who knew that her father had a living wife, would say nothing. She had after all asked Sister Madeleine, and Sister Madeleine had said to do what she thought was right.

It was a huge responsibility but she would do it.

Kit settled into the College of Catering with great ease.

The very first week she met a girl called Frankie Barry with dancing eyes and a sense of rebellion. Frankie was going to go to America eventually and travel coast to coast, managing a hotel here and there along the way.

"Would we be able to do that, do you think?" Kit was doubtful.

"Certainly we will. Aren't we going to do the City and Guilds Exams? That's the highest qualification in the world," said Frankie confidently.

Kit was pleased about this. There would be no fear of ending up jobless after two and a half years and having to go meekly into the Central Hotel and work with Philip's parents and maybe marry him just to keep everyone quiet.

Philip was enjoying the college too. He showed her proudly how he had sewed on his own name tapes. "Aren't you the little treasure," Kit had teased him. "A prize for any girl." But he had flushed and she felt ashamed. Wouldn't it be wonderful if he fancied Frankie. She tried to bring them together, but it didn't work. Frankie had a flat with two other girls, Philip lived in his uncle's house, Kit was in the hostel.

Dublin was filled with things to do. The problem was to choose. She arranged to go and meet Rita. Philip was waiting patiently for her after the lecture as she knew he would be.

"No, Philip. I have arranged to meet someone, honestly."

"Who?"

"I beg your pardon?"

"I mean is it anyone I know?" Philip realized that he had been too proprietorial.

"It is actually. It's Rita Moore."

"Rita, your maid from Lough Glass?"

"Yes." Kit didn't like the snobbish way he said it, it was very like his mother.

"I mean you're meeting her in a cafe . . . and everything," he said, astounded by the democracy of it all.

"No, of course not . . . I'm going to sit down at a table and ask her to serve me and then eat on her own."

"I only asked."

"And you were told," Kit said shortly.

Rita wanted all the news, and details of how Peggy, the daily who came for a few hours, was doing her job.

"Will Miss Hayes make any changes, do you think?"

"I hope so . . ." Kit said. "I mean I'd like her to make it into her place, you know, not just move into our place."

"She's going to ask me to the wedding," Rita said.

"I know . . . what are you going to wear?"

"I saw a suit in Clery's. It's the very thing. And I might get shoes to match. It's a sort of light green. What'll you wear yourself, Kit?"

"I don't know. Daddy gave me money to buy an outfit. I haven't seen anything I like yet."

Next morning at the college Kit was told that there was a parcel for her.

When she saw that it was from London she took it to the ladies' cloakroom, where, heart beating like a hammer, she opened it. What could Lena Gray be doing now? What awful secret was there here that was going to upset them all?

She unpacked the gray and white silk dress in amazement and read the note. The dress didn't look like much, but that wasn't important . . . what was important was the note.

I thought you might like this to wear at the wedding. L.

She read it over and over.

What it meant was that she was giving her blessing to the wedding. Helen McMahon was saying that the marriage would go ahead and she would not interfere. Tears came down Kit's face, tears of pure relief.

She looked at the dress again. It was silk, maybe even pure silk. It must have cost a fortune. She would try it on tonight and then she would think of what she would write.

That is if she did write.

But you'd have to write to thank for something like this. Which was probably what Lena wanted.

Clio's hostel was near the university. There were girls from all over Ireland there, some of them from very posh families. Most of them had never heard of Lough Glass. Lots of them had been to boarding schools and knew each other. It wasn't as easy as Clio had thought to make friends. And it was the same at lectures. In some magical way other people seemed to know each other.

Clio found her first days at University College Dublin much less fun that she had hoped they would be. For the first time in her life she was a little bit lonely. For the first time she realized she was a very small fish in a pond so big she couldn't even see the edges.

She cheered herself up with the thought that however bad it was for her it must be worse for Kit with all those hotel people from everywhere. And down at the other end of O'Connell Street, miles away from where all the action was.

Kit went out to supper with Philip O'Brien. She invited *him* and said it was her treat.

"What's this about?" Philip was suspicious.

"I want to talk to you properly and if I am your guest then I think you've invited me out, like asking someone out."

"Well, you're asking *me* out, isn't that the same?" he grumbled.

"You know it isn't," Kit said firmly.

He was tall, Philip, and his freckles seemed to suit him more, his hair had stopped standing up at odd angles, he didn't have that slightly puzzled look he'd had as a youngster, he had a sense of humor. In most ways he was the perfect friend. Apart from one way, and that's what Kit wanted to talk about.

"I'm going to have spaghetti," she said, looking at the menu.

"It's probably tinned," Philip said.

"Good. I loved tinned spaghetti. It's much easier to eat."

"Don't let them hear you saying that in the training college. They'll think we're a couple of yahoos."

"That's exactly what I wanted to talk to you about," Kit said.

"What? Spaghetti?"

"No, the word you said, a couple of yahoos . . ."

"A lot of them are from Dublin or from big cities. They think everyone from a place like Lough Glass would be a yahoo."

"I'm not talking about the word 'yahoo,' it's the word 'couple' that worried me."

"It is what you call two people." Philip was aggrieved.

"It's not what you call us. I have my whole life to live and things to worry about. I can't find myself sliding into a sort of pairing with you as well as everything else . . ."

"I don't see what's so terrible . . ." he began.

"It's not terrible, it's just something that has to be agreed between two people, not assumed

446

by one and the other go along without thinking."

"Then, will you be my girlfriend?" Philip asked.

"No, Philip."

"Why?"

"Because I want to be me. I want to be without a boyfriend."

"Forever?"

"No, not forever but until I meet one, and it might be you, and we both agree."

"But you have met me." Philip was very confused now.

"Philip, I'm your friend, not your girlfriend. And if you say *But you are a girl* I'll stick my fork in your eyes."

"I'll always want you as my girlfriend," he said simply. "You can go off with whoever you like, but I'll always be there for you in Lough Glass with the hotel, and maybe we might even get married."

"Philip, you're eighteen. Nobody gets married at eighteen." The waitress was standing there.

"People who love each other get married at eighteen," Philip said, totally ignoring the girl standing with her little order book.

"They don't unless they're pregnant," Kit said with spirit.

"We could get pregnant. That would be a great idea," Philip said.

"Jesus!" said the waitress. "I'll come back when you've something less dramatic on your mind, like what you're going to have for your supper."

"Are they a terrible crowd of hicks down there?" Clio asked. She and Kit were having coffee in Grafton Street.

"Stop talking about down there. It would take me less time to walk to my college than you to yours."

"Yeah, but what are they like?"

"Very nice mainly. It's quite hard work. You have to concentrate a bit, but I suppose I'll get the hang of it."

"And what will you do in the end, I mean where will it take you?"

"Christ, how do I know, Clio? I've only been in it a week. How about you? Where's a B.A. going to take you?"

"Aunt Maura said it's a great basis for meeting people."

"Maura says she never said that."

"I wish you wouldn't talk to her behind my back about things I told you. She is my aunt, you know."

"And she's going to be my stepmother." They both laughed. They were squabbling the way they did when they were seven years of age.

"Maybe we'll always go on like this," Clio said.

"Oh yes. When we're old ladies holidaying in the South of France, fighting about our deck chairs in the sun and our poodles," Kit agreed.

"You getting away from Philip O'Brien, crotchety old owner of the Central Hotel."

"Why don't you see me as the owner of a string of hotels of my own?"

"It's not what women do," Clio said.

"And what about you? Will you have married some suitable fellow from First Arts?"

"God no. There's no one suitable there. I'll

be looking amongst the lawyers and the medics."

"A doctor's wife? Clio, you'd never have the patience. Look at what your mother has to put up with."

"A surgeon's wife, a specialist's wife . . . I'm planning this properly," Clio said. Then she asked: "What are you wearing anyway?"

"A sort of gray and white dress," Kit said.

"What material?"

"Silk, sort of silk."

"No! Where did you get it?"

"In a small shop on a side street." Kit was evasive.

"You're not exactly killing yourself then, are you?"

"It's quite nice, it looks weddingy." Kit defended the dress.

"Gray and white, it sounds like a postulant nun to me."

"Well, let's wait and see, will we?"

"Does it feel funny, your father getting married again?" Anna Kelly asked Emmet as they met at the sweets counter of Dillon's grocery.

"What do you mean funny?" Emmet asked. Anna was pretty. She had blond curly hair and a gorgeous smile. They were going to be sort of related after the wedding.

"Well, will you call her Mummy?" Anna wanted to know.

"Lord, no. We call her Maura already."

"And will she sleep in your father's room or your mother's room?" Anna wanted to know all the details.

"I don't know. I didn't ask. Daddy's, I suppose. That's what married people do."

"Why didn't your mother then?"

"She had a cold, she didn't want to give it to Daddy."

"A cold? The whole time?"

"That's what I was told," Emmet said. He spoke without guile.

Something changed in Anna. "Yes, well, some people do," she agreed, and companionably they discussed the relative merits of Cleeves toffees, which were flatter, and Scots Clan, which were more chunky but dearer.

Mrs. Dillon watched them. At least these two didn't look likely to pocket half the display when no one was looking, but you couldn't be too careful.

Maura hadn't wanted an engagement ring. "We're too mature for that," she said to Martin.

"We're not old, don't say that."

"I didn't say old, I meant we didn't have to get engaged . . . we had an understanding in the real sense of the word."

"I don't know how you waited so long and were so understanding when I was such a ditherer," Martin said.

"Shush, we've been through that before. You had much more to sort out than I did." Maura could afford to be generous now, she told herself. Her months and months of coping with Martin's indecision were over. He was now deeply committed to their marriage. He would make it work, he would make her happy. He knew these things were possible. And as for Maura herself, she could hardly believe her good fortune in having chased the ghosts of the beautiful, restless-looking woman who was her predecessor. Martin and Maura could walk by the lake of an autumn evening now without pausing, stricken, to remember that this was where Helen's life had ended.

"I want the wedding day to be the best day in the world for you."

"It will," Maura said.

"Then let me get you some jewel if you won't have a diamond engagement ring. I want you to have more than a plain wedding ring. Would you like a diamond brooch, do you think?" His face was eager to please her.

"No, my love. Truly."

"There are jewels of Helen's in a box. You know that. Suppose I were to bring them to a jeweler in the town and ask him to make something completely different, then you wouldn't worry about cost." He was able to speak of Helen naturally now, without his face contorting.

"No, Martin. Those belong to Kit. She must have them someday. When she's twenty-one, maybe. You must give them to her. She should wear them with pleasure. Don't have them altered for me. I have enough."

"They're all there somewhere, I never even looked at them."

"Fine. Let's leave them for Kit's twenty-first." Maura had looked at them though. She had fingered them sadly. A marcasite brooch, a locket, a diamante clip, a pair of earrings that might have been real rubies and might not.

But mostly she had noticed two rings, an engagement ring and a wedding ring. Helen McMahon had not taken those with her on the night she went out in the boat on the lake. Maura wondered whether Sergeant Sean O'Connor or the detectives from Dublin had inquired about that at the time. It surely must have been a pointer to the state of mind of someone who might have been thought to end her own life, if she had carefully removed valuable jewelery and left it behind.

"Are you asking Stevie Sullivan to the wedding?" Clio asked her aunt Maura.

"No. There was a lot of debate about that. He is my future boss, that would mean a yes, but then think of his mother and that means a no. And he is a neighbor but think of his terrible little brother."

"He is a single man and quite good-looking," Clio added.

"Yes, but he also has a reputation for disappearing from public functions with young ladies in tow." Maura knew the whole world of Lough Glass now. "Martin and I added it up and it came out against asking him."

"Imagine you working for him, Aunt Maura. He came from nothing."

"Imagine you using an expression like that . . . a young girl like you." Maura's eyes were cold. Clio realized too late that she often misjudged her aunt. Aunt Maura didn't have the same cozy, gossipy way of looking at the world as her own mother did. There was very little gossip, and ab-

solutely no feeling that some people were acceptable and some were not.

The week before the wedding gifts poured into
the chemist's shop. And even more important for
Maura and Martin were the accompanying notes
wishing them well. People said that it was good
to see two such nice people finding happiness.
Maura was a known visitor to the town in recent
years, and as a child had grown up only a few
miles away. It wasn't as if Martin McMahon was
looking outside for a stranger.
As he had before.
Mona from the post office gave some Belleek
china. She said she thought there was something
gracious about it which would suit the new Mrs.
McMahon. Mildred O'Brien chose a small set
of silver coffee spoons. The Walls sent a glass
bonbon dish with a silver handle. The Hickeys,
who had been intending to send meat as they
always did if the event was being held in Lough
Glass, stirred themselves and sent something
which looked suspiciously like a pram rug.
Paddles sent four bottles of brandy and four
bottles of whiskey, on the grounds that the groom
and the bride's brother-in-law would consume
that amount easily in any given year. There was
an embroidered sampler from Mother Bernard
and the community, a history of the county from
Brother Healy and the Brothers' school, a set of
saucepans from Mrs. Hanley in the drapery and
from Sister Madeleine a great clump of white
heather and a tub to plant it in. She said that
although it was superstitious to believe that white

heather was lucky, at least it might be nice to have this as a symbol of their marriage, and that when it grew every year it would remind them of their good fortune in coming together.

Kit looked at the heather thoughtfully. Sister Madeleine knew that there never had been a Lena Gray writing to Helen McMahon, and so this was a new relationship. Therefore she suspected this was not a marriage in the eyes of God and yet she was going along with it.

Sometimes Kit felt the world was tilting.

א א א

"You never tell me anything about Lough Glass," Louis said to Lena on Saturday morning.

"I used to my love, but you said it was very trivial."

"Well, some of it was . . . you know, the petty things . . . but I'm not totally insensitive. I know you must think about the children and about Martin."

"From time to time," Lena agreed.

"Well, don't shut me out . . . I mean, I am interested in everything that concerns you. I do love you." He sounded defensive.

"I know."

"How do you know?" He seemed to doubt the rather flat tone of voice.

"I know because you came back," she said. Again it was if she was saying something by rote. In fact she was repeating his own words to her. *Why would I come back to you if I didn't love you?*

454

"Well, that's all right then." But Louis was watchful. Lena didn't seem herself this morning.

"What do you think the place is like now?"

Lena looked at him for a long moment. She debated for a wild moment whether to tell him that her husband was marrying Maura Hayes at eleven A.M. and that she had spent a week's salary on a dress for her daughter Kit to wear at the ceremony. She wondered was it possible that, if she were to fill him in on the important areas of her own life, he would be able to feel involved with her to such a degree that he could put aside all the many distractions of his world. But the moment ended. She knew it would not be possible. She would not get the reaction she hoped for. Instead, she would get blame and recrimination for having hidden the fact that she had written to her daughter for years and then met the girl in London.

"Oh, I expect it will be like any other day," she said. "Any ordinary Saturday in Lough Glass."

אׁ אׁ אׁ

Steve Sullivan said once he'd be in Dublin anyway he'd drive the bride to the church, and drive them both to the reception.

"We can't accept that, Stevie . . ." Martin began to protest.

"Jesus, Martin, isn't it a grand easy wedding present? Let me do it for you." Stevie was a handsome young man now of twenty-one, with his long dark hair falling over his eyes and his tanned skin. When Stevie was a boy he had often heard part of his father's drunken rages include the possibility that his mother had lain down with the tinkers . . . how else could she have produced such an unlikely-looking son for him? Stevie had heard her reply that since it had been such a hellish thing to have to lie down for her own husband she was unlikely to want to repeat the experience with anyone else, tinker or no tinker. His own experience of sex had made him think that his mother must have missed out a lot on life if this had been her attitude. But it was a view he kept to himself.

"Anyway you can rely on me, Maura. You wouldn't want to be having any truck with these Dublin fellows."

She was grateful. It would be good to have a friendly face beside her as she set off to the church. She had packed the possessions that she needed from her flat in Dublin and brought them in advance to Lough Glass. The flat had been painted and let to a young couple who had already moved in. Maura had hoped that in the future Kit and Clio might be able to live there. It would be handy for them; it had two bedrooms, it was central. But she thought that they might not be temperamentally suited to sharing a flat. There was an edge between them that did not suggest a real friendship, more a wishing to score off each other. She wouldn't suggest the idea until they had made up their minds more about life.

Stevie wore a dark suit, which could almost have been a uniform, when he came to the hotel to collect Maura.

"You look lovely, Maura," he said.

He was the first to see her and even though he was little more than a child still, she was pleased. A flush came over her face and neck. "Thank you, Stevie."

"I'm pleased to see my staff know how to kit themselves out," he said.

Kit and Clio stood side by side in the big church.

Clio hadn't ceased to gripe about the dress since she arrived. "What kind of a shop did you say it was, that shop?"

"Oh, I told you, in a side street."

"You're lying in your teeth."

"Why would I lie?"

"Because that's the way you're made."

"Ask anyone. Ask Daddy. Ask Maura."

"You lied to them too. This is a really good smart dress. It cost a fortune. Did you steal it?"

"You have a very diseased mind. Will you shut up and let me enjoy my father's wedding."

At that moment they saw the small congregation turning around. Maura Hayes was walking up the church aisle with her brother. Martin McMahon stood beaming at the altar rails.

"She looks great," Clio whispered. "That's a terrific outfit."

"She probably stole it. Most of us did," Kit said loftily.

Stevie was outside the church holding open the door of the car. "I didn't know he was coming," Philip said to Clio.

"Oh, he gets anywhere," Clio said. "If you have a brass neck and flash good looks like that, the world is open to you."

Philip seemed disappointed by this. "Is that his car?" he asked.

"Yes." Clio still sounded scornful. "Part of the Sullivan Motor Service is to realize that there will be times in people's lives, functions, when they'll need a bit of class. Stevie's ahead of the game."

"Do women like him?"

"Yes, but only in a very obvious kind of way. I mean, I personally wouldn't touch him with a barge pole. He's been with every maid and skivvy from here to Lough Glass and back."

"Slept with them, you mean?" Philip's eyes were round.

"So I hear."

"And none of them got . . . um . . . pregnant?"

"Apparently not. Or if they did we didn't hear."

Maura had chosen the hotel well. There was a sherry reception in a big bright room with chintzy covered couches and chairs. The waitresses moved around efficiently, making sure that glasses were well filled. When they went in to sit down the late autumn sun was slanting in the windows on the group.

The seating plan had been carefully thought out. Kit and Emmet sat on either side of Rita. The O'Briens were divided up so that they could not glare at each other. Lilian Kelly was put beside two of Maura's work colleagues so that she could talk about shops in Dublin and the races.

There was a grapefruit cocktail, then chicken and ham, and an ice cream with hot chocolate sauce. The wedding cake was small, one tier.

"There won't be any need to keep a tier for

458

the christening," Mildred O'Brien explained to her neighbor, who nodded, bewildered.

The speeches were very simple. Peter Kelly said how this was the happiest day for a long time. And how great it was that his good friend had found a partner for the rest of his life. Everyone clapped.

Martin thanked everyone for their support in coming to wish them well. He said it was particularly gratifying that Maura had so many friends already in Lough Glass, and it would in many senses for her be like coming home. They thought the speeches were over but Maura McMahon stood up. A little ripple went through the group. Women so rarely spoke in public. Brides never.

"I would like to add my thanks to Martin's, and to say this is the happiest day of my life. But I want to thank most of all Kit and Emmet McMahon for their generosity in sharing their father with me. They are the children of Martin and Helen, they will always be that. I hope the memory of their mother will never fade. For them or for any of us. Without Helen McMahon, Kit and Emmet would not have existed. Without Helen, Martin would not have known his years of happiness in a first marriage. I thank her for all she gave to us, I hope her spirit knows what a feeling of warmth there is toward her this day. And I assure you all that I will do my very best to make Martin as happy as he deserves to be. He is a truly good man."

There was a silence as people took in the depth of feeling in her words. Then they clapped and clapped and raised their glasses. And the pianist in the corner began to tinkle so that a few songs could be called for. Maura had checked. There had been no singing at Martin and Helen's wedding.

Stevie Sullivan stood outside the door. Maura had not changed her outfit. The wedding dress and jacket were quite suitable for traveling. The cases were packed and had been put in the back of the car.

"You're looking fairly irresistible, Kit," Stevie said.

"Better resist me, though," Kit said. "I believe you're taking them to the train."

"That's not what I heard," he said.

"But aren't you going to take them off to start their honeymoon?"

"Right in one."

"So?"

"So, it's not the station, it's the airport."

"The airport?" Kit had thought they were going to Galway.

"They're going to London," Stevie said. "Didn't they tell you?"

CHAPTER SEVEN

Ivy could hardly believe it when she saw the letter with the Irish stamp and the foreign-looking postmark that nobody could read. She twitched her curtain as Lena ran downstairs on her way to work.

Lena scarcely dared to hope. She sat down in Ivy's kitchen and read it. It was one page. It had no beginning, no greeting. But then neither had her note to Kit.

> *Thank you very much for the beautiful dress. It looked very well and was much admired. It arrived at the college over a week ago but I waited until now to write.*
>
> *So that I could tell you the ceremony has taken place. It all went very well and they have gone to London today. I thought it was Galway that they were going to, but apparently it's the Regent Palace Hotel, London.*
>
> *I know London is a huge city but I thought you would want to know. Just in case.*
>
> *Once more, thank you for the dress.*
> *Kit.*

Lena sat holding the letter.
"Is it bad news?" Ivy asked.
"No. Not bad news, no."

"Well, is she speaking to you?"

"No, not really speaking to me. Not yet, no."

"Oh come on, Lena. Don't make me beg . . . what is it?"

"It's a sort of contact, sort of warning me off something . . . but I haven't told you the whole background. Can I do that some long, lonely evening?"

"There'll be plenty of those ahead of us," Ivy agreed.

When she got to the agency she found Jessie Park waiting in her office for her. Jessie was a changed person to the tired, flustered woman in a cardigan whom Lena had discovered the first day. Now a trim smart woman of forty-seven, Jessie exuded confidence. Her mother played racing demon with the other tenants in the sheltered accommodation and seemed to have forgotten her digestive problems.

They had set the date, were going to have a small wedding. Just eight people to sit down to a lunch in a hotel. Could Lena be one of the witnesses? Jim Millar's brother would be the other. And they would love Lena's Louis to come as a guest to the wedding, of course. Lena embraced her and said how happy she was. She very much hoped that Louis would be free. His hours were so difficult. She said all the right things. But her mind was far away.

She was breathing up a prayer of thanks to Kit for having warned her about Martin and Maura's being in London. Suppose, for example, that Jessie's wedding lunch had been in the Regent Palace Hotel? There had been stranger coincidences. To be forewarned was very useful indeed.

She knew that Louis wouldn't want to go to the wedding.

"Darling heart, don't I get enough of this every day at work?" he said, smiling at her despairingly and holding his hands out as if to show that it was raining weddings on him every time he moved.

The Dryden did a very scant wedding business indeed. But Lena didn't make an issue out of it. "I know, just to let you know that you're welcome and they'd love it if you could get away. That's all."

"Can you get me out of it?" He seemed pleased.

"Easily," she said.

She saw the little tension lines around his eyes relax. Perhaps Louis Gray didn't like the idea of going to weddings with her, watching other people making promises for a future together. And Louis was in such good form these days, so light-hearted and happy. It would be ludicrous to make a fuss over his attending the function. It would of its very nature be as dry as dust. Louis would hate it.

Because she hadn't forced him or complained that he wouldn't give her support he was even more loving than ever. And he called unexpectedly at the office one day with a bottle of champagne for the happy couple.

"I'm so sorry I can't be there," he said. There was a real regret in his eyes and voice.

Lena stood listening to him and even she felt that there were ways in which Louis Gray *was* sorry he wouldn't be attending.

Jim Millar and Jessie Park were, of course, delighted with him. "He's a great man, that husband of yours. I'm sure he's a top businessman," Jim Millar said.

"I think they value him a lot at the Dryden," Lena agreed.

"I'm surprised he doesn't run his own hotel," Jessie said.

"He may one day," Lena said. But she didn't think that far ahead. She had discovered that you got by better taking life in short bursts.

She dressed in front of Louis, he lay making admiring sounds from the bed. It was one of his late mornings.

"You're far too glamorous for that crowd," he said. "Let's you and me go off somewhere and dazzle the world."

"I'll see you later." She blew him a kiss.

"Come home sober," he called after her.

"I think that's fairly likely," she laughed.

The wedding luncheon ended nice and early as everyone had known it would. Mrs. Park was brought back to her new friends, Jessie and Jim caught the train for St. Ives. They were going back to Cornwall where their romance had begun. Lena assured them she had many things to do.

Without her realizing it her feet took her toward the Regent Palace. She stopped and studied hard her appearance in a shop window mirror. She was wearing a cream suit with lilac trim. Her hat was in velvet to match the trim. She had a large black bag, black gloves, and very high-heeled court shoes. She wore a fair amount of well-applied makeup. Surely she could not look like the woman in the dirndl skirts and loose flowing dresses that they had known years ago.

Her eyes might give her away. People often recognized others by the eyes alone. She stopped in Boots and bought a pair of sunglasses. "Not much call for those these days," said the young girl selling them.

"I'm going to rob a bank," Lena explained.

"Want anyone to help you carry it all away?" the girl said. Louis was right about the English. They were dying to talk, it was just that they needed someone to start them off.

Lena studied herself in the sunglasses. That was just the trick. She positioned herself in the lounge of the Regent Palace. She had no other plans for the rest of the day, she would wait here until she saw them going in or coming out.

James Williams couldn't believe it. He had thought that the well-dressed woman in sunglasses was Louis Gray's wife. There weren't many with that hair and those legs. But what on earth was she doing sitting in the foyer of a huge hotel like this? It was almost as if she were waiting to pick someone up. But perhaps she was just waiting to meet that handsome if feckless husband.

James Williams wondered whether Mrs. Gray had any idea of her husband's popularity with the ladies. He declined to listen to whispers in his own hotel, thinking it beneath him. But he would have to be deaf not to have known that

Louis Gray had gone off with some rich spoiled young American to Paris not long ago. Possibly Mrs. Gray put up with it.

He looked over at the elegant figure sitting in front of a drink, which she was studying through sunglasses. Perhaps she might even be here consoling herself. It was an attractive thought, but James Williams had a meeting in one of the conference rooms.

When he came down through the hall again he saw she was still there. "What's the lady drinking?" he asked a waiter.

"She's refused other drinks that were offered."

"She won't from me, I know her." He learned it was gin and orange. He ordered one for both of them and just as the tray arrived he appeared at her table. "Really, Mr. Williams," she said.

"Really, Mrs. Gray." It was always their joke to be so formal.

"Were you waiting here by any chance hoping I'd turn up?" He was playful, flattering, flirtatious.

"No, I'm sorry to disappoint you. I just came in to take the weight off my feet," she said.

"Just came in? Wasn't I lucky!"

"Just this minute," Lena Gray said. He looked at her with interest. She had been in this lounge for more than two hours. What on earth was making her lie to him like this?

They talked away, Lena and James, about the world in general and hotels in particular. At no stage did either of them mention Louis Gray, who was the only person they had in common. They had another round and another.

Three gin and oranges with him, and perhaps more before he arrived. James was wondering if by the most amazing good fortune he had got lucky with this attractive Irishwoman. Her voice was not slurred. He couldn't see her eyes because of the ridiculous glasses, but she said she had an eye infection and needed to wear them. He thought there was something a little odd and light-headed about her behavior, and at one stage she stood up and excused herself very suddenly. She didn't go to the ladies' as he expected, she went inside to stand by the gates of the lift. She stood quite near a middle-aged couple who were carrying a lot of shopping — typical out-of-town tourists and shoppers. If it hadn't been so ridiculous James Williams would have thought that the elegant Lena Gray had gone over to eavesdrop on what they were saying.

It was five years since she had seen them. Her head was slightly dizzy. She must remember this moment.

Martin was still in a bulky suit. It looked new, this one, but it had not been made by a tailor. He was forty-five, a year older than Louis, but he could have been ten or fifteen years older. His stance was the same, slightly stooped, his good-natured smile was there. His arms were full of bags, from British Home Stores, C & A, and even Liberty's. Was anything different? He looked happy, he looked like he used to when he had been playing with the children or had pushed the boat out on the lake. He looked less anxious to please.

And Maura Hayes. Maura, whom she'd hated to meet because she was the jovial sister of Lilian, the woman who made it very difficult to refuse an invitation. Was she older or younger than Lilian? Had she been told? Had she ever listened? She looked flushed and happy.

"I'd love a cup of tea," Lena heard her say. "Is that a real country hick thing to want?"

"And this from the city sophisticate working in Dublin all those years?" he said, laughing. "But I imagine that they'll have no difficulty in bringing a tray to the room."

"Do you think so?" She looked eager and as if all her problems had been solved at a stroke.

"This isn't the Central Hotel in Lough Glass, you know," he said.

She was so near she could touch them, the ghost of the wife they had thought was dead. Her appearance would destroy so many lives. Filled with the self-pity that gin can often bring, Lena started to weep. Perhaps it would have been better if she had died in the lake that night.

She looked flushed when she came back. James Williams leaned across the table. "If you're in no hurry home . . . ?" he asked. His tone was polite, it was not remotely like a proposition.

"If I'm not, Mr. Williams . . . ?"

"Then I was wondering what we might do . . ." He was walking on eggshells now; her voice had got shaky, there seemed to be glistening tears on her face.

"I was wondering if you might like me to give you a lift in a taxi . . . perhaps?"

"To where?"

"To wherever you'd like to go next. Somewhere for another drink possibly? A bit to eat? Home to your doorstep? To the Dryden Hotel?"

"Anywhere you say." She took off her glasses and looked at him. She had been crying, but her eyes did not look infected. She was very upset. "You're a very intelligent man, James Williams, very smooth, very polished. I'm no match for you. I think I'm so capable and in control, but I'm only a poor country hick. That's the word I heard two people using a few minutes ago. That's what I am, a hick."

"No. No," he protested. "Please tell me. What can I offer you?"

"A chance to go now while I still have two legs to carry me to the door," she said.

She put on her sunglasses. She was a very attractive woman. If ever he saw anyone who needed a strong shoulder to cry on over something, it was Lena Gray. After she had cried she would feel grateful to him. He considered it for a moment. But only a moment. "Off we go then, I'll find you a taxi." His hand tightly on her arm, he steered her out into the traffic of Piccadilly Circus.

"I see you didn't take my advice," Louis said as Lena stumbled in the door.

"What advice wash that?" Lena couldn't get the words out.

"I thought I said you should stay sober, and you said there was no question but that you would." He looked at her quizzically.

She had flung off her shoes and her hat was

at an awkward angle on her head. "Yesh," she smiled at him. "That's what I thought. But I wash wrong."

"You're a sweetheart," he said. And peeled off her good suit, hung it carefully on a hanger, and steered her to bed.

Twice in the night she got up to be sick.

If Louis heard he made no sound. He lay breathing gently. He never dreamed, or at least he couldn't remember his dreams. A man who had so much to remember, why did none of it come out in dreams?

Lena had dreamed incessantly of James Williams and what might have happened if she had accepted the offer he was so definitely making. She shuddered to think she had been so near to saying yes.

Louis was on an early shift. *I didn't wake you,* he wrote in a note. *Your lovely little snores sounded as if they deserved to be allowed to continue. See you tonight.*

She had never felt worse. Why did people drink too much if this was how it left them feeling next morning? She wasn't at all sure that she could make the office.

She called in on Ivy.

"How did the wedding go?" Ivy said, pouring coffee.

"They seemed to be happy, buying lots of stuff in Oxford Street and going back to the hotel to have tea served in the bedroom."

"You went on their honeymoon with them?" Ivy asked, shocked.

"No, that was something else. Ivy, do you think I should have something like a prairie oyster?"

"A what?"

"It's to cure a hangover."

"What is it?"

"You're the one with the contacts in the pub."

"Not anymore," Ivy said.

"Well, I need to know. Would Ernest know?"

"I expect he would."

"What's his number?"

"Lena, you're mad. It's only nine-thirty in the morning."

"Yes, I'm half an hour late for work already. I can't go in like this or I'd collapse. Give me his home number or I'll ring directory inquiries."

"I've always said you're *mad*."

"Hello, Ernest, it's Lena Gray."

"Yes?" He sounded cautious.

"You do remember me?"

"Well, yes."

"Ernest, very simply, what's a prairie oyster? It's got something to do with raw eggs and nothing to do with oysters, am I right?"

"A raw egg in a glass, a tablespoon of sherry, some Lea and Perrin's, shake like mad and swallow in one."

"Thank you, Ernest."

"Have you got all the ingredients?"

"Yes, I think so. Thanks."

"Will she be all right, do you think?"

"Who?"

"Ivy. I presume she's been overindulging."

Lena paused for a moment. Perhaps this was a way to get Ivy back with Ernest. "I do

471

hope so, Ernest. She doesn't tell you, but it's all hitting her very badly."

"Could you — um — tell her . . . ?"

"Yes?"

"Tell her . . . to take care."

"Maybe you should tell her yourself, Ernest."

"It's difficult."

"No, it's not. These things are easy."

"But she's always pissed drunk."

"No, she's not, last night was special. It was some kind of anniversary between you both. I don't know exactly. But whatever it was it hit her hard." Lena hardly dared to lift her eyes to meet Ivy's.

"Yeah, well, it's about this time of year that she and I . . . But you don't want to bother."

"It's none of my business. All I know is that she won't hear a word against you, Ernest. I have tried, God help me I've tried to say a few, but she won't listen."

"You're a very good friend, Lena. Even with you being Irish and not understanding any of our ways," he said.

"Thank you, Ernest," she said humbly, and hung up.

"I'll kill you here and now in my own kitchen," Ivy said.

"No, get two eggs, sherry, Worcestershire sauce, and a saucer to put on top of the glass."

"Why?"

"So that it won't all fall out when I shake it."

"No, I mean why should I do any of this for you?"

"Because I think I may have saved your great

romance for you. Hurry, Ivy. I might be about to die."

"Was it a great wedding?" Dawn asked.
"Simply lovely," Lena said.
"I was hoping I might be asked."
"There were very few of us there. Honestly it was only a handful."
"Was your husband there, Mrs. Gray?"
"No. Louis wasn't able to go, sadly."
Dawn went back to her work.

Lena looked over at her blond head bent over the papers at her desk. Dawn was a spectacular-looking girl. Lena and Jessie had arranged that she take public-speaking lessons and it had been a wise investment. Now Dawn could stand up in front of any gathering of school seniors. Lena knew that the students would listen to the words that came from a slim young glamour girl only a few years older than themselves. If Dawn talked about the need to get good typing speeds, exact shorthand symbols and office routine, then they would accept it. Such advice coming from Jessie or herself would carry little weight.

Lena felt her head heavy and she had an in-explicable thirst. She must have drunk six glasses of water by lunchtime. Is this the way all heavy drinkers felt? The regulars in Paddles' and Foley's back in Lough Glass? The regulars in Ernest's bar? Did they all have to rehydrate themselves the next morning? What a pointless exercise it was. She would never get drunk again.

"Ernest is coming around tonight," Ivy said.

"Great stuff. Have you said 'Thank you, Lena'?"

"No, I haven't. I've said I wonder why I am now cast in the role of a screaming alcoholic."

"You could be a reformed alcoholic. Men love that," Lena suggested.

"I'm actually pleased," Ivy said.

"I know you are."

"But I don't want to put too much hope in it."

"No, of course not." Lena lay down on her bed and drifted off to sleep.

When she woke Louis was standing beside her. "How's my poor drunk?" he said, full of sympathy and love.

"I'm so sorry, Louis, was I disgusting?"

"No, you were sweet, you were like a floppy bunny, you couldn't sit or stand or anything . . ." He handed her a cup of tea which she drank thirstily.

"And what was I saying?" She was ninety percent sure she hadn't mentioned the Regent Palace Hotel, the journey to spy on the newly married couple.

"Nothing too intelligible, great difficulty in pronouncing words with an 'S' in them." He stroked her forehead. "More tea, then I'll scramble you some eggs . . . that's all you'll be able for. Trust Uncle Louis."

Lena closed her eyes. How strange it all was. Here she was lying in bed while Louis Gray got her a cup of tea. A couple of miles away Maura Hayes was lying in bed while Martin organized the hotel to get them tea also.

Lena let her mind wander back to the way they looked . . . Martin and Maura. At ease together, like people who had been friends and loved each other for years and had only just realized it. Martin wasn't straining and struggling to please her as he would have been with Helen. Maura was making no effort to concentrate.

They were well matched.

Lena wondered whether there was any passion between them. There must be some sexual love. They would hardly enter into a relationship unless they had planned to consummate it.

But she found herself unable to imagine it.

She could hardly remember her own coupling with Martin. Sex had always meant Louis, from the very first time she had known him and known he was for her. It didn't make her uneasy thinking about Martin and Maura making love on their London honeymoon, nor about Maura sleeping beside Martin in the bedroom that Helen McMahon had abandoned early in their marriage.

It was just that she couldn't imagine it at all.

Jessie and Jim came back from their honeymoon. They were anxious that the wedding party had been a success.

"I think everyone enjoyed it," Jessie said.

"Oh yes, it was wonderful," Lena assured her.

"My brother didn't say much about it, but then he's a silent man," said Jim Millar.

This was an understatement, he had been almost wordless through the ceremony and the lunch that followed it.

"My mother enjoyed it though?" Jessie was

hoping it had been the great social event that she wanted to remember it as.

"It was a wonderful day," Lena said. "A marvelous happy occasion. We won't ever forget it."

She was rewarded by the relief and pleasure in Jessie's eyes, and in Jim's when she looked at him triumphantly.

The truth was that Lena had hardly any memory whatsoever of anything that day except standing beside Martin and Maura as they waited to go upstairs.

Ivy grumbled from time to time that Ernest had taken a very strong stance about things like sherry trifle. He said it could be the beginning of the slippery slope. But still it seemed a small price to pay to have him back in her life.

He called regularly. Sometimes Lena spoke to him. "I owe you a great debt of gratitude," he said once conspiratorially. "I always thought that Ivy was a woman who could take care of herself, run her own life. I never knew she'd gone to pieces."

The months passed in Lough Glass as they did everywhere else, and people were so accustomed to seeing Martin McMahon and his wife Maura walking together exchanging affectionate smiles that the memory of Helen had faded from the forefront of every mind.

"She's a lot dumpier than her predecessor," Mildred O'Brien said, looking out the hotel window at the McMahons striding along with Rusty, their red setter puppy. Mildred had never liked

476

Helen when she was alive, but she didn't seem to be pleased either with the second Mrs. McMahon.

Dan sighed. "She doesn't have Helen's way with her, that's true," he said, thinking back wistfully on the slow swish of Helen McMahon's skirt as she walked down the lane behind the hotel, her hair tumbling down her back, her eyes restless.

Maura went from time to time to see Sister Madeleine. Once she brought a pane of glass and some putty. "At least you won't give this away," she said, knocking out the broken window with a hammer and collecting the shattered glass on old newspapers.

"Don't be too sure of it. There are plenty of people worse off than I am," said the hermit.

"This is the first window I've ever put in, you wouldn't destroy my faith in myself by taking it out to give to some ne'er-do-well."

"You sound very happy, Maura."

"I am, thank God, very happy indeed. And what's more, I'm blessed in those two children."

"You wouldn't be if you weren't so good to them."

"I was wondering . . ." Maura lined the window frame with the putty as she spoke. "I was wondering whether you'd put my mind at rest over something . . ."

"My own mind is so confused, Maura, I'm never one to set myself up as an adviser to other people's minds."

"It's just, you know, dreams, and superstitions, and sort of thinking you see things . . ."

"Go on."

"Would that be real at all, or would it be just from being overtired?"

"Would you tell me a bit more and maybe I'd know the drift."

"It sounds very silly."

"Things always do." Madeleine went to the fire to move the old black kettle over the flames.

Maura eased the glass into place. "There now, isn't that a dream," she said, standing back to admire the slightly crooked window which was a great deal better than the cracked frame with several pieces out of it which had been there before.

"It's beautiful, Maura. Thank you from the bottom of my heart," said Sister Madeleine, looking at it with admiration.

"I've put in an extra bit of putty at the top, where there was a bit of a gap on the top corner. I don't think you'd see it." Maura bit her lip looking at it.

"I only see a lovely clean shiny window keeping out the wind and rain. Thank you again, Maura." The tea was poured. "And what did you see or dream that disturbed you."

"It's so odd. But it was when we were in London . . . a woman came and stood beside us . . ."

"Yes?"

"And I was absolutely sure it was Helen."

They were having dinner at the golf club as they did every Saturday. It was such an easy foursome and sometimes they were joined by other couples. The talk turned to the hermit.

"She won't let me listen to her chest," Peter

Kelly said. "I don't think she has any truck with modern medicine, you have to be a mystic or a gypsy for her to take any notice."

"She's warm enough in there, the place is quite snug," Maura said.

"Ah yes, it's warm all right, but what's she inhaling? Turf smoke, and her bedding could be damp. Still, you might as well be talking to the wall, she was always full of cracked notions. She'll live and die by them."

"I tried to give her a preparation for chilblains last year and she thanked me and said they'd go in their own time." Martin shook his head about her.

"But I think she's fairly sound in her own head," Maura said.

"She certainly cured Emmet's stutter," Martin agreed.

"And she calmed Clio down when she was behaving like someone bound for the gallows," Lilian added.

"She doesn't encourage foolish fantasies. She's as practical as Mother Bernard in many ways," Maura said.

They talked about Mother Bernard and her drive to build a new wing on the convent; her fund-raising activities had Lough Glass demented.

Maura's mind wandered away from the conversation.

She thought of the way the nun had been so adamant it couldn't have been Helen McMahon she had seen in London. What it undoubtedly must be was the imagination playing tricks. Like a tree can take on the image of a dangerous bogeyman if you're frightened, like a shadow on the windowpane can look like an intruder rather than a branch waving. So it was when Maura had been thinking of Helen she would automatically think any woman of the same age and size might be she.

"I wasn't thinking about her, you see," Maura had countered.

"How was she dressed?"

"She had dark glasses and a little hat. Purple feathers. It was *so* like her, Sister Madeleine." The nun threw back her head and laughed away Maura's anxieties. "Well now, don't you believe me?"

"Helen McMahon in sunglasses? Indoors? And in a hat? In all the years I saw her here she never wore a hat . . ."

"But suppose . . ."

"You see, even though you weren't thinking of her consciously, you must have been on another level. That's why you transposed her features onto a totally different stranger standing beside you." Sister Madeleine had beamed at the obvious explanation.

And of course Maura knew she must be right.

א   א   א

They learned a lot in the catering college, but there was still some free time. Often Kit went to the cinema with Frankie, who was always planning some devilment and was great at negotiating late passes from the hostel for her friend Kit.

Frankie was cheerful and casual. She didn't have the hothouse intensity of Clio, nor did she criticize with such outrage if Kit didn't do exactly what she wanted. She invited Kit for a weekend to Cork to stay with her family. Kit would have loved to have gone but it was at the end of the month and she had spent most of her allowance. She literally didn't have the train fare. Frankie shrugged. Another time. It was a relief. Kit thought of all the cross-questioning and analysis that she would have got from Clio.

There were some parties in flats, some of them marvelous with people singing and laughing way into the night, some of them messy evenings that shouldn't have been parties at all because they were just excuses for groping. Kit and Frankie thought that it was badly behaved to go in search of groping to a public place. This was a private matter, they said, and clucked at each other pretending to be nuns until they fell about laughing.

"What do you do all the time? I never see you," Clio complained. Kit tried to explain but nothing she said met with any approval. "It sounds awful," Clio said dismissively.

"Then you're just as well out of it." Kit was unconcerned. "But I would like to meet you for coffee now and then. We are meant to be friends."

Clio stopped sounding like a fourteen-year-old. "Let's go to Bewley's in Grafton Street tomorrow."

"Have you gone all the way yet?" Clio asked Kit.

"Are you out of your mind?" Kit asked.

"Does that mean out of my mind, yes, or out of my mind, no?" Clio had an infectious grin. That was why their fights had never lasted long when they were young. They didn't have fights now. They were much too old for that sort of silliness.

"The answer is no, as you know very well," Kit said.

"Me neither." Clio was sheepish.

"I didn't ask, remember that. I am mature enough to think it's people's own business."

"I wonder are we just the odd ones out. Like, is everyone else doing it and being mature and not telling?" Clio sounded very unsure.

"Well, we know Deirdre Hanley does it with everyone she sees. We know that Orla Dillon from the newsagent's at home was stupid enough to do it with that man from the mountains and is married to him now, which is about as bad as could happen."

"I don't mean people like that," Clio said. "I mean people like us."

"Well, they are like us. They come from Lough Glass."

"No, you know, middle-class people, upper-class people."

"Clio, you sound like Margaret Rutherford in a film." Kit pealed with laughter.

"I'm being serious. How would we know?"

"Well, I suppose people like us do if we want to and don't if we don't want to."

"We don't if we're afraid we'll go to hell, or people might talk about us and give us a bad name."

"I don't think it's simple as that."

"Simple? I've spelled out every possibility for you, every eventuality. What do you want?"

"It's just that Michael O'Connor, you know the fellow I was telling you about . . ."

Kit did know. A tall, unattractive commerce student with a very irritating laugh, a brother of Kevin O'Connor's in her own catering college . . . sons of a very wealthy family, each with his own car in Dublin, something unheard-of as regards luxury. Clio had spoken several times about Michael O'Connor.

"Yes, what about Michael?"

"He says everyone does it, and that I'm only being a foolish provincial. Out of step with the world."

"And does he say it's good-bye unless you have sex with him?"

"He calls it making love."

"Whatever it's called."

"Well, he doesn't quite say that, but you'd know that's what's meant."

"It's blackmail."

"He says you can't love someone properly without . . ."

"I bet he does." Kit sounded sarcastic.

Clio's eyes flashed. "He also says his brother Kevin did it with you."

"He *what?*"

Clio looked alarmed at the emphatic response. "That's what he said, after some party apparently."

Kit got up from the table, her face red with rage. "I have some advice for you, Clio . . . take

483

it if you like or ignore it. That is a great big lie, his stupid ox of a brother did try to take the knickers off me one night and I refused, because whenever I lose my virginity it will not be with one of those pig-ignorant O'Connors, with their stupid laughs and their lies and thinking they're God-all-bloody-mighties in their cars going vroom vroom."

The people at the other tables looked up with great interest as the handsome girl with the long black curly hair and the smart red jacket flung some coins on the table and stormed out of the restaurant. It wasn't every day that you overheard a conversation that covered lies and virginity and knickers and God-all-bloody-mighty.

Dublin was changing.

א א א

A hundred times Lena thought of an excuse to send Kit a short letter, a postcard even. But she always dismissed it as being too flimsy. The girl would shy away again if she were to attempt to contact her. After all, Kit's note had only been a belated thank-you letter for the dress and a warning about the presence of Martin and Maura in her city. It had not been a letter with any warmth or wish to rekindle a friendship.

But there might be something. Some possible excuse she could find that would give her a reason. Lena raked the local newspaper for any item of interest, something that might reasonably trigger a communication. She saw an item about the difficulties of getting employment in the hotel industry. She cut it out and pasted it on a sheet of paper. Then she added the Millar's Agency brochure on opportunities in the hotel trade and posted them to Kit at her college.

Kit was in her second year now. It would be time for her to think about positions and jobs. Surely she could not take offense at this.

Lena wrote the note over and over until she was satisfied with it. She made sure that the address was still the same, care of Ivy Brown. She wanted neither Louis nor her office colleagues to know of this correspondence with Ireland. In the end the note she wrote said:

Thought this might be of some interest to you and your fellow students.
Hope the course is going well.
Sincerest wishes for your success and happiness

And she signed it *L.*

א   א   א

It was Maura who noticed that there was something the matter with Emmet.

He didn't want any fuss, he said. Anyway he was playing in a match. Brother Healy wouldn't take kindly to his crying off.

"I'll get Peter to have a look at you, if you don't mind," Maura insisted.

"I'm quite grown up really, Maura. I'd know if there was something wrong with me." They looked each other in the eye. This was their first confrontation.

Emmet was a handsome boy, slim and sometimes frail-looking. He was a wiry hurler and much in demand on the team. Maura knew that missing a match wasn't something that would be countenanced except in case of dire emergency. But the boy had aches and pains, his skin looked sallow, and the whites of his eyes were yellow.

She wasn't going to back down. "I know you are an adult, Emmet, believe me I do. And if it were a matter of asking you to come up and wait in the surgery and waste time and make it all official I wouldn't try to force it on you. But Peter is my brother-in-law . . . Is it all right if I ask him to look at you, just look, this evening?"

Emmet grinned. "You're too reasonable, Maura. That's the problem."

Peter Kelly said that Emmet McMahon had acute jaundice. It could be cured at home. A darkened room, a lot of barley water, a heavy dose of those M and B tablets, examination of the urine, which was as red as port wine.

Maura came across twice a morning from her job in Stevie Sullivan's. His father came up twice a morning from the chemist's below. Anna Kelly was home from school recovering from measles. She called in too and read to him.

"What would you like? You wouldn't like *Desiree*, it's a great story about Napoleon's girlfriend."

"No, I'd prefer something else if you wouldn't mind, poetry maybe."

"Will I do some from our textbook? It could

be revision for the exams."

"No, the only good thing about all this is not having to think of revision or school. Do you know any funny poems?"

"Not by heart, no," Anna said. They seemed to be at a loss. "I have a book of funny poems at home though . . . Ogden Nash . . . would that do?"

"Well, if you're passing."

"I'll go and get it," she offered.

"I don't want to waste all your time off." He was solicitous.

"No, heavens no. Anyway, you're the one with the bad sickness, I only had measles."

Emmet felt important that he had a serious illness, and was flattered that Anna had gone all the way up to Lakeview Road to get the book.

They loved Ogden Nash. The house rang to the sound of their laughter as they read to each other.

When Kit came back from Dublin she found them there together day after day — her brother Emmet with the yellow skin and the yellowed eyes, Anna Kelly with the dark brown rash of fading measles spots. They looked quite companionable together.

Kit debated for a long time about writing to Lena. The brochure had to be acknowledged. But did Lena not have a right to know that her son had been very ill and had recovered. Of course she had forfeited any rights when she went away. But if she had been able to have the letter she left delivered . . . then she would at least have had some knowledge of her children and their well-being. If the letter had been delivered rather than burned . . . then Father and Maura could never have married.

It was always the same circle of thoughts. Kit never got any further in her understanding of them. You just had to make it all fit in with the way things were rather than wishing and wondering.

Thank you very much for the brochures, she wrote eventually. *It's interesting the range of opportunities that are on offer in Britain. We do the same examinations here so anyone from our college would be qualified. We hear all the time of the huge opportunities which will come our way as soon as tourism in Ireland begins to take off properly, but it is very interesting to read about the specialization that is already happening over in England.*

Emmet is now recovering from a bad bout of jaundice. He was well looked after and cared for, and he should be back in school in two weeks.

I just thought you would want to know.

> *I too send you kind wishes,*
> *Kit.*

Lena read about her only son lying in bed with jaundice, which after all was a form of hepatitis.

She felt jealous too. Jealous of Maura Hayes, who got to bring him beef tea and chicken broth, who made a little gauze cover for his jug of lemon barley water. Lena would have done all that and more. She could have stroked his forehead and changed his pajamas. She would have sat and told him stories and read poetry to him. Her mind was far away thinking about it.

Louis touched her hand. She always arranged that they had a relaxed breakfast together. Real coffee, a warmed roll and honey. She set the table nicely with a pink cloth. It helped to give him a good start to the day.

"And what were you dreaming about?" he asked.

"I was thinking that my son has jaundice . . . and I hope he'll be all right," she said before she could check herself.

"How on earth do you know that?" He looked alarmed.

But she had recovered. "You asked me what I was dreaming about. That's what I dreamed." Her smile was reassuring.

He looked sympathetic. "I don't go on about it because there's no point in speculating. But I *do* know how hard it is for you."

"I know, Louis. I know you know."

"It's a pity we never had a child, you and I."

"Yes, it is." Her voice was dead.

"But still, you must think of the boy and girl . . . I know that." It was as if he was forgiving her, excusing her for harking back to her son and daughter.

"From time to time, yes."

"You're not sorry ever that you left?" He knew what the answer was going to be.

She paused before she said it. His face had a

flicker of anxiety but then it creased into a great smile. "You know, Louis, that I loved you all my life, any time away from you was wasted time . . . how can you ask me do I regret doing anything that meant I had the chance to be with you?"

He seemed moved. Did he ever feel any guilt at having jilted her, abandoned her all those years ago? About being so constantly unfaithful to her now? He said over and over that she was the only woman with the power to hold him. But that could easily mean she was the only woman foolish enough to stay with him through such a series of humiliations. Was that what he considered holding him?

Years ago when she had told Martin McMahon that she couldn't marry him because she still loved the memory of another man . . . he had said in a puzzled way that surely this wasn't love, it was infatuation. At the time it had irritated her terribly. It was so silly to try to define things by words, she had said. What did one person mean by infatuation or obsession and another mean by love. The whole thing couldn't be tidied away with neat little labels.

She still believed that. She looked at the line of Louis Gray's jaw and the shadow of his eyelashes, and wondered what a different turn her life might have taken if she had been able to forget him when he had gone away and left her the first time, if she had been able to say no when he came back to collect her.

"What would you like to do this weekend?" he asked her.

What she *really* would like to have done was to have flown to Dublin, put on her headscarf and dark glasses, got the train and bus to Lough Glass, let herself into the house and gone to her son's room. She would like to have come in, during the afternoon when he might be asleep, and have touched his forehead, whispered to him that his mother loved him and knew all about him . . . every heartbeat . . . then she would have kissed him. And when he woke he would remember it all, but as if it were a dream.

She would have gone down to Sister Madeleine's cottage and thanked her for being a lifeline for so long. She would have told the old nun that she had found happiness. Then she would meet Kit and walk a bit by the lake. It would make her so free. It was such a fanciful idea. And she knew it was dangerous to think of it even for a few moments. It was to contemplate betraying even more people than she'd betrayed already.

"Do you know where I'd love to go? I'd love to go to Oxford or Cambridge and stay the night." She sounded like an eager child.

He thought about it. "Well, they're not far on a train, certainly."

"And then we could take a tour and see the way they live their lives there . . ."

"And we could be up for one of them in the boat race because we'd been there," he said, entering into the spirit of it.

They picked Oxford. He'd inquire at work about a nice hotel. It was easy to be the only woman in the world who could hold Louis Gray. All you had to do was walk around with your eyes closed and your mind open. Oxford and Cambridge were two places he had never gone on business trips. They would be safe places to go to.

א א א

"How's the young lad?" Stevie asked.

"Over the worst of it. He's as yellow as a duck's foot but he's on the mend." Maura spoke with relief and concern. She had been worried by the illness.

"That's good. Listen, Maura. I'll be out for a few hours this afternoon. In fact, I mightn't be back at all. It's all under control, isn't it?"

"The *business* is, Stevie yes."

"What on earth do you mean by that?"

What she had meant was that Stevie Sullivan's private life was in no way under control. Maura McMahon had eyes in her head. She knew about the pretty little Orla Dillon from the newsagent's shop. Orla who had married in great haste a couple of years back and lived with her husband's family in a faraway parish.

Orla had been spotted with Stevie a couple of time in places which were, to say the least of it, unwise. She had telephoned this morning — even though she gave another name Maura knew her voice. Obviously an afternoon meeting was planned.

"I don't mean anything, Stevie." She lowered her glance.

"Great. Well, I'll be off then. The two young lads are okay on the forecourt, and take the phone off the hook if you look back in on Emmet . . ." He stood at the door swinging his car keys, a tall handsome young man. Far too intelligent and full of promise to get into a messy situation with that little Dillon girl, and all her in-laws from the back of the mountains.

"I know I'm not your mother . . ." she began.

"Thank God you're not, Maura. A younger, classier, smarter person entirely . . ."

She looked after him in despair.

His mother indeed was unlikely to give him any constructive advice. She was a sour woman, hardened by the life she had led, but unable to realize that its quality had improved. She passed her time by making jibes at Maura. She would have thought the pharmacist would be able to support a wife himself. And she managed to mention many a time that the first Mrs. McMahon never saw any need to burden herself with a job outside the home. Maura took no notice. Kathleen Sullivan was a pity. That's what people said about her, she was a poor pity.

She couldn't have been more than fifteen minutes across the road. Long enough to change her stepson's pajama jacket, to give him a wet flannel to wipe his forehead, neck, and hands, and a bar of Kit Kat as a treat. He was well on the road to recovery. She let herself out quietly and didn't even pause to go in to Martin in the chemist's.

As soon as she went into the office she saw the safe door open . . . things were knocked from every shelf, and the desk drawers were upside down on the floor. Maura had often heard of people saying they were rooted to the ground by a shock, and she realized it was a good description. Her feet were not able to move. Not until she heard the sounds of groaning . . . a faint sound coming from beyond the door into the Sullivans' house. It was then that her feet began to move and she ran to find Kathleen Sullivan lying on the floor, her two hands raised for help. She had been savagely beaten, her face and hair were covered in blood. Somebody had attacked her in a frenzy, and had very nearly killed her.

They all praised Maura for being so level-headed, but she pushed away the praise. It was easy, she had her husband in the chemist's shop a few yards away, her brother-in-law at the other end of a telephone. If anything she blamed herself for having left the office. Had she been there Kathleen might not have been attacked.

"Don't say that," Martin whispered. "It might have been you. God, Maura. Suppose it had been you . . ."

She had been tactful too about Stevie's absence. He had told her that he had a meeting. It was with financial advisers, she assumed. No, not the bank, not the accountants. He would be back.

She insisted on staying on the premises until he returned. Kathleen had been taken by ambulance to the hospital in the town. She had lost a great deal of blood and needed to be examined for broken bones. Her wounds were too deep to be stitched without anesthetic.

Peter's face had been grim. "You don't look all that well yourself, Maura. Go back across the road home," he suggested.

"That's what I keep telling her."

She knew she must keep the shrill note out of her voice, lest it sound like a tinge of hysteria. "Let me stay, please. I was minding the place for Stevie Sullivan. I want to be here when he gets back."

Sergeant O'Connor said he'd stay too.

"Ah, Sean, can't you go back to the station, for God's sake. I'll tell Stevie to call when he gets back."

"No, I'll wait too." Sean's face was set.

"I can tell you what's missing . . ."

"I'm waiting too, Maura."

"We'll have a bit of a wait."

"Is it young Dillon?"

"I've no idea who Stevie's meeting . . . he said . . ."

"Okay, Maura, leave it." The sergeant sounded weary. "Only, if it's Orla Dillon, I hear they usually go to an empty house up behind the churchyard."

"How would you hear things like that?"

"It's my job."

"It's not, it's a gossip's job, a scandalmonger's job."

"Would I be wasting my time going up there, would you say?"

"You're not going to get me to say . . ."

"No, it was shortcuts I was thinking of really. Like, it would mean we'd all get home hours earlier."

"Well then . . ."

Sean stood up and took out the keys of the Garda car.

Nobody knew where they could have come from. There hadn't been any other burglaries in the area. There were no fingerprints.

Could it have been a professional gang? Sean O'Connor didn't think so. Professionals might have left the place in such a mess but wouldn't have missed so many car documents that could have easily translated into money — registration certificates, endorsed checks, and even number plates. It hadn't the hallmark of an organized gang.

Kathleen Sullivan, recovering in hospital, couldn't remember how many there had been among her assailants. Sometimes she thought it had only been one, a big fellow with coarse black eyebrows and a smell of sweat off him. Other times she thought it must have been two, because something hit her from around the back and the dark-faced fellow was in front of her.

"It could have been the desk," the sergeant suggested. She had hit her head on that.

"Yes, but it hadn't risen up to hit her."

She felt there were two. Whoever it was hadn't come in a car, the lads who filled up with petrol knew that. They could account for who had been in and out. None of them had left to go into the house. It must have been someone who came in the back, someone watching who had seen Maura cross the road to the pharmacy. Someone who hadn't expected to find Kathleen in the office.

What had she been doing in the office anyway? There was no need to ask. Everyone from Maura to Stevie to Sergeant O'Connor knew that she had pounced on the opportunity of Maura's going back across the road to come and have a rummage around, probably in Maura's handbag too. Not to take anything, mind, but to get information . . . find out how much there was in a post office book, see the age on a driving license, know what kind of letters she carried.

They didn't even bother to ask Kathleen why she was in there. Which was a relief to the older woman as she lay in the hospital recovering from her injuries and accepting the sympathy of Lough Glass.

"I shouldn't have gone across the road," Maura said to Stevie.

"I shouldn't have been where I was." He grinned.

"They mightn't have gone for me, fine strong woman that I am," she said. Her voice was still shaky.

"My life is bad enough, Maura. If they did have a go at you I'd have to be looking at Martin McMahon for the rest of my life. I wouldn't have liked that. Just as the man has got a bit of a life for himself at last."

Maura smiled with pleasure at that remark. "Did you know Helen?"

"Not really. Who knew her? She was, as they say, a looker, but even with my enthusiasm for ladies I think I probably felt a bit young for her."

"I pity the woman you marry, Stevie Sullivan."

"No you don't. People who say that have an insane urge to be part of the excitement."

"Aren't you full of yourself! Will we start the cleanup tonight? Sean is finished with everything."

"Oh God, no. Let's not go within a mile of it. Will you come down to Paddles' and I'll buy you a drink to help us recover?"

"No, Paddles doesn't like females. They upset the even tenor of his ways."

Stevie laughed. "The Central then?"

"No, honestly, I'll go back across the road. Poor Emmet doesn't know what's happening. Come with me there, Martin would be delighted."

"I will. My legs are a bit shaky." A lot of Stevie's shakes had to do with the fright he got when the love nest was so suddenly interrupted by the sergeant. He thought he was going to have to deal with all Orla Dillon's in-laws, and it would not have been an engagement he would have come out of alive.

He needed a drink. Anywhere.

Anna Kelly was sitting beside Emmet's bed. She wore a white cardigan over a pale blue dress, her blond hair, like Clio's, was shiny and the color of corn.

Stevie hadn't realized that she was such an attractive little thing. "Well, well. Lucky Emmet. His own little Florence Nightingale," he said admiringly.

"We're playing Old Maid," Anna explained.

"Never a fear that you'll be that, Anna," Stevie smiled.

"Oh, I don't know, it could be worse. Imagine marrying anyone from round here."

"You don't only have to choose from round here," her aunt Maura said.

"You did," Anna said.

"Yes, but that was when I was mature, shall we say, and knew that this is where I wanted to be. Now, Emmet, I was coming in, in case you were lonely . . . but you're not."

"Have they caught them?" Emmet's eyes were eager and bright.

"Not yet," Stevie said. "But don't worry, they're not hanging around. The guards think they have gone off out the back again, the way they got in. Up the lane and out by the church. They're between here and Dublin now."

"Why did they choose your place?" Anna asked.

"Fastest growing car business in the land," Stevie said.

Anna looked at her aunt to confirm this.

"You don't think I'd be working there otherwise," Maura said. "Come on, Stevie. I'll get you that drink I promised you."

They went into the sitting room. Martin was on the phone to Kit. The robbery had been reported on the news. She had heard Lough Glass mentioned and wanted to know was everyone all right.

"Talk to her." He gestured eagerly to Maura.

"Oh, Maura." Kit burst into tears. "I was so afraid something might have happened to you. Thank God it was only batty old Kathleen."

Maura held the receiver for a while before replacing it. She was hardly able to speak with the emotion she felt, that her stepdaughter should cry over her possible safety. It was more than she had ever hoped for. That, and the look of relief and love in Martin's eyes as he poured them all a large brandy. Purely medicinal of course.

Sister Madeleine poured out a cup of tea for Mrs. Dillon. "It's a hard world to understand all right," she said.

"I came to you, Sister Madeleine, because you know all about the wickedness that goes on and you're not above in a pulpit preaching about it and forgiving people or not forgiving them as the case may be." Mrs. Dillon from the newsagent's and confectioner's nodded her head vigorously as she spoke. This was serious praise for the hermit.

Sister Madeleine accepted the high regard. She didn't say that it wasn't actually her position to forgive sins or to ascend a pulpit. It was easier to let people think they had a second line of approach. An alternative confession, if you liked to put it that way.

The woman was very worried about the behavior of her daughter Orla. "Maybe she should never have married into that clan," Mrs. Dillon said. "But Father Baily was very anxious that it should be done as quickly as possible not to give scandal, or 'any more scandal,' as he put it." Madeleine murmured and sighed as she always did, and people always took great comfort from it. No blame was being attributed. That was why people loved to come and see her. It was more soothing than anything. But when advice was being sought, she let you work it out.

"I fear that Orla may be neglecting her child and that I will not stand for." Mrs. Dillon's head bobbed up and down. "But Sister Madeleine, you can't talk to young people these days. They're not afraid like we were."

"She might be afraid of her husband's brothers though," Sister Madeleine said eventually. "If you were to hint that they had been drinking somewhere and that a rumor had come to their ears. You might find that that would work wonders."

Mrs. Dillon left, thanking the nun as if she had performed a miracle. This is exactly what she would do. That was precisely the route to take. Neither of them commented on the fact that it was a trick, a lie even. It would work.

Alone now, Sister Madeleine poured a saucer of milk for the blinded kitten that some children had brought her. The vet had said that it would be kinder to have put the animal to sleep but Sister Madeleine said that she would care for it, point it at the food, and keep it safe from anything that might be a danger. It was a frail little thing, trembling as well it might after all that had happened to it in its short life. But she was rewarded with the purring when it realized that its face had been pointed toward something as comforting as bread and milk.

Then she heard the sound. It was a rough, gasping breath. And very near her door. At first she thought it was an animal; once a deer had come right up to the water's edge In front of her cottage. But there was a grunt as well.

Sister Madeleine never felt fear. When the big

form loomed up at the doorway she was calm, calmer than the man with the bushy eyebrows and blood-streaked arm, a man who had been in some fight and had been injured. He had very wild eyes and he was more startled to see her than she him. He had thought that the cottage was empty.

"Don't move and you won't get hurt," he shouted at her.

Sister Madeleine stood without stirring; her hand was at her neck fingering the simple cross she wore on a chain. Her hair was pulled as always into a short gray veil. Her clothes marked her out as a nun. Not one that lived in a convent perhaps, but with the gray skirt and cardigan, the sensible laced shoes, she could be nothing else. The most nunlike thing about her was the fact that when asked not to move she stayed so utterly still. Her eyes never left his face.

After what seemed like a very long time his face began to crumple. "Help me, Sister. Please help me," he said. And the tears began to pour down his face.

Very gently so as not to frighten him Sister Madeleine moved toward him, and motioned him to a chair. "Sit down, friend," she said, in a slow calm voice. "Sit down and let me look at your poor arm."

"At least it's not the tinkers," Sean O'Connor said to his wife.

"Why should it be the unfortunate tinkers?" She defended them.

"That's what I'm saying. No one can say it was them, they've all gone off on some outing

502

or horse fair, or whatever it is they do."

"If you talked to them more instead of frightening the daylights out of them you'd know what they do," said Maggie O'Connor.

"Jesus, isn't it hard to say anything to anyone these days without being taken up wrong," said Sean O'Connor, feeling very hard done by.

They had no idea who had robbed Sullivan's and battered Kathleen so severely. It looked to be the work of a madman. But how had a madman got away so skillfully? It wasn't as if anyone in the neighborhood would hide him.

"It's no concern of anyone else's," Sister Madeleine said as she washed the man's wound.

He kept asking her to look out the door, fearing that she would run off and tell someone that he was here. "Don't get out of where I can see you," he said, his great frown darkening even further.

"I have to get more water." Sister Madeleine spoke simply, without fear or any sense of making excuses. "It comes from the pump outside and then I have to boil it." He lay back in the chair. There was something about her that made him feel she wouldn't turn him in.

"I'm in trouble," he said eventually.

"I'm sure you are." She said it mildly as if he had said he was from Donegal or from Galway, a matter of no huge concern. She said that the wound didn't need to be stitched as far as she could see. If she bandaged it up the skin would probably knit together. "You might like to give yourself a bit of a splash out at the pump there. Mind your poor arm of course, try not to wet it . . . but it would make you more comfortable before we had tea."

"Tea?" He couldn't believe it.

"I was going to put a lot of sugar in it, it gives you energy when you've had an accident."

"It wasn't an accident."

"Well, whatever it was. And I have some nice fresh bread that Mrs. Dillon brought . . ."

"People come here?" He was alert and watchful.

"Not at night. Go on now." She was gentle and firm at the same time.

Soon he was sitting, half washed and more relaxed, at her table swallowing cup after cup of sugared tea. He had gulped slices of warm buttered bread. "You're a good woman," he said eventually.

"No, I'm the same as anyone else."

"You wouldn't want to let people like me come in and take a loan off you like this. Some of them wouldn't be decent men like I am."

If she was hiding a smile he didn't see it. "No, I generally find people are generous and decent if you let them be."

He pounded on the table with his spoon in agreement. "That's exactly it, but people *don't* let them be. That's where you're right."

"Would you care to sleep the night here by the fire? There's a rug and a cushion."

His big face almost crumpled. "You don't understand . . . you see."

"I don't have to understand. The fire is there if you'd like to stay rather than going out into the wind."

"Well, you see, Sister. There's a possibility that people would come looking for me."

"Not in my house, not in the night they wouldn't."

"I wouldn't sleep easy, I really wouldn't."

She sighed and took him to the door. "Do you see in a straight line from here a big tree on its own away from the others?"

"Yes." He squinted into the night.

"There's a tree house up there. Steps in the trunk and up there a secret tree house. Children made it a long time ago."

"And would they want it now?"

"They're grown up and away from it now."

It was the talk of the town. For days Mona Fitz said that her heart was in her mouth because those kind of gangs came back and did post offices, she had read of this happening. Wall's Hardware put padlocks on every door. If the gang had made their getaway down the back lane they might have seen all the pickings that lay waiting for them in Wall's. They could come back again another day.

Dan and Mildred O'Brien in the Central Hotel were depressed. The place was bad enough, they said, without having the reputation of a town where there were armed robberies. And of course it was written up in the local press.

א   א   א

There was extensive coverage in the paper that Lena bought every week. She read the details of

505

what seemed a violent and senseless crime. Without having to be told she could sense the town's relief that Maura McMahon had been on an errand of mercy and was not in her customary position. Reading between the lines she knew that Kathleen Sullivan would have been snooping.

It was not news that gave her any pleasure to read but at least it provided an excuse to write again to Kit.

I read with concern about the events in the garage across the road from where you live. I just wanted you to know how sympathetic I feel and how I hope everyone has recovered from the shock. I do not wish you to feel that you always have to acknowledge every note I write to you. But when I feel such an urge to let you know how very involved and concerned I am, I'm sure you will forgive me for writing.

She signed it *Lena.*

א   א   א

"Kit, I was going to sort of say that you and I were going off together for a weekend," Clio said on the phone.

"Why were you going to sort of say that?"

"Because I'm going off for a weekend."

"And . . ."

"You know the way Aunt Maura's always poking her nose into things and asking am I all right . . ."

"Yes." Kit didn't mind it, as it happened.

506

Maura only asked enough to make sure that they had enough money, entertainment, sources of clean clothes. She didn't question them about their friends. But then, of course, Clio was probably up to no good and felt threatened by even the simplest request for information.

"So I thought I'd say you and I had gone to Cork. It's the kind of thing we might do."

"It's nothing like the kind of thing we might do."

"Well, will you go along with it?"

"When for? Where *are* you going, Clio?"

"I don't know exactly."

"You do. You're going off to lose your virginity with that terrible Michael O'Connor, aren't you?"

"Kit, really!"

"Aren't you?"

"Well, possibly."

"Oh, you're such an eejit."

"Sorry, Sister Mary Katherine, I didn't realize I was talking to a fully professed nun."

"I didn't mean it, I mean him."

"Just because you don't like his brother . . ."

"I don't like him and neither do you, Clio. You only like that they're rich."

"That's not true. I've met his family and I like them. I don't care whether they're wealthy or not."

"I've met a bit of their family in that fellow Kevin and I don't like him at all. I especially don't like what he's been saying about me. I wish I could get back at him . . . I'll think of a way."

"Oh, don't make such a drama out of it," Clio

complained. "They're very nice really. They have this elder sister, Mary Paula. You never saw anything like her clothes, you wouldn't believe it. And she's been everywhere . . . hotels in Switzerland, France . . . everywhere."

"Did she train? As a hotel manager?"

"No, I think it was just experience. She was in this great skiing place."

"Lots of opportunities for skiing jobs in Ireland," Kit said sarcastically.

"Oh, stop condemning them all. Listen, what are you doing that weekend anyway?"

"As it happens I *am* going to Cork to stay with Frankie," Kit said. "But you can't come, either of you."

"That's all right, I'll just say I'm going there and that will provide some kind of smoke screen. What's her second name?"

"Who?"

"Frankie?"

"I don't know, I never asked."

"Oh, don't be such a pain and a prig, Kit . . . I'll make up a name. God, you're so uncooperative. Sometimes I think you're getting as mad as your mother." There was a silence.

Kit hung up.

Frankie and Kit laughed all the way down to Cork on the train.

A fat old man bought them fizzy orange drinks and chocolate biscuits. He said he loved to see young girls eat and drink and laugh.

"That's all he's going to see," Frankie whispered to Kit.

"We can't take another one. Stop, Frankie, you're going too far." Kit felt guilty as the man looked at them excitedly, hoping for something . . . possibly a squeeze . . . in return for his heavy investment.

"It's his choice," Frankie said.

They got a bus to the town where she lived in County Cork. It was bigger than Lough Glass but not much. Frankie's father ran a pub . . . he said that when he had a daughter a hotel manager and a son a solicitor he was going to retire, sell the pub and that was his plan. Frankie's mother said he would never retire. He would be carried out of the pub with his arm still up in the position of pulling pints. He had done it since he was eighteen years old, he knew no other life.

They were happy, easygoing people. Much less full of nonsense and questions about her background than the Kellys would have been, but somehow less stylish and elegant than her mother would have made her house for a guest. Kit wondered why she thought of her mother suddenly. The house in Lough Glass had been run by Maura for a sizable time now. Why did she think of it as her mother's place still?

She wondered if she should write to Lena again but there wasn't a reason. She was not going to start a correspondence all over again. Not after all the lies. All the deception.

Frankie's brother Paddy came home from Dublin too. He had got a lift from a fellow who had a hopeless car; he wasn't in until nearly midnight.

"Oh good," he said when he saw Kit. "A nice

bird for the weekend."

"Not really," Kit said loftily.

"You know what I mean, it was a term of admiration," he said.

"Oh well, thank you then," she said good-naturedly.

Paddy was a law student. He attended lectures in the Four Courts, he said. And that was the bit that had some freedom about it, the rest was being apprenticed to his mother's brother, which was like being a galley slave.

"He's not that bad, is he?" Frankie defended her uncle.

"Easy to say if you don't have to work for him . . . still, it's a good training."

They sat companionably in Frankie's father's pub. Paddy was drinking half pints of stout, the girls were drinking bitter lemon. A few regulars who didn't feel it necessary to observe the licensing hours were sitting around with the air of people who had a perfect right to be there and wouldn't cause any trouble just as long as they were left in peace.

Paddy told the girls about some of the work he had to do.

Debt collecting was the side of it he hated most. It meant going into houses where women with children in their arms tried to explain why money hadn't been paid by a man who was not there to make the explanation himself.

You saw all of life in a solicitor's office, he said. They had people with no lights on bicycles, applications for publican's licenses, a woman who had choked eating a piece of poultry that had not been properly carved. Now they'd better watch out for that sort of thing when they were hotel managers, because she had got quite a lot of compensation, as it happened.

And there was a claim for damages for a woman who got a big scar on her face. It diminished her chances of marriage so she would get a lump sum.

"Is it only women who get that money for disfigurement, or is it men as well?"

"Only women, in terms of losing marriage prospects," Paddy said cheerfully. "Men could get married if they had faces crisscrossed with scars, it wouldn't affect their chances at all."

"That's very unfair, isn't it?" Kit said. "It sort of says that women can only get married if they look all right."

"It's true," Paddy said. "And this woman is entitled to big compensation. What does a woman have to offer anyway except her appearance and her reputation?"

Frankie laughed. "That's straight from the nuns," she said.

"Well, it's case law, as it happens," Paddy said. "If you take a woman's reputation away falsely you have to pay."

"Tell me more about that," said Kit, her eyes shining with excitement. "Tell me all about that, I'm fascinated."

They had great fun during the weekend writing the letter. Paddy said that the more threatening you made it, the greater the chance of there being a craven response.

"We're looking for high compensation here,"

he said. "That fellow is the son of Fingers O'Connor. He's very well known, he wouldn't want any scandal getting out. He'll pay all right."

"I don't expect him to pay," Kit said. "I just want to terrify him."

"Anyway, you're not a real solicitor," Frankie said.

"He won't know that if we use the other stationery," Paddy said.

Kit sent a postcard to Lena. It was a picture of the Blarney Stone in Cork, the place you were meant to kiss and then you got the gift of the gab forever, or so they told the tourists.

Having a nice weekend here with friends. Thank you for your inquiry about the drama in Lough Glass. It's all passed over now, though nobody has a clue who did it or why.

> *Look after yourself,*
> *Kit.*

"Who do you know in London?" Frankie asked as Kit posted the letter.

"Oh, just a woman I got to know. She's been very good about writing. This seemed an interesting place to send her a card from."

"Sure, and you don't have to say too much on a card," Frankie agreed.

After Clio, Frankie was a very restful friend.

He lived very peaceably in the tree house. It was a quiet place, but he liked the sound of the lake lapping below, and the call of the birds. The nun was a very reasonable woman. She said she was an outcast herself in her way and she understood. He had tried to tell her that first night, but she wouldn't listen. Then the next day he knew she had heard because her face was different.

"Where is the other man?" she had asked him. "The people of the village had said there were at least two, maybe even a gang."

He became very agitated when he heard this. Now they would be definitely after him and maybe with tracker dogs. He told her he had done it on his own. He had needed money and he had waited in the lane until that woman had left. How was he to know that the old one was going to creep in as soon as she was out of the place? And the screaming and roaring and . . . well, he had to hit her just to shut her up. He hadn't intended it to be so hard.

"What's your name?" Sister Madeleine had asked him.

This conversation was carried on the whole length of a tree. The man sat in the tree house, wrapped in the rug she had given him, Sister Madeleine sat on a tree trunk.

"You're asking me to give my name?" he said in disbelief.

"I have to call you something. I'm Madeleine," she said.

"I'm Francis," he said. "Francis Xavier Byrne." There was a silence. She thought of the day he had been baptized and someone had considered this was a fine, fitting name.

"And where do you live . . . usually, that is, Francis?"

"I live . . . I live . . ." He stopped. She was still. "I used to live in a home, Sister Madeleine, but I got out of it. The trouble was I needed money. I hated the home . . . they should never call it that. This place is more of a home than that was."

"Then stay here," she said simply.

"You mean that? After what I did!"

"I'm not a judge and a jury, I'm just another person living on the same earth," she said.

He spent most of the day sleeping in his tree house.

Sergeant O'Connor came later that day. He said they were searching the area. "You'd tell us if you saw or heard anything, wouldn't you?" He looked at the woman's unsettling eyes.

"Well, sure I never go up to the town at all, Sergeant. And who do I see but friends dropping in?"

"Well, if you saw something unusual you'd tell . . . your friends, wouldn't you?" He was in some doubt as she looked back at him directly.

"You see all there is to be seen here, Sean. Just a two-room cottage." The door of her simple bedroom was open, with its white coverlet and its crucifix on the wall. Was it his imagination or had she always kept that door closed before. It was almost as if she was showing him that nobody was harbored here.

Sean knew he was becoming tired and fanciful about this. "I'll leave you on your own, Sister. God, I nearly stepped on that little cat of yours. Is it sick?"

"It's blind, poor little thing." Sister Madeleine picked it up and stroked it.

"Not much of a life for a cat if it can't see where it's going. I'm surprised you wouldn't do the right thing and let it be put to sleep," he said.

"We don't always know what the right thing is," Sister Madeleine said.

"No? Well, the right thing if any group of men turn up here is to let us know where to find them and not to be making them tea and sandwiches."

"Is it a gang, it's not one person then?" Her face was bland.

"It's a gang. I'll be seeing you, Sister." He was thoughtful as he walked away. He looked around him, but there was no sign of a boat in or out, no blood around the place, and the one thing they did know was that one of them, or maybe indeed the only one, was bleeding like a stuck pig.

Sister Madeleine smiled and stroked the kitten. She was glad that she had thought of burning all the torn bits of shirt and sheet that she had used to mop up the blood.

She sat for a long time looking at the lake, wondering was she doing the right thing. Usually she was fairly clear about what to do, you did what hurt nobody. But this man had beaten poor Kathleen Sullivan and might have killed her. Was he a dangerous person who should be handed over? She didn't think so, but for the first time in a long time a shadow of indecision came across Sister Madeleine's mind.

"All the yellow look has gone off you now,"

Anna said proudly to Emmet, as if it had been entirely her own doing.

"I know, I don't look so like a rat."

"You never looked like a rat." Anna ruffled his hair. "You're very good-looking actually." There was a pause. "As it happens," Anna added so that he would be sure.

"Yeah, of course."

"I wouldn't say it otherwise."

"It's just that I'd like to look . . . well, okay, if I were to be a bit around with you."

"What do you mean, 'a bit around'?"

"Well you know, the pictures, or a walk or something."

"Are you asking me to go out with you?" Her eyes were dancing, she seemed eager.

"You know my stutter is inclined to come back at moments of high emotion and drama like this," he said.

"Oh, is that what we're in the middle of?" Anna cocked her head and looked at him quizzically.

"Very much so," Emmet said. He was making fun of himself in case she might ridicule him. Everything depended on what she said now.

"Well, it would be very inconvenient," Anna said after a time.

"How's that?"

"If your stutter came back, say, when you were trying to say I was beautiful or something . . . too many stammers over the b-b-b-b-b would have me very uneasy."

"Why might I say you were beautiful?" He still didn't want to believe that she might be taking him seriously enough.

"Because I said you were very good-looking, it might have been a nice way to return the compliment." Again her smile was arch. But he thought he read enthusiasm in it.

"You're very beautiful, Anna," he said.

"There now, not a stutter or a hesitation . . . perhaps it's not a moment of high drama or emotion at all."

She blew him a kiss and he heard her feet running down the stairs and out onto the street.

Emmet McMahon hugged himself. He had never felt so happy in his life.

Emmet was almost ready to go back to school but he still looked a little shaken. Maura decided to suggest a family holiday . . . a week in one of the big seaside resorts, which would be quiet now that the summer was over.

She looked up prices and presented Martin with the idea. "Maybe we could even get Kit to come for a long weekend. She has the Monday off anyway . . . suppose she was to take the Friday as well . . . ?"

Maura was so enthusiastic about her new family and this was hard to resist. "I'd say she'd love it," Martin said. "But aren't you going to have great difficulty in prising young Romeo away from the scenes of his conquests . . . ?" They had been observing discreetly the romance of Emmet and Anna from a distance and without comment.

"Aha, but suppose the object of desire is coming with us?" Maura laughed. "Peter and Lilian say it's just the sort of thing they could do with too . . . and there are these two little houses side by side. It will be like magic," Maura said.

Emmet was very sorry but he didn't really want to leave Lough Glass. With an earnest face he spoke of having to do his revision and get back to school. He had no idea how transparent he was being. Anyone could have seen that he didn't want to leave the place where Anna Kelly lived.

Martin teased him for a bit. "It would be a great rest you know, probably the last time anyone will ever pay for a holiday for you and order you not to work," he said.

"I know, Dad, and it's very kind . . . but just at the moment . . ." He looked embarrassed refusing the generosity.

"Oh go on, Emmet, if you don't want to go she won't take me." Martin often pretended that he had no standing at all in the family.

"Oh, I have to take you, I promised Peter and Lilian when we all arranged the trip that I would make you take a rest and I've got the time off myself from Stevie, and you can have that nice fellow who did relief before for you . . ."

"Oh, are the Kellys going?" Emmet said eagerly.

"Yes indeed they are, and I'm sure Anna'll be very disappointed you're not going to be there."

"Maybe it would be disappointment for you then if I didn't come," he said to Maura.

"Yes, it would have been a bit of a disappointment all right," Maura admitted.

His face was radiant at this stage. "Maybe I'll just stroll up to Kellys' and discuss it a bit," he said.

"Put on your jacket," his father said. "You're not totally cured yet."

"Oh but I am. I'm absolutely better."

"I was very surprised when Clio said she'd come with us," Lilian Kelly said to her husband.

"Don't look a gift horse in the mouth." Peter Kelly was glad that his elder daughter had shown an interest in going to a quiet holiday resort off-season.

"It won't be glittering," he had said, in case there should be any misunderstanding.

"You can get a bellyful of glitter," Clio said mysteriously.

Philip heard about the trip. "I might be there, as it happens, at that time."

"No you won't," Kit said. "It never crossed your mind to be there at that time. If you turn up I shall take it as definite proof that you followed me."

"I only do it for your own good." He was defensive.

"What?"

"Follow you."

"You dared to follow me. Where did you follow me?"

"To the station when you were going to Cork."

"To Cork? You followed me to Cork!" Her face was white with rage.

"No, only to the station. To make sure you weren't going off with that great ape . . . ."

"What great ape? Not that I'm not entitled to

go off with any great ape, but which one do you mean?"

"I mean Kevin O'Connor. He told us all he slept with you and that you were mad to do it again . . . I knew it wasn't true but I didn't think he'd talk like that unless he had some hopes." Philip was very upset.

"Why are you telling me all this filth and madness?" Kit shouted at him.

"You asked."

"I did not ask, I just asked you not to follow us to the seaside. I had no idea about all this rake of lies . . . I was thinking about getting a solicitor's letter written to that Kevin O'Connor . . . there's a crime saying you did when you didn't. By God he'll suffer from this . . . I thought it was just Clio exaggerating."

"Well, don't tell him . . ."

"Yes I *will* tell him, you weak, yellow coward . . . That ape is going to be sorry he ever met me."

Clio and Kit walked along the beach. It was a lovely time of the year to come. Just too cool for anyone to expect them to be Spartan enough to try out the cold Atlantic waters; warm enough to walk easily on the damp, firm sand without any sense of discomfort.

"Before you tell me all about it in glorious Technicolor I have to tell you something about that family," Kit said.

"What makes you think I'm going to tell you anything at all? You were so unhelpful about the weekend," Clio grumbled.

"And I'm going to be even more unhelpful now," Kit said with some pleasure.

"Tell me."

"I'm going to sue his brother." She stood away to observe fully the reaction on Clio's face.

"Sue him? What in the name of God for?"

"For impugning unchastity to a woman, that's what it's called."

"What?"

"I told you, he tells people like his own brother that he has had relations with me. That is not true. I am an unmarried woman; to imply I had sexual relations is implying I am unchaste. It is diminishing my marriage prospects. He'll have to pay for that."

"Jesus . . ." Clio began.

"And it's not only you. Stop panicking, you're not the only one who heard. He told Philip O'Brien too, which is like putting it on the six-thirty news on Radio Eireann." Kit's eyes blazed at the injustice of it all.

"And will it go to court?"

"Oh, I hope so."

"Oh God. When?"

"Well, if he doesn't apologize and pay full costs and give me a sum of money to compensate for my reputation being taken away . . ."

"Your reputation hasn't been taken away."

"Yes it has. If his awful brother tells you . . . if he tells Philip . . . what's that but taking away a reputation?"

"No, Kit, don't do it. I beg you."

"It's too late. It's done."

"You've sued him? You've sued Michael

521

O'Connor's brother?"

"I've sent him a solicitor's letter."

"You can't. You're not old enough. You have to be twenty-one."

"No I don't."

"It's posted?"

"Yeah, nothing to it. He says they're three a penny."

"That can't be true. I never heard of it. You never heard it until this time."

"No, solicitor's letters about anything, I mean. They told me I had to be prepared to go through with it if he said that I was a tramp and all. So I said I'm a virgin, I can prove that, so he's a liar."

Clio was sitting on a rock looking greener than the seaweed around her.

"You've ruined everything for me and Michael, ruined it."

"Not at all, quite the contrary. You can warn Michael that if Kevin challenges this I'm going the whole distance to fight him. I'm very, very interested in having sex with someone when the time comes, and I will not have that great, drunken, ignorant ape who I wouldn't sleep with if he were the last man on earth and I was about to die wondering . . . going around saying he did it with me. You can tell him that. I'd actually enjoy it."

"Kit, your father, Aunt Maura . . . what would everyone say?"

"They'd say that I was terrific and I set a high store by myself. Now, tell me about your weekend with Michael."

The Kellys and the McMahons had rented two adjoining lodges. There were three bedrooms in each. There were little verandas on the front that looked out on the beach. They saw Emmet and Anna walking very close together but not hand in hand, that took place when they were around the corner and out of the veranda's view.

They saw Clio and Kit talking intensely.

"They seem to have remained friends in spite of all the ups and downs," Lilian Kelly said.

"They seem to, all right," said Maura, who watched the way the two girls spoke. It wasn't the easy laughter of girls finding everything funny, it was much more intense than that.

The rains came and the tree house was very damp. It needed a firmer roof. Tommy Bennet the postman was a helpful man.

"Do you know what would be a great ease to me, Tommy, is a couple of sheets of lino or tarpaulin, something that would keep that rain out of a caravan."

"Now, Sister, I've told you a thousand times they could buy and sell us, those tinkers."

"I'm not talking about the traveling people across the lake who are good friends to this community but about another friend who has a caravan. You often ask if there's anything you could do for me. This is something I couldn't thank you enough for."

"Say no more." Tommy Bennet hated these people taking advantage of the kind nun. "I'll have it for you in a day or two." As he left the house he put on his cape. The rain was lashing against the door. "Ah, would you look at that," he said. "The poor little kitten is half drowned in a big dish of water."

"What? Where?" Sister Madeleine ran out in the rain, mindless of getting wet.

There it was, panting and struggling for life but obviously nearly gone. "Let me finish her off in the barrel, poor little thing. She's not going to make it." Tommy had a kind heart.

"No," Sister Madeleine cried.

"Ah, look at it, Sister. It's gasping for breath, it's dying. Be kind to it. We can't will it back to life. Be fair to it, Sister. It was blind anyway, always hitting into things. Maybe we should have let it go at the start."

Tears were mixed with rain on Sister Madeleine's face. "Drown it then, Tommy," she said, and turned away.

It only took a few seconds for the small wet limbs to stop moving.

"There, Sister. All at peace now," he said.

He wondered at the nun. She took the body and put it into a box that had once held cornflakes. "I'll bury her later," she said. Other animals had died — she had the place surrounded with little crosses, she knew what foxes and tame hares and elderly dogs lay under each simple marker. Why was there such a fuss about a poor blind kitten that everyone had said she was mad to have kept in the first place? He wasn't to know that she saw the kitten as an omen, some kind of sign that she hadn't always done the right thing.

"I've stopped saying my prayers but you're the kind of woman that would bring me back to them," said Francis Xavier Byrne as he chewed the lamp chops down to the bone.

The young Hickey boy had been so grateful for a reference that Sister Madeleine had written him, he had agreed to do anything for her. "Just the odd bit of meat, whenever you think there's some your parents don't need. I don't want you to take from their earnings," she had said. He understood that he wasn't to tell them about it either. "Is it for the gypsies?" he asked. "It's for someone who needs meat to make them strong," she said.

"We could always say a prayer together, Francis," she said.

"What would we pray for?"

"We could give thanks that Kathleen Sullivan is out of hospital and back in her house again."

"I don't have all that sympathy for her, to be honest. She came at me herself like a demon out of hell."

"Well, you were attacking her and robbing her son's premises. Just because you stay here I don't want you to think that I approve of everything you do."

"But you know why I did it."

"Do I?"

"You know I didn't mean to do it. I needed something to keep going. I couldn't be cooped up. You said yourself that you hated the feeling of being cooped up."

"I didn't rob and steal and hit people to get out of it."

"You didn't need to, Sister," he said.

And again the sureness came back that she was doing the right thing.

"Do you know I think you got a suntan even in this weather," Stevie said admiringly to Anna Kelly.

"Well, they always say it's the wind that tans you," she said, smiling.

"Only one more year and then you'll be a free woman," he said, looking up and down the tall blond girl with the perfect teeth and the bright smile.

Anna liked the admiration. "Free from school, but not what you'd call free, Stevie Sullivan," she said.

"And what would I call free?"

"Oh, something much racier than me altogether," she said.

She went home pleased with herself. It wasn't bad to have the two best-looking fellows in Lough Glass interested in her. Not that she'd pay any attention to Stevie. Everyone knew what he had been up to.

They were old enough now to have a flat in Dublin. Everyone thought that Kit and Clio would share. Everyone in Lough Glass, that was. Except perhaps Maura.

"Won't you be lonely in a little bed-sitter of your own?" Martin worried about his daughter.

"No, Dad, and it's so near college and everything . . ."

"But if you were to share with Clio . . . you could both afford somewhere nicer."

"We'd do no work . . . we'd be laughing and talking all the time. Anyway, we have different friends in Dublin."

Maura glanced at him and Martin let the matter drop.

Frankie helped Kit to move into her little room.

"I wish there was room for you in our place," she said. "But I was the last one in so I can't throw any of the others out."

"No, I mean it, I like being on my own."

And mainly Kit did like being by herself. She could study when she wanted to and if she needed friends she could go to Frankie's flat or to see Clio, who had also got a place on her own. But Michael O'Connor spent a lot of time there. Clio's need to be without flatmates had a lot to do with Michael O'Connor's idea of entertainment. Not that she would ever let on to them back home.

"Now, isn't that fine." Frankie admired that way she had tacked a brightly colored bedspread to the wall and fitted linoleum onto the little shelf where the kitchen things assembled by Maura were arranged.

Frankie's brother Paddy, the law student, had helped them too. "I pretended I was delivering a summons," he said.

"You'll get fired one day." Kit was amazed at how casually Paddy took his job.

"Nephew of the boss! Not a chance," he said cheerfully.

"Oh well then," Kit laughed at him.

"Hey, why don't I just put in an appearance in the office, show them I'm alive, and then take you girls to beans and chips?"

He made it sound a great outing. Kit and Frankie said it was the best offer they had had all week.

He was back in fifteen minutes, racing up the stairs waving a paper and so excited that he could hardly speak. "You won't believe it! He's paid, he's paid. I have the check here for you!"

"What, what?"

"Fingers O'Connor. A check from him in absolute settlement. He fell for it . . . he's paid what we asked for . . ."

The girls looked at him in disbelief. "But isn't it illegal . . . I mean it's not a real demand . . . from a real solicitor," Kit said.

"Could you get struck off the rolls before you get onto them?" Frankie wondered.

"No, it's all legitimate . . . look at what he's written . . ." The letter was addressed to Paddy.

Dear Mr. Barry,

I am sure I can rely on your discretion in this matter. The statement attributed to my son Kevin is agreed to be entirely false and shall never be repeated. I am enclosing a check made payable to Miss McMahon, who has my son's assurances that no further statement of this nature shall ever be made concerning her character or behavior to any other person.

If there are legal fees above and beyond this I shall be happy to pay them. Please mark any correspondence in this matter STRICTLY PRIVATE.

I look forward to hearing from you.

Yours,
Francis Fingleton O'Connor

They whooped with delight when Paddy finished reading it out.

"Can we keep it, do you think?" Kit said.

"You can . . . you earned it by being reported as unchaste."

"I'll take you out to something better than beans and chips," Kit said.

"We have to cash it first," Frankie said.

"Fingers's check won't bounce," Paddy said.

"What will you do about fees? You can't get your office to send him a bill when they don't know they've sent him this." Kit hardly dared to think it was true.

"Oh, I'll write him a generous letter and say that since he paid so promptly and that since you are a personal friend of mine I will not charge any fee. That leaves me in the clear."

"You're terrific, Paddy," Kit said.

He looked embarrassed. His freckled face reddened and he didn't know how to take the compliment.

"What's this about a slap-up meal?" he said.

"Anywhere you like," Kit said. Paddy Barry's letter had got her the kind of sum of money she would never have dreamed of. The whole year's allowance for pocket money that she got from her father.

Weren't these old-fashioned laws about women's reputations absolutely marvelous.

"Hi Philip, it's Kit."

"Yes?" His voice sounded fearful. What was she going to throw at him now?

"I'm going to take you out on the town for a great night out," she said.

"You are?"

"Where would you like to go?"

"Don't make fun of me, Kit. Please."

"I swear I want to take you on a treat. Suppose someone asked you, what would you say? Don't think what I'd like, think what you'd like."

"I'd like to go to the pictures first, to *Mon Oncle*, the French one, you know, like *Monsieur Hulot's Holiday* we saw, then I'd like to go to Jammets for just a main course, not a full meal. I'd love to see the way they serve it."

"Done," said Kit. "Where'll we meet? Let's look up the times at the cinema."

"Why, Kit?"

"Because you're my friend."

"No. Why really?"

"Because thanks to you I got a fortune from awful Kevin O'Connor. A fortune."

"How much?"

"You'll never know, you'll have your night out and that's it."

Kit went to Switzer's in Grafton Street and

bought a lace nightdress for Clio. She gave it to her in a box all wrapped in tissue.

"What's this?" Clio was suspicious.

"The ape paid, the big bad ape, he ran for cover. I owe it to you."

"They all think you're cracked, you know. A screw loose is what they say."

"Good. Then I won't have to be bridesmaid."

"Stop making jokes. What did he say when he gave you the money?"

"He said nothing. It was all done through solicitors with mutual assurances of confidentiality."

"So how much did you get?"

"You heard me, assurances of confidentiality."

"I'm your friend. I'm the one who put you on the track."

"You get a nightie. Enjoy it, though how you could I do not know."

"You're no authority on anything."

"I know. Don't you keep reminding me."

"Why can't Emmet come up to Dublin for a weekend? I'll show him the ropes," Kit said.

"We might all go together sometime," Maura suggested.

"No, I'd love to show my little brother Dublin. Go on, Maura. Let me feel like a big important person," Kit pleaded. Maura's smile was so warm and nice Kit felt a heel.

Maura gave in at once. Emmet was to come to town.

Philip lived in a flat now so there would be a bed for Emmet there. "Only if you don't hang on and spy, and follow and do all those awful things," Kit said.

"I told you that phase of my life is over," Philip said. He was much nicer now. The night at Jammets, Dublin's poshest restaurant, had been a huge success. Philip had discussed wines with the waiters as if he were a regular visitor.

"What are you going to do to entertain him?" Philip asked.

"I warned you, no spying," Kit threatened.

"What do I care what you do?" Philip asked. "Even if my future brother-in-law is shown none of his capital city I'll say nothing."

"That's the boy," Kit said approvingly.

א   א   א

The postcard from Kit of the Blarney Stone had been a breakthrough as far as Lena was concerned.

There was no reason for it. It wasn't thanking for anything . . . not in any real sense. And Kit had asked her to look after herself. The girl who had run from her in disgust all those months ago had softened enough to ask her to take care. It was a ray of hope. Lena kept these letters carefully in a drawer in Ivy's kitchen. Sometimes she took them out to read them again. The last one was definitely full of promise.

Lena waited until she left London to send Kit a card. She and Dawn went to talk to Sixth Formers in four different cities. It meant spending the night in Birmingham. Lena bought a postcard of the Bull Ring and addressed it.

I'm here spreading the good news of our agency to schoolgirls. Very exhausting but satisfying all the same. I think maybe I should have been a schoolteacher. All I know is that I was extremely foolish to have had no career for so long. Have you got a date for your exams? And I'd be so interested to know about your brother's too, of course.

I hope you are well and happy.
Lena.

She debated putting "love" but decided against it.

"Are you sending a card to Mr. Gray?" Dawn asked her.

"Hardly, Dawn. I'll be home to him tomorrow night."

"He's so nice, Mr. Gray. Great fun and everything . . . he was the life and soul at the Dryden."

"I forgot you knew him then."

Lena had forgotten. Dawn had been with her so long in Millar's she had almost forgotten the tempestuous short-lived series of appointments they had found for her in offices and hotels, and where there was some incident of Dawn being highly fancied by the most unsuitable men in the company. As far as she knew that hadn't happened in the Dryden. James Williams was not the type.

"Did you like Mr. Williams?" she asked Dawn.

"I can't say I remember him, Mrs. Gray." Dawn's big blue eyes were unaware of a lot of people who had passed through her life.

"Oh, well, it's a long time back now."

"That's true."

Dawn looked around the dining room in the hotel. They were the center of many appreciative glances, the blond girl and the dark handsome woman. Nobody could quite place what they were doing there. They looked too respectable to approach and yet surely Dawn's eyes promised a lot of fun.

Lena smiled to herself to think how the great James Williams would feel to be so instantly forgotten by a pretty little secretary like Dawn Jones.

But then with the familiar turn of her heart she remembered that Dawn hadn't forgotten Louis Gray or what fun he had been. "The life and soul at the Dryden" was how she'd put it. . . ."

Back in the office she found herself looking speculatively at the blond girl she had thought was such an asset to Millar's Employment Agency. She had, of course, been quite right in insisting that a young attractive girl would sell the whole idea better than any other approach from a different generation. She must beat down this absurd and dangerous suspicion. She could not be jealous of every single woman who had ever worked with Louis.

Pausing to pick up some papers in an outer office, she heard Dawn talking to Jennifer, the receptionist on the desk.

". . . honestly she was so nice, and she's done so much for me. Sometimes I feel guilty, dead guilty about her husband."

534

Dawn noticed Jennifer staring horrified over her shoulder and she met Lena's smile. "Oh, Mrs. Gray . . ." Dawn's face reddened. Lena said nothing, just stood there with the smile nailed on her face. "Mrs. Gray, you know what I mean. It was all a bit of fun, nobody meant anything by it."

"I know indeed, Dawn . . . a bit of fun is what it was."

"And you're not upset . . . ?"

"About Louis having a bit of fun . . . heavens, what do you take me for?" she said, and left them.

She barely got to the bathroom basin in time to throw up. Louis and this girl, this girl whom he knew had been sent to his hotel by Lena. Lena rinsed her face and reapplied her makeup. She returned to her desk and managed to avoid Dawn for the rest of the day.

That evening she went to Jessie's office and said she would like to dismiss Dawn Jones.

"I missed you when you were in Birmingham," Louis said that night to her.

"I wasn't away for long."

"No, but any time is long."

"It was hard work," she said. "Dawn and I were almost hoarse at the end of it."

"Dawn?" he said.

She looked at him. He probably didn't remember Dawn. Truthfully. The bit of fun had been so passing, so fleet, that it had not stayed in his mind.

"Dawn Jones, remember she used to work for

James Williams once?"

"Oh, yes." Now he did remember. "And how did she get on there with you?"

"Fine, just fine. I think she's leaving the agency though."

"Oh, is she? Why's that?"

"I'm not really sure," Lena said, turning off the light.

א א א

Rita was well established now in the car-hire company in Dublin. She was walking out with one of her colleagues. He came from Donegal, far far away. She thought of the gypsy who had said she would marry a man from far away. His name was Timothy and one day soon he was going to introduce her to his mother.

Rita had told him she didn't come from important stock. Not from any people you could speak of. Her father and mother had lost interest in her when she had gone as a girl to work as a maid for the McMahons. She didn't want Timothy to have any false impressions.

Timothy told her that nothing mattered less. He said that all that old nonsense was changing in Ireland and about time too. Once or twice Rita wondered whether she should ask Kit if she might meet Timothy. It would give her a bit of standing if a lovely, confident young hotel management student appeared as her friend.

But Kit had enough to do and Rita would not abuse their friendship. One day she would meet Timothy and that would be fine.

Emmet went up to Kellys' to tell Anna about his trip to Dublin. Kit was going to meet him at the train and he would stay with Philip O'Brien, who had improved beyond all measure apparently. They were going to the pictures and on a little train out to Bray to the amusements. And Kit had a friend who was a law student who was going to take them to see a prison and a tattooist.

It was going to be a fantastic weekend, everything he'd want to do. He hated leaving Lough Glass and Anna, of course, but then she'd had so many outings recently . . . there was a school trip here and a careers talk there and he had not really seen her for ages.

Lilian Kelly opened the door. "Hello, Emmet," she said, surprised. There was something about her voice that alerted Emmet. He said nothing, just grinned. "I thought Anna was with you," she said.

It was awkward telling Father and Maura that she didn't need any money to entertain Emmet in Dublin. Kit would've liked to buy them presents too with her unexpected windfall. But she thought it would cause too much trouble if she explained it.

She waved and he saw her. "Come on, we'll get the bus back. Quick, to the front seat," she said, taking his hand, and they ran together to board the bus for the city center.

"Imagine you knowing Dublin so well." He seemed wistful.

"Well, you will too next year, won't you?"

"Yes." His voice sounded a bit down. But perhaps he was just tired after the journey.

"I'll show you my flat first," Kit said, determined she wouldn't start looking for problems where none existed.

Emmet said he thought it was great. Imagine all this whole place of her very own. Kit was touched by that.

It was so small, even her bedroom in Lough Glass was bigger than the area where she slept, sat, ate, studied, and washed at a sink. But it was very central, there were no bus fares, she was even so near one of the cinemas that she could look out her window and see whether the queues were lessening.

"We could go to a dance, seeing it's Friday night," Kit said. "And I'd be happy to bring you to one of the places we go, but they're very hot and sweaty. And honestly, as it's your first night I thought we might go somewhere less noisy."

"That would be nice," he said.

He did sound flat. Kit was not imagining it.

"What do you think of an Indian restaurant?" she suggested. "There's one up in Leeson Street. It's great, and I've been there a couple of times so I know what to order. And then we'll meet Philip and he'll take you home."

He said it sounded great. They walked together through O'Connell Street, past crowds of people.

"I've never been here at night," Emmet said.

"No. It's changed completely." They stopped and looked at the Liffey flowing under O'Connell Bridge.

"It's not smelly," Emmet said. "People are always saying it is."

"It is a bit, to be honest, in the summertime but not now," Kit agreed.

They went past Trinity College, and Kit pointed out students coming and going through the main gate.

"Are they very posh? English and upper class?" Emmet asked.

"I don't think so, I used to think that, but apparently it's just lots of foreigners and people who aren't Catholics . . . but ordinary just the same."

"It's cracked Catholics not being allowed to go there. Brother Healy says it's right, he says that for years when we wanted to they wouldn't let us in."

They walked up Grafton Street and looked at all the expensive things in the windows. They went by St. Stephen's Green, all dark and shadowy now at night, and then up to Leeson Street.

"There's a student pub here on the corner. This is where we'll meet Philip afterward," Kit explained.

"I'm glad he's not coming to dinner with us," Emmet said unexpectedly.

"Yes, well, he has improved but not so much as you'd want him round all the time. It's just his parents are so awful it rubs off on him, you know."

They went into the Indian restaurant and Kit picked a corner table. She advised Emmet about the menu.

"Suppose you have the mutton and I have the kofta curry — that's meatballs."

He nodded. His eyes were fixed on the menu as if he were trying to summon up the courage to say something. "This is quite dear, Kit. Are you sure we can afford it?" he asked.

"No problem," she said.

"But all this and the pictures tomorrow and the tattoo parlor."

"That won't cost any money. Honestly, Emmet, don't worry." She put her hand to pat his as reassurance and to her horror his eyes filled with tears. "Oh, Emmet, what's wrong?" she cried.

"Kit, I want you to do me a big favor. Will you do something for me, it's a huge thing?"

"What is it?"

"Promise first."

"I can't promise until I know. That's not fair. I'll try, you know I will."

"You have to promise . . ."

"What *is* it?"

"It's Anna. She's keen on Stevie Sullivan and he's taking her out. She doesn't want me anymore."

"It's only a crush, she'll get over him."

"No, they meet all the time, she's crazy about him."

"He's too old for her. Much too old."

"I know, but that makes him more interesting than ever."

"But he can't feel the same about her, can he?"

"Yes, he's crazy about her."

"What about Dr. and Mrs. Kelly? I bet they're furious."

"Yes, but all this makes it even more . . . I

don't know, dramatic."

"What can I do . . . tell me what kind of favor could I possibly do you? Hypnotize her? Kidnap Stevie Sullivan?" Kit looked at him mystified to know what role he could see for her in all this.

"You're not bad-looking, Kit. Fellows are always saying that you look terrific. Could you sort of set yourself at him and get him? Distract him from Anna . . . then she'd come back to me."

Her first instinct was to laugh. Kit McMahon a Mata Hari who could attract the desire of any man away from a little blond beauty like Anna Kelly!

Then she saw his face and she didn't laugh. Emmet was near breaking point. And he really believed she could do it. Poor, poor Emmet. Imagine feeling so strongly as this.

Kit had never loved anyone to the extent that she would admit it so openly, so wretchedly. She didn't know anyone who could, except in books. Then with a shock she realized the only other person who had loved so foolishly and recklessly that she didn't consider anyone else was Helen McMahon. Their mother. She looked at her brother, stricken.

"Will you do it for me please, Kit?" he begged.

"I'll try," she said.

The least she could do for him was try.

CHAPTER EIGHT

Paddy Barry apologized profusely. The man he had been going to visit in prison had been released.

"It was very bad luck," he said over and over.

"Good luck for him, I suppose," Kit had said.

"Yes, but bad for your brother."

"I don't mind," Emmet said. "Is the tattooist still there?"

Paddy's cheerful freckled face lit up. "Emmet boy, he is still there and we're going to meet him this morning."

"There's no question of any of us getting things done on our arms is there . . . ?" Kit regarded Paddy with some awe and anxiety. Anyone who could trick Fingers O'Connor into such craven submission was a force to be reckoned with.

"I might have a very small anchor done myself. . . . I'll see," Paddy said. "No obligation on the rest of you, of course."

"Does it hurt?" Emmet asked.

"Excruciating, I believe," Paddy said.

The tattooist was a very small man with an anxious face. "Any friends of Mr. Barry's are welcome here," he said, looking doubtfully at Kit and Emmet.

"See, I told you." Paddy was triumphant.

It had never been clear what particular service Paddy Barry had done for the tattooist. Kit didn't really want to know. She felt it may not have been on the right side of the law that he was learning to uphold. It had something to do with giving him a warning about smuggled cigarettes from sailors. Whatever it had been it had been a matter deserving great gratitude.

"Would you all like tea?" the tattooist offered, and provided it out of grimy enamel mugs.

He showed the needles and the fluids and a book of designs, as well as letters from satisfied clients.

Kit looked at Emmet. He was utterly delighted with the experience. This had been a brilliant idea. She could hardly recognize the troubled face that had sat opposite her last night in the Indian restaurant as Emmet toyed with his food and begged her support.

They had agreed that Kit would give it her best. But in her own time and in her own way. Emmet must not keep inquiring how it was going, he must make no efforts to help. They had shaken hands on it and he had cheered up in time to meet Philip in the pub.

Philip had wanted to come to the tattooist as well but Kit had said that the thing was sufficiently like a circus already . . . they didn't want to have to sell tickets for the visit. What about lunch? Philip had wondered. That was no use either. Emmet and Kit were meeting Rita and her boyfriend.

"Rita who worked for you?" Philip said.

"The very same."

"What would you have to say to each other?" he asked. It was uncanny the way he sounded like his mother. You really could hear Mildred O'Brien in some of the things he said.

"We have lots to say to each other," Kit explained. "Rita brought us up."

Philip had felt the reproof and regretted his attitude but it was too late. He wouldn't be able to see Kit and Emmet until the evening when they would meet for the pictures.

Kit brought her mind back to the conversation taking place in the tattoo parlor. Emmet seemed to be pricing a small heart with a four-letter word inside it.

"Don't consider it for two seconds, Emmet," she cried.

"It would be discreet," the tattooist said.

"And a sign of how much I cared," Emmet said.

"You wouldn't want to commit yourself to one name at too early a stage though." Paddy Barry was wise in the ways of the world.

"I'll never want any other name," Emmet said in a voice that chilled Kit to hear it.

"This is my friend Timothy," Rita said, and introduced the man from the car-hire firm.

Rita looked well. She had her hair cut smartly and she was wearing makeup. She wore a bright uniform jacket, as did Timothy. They worked Saturdays so were only free for a short lunch hour. Rita asked Kit all about the people in Lough Glass and Timothy told Emmet about the cars.

"Not a sign of his stammer. Isn't it wonderful," Rita said when she knew she couldn't be overheard by Emmet.

"It comes and goes when he's upset," Kit said.

"Well, there's probably not too often that happens. And Maura's running the house all right with Peggy?"

"Nothing to the way you did," Kit laughed.

They both knew that was only a politeness. Maura McMahon managed their home magnificently.

"Is this the real thing?" Kit jerked her head toward Timothy.

"I hope so, Kit, he's very good to me. He's mentioned marriage several times." Rita looked pleased and proud.

"Can I come to the wedding?" Kit whispered.

"Of course you can, but it may not be for a while, we have to save a bit first. Perhaps I'll be at yours before then."

"I doubt it," Kit said. "I'm not great with the fellows at all."

"Too choosy more like it, you have them all admiring you."

Kit hoped this was true. If she could just get Stevie Sullivan to admire her for a bit, that would honor her promise to Emmet. She wondered would it involve going the whole way. Kit swallowed nervously at the thought of it. Surely nobody could be expected to do that just for a childish promise to a brother.

"I often meet Clio on a Sunday," Kit said to Emmet. "Would you like that or not . . . ?"

His eyes lit up. Even the thought of being close to Anna's sister was a delight. "And don't forget, her family know nothing of her meeting Stevie . . ."

"So why don't we let her get caught, make more trouble for her? Clio would help with that."

"No, you don't understand." Emmet's face had the tight tense look again. "She came and told me honestly, she made me promise as a friend that I'd not tell tales on her."

"And you promised?"

"I did of course," Emmet said.

"Heigh-ho," said Kit.

"I hope my mother doesn't hear you've had Emmet up here for a weekend," Clio grumbled on the phone when Kit rang.

"You can be sure she will, they hear everything in Lough Glass," Kit said.

"She'll think I should be having the dreadful Anna."

"Well, why not? It would be nice for her." Kit was being very cunning. Perhaps it was an opportunity to get Anna away from Lough Glass and Stevie.

"I've always said that she and Emmet are two different species. Are they still in love with each other, by the way?"

"Hard to say," Kit lied. "You know boys don't talk much about that sort of thing."

"Anyway she's working very hard. Horrible little sneak that she is, she'll get much more honors in her Leaving than I did. Apparently she's off studying all the time."

Kit nodded glumly. She knew about all this studying and what form it took.

Clio couldn't stay long, she said as soon as she arrived. She was going to Michael O'Connor's house. It was his sister's birthday and there was a family lunch party for them.

"They're very family-conscious," she said proudly to Kit. Clio loved being included in the O'Connor rituals. "Mary Paula is allowed to choose what she wants for lunch and it's made in one of the hotels and then served in the house."

"Will there be champagne?" Emmet wanted to bring news home to Anna when he saw her as a friend.

"No, I don't think so. Mr. O'Connor has probably had to make a few economies recently. He had to pay out unexpected sums of money."

Clio glared at Kit, who giggled, pleased at the joke. It was as far as Clio would go, she would not risk the story getting home. It would reflect no credit on the beloved O'Connor family.

Philip and Kit said that Emmet would have to be on the train in good time, it got crowded early and there were a lot of people going home after spending a Sunday in Dublin. They went to have chips in a cafe first.

The girl at the cash desk in a bright green tent-like dress looked familiar. All three of them looked at her with interest and then they spoke at the same time.

"It's Deirdre," said Kit.

"Deirdre Hanley," said Philip.

"And she's pregnant," said Emmet.

Deirdre was delighted to see them. "Imagine

you lot being old enough to go out on your own," she said. "I'll get them to give you bigger helpings." She called to the man in the white apron: "Gianni, these are friends of mine, huge helpings."

"*Molto grande,*" Gianni cried enthusiastically.

"That's my Gianni," she said proudly to Kit. "He owns the place."

"He's very nice-looking," Kit said admiringly.

"Yes, he's not bad," Deirdre said.

"Emmet came up for the weekend, Philip and I are doing hotel management." Kit felt that Deirdre might not be up-to-date with all the details of their lives.

"You're in Patsy's year, Emmet, aren't you?" Deirdre said. Patsy was the entirely different younger sister. All the mistakes Mrs. Hanley considered she had made with her eldest were being righted in her second daughter. Patsy was watched like a hawk.

"That's right, I often see her," Emmet said. He hardly noticed Patsy Hanley, if the truth were told, but he was being polite.

"When did you and Gianni get married?" Kit asked. It was something she had never heard at home, and Mrs. Hanley was great with news and information. Surely the eventual settling down of her troublesome daughter with an Italian who ran his own restaurant was worthy of mention.

"We didn't actually get married," Deirdre said. "You see, there's this business . . . Gianni has a first marriage which has to be annulled. It will, of course, but it all takes time."

"I know, I know." Kit nodded sympathetically.

She wished she hadn't mentioned the word.

But Deirdre didn't seem at all put out. "So the bambino may well be able to come to the wedding," she laughed.

Emmet and Philip were amazed at the conversation that was taking place.

Gianni came to shake hands with them. "Deirdre tells me everyone in Lough Glass is old and old-fashioned," he said, stroking the bump on her stomach. "But this is not so."

"Not at all," gasped Philip.

As they went to the station Kit said to Emmet: "Maybe you shouldn't necessarily mention . . ."

"About Deirdre? I wasn't going to," he said.

"No, indeed. Wiser not," Philip said.

But Kit knew that Mildred and Dan O'Brien would be told.

א א א

"Isn't 'Slough' a funny word?" Lena said to Louis, shuffling some papers around. Normally she took very little work home, he hated to see her working.

"Why is it funny?"

"I thought it was pronounced *sluff*, you know, like enough, like to slough something off . . ."

"And what made you think of it?"

"I have to go there on Saturday to talk to a couple of schools."

"Dawn going with you?"

"No, she left. Remember?"

"Oh that's right." He hadn't remembered. But at least it meant that Dawn hadn't contacted him

549

and said that she had been fired because of her past.

Dawn had more style than that, Lena thought regretfully. The girl was a loss to them. They were grooming Jennifer but she didn't have the same appeal.

"I'm going on my own . . . but you're off that day, why don't you come with me?"

"Much as I'd love to wander round a few girls' schools I don't think it's really my scene."

"No, it's only a couple of hours for me . . . then we could go and stay somewhere."

"It's all buses and trains," he grumbled. He would love to have had a car.

"There must be nice places . . . we deserve a bit of a treat, a night out, a night away. The two of us."

"All right, I'll look into it. I'll ask James, he knows everywhere and everything."

Louis sounded a little restless these days. She had hoped that the mention of a change in their routine would brighten him up, but it seemed just another wearying chore. She wished that her location had been somewhere more glamorous than Slough.

She had forgotten how unpredictable Louis was. Next day he telephoned the office. "James knows the perfect place. He's lending us the car, it will be a great weekend."

"Where are you off to?" Grace asked.

"I don't know. Louis found a hotel. We're spending tonight there and tomorrow."

"A real holiday," Grace said admiringly.

"The nearest we get," Lena said.

"Why don't you go abroad?" Grace wanted to know.

"Too many complications."

"Still, Buckinghamshire is nice."

"I hope so." Lena sounded a little unsure of herself.

"And you look lovely as always."

"Ah, Grace . . ." Lena caught her eye in the mirror.

"Look at yourself, woman." Grace was impatient. "You're fantastic. Slim as a reed . . . gorgeous. But you're not if you don't believe it."

"Sound advice, Miss West," Lena said, laughing a real laugh and banishing all the strain from her eyes.

They had dinner at the elegant country hotel where James Williams had got them a fifty percent reduction for bed and breakfast. A wine bucket came to the table as soon as they sat down.

"We haven't ordered anything yet," Louis said.

"It has been ordered for you," said the waiter. James Williams had wanted them to have a good weekend.

There was a small dance floor, a pianist and a saxophone player made music for the diners. Sometimes there were only two or three couples dancing. Louis and Lena held each other and danced to the music. They were a handsome couple. Anyone looking at them would have thought it might be an anniversary or an illicit weekend.

They didn't look like an ordinary married couple having a night out.

Lena was tired and aching next morning after a long night of love. She would have liked nothing better than to lie on in their hotel bedroom with a breakfast served in bed, but she had work to do.

She slipped out quietly so as not to wake Louis. He lay with his arm behind his head, his long lashes casting a shadow on his face. He was so handsome and she loved him so very much. Nothing he had done or might have done could ever change that.

When she got back to the hotel by taxi after two exhausting but hopefully profitable sessions he was waiting in the coffee lounge.

"You should have told me," he said. "I'd have driven you. The car was for both of us, but I had no idea where your schools were." Of course, if he had really wanted to know he could have phoned Millar's. "Come on," he said. "We're off. I've planned a trip."

They drove through the English countryside past farms and villages. Louis and Lena never compared the English countryside to the places they knew back home. It meant too much of a journey into what was over, what was best forgotten.

"Where are we going?" she asked.

"You'll see," he said, and he placed his hand on her knee. He looked so right driving James Williams's car. Louis Gray was a man born to style and gracious living no matter what his original circumstances had been.

She saw the name of the village of Stoke Poges.

"But isn't this where . . . ?" she began.

"Yes . . . I wanted you to see the family's pride and joy."

"What!"

" 'The curfew tolls the knell of parting day' . . . er . . . Gray's 'Elegy Written in a Country Church-Yard' by my ancestor Thomas Gray," he said, and parked outside the gate of an absurdly picturesque churchyard.

"But you're not a relation of that Gray . . ." she laughed, half believing he might be.

"Of course I am."

"You never said."

"You never asked me."

"But not seriously!"

"We are who we say. I'm upset you don't believe me," he said.

"But Louis, you're not from these parts . . . you're from Wicklow . . . you're not from Buckinghamshire in England."

She knew scant details of his background. His father had died when he was young . . . he had older brothers and sisters who had all left home, gone abroad to work. They had not stayed in touch, he had not sought them out.

Because Lena had no family herself she always thought that people would rate a family highly.

Not Louis. He spoke little of his childhood, he neither blamed it nor harked back to it. It was now that mattered, he said. Now, not the past.

They walked to the poet's tomb, they stroked the flat top of his grave. They read the poem to each other, remembering little bits of it from what they had learned by heart at school.

" '. . . and leave the world to darkness and to me,' " read Lena.

"That's it, Uncle Thomas," Louis said.

"He wasn't a relative really?"

"We are what we think we are," Louis said.

"I love you, Lena," Louis said later that night. He had woken up and found her sitting in her dressing gown by the window, smoking and looking out into the night.

"Why do you say that to me?" she asked.

"Because it's true. And sometimes you look sad as if you had forgotten that it's true."

א   א   א

Stevie Sullivan's mother, Kathleen, was discharged from hospital and came back to Lough Glass.

"Don't end up getting her cups of tea, Maura," Peter Kelly advised his sister-in-law. "They can well afford to get a woman in to do it."

"Who knows better than I what they can afford?" Maura answered. She did the books and knew exactly how well the motor business was working for the Sullivans, thanks entirely to the flair and hard work of Stevie. If he gave his full mind to it she didn't dare to think how successful he would be.

He toured farms and explained to farmers who might be slow in making decisions the wisdom of improving their farm machinery and their pickup trucks before they had been run into the ground. Then he did up their original vehicles and sold them on to others. Nowhere did he break the law or indeed break faith in his clients. His success came from knowing how to suggest, rather than waiting for business to fall into his lap.

"Do you think we should arrange for someone to come in and look after your mother?" she asked Stevie.

"Oh I don't know, Maura. She mightn't want it. You know she'd say she's the class that should be serving people rather than having people serve her."

"You've changed all that, you're in a different setup now."

"Yes, I know that, you know it, my mother might not."

"Let her benefit from it. I know a friend of Peggy's who could come in."

"Set it up, Maura. That is, if you haven't already."

She smiled at him. They liked each other. "No word yet on who did it?" Maura knew that Stevie had been talking to Sergeant O'Connor earlier on that day.

"No, they seemed to have gone off a flying saucer, whoever they were. Maybe it's for the best, Sean says. It might put my mother into a trauma. He says it might make her worse than she is already if she had to identify them . . . pretty relaxed attitude to detecting crime if you ask me."

"Very human attitude as well," Maura said.

555

"He may be kind but he's not a fool, Sean O'Connor."

"I know that, he gets inspired about lots of things. I know nobody gave him a hint." Stevie looked hard at Maura, as if trying to get her to admit that she had ratted on his being with Orla Dillon.

"He knew chapter and verse, Stevie. I wouldn't have told him but he knew already, and where to find you."

"He knew how to frighten the wits out of me too," Stevie said ruefully.

"Yes, well." Maura pursed her lips.

"But by amazing chance Orla's mother came up with the same argument at the same time. Beware the mountainy men. Orla's so afraid of the troop of brothers-in-law coming for her with scythes and hatchets she won't raise her eyes to greet me. So that little episode is over." He looked for a moment like a small boy who has been told he can't play football that afternoon. His lower lip stuck out mutinously.

"I'm sure you'll find other distractions," Maura said unsympathetically.

"I suppose so," Stevie said. There was no reason to tell Maura McMahon that her sister's daughter, her own little niece Anna Kelly, had proved to be a very great distraction indeed.

"You can't stay here forever, Francis," Sister Madeleine said.

He sat shivering by her fire. With damp sacking hung ineffectually around it, the tree house was no protection against the start of a wet winter in Lough Glass. "Where would I go, Sister?" he asked. His face was thin and white. He had a hacking cough.

She had asked young Emmet McMahon for a cough bottle from his father and to her irritation Martin McMahon had sent back a message saying that it was going to be a harsh winter and he would very much prefer if Sister Madeleine went to visit Dr. Kelly and had herself and her chest looked at and listened to. She had got lozenges, but still Francis coughed and barked and looked like a man who should really be in a hospital bed.

"Sleep in my bed, Francis," she said.

"But you, Sister?"

"I'll sleep by the fire."

"I can't, I'm too dirty and shabby and bad. Your bed is snow-white." But he craved a night in the warmth and peace.

She knew that. "I'll give you some hot water to wash."

"No, you often do that. But there's too much of me."

"Suppose I put a kind of cloth on the bed, in it even, like that you could wrap yourself in."

"And something for under my head, Sister."

She found an old bedspread which she warmed by the fire, and put some tea towels on her immaculate pillow slips. He was asleep in minutes, breathing coarsely and with a gurgle, as would a man with a chest infection. She sat at the open door watching him for a long time. Francis Xavier Byrne, somebody's son. A man not right in the head, who should be allowed some freedom like

557

the wild animals. He should not be chained up and fenced in. He couldn't do any harm here, and he was learning to trust again. Soon, when he was better, she would give him his bus fare and he would go far away.

Kathleen Sullivan was better now, they said. Back from the hospital with a woman going in and out to look after her. Surely a loving God wouldn't want to work out any revenge on poor Francis, that man sleeping there in his fitful turning sleep, shivering and coughing as he tossed in her bed.

Sister Madeleine knew that she would have to work something out about the bag of possessions, as he called it. Normally he never left it out of his hand. Tonight it was laid casually in her simple wooden chair. He was learning to trust, he couldn't be handed over now. She would make it clear that he would have to return whatever money he stole from Sullivan's garage. She would be responsible for doing it herself.

"What did you eat at the Indian restaurant?" Maura asked Emmet.

"I can't remember, Maura. I'm sorry."

"Was it fish or meat . . . or what?"

"I don't know. Meat, I think."

"Lord, and that girl saving her money to take you to a special meal." Maura shook her head in mock despair.

"We had Knickerbocker Glory in Cafolla's," he said, desperate to sound as if he had been appreciative.

"Good, at least we know what remains in the

mind," Maura laughed.

"It's just we were talking rather a lot and I ate without thinking."

"I know, I know." She was sympathetic. There was something bothering Emmet McMahon, but she wasn't going to find it out.

She thought it might be the absence of Anna Kelly, but Emmet went out as soon as meals were over so perhaps he was meeting her then. She hoped they weren't going to get too serious, and debated whether she should discuss it with her sister, Lilian. But Lilian had a poor track record as regards coping with either of her daughters' emotional adventures. Maura thought that, as so often in life, the best thing to say was nothing.

"Hello Emmet."

Anna Kelly had never looked so lovely. She wore a green coat with a white angora scarf around her neck. She was flushed and excited-looking, her blond hair held up by a green clip in a ponytail. She looked like a film star. Yet here she was in Lough Glass. Anna Kelly, who only a few weeks ago had been happy to kiss him and let him stroke her. Now she said that this couldn't go on anymore, but that she wanted very much to be friends. She didn't know how very, very hard that was for him.

But it would gain him nothing if he were to sulk. "Hello, Anna, how are things?" he said cheerfully.

"Awful . . . it's like living in a German prisoner-of-war camp," Anna grumbled.

"Oh, why's that?"

"Where am I going, what am I doing, where

will I be, who am I meeting, what time will I be back?" Anna groaned. "Jesus, Mary, and Joseph, it would make you want to throw yourself into the lake." There was a silence. "Oh Emmet, I'm so sorry," Anna said.

"Sorry for what?" He was cold.

"What I said . . . like your mother and everything."

"My mother drowned in a boating accident in the lake, she didn't throw herself in because people kept asking her questions," he said.

Her face was dark red.

He longed to reach out and hold her close to him, tell her that of course he knew that was what people had said and that he understood her embarrassment and that it didn't matter one little bit. But he had been told they were no longer close, they were just friends. So he kept his hands in his pockets instead of reaching out for her. And he looked away.

She laid her hand on his arm. "Emmet?" she said in a small voice.

"Yes?" She had been going to ask him a favor; he knew that tone of voice. But her eyes met his and something in Anna Kelly's mind told her this was not the time to ask a favor.

"Nothing, nothing at all."

"Well, okay then. I'll see you, I expect." His heart ached to tell her that he would always be here, whatever she wanted. But it would be wrong. Anna hated people who were weak, she had told him that. She liked the strong things about him. So he had to be strong now.

He saw Kevin Wall and shouted to him.

Kevin was pleased to see him. "What about your one?" he said jerking his head back to where Anna stood forlorn on the road.

"Oh Anna, she and I were just having a chat."

"I thought you were soft on her."

"Don't be mad, Kevin. She's only a friend," said Emmet McMahon, and walked off with his schoolmate without a backward glance.

Kit was doing her practical work in a Dublin hotel where they took a serious interest in the trainees. One week she was on the reception desk, and the next in the bar. Then she could be waiting tables, or supervising chambermaids. It wasn't easy but she knew from the outset that it wouldn't be.

"You must be mad," Clio said when she came to call one day.

"You say that about every single thing I do."

"Why be different this time?" Clio was sitting up at a high stool at the bar. "Do I get free drinks for knowing the barwoman?" she asked hopefully.

"Not a chance," Kit said.

"Okay, I'll buy one then. Can I have a gin and lime?"

"Gin! Clio, you're not serious."

"Why not! Are you an apostle of temperance masquerading as a barmaid?"

"No, it's just that we don't drink gin."

"You don't. I do."

"As you wish. The customer is always right." Kit turned and filled the optic measure. In the mirror she saw Clio's face. Clio was biting her lip; she looked very unhappy. Kit carefully put the ice lumps in with her silver tongs and pushed the lime bottle and the jug of water toward her friend. "Help yourself . . ." she said with a smile.

"Will you have one too?" Clio asked.

"Thanks, Clio. I'll have a Club Orange."

They drank companionably for a few moments. "Aunt Maura is becoming a bit nosy," Clio said eventually.

"Ah, she's only making conversation, asking us what we're doing," Kit defended her stepmother.

"I think she knows about me and Michael."

"Well of course she does, you never stop talking about him."

"No, I mean about the other bit, about sleeping with him and everything."

"How could she know that?"

"I don't know." Clio bit her lip again.

"Well, stop looking at me, I didn't tell her."

"No, I know that." Clio did know that much.

"What makes you think she knows?"

"She says things like . . . oh, I don't know, awful cautionary tales about lack of respect, and girls not needing to do more than they want to . . . to keep men."

"Well, you're not doing more than you want to," Kit said briskly. "According to yourself you're only doing what you love doing."

"Yes, that's true but it's not something you'd say to Aunt Maura . . . and apparently she knew Michael's father."

"Well, isn't that good? They love knowing people and who people are."

"I get the feeling she didn't like him."

"Oh?"

562

"And when I was in Michael's house Mr. O'Connor said he sort of remembered her."

"But not enthusiastically?"

"No, kind of furtively, if you know what I mean."

"Maybe they had a romance."

"I doubt it. Michael's mother and father have been married forever."

"I'm sure you're imagining it," Kit said, trying to console her.

"I wish we were young again. Things were easier then."

"You're not even nineteen, a lot of people think that's still young."

"No, you know what I mean. It's easy for you, Kit. It always has been. You'll marry Philip O'Brien and run the Central and boot awful old Mildred and Dan down into some kind of cottage and be the real queen bee of everything."

"As long as I remember you, you've been saying that and I've been saying I won't. Why won't you believe me?"

"Because we all do the same as our parents in the end. Your mother was glamorous and could have gone anywhere and done anything and yet she married your nice, safe father and came to live in a one-horse town like Lough Glass for security; you'll do the same."

"And what about you? Do you love Michael, Clio?"

"I don't know. I honestly don't know. What's love?"

"I wish I knew that too," Kit spoke absently. She wondered if there was any truth in what Clio said, that people did what their mothers did. If so, there was a stormy future ahead for Kit.

Kevin O'Connor brought some friends into the bar of the hotel where Kit was working. As she served them one of his companions put a familiar hand on her bottom.

Kit tensed up immediately and looked him straight in the eye. "Remove your hand," she said in a staccato voice like shots from a gun.

The boy dropped his arm immediately.

Kevin O'Connor looked at her, horrified. "Kit, I'm sorry, I swear . . . I mean . . . I swear . . . Matthew, why don't you fuck off out of here if you can't treat a woman with respect."

Matthew, the offender, looked at his friend Kevin in open amazement. This was not the response he had expected. "I was only being friendly," he blustered.

"Leave the company," Kevin O'Connor ordered.

"Jesus, O'Connor, you're an ignorant bollocks," he said, aggrieved.

"If there is one more word of that language nobody will be served," Kit said. She was confident and secure. Not only did Kevin respect her but he made sure that his loud-mouthed and ignorant friends did so too.

"Sorry, Kit," he said to her sheepishly, as a bewildered Matthew left the hotel.

"That's all right, Kevin. Thank you." She gave him a warm smile, and he looked pleased. She felt cheap practicing on him this way, but she had to do something to rehearse for Stevie Sullivan in order to keep her faith with Emmet.

Dear Kit,

Your card about working in a bar was most entertaining. I found this book on cocktails to send you in case there might be anything in it that would be of use. It does seem a very odd thing to send you. I suppose in other circumstances someone in my position would be warning you of the evils of drink rather than sending you a book detailing ways to make even stronger concoctions. But then these are very unusual circumstances by any standards and I want to thank you for everything. It makes a huge difference.

Love Lena.

Kit read the letter that came with the cocktail book a dozen times. She wondered what exactly Lena was thanking her for. For not blowing the whole situation wide-open?

Possibly Lena, too, missed the happy carefree correspondence when she and Kit wrote as friends. Kit certainly missed it. There were so many things she would have written to Lena, had she continued to be the friend she had once been.

And not the mother who had lied to her.

"Stevie? It's Kit McMahon." She had rung deliberately when she knew Maura would have gone across the road to have lunch with Father.

565

"Oh sorry, Kit, you just missed her. She'll be back at two."

"No, it was you I wanted."

"Great. You've saved enough to get a car?"

"No, not work. Leisure I'm afraid."

"Leisure is always good with me." She could see him smiling lazily and leaning against something as he held the phone with his shoulder raised and looked for his packet of cigarettes at the same time.

"Would you like to come to a dance in Dublin next Saturday?" she asked.

"Say that again."

If she had been keen on him, if she had waited in panic for his reaction, she would never have been able to do it. But because she was so casual she was playing it just right.

"What kind of dance?"

"Aren't you choosy?"

"Wouldn't you be if somebody phoned you out of the blue with a notion like this?" He was laughing, and playing for time.

"Yes, I would be." Kit was being fair. "It's one of those dances where we all pay for our own ticket in the Gresham on a Saturday night, tables you know, and a great band."

"I've not been to one of those," Stevie said.

"No, neither have I, and we got up a party but we're a couple of fellows short and I was wondering . . ."

"Why don't you ask Philip O'Brien? He'd go like a shot."

"If I asked him he'd think I fancied him."

"And what about me? What might I think?"

566

"Oh God, Stevie, you've known me long enough to say yes or no."

"Would I like it?"

"You might love it. Loads of great girls, music, drink even. Wouldn't you love it?"

"And I'd be getting you out of a problem."

"Not just that. I think you'd like the people going. I think they'd like you too, you're great fun."

She tried to remember whether he was or not. He always seemed so jaded and cynical and eyeing people up and down. But he did have a kind of laughing way with him.

"Okay, it's a deal," he said.

"Thanks, Stevie." She told him where they were going to meet and how much it was going to cost.

"And do I say anything about this to your step-mother or not?"

"I leave this entirely to you whether you do or not."

"May I put this another way, do you intend to tell her?"

"I'll probably mention sooner or later that we organized a party, but I don't believe in burdening people with every detail of life, do you?"

"I get your drift," he said.

Kit hung up and let out a breath of relief. 'Well, Emmet. Your old sister is beginning to deliver the promise for you,' she said to herself. This at least would mean that the awful little Anna Kelly would be at a loose end for Saturday night. But she wouldn't tell Emmet yet, she didn't want him rushing in too early and ruining it all.

Stevie Sullivan hung up and looked at the phone in surprise. That McMahon girl was remarkably attractive nowadays. Imagine her asking him to make up a party. He had always wanted to go to one of those Dublin dress-up affairs. It would mean telling Anna Kelly that the pictures were off. But he'd tell her nicely and she'd understand.

Anna Kelly didn't sound very understanding. "I just got permission from my parents to go into the big town for the pictures. I told them a whole group of us were going."

"Well, go then. I have to go to Dublin for work," Stevie said.

"No, if I go it'll waste an outing I could have had with you." Why didn't he understand?

"Well, I'm sorry too." He gave her his lopsided grin, but it didn't work.

"You couldn't change it, I suppose," she pleaded. Stevie looked impatient, and Anna caught the mood. "No, I'm being silly, of course you can't. Okay, another night, right?"

"Right," Stevie smiled. It was easy in the end if you were just nice to girls. That's what lots of people didn't understand.

"I could go to the pictures with you this weekend if you liked, Emmet . . ."

"Thanks, Anna, but no."

"Are you sulking?"

"Absolutely not. Remember I said I wouldn't sulk. You said you and I were to be friends, that's what I'm doing." His smile was bright.

"Well, friends go to the pictures," Anna complained.

"That's what I said to you, but you said no, it would interfere with what there was between you and Stevie." Again his glance was innocent.

"Yes, but as it happens Stevie is not going to be here this weekend. He's got to go to Dublin on business."

Emmet smiled warmly. Kit had begun to do her stuff for him. "But he'll be back of course," he said in false consolation.

"Yes of course he'll be back," Anna snapped. "But I thought that since . . ."

"You weren't asking me to come just because you were at a loose end suddenly?" Emmet shook his head in disbelief. "We're friends, you and I. That wouldn't be the action of a friend. Just using somebody."

She turned and walked away very fast.

"I could get all the things in that bag back to the garage for you, Francis." Sister Madeleine was being helpful.

"I don't want to give them back, Sister." He clutched his bag tightly.

"But it would be for the best." Her voice was gentle.

"They're mine now. They're all I have to help me get away and make a new life."

"If we gave them back then they might stop looking for you, and you wouldn't have to live up in the tree house . . ." Her voice trailed away. She knew when she was talking to someone who wasn't listening.

"It's all I have," he said again, and held the bag close to him.

"What are we going to do with you?" she asked the air around her.

"You said you'd look after me." He was plaintive now.

"I know I did, and I will." Sister Madeleine felt less confident than she usually did.

It had always been right to do the things she had done in the past. There had not been a moment of doubt about any of these.

But recently . . . perhaps she had not been right to save the little blind kitten. Or to keep this mentally ill man here for so long living in her tree house. Should she have just tended his arm that first night and sent a message so that he could be taken into custody? But for Sister Madeleine any uncertainty was impossible. She had to believe in what she was doing and that it was for the best, otherwise her life had no center.

"Very well, I won't force you obviously," she said.

"Will you still be nice to me?" He had the mind of a child.

"Yes, of course I will." She dipped a metal mug into the pot over the fire and gave him soup. "Will you want to go and look around . . . for a new life?" she asked him.

"Yes I will, soon," he said.

"Perhaps I should cut your hair for you, make you look more . . ." Sister Madeleine paused. What was the word she was looking for? "Normal"? "Noncriminal"?

But he nodded eagerly. "Please Sister, that would be good."

She tied a cloth around his neck as if she were running a barber's shop and trimmed his hair, his eyebrows, and his beard. He looked far less frightening, far more ordinary, nearly normal in fact.

"When you go out, Francis, if they see you with that bag they still might put two and two together."

"I could leave it here, Sister, for a bit."

"You'll be back then?"

"Well, I will. I'll come back and tell you when I get settled. I think I'll just take the money."

"Francis, might you not be better to . . . ?"

"I'll trust you, Sister, like you trusted me. You were never afraid of me, I'd not be afraid of you either."

She gave him her hand even though her heart was troubled.

"That's right, Francis, you can trust me. In a world full of people you don't know about you can rely on me." And she was rewarded by the big and foolish smile of a slow child. A child in a big, strong man's body.

א א א

"I wish we had a car," Louis grumbled as they were getting dressed.

"Let's get one then."

"Easy to say." He spent a time fixing his tie.

"Easy to do. We haven't bought a house, we've

571

no mortgage, no children. What are we saving for?"

"We're not saving much," he said.

Which in Louis's case was true. But he didn't know how carefully Lena put away money. How her account in the Building Society was mounting, how shares in Millar's were increasing every year.

"Well, let's see how much you could afford a month," Lena began.

"Not much."

"I'll see if I can raise a deposit. You know, get it a bit as a perk from my work."

"Could you?" Louis looked at her, his eyes were alight.

For a man so clever at deceiving, at attracting people, and knowing what a customer in a hotel might want, he was remarkably innocent and naive about other things. It didn't even occur to him to inquire why Mr. Millar might give her a car allowance since she lived five minutes away from her job and went there on foot every morning.

"Yes, it's a possibility, isn't it," he agreed.

"So this is the last time we head out for the Home Counties by train," she laughed.

"I love you, Lena," he said, and came across to kiss her as she sat at a smaller mirror in a poorer light, fixing her earrings. He hadn't noticed that there was new color in her hair, but he did think she looked well.

Grace's salon had come up trumps again.

The taxi driver at the station said he knew the road. "That's where the nobs live," he said.

"Great," Louis said. "We wouldn't want to be going anywhere downmarket." He had such an infectious way with him.

The driver, in his shabby coat and his nicotine-stained fingers, who would never be allowed inside the gates of these houses unless he was driving a taxi, seemed pleased and enthusiastic. That was Louis all over, he made other people glad that he was around.

James Williams was divorced, Lena knew. But he had a friend, a lady who had great designs on being the next Mrs. Williams, Louis had said.

"Will she?" Lena had wanted to know.

"No, I think he's too clever for that," Louis had smiled.

Lena smiled too. How innocent of Louis to admit to her that a clever man avoided marriage, commitment of any kind. As if she didn't know already that this was his view.

James Williams was delighted to see them. A kiss on each cheek for Lena. "You look younger every day."

"You're too kind."

"No, I mean it. Come in, come in and meet everyone . . . Laura, come here and meet Lena Gray."

Laura was hard as nails. Shiny red lipstick, shiny metallic black hair, a satin blouse with a sheen and a tight black shiny skirt. Her shoes were patent-leather high heels. She looked as if she had been polished and burnished. "The famous Mrs. Gray," she said, looking Lena up and down.

"Ah no, it's my husband who's the famous one

in the hotel business."

"James always brings your name into the conversation . . . if I didn't know better I'd think he fancied you . . ."

James Williams had turned to welcome Louis.

Lena looked at Laura long and hard. "But you know better."

"Oh I know better." She paused. Her eyes flickered over toward Louis and away again. Lena thought she was going to say that she realized Lena had a very fanciable man of her own. But she wasn't looking at it from that point of view. "I know better, because if James had fancied you he'd have done something about it."

"And what's your second name, Laura?"

"Why on earth do you ask?" Laura looked at her as if Lena had committed the greatest social faux pas of all time.

But Lena had not been idle in her years of dealing with people through Millar's Agency. She was not easily put down. "Because it wasn't given to me," she said, in the coolest tones possible.

Their eyes held each other.

"Evans," she said eventually.

Did James Williams sense the mood? Or was it by pure coincidence that he turned and placed an arm on each of their shoulders. "Now let me take my two favorite ladies to meet the rest of the guests."

Lena didn't look at Laura, but she knew that in this unexpected and unimportant battle that had suddenly flamed up she, Lena, had most definitely won.

They had never been to a party like this before,

but Lena knew how it was going to turn out. She could see from the outset the two women who would vie for Louis's attention. And she knew now which would win.

Let them fight it out. Let him ply one with plates of tiny cocktail sausages on colored sticks, let him fill the other's glass. Let him laugh, delighted, into both their eager faces. That was part of the fun. This was probably the only fun.

Lena pretended the party was a conference. She told the stockbrokers and their wives that she worked in an employment agency. She refused to give business cards; it was a party in someone's house. But she did say the name Millar's so often that nobody would have forgotten it. She advised them about their daughters, their mature, unmarried, own hopeless office staff, none of whom could spell "sincerely" or "faithfully" so all letters had to end simply "yours."

And as she moved talking animatedly but not stridently she knew people were interested in her. A groomed handsome woman, in charge of her own life, unaware or possibly indifferent to the fact that her handsome husband was being overtly flirtatious with two of the other guests. And Lena knew that the eyes of James Williams were on her all night.

And that Laura Evans who might never be Laura Williams was drinking far too much and far too quickly. Already there was a stain down the shiny cream satin blouse, a stain that looked ugly and out of character with the elegant woman who should have been acting as a hostess for James tonight.

It was only when everyone had gone that Laura seemed to remember any hostess duties. "Better clear up all this mess," she grumbled, staggering toward a table with glasses on it.

"Leave it, Laura. It'll all be done."

"I don't mind. I do stay here. I don't want the place looking like bedlam." She looked at Lena to make sure the part about staying here wasn't lost.

"Yes, well. Everyone's staying here . . ." James was easy. "Let's have a last drink and a post-mortem."

But Laura was having none of it. She lurched toward the glasses and missed her footing then fell, spilling dregs of wine and splintering some of them on the floor.

"Now will you leave it, Laura." James was ex-asperated, as you might be with a small child, but not angry.

"I'll pick them up, let me."

"Maybe it'd be better to wait for the day-light," Lena suggested mildly. "Easier to see all the little bits of glass then, than in the artificial light."

"I can see perfectly well," Laura said, and fell, cutting herself on both palms on the broken glass.

Lena took her to the kitchen and silently picked the particles of glass from Laura's hands. Then she dabbed the cuts with TCP. "There, you're fine now," she said eventually.

"Stop being so bloody patronizing," Laura said.

"She means, thank you very much," James said.

"I meant stop being so bloody patronizing," Laura said.

"Those look very slight, but they can sting a lot," Lena said, referring to the marks on Laura's hands.

"You're a proper pain in the arse," Laura said, flouncing to the door. "No wonder he never made a move on you, Lena Gray. You were too po-faced. You'd have frozen him out of it."

"Good night, Laura," James Williams said coldly.

They sat by the fire the three of them. They talked about the party, the neighbors, the things people had said about *Room at the Top*. Some had thought it very vulgar, others had said it was realistic about England at last. They talked about Cliff Richard and Yves Saint Laurent. "Would many of the guests have met either of them?" Louis asked his boss respectfully.

Lena knew that Louis realized, just as she did herself, that nobody visiting this house had ever been within an ass's roar of either Cliff Richard, or Yves Saint Laurent, who had shortened skirts again. But she said nothing. It was part of Louis's charm to look innocent and vulnerable when it mattered.

What she found a little uneasy-making was the way James Williams caught her eye. It was as if he understood not only the crassness of Laura Evans, who would, after tonight, never become Mrs. Laura Williams, but also the naiveté of Louis Gray, who would never in a million years be as smart as his wife, Lena.

It was an awkward moment. Lena let her glance

577

fall to the floor. "Well, do you think . . . ?" Louis suggested.

"You must be exhausted, James . . . how lovely to have met all your friends," Lena said.

He showed them up the stairs to the room, the big guest room with a bathroom of its own adjoining. It was more elegant than anywhere they had ever stayed. The sound of snoring came from an open door, and a glance showed Laura Evans asleep on a bed, one shoe on the floor, the other dangling. It was unlikely that James Williams would sleep beside her.

When the door was closed Louis reached for Lena as she had known he would. There was nothing that excited him so much as knowing that two women had left that party unwillingly. Both of them would have given anything to have been with Louis Gray that night. Lena knew that this would make Louis desire her very much indeed.

"You're beautiful," he whispered into her ear.

"I love you," she said truthfully.

"You're a queen among the women here tonight," he said.

Lena closed her eyes. Well at least she wasn't lying drunk and snoring like Laura Evans, the woman who had hopes of the host, and she hadn't gone home to her own house as had done the ladies Louis had found attractive. She was here, sober, and not looking her forty-five years. Yes, she was certainly queen for the night.

"I was wondering, that is *we* were wondering, if you'd do us the honor of being a witness."

"In a case, a court case?"

"In a registry office, you dolt. I'm asking you to be my bridesmaid."

"You're getting married?" Lena looked at her astounded.

"Well, I did all the things you told me to."

"Oh Ivy, I'm so happy for you. When did you decide this?"

"Last night."

"And is Ernest all delighted too?"

"Of course he's not, let's not ask for the moon. But he says it's what we should do. And it's most certainly what I want to do. Always wanted to do." Her eyes were very bright.

"Isn't that great!" Lena hugged her tight and over her friend's shoulder, as she saw the walls with all their postcards, clippings, cuttings and little pictures, and thought how much Ivy deserved good luck and happiness.

א א א

"There you are, Mona." Martin McMahon handed her a bottle of tablets across the counter.

Mona Fitz from the post office was on a mild blood pressure medication. Martin could have prescribed for almost everyone in the town even if Peter wasn't there, he knew their complaints and symptoms so intimately.

"These keep me alive, Martin." Mona was very dramatic.

"Indeed they do," he nodded gravely.

That's the way she liked to play it. No point in telling her how slight their strength and how

579

unimportant it would be if one or indeed several days were missed. Tablet-taking and spooning from a bottle had almost magic powers. No one knew this better than the local pharmacist.

"Tommy's cut heal up all right?" he inquired about the postman, who had ordered a lot of bandages and sticking plaster, as well as disinfectant.

"I didn't know he had one," Mona said.

Martin McMahon often wished he hadn't made some harmless remark. It could lead to endless speculation. He could see Mona Fitz looking puzzled.

"He could have hurt his leg but he never said a word. I might be wrong, I'm often wrong about things." He looked apologetic.

But Mona was having none of it. "Of course you're not, Martin. Would we all be able to take our pills and bottles from you if you were wrong about things?" Her tone was most reproving indeed. And she went off puzzling why Tommy Bennet would have needed to buy bandages.

The house seemed oddly empty when Francis Byrne had left. Sister Madeleine felt no need to build up the fire that evening. When she went out to her door there was no cause to look up and over at the tree house with a friendly wave. When people brought a cake of bread she knew that this time she would have to walk over to the travelers' to make sure that it got a proper home. Francis Xavier Byrne could eat an entire loaf of bread from which she had cut one slice for herself.

In a bizarre way, even though he was disturbing

and a worry, he was company for her. The nights strangely now seemed very long. She prayed that he would make his way all right. That he would come back in some months for the rest of his things. To tell her that he was well settled now, under another name, working for a farmer. Or maybe as a chopper of wood in a big monastery where the monks would be kind to him. Better, he might write and say that she could give the bag of items taken from Sullivan's garage back. He couldn't write, of course. But someone would do a letter for him. Some kind person who was looking after him now as she had looked after him.

Philip had come home for the night, he brought all his washing with him on the bus.

"You look like Dick Whittington," Kit had said.

"Don't you bring your washing home?"

"I most certainly do not, I wash it myself."

"You're a woman."

"That's very true, but even if I were a man I would too."

"You only say that because you're not," Philip said.

"Not true."

"Or to fight with me," he said glumly.

"Now that's certainly not true." She laid her hand on his arm. "I think you're terrific, you got rid of all this lovey-dovey bit and we've been great friends, you and I, haven't we?"

"I only got rid of the lovey-dovey bit on the outside," Philip said sadly.

For a moment he reminded her of her brother

Emmet and the way he talked about Anna Kelly. Wouldn't it be extraordinary to feel so strongly about someone as that. She was brisk with Philip. "Nonsense. It's gone totally," she said.

"It's not, Kit. It's there in aches a lot of the time, like a nagging toothache; it keeps asking me questions."

"What does it ask?" She couldn't be harsh or flippant with him. He was far too like Emmet.

"Things like . . . why didn't you ask me to join this group for the dance you're setting up for Saturday?" His disappointment was naked.

"*I'm* not really setting it up, it's other people too."

"If you wanted me there you'd have asked."

"Well, you're going home." She was desperate not to have him hurt.

"I'm only going home so as not to be around. If you asked me to the dance I'd not be going home."

She wanted desperately not to disappoint him. But she couldn't have him there while she was making her play for Stevie Sullivan, that would be even worse. "It'll all work out all right in the end, Philip," she said.

"It better had," Philip said. "It sure as anything isn't working out well now."

It was dark when Philip got off the bus in Lough Glass. He didn't know why he had come home. His mother was bound to complain that they saw so little of him. His father was going to tell him that he had chosen the world's worst trade, that the hotel business was over. Kit was in Dublin

582

organizing a gathering of her friends of which he apparently wasn't one.

The porter in the hotel welcomed him in a half-hearted way. Philip knew that was the way Jimmy would greet anyone. The boss's son, a regular customer, a new American visitor; the half shrug and grunt and weary sigh would be your welcome to O'Brien's Central Hotel.

"I'll leave my things here of a bit and go down and have a walk by the lake," Philip said, a heavy unwillingness to go into his family home coming on him suddenly.

"Suit yourself," said Jimmy.

Philip went down the lane to the lakeside. He looked back up at the hotel. One of the best front-ages in Ireland, they should be doing much more than they were. He sighed, and walked along moodily by the shore, watching the winds whip up the lake into what looked like waves. He often thought about Kit's mother dying here alone that night. He had tried to mention it to Kit to show he understood, that he wasn't just an insensitive hulk like so many men. But she never wanted to talk about it.

Without his realizing it, Philip's walk had taken him toward Sister Madeleine's cottage. He knew the hermit, of course, like everyone did. But he had not been one to go in and give her his confidences. He was about to turn away when he saw her standing at the door. She clutched a shawl around her thin shoulders, and there was something about the way she hugged herself to make Philip think she was in distress.

He debated slipping away. After all, she had

not seen him. She had chosen to live this strange hermit existence. There was probably nothing wrong at all, just his imagination. But something made him call out. "Are you all right, Sister Madeleine?"

She squinted out into the dark. "Who is that? It's so dark."

"Philip O'Brien," he called back.

"Isn't that grand, the very person," she said. Philip's heart sank, she wanted him to do some errand. "Would you like a cup of tea? It hardly seems worth making one for myself."

It was an odd thing to say. She lived by herself. For heaven's sake she must always be making cups of tea on her own. Still, it would be welcome; he was stiff and tired after the journey. He followed her in. "How's the kitten, the little blind one?" he asked. He remembered Kit had told him that the hermit had insisted she could give it a good life.

"It died. Drowned there in three inches of water outside my door." Her voice was curiously flat and dead.

"Oh, I'm sorry."

"It should have died the first day, the vet was right."

"Maybe it had a nice life."

"No, it had a stupid life, hitting its poor little head off things."

Philip had no idea how to contribute to the conversation so he said nothing, just settled himself on a three-legged stool to await tea.

She cut him a slice of currant bread and spread it with butter. "You're an earnest fellow, Philip.

It's the kind of thing that will stand to you in the future."

"I hope something will stand to me in the future." He was morose.

"So life isn't good?"

"I want to marry Kit McMahon," he said suddenly. "Not now, but in a couple of years time maybe. And I've always known that. I've known it since way back the night her mother died, and that's years ago."

"Yes," Sister Madeleine said, looking into the fire.

"But being patient isn't enough. She must like someone else and she hasn't told me."

"Why do you think that?" The old nun's voice was gentle.

He explained about the dance. If there hadn't been someone else special she wouldn't have kept Philip out so deliberately. "I just don't know who it is," he said, his face sad and resigned.

"There might be nobody."

"No, her mind's very caught up with somebody."

"I'm going to tell you something . . . I know Kit very well and she does have problems on her mind . . . and something which takes up a lot of her attention, but I assure you it's not another boy. You have no rival. She's just not ready to think about men yet. Trust me." Her eyes were very bright and very blue. They almost bored through him. He believed her and he trusted her. His heart felt light. "Go on back to the hotel, Philip. Your mother and father will be looking out for you."

"They know I'm back, I left my stuff with Jimmy. Bundle of fun, Jimmy. A hundred thousand welcomes to Lough Glass written in his face."

"If you had Jimmy's life you might have a few less welcomes written in your face too." She spoke in general tones. He would never know what she had learned of Jimmy's life, but it made him feel a small wave of sympathy. It can have been no picnic working for the O'Briens, chopping wood, filling coal scuttles in rain and heat.

"You're very good for people, you know," he said as he left.

"I used to think so, Philip. Nowadays I'm not so sure." She shivered although she was in no draft.

"Good-bye and thank you . . . thank you again."

She made no reply, she was sitting looking into the fire. He pulled the door after him and fastened the latch. He walked back along the lakeshore with a smarter step. Kit didn't love anyone else. She would have told the hermit, they were great friends altogether. This was very good news, very good news indeed.

On that Saturday in November Martin McMahon told his wife Maura that they were going to get a new car. He had been discussing it with Stevie Sullivan but it was a surprise until now.

"That's the one the great spit-and-polish job was being done in." Maura was delighted. "I can tell you we're not getting anything half looked at. Stevie was under the hood and lying under the chassis, examining every inch of it."

"Are you pleased? We'll be able to go on outings without fearing that it'll never start again." He was like an excited child.

"You're the best husband that ever lived," she said.

"I wasn't always a good husband." There was a shadow on his face.

Maura was annoyed that it had come back. "To me you always were, and are."

"Yes, but I don't know." He tried hard to shrug off the mood.

She could see him almost physically struggling. She laid her hand on his arm. "Wherever Helen's soul is today it's at peace, Martin. We've told each other that so often . . . and we believe it. None of us can look back on any year, any hour even, and not wish that we had done something differently. But remember, we worked all this out. Time spent regretting is time wasted."

He nodded. She could see the shadow beginning to lessen.

אׁ אׁ אׁ

Lena Gray was explaining to Jim and Jessie Millar that she would be buying the car through the firm.

"But of course you can have a car," Mr. Millar said. "Haven't I asked you a dozen times to take something out of this firm that you built up to be what it is."

"I won't use it, Jim. It's for my husband, so I want to pay for it."

"No, the principle is still the same."

"You don't take things out of the firm for your own personal use, I will not either."

א א א

Kit arranged that they should have a little party in Frankie's flat. The girls would provide some wine, and cheese on biscuits. Later on at the hotel the boys would pay for drinks, so this sort of evened it out.

"They're not coming back for coffee," Frankie explained very firmly. "The landlady here has her hand on the phone to all of our mothers if a fellow comes into the house after ten o'clock."

The others agreed. Bringing guys back to a flat afterward was asking for it. It was cheap.

Clio heard about the party and came down to challenge Kit.

"Why was I excluded?" she asked.

"You weren't included, that's a totally different thing. This is just friends to do with catering."

"Kevin O'Connor is going," Clio said.

"Yes. It may have escaped your notice and probably everyone else's but he *is* meant to be in catering, you know."

"Well, it may have escaped your notice that I happen to be going out with his brother," Clio said.

"Clio, you and Michael can afford to go to the Gresham to a dance every night they have one," Kit said.

"I wish I knew what you were planning to do with your life, Kit McMahon," Clio said.

"So do I," Kit agreed fervently.

The Blue Lagoon was showing in the town. It would have been great to go with Anna, but Emmet knew he mustn't weaken. He saw Patsy Hanley walking disconsolately down the main street of Lough Glass. "Would you like to go to the pictures tonight?" he said quickly before he could change his mind.

Patsy blushed with pleasure. "Me? Just me, like a date?"

"Sure."

"I'd love that," she said, and scampered home to get organized.

Anna Kelly had intended to go to *The Blue Lagoon* with some of the girls from her class, but fortunately for her pride she heard that Patsy Hanley was going to go with Emmet. They would all be on the same bus.

She wouldn't let anyone see her being a wallflower. She would stay at home. In fact, she would stay at home alone because her mother and father would be having dinner at the Golf Club. Anna felt this was a very bad way of spending a Saturday night.

Philip sat with his father and mother in the dining room. The walls were a mournful brown, the tablecloths were stained with the memory of too many sauce bottles. The lighting was poor, and the service was slow.

Philip knew that this was not a hotel that would tempt anyone to make a return visit; it was not the place that would invite a business traveler to come back with his family. It was going to be a long and uphill road to transform it. He had hoped to have Kit McMahon at his side. And perhaps that hope was not so far-fetched. Sister Madeleine had been very confident and sure when she spoke. She had extraordinary piercing eyes; you believed everything they said, and she had assured him that Kit McMahon had no other love.

Philip sat trying to work out what other problems Kit might have that took up her time and attention. His parents looked at him without much pleasure.

"You're gone for weeks on end and then not a word out of you when you come home," his mother complained.

"You know, Son, if you're ever going to make any kind of a fist out of the hotel business you're going to have to be outgoing, greet people," said Philip's father, Dan O'Brien, who had never been known to begin any conversation except with a list of moans and complaints.

"You're right," he said agreeably. "I'm luckier than a lot of the others, I have a hotel in my family where I can learn."

They looked at him suspiciously, in case he was making fun of them, but could see no sign of it.

Philip nailed a smile to his face and wondered whether any other young man of his age was having such an appalling Saturday night.

"Who'll be first?" Frankie wondered as they admired the table.

It looked very festive with its colored candles

and paper napkins, and plates of food. They had speared an orange with little cocktail sticks, each one bearing a cube of cheese and a portion of pineapple. They had stuffed hard-boiled eggs, where the yolks had been taken out, mixed with mayonnaise, and put back. There were bottles of beer and glasses of red and white wine.

"I bet you it'll be that Kevin O'Connor," Kit grumbled.

"I don't think he's all that bad," Frankie said. "You have him actually crawling on the ground he's so afraid of you, and still you won't be civil to him."

"He has been very uncivil to me indeed in the past," Kit said. "It's hard to forget that sort of thing."

"You have to forget," Frankie shrugged. She almost shrugged herself out of her strapless taffeta dress and made a note not to raise her shoulders again.

"Do you, though?" Kit was wondering.

"Do you what?"

"Do you have to forget?"

"Jesus, Kit, of course you do, otherwise wars would be going on forever and women would be committing suicide over fellows they loved."

"But what's the point of anything if it can be forgotten, wiped out, start again?" Kit asked.

"Listen, we're having a party, not a debate," Frankie said. "Who do you hope to end up with tonight?"

"I don't know. Maybe the fellow from my own hometown. He's very good-looking, Stevie." Kit said this partly to put the glamorous Frankie in the position of knowing that Stevie was out of bounds, partly to convince herself in her heart she knew that Stevie was cheap and obvious.

The doorbell rang. "Here we go," said Frankie, bouncing off to answer it. Frankie came back in, eyes rolling up to heaven and followed by the most handsome man that any of them were ever likely to see in a long time.

In his dinner jacket and his hair longish but clean and shiny, with his outdoor look from working all weathers, more fit than any of the college sportsmen, and with a smile that would stop a hundred women in their tracks, Stevie Sullivan was like something that stepped down from a poster outside a cinema.

"Well, don't you look great!" Kit said before she could help herself.

"You beat me to it," he said. His eyes were warm and admiring on her bare shoulders and the peach-colored silk dress with its halter neckline.

Kit had been worried about not wearing a bra, but the girl in the shop had assured her the dress was so well formed in the bodice that no undergarment was needed. She thought she felt Stevie Sullivan's eyes examining the bodice as if he were making the assessment too, but then she was sure she imagined it.

The doorbell rang again at that moment and several more guests arrived. One was Kevin O'Connor. He made straight for Kit. "I just want to say that Matthew is here, but he's under observation from all of us. Anything untoward and he'll be sent home. Just so that you understand."

"Matthew?" Kit said, confused.

"Yes, who made the unfortunate mistake and behaved in a manner that was unseemly when you were working in the bar. That's him over there at the door. I said I'd come in and clear it with you. He's replacing Harry, you see."

"It's all right. He may stay," Kit said regally. "As long as everything is under control."

"You have my word on that," Kevin assured her.

"My God, Kit McMahon, don't you have Dublin brought down to size," Stevie said admiringly.

"Ah you don't know the half of it, Stevie." She tucked her arm companionably in his and brought him around to introduce him. She saw from the looks he was getting that she wasn't alone in her admiration. Stevie Sullivan dressed up and in a place like this was a knockout. Far too good for Clio's horrible little sister. Suddenly Kit remembered the purpose of the whole evening. She must distract him from Anna, so that Anna would go back humbly to Emmet. She must dazzle the eyes out of him at this dance. It mightn't work but she was certainly going to give it her best try.

It was the usual Saturday night in the Golf Club and the Kellys and the McMahons were finishing their dinner as they did so many weekends. It seemed impossible to believe that this had not always been the way things were.

They talked about the children. Clio wasn't studying that much, they knew. When she came home for visits it was always to sleep. "I don't think she sleeps at all in Dublin." Lilian worried about her elder daughter. Maura McMahon worried about where Clio slept but this was not the time or the place to bring up such a subject.

"Apparently Kit is going to a dance tonight," Peter Kelly said. "Clio was on the phone full of envy about it all."

"That's right. They were having a party in some girl's flat first, I think it was the College of Catering people." Martin was always a peacemaker.

"Oh I'm sure. Anyway, Clio said that if she could get a lift home she'd come tonight."

"That would be nice," Maura said, a little insincerely. She found her niece trying and unrestful. There was always some hidden tension there.

"I left a plate of sandwiches out for her," Lilian said, fussing. "Anna's not going to eat ever again she says, she has this belief that she's as fat as a pig. Lord, they can be very hard to cope with sometimes."

"I see young Philip's home," Martin said. "They could have come down together for the company."

"Oh she's full of some boy with a posh car. He might drive her." Lilian sounded worried.

"Will he want to stay?" Peter asked.

"That wasn't mentioned. And you know Clio, she'd snap your head off if you asked a question. We'll have to wait and see. I did leave out some clean sheets and pillowcases in case."

Maura said nothing. She knew the boy in the posh car was the son of Fingers O'Connor.

Francis Fingleton O'Connor was a legendary hotelier who had made a fortune through his four strategically placed hotels in Ireland. But he was even more legendary in his belief that he was attractive to all women, and that all a woman needed to make her feel feminine and desired was a grope and a feel, and a few suggestive remarks. Maura had met him on more than one occasion through her work and had disliked him intensely. She had kept her hostility until she was sure she was not observed and then had told him that his attentions were unwelcome, in such a firm tone that even Fingers O'Connor understood. But about this, as about so many things, she kept her own counsel.

Kit had mentioned that a son of his, Kevin, was in Cathal Brugha Street with her. An unpleasant lout, Kit had said. Maura told no tales, but was glad to hear it. Clio, on the other hand, seemed very involved with the boy's brother. Maura felt sure it was the lure of the car and the lifestyle.

She brought up the subject of Emmet; there would be no dissension here surely. "He's gone to the pictures tonight. Aren't they all getting very grown up, all four of them with their own lives to live," Maura said admiringly.

She thought that the Kellys didn't seem particularly confident that their daughters were leading their own lives very well. One was coming back discontentedly from Dublin to sleep for hour after hour. The other was sitting at a kitchen table on her own, refusing to go to the pictures or to eat. And both of them such beautiful girls, Maura thought.

For the first time for a long time she thought

of Helen McMahon. Her beauty had brought her nothing but tragedy.

אאא

"They're too old to get married," Louis said about Ivy and Ernest. His tone was dismissive.

"Why not if they want to?" Lena knew that Louis would take this line. She had prepared herself for it, and was determined not to sound defensive.

"Ah come on, it's ridiculous. Everyone knows they've been at it for years, why doesn't he move in or she move in, not all this love, honor, and obey bit?"

"It's a sign, that's all." She knew she was short.

"It's a sign of nothing."

"Not to people like us," she said as if it was obvious. "We don't need things like that, you and I . . . because I think we know, but other people often do need them. You're usually so tolerant of the things people do that we don't understand. Why can't you be glad for Ivy and Ernest that they're making a bit of a thing out of it?" It was exactly the right tone.

"Well yes, when you look at it like that . . ." It was as if he felt a burden, a threat, lifted from him. "Hey, let's buy them a bottle and go down tonight. Make a bit of a party of it, remind them that it's their last Saturday as free people." He was all smiles now. He would charm them to bits.

Lena was right. Louis was the life and soul of the party. He had invited all the tenants to come in and wish the happy couple well. Each one had brought a little gift. Ernest and Ivy were over-come with the emotion of it all.

"How did you know?" Ivy whispered to one of the New Zealanders.

"Mr. Gray told us. He wanted it to be a bit of a celebration," she said.

"You've got a good man there," Ivy said to Lena.

"Yes," Lena said.

Ivy looked at her sharply. "Deep down he's full of heart," Ivy insisted.

Ivy, who knew how unfaithful he was, how hard she tried to entertain him. Ivy, who alone knew that they were not married, could be fooled by this little gesture of goodwill.

Lena felt that life was all an act. "I know," she said, in a voice that had no life in it. She felt that she had stepped outside herself and that she was watching this whole scene without being a part of it. It was she who had thought of having a celebration to mark Ivy's happiness. She had swallowed her own feelings of jealousy and envy at Ivy's sudden rush of luck in the security of her man. Ivy deserved this, and Lena was glad for her neighbor and friend's moment of hap-piness.

She watched the others looking at Louis, an-imated, handsome, and the center of attention. He is a sham, she thought angrily, he is a fraud and a con trick. Why had she wasted her life on him? Why was she not back in Lough Glass where she belonged with her family, with her children who needed her?

What was she doing in this ridiculous house

in London, working her guts out for an employment agency up the road, drinking a toast to Ivy and Ernest in a roomful of people she hardly knew? This was a Saturday night, she should be at home in Lough Glass.

A terrible emptiness took hold of her. At home in Lough Glass doing what?

א א א

Michael O'Connor and Clio drove through the night to Lough Glass.

"You do know we can't sleep together at home," Clio said.

"So you keep saying."

"No, so I keep insisting. I wouldn't have to if you didn't just take it as a joke."

"Peace, peace. We start the night in separate places and then you creep along to me. Right?"

"No, Michael, not right. This is the house that I was born in and grew up in. My parents are there with ears sharpened, waiting for every creak of the floorboards."

"We'll find a way around them."

"No!" She sounded very angry.

He pulled the car into the side of the road. "What's this, what are we fighting about?" he asked.

"About the fact that I did say to you before we left Dublin that this wasn't on. I didn't want you to be under any false impression." She looked very troubled and very young. Her blond curls looked babyish and her lower lip was trembling like any toddler's.

He softened. "Okay, okay. I take your point."

"But will you take it when you're in the spare room, Michael?" she asked.

"I don't know. It depends on how eager I feel."

"Unless you know that it doesn't matter how eager you feel, we're not going any farther. We stop right here," she said.

"Oh really, and what would you do in the middle of nowhere?"

"I'd either get out and hitch or I'd come back to Dublin with you." She sounded more confident than she felt.

"Aw to hell, we're halfway there. I'll drive you to Loughwhatsit and then go back to civilization."

"It's too much to ask."

"The lady must be obeyed."

"Honestly, Michael."

"No, I want to see your place anyway. I have to report on whether my girlfriend is my social equal." She assumed he was joking and laughed. "I'm deadly serious," Michael said. "My father keeps asking me what class of a girl Maura Hayes's niece is. I think your aunt was quite a goer."

"A goer?"

"A flier."

"Aunt Maura? You have to be joking."

"That's what he says, or sort of doesn't say. A real party girl."

"Is that good or bad?"

"It's great. Like you, a party girl, full of fun." He gave her a squeeze and then reminded himself that this was not the place or time. "No point in getting myself going, especially if nothing lovely lies ahead for me."

They drove through the dark Irish countryside, through small villages, and past farmhouses with lights in the windows, past herds of cattle looking at them over hedges. Past wayside shrines to Our Lady of Lourdes. But they spoke of none of these things they passed. They had little conversation, Clio realized, it was not a life that involved much sitting down together and chatting about the way of the world.

But then they had something much more important, they had a very passionate love life. Most people weren't lucky enough to have that. Ever. Clio knew now how hard it was to define love in poems or in paintings or in music. It was all about . . . well, closeness, being intimate. That kind of thing was impossible to describe.

She looked at Michael's face as he drove. She wondered was he thinking something on the same lines. She placed her hand on his leg.

"We're very lucky, aren't we?" Clio said.

"No, we're bloody not . . . your parents are there waiting like grizzly bears to catch us."

"They're not at home yet, they'll be up in the Golf Club," Clio said.

Michael's face brightened. "Maybe we'd have time before they got back," he said.

Clio looked at her watch. It was ten o'clock, they were half an hour from Lough Glass, but her mother and father rarely left the Golf Club before midnight. "Drive faster," she said, and was rewarded by Michael's whoop of delight.

Sister Madeleine was restless. Yet again the evening seemed long and lonely to her. This was something she must not allow to happen. She had craved to be away from the ceaseless chatter and business of other people's lives. She had always been proud to live comfortably with her own thoughts. But maybe that was in the days when she had faith in her own thoughts. Recently she was less and less sure of everything, and when the certainty had gone a lot of other things went too.

The shadows of evening over the lake seemed a little menacing now: the creaks and sounds in the trees around, the rustle in the undergrowth. She could see the lights of the travelers' camp in the woods. They had a fire and they would make her welcome but she would cast a quietness on them. She would change their mood. She looked through the trees up at Lough Glass, and saw the lights of the one long street. In those houses were settled people, not travelers, not hermits like herself. She knew most of their stories, their secrets. There was hardly a home where they wouldn't reach out a hand and pull her warmly into the house.

But there was something holding Sister Madeleine back. If she went calling, if she gave up this life of independence, she would be lost. She told herself that she was being full of fancies. She tried to imagine that she was one of the many who filed to her little cottage for advice. What would she have said?

"The great trouble with most of us is that we think too much about ourselves, that's what makes our problems seem so much more important than they are. Now if you were to think about someone else . . ." Very good advice, but the only person she could think of was poor Francis with his scattered wits wandering somewhere in the night. She wished she could believe he was settled and safe. He had been gone for three days. She shivered as she tried to imagine where he was laying his head this Saturday night. She wished it was still on the settle bed beside the open fire in her little cottage.

There was a buzz of conversation in Frankie's flat. The party was going well. Frankie and Kit looked at each other in delight. It was working better than they had hoped. It would be magic when they got to the ballroom. Kevin O'Connor was standing beside Matthew, the one-time foul-mouthed friend, as if he were a bodyguard. Kit had to smile her amusement. Boys were so young really compared to girls. Those two were behaving as if they were Emmet's age.

Thinking about Emmet, she realized she had been neglecting the night's mission. It wasn't enough to lure Stevie to Dublin for just one Saturday night, she must try and let him think she was interested in him so that he would forget Anna and concentrate all his attentions on her.

Really, those Kelly girls were very tiresome, Kit said to herself. Clio had behaved like a wounded deer just because she wasn't included, but it would have been impossible to have her. The whole of Lough Glass would know that Kit McMahon had behaved disgracefully with Stevie

Sullivan, which was what she was now about to do.

She smeared a little Vaseline over her lipstick to make her mouth look more shiny and moved over to where he was standing talking cars, relaxed, at ease, as if he spent every Saturday night in the company of people in evening dresses and dinner jackets. He was far more comfortable there than some of the guests. Kit decided that he might not be as rough a diamond as she had thought or perhaps he was just a very good actor.

"We're thinking about who'll go in whose car down to the Gresham," she said. "Do you have room for a few in yours?"

"Sure," he smiled easily.

Kevin was beside her blustering. "I'll take you, Kit. I've got the Morris tonight, plenty of room, we can get four in the back."

"I have to help Frankie as hostess and sort of be in charge." Kit smiled at him sweetly. Kevin beamed back idiotically. He seemed to have been forgiven, welcomed back to the fold. She laid her hand on Kevin's arm. "Hey, why don't you be a sweetheart and get Matthew in the front seat where you can keep an eye on him and take those four girls over there?"

Kevin was delighted to oblige. Kit did rapid mental arithmetic and saw to it that Stevie was driving her and her alone. When they locked the door of the flat behind them Paddy and Frankie had been installed in one of the other cars, Stevie and Kit were left together.

"So nobody wanted to come with us?" He looked at her playfully.

"That's the way it turned out," she said.

He opened the door of a very smart car indeed.

"What is it?" she asked in wonder.

"It's an E-type," said Stevie casually.

"Well now, if they'd seen this we'd have been killed in the rush," she said.

"No good, Kit, if they just want you for the car. They have to want you for yourself," he said.

He was easy company, semi-flirting, more admiring really. She found it easy to play her role.

"Ah, I'd say you have no trouble in that department," she said.

"What department?"

"The department where they want you for yourself. Queuing up, from what I hear."

"Come on out of that, you're the girl next door, remember. You never saw any queues form at the garage."

"I saw enough," Kit laughed.

He looked at her and she smiled quite deliberately, like people did in films. It felt corny inside but he liked it. "You've certainly changed since those days," he said.

"Have I? I feel just the same."

"No you don't. You were a silly giggling schoolgirl with Clio. You laughed at everything and everyone."

"And now I'm all morose, is that it?" Again she looked up at him from under her eyelashes. Kit wondered was she overdoing this.

Stevie wasn't a fool, he would know what she was trying on, and despise her. But apparently not. "That's a nice crowd of friends you have,"

604

he said. "Yes . . . that's the great thing about Dublin, isn't it. There's a chance to meet so many more people than at home. Is the big blond guy your boyfriend?" He was very direct.

"Why do you ask?" She had raised her eyebrows. Surely he'd tell her to stop playacting. He seemed very attentive. "He's in my year at the catering college."

"Is he that O'Connor, of the hotels?" How quick he was. He had learned Kevin's name, and put two and two together.

"That's it," she said. She had an urge to tell him that Kevin O'Connor was a great ignorant loudmouth who had told all his friends that he had slept with her, and paid dearly for it. That he was afraid of his life of her now. That he would probably run one at least, if not all, of his father's hotels into the ground by the time he had finished with them.

But that wasn't part of the game. The game had to do with making him just a little jealous. Letting him think she was rushed off her feet. So she said none of these interesting facts about Kevin. But then, going out with a fellow like Stevie wasn't like going out with a friend.

"So he's the one, is he?"

"Frankie's brother the law student? No, just a pal but as you said, he's attentive. I think that describes it well."

"And young Philip O'Brien from the hotel, attentive as well! Lord, you're notching them up, Kit McMahon."

"Oh no. Philip's just a friend."

"And why wasn't he at tonight's do?"

"I think he had to go home," Kit lied. She felt sure he could see through her like glass.

"Well, I'm glad you asked me. I'm having a good time," said Stevie. He swung the car around and parked it in a place that looked as if it were reserved for visiting celebrities. Hardly anyone visiting tonight would have a smarter car, so a judicious discussion with a porter made sure that it was all organized.

Then, with his hand under her elbow, Stevie Sullivan led Kit into the hotel where the others in their party were gathered, looking open-mouthed at the car that Stevie had parked so casually.

"That's some motor," Kevin O'Connor said, the envy oozing from his every pore.

"Oh, I don't know, they're a bit flash. I think you're just paying for all that chrome. You say you have a Morris? I think they're the best thing on the road these days, fast too if you need it."

Kevin was appeased. "Yeah sure. That's what I thought." They came nearer to the ballroom and they heard the music of the band. "Kit, can I book you for the first dance?" Kevin said.

It was loud rock and roll. It wasn't a seducing number. Nothing she would need to concentrate on with Stevie. "That would be great, Kevin," she said in a low breathy voice. Kevin straightened his bow tie and led her by the hand onto the floor.

Men are such idiots, Kit said to herself. And for some reason a vision of her mother flashed in front of her.

606

"Are these the bright lights of Lough Glass coming up ahead?" Michael O'Connor asked Clio.

"You're not going to make me defensive about my hometown," she laughed at him.

"No, it must be very deep and important, coming from a place the size of this," said Michael O'Connor.

"Okay, so you were born in Dublin, but your father wasn't, nor your mother. Everyone came from a place like this, it's just a question of when," Clio said.

"I love you when you're angry, Miss Kelly."

"I'm not angry," Clio said.

"Good, so you're going to be real nice to me . . ."

"Yes, but we'll have to be quick."

They parked the car in the drive. As she had expected, her parents' car was not there. They would be another hour at the Golf Club.

She opened the door and saw Michael O'Connor's eyes take in the house. It was comfortable and she felt no sense that it was not worthy of them. Her mother spent a lot of time and money choosing furnishing fabrics. The hall had an antique mirror and two old tables of elegant design. There was a light in the kitchen.

Clio saw the glum figure of her younger sister sitting reading at the kitchen table. "Oh shit," said Clio. "It's Anna."

"What does that mean?" Michael asked, peering over her shoulder.

"What you've guessed it means," said Clio with

607

her mouth a hard line.

Anna looked up from her book. "Oh hallo," she said. "I thought it was them, back from tombstone city a bit early."

"Why aren't you out?" Clio snapped. "It's a Saturday night."

"Why aren't *you* out?" Anna retorted.

Michael just stood there.

"I am out," Clio said foolishly. "I'm out from Dublin."

"Great." Anna went back to her book.

"Anna, this is Michael O'Connor, a friend of mine from Dublin. This is my younger sister, Anna, who's at school."

"But not at the moment," Anna said. "At the moment I'm committing what is apparently the worst crime in the book, I'm in my own house, sitting here reading my own book, and for some reason I have offended my big sister greatly by doing this."

"Oh shut up, Anna. You're a pain in the arse," said Clio.

"Well, I think I should be . . ." Michael was anxious to be far away from this kitchen.

"No, heavens, you must have a drink, a coffee or something. You can't drive me all this way and just . . ."

"Well, it looks as if I have driven you all this way and then just . . ." he said. And there was a look of real annoyance on his face.

"Perhaps, Anna, if I could ask you to go to your own room and read, Michael and I could . . . um . . . talk here with more comfort?" Clio didn't hold out much hope.

"There are six chairs." Anna looked around as if to reassure herself. "And there's the drawing room and the dining room. I don't remember anyone saying that when I read a book I had to be confined to my own room."

"Jesus," Clio said to her, with a look that would have weakened a lesser sister.

"It's been great," said Michael icily.

"Listen, come back. I'm sorry."

"Come back for what exactly? For repartee in the kitchen? No, I'll just drive back to Dublin. It's what I love to do on a Saturday, drive to the middle of nowhere and back." She heard the bang of the car door and he was gone.

With a look of murder in her eyes Clio returned to the kitchen.

Emmet had thought *The Blue Lagoon* a bit soppy and sentimental, but Patsy Hanley had liked it. She giggled a lot when she talked about it afterward and said *You know* and *I forgot what I was going to say* a lot. Maybe she was shy and that was why she talked so much. Emmet knew how hard it was to mean to say one thing and have another come out. But really Patsy was hard going. If it had been Anna . . .

If only it had been Anna. They could have talked about it properly . . . Anna was so bright, she had such imagination. Her mind went everywhere.

As he sat beside Patsy, who was prattling on about the film on the bus, he thought of Anna. She wasn't going out with that greasy Stevie, that was good. But had he been right to pass up the chance of taking her out tonight? Was it wise to take Patsy and make her jealous? Why did life have to be such a series of games?

When the bus stopped outside Paddles' bar Emmet and Patsy walked together along the street in Lough Glass. "Wouldn't it be great if there was a place to go for coffee or ice cream here?" Patsy said.

"Yeah." Emmet didn't think he could take any more of Patsy and was quite relieved that there wasn't anywhere to go. They passed the Central Hotel and looked at it without enthusiasm. "It's a real mausoleum, isn't it?" said Emmet.

"A what?" Patsy asked.

Emmet dug his hands into his pockets.

"Were you at the pictures?" called Philip O'Brien.

"It was terrific, *The Blue Lagoon*," said Patsy.

Philip was always nice to Emmet McMahon. One day Emmet would be his brother-in-law; he wanted them to have a history of being friends. "Anna Kelly not with you?" he asked conversationally. He thought Emmet would be pleased to know that he, Philip, a much older man, would even know who his friends were.

He was unprepared for the glower he got from Emmet. "No, she's not," he said with his stammer returning. He struggled out the words that people were free to come and go as they wanted to and then marched off with a red face. Patsy Hanley shrugged at Philip and followed. She didn't know what was wrong either.

"Well, I'm home," Emmet said gruffly as they got to McMahon's pharmacy.

"Aren't you going to escort me home?" Patsy said. "You did ask me to the pictures."

Emmet had opened the door, but he realized that it was just pure annoyance and bad temper on his part to dart into his house. Of course he should have walked her across to her house over Hanley's Drapery. "Sorry," he muttered.

They walked through the quiet town. There was never much sound coming from Foley's bar up at this end, all the activity seemed to be down at Paddles' place.

Mrs. Hanley was waiting. "I thought the bus should be in about now," she said. She had no intention of allowing her second daughter to follow the path of Deirdre and be regarded as an easy conquest. "Come on in, Emmet. I'll give you a cup of drinking chocolate," she said.

"No really, thanks, Mrs. Hanley."

"Ah, come on up, can't you? I've chocolate biscuits."

Emmet went up. There would be nobody at home. His father and Maura were at the Golf Club and he didn't want to be alone thinking about Anna. This was more companionable.

Kit discovered that Stevie was a great dancer. She wanted to ask him where he had learned. She had learned at special lessons, an optional class provided by Mother Bernard on Friday afternoons up at the convent. They had mocked the teacher at the time but always looked back in gratitude.

But Stevie now. All his life spent in overalls, tinkering with engines. Living with that awful moaning mother of his and a wild young brother. Where had he found time and interest to make himself so smart and so skilled? When they danced to "Smoke Gets in Your Eyes" he laid his cheek against hers. Kit moved slightly away but only very slightly, so that he could follow.

"Do you know something?" Stevie said.

"No. What?" Kit was giggly and coy. It seemed to be working.

"The words of that song are utterly ridiculous. It's about some guy who had laughing friends deride him . . . listen . . ." They listened to the words. It was as he said. "What kind of a shower of friends would they be?" Stevie asked.

Kit agreed with him. She was about to give her views then she remembered her role. She was here to make him fall for her. What that involved was not having views yourself but talking entirely about the boy.

"Do you have friends?" she asked, looking up at him.

"You know bloody well I don't have friends. Haven't you known me all my life? What time have I for friends? Where would I find them?" He sounded bitter.

"I don't know you all my life," she came back with spirit. "I hardly know you at all. You're a different man tonight, a person I don't know at all. For all I know you could have friends in Hollywood or the South of France. You look the part." She realized she sounded angry.

But he took it as admiration. "Thank you," he said. She longed to talk to him. But there was no time. "And have you many friends?" he asked as they stood on the dance floor. They didn't even bother returning to the table where the wine and the others were, they knew they would be dancing again.

"Not all that many really." Kit was thoughtful.

"I thought you and Clio were still Siamese twins."

"No, not at all. She's not here tonight, for example."

"Anna says you're as thick as thieves."

"Anna!" There was the word. This is what she must get back to — outsmarting Anna. "Anna knows nothing." She put all the scorn in the world into her voice.

"She's brighter than you think, she's got a mind of her own," he defended her.

Kit knew that this was true. Anna was bright and imaginative. She remembered that from when Emmet had been so sick and she had come to mind him. She mustn't protest too much. "She's pretty, mind you," Kit said in a coquettish way that felt horribly alien. "I can see that people would think she was a little attractive, but bright . . . I don't think so."

"She's only pretty in a schoolgirl way," Stevie said. Then the band began to play "A Fool Such as I" and he held her close to him for the slow swaying number. He held himself back from her to look at her face, flushed, eyes sparkling. "Now you, Kit McMahon, you are seriously good-looking," he said.

She understood in those seconds why people had found him so sexy and attractive, why even married women had gone off with him and taken terrible risks. But of course he would be a ridiculous person to fall for, Kit told herself. Thank heavens she was only doing this ludicrous charade as a favor for her little brother. She reminded herself of this again as his arms tightened around her when they danced.

"You behaved like a spoiled brat," Clio said to Anna. "I want you to know that I will never forgive you for this as long as I live."

"Did I spoil your plans?" Anna asked.

"You were extremely discourteous to a friend who kindly drove me the whole way from Dublin."

"And was about to drive you upstairs to bed if only little sister hadn't been here to guard your reputation."

"Don't you dare even suggest such a thing." Clio was white with rage.

"I think we're quits," Anna said calmly. "You don't mention my bad manners, I don't mention your intentions." She went back to her book.

Clio saw it was *Wuthering Heights*. "Poseur, affected show-off . . . pretending you read books like that for pleasure . . ."

"But I do," Anna said. "There's real passion in this book, not just gropes and feels in motorcars. And anyway, aren't you the one studying English for a degree? I thought you would read a book a day, a classic I mean, for pleasure."

"I could stab you with the bread knife and pretend it was an intruder that did it," Clio said.

"Yes, but it wouldn't be worth it," Anna said, going back to her reading.

Martin McMahon was annoyed when they got home. The door was open. "That's very careless of Emmet," he grumbled. "Leaving a door swinging open on the street."

"Maybe he's just gone upstairs," Maura said, ever the peacemaker and wanting to find an excuse.

"Let me check the chemist's." Martin always feared that people would break in, in search of his medicines and drugs.

Maura went up the stairs without him. There didn't seem to be any sign of Emmet, but the light was on in the kitchen, so Maura went in there.

But it wasn't Emmet who sat there. It was a tramp, she thought first, a man with a torn coat that had been wet through. His shoes looked as if they had let in water and he was unshaven, and wild-looking even though he was asleep with his head lolling to one side.

Maura's hand flew to her throat. "Oh my God!" she said before she could stop herself. Her voice woke the man and he leaped to his feet. Maura saw that his eyes were wild and she clutched her throat in terror. "Please," she said. "Please."

The man stood up unsteadily. He looked around him for something that would serve as a weapon.

Maura knew with relief that the knives were at the very back of a drawer. He wouldn't find one easily. She was surprised at how rationally her mind was able to work. She prayed that Martin would come up the stairs, and then she prayed at the same time that he wouldn't. The man was like a wild animal who would see himself trapped by two people and flail even more dangerously. "I won't hurt you," she said.

He gave a strangled cry, a sound that wasn't any words. But at the same time he picked up one of the kitchen chairs and lunged at Maura.

She moved away from him, leaving him the doorway free to make his exit. Please, please, God, may Martin not be coming up the stairs. "Go now. Run away, I'll say nothing," she said in a voice a bit above a whisper. He looked at her, confused, and seemed to come after her again. She fell on her knees trying to avoid him.

When Martin came in and stood frozen in shock, blocking the doorway, he saw the tableau of his wife kneeling, cowering in terror from a wild man about to batter her with a chair. "Get off, get off her," roared Martin, flinging himself on the man with the wild eyes.

The man raised the chair and beat Martin with it as Maura dragged herself to her feet to come and pull him off. Only the sound of Emmet's voice as he ran up the stairs shouting "What's wrong, what's wrong, what's happening?" broke the remorseless series of blows.

Now that there were three of them the man with the wet coat, the straggly hair, and wild, mad eyes realized he might be outnumbered. Grabbing up a soaking-wet bag of possessions he pushed his way past Emmet and down the stairs.

"Daddy, D-Daddy," Emmet stuttered out

the words in his grief.

"Get Peter," Maura said. "Phone him this minute." Then she ran out the door and down the stairs.

"Maura, come back," Emmet cried.

"He's not going to get away . . . he's not going to do this to Martin and get away." In seconds she was at the door and looking out on the dark quiet street of Lough Glass. "Help!" she called. "Help! Get help, there's a man running down the road. Stop him, stop him. He's attacked Martin."

Almost at once lights went on, doors opened. Maura saw young Michael Sullivan come out of the garage across the road, and the Walls in the hardware shop followed.

"Which way?" called Mr. Wall.

"He's gone down toward the Brother's." The Walls started to shout too and roused the Hickeys over their meat shop and by the time the noise came to Foley's pub there were people out in the street running after the figure they saw staggering and stumbling away.

When Sergeant Sean O'Connor arrived on the scene the man with the wild eyes and the words that were hard to understand was firmly held. Held, it had to be said, by the after-hours drinkers from Foley's bar and some who had crossed the street from after-hours drinking at Paddles' place. But such niceties as the licensing laws were unimportant now.

"It's one of the knackers, bloody tinkers always the same," said Mrs. Dillon from the newsagent's shop. She hadn't known such excitement in years as to witness the capture of a criminal just outside her door.

"It's not," said Paddles.

Sergeant Sean O'Connor was indifferent as to who the man was. He moved him firmly into the Garda car under the efficient armlock of the young Garda who was with him. The sergeant was giving the impression that the fun was over. "You'll all be on your way home now," he said mildly, looking at the two open licensed premises beckoning warmly if illegally in the night.

People shuffled around noncommittally.

"Is Martin McMahon all right?" asked Dan O'Brien, who had run from the hotel to see the cause of the commotion.

"The doctor is with him now, he won't want a flood of people in on top of him. So I won't detain any of you from your beds," said Sean O'Connor, taking his prisoner into custody.

"It's not very deep, Maura." Peter Kelly knelt on the floor beside his friend Martin.

"But he's unconscious."

"That's because he hit his head falling down.

"Has he concussion?"

"I don't know. We'll get him to hospital."

"My God, Peter, what'll we do? I will kill that madman with my own bare hands if Martin's badly hurt."

"No, his pulse is fine. He's going to be fine."

"Do you mean that? Or is it just to make me feel better?"

"Maura, he'll be grand."

"Can he hear me?" she asked.

"No, I wouldn't think so. No, not now. But

he'll come around, he'll be fine."

Just in case Maura knelt beside him and kissed his bloodstained face. "You're going to be fine, Martin. I've seen Peter's eyes, he means it. And I love you, I love you with all my heart. You make me sing with happiness."

Emmet McMahon and Peter Kelly exchanged glances. They knew they weren't meant to hear such a declaration of love. It was very private and neither of them would ever refer to it again.

It was a long night in the cell. Sean O'Connor got dry clothes for the dirty and shivering man in his charge. He even gave him a cup of tea though his heart wasn't in it. He had seen the blood on the floor of the McMahons' kitchen and was still awaiting news from the hospital about Martin's condition.

The man was deranged and made little sense. He spoke a lot about his sister. Or was it his sister? She'd want to know where he was and what had happened to him. Mostly he rambled and moved from sentence to sentence without finishing the first. His words were confused. He needed to be in a psychiatric home, Sean O'Connor guessed. Perhaps he had even come from one. As he left the cell he saw the man curl up to sleep on the bench-style bed. He was mumbling names over and over. None of them made any sense to Sergeant O'Connor.

Lilian was still up when Peter Kelly got back from the hospital.

"It's all right," he reassured her from the door.

"It's all right. He's regained consciousness, they're testing him for concussion, and he's had a lot of X rays. No, he'll be fine."

Lilian let out her breath in relief. "And Maura?"

"Insisted on staying in there in the hospital with him. Brought Emmet with her. They found them beds."

"Was it necessary?"

"It was what she wanted to do," Peter said, pouring himself a brandy.

"I had some tea ready."

"I'm past tea," Peter said. He sat down at the kitchen table. "The girls in? Did Clio come home?"

"Yes, both of them like vipers. You could cut the atmosphere. They had some huge row which was still simmering."

"What else is new?" Peter sounded weary.

"Who was he? Was it one of the tinkers?"

"No it wasn't. Why do people automatically blame them?"

"Because they're different, that's why. What was he then?"

"God knows . . . some tramp who came in."

"There aren't any tramps in Lough Glass. Anyway how did he get in?"

"Emmet left the door open. The poor lad is nearly dead with grief. He thinks it was all his fault. That's why Maura brought him with her."

They were silent. Lilian was thinking that Maura seemed to get on much better with her two stepchildren than she, Lilian, did with her natural children. She looked at Peter and wondered if he had any of the same thoughts running through his mind.

Kevin O'Connor danced with Kit. "Eventually I was able to prise you away from the lounge lizard," he said.

"Whatever else he is he isn't that," Kit said.

"Oh really? He looks as if he'd stepped straight from the pages of a glossy magazine . . . with all the shine intact. Years of escorting ladies through crowded dance floors."

"No, years of working long hours getting rust out of cars, tuning engines, selling tractors . . ."

"How do you know all that?"

"He's the boy next door, he's from Lough Glass."

"Jesus, half of Dublin seems to be from that one-horse town. Clio as well. Well, it sure breeds fine looking women." His arms tightened a little around her.

Kit was about to pull away when she saw Stevie Sullivan looking at her over Frankie's shoulder. She didn't pull away, instead she smiled up at Kevin. "Any tighter and I'll put my knee up with a sudden jerk," she said, still smiling sweetly.

"You'll what . . . ?" He looked alarmed.

"You won't be able to walk for a week," Kit said, her face never changing. She could see Stevie watching them with interest, but with no idea of what was being said.

It wasn't all that difficult to get men to fancy you if you tried, Kit decided.

The dance was over at midnight. All Saturday night dances in Dublin had to end then, it was so that it wouldn't go on into the Sabbath Day. The national anthem was played and they went for their coats. Kevin O'Connor and his friend Matthew wondered casually if people might like to come around to their flat for a beer or a coffee. And to play records. Matthew managed to put such a leer of suggestiveness into the words "play records" that nobody was in any doubt about what he meant.

"I'll walk you back to the hostel," Stevie suggested to Kit.

"It's not a hostel actually, it's a bed-sit," Kit said.

"Well, if I'd have known that, then I might have had somewhere to lay my weary head." He smiled at her.

"Oh no, no weary heads, only my own," Kit was relaxed. This was surely going well.

"I might have tried to persuade you." He smiled.

"I wouldn't have counted on it. No, better to have made your own arrangements."

"Mine are simple, I drive back to the ranch, now."

"Now, at this time?"

"No rest for the self-employed."

"But tomorrow's Sunday."

"What other day do I have of meeting farmers, when they come in to Mass, telling them all about new equipment?"

"You're really determined to make that place a success, aren't you?"

"Well, it would make a nice change from the way it was handed to me, I can tell you that."

His voice sounded bitter for a second.

"Your mother must be very proud of you . . ."

"You know my mother, she's proud of nothing. Oh God, that reminds me . . . could you hang on till I make a phone call." They were just coming out of the hotel door but he searched his pockets for change and headed to the phone. He turned back to say, "I totally forgot that my mother's staying with her sister . . . and I'm meant to be responsible for that young hooligan Michael."

"How can you be responsible for him from here?"

"A good question. But I said I'd phone him at midnight to check that he was home and I'd kick the arse off him if he wasn't."

Kit laughed. He didn't have to tell her whom he was phoning, but somehow it was a relief. Stevie Sullivan must have had a lot of telephone numbers he could call. Even this late on a Saturday night.

She watched the dancers leaving and the hotel wind down. Kit thought that it had been about as successful as it could possibly have been. She had definitely taken his mind off that baby-faced Anna. Anna would go back to Emmet for consolation. It was all going according to the plan.

Stevie was walking over to her, but there was something different about his face. "Hey, let's sit down for a minute." He indicated a group of chairs.

"But aren't we going to go? They're cleaning up."

"It'll only take a minute . . ."

"Was Michael not there?" She knew something had happened.

"No, he was there all right, but . . . ."

"But what?"

"But he said that there had been an accident, that your father had got hurt."

"Oh my God, a car crash, the new car. They weren't used to it?"

"No, nothing like that, an intruder. But he's fine, your father. He's in hospital, but he'll be out in a day or two, truly."

Kit thought of scatty young Michael Sullivan and didn't put very much faith in his judgment. Kit's face was white with anxiety, she felt light-headed as if she were going to faint. Father in an accident with an intruder . . . what did it mean?

"Please, I tell you, it's going to be all right." She didn't even have to say it, Stevie realized. "No, I didn't take Michael's word for it, I went back through the exchange to Mona Fitz in the post office. There was some kind of madman, they caught him. He hit your father but it's going to be all right . . . ."

"It might have been the same people who hit your mother."

"Yes, it might."

"I feel sick with shock thinking about poor Father," Kit said.

"It's all right, go home and get on a nice warm coat and I'll drive you back to him."

"Will you?" She looked at him trustingly. All flirtatious behavior was long forgotten now. He put his arm around her shoulder and walked her to the car. "Maybe I'm only delaying you. I'll go like this," she said.

"No, you can't go like that, not into a hospital. You'll frighten the wits out of them." Yes, he was right. "And another thing, I couldn't drive all those miles beside you dressed in that getup. It would be more than flesh and blood could bear to keep my hands off you."

"Then I'll get changed," she said, her tone mute.

And he seemed sorry to have made the remark. Kit was worried about her father, it had been a coarse sort of thing to say. "I'm sorry, Kit," he said simply. "Sometimes I'm very rough, I disgust myself."

"No, it doesn't matter," she said. They were talking like friends, real friends who knew each other very well. He sat in the car while she went in to change.

She hung up the dress that had worked such wonders and looked at her pale face in the mirror. It all seemed very childish and unimportant compared with poor Father. She wished she knew more about what had happened. Wasn't it lucky that Stevie had phoned home. She had never known that he was the kind of fellow who would actually mind his younger brother. There were a lot of things she hadn't known about him until tonight.

The towns and the fields, the woods, the crossroads and the farmhouses, slipped past in the night. Kit felt it was all so unreal.

"Try to sleep," Stevie said. "There's a rug there, you could put it under your head like a cushion." She sat, small and frightened in her black polo-necked sweater and her black and red skirt. She had taken a jacket and a warm woolly scarf too but she didn't need them. The luxurious car was very warm.

"Did Mona Fitz say any more?" she asked.

"No, I didn't keep her on the phone, I thought it was better just to head out there."

"Much better," she said. Her voice was small.

"You'll be fine," Stevie said.

"I know."

"These things don't happen," he said.

She looked at him, his face was very handsome in the moonlight. "What things?"

"There's some fairness in the world," Stevie Sullivan said. "I mean, they wouldn't let you lose your mother *and* your father. He's got to be all right."

Sergeant Sean O'Connor woke with a start. It was seven-thirty in the morning. He had suddenly made sense of all the jumble of names, and of the man talking about his sister. He went into the cell, he kicked the bed and the man sat up alarmed.

"Tell me about Sister," he said.

"What, what?"

"Sister Madeleine. Did you hurt her? Did you lay a hand on her? If you touched her I'll have you beaten to death in this station and then give myself up."

"No, no." The man was frightened.

"I'm going down to her house this minute, and you'd better pray to your God that you didn't harm her. That woman is a living saint."

626

"No, no." The man was like an animal crouched and frightened. "She was good to me. I stayed with her. She hid me, you see. She hid me in her house, first up a tree in the tree house, and then in her own cottage. I wouldn't hurt Sister Madeleine, she's the only person who was ever good to me."

He parked the Garda car outside Paddles' bar and walked down the narrow path to the hermit's cottage. He stopped outside the window and peered in. The small bent figure was lifting her heavy black kettle from the hook over the fire. That at least was good timing. They could talk over tea.

She was pleased to see him. "This is a real treat for me now. I was thinking wouldn't I love a friendly soul to come in and have something to eat and drink with me. Not to be doing it on my own."

"But don't you choose to live on your own? Aren't you a solitary person?" His eyes were narrow as he looked at her.

"Ah, there's solitude and solitude." A silence fell between them. Eventually the hermit said. "Is there anything troubling you, Sean?"

"Is there anything troubling *you*, Sister Madeleine?"

Her eyes seemed to see through him, right across the corner of the lake and up to the prison cell where the frightened madman had lain on his bunk bed babbling her name. "You found Francis, Sean, is that it?"

"I don't know what his bloody name is, but he said he'd stayed here, that you looked after him."

"I did what I had to."

"Harbor a lunatic?"

"Well, I couldn't let him off on his own, he was wounded. And anyway he was frightened."

"What was he frightened of?"

"That you'd catch him, and punish him."

"But he hadn't done anything yet, had he?"

"The garage, Kathleen Sullivan . . . you *know* all this, Sean."

And suddenly it all clicked together in Sean O'Connor's head. "You knew he had beaten that woman and still you hid him. You harbored a criminal."

"That's being too harsh."

"For God's sake, he's put two people in the County Hospital. What do you call that, peace and light?"

"Two people?"

"Yeah. He beat Martin McMahon senseless last night."

Sister Madeleine's hands went up over her face, her shoulders shook. "The poor man," she said. "The poor, poor man."

Sergeant Sean O'Connor sat there, grim-faced. He would have liked to believe that the poor man she was feeling such sympathy for was Martin McMahon, coming innocently up his own stairs into his kitchen and seeing his wife being attacked.

But he feared it was the disturbed mind of the prisoner in his cell, the man she called Francis. "Tell me about Francis," he said wearily.

"You won't hurt him?"

"No. We'll get him looked after."

"You promise?"

Sean got a wave of impatience. Why did he have to do deals with people over something as basic as this? "Did he tell you where he came from, Sister?" he said slowly and deliberately.

"He said he'd come back when he got settled. Come back for his things."

"How long has he been gone?"

"Only three days."

"Well, he didn't get far, up to the main street of the town, it seems. Into the kitchen of the McMahons to beat them all with a chair."

"I can't believe it," she said.

"Where did you think he was going?"

"I didn't know, he said he wanted to be free." She looked very upset.

Sean O'Connor forced himself to lower his tone and be gentle. "And how long was he here altogether, would you say?"

"I suppose about six weeks . . . who can tell? Time has no meaning."

"Immediately after the garage, and Kathleen being taken to hospital, would it be?"

"I expect it must have been." Her voice was very flat.

"And you never thought of telling us he was here?"

"Never."

"You have a strange sense of responsibility to the community, if I may say so, Sister Madeleine."

"I felt he couldn't do any harm while he was here." Her eyes were clear in their sincerity.

"True, but he sure did the very moment he left you."

"I didn't know." There was another long silence. "I'll get you his things," Sister Madeleine said. She produced a blue carrier bag with money, checks, motor registration books, and the few cheap ornaments he had taken from the office in Sullivan Motors.

Sean O'Connor looked through them in disbelief. "We've had half the country searching for all this." She said nothing. "How did you hide him? People come in and out. I've been in and out myself, for God's sake!"

"He lived in the tree house during the day," she said simply, as if it were a perfectly natural thing to do.

The sergeant stood up. "It wasn't the right thing to do, Sister. He's not a fox or a rabbit, or a poor little duck with a broken wing. He's a man, a disturbed man who injured people badly, who could have killed them. You did him no service by giving him this Alice in Wonderland place to live."

"He was happy here," she said. Sean O'Connor didn't trust himself to speak. He was afraid he would lose his temper and say something he would regret. "Sean?"

"Yes, Sister?"

"Can I come and see him? Up in the station?" There was a long pause. "It couldn't do any harm, it might possibly do some good."

Stevie Sullivan had left Kit at the door of the hospital.

"Aren't you coming in?"

"No, I'd be in the way, he's all right I tell you. I wouldn't leave you to face things if he weren't."

"Thank you very, very much, Stevie. You've been wonderful to me."

"Glad I was there," he said. She didn't want him to leave. And she felt he didn't want her to go. "I'll see you later in the day," he said.

"When you've talked the Mass goers into buying tractors," she said with an attempt at a watery smile.

"That's the girl," he said, and drove the E-type out of the hospital grounds in a flourish.

"Your mother and brother are with him, he's talking now," the nurse said.

Kit got a shock for a moment. The wild idea that Lena had flown over from London to be at his side crossed her mind. Then she realized. "He's going to be all right?" she said, searching the nurse's face.

"Oh definitely," the nurse said. "Come on and I'll bring you up there."

Maura and Emmet jumped up with shock and delight to see her. She went straight to her father. He was on an IV, there was a lot of bruising and bandaging around his head. "I look worse than I am, Kit," he said.

"You look grand to me," she said and put her head on his bed and burst into tears.

They knew that he was in no danger but they wanted to stay nearby. The hospital provided beds for them all. Kit lay under her rug and tried to sleep. Her mind was too full of images. There was the dance. The shock of Father's face with the bruises and cuts. There was Emmet crying that it was his fault, if only he had closed the door. There was Maura holding Father's hand with such love in her eyes that Kit almost had to look away.

And there was Stevie Sullivan's handsome face as he leaned out of the car, still in his dinner jacket but his white shirt open at the neck. "I'll see you later in the day," he had said. Later in the day.

Finally she fell into a sort of sleep.

When they got back to Lough Glass, they all hesitated before going up the stairs to the scene of all the violence the night before.

Sergeant O'Connor had said that the place would be tidied up a bit for them. And so it was. The broken chair had been removed. Someone had washed the blood from the sisal floor covering. There was a dark damp stain but at least it didn't look like blood. The place seemed gray and empty.

Maura opened a note that had been left through the door. "That's very kind," she exclaimed. Philip O'Brien from the hotel had invited them to come and have breakfast when they returned. They wouldn't be in the mood to cook anything for themselves. "Will we do that?" she asked Emmet and Kit. "It would give us energy to face the day." They knew she wanted to, so they agreed.

Philip hadn't expected Kit to be home. He was delighted to see her. "You missed the dance then?" he said with barely hidden delight.

"No, I heard afterward," Kit said.

"And how did you get down?"

"You're very good to ask us to breakfast, Philip," Kit said quickly.

Maura was agreeing, and soon the smell of bacon and sausages came from the kitchen. They sat by the window. Morning had come up and the lake looked very beautiful.

"Don't you have a wonderful view?" Kit said to keep the conversation going, and away from both her father's injuries and how she had got back from Dublin.

"Yes . . . I suppose like everyone here we get used to it. It's only because you and I have been in Dublin we appreciate it." Philip was trying to find a common bond with her, something which marked the two of them out as sharing something special. Even if it was something as ordinary as both living in Dublin.

"That's right, Philip," she said kindly. "In fact, if you were to cut down some of those bushes over there it would be really terrific, like a kind of panorama."

He had been suggesting that to his parents for more than six months, but as always they resisted change. He smiled at Kit, a warm smile of recognition. They were indeed kindred spirits. And perhaps he had been right to believe Sister Madeleine that she was not taken up with anyone else. After all, the party or dance or whatever it was couldn't have been that special if she had been able to leave it so quickly.

"I'll leave you to get on with your breakfast without having to make conversation all the

633

time," he said to them all, and Kit flashed him a grateful look.

As he left he heard Kit say to Maura, "Philip is the kindest man at any crisis. I always remember that."

If Maura realized what previous crisis Kit might be thinking of, she said nothing. "I promised your father that we'd go on as normal, but this isn't exactly normal, is it? A real hotel breakfast with lashings of everything."

They heard the sound of relief and happiness in her voice, the delight that their father would soon be coming home to them.

Sister Madeleine walked quietly along the lakeshore. She did not come up by Paddles' bar, nor by O'Brien's hotel. She waited until she had passed the Garda station. This way she would meet fewer people.

The small gray figure stood humbly by the desk. She had a packet. "He likes a bit of soda bread, Sean," she said diffidently.

"I'll make a note of it," he said flatly.

"Maybe we could both have a cup of tea and I could serve it to him. It would be like old times."

"You're not going into the cell with him." Sean O'Connor was appalled. "Whatever way he was when he was with you, he's like a caged animal now, he hits out at everyone."

"I'll be all right," she said.

He handed her two mugs of tea and put the buttered bread on a tray. He had never called the man by his name. "Listen, you," he called into the cell. "I've brought a friend of yours. She wants to come in and sit with you, the Lord knows why. If you touch her, you'll get such a pasting you'll have to be scraped off the walls."

The man seemed not to understand, then he saw Sister Madeleine. His eyes filled with tears. "You came to take me home," he said.

"I came to bring you breakfast," she said.

They sat in the cell, the nun and the wild man, sipping tea and eating thick slices of buttered bread. Sean O'Connor watched them from a distance. They talked about the trees by the lake, and the way a bit of the tree house had fallen down in the wind. Sister Madeleine spoke about the birds going away for the winter, they would be back next year. They always came back too.

She called him by his name, she said the word "Francis" so gently and with such respect that Sean felt ashamed of having called him *you*.

Francis replied, coherently now; you could understand his words. He asked about the old dog, he asked did she have trouble getting wood for the fire. He said he had got very wet and had wanted to sit by a fire.

"And did you go far when you left me?" Her voice was low and interested. There wasn't a trace of hectoring him or doing an investigation, but she knew that the sergeant was listening.

"I slept in the fields, Sister. It was cold and wet. I couldn't find anywhere. I got a pain in my head."

"And why didn't you come back to me? There was always a home for you with me."

"I'll go back now," he said eagerly. Like a child.

"And at night did you have to sleep in the rain?"

"I found a barn one night, but there were animals in it and I was afraid. And another night I was under a tree. I didn't go far. I was tired walking."

"But you found a kitchen and a range to sit at in the town, didn't you? In a house?"

"Yes." He hung his head.

"And why did you hit the good people . . . they wouldn't have hurt you."

"They were going to get me locked up again," he said.

"You hurt Mr. McMahon, he's a very good man. He's the one who got you the bandage and the throat sweets and you hurt him."

"I was frightened," he said.

"Poor Francis, don't be frightened." She held his hand. "Fright is only in our heads."

"Is it, Sister?"

"Yes, it is. I know that, I feel it in my own head."

"Am I not coming home with you?"

"No, you'll be taken where people can look after your head and take a lot of the fright out of it. I wasn't good at doing that." She stood up.

"Don't go," he pleaded.

"I must. I have a lot of things to do."

"My bag of things, it's in your house."

"Sergeant O'Connor has it. He found it when he came to tell me you were here."

It was a slight bending of the truth, Sean O'Connor observed. He hadn't found it, the hermit had gone to find it for him, but he un-

636

derstood. She had to leave Francis with the belief that she had been faithful to him.

"Will you come to see me?" he asked.

"I'll be thinking about you, and praying for you. I'll think about you every single day, Francis Xavier Byrne, so I will. Wherever I am."

"You'll be in your cottage, won't you? For when I get better."

"I'll be thinking of you wherever I am," she said.

After Mass everyone crowded around the McMahons; the whole place had heard the story of the night before. The good wishes to Martin were overpowering.

Through the crowd Kit caught sight of Stevie Sullivan. Dressed now in his brown belted coat and wearing a tweed cap, he looked a different person. He was talking to a group of men. It was a few minutes to opening time. They would walk together down Church Road and turn into the main street, then they would move to Foley's bar or O'Shea's, or even Paddles', to do the kinds of deals that he had told her about.

He wouldn't appreciate her coming over to join him now. Their eyes met. She smiled and waved but made no move to join him. He excused himself for a minute from his group and moved over to her.

"He was fine?"

"Exactly as you said. Go on back to business, no rest for the self-employed! And thanks again, Stevie. I'll never forget."

She could feel his eyes still on her as she moved back to Maura. There was a hooting of a car

637

horn. Peter and Lilian Kelly had come to take them to lunch.

"I wanted to go back in to see Martin," Maura protested.

"I've been on to the hospital. He's having a doze, better let him rest. You can go in during the afternoon. Come on, all of you pile in."

"Seven of us in one car?" Maura laughed at the idea.

"Why do you think doctors have station wagons?"

Emmet and Anna looked at each other in a guarded way. "Did you like the pictures, Emmet?" Anna asked finally.

"Yes, but it's rather gone out of my mind now with everything that happened since," Emmet said.

Anna was instantly sympathetic. "Yes, that was stupid of me. It must have been an awful shock. Were you frightened?" There was a lot of warmth in her voice.

Kit could see Emmet responding. Stevie Sullivan had been right about one thing. Anna Kelly was a bright little thing, not just a pretty face under a mop of blond curls.

After lunch at the Kellys', Kit went up to Clio's room. "What's wrong, Clio?" she asked.

"What do you mean? Don't come this nanny bit with me. What should be wrong?"

"You look very fed up."

"Well, I am fed up. My best friend doesn't invite me to her party. Then Michael gave me a lift home last night and bloody Anna was down there behaving like some kind of dervish spitting fire at us, and he had to go back to Dublin without . . . well, you know, without coming up here."

"Jesus, Clio. You were never going to go to bed with him in your own house."

"There would have been time before the others came home from the Golf Club."

"You must have been off your head. Thank God Anna was here. You must be losing your marbles."

"I've probably lost my boyfriend."

"Well, he can't be much of a loss if he's only staying round because of the pouncing."

"It's not just pouncing. He could pounce on anyone in Ireland. It's me he likes, and also pouncing on me." Clio seemed very aggrieved.

"Well then, he'll wait until you're free to pounce, which would appear to be most of the time."

"God, you sound like Mother Bernard."

"No, I'm not. I'm just hoping you don't get caught. Honestly, I'm out for your good," Kit said spiritedly.

Clio was a little reassured. "Yes well, maybe you are. I don't know, Kit. I don't. It's so bloody confusing. Do I ring him and say sorry about this little hiccup, or does that look pleading and pathetic? Would it be better to say nothing and hope he'll come back?"

"Lord, isn't that the question!" Kit had been pondering exactly the same problem about Stevie Sullivan. She must leave the next move to him, but suppose he didn't make one? What then?

"Remember in the old days we used always

go down to Sister Madeleine and ask her about things like this."

"Not exactly like this," Kit said.

"No, but she always had some sort of answer," Clio said.

It was an idea. Kit decided that when Maura went to see Father this afternoon she would go down on her own and talk to the hermit.

There was something different about the place. A lot of the old boxes that had held various animals in their different degrees of convalescence were gathered in front of the door. Inside, the house had changed too. Almost all the few possessions that Sister Madeleine had were laid out on her kitchen table. An old kettle, the three cups, the tin that held biscuits or cake.

The little can that she kept the milk in was there, a few plates, one or two little boxes. Sister Madeleine was in the bedroom looking around.

"Are you all right, Sister?" Kit called.

"Who is that?" The voice sounded flat and dead, not like the usual enthusiasm that greeted any caller.

"Kit McMahon."

"I'm so sorry, Kit." Sister Madeleine stretched out both her hands. "To the end of my life I'll pray for you and your family that you'll get over this, and understand."

"But he's going to be fine, Sister Madeleine. I saw him last night and this morning. He'll be out of hospital in two days."

"That's good surely. That's good." The whole place had changed. Sister Madeleine looked unbelievably as if she were packing, as if she were closing up her cottage and going to move somewhere else. "He was a poor man out of his mind, you know. He should have been in a mental hospital. They'll put him back in one."

"I know, I know. Clio's father told us."

"He didn't know what he was doing. It doesn't make it better on your poor father, or poor Kathleen Sullivan . . . but that's the only way we can look at it. His mind wasn't right."

"Was it the same man who hit Mrs. Sullivan and stole the things from the garage?"

"Yes, didn't Sergeant O'Connor tell you?"

"No, no. He told us nothing . . ."

"He will, everyone will know."

"But where was he between? That was ages ago, months ago."

"He was here, Kit. Here in your tree house."

"*What?*" Kit couldn't believe it.

"I minded him because he was sick, you know. Just like the poor Gerald there with his broken wing." She indicated a bird that normally lived in a box but was struggling to walk outside.

"He was here all the time?" Kit asked.

"That's what I'm so sorry about." Sister Madeleine's eyes were full of tears. "While he was here he was safe, he couldn't harm anyone or come to any harm himself. But he wanted to go, and I never keep anyone if they want to go." She looked up at the sky, remembering birds that had flown off when their time had come.

"Oh Sister Madeleine."

"And if I hadn't kept him, minded him, been good to him, then things would have been different. He wouldn't have hurt your father, he would have been in a hospital now, the Sullivans would have had their money back . . . why did I have to interfere?" She sounded many years older and much more frail. She wasn't sure of herself anymore . . . there was a long pause.

"You did what you thought was right," Kit said.

"Even though it meant your father ending up in hospital. Suppose he had killed him. Suppose your poor father was dead. It would all have been my fault."

"It didn't happen."

"You have no hatred for me for playing God? For thinking I knew better than everyone else?"

"None. I could never hate you. Look at all you did for me — for all of us."

"I used to have good judgment. Not anymore." Her once piercing eyes seemed dim.

"What are you going to do?" Kit spoke in a whisper.

"I'm going away to somewhere where people will look after me, where I can be safe and obey rules and not be allowed all the freedom to make wrong decisions."

"Where will that be?"

"A convent. I know a place where they take in people like me. I could clean floors and help in the garden or the kitchen, and have my meals and a little cell."

"But you said you hated being with people and living to rules."

"That was then, this is now."

"How will you make arrangements, will you ring them or write to them?"

"No, Kit. I'll just go on the bus."

"You *can't* go away, Sister Madeleine. People love you here."

"Not after this, they won't. The person who sheltered the villain who attacked Kathleen Sullivan and said not a word, then let him loose to attack Martin McMahon. Love turns to scorn very quickly."

"Please don't go."

"I have to go, Kit. I'm just so glad you came in to say good-bye."

"But there'd be a procession of people coming to say good-bye if they really thought you were going. In fact, they wouldn't let you go." Kit's eyes were blazing.

"If you want to be my friend, Kit, you won't tell them."

"Have you any money, any cash to tide you over?"

"Yes, your mother sends me English five-pound notes from time to time."

Kit looked at her openmouthed. Sister Madeleine had never acknowledged that she knew the identity of Lena Gray.

"My mother . . ." she began.

Sister Madeleine took no notice. "She doesn't say it's from her, but I know. It just says *For Emergencies* and this is an emergency."

"People will be so hurt, Sister. They've come down here time after time, they've told you their life stories, and you leave without saying good-bye."

"It's the best."

"No it's not. What about Emmet, for example?

You taught him to speak, to read, to love poetry. What about Rita, when she comes back to Lough Glass and comes to see you she'll find an empty cottage . . . I know Maura thinks the world of you, she wouldn't blame you for what happened to Father. And I heard awful Mrs. Dillon, who never said a nice word about anyone, saying you should be canonized . . . you can't walk out on everyone."

But Kit knew that her words were in vain. "When are you going, Sister?" she asked.

"This evening, on the six o'clock bus. I have a lot to do, Kit. May God bless you, and guide you." She paused and then spoke again. "May your mother find peace and fulfillment in the life she has. Is it a good life?"

"Only sort of," Kit said.

"It must have been what she wanted." Sister Madeleine's eyes were still misty.

"I could tell you all the story if you stayed . . ." Kit pleaded.

"No, I don't want to hear a story of someone else. People should tell their own story. God go with you always, Kit McMahon." She turned away.

Kit dashed out of the cottage in tears. She ran by the lakeside until she came to the path that went up by the hotel. Looking into the neglected grounds and gardens of the Central Hotel, she saw Philip sitting in the old summerhouse. It was rotting and needed great repairs and a coat of paint. He wore his thick coat, but still it must have been a cold place to sit and read.

"Can I come and join you?" she asked.

He closed his book. She saw it was one of their textbooks. "Will you be warm enough?" He was kind, out for her good.

"Imagine you reading this. That bonehead Kevin O'Connor hasn't even opened it."

"He doesn't need to with his hotels," Philip said.

"No. Life's not fair, is it?"

"Were you down with Sister Madeleine?"

"Yes, how did you know?"

"Well, you came in the side way, where else would you have been walking on a Sunday afternoon?"

"She's leaving," Kit said. And she told him the whole story.

There was a wide bit of road outside Paddles' bar. The bus came in about ten to six. The small figure of Sister Madeleine came up the lane. She carried a bag, a torn bag held together with twine. Somebody must have brought it to her once. It was one of the few things she had not been able to pass on to anyone else.

A lot of people stood around, many more than would have been traveling on the bus. Or indeed going into Paddles' bar. Or knocking on the back door of Mrs. Dillon's to ask her to give them a tin of beans or a packet of Gold Flake on the quiet. They had come to see if it was true that the hermit was leaving.

Clio was there, and Anna. Michael Sullivan, Patsy Hanley, Kevin Wall standing beside Emmet. Patsy Hanley eyed them speculatively as she sucked her finger, and tried to take in all

645

that was going on. There were some older people too, Tommy Bennet the postman, and Jimmy the porter from the hotel. They stood silently shuffling as if waiting for someone to say something. Something that would stop the hermit from leaving town.

Sister Madeleine seemed to be unaware of the people standing around.

Tommy Bennet stepped forward. "Where are you going to, Sister? I'd be glad to pay the fare."

"It's nine shillings, Tommy," Sister Madeleine said in a low voice. She didn't want the name of the place she was heading for to be said aloud.

"But you'll be back, Sister," he said, paying the fare and accepting the ticket for the hermit.

Shadowy forms in the background meant that other people were there too to see the departure.

"She can pay you with the money that came from Sullivan's garage," someone called. And there was a half laugh. Kit looked around her in disbelief. These were the people who had loved Sister Madeleine. How could they have turned on her like this?

The driver, who was not from around this part of the world, shivered. There was something happening here that he didn't understand, but he didn't like it. He saw various youngsters come and shake the hand of the small woman who was most probably a nun. He saw a lot of others hang back, and look at the scene as if they were watching a play.

Just before they heard the Angelus begin to ring out at six o'clock the conductor was in the bus, and had the driver ready to move. He looked

646

hastily up and down the long main street of Lough Glass. He didn't want to miss any stragglers by leaving too early, but he felt a wish to be gone. The bus went down the dark street.

And nobody at all waved good-bye.

CHAPTER NINE

James Williams had been debating for a long time whether he should invite Mrs. Gray to lunch. If he telephoned to make an arrangement she would certainly say no. He could hardly run into her casually again.

He decided to call at the agency. To say that he had been passing. He would say that he had found himself in the area and wondered if he could tear her away from her work for an hour. If she said no, then he would find another opportunity. He wanted to talk to her very much indeed, and lunch seemed the right time to do it.

The place was much bigger and smarter than he had been led to believe. Why did Louis live in a rundown street in Earl's Court if his wife ran a place as prestigious as this? And run it she did, there was no doubt about it.

She was well guarded from the casual passerby. He was offered an appointment. If he could wait for half an hour, Mrs. Millar might be free. There wouldn't be a chance of seeing Mrs. Gray he was told. Several times.

"But it's only for a moment," he begged, putting on a mock despairing face.

"In what connection?" the receptionist said.

"I am so anxious to take Mrs. Gray out to lunch," he said with his practiced charm. "I wonder could I ask you to go in and intercede on my behalf."

"Does she know you, Mr. Williams?"

"Ah yes, she does. But that alone might not make her say yes." He looked suitably humble and hopeful, and sat in the blue and gold waiting room admiring the professionalism that had been brought to bear on this place. It was all a credit to Lena. Millar had made nothing of it for years, and there was no other explanation for its success since Lena's arrival.

Lena came through the door. "James, what a surprise," she said, both hands out to meet him. He thought she looked thinner than when he had seen her last. And a little pale. Perhaps it was the dark red outfit that took the color from her face.

She was very smart in a red-check dress and jacket, her shoes were black and red . . . she was the role model for every young office worker. If they could look as good and confident as this at Mrs. Gray's age, then life would have been very satisfactory.

"It's twelve forty-five, I was passing the door . . ."

"You never pass doors," Lena said, laughing at him.

"I'd never pass yours. Say yes, a little lunch, I'll have you back well before two."

"I should think so too. We don't take huge long lunch breaks at Millar's, not like your world, James."

She hadn't revealed what his world was, neither did he.

649

They made small talk, polite banter, each accusing the other of knowing much more about wines than they claimed. Then the fish had been ordered, and the chat was over. A little silence fell between them.

"Have you any idea why I wanted to see you?" James asked.

Lena was thoughtful. He had lost his air of mock gallantry now, he seemed more serious. She decided not to be flippant. "Something about Louis, I imagine."

"Yes. It's not easy. Do you have any idea what it is?"

"No. Has he been unreliable? Not turning up?" Her eyes were troubled.

"No, no. On the contrary, he has been working almost too many hours. Surely you must have noticed that."

"Well he's away from home many hours, that's true certainly." She spoke without bitterness, with a sort of resignation.

"And has he said anything at all to you about a new post?"

"No, nothing at all." She looked up at him, bewildered. Louis always discussed work with her — his wilder ideas from which she had to turn him so gently and tactfully that he thought it was he who had made the decision; his disputes and indignations with fellow workers . . . they had talked them through, often late into the night. Lena would bring about a situation where Louis would see that confrontation would be a loser's game. Diplomacy meant playing at being careful.

But what new position could there be? He was manager of the Dryden. It must be somewhere else. There was no higher he could go where he was. God, had he entered into negotiations without telling her? Was there some plan afoot to go to Scotland? Had he decided not to consult her in case she threw obstacles in his path?

She looked at James Williams's face and tried to read it. He could read hers easily — ignorance and hurt.

But James Williams had a face that was hard to understand. A gently flirtatious smile seemed to be coming back to play about his lips. The admiring, distant stance that he always had with her had replaced what looked like being a serious discussion. "Well, I suppose he's absolutely right not to drag boring old hotel politics home with him . . ." His smile was broad.

But Lena thought he had deliberately decided to change the direction of the conversation. "What post exactly?"

"In hotels there are always debates, discussions, worryings about this post and that . . . it obsesses us, it's surprising we have any time to look after clients . . ."

Lena looked at him with respect. James Williams was very smooth. Look at how effortlessly he moved away from the topic once he realized that Lena knew nothing of any new position. She would play the same game and help him to change the subject.

"Tell me about Laura Evans, that friend of yours we met when we came to stay?" Lena said. She heard the question almost echoing in her ears, and could hardly believe she had asked it.

"Laura?" he said, in well-bred disbelief that she should have brought the name up.

She did not let her glance drop from his. "That's right." She was bright, eager, interested.

"Oh, I think she's fine. I haven't seen her for some time," he said.

"I see," said Lena.

He laid his hand on hers. It was a long moment. "It's a funny old life," he said.

"How do you mean?"

"You could have met someone like me, I could have met someone like you."

Now Lena decided to be the one who changed the direction. "Ah but the world is very small. We did meet eventually. Now, let's pay great attention to this very decorated dish of plaice I see coming toward us."

Her eyes were bright in her face, which he realized was indeed thinner and more drawn than before. James Williams wondered what it would be like to be loved so passionately and uncomplainingly by a woman like Lena Gray.

The afternoon seemed very long, which was rare. Normally the time flew by.

"I told you twice already we went to Julio's and I had plaice Florentine. Now, can you get on with your work and let me get on with mine." She rarely snapped at people.

Jennifer, her secretary, looked up startled. "Was it bad news, Mrs. Gray?" she asked.

"Why on earth do you think it was bad news? Now, might I add that at Millar's we actually publish guidelines for our clients. We advise office workers not to interrogate their employers about their private lives, especially having been advised to get on with their work."

She knew she had behaved badly. Why could she not have spent two minutes saying that Mr. Williams was a friend of hers and her husband's outside work, and said that they had a delicious lunch in a place where the waiters called you Signora? That way Jennifer, who was only being friendly, would have gone happily back to her desk. Why could Lena not have pretended to be calm as she did so often?

Because she didn't feel bloody calm, that was why.

"I won't be having lunch with you on Saturday, I'm a witness at Ivy's marriage," Lena told Jim and Jessie Millar.

"That's nice, a wedding's great," Jessie said, looking back affectionately at her own wedding day.

Lena shuddered, remembering.

"You're looking tired," Jim Millar said. "Perhaps we're working you too hard. Take a few days off for your friends' wedding."

"No, Jim. I'm better working," Lena said.

"You are tired, I said only the other day you were, and Jessie was saying it too."

Lena knew that tired meant old. People didn't know that's what they were saving but that was it all the same. Well, she was in her forties, well into her forties. What could she expect to look but old. This wedding was probably the last time

653

she would dress up and put on the style. After this she would wear sedate clothes, dove grays, navy with a little touch of white. Mother-of-the-bride outfits.

With a lurch she realized she would not be there at Kit's wedding, no matter what kind of outfit she wore. Plump, generous, spirited Maura Hayes would go to Dublin with her sister Lilian and buy something suitable, something that would see her through other social events during the years that followed. Unexpected tears came to her eyes.

"Are you all right, Lena?" Jessie was concerned.

"I'm fine, never better," Lena said with a smile that was much too bright.

"What'll we give Ivy and Ernest?" Louis asked. He was home just for an hour. It was all go at the Dryden these days. They had a function again tonight, he needed to be there to oversee it.

"You shouldn't have come all the way back," Lena said, solicitous that he was rushing too much.

"I wanted to see you, say hallo anyway."

"Well, will it be a late do?"

"Makes no sense my coming back, darling. I won't be out of it until four, and then start again at eight. No, better that I sleep there."

The old familiar dull thud came in her heart. "Sure," she said brightly.

Louis stood there smiling at her. He had taken his shirt off and he patted his stomach. "Terrible middle-aged spread . . . I'm pathetic," he said.

"Come on, flat as a board . . . you'd think you were playing tennis all day, you're so fit." She loved to praise him, and see the light dance back into his eyes.

"Oh, I don't know, I don't think I'd cut much of a figure on the beach . . ."

"Let's go to a beach somewhere for our holidays next year," she said suddenly.

He looked caught unawares. "Who knows where we'll be next year?" he said.

"Exactly, we could go somewhere smashing. I'll start looking up brochures."

"Yeah, well, we'll talk about that later. Now let's think what we'll give love's young dream downstairs."

She wished he didn't make such fun of their ages. When she and Louis got married someday they too would be old. When they got married.

He was fastening his clean shirt and looking critically at his face in the mirror. She knew with a certainty that they would never marry. Why had she kept this foolish notion, like a child's toy, in her mind? She also knew that he was about to start an adventure tonight. Or perhaps he was in the middle of one. She knew the signs by now.

"I thought we'd get them a mirror, a nice antique mirror," she said. She heard her voice as if it were coming down a tunnel.

Louis smiled at her. "Would there be room for it on the wall, with all Ivy's rubbish?"

"Oh yes. They're doing the place up, haven't you noticed?"

"No, I didn't see any difference." He hadn't been into Ivy's since the night he had taken over her little celebration for them.

"I think they'd like it."

"Sure, get it then, as long as it's not too dear."

He wouldn't pay a penny toward it, nor would he ever know that her real present to Ivy had been an outfit, a maroon velvet suit, and a hat to match. She had arranged a facial and a hairdo at Grace's salon. She had spent maybe ten times the cost of the mirror already.

Was Louis mean? He had always seemed the very spirit of generosity. When he had hardly sixpence left he would spend the coins he had on a bunch of violets. She couldn't bear to think of Louis as mean. Anything else but that.

"And you're all clear to come to the wedding on Saturday?" she said.

"Yes, I wouldn't miss a good feed and booze-up. Funny he's not having it in his own pub."

"No, that wouldn't be good for the people who remembered Charlotte, or for his sons . . . more tactful to have it elsewhere."

"But a bloody railway station! Really, Lena." He was so scornful, so full of ridicule. And yet she knew he wouldn't say anything of the sort. He would tell Ivy and Ernest that it had been an inspired thing to have a party in a pub by one of the big railway stations and then leave for a honeymoon. His pity and ridicule wouldn't be seen publicly. The public Louis was a man you couldn't fault.

"We have to be at the registry office at twelve," she said.

"I know, I know. I'll be there. I've arranged a split shift."

"You mean you have to go back to work after it?"

"Some of us have to work," he said, hurt.

She remembered James Williams saying that he worked almost too hard. She felt very uneasy. "I met James Williams today," she said suddenly.

Was it her imagination or did he look wary. "And what did he have to report?"

"Not much, mainly wine conversation, fish conversation. The fact that Laura Evans has gone the route of all other ladies before her, and probably after her."

"She was a drunken tramp," Louis said. "I can't think why a man like that bothered with her."

"Perhaps he was lonely."

"With all that money! You saw his house, how could he be lonely?"

Lena didn't agree at all. But he was on the point of leaving, she didn't want an atmosphere, a silly row over something that mattered not at all.

"Why was James talking about fish and wine anyway?"

"We were in a restaurant. He brought me to lunch, he was passing by."

"When was James ever passing by?"

"Funny, that's just what I said to him."

"So what was it then?" He really did look ill at ease.

But she was light. "Well, that's what I'd like to know. He looked as if he were going to tell me something, and then he seemed to decide against it."

"What kind of thing?"

"I haven't an idea. Maybe he has a new Laura Evans installed. Who knows? He went back to talking about fish and wine and all."

"And did neither of you talk about me at all?" His voice was light, but he was poised. She could sense it.

"Only to tell me that you work all the hours God sends."

He came over and put both his hands on her shoulders. He kissed her on the forehead. It was a solemn sort of thing to do, like a ceremony, or someone acting in a play. "See you at the wedding tomorrow," he said.

"Try to get some sleep," she said to his back as he ran lightly down the stairs.

She went in to Ivy as she had promised.

"Is he out or in?" Ivy asked.

"Out."

"Good, I have you for longer then." Again Ivy took out the wine-colored velvet suit. Again she thanked and blessed her good friend Lena. "Without you none of this would have happened. None of it," she said in a choked voice.

"Give over, you'll have me crying now."

"Ernest's out with some of the lads, we can have a drink, you and I."

"Don't tell me you're still meant to be on the wagon?" Lena laughed.

"Ah yes, but wait till I get my lines, as they say. When I'm a Mrs. again, then I'll introduce alcohol slowly back into our lives." They raised a glass to the future.

"And what are your plans, Lena? You who sort

out everyone else's life."

"I don't know. Louis and I were talking about going to the seaside for a holiday next year."

"Imagine. That would be great!" Ivy was very impressed.

"It's not definite yet, of course."

"No, of course."

Lena longed to cry on her friend's shoulder, to tell her that she thought there was something serious afoot. Something which James Williams was about to tell her though he had chickened out at the last moment. Something she had read in Louis's eyes when she had spoken of the holiday next year. And when he had come and put his hands on her shoulders.

She couldn't think what it might be. What could be worse than the affairs he had hidden from her over the years? But this was the night before Ivy's wedding. This was no time to sit and drink and cry that there ain't no good in men.

"Do you think it's silly having the few drinks near the station?" Ivy asked.

"No, I think it's brilliant. You said Ernest doesn't want a big formal sit-down thing. This way it's a nice familiar setup that we all know and like. I've been in and arranged the sandwiches." She had also arranged a small wedding cake but that was to be a surprise.

"When I married Ron," Ivy said, "I had a girl called Elsie as my bridesmaid. I haven't an idea where she is. I don't know what happened to her."

"I don't know what's become of my bridesmaid

first time around either," Lena said. "I suppose she came to my funeral. I forgot to check." Her smile was a little watery.

Ivy always felt uneasy when Lena joked about the events of long ago. To her it was unfathomable that someone should have to pretend to be dead instead of getting divorced properly. "But I'll never forget you, Lena. I mean it. You're truer than any friend I ever had."

"I think this port is making you weepy," Lena said. "I think I'm going to have to side with your husband and keep you off it altogether."

"My husband," Ivy said in wonder. "Imagine, tomorrow I'll be Ernest's wife."

"It's all you deserve," said Lena.

Her heart felt like a cold, heavy stone.

א א א

The letter from Kit was three pages long. Lena's first reaction was anxiety. Why was she saying so much, was there something that had to be told . . . but as she skimmed it quickly it seemed to carry no terrible message.

Kit wrote about the man called Francis Xavier Byrne who had been the one responsible for the events in Sullivan's garage and how Sister Madeleine had harbored him as if he were a runaway fox.

She wrote very simply about how her father had been beaten but had recovered well.

I know you'd be glad to hear Maura looked after him so well that he's as good as new again, and back making jokes and laughing like always.

I tell you this because if you just read about it in the paper that you get you might think it was worse than it was. It's strange that you read news of Lough Glass still. I don't know what kind of things to tell you about the place.

The Hickeys have extended their shop. Mr. Hickey has taken the pledge and Mrs. Hickey says that this means with the money they save they'll own a fleet of butcher's shops all over the country. Sister Madeleine's house stands empty, the door swinging open. I went to see it last week, there were rabbits inside and a couple of very tame-looking birds I expect they thought she was coming back to feed them. The worst thing is that people say she was never any good, that she was more superstitious than saintly. I always liked her anyway and I'm not going to change.

Clio feels the same. I don't see a great deal of Clio these days. She's very much "in love" as she says with an awful fellow called Michael O'Connor, whose father owns a lot of hotels. He's very rich. His brother is in our class at Cathal Brugha Street and is even worse. I'm not "in love" with anyone yet.

Stevie Sullivan in the garage turned out to be much better than he looked as if he was going to be. His brother is still a monster though.

Some things haven't changed. Father Baily is the same, and Mother Bernard and Brother Healy. They were always like that I suppose and always will be. Farouk is the same, he doesn't mind Dad and Maura's dog, he just ignores it and walks loftily out of the room if the dog comes in. I don't know why I'm telling you all these things. I suppose I thought if you go every week to buy the newspaper you must still care about what's going on.

All the very best to you,
Kit.

Kit was pleased that she had written. She didn't know why she had changed the nature of her usual curt little notes. It was as if she felt somehow that Lena Gray must be lonely and it didn't cost much to write a few lines.

Kit,

I can't tell you how much I love to know what's going on. Anything you have time and energy to write is interesting. I'm deliberately making this a short note so that you will not think I am burdening you down with correspondence.

And you were quite right in thinking that I would be glad to hear how well Maura looked after your father. I was very happy indeed to hear that and to know of his recovery.

Love from Lena.

Lena did not sleep. At two A.M. she was wider awake than she often was in the middle of the day. She got up and made herself some tea. It didn't work. She had read that you should do some physical work like cleaning silver. That one was easy; they didn't have any silver. The flat was tidy. She always kept it immaculate so that he would never say they lived in a poky place. She wandered around, restless, opening cupboards and drawers. They were all tidy.

It reminded her of the time those years ago when she had been about to leave Lough Glass.

She had spent so long leaving everything so that it would be perfect. She wanted Rita to be able to dispose of her clothes for her. She had even got all her shoes mended so that they could be given away. How was she to know that they would think she was dead? Why had Kit taken it into her head to burn the letter?

She looked at the wardrobe where Louis's clothes were kept. They hung there, the jackets she had bought for him, the shirts that she took to the Chinese laundry each week, the shoes that she polished until they shone. "Oh nonsense, I'm doing my own," she had said the first time he protested, and he hadn't protested again.

Of course she had done too much for him. But if she had done any less it would have ended long ago. Long before now. She felt a chill. Why did she think it was ending now?

The phone was on the landing, the public telephone that any of the tenants could use. If she spoke in a low voice no one would hear her, no one would know her shame. She dialed the Dryden Hotel. A voice answered. She knew it was the night porter. "I just wanted to inquire about tonight's function," she said.

"I beg your pardon?"

"Just a quick question. What time do you expect it to be over?" she asked.

"I'm sorry, madam. There's no function tonight," the voice said.

"Thank you, thank you very much," she said.

She saw the dawn come over the city. She knew how to do small miracles with makeup, but not major miracles. Nothing that would hide black hollows in her face, nothing that would give a shine and sparkle to haunted eyes.

She remembered hearing a coal miner, who had managed to hack his way out of a pit disaster, saying on the radio: *I tried to think of something else, not the big thing. I wouldn't allow myself to believe that I might be dead, so I thought about the garden shed I was building, and I went through all the wood I'd need and the nails and the roofing. It saw me through.*

That's what she would do, Lena decided. She would throw herself so much into Ivy's wedding that there would be no time to think that her own life might be about to end.

She made a pot of tea, and toast with honey, and brought it down to Ivy.

"I don't believe you." Ivy's delight was so great she didn't notice the hollows and lines in the face of her bridesmaid. Anyway on a wedding day people only look at the bride. "You're going to have every single thing you want today," Lena said, her smile so wide it made her face ache.

She walked up to the Grace West Beauty Salon and handed Ivy over to their care. "I'll be back for you at ten-thirty," she promised.

"I think Louis Gray will be glad to see me off your hands. I'm taking up so much of your time," Ivy said.

"Oh don't mind about Louis."

Grace gave Lena a sharp look. "Do you want anything? A bit of a comb-out, eyeshadow?" she asked Lena quietly.

"No, it goes deeper than that." Her voice to Grace was bleak.

"You've been there before and back," Grace said.

"Not this time." They had moved away from Ivy's hearing.

"I don't believe you, I'd bet you five to one."

"I'm not a gambling woman . . ." Lena's voice was flat.

"Oh yes you are, you gambled on that man of yours."

"If I did I lost."

Grace said nothing.

"By the way, Ivy doesn't know," Lena said.

"Nobody knows," Grace said. "You're just overtired, imagining things."

"Yes, sure."

She went home and dressed. She made no telephone call to the Dryden to discover whether there had been a split shift or not. She put the film in her camera, she prepared four envelopes of rice in case other people might like to throw it as well.

She emptied the wastepaper baskets into a paper bag so that she could take it down and put it into the dustbin. There she found a printed paper with the times and prices of flights to Ireland. It was crumpled up and thrown away. But it was not something she had ever had. So many times she had thought of flying there, but she had never gone so far as getting a brochure with the times of the plane departures.

Louis couldn't have been thinking of going to Ireland without letting her know. It couldn't possibly mean that his latest fling might be someone from Ireland. That would be too hurtful to imagine. Or someone that he was taking to Ireland on a magic trip. Some girl that he was going to impress with his fairytale ways in the Emerald Isle. She left it in the basket, just where it was, and straightened up her back. This day was going to be very long and very hard.

And now it was almost time to go and collect Ivy.

Ernest was nervous too, and his friend Sammy was no help. Just a stream of jokes in rapid-fire delivery. Nothing reassuring. Nothing to calm the nervous Ernest down and tell him that it was a few words said at whatever volume he wished to say them.

"I feel such a fool in front of all these people," Ernest complained.

Lena wanted to smack him very hard.

There were going to be sixteen people there altogether. All friends who wished them well. His two sons had accepted that Ivy would now be his wife. They would be there. He had nothing to do, nothing to organize, all he had to do was be bloody grateful that Ivy saw fit to marry him.

Lena wondered was she becoming very anti-man. But that was not so. Mr. Millar was an angel. James Williams was a gentleman. Martin had been a sort of saint. Peter Kelly had been a good and loyal friend. There was so many around her who were giving. And Ernest wasn't all that bad, he was gruff and inarticulate, he didn't have the silver tongue of Louis Gray.

Louis, who would come and join them and lie his way into their hearts. When the day was over they would remember him and the lovely mirror he had given and the jokes he had told and how he had made people happy.

She saw that Sammy was perspiring heavily, the man really was nervous. These were timid people, she remembered, people who feared ritual and occasion. They didn't realize that they controlled it, and they could run it. They thought it controlled them.

"Well, are we ready for the road?" she asked the two men. "The taxi is outside the door." She had arranged that too. And paid for it in advance. Otherwise they might have been searching the streets of London for one when they were all assembled.

"The bride?" Sammy said, as if he had only just thought of her as an essential part of the undertaking.

"Is in the bedroom. She'll come out when we're all set to go." Lena went to fetch her. "You look absolutely lovely," she said. "You never ever looked better."

Ivy's lined face lit up with pleasure. Her hat was at an angle, her cream and maroon scarf was tied jauntily. She looked years younger and about four social classes higher than she looked normally. She was the kind of lady you might see coming out of the Ritz Hotel.

Ernest and Sammy looked at her in awe. That was Lena's reward, the pure undisguised surprise and delight that their Ivy had smartened up so well. And the slight fear that they might not look her equal.

"Where's Louis?" Ivy said. As almost anyone who had ever met Louis always said.

"He'll meet us there, he has to get away specially." She linked Ivy's arm and escorted her out to the taxi. "Caxton Hall please," she said at the top of her voice, so that nobody could be in any doubt where they were heading.

Louis slipped in beside Lena just before the ceremony. He smelled of lavender soap. Of course, they could have lavender soap at the Dryden. He smiled at her warmly. "You look gorgeous," he said appreciatively. The tan and cream outfit had cost a lot, but she could wear it for giving lectures, for meeting important new clients. For the many work engagements that stretched ahead of her as her future. "Sweet little hat," he whispered.

The function might have been canceled. And he might have had to stay and work on late anyway so that it seemed a waste of time to come home. Don't ask, Lena told herself. Leave yourself that escape route. You can always think it. If you ask then you'll know. "How was the function?" she asked before she could stop herself.

"Don't ask," he sighed, rolling his eyes to heaven. "Interminable, I suppose that's the best way to sum it up."

"What was it, a conference, a golden wedding or what?"

"A crowd of salesmen on the piss."

"Still, it's good money for the hotel."

"I'm getting a bit sick of doing things so that the hotel will make money."

She looked at him. This was her cue to soothe him, persuade him to stay, tell him what a good position it was, how highly they thought of him . . . how unwise it would be to make any move.

This time she did it differently. "Well, you should move, Louis."

"What?"

They were whispering, waiting for the little group to assemble itself. Lena should be up beside Ivy. "Don't let them use you, take advantage of you, there must be some new positions coming up. You should think about them seriously."

He was staggered. "But I thought you would . . ."

"Never assume you know what I'm going to do or think . . . which reminds me, I'm meant to be a witness here."

With perfect timing at the arrival of the registrar she went to stand beside Ivy and Ernest and Sammy, and take part in a ceremony which felt as if it were a million miles away. Like a little pinpoint down there on earth. Far below where her mind had gone to try and take in the whole situation.

Once the formal bit was over, Ernest and Sammy relaxed to the extent that Lena thought that the couple might never leave on their honeymoon. The pints were bought, the brandies-and-gingers. Plates of sandwiches circulated in the corner of the pub that had been reserved for them. Passersby came to wish them luck and were offered a sandwich and even a drink for their trouble. Then the little cake came in and Lena photographed them cutting it.

She took some time to pose this picture. It would be the one on the wall. She straightened Ivy's hat and Ernest's tie. She even got them to put their hands together on the knife so that it looked like a real wedding picture.

"I'm surprised you didn't have her in white with half a dozen trainbearers," Louis said under his breath.

Lena flashed him a smile as if he had said something warm and encouraging instead of sneering. Ivy was very quick on the uptake, she would notice if Lena glowered.

Then they asked the barman to take a group picture and the bride and groom ran in a shower of rice across the station. They were going to spend three nights in a town thirty miles and one hour from London. Their friends waved them good-bye from the platform. The pubs were closed now, the little group wandered back through the barrier.

The good-byes were lengthy, Sammy wanted everyone to come to a drinking club he knew down in the City but their hearts weren't in it. Lena knew that she could have invited them back to the flat, a couple of bottles of wine would have kept the party going until opening time. But she had no intention of doing it. Not for Ernest's two sullen sons, not for Sammy and the handful of people who couldn't organize anything for themselves.

With huge regret she said she had to go back to work and she dragged Louis away with her.

"You don't really have to go back to work?" he said.

"No, but you do. I wanted to get you out of it without having the lot of them descend on the Dryden."

"I don't have to go back to work," he said.

"You said you had a split shift, didn't you?"

He looked at her searchingly to see was he being tested. "My God, of course I did." He hit his forehead.

"Well now, who's a good secretary to you then?" She was playful.

"I work too hard, Lena," he said.

"I know you do." She was insincere but he wouldn't know it.

"Maybe you're right. Maybe I should leave the place."

"Not in the middle of a Saturday split shift. Wait till there's something better on offer. You could do any job." They had walked as far as a tube station by now.

"Where are you going?" he asked.

"Well, if you have to go to work so will I. It's no fun without you at home."

"Do you really think that?" He looked troubled.

"Come on, handsome, you know I do." She kissed him on the nose and looked around once to find him still standing at the top of the steps looking after her as if there were things to be said but he hadn't said them.

Lena picked up the post. It always seemed a total luxury to her to have a postal delivery on a Saturday. Imagine if there had been such a thing in Lough Glass. Mona Fitz and poor Tommy Bennet would have had a fit if anyone had suggested it.

She divided it up expertly, marveling as she often did at the way the business had blossomed. When she came here first the mail had been hardly worth talking about and there had been only Jessie sitting bewildered and confused with overstuffed drawers full of papers that would take hours to sort out. If she had done nothing else in the years of life in London then at least she had built this monument to working women, their needs and hopes and chances.

She made herself a cup of tea, took off her wedding hat with its little tan feather, and her shoes. She sat back in her office chair and wondered what she would like to do now. She decided she would like to write to Kit. She must be careful, she thought. It was fragile, the peace between them; she must not rush the fences and destroy it again.

But this was the first time today that she had asked herself what she, Lena, would like to do. And she was going to do it. After hours of encouraging Ivy, calming Ernest, making conversation with Ernest's sons, taking pictures, throwing rice, smiling at everyone, telling Louis that she knew he had to go back to work, she bloody deserved to do what she wanted to do.

She wrote to her daughter about the wedding

she had just come from. About how well Ivy had looked and how nervous the groom had been, about the people in the pub who had all joined in and the passersby who had waved as the happy couple got onto the train. She wrote light-heartedly and read through it many times to make sure that there was no telltale sign of bitterness or self-pity. Nowhere in the three closely typed pages had she mentioned Louis Gray.

It was as if he did not exist.

"Hello Maura, it's Kit."

"Oh Kit. I'm so sorry, your father's just gone down to Paddles' with Peter. He'll be so sorry you wasted your money on the phone."

"Will you come on out of that, wicked step-mother. I didn't waste my money. Didn't I get to talk to you?"

"We're all fine here, he's totally back to his old self again. And Emmet's cheerful too, head down studying hard. You won't know this house when you get back at Christmas."

"Is Emmet there, Maura?"

"No love, you've missed him too. He's gone to the pictures with Anna. They seem to be pals again, really they're as bad as you and Clio used to be. How's Clio, by the way?"

"I don't see her that much, Maura, but she's fine."

"Ask her to ring home a bit more, will you? I feel ashamed telling Lilian that you ring twice a week, it's like I'm boasting."

"So you should, you're much nicer than Lilian," Kit said.

"Stop that. Do you want me to give them any messages?"

"Yes. Tell Father that his only daughter was distraught to hear he was out drinking his skull off, and tell Emmet I'm keeping my promise."

"I don't suppose I'm going to be told what promise."

"No, but he'll know."

"You're a great girl, Kit."

"And you're not the worst either."

"Clio, will we go out for chips?"

"Lord, who stood you up that you have to phone me as a last resort?"

"Did you go to special classes in how to be charming, or did you just read a book?"

"Sorry, I'm in bad form."

"Would chips help?"

"When did they not?"

"This is Philip. Kit, I was wondering would you like to go to the pictures. Normally like, you know the way people often go together."

"I know the way people go to the pictures, Philip. But I can't, I've just said I'd meet Clio for chips."

"Oh." He sounded very disappointed.

"Come with us if you like," she offered.

"Won't you want to giggle and laugh?"

"No, we're too old for that now. Come with us."

"It would make life so much easier if you fancied Kevin O'Connor," Clio said.

"I told you what I felt about him, I even told him by solicitor's letter, for God's sake. There's no use going after that particular fantasy."

"A person can wish," Clio said.

"I told Philip O'Brien he could join us, he seemed a bit at a loose end."

"Of course he's at a loose end until he can take you to the Happy Ring House and buy you a miserable small diamond and chain you to his side."

Kit laughed. "Where on earth is Michael? What has he done to bring on all this fit of the miseries?"

"He wants me to go to England with him for Christmas and New Year. His sister's having a big party or something."

"Well, isn't that great."

"They're not letting me go."

"Oh ask them nicely, Clio."

"No, it's a brick wall. And Aunt Maura is in it too, up to her eyes in it."

"But you're grown up. They'll have to see that."

"They don't see it. It's just an ultimatum. We expect you to come home to us for Christmas and New Year, Clio, like any nice girl from any nice family would do." Her face was full of tragedy.

"He won't take anyone else," Kit consoled her.

"But it makes me such a fool. The one time he does see my home it's got that mongrel Anna sitting hissing insults at him in the kitchen, now he hears that they're such jailers they won't let me accept a perfectly reasonable generous invi-

675

tation to a friend's house."

"Have you told him that you're not allowed to go?"

"No, I'm too ashamed. I'll pretend to be sick or something, or I may just go."

"You won't do that." Kit knew Clio well enough to realize that she wouldn't defy her family this way.

"No, I want to have some kind of family left to present him with when we get engaged."

"You really will get engaged, the Happy Ring House and all?" Kit was surprised.

"Oh, eventually, not yet. Not the Happy Ring House."

Philip came in.

"We're talking about the future," Kit said.

"Shut up," Clio said.

"I knew you'd have things to giggle about," Philip said defensively.

"Giggle?" Clio said. "I haven't giggled in years. Will we have double chips?"

"Yes, and cappuccino," Kit said.

"I want your advice." Philip had never asked their advice before, he had always offered it. They leaned forward, interested. "The floor in the Golf Club is banjaxed," he said eventually. Clio and Kit looked at each other mystified. "Banjaxed completely," he confirmed. "So you see, they won't be able to have their New Year's Eve Dinner Dance there, and I thought . . . well, I thought I'd try to have it in our hotel. In the Central."

"In the Central?" cried Clio and Kit in such disbelief that Philip felt defensive.

676

"At least the floor isn't subsiding," he said, hurt.

"No of course it isn't." Kit felt they should look less astounded. "But a dance, a dinner dance."

"The dining room is very big," Philip said. It was indeed, a great gloomy barn of a place. Kit had only eaten there once, the day Philip had invited them for breakfast. Despite all Maura's praise it had seemed a cheerless kind of room. "And the band could be up in the bay window. We could have the curtains pulled back and if there was a moon the lake would look great."

"They might all freeze to death watching it though," Clio said.

"Philip would get proper heating," Kit said.

He gave her a grateful look. "Yes, but I've only a few weeks. I'll have to tell the committee in the Golf Club that it can be done, and that it will be right . . ."

"They might take a bit of convincing," Clio said.

"It's your father, Clio, and yours, Kit. They're kind of the ones who could make it happen." The girls were silent. In neither home had much good ever been spoken of the Central Hotel. "And there's no floor, remember that."

"They might mend their floor rather than go somewhere different," Clio said.

"No, there's going to be a court case and all about their floor, the fellows that put it in gave them a guarantee and now it's falling to bits . . ."

"What do your parents say?" Kit cut through all the inessentials.

"They don't know yet."

"They'll say no," Clio said.

"Well, they will at first, but they might say yes later."

"Six weeks after the dance is over." Clio saw no good in anything or anyone in Lough Glass.

"So we must make them see it would be a great thing," Philip said.

"Who's this 'we'?" Kit asked suspiciously.

"Well, you, Kit. You could help me, I mean you're nearly qualified too, and you got such good marks . . . and if they hear you saying it could be done they'd believe you more than they would just me. No one ever thinks their own children grow up."

Kit was thoughtful. There was the danger of being drawn into something which was doomed from the start. Who wanted to lock horns with Mr. and Mrs. O'Brien?

Philip looked so full of hope.

And wouldn't it be wonderful if it worked. A real glittering dance on their doorstep. A dance where she and Stevie Sullivan could whirl around together under colored lights. Where Emmet could get together with Anna Kelly again. Where Philip could show his gloomy parents that he was indeed a grown-up man with ideas of his own.

"Well?" he said, hardly daring to let out his breath.

"I can hear the tinkle of trays of very small stones at the Happy Ring House," Clio murmured to her.

"I think it's a great idea, Philip," cried Kit. "And this will solve all your problems too, Clio."

678

"How's that?" Clio was suspicious.

"If there was a great dance that we'd all be helping at, a great smashing gala affair . . . then you could ask the magnificent Michael to come to that instead of you going to England."

"It wouldn't work . . ."

"Yes, it would." Kit warmed to the idea. "And I'd ask the awful dreadful Kevin too, just to make a party out of it. Oh stop looking at me like that, Philip. You know I can't stand Kevin, it's only to be sociable and make it good for Clio."

Clio was beginning to see the possibilities. "Where would they stay . . . ?" she asked.

"At the hotel," Kit said.

"I'm not sure if they'd think . . ."

"The hotel will be terrific . . ." Kit insisted.

"It's only a few weeks," Philip said in a panic.

"Then we've got to work very hard. On everybody."

"Everybody?"

"Yes, Clio's got to tell her parents and I've got to tell mine, and we'll get your father enthusiastic and awful Mrs. Hickey, she's a great organizer."

"She's not in the Golf Club though, is she?" Clio found a flaw.

"No, but she'd love to be in with that crowd so she'll work like the divil."

"When will we start?" Philip's eyes were shining now.

"This weekend. We'll all go home on the train on Friday night. They won't know what's hit them."

"I don't think Dan would be able to take on

the Golf Club Dinner Dance," Kit's father said. "Haven't you always said yourself that the place smells of stale gravy?"

"I've got a few weeks to get that smell out of the place," Kit said. "Oh, go on, Father, be enthusiastic. It's people like you and Clio's father we need to push it that way."

"I'm not the leading social light in the town . . ."

"No, but you could bring all the Golf Club crowd with you . . . otherwise it'll all be in the big town in some well-known place and the poor old Central will never get a chance to show what it can do."

"You've always said that the best thing it could do was fall to the ground." Martin was shaking his head at the complete change of attitude.

"But I've grown up a bit. I want something that will be good for Lough Glass. And for Philip. He's been my friend for years."

Maura intervened. "It would be much handier, Martin, if it could be here . . . and wouldn't it be lovely if we were all there. Emmet's keen to go, and Clio and Anna . . . it would be a family outing for us rather than just the four oldies up in the Club."

"And you can't be in the Club anyway because of the floor," Kit said.

"Well, I'd be very glad to give Dan and Mildred the turn . . . but do they want to? I mean they never want to do anything new."

"If they thought that all you lot were coming . . . the quality . . . they'd agree."

"We're not the quality," Martin said.

680

"No, but we're as near as it gets in Lough Glass," Kit sighed.

"Will we help them, Philip, Kit, and Clio?" Emmet asked Anna.

"I don't want to do anything to help Clio. I'll take part in anything at all that might lead to her downfall," Anna said.

"You don't mean that."

"Oh but I do. Just because you get on with Kit doesn't mean it's the normal thing to do."

"I know." Emmet did know. Very few people had a sister as marvelous as Kit. Someone who promised to help him and did. She had been very successful indeed at distracting Stevie Sullivan's attention away from Anna Kelly.

Emmet thought that Kit was reasonably good-looking. Of course, being her brother it was hard to look at things objectively, but he couldn't understand why Stevie would feel drawn to her instead of the beautiful Anna.

But whatever Kit was doing it was working. "I hope it's not an awful bore for you," he had said to Kit.

"No," Kit had assured him. "I'm quite enjoying it actually. But don't assume it's working totally. I wouldn't rush in there to Anna, you know."

"You're right," he said sagely. And he had been cautious.

He could see that Anna was still hanging around hoping that Stevie would be available, but he always seemed to be in Dublin these days, she grumbled.

"Never mind, I'm sure he'll be around at Christmas." Emmet was encouraging.

"Yes? Well, I hope so."

"So you'll help in the dance . . . it's a place you could go with him."

Anna hadn't thought of that. It was indeed a heaven-sent opportunity, a glittering dance on their doorstep. She began to think of what she would wear. "You're very kind, Emmet. I really appreciate it, what with you fancying me and all that."

"That's all right." Emmet was courteous. "After all, you fancied me too for a while, maybe we might get back to the way we were, but I understand that's not the situation at present."

"You deserve someone terrific," Anna said. "Someone much more worthy of you than Patsy Hanley."

"Patsy's quite nice to talk to when you know her," Emmet lied.

Clio knew just how to play it. She wouldn't plead with her parents to support the Central's bid to get into the big time in terms of entertainment. Instead she put on the look of an early Christian martyr.

"Clio, sweetheart, please cheer up. We were looking forward to your coming home, now you just sit there as if the world were coming to an end."

"It is as far as I'm concerned, Daddy."

"We can't leave you off there to England with people we don't know."

"So you said. I gave in, you've won. But I'm

682

not expected to be happy about it."

"We all have a life to live, Clio. Your mother is very upset by you."

"And I'm very upset by her and by you. These are facts, Daddy."

"You'll have a good Christmas here."

"Sure."

"And perhaps your friend Michael would come here and see you, see us all."

"I can't invite him here; nothing ever happens in Lough Glass. You'd have to give a person a reason for driving from Dublin."

That night in Paddles', Peter Kelly heard about the plans that were afoot.

"I suppose we should support them," Martin McMahon said.

"God, this might be the direct answer from God that we were looking for." Dr. Kelly seemed very pleased. "Count us in, Martin, and if this doesn't put a smile on Clio's face nothing will."

Clio didn't sound enthusiastic.

"I thought you'd be pleased," her father said, disappointed.

"Yes, but it probably won't happen. You know all the old Golf Club fuddy-duddies won't think the Central is good enough for their precious party on New Year's Eve."

"It's not, it's a terrible hotel . . . you and Kit have always been to the forefront of saying what a desperate place it is." He was bewildered now.

"Things will always be desperate while old people don't make any move to change them," Clio said.

"Yes, I know that's your view. We've ruined

everything for you, but what are your lot doing? Tell me that, except sitting around complaining and sulking."

"I'd help Philip get the hotel into good shape if his awful old parents and everyone else's awful old parents didn't go round shaking their shaggy locks and saying that things should just stay as they were."

Peter Kelly ran his hand over his rapidly balding head. "It's very nice of you to refer to my shaggy locks," he said, hoping to coax a smile out of her.

Clio gave a watery smile. "You're not the worst, Daddy."

"And you all would like us to have the dinner dance there . . . even though we're crumbling old geriatrics . . ."

"Yes. The rest of us would be normal," she said.

"I hope you have a daughter yourself one day and you'll know how much you'd love her to praise you instead of always finding fault," he said, in a rare mood of admitting his affection for her. Normally they had a joky sparring relationship.

"I'm sure I'll be a terrific mother when the time comes," Clio said.

But she spoke with a slightly hollow note. She was five days late with her period, she fervently hoped the time to be a mother hadn't come yet.

"They won't come here," Philip's father said, sniffing.

"They've had many a year when they could

come, but they preferred their great ugly concrete barn of a Golf Club," Mildred said.

Philip gritted his teeth. He would not lose his temper. Part of a hotelier's training was to remain outwardly calm when inwardly seething. They had been told that often enough. He had to practice it often enough in the various establishments where he had done his practical work.

"They have nowhere else to go," he said.

"And we'd put ourselves out for one year, then they'd go back next year to their old shed out there." His mother felt very keenly the fact that she was not part of the Lough Glass golfing set. The fact that she didn't play the game seemed to her irrelevant.

"It could be such a success that they'd want it here next time, and so would other people."

"How would they know?" Dan O'Brien asked. "That it had been a success, if it was a success?"

"We'd take photographs. Send them to the papers, magazines even."

"You'd be off back to Dublin and we'd be left with the work of it."

"No. I'd come back, every weekend, and I'll be home for the Christmas holidays."

"And what would you know . . ." his father began.

Philip sounded weary, but he knew that Kit and Clio were having similar arguments in their families. "I don't know everything, but we're hoteliers, Father. All three of us, isn't that right, Mother? And if we're ever going to get a chance to do something different, a bit exciting . . . isn't this one being handed to us on a plate?" He didn't

685

know why or what words he had used but it worked.

They looked at each other, a flicker of life and enthusiasm in their eyes. You would have to be quick to see it, but it was there. "How will we heat the place?" his father asked, and Philip knew the battle had been won.

They had a little committee, and they met in the hotel. Kit took the minutes of the meeting in a big notebook, then she would type the notes up afterward and give everyone a copy so that they would all know what they had agreed to do. They sat in the freezing cold breakfast room, a square unattractive place only marginally touched by the small smoky fire that sent all its heat up the chimney.

They were very businesslike, even though dressed in their outdoor clothes to keep warm, Kit in her navy duffel coat and white angora scarf, Clio in her gray flannel coat with its peach-colored blouse showing at the neck. She had read that peach gave a good glow to the face. Anna in her tartan jacket, Patsy Hanley belted into her navy gaberdine coat that was too small for her and also not smart enough. She made a resolve to tell her mother that there was no point in being the daughter of the drapery if you ended up the least well-dressed girl in Lough Glass. Emmet in his thick wool polo-neck sweater and belted brown jacket. Michael Sullivan with his long dark hair below the collar of his gray overcoat. Not as good-looking as his elder brother, but one day, when the pimples were gone and his face and shoulders filled out, he might well turn into the same kind of heartbreaker.

The young people of Lough Glass determined that their New Year's Eve would be the kind of success they saw when they went to the pictures. The kind of happening that other people had and that they would have to create themselves if it was to come to Lough Glass.

Philip decided that he had to wear indoor clothes as some kind of act of faith in his hotel. It might be seen to be letting the side down if he too was dressed in a kind of lifeboatman's outfit that would make the place tolerable.

He was doing quite well as chairman . . . he seemed to know at the outset that he should never think of it as his hotel or his dinner dance, but as theirs.

"Have any of us ever been to anything up in the Golf Club?" he asked.

Nobody had. That was the first priority; they were to find out what aspects of the place had been good, and what had needed improvements. Everyone had a specific job to do. Even Patsy Hanley, whose mother wouldn't have been there, Philip was able to find her a responsibility.

Patsy was to discover what kinds of facilities they had in a ladies' cloakroom; were there mirrors, how many lavatories, did they hang their coats on a rail or did they have a lady who gave them cloakroom tickets? Would it be better to use one of the hotel bedrooms for this purpose? Patsy was to come back with her report on Sunday afternoon.

"How will I find it all out?" she asked.

"Research," Philip said.

"You'd be in the way of asking people things. You're good at chatting to people," Emmet said.

He noticed Anna Kelly jerk up her head as he said this. Then Emmet himself would be in charge of what the gentlemen would require. He would ask his father and Dr. Kelly and Father Baily and anyone who went to the Golf Club.

Clio was going to come back with her ideas on decoration. It was very important, the first look of a place. Her ideas would be put to the group and they would vote on what they could do and what might be beyond them. Clio was flattered that people thought her ideas might be beyond them. She made up her mind to look at magazines and study the thing properly.

Michael Sullivan and Kevin were deputed to find out how the front of the hotel could be altered so that it looked more splendid. Michael, because his garage had improved its appearance and secured troughs of plants and flowers to smarten it up, Kevin, because his brother was a jobbing builder, and the materials would naturally be bought from Wall's. They were to come back with an estimate.

Anna Kelly was to concentrate on curtains and lighting. Hers were to be practical suggestions, the matter of image was left to Clio. "How will I know what we should do with curtains until I know what the artistic designer has dreamed up for the whole hotel?" Anna was being heavily sarcastic.

Philip didn't appear to see it. "Ah but that's the hard part, Anna. Whatever you come up with will have to be sheer genius, there's no question of there being any money to coordinate anything with anything else . . . you're on your own." Anna seemed pleased by this.

Kit looked at Philip with admiration. He did seem to have the thing under control, and he was far more diplomatic than she would ever have believed. "What will I do?" she heard herself asking, almost too eagerly. After all, she had been the moving force behind it. "Will I just keep the notes?"

"Kit and I will do the food," Philip said. "We are the trained folk after all, and we want them to have a meal they'll never forget."

"They'll never forget the night anyway," Kevin said. "Most of them will be taken to the County Hospital with frostbite."

"My father's going to tell us by Sunday just how much he can afford to spend on storage heaters and radiators." Philip was unperturbed. "Will we meet here at three o'clock?"

And they went their ways, each with a dream. Clio, with great relief that motherhood did not seem to be imminent, was in high good humor. She thought about the New Year's Eve Dance. She would see that at least one of the Central's ugly plain rooms would be properly done up, one that would be away from prying eyes.

Patsy Hanley left happy. Emmet McMahon had made much of her in front of that stuck-up Anna Kelly.

Kevin Wall and Michael Sullivan wouldn't have admitted it to anyone but they were flattered to be part of something new. It hadn't been long ago since they were regarded as the young thugs who would have to be kept away from any function rather than invited in to help run it.

Philip was pleased with how it had gone. They were all offering to help. If it failed it would be a group failure, and Kit in particular would be at his side, win or lose.

Emmet McMahon knew that this dance would be the great opportunity to let Anna Kelly come back to him on his terms in his own town.

Kit McMahon and Anna Kelly looked over at the garage where Stevie was talking to a client. Neither of them would interrupt him during working hours. Both of them had huge hopes of him when the dance came to town on New Year's Eve.

Lena did not know how she had managed to survive the days after Ivy's wedding. How she had gone on acting normal to everyone? Someone had told her that chickens did this; if you cut off their heads they still ran around for a while, just as if they still had heads. Nobody said what happened then. They probably just fell over and died.

There had been so many discoveries in the past week. Things she had not set out to discover. And did not want to know. She knew that Louis must be about to leave the Dryden. That he was going to leave her and go far away. Sometimes she suspected that he was going to Ireland. He came in so rarely, often to pick up mail which had suddenly started arriving at the flat rather than at the hotel. She never remembered him getting any letters at home before. There were references to Ireland in the conversation. Not the Ireland of long ago that they had known . . . but today's Ireland. He never stayed the night. She never asked for details of functions or late shifts. It was as if they were both waiting. Waiting for the day when he would tell her.

Lena felt very frail, the thread that was holding her together was so fragile, it could easily break. When she saw the envelope from Kit so soon after she had written her heart turned over with fear. Please, may her daughter not say anything scathing to her. Not just now, not at this point.

Please, God . . . Lena said as she opened the envelope.

She realized it was a long time since she had asked God for something. Why should it work now?

Dear Lena,

That sounds a great wedding. It was like seeing a film, I could imagine everyone, especially the terrible Best Man.

I realize how much I have missed your letters from the time when you were just Lena, mother's friend. And I missed writing to you too, though these days there's hardly time to breathe let alone write. You'll never believe what we're going to do, sit down before you read this . . . we're going to try to have a glittering fabulous New Year's Gala at O'Brien's Hotel . . .

Hardly daring to believe her luck, Lena read

with shining eyes the tale of the hotel's transformation and the committee hard at work.

Even Clio is taking part, Kit wrote. *It's only because these terrible O'Connors that she is so taken with are going to be there. She thought they were going to be in London and miss it but once the almighty Michael said he was going to be present, then it all had Clio's blessing.*

Lena hugged herself and laughed aloud to read this. She could hear Kit's voice . . . just as she had been at nine, ten, eleven, twelve . . . always complaining about Clio's airs and graces, and yet always involved with her as well. The letter sparkled with life and enthusiasm. In the last paragraph it changed its tone.

You didn't mention that Louis was at the wedding. Don't feel that he can't be mentioned or anything. I wouldn't want you to think that he has to be cut out of what you tell me.

Warmest wishes always, Kit.

She couldn't tell Kit about Louis. All she had left in the world was Kit, and Lena was going to be some kind of person in the girl's eyes, not a worn-out, thrown-aside fool, which is actually what she was.

She read over and over and over her daughter's plans for the hotel. Some of them ludicrous, some of them well within anyone's power. She wondered how much money she had, she would love to have invested it there and then in a refurbishment program for the Central Hotel, Lough Glass. After all, hotels were doing very well in Ireland. Their time was coming.

Lena had reason to know this very well.

אאא

"We'll have to come home again next weekend," Kit told Philip.

"I can't ask you all to do that."

"It's only Clio and myself. The others are there already." They sat companionably in the summerhouse, which they had agreed to paint and surround with fairy lights for the occasion.

"Well, it's taking you away from whatever keeps you both in Dublin." He was a bit diffident. He was so much nicer than when he had acted as if they were foreign prince and princess, promised to each other from birth.

"Oh, better for Clio to come home, let me tell you. That eejit she is stuck on values her much more when she makes a move out of Dublin instead of waiting on his every move."

"And what about you?"

"I told you. I have no romances. Hand on heart, there's nothing to keep me in Dublin."

And she spoke the truth. Stevie Sullivan was home running his business every weekend. She made no move to contact him, but she was there like a sentinel in case he might make any step in the direction of Anna Kelly.

The O'Connor hotels all had a Christmas program. It was becoming quite a smart thing for a family to go and stay in one of their hotels. Everything done for you, wonderful atmosphere, people said. Those who said it didn't have the real spirit of Christmas were almost always those who didn't have the money to afford it.

"Will you be helping out at one of them?" Kit asked Kevin O'Connor.

"Jesus, no. I have enough work to do all term without taking that lot on in my holidays," he said.

Again Kit wondered how two boys could have been brought up in such a way that they seemed to have no interest at all in what was after all going to be their inheritance.

"So where will it be then?"

"My sister in England has a new fellow, a fiancé, I think — oh, heavy, heavy secrecy — but I gather the ring's being bought and we're all to go over there."

"Is he English?"

"I don't know. I suppose so." The O'Connors knew very little of each other's business.

"Do your father and mother approve?"

"I'd say they're so relieved that Mary Paula's getting hitched they don't care . . ."

"I'm sure that's not so . . ."

"But it is. She's getting very long in the tooth."

"How old exactly?"

"Wait till I see. It's always a gray area, but she must be nearly thirty. We're the two youngest by a lot, Michael and I."

"Little afterthoughts . . . how sweet," Kit said.

"Do you have a big family?"

"Just one brother." Kit had told him before but he hadn't remembered.

"Oh, very posh. Like Protestants, small families."

"Clio has only two in her family also."

"Yea, Michael told me there's a really frightful sister."

"She is a bit of a pain all right," Kit agreed. "Good-looking though. Do you like Mary Paula, the one in England?"

"I hardly remember her," said Kevin O'Connor. "She was okay, she always had friends round the place. I think she thought we were dead boring. She's only keen on us going over to England for this party so that she can field a team."

"You're not all mad keen to go then, are you?"

"No. I'm not particularly. Why? Are you arranging another party?" He moved closer to her.

"In a way I am. It's going to be fabulous, we've taken over Philip's hotel, everyone will stay there."

"But that's in the arse end of the world." His enthusiasm died.

"It's in my hometown, and Clio's, and Stevie's and Philip's. It's a beautiful old Georgian house, not a big ugly modern concrete block. We're going to have a fantastic New Year's Eve there. I was going to ask you, but if you're so dismissive . . ."

"I'm not dismissive." He was full of contrition now.

"Yes, well, maybe it's too late . . ."

"Will Michael be going . . . will there be a

crowd from Dublin?"

"I've no idea whether Michael will be going or not, presumably if he answers Clio the way you answered me he won't. But don't worry, we'll have plenty who will."

"No, you got the wrong end of the stick . . ."

"Listen, our New Year's Eve Dinner Dance can well do without the O'Connor brothers . . . just know that . . ."

He blustered for a while then went away to make a phone call. Kit smiled to herself. She didn't even need to listen to know who he was calling and with what advice.

"Listen, Michael. Kevin here. Did Clio say anything to you about a big dance in this god-forsaken place they live in? No? Well, ask her. And for God's sake be nice about it. Say you do want to go. We'll be staying in a hotel, it won't be like last time . . ." He paused. "Mary Paula won't give a damn. I'll stay for Christmas, that will be enough. Anyway, this will be a lot of fun."

"We must get spot prizes," Philip said to Kit.

"Of course we must. Let's ask Anna to collect them."

"Why Anna?"

"She's good-looking, she's kind of charming. People won't say no to her."

"You're good-looking, they wouldn't say no to you either," he said.

"Jesus Christ, Philip, I've got enough to do . . . let Anna loose on them. Anyway she's there the whole time, I'm not. Make it a point of honor that she gets a lot, say it out in front of everyone that she'll have a hard job extracting them. She'll kill herself."

"You don't like her, do you?"

Kit looked at him thoughtfully. She must be careful not to let anyone get this idea. "I'm still inclined to think of her as Clio's awful little sister at times. But usually I think she's terrific, that's why I suggested she'd be a good one to wheedle the prizes out of people."

"Stevie Sullivan thinks she's the bee's knees," Philip said.

"Go on, he's years older than she is."

"That's what I hear anyway," Philip said. He looked like his mother when he spoke like that, prissy, mouth pursed, a real village gossip.

"I hear Stevie Sullivan fancies everything that moves," she said. "But let that not detain us. We have a banquet to organize."

She took his arm companionably and Philip straightened up with pride. Everything was going his way at last. He had been right to take things slowly and not rush in foolishly. Here he was in Dublin with Kit's arm in his, making plans for his hotel, their hotel. It was exactly as he had hoped.

"The O'Connor boys will be coming down to stay over New Year, I gather." Maura spoke in that very overcasual voice she used when she was anxious about something. She was standing at the door of Kit's bedroom.

"That's right, they're going to stay in the hotel. Quite a few from Dublin are coming, Philip's giving us a special price."

"He should give it to you free after all you're

doing." Maura had seen the frenzied activity.

"It'll be great, everyone's really putting their hearts into it," Kit said.

"The O'Connors?" Maura said.

"Yes?"

"Clio's going out with one of them, isn't she?"

"Oh you know Clio, half of Dublin admires her."

"It's not just idle curiosity, Kit. I never ask you about your friends or Clio's."

"You do ask about the O'Connors though," Kit said.

"Yes, that's perfectly true, I do. And I'll tell you why." Maura's face had got a little pink. She stood in the doorway slightly at a loss.

"Oh come on in, Maura, sit down." Kit moved her notes and folders from a chair to make room.

"In the olden days I used to know their father, and I never liked him, but that's not the reason. Poor Mildred O'Brien is like a wet week and look at how well Philip's turned out."

"Yes, I know." Kit waited.

"Well, I was in Dublin last week . . ."

"You didn't tell me . . ."

"I just went for an examination, tests."

"Oh Maura!" Kit was stricken.

"No, please, Kit. This is why I didn't tell you. I'm a middle-aged woman, all kinds of bits and parts of me aren't working anymore, I thought it best to go quietly."

"And what did they find?"

"They didn't find anything yet, and probably may not find anything at all. Let me finish . . ."

"What were they looking for . . . ?"

"They were looking at my womb; I may have to have a hysterectomy. Apparently it's a great operation; you feel better than you ever felt after it, but it's a long way down the road. I didn't intend to tell you any of this, I haven't even told your father."

"You must let us share, we're your family."

"I know, and was ever anyone more grateful for the family they got than I am. But believe me that's not what I was going to say . . . you've wormed all this out of me. Now can I tell you what I wanted to?"

"Yes, go on . . ."

"When I was in Vincent's, it was just overnight you know, who did I meet but Fingers."

"Fingers?"

"Well, Francis O'Connor, the father of the twins."

"Was he in hospital?"

"Or visiting someone . . . anyway he was the last person I wanted to meet, I can tell you. And he was full of chat and wanting to take me off to the Shelbourne for coffee."

"Well, look at the antics you get up to from your sickbed in Dublin."

"I tried to get away from him but he insisted that we sit and have a chat over old times . . ."

"And?" Kit waited.

"And Kit . . . he's a very vulgar man, he always was and always will be . . . but he said, well, he as good as said, he implied . . ." Kit waited. "I can't remember his words exactly, I suppose I sort of deliberately didn't want to remember them, or to be talking to him at all, I had my own worries . . ." She paused.

"Poor Maura," Kit said sympathetically.

"And he sort of said, he as good as said . . ."

"Oh come on, what did he say, Maura?"

It did the trick. It shocked Maura into saying something at last. "He said his two sons were having their way with you and Clio, and they'd been invited down here for a week for more of it after Christmas, and he's very annoyed because he wanted them all to go to England to one of his other children who's just got engaged to someone, and is coming home to run one of his hotels . . ."

"He said *what?*"

"I knew I wouldn't say it right, but that's what he said."

Kit's face was white with rage. "Now, Maura. I'm going to tell you something that will cheer you up greatly. I am a virgin, I have never been to bed with anybody, but if the survival of the human race depended on it I wouldn't go to bed with that great misshapen oaf Kevin O'Connor."

Maura was startled by the strength of Kit's reaction. "I wish I hadn't said anything . . ." she began.

"Oh, but I'm glad you did, very glad." Kit's eyes flashed with anger.

"Perhaps we should leave it." Maura knew she had opened floodgates.

"No, I can't leave it. They made an undertaking, those disgusting creepy O'Connors. They signed a legal document promising not to tell any more of these lies, and now they've bloody broken it."

"They signed a what?" Maura was horrified.

"I sent Kevin O'Connor a solicitor's letter because he imputed unchastity to a woman, and he apologized and his father did and they paid me compensation for the slight on my reputation, and for casting aspersions on my virtue and possibly minimizing my marriage chances."

Maura's eyes were wide in disbelief. "Kit, you're making this up."

"I'll show you the letter from Fingers," she said, smiling broadly.

"A solicitor's letter! You consulted a law firm?" Maura felt weak at the shock.

"Yes, well, to be strictly honest it was Paddy Barry, you know, Frankie's brother, but it was on real solicitor's paper and it looked legal . . . anyway it frightened them to death and they paid up." Kit grinned with pleasure remembering it.

"You got a friend . . . a student . . . to demand money with menaces from the O'Connors. I can't believe I'm hearing this."

"Look what he said . . . look what Kevin O'Connor said! He said I was anyone's, that I'd do it with anyone and I'd done it with him. He told his brother, he told Philip O'Brien, he could have taken an advertisement in the *Evening Herald* for all I know . . . and I'm meant to ignore that and say it's just his little way of having fun?"

Maura had never seen Kit so angry. "No of course not . . . but . . ."

"But nothing, Maura . . . there are no buts in this. His father who paid out good money obviously thinks it's a tale worth telling and trots

it out to my stepmother . . . after all his undertakings . . ." She looked very determined.

"What are you going to do?" Maura asked anxiously.

"I may ask my lawyer to remind him of his
obligations." Kit sounded lofty.

"You and your lawyer will get caught," Maura
warned.

"Right. I think you are right actually. I'll tell
him I'm approaching him personally before placing it all in the hands of solicitors again." Kit
smiled at the challenge ahead. Her enthusiasm
and sense of outrage was infectious.

Maura began to share it. "I agree it is appalling
that he should be allowed to say such things about
you and Clio." Maura's eyes met Kit's for a long
moment.

"I'm fighting my own battles on this one,
Maura," Kit said. "Clio can fight hers."

And Maura knew without having to be told
that her sister's daughter would not be sending
any solicitor's letters.

She marked the envelope STRICTLY CONFIDEN-
TIAL.

Dear Mr. O'Connor,

*My solicitor would probably disapprove of my
contacting you personally but I am doing so because of family connections. You will remember
the letter you sent to me (copy enclosed) and
the undertakings it contains. Unfortunately
grave news has reached me that you spoke in*

*the very terms that caused my having to seek
legal redress in the first place, and you addressed
these remarks to my stepmother Mrs. Maura
McMahon (née Hayes).*

*I demand that you write a letter to my step-
mother at once retracting every word that you
said in this regard, and that you also give me
your assurance that I do not have to have re-
course to further legal action.*

*Normally I would have done this but my
friend Cliona Kelly is friendly with your son
Michael and I would not wish to make trouble
between the families.*

I look forward to hearing from you tomorrow,

*Yours faithfully,
Mary Katherine McMahon.*

"Kevin?"

"Is that you, Pa?"

"Turn off that bloody rock and roll and you'd
know who was on the phone. Do you do any
work or do you just fill your head with that jungle
music?"

"You don't often ring me, Pa," Kevin said uneasily.

"No, is it any wonder? You know this girl Mary
Katherine . . . ?"

"Who?"

"The McMahon girl from Lough Glass."

"Kit, yes. What about her?"

"What about her, what about her? Didn't I have
to pay out good money to shut her up when you
said you'd ridden her more often than Roy Rog-

703

ers rode Trigger . . . ?"

"Yes, but that's all over now, Pa. You know I told you there was a misunderstanding."

"I tell you there was a misunderstanding . . . is she cracked, off her head or something . . . ?"

"No, she's not, she's terrific. Why do you ask?" There was a silence. "What is it Pa? We apologized, well, I apologized and you paid and Kit accepted it and that was that. And we're quite friendly now . . ."

"Yes. Right." Fingers O'Connor saw that the blame must be entirely his. He had thought it would make that nice plump Maura Hayes more pliable. What a mistake it had been. "And this girl and her friend . . . are they the halfwits you're going to cancel the whole arrangements for Christmas to go and see, down in Bally mac Flash or whatever it's called?"

"Lough Glass, and it's only for the New Year. Ma told you. I'll be in London for Christmas."

"I can't wait," said his father, and hung up.

"Kit, it's Maura. I can't talk long, I'm ringing from work."

"Hello, Maura. Tell Stevie that the laborer is worthy of her hire, you're entitled to the odd phone call."

"He's out of the office."

"Do you have any results of your tests?" Kit sounded anxious.

"Perfectly normal — as I told you they would be."

"Thank God." Kit closed her eyes with relief.

"That's not what I'm ringing about. Kit, I got the most extraordinary letter from Fingers O'Connor."

Kit giggled. "I thought you would. I got one too."

"Kit, you didn't, you didn't . . ."

"That's it, Maura, I didn't. And I'm damned if that madman of a son of his is going to say I did . . ."

"Clio?"

"Hello, Michael."

"Can I come round and see you?"

"No, I've got loads to do. I'm trying to work out a plan for decorating a big barn of a room."

"Is this down in the hotel in Lough Glass?"

"Yes, how did you know?" She had said nothing to Michael about it yet, she wanted to be sure it was going to work before she began to persuade him.

"Kevin told me, and my dad."

"Yeah, it should be great."

"Why didn't you ask me?" Michael was aggrieved.

"You're going to be away in England, staying with Mary Paula, remember?"

"I don't have to, Kevin's not going."

"Well, then."

"Well, what? Why didn't you ask me?"

"You didn't seem to rate Lough Glass very highly when you were there last."

"That's because everything went wrong and your sister was behaving like an Alsatian with distemper."

Clio laughed. "That's good. I'll remember that."

"Can I come then? To Lough Glass?"

"I'd love if you would. I didn't want you to be bored, that's all."

"And Clio, another thing . . . you know Kit?"

"Of course I do. I've known her since I was six months old."

"I might not have been right about her and Kevin being at it like knives."

"I know you weren't right."

"Maybe we'd better not say that she was, you know?"

"I never said she was. Jesus, you didn't say it, did you?"

"This is becoming more like a police state," said Michael.

"You're telling me," said Clio.

Peter Kelly and Martin were in Paddles' bar.

"I see that Fingers O'Connor has bought a new hotel . . . that'll be his fifth," Dr. Kelly said.

"I wonder how he got a name like that." Martin McMahon was thoughtful.

"It's not a good one for a businessman, sounds as if he's into shady deals."

"But these names stick. Do you remember Arse Armstrong?"

They laughed like boys.

"Where is he now? Didn't he join the priesthood?"

"Oh, I think Arse is a bishop or something out in Africa. Maybe he wears a long white frock. You wouldn't know the reason for the nickname."

"Well, however Fingers got the name, it seems that everything he touches turns to gold. Our Clio seems very friendly with his son. We haven't met him yet, but apparently he's coming down here for all the Versailles Ball activity up in Dan O'Brien's."

Martin McMahon smiled. "Isn't it great that they all come home and seem so wrapped up in it. Our house is draped high and low in recipes and table decorations . . ."

"You're lucky, we have branches of trees in ours," said Peter Kelly.

"God, what's that for?"

"Search me. 'Decor' is the word Clio uses. Still, I'm happy she's not gone gallivanting with young O'Connor. Maura always gives me the impression that the father was a bit wild and his sons could be the same."

"Ah, Clio's well able to look after herself," said Martin McMahon.

"I hope so. God, it's one thing I couldn't bear, some fellow taking advantage of one of my girls. I'd kill them you know, not that I'm a violent man."

"When am I going to see you, Kit?"

"Well, Stevie, aren't you looking at me now?"

"I am for two minutes, then you'll be off down to your committee meeting in Dan O'Brien's mausoleum."

"Never to be called that again . . . 'all is changed, changed utterly.' "

"That's not fair, I haven't read Yeats."

"At least you knew it was Yeats."

"So where'll we go and when?"

"You could take me out to dinner in the Castle Hotel."

"You're joking!"

"I'll pay for myself."

"It's not the money. What would we want to go to the Castle Hotel for?"

"To see what competition we have."

"But that's ludicrous. It's an ordinary Saturday night, it's not a New Year's Eve ball, you'll not be comparing like with like."

"I'd consider it research, Stevie . . ."

"Oh yeah?"

"And great fun . . ." She smiled up at him. "I'll never forget how well you looked that night in Dublin."

"You don't want me to put on a monkey suit?"

"No, but you're super when you're dressed up."

"Will you dress up too? I haven't forgotten that nice backless number."

"No, I haven't got any backless things down here, and anyway we don't want . . ." She paused.

"You're right, we don't want . . . but let's go there anyway. It's research, remember."

"If we're caught . . ." Kit said.

"Yes, and we don't need to be." They both recognized the need for their outings to be secret.

The committee meeting on Sunday went well. Everyone had brought news of some sort. Kevin and Michael Sullivan had technical details to blind everyone, but the estimates about the cost of labor were depressing.

"We can't afford that," Philip said firmly.

"It's a pity, though, the front would look very well if we had all these shrubs in containers and a new sign painted." Clio was keen that the place should not look like a hick town when the guests approached.

"We could plant things ourselves, I suppose," Michael Sullivan suggested.

"In what?" they asked. They were not dismissive, they wanted to know.

"Barrels," Michael Sullivan said.

And that was agreed. Everyone would get at least two barrels. They divided up the public houses between them so that the same people would not be asked over and over. This was regarded as men's work. They would dig shrubs and greenery from the lakeside.

"Are we allowed to?" Anna Kelly asked.

"We'll ask later," Emmet said.

Clio had a friend who went to the College of Art, she could do a new sign. She would have to be paid for the materials. Kevin said they could get the paint from the hardware shop. No one asked in too great detail how this would be negotiated with his father, they agreed that Kevin would deliver the paint to Clio's house and the friend would come down and paint it before Christmas.

Anna Kelly had drawings of the curtains. They would be looped back from the window and tied with red and white ribbons. Huge bunches of holly would be pinned to the ribbons. Anna said that the frames needed to be painted white. She would organize a painting team if there were volunteers. She had ideas for the lighting too, wine bottles with candles in them. They must be high on the mantelpieces in places where they couldn't be knocked over. Each bottle would have a spray of holly attached to it. The main center lights should not be on at all, in fact Philip should see the bulbs taken out of them in case they be switched on accidentally.

Everyone was pleased with Anna's industry. Kit watched her accept the praise. She was strikingly pretty, much more glamorous than Clio. Kit must remember the way she looked at people, it was minxlike. She half looked and then looked away. It made her seem shy and vulnerable when in fact she was nothing of the sort. Kit noted every glance and filed it for further use.

Patsy Hanley had none of those skills but she read eagerly from her notebook that in a gathering where there might be sixty or more ladies they would need at least five lavatories. This caused some gloom.

"You see, they'll all want to go at the same time," Patsy explained. "That's what I found out."

"Why can't they go like everyone else, when it's time?" complained Kevin Wall.

"Because you can't have them hopping about holding on, it would spoil the atmosphere," Patsy said.

"We're going to have to get new facilities sometime," Philip said. "Leave that with me."

"You'll never get your father to agree to five toilets in the next few weeks." Kit was concerned.

"No, but that's my problem. Patsy's done the

research, we're grateful for it."

Emmet gave the good news that men were much less fussy. Two cabinets and a urinal would be fine. He also had learned that men loved a place where there could be pints as well, so maybe the bar would broaden itself out a bit for the night, and have a couple of extra barmen on there to serve . . . the money would be taken in pints . . . otherwise Emmet had learned they might all be slipping out to Paddles' or across to O'Shea's.

"They don't do that up in the Club," Clio said.

"No, that's because the Club is as deserted as the Bog of Allen," Emmet said.

Anna Kelly looked at him admiringly. Emmet noticed and reddened with pleasure.

Clio spoke about the hotel's image. She was glad that the new sign had been agreed, and thought that some money might be diverted to have a light which would illuminate it.

"But doesn't everyone know where it is? It's not as if anyone would be looking for the Central," Kevin said.

Philip agreed with Clio. "It's a statement, isn't that what you mean?" he said.

"That's exactly what I mean." Clio was mollified. She thought that a lot of the somber dark brown pictures in the halls should be replaced with garlands of ivy. There were literally miles of it by the lake, nothing would make a better decoration. And that the guests should be greeted in the vestibule with a glass of warmed wine with cinnamon in it. Something to make them feel welcome.

711

"I hope I'm not venturing into Kit's territory here," she said tentatively. "I know you're in charge of food and drink . . . but it is part of the image. The statement."

"Perfect," said Kit with gritted teeth.

And it was a good idea. In one stroke Clio had managed to conquer the very worst bits of the hotel, the ugly entranceway, the hideous sepia pictures in their ugly frames, and also give an illusion of warmth by offering a warm drink.

"And now the food." Philip pointed at Kit.

She drew a deep breath. Her idea was to have a buffet. She knew it would meet with huge resistance from the diners and wanted to try it out on the audience here. It would be self-service where you could come back to the table again and have seconds or even third helpings. She showed them her costings. It would be less than for a traditional sit-down supper. For one thing you would save on waitresses. You wouldn't need as many experienced people to attend tables, and serve, anyone could clear. "Kids from the convent could clear," she explained.

"Or from the Brothers," Kevin said.

"Yes, possibly." Kit had her doubts.

She said that at a formal meal there would be soup or melon, and then always chicken and ham. There would have to be potatoes, gravy, and two other vegetables, it would be a lot more work than preparing a buffet.

"But will they think they've had a dinner?" Emmet wanted to know.

"They'll have had three helpings, some of them," Kit assured him.

712

"But suppose everything gets finished, suppose they all eat the chicken in wine sauce and no one eats the cold tongue, what then?" Patsy Hanley spoke with the intensity of someone who would never have eaten cold tongue but feared with her luck it might be all that was left on when her turn came.

Patiently Kit pleaded her case. As she had suspected they all objected. "But that's what all the places in Dublin are beginning to do," she said.

"It might be too Dublinish for people round here," Anna said.

The others nodded, they were much more conservative around here than up in the capital city.

"They have it in the Castle Hotel," Kit said.

"Are you sure?" Philip would be convinced by anything they did in the Castle Hotel.

"Yes, I was there last night," she said. If she claimed to have visited the planet Mars they wouldn't have been more surprised.

"You never were." Clio was green with envy.

"Yes, and they find it works very well. I was watching, it actually looked much more lavish than it is, if you know what I mean . . ." She was anxious to define how the buffet would work for them but they were looking at her open-mouthed.

"You went to dinner out in the Castle Hotel!" Philip said.

"Yes, to look." Kit feigned surprise. "We said we'd do research, didn't we."

"Yes, but the cost of it."

"It wasn't too bad, I didn't have anything to drink, that's where they make the profit. Oh, and coffee's extra. I didn't have any of that. They serve it in their drawing room, you see, to get you out of the place so that they can clear up."

"You never went in by yourself and sat down to have dinner in the Castle Hotel." Anna Kelly's eyes were narrow with suspicion.

Kit smiled at her. "But look at all you've done, Anna. All those spot prizes you've been promised and all the bottles with the holly and candles." Kit looked admiringly at the Chianti bottle decorated as an example of how things could be done.

"How did you get out there?" Philip asked.

Kit caught Emmet's eye. He was even quicker than she had hoped. "Hey, the point is were they the kind of people who'd be coming here or were they lords and ladies and things?"

"They weren't lords and ladies. I talked to the waitresses. They were kind of middle-class people like the ones who'd be coming to our do."

Philip was so pleased with her calling it "our do" that he forgot to worry about who had driven her the fifteen miles to the Castle Hotel.

"Let's make a list of their possible objections. Come on, everyone say what they think's wrong with a buffet and we'll see does it sound reasonable."

As they began their list Kit glanced over at Emmet again. He was looking at her with awe. Things must be really moving if Kit and Stevie Sullivan had gone to the Castle Hotel. Soon Anna wasn't going to have a look in. Anna would come back to him and everything would be the way it was.

"How are you, Martin?"

"Oh, come in, Stevie."

"No, I won't I'm rushing. Listen, has Kit gone back yet?"

"No, she's going down on the six o'clock bus. Why, did you want to see her?"

"It's just that I have to take a car to Dublin, I wondered did she want a lift."

"Well, I'm sure she'd love it, you'll have a full car. Clio and Philip are going back too."

"It's only a sports car, a two-seater. I thought I'd ask Kit since she was a neighbor's child." His smile was winning. Maura was at the top of the stairs.

"I think they all travel as a team, Stevie. They're all so involved in this dinner dance they're organizing."

His eyes met Maura's. She knew exactly what he was offering. And on Kit's behalf she was refusing it. He was going to have to get Maura McMahon on his side.

It was a long journey back to Dublin. The bus to the town, the train to Kingsbridge Station, and then a bus back to O'Connell Bridge.

"Will we go and have chips?" Philip said hopefully.

"I'm too tired, Philip." Kit looked tired and pale.

"Wouldn't it be great if we had a car?" he said.

"You will, one day. Wait till we make your hotel into the 'in' place in all of Ireland."

He hated her calling it his hotel, it had been their place and their do earlier on. But he knew

715

better than to give any hint of it. "Kevin O'Connor's father's bought another place."

"That's because his daughter's getting married. He's bought a hotel for her husband. It's like a game for him . . . they're not people we want to be like."

Philip waved her good-bye as he got his bus one way and Kit ran lightly down O'Connell Street in the other direction.

Stevie Sullivan was parked outside her door in a small red sports car.

"I don't believe you," she said.

"I got an urge for a Chinese meal. Come on, get in." She got into the car and they drove to a restaurant.

"Aren't you very fussy about your food. Imagine a good ham sandwich in Lough Glass wouldn't do you."

"Not a bit, I fancied sweet-and-sour chicken, and if you've been out with the lovely Kit McMahon in the Castle Hotel one night, you somehow want more of the same the next night."

The Chinese restaurant was fairly basic and simple. Kit looked around her. "Better not let them know in the Castle Hotel that you think this is more of the same," she said.

"I want you, Kit," he said.

"You can't have me, it's as simple as that."

"That's very harsh."

"The way you put it is harsh and demanding also." She realized she was speaking to him as a real person, there was no simpering and play-acting involved.

"What way should it have been put?" He was

being serious also. Not falsely flirtatious. Not the Stevie Sullivan she had watched for years around her hometown.

"Well, it's a question of people wanting each other, isn't it? One doesn't say I want you, implying I mean to have you, as if you were a cowboy taking your head of cattle, or your ranch, or your woman from the saloon . . . that's not the way things should be done."

"Okay, but I don't believe in a lot of fancy phrases either. I drove all the way up here to tell you that I want you, I want to be with you. I want to be with you properly, not just kissing and stroking each other in a car like last night."

"Was it only last night, it seems ages ago." She looked at him with surprise.

"Yes, it seems a lot longer to me too," he said.

She lifted her eyes and looked at him. His face was absolutely sincere. She could see that. But then this was the whole secret of Stevie Sullivan's charm. Everyone thought he was utterly sincere. Anna Kelly, Deirdre Hanley, Orla Dillon, dozens and dozens more that she could name, hundreds that she had never heard of.

He probably was sincere at the time. He just wasn't exclusive. That was his winning streak. He meant it, he meant it with everybody.

"I didn't mean to feel this way," he said to her.

"No," she agreed.

"It isn't at all what I thought would happen."

"No, indeed."

"Kit, stop yessing and noing and three-bags-fulling. Do you feel the same or don't you?" He was angry.

"I'm very fond of you . . ." she began.

"Fond!" He snorted.

"I was going to say unless I was very fond of you I wouldn't have been so warm and loving to you last night . . ."

"I don't believe this," he said.

"What don't you believe?"

"I don't believe you're sitting here cool as a cucumber explaining your behavior, explaining it as if I were someone who had demanded an explanation. We held on to each other last night because we wanted to, and wanted to do a lot more. Why can't you be honest enough to admit it?" His eyes were hurt and his face very upset.

But then this must be new for him. Everyone else including that little baby-face Anna still in her gym slip had probably gone along with his line of persuasion so easily. It must be strange if you were the great Stevie Sullivan. It must be strange and unpleasant to find yourself refused. Especially if you have just driven up from Lough Glass to Dublin, overtaking the bus and the train and then to be refused. But refuse she would.

"Why are we fighting?" she asked him.

"Because you are being so prissy and dishonest."

"Prissy maybe, it's just the way the words come out, but dishonest no."

"You sit there and say I mean nothing to you."

"I didn't say that."

"I've told you what I feel. I need you."

"No, you don't."

"Don't bloody tell me what I need and what I don't need."

"I'm trying to say, without being cheap and vulgar, that anyone, just *anyone* would do."

"And I'm trying not to sound cheap and vulgar either but you are a right prick-tease."

Her coat was on the back of her chair, Kit began to put her arms back into it. "I'll go now, and let you finish your meal." Her face was white. She was shaking with anger. At the words he had used, at the fact that she had let Emmet down, he would be back to Anna Kelly within twenty-four hours. And also the fact that she wanted him so much. She did need him. She would like nothing more than for him to go back with her to her little bed-sitter tonight.

How had it all gone so terribly wrong?

He put his head in his hands. "Don't go," he mumbled.

"I'd better." Her voice was shaky now and he looked up.

He saw her lip trembling and reached out his hand for hers. "I'm very, very sorry. I wish more than anything I could have the last minute back so that I wouldn't say that. I'm so sorry."

"It's all right, I know. I know."

"No you don't know, Kit," he said, and she saw he had tears in his eyes. "You don't know. I've never felt like this before. I want you so much I can't bear it." She looked at him distressed. "Listen. This is the worst thing that could have happened. I just meant to go to a dance with you, to have a little fling if you felt like it. I didn't mean all this."

"All what?" She marveled at how calm her voice was.

"All the way I feel. I suppose it's love, I haven't ever loved anyone before . . . but I'm so eager to see you and to know what you'll say . . . and to touch you and see you laugh . . ." His words came tumbling out. "Is that it, do you think?" he asked her. He really wanted to know.

"Is that what?"

"Is that love? I didn't love anyone up to now, so it's hard to recognize."

"I don't know," she said truthfully. "If that's truly the way you feel then it might be."

"And you?"

She had forgotten her coat now, now they talked as equals. "I suppose it's the same, I didn't mean this to happen either. I thought, I thought . . ."

"What did you think? You started it, you asked me to the dance."

"I know." She was guilt-ridden. She could never tell him why she had done that. They were much too far in for that ever to come to the surface.

"So what did you hope? What did you think would happen?"

"That you'd be a nice man to join our party . . . which you certainly were . . . but I didn't expect that I'd get so close to you, so involved."

"You won't say *love*."

"I haven't loved anybody either," she said. "So I don't know."

"Aren't we a real pair of cold zombies. Most people of our age have loved dozens of people."

"Or what they say is love," Kit said.

"Or what they think is love," Stevie said. There was a silence. "I'm sorry for what I said," he spoke up eventually.

"And I'm sorry for saying anyone would do, that was coarse." She was apologetic.

"I'm not hungry anymore." He pushed his plate away.

"Me neither."

He was cheery and apologetic to the Chinese waiter, who seemed impassive about the whole business.

"They must be mystified by us, coming from as far away as they do," Kit said.

"Anyone would be mystified by us," Stevie said. He helped her into the tiny, low car.

He dropped her at her door and leaned over to kiss her cheek. "I'll see you again during the week, I hope." He looked at her, his face a question.

"I'd love that if you're going to be up here again."

"I'll be here tomorrow night, for example."

Her voice was still shaky, she didn't know whether to make a little joke or not. "Lord, you'll have the road worn out with all that traveling up and down."

"I'm not going back tonight, I'll wait until tomorrow night."

"And who'll mind the little shop?"

"Your stepmother. And we'll start with a clean slate tomorrow." He looked like an eager nervous schoolboy. He reminded her of her brother Emmet when he was struggling and hoping that the right words would come out. Not like the great Stevie Sullivan.

"A shiny clean slate," she said.

"I love you, Kit," he said, and turned the car and was gone.

Kit lay awake all night. There was a church clock that struck every quarter of an hour. She wondered why it hadn't driven her mad before. She got up and made herself some tea. She looked around the room, small, untidy, but full of character, her good dresses hanging on hooks on the wall because the wardrobe wasn't big enough. Shelves of books, a little homemade desk with a small red lamp. She had blue-and-white pillowcases. It would have been a lovely warm friendly place to have brought Stevie Sullivan back for the night.

As the clock chimed on and Kit sat hugging her knees she wondered why she had been so adamant. It wasn't such a big deal. She had been the one making it so. Look at Clio, the skies hadn't fallen on her. She sat there, confused and lonely. She wondered could she ever tell Lena about it. She might. Lena had been through all this kind of thing, she would know what it felt like.

א א א

Lena always organized the office party. That way she could keep control of it. It would be dangerous to leave it to one of the younger, giddier girls or even Jennifer. They would pick an entirely unsuitable place with a wrong atmosphere.

Lena always found a restaurant with atmosphere, somewhere that Italian, Greek, or Spanish waiters would join in the fun but where there would be no silliness.

She had seen office parties go so wrong. She had heard stories from the girls who had moved on from perfectly satisfactory posts only because they had been compromised or done the wrong thing at the annual office party.

"Lord, I'm so sensible," Lena said to Grace.

"You look too good to be sensible." Lena looked at Grace's reflection in the mirror. They had been friends for too long to let Grace lie without being caught. The look of reproach was enough. Grace began to backtrack. "Too thin of course, too tired, but still good."

"I'm a scrawny old turkey, Grace. I used to see them in Lough Glass, they were survivors. They looked so woebegone and bedraggled at Christmas no one would kill them. They escaped the oven year after year."

"So will you," Grace said tenderly.

"Not this year. No, the time comes for every old turkey, even if the bones only make soup."

"Will you and Louis join us for Christmas dinner?" Ivy asked her on the stairs.

"You're very good, Ivy."

"That means no." Ivy looked at her shrewdly.

"Why do you say that?"

"Because I know you so well."

"It doesn't mean no, it means I don't know." There was a silence. "It sounds very rude."

"No, love, it sounds very sad."

"That's exactly what it is, Ivy, very sad." Lena

723

walked up the stairs with a heavy tread.

Jessie Millar was spending the evening with her mother. Every Thursday she went around to Mrs. Park while Jim went to the Rotary Club. Every weekend they took her mother out to Sunday lunch.

Jessie Park's life had changed in so many ways for the better the day that Lena Gray had walked in her door. She would do anything to help Lena through what was obviously some huge crisis. But Lena was so private she would freeze you out if you dared suggest that anything was wrong.

"I suppose it's her husband," Jessie said to her mother.

"It usually is," Mrs. Park nodded sagely.

"I have to do something. I have to tell her that I'd do anything."

"Well, if it is her husband what could you do, Jessica? Go and meet him and say, 'You're upsetting Mrs. Gray, desist this minute.' "

"No, but I could give her some comfort."

Mrs. Park shook her head. "You could only tell her you are sorry for her. She's a proud confident woman, she wouldn't want that."

"She comes to see you from time to time, do you get any hint of anything . . . ?"

The old woman was thoughtful. It was true that Lena Gray found time to call and see her at least once a month. She always brought some small useful gift, an airtight biscuit tin, a foot cushion, a cover for the *Radio Times*. It was amazing that such a busy career woman as Lena should make the time to visit her. But then Mrs. Park remembered that when she was young they used to say if you want something done ask a busy man. Woman in this case.

"She never talks about herself at all," Mrs. Park said eventually.

"I know, but what do you think?"

"I think she has children, grown-up children of her own from a previous marriage."

"Oh, that couldn't be possible," Jessie said.

"Why not?"

"Well, if she has where are they? No normal woman would have children and leave them."

"I wish it was an office lunch, not a dinner," Jennifer complained.

"The lunch would go on all day . . ." Jessie said.

"Yes, I know. Wouldn't it be marvelous, everyone going mad, and we'd get to know other tables having lunch . . ."

That was exactly what Lena had been trying to avoid, Jessie realized. At least at a dinner there was some end to the evening. People had to go for trains and buses. They weren't left high and dry and drunk at five o'clock waiting for the pubs to open and to carry on the foolishness.

"We're lucky we don't have to pay for our party," squeaked the new receptionist. "In the last place we all had to contribute."

"Lena set that up years ago when she came first. She was always making little savings on this and that in a tin called Office Party." Jessie remembered it with affection.

"Has she been here for years and years?" asked the receptionist.

"Eight or nine years, that's all. But of course I can hardly remember what it was like before she came."

"So you never knew her when she was young?" Jennifer said.

"Not really young, no." Jessie shifted on her feet, annoyed by the dismissive ways of youth.

"I'd say she was a stunner," Jennifer said. "She must have been to get that dreamboat she married."

Jessie felt they were on dangerous ground now and wanted to move.

"Yes, I'm sure she had the pick of the bunch," she said, in a tone that brought the conversation to an end.

"We can't persuade you to change your mind, Louis," James Williams said.

"No, James. Many, many thanks for everything. I came here with nothing nearly a decade ago and I have the world at my feet now."

"The Dryden didn't give you that. You built it yourself. We'll be very sorry to lose you."

"Well, you know I'll see you over the season. I won't be off until we've New Year's Eve well over us."

"That's good of you, that's certainly a relief."

"Come on, I wouldn't do that to you."

"And I imagine Lena is delighted to be going back to Ireland . . . I think her heart was always there despite her great success here." The inquiry was made with a bland face and innocent eyes.

Louis Gray took a deep breath. "Ah James,

now there's something I have to tell you about that . . ."

For weeks she had taken work home and listened for his key in the door. At the sound she would slip off her glasses which made her older than ever, and sweep away the paperwork. She would get up to greet him, fresh and fragrant as she always was. Sometimes she would suggest he have a bath and that she'd bring him a drink.

She never asked where he had been or why he was so late. She knew that he would tell her one evening. Some warning had told her it would be tonight. Habits die hard. She put on her best cream blouse and her pencil-slim red skirt. She put a red glass necklace around her throat and then replaced it with a red scarf.

The scarf hid more of the lines, and anyway the red necklace had been bought in Brighton when he had said that one day he would buy her rubies.

She sat at her table for three hours.

But her eyes were too tired and her head too heavy to concentrate on any of the work she had brought home. Instead she waited and waited for the sound of his step on the stair. She had a bottle of wine in the fridge, and she had coffee at the ready. This was going to be a long night, they would need both.

When he came in she stood up. Her feet seemed stuck to the ground, she didn't go toward him as she normally did. Instead her hand flew to her throat and fiddled with the red scarf.

"I'm sorry I'm late," he said.

It had become an automatic greeting. Usually she said, "Well, it's great to see you now." Tonight she said nothing. She just looked at him. She knew her eyes were wide and staring as if she had never seen him before. She tried to relax the muscles of her face, but nothing would obey her.

"Lena," he said. She still looked. "Lena, I have something to tell you."

Ivy and Ernest were looking at television downstairs, but Ivy's glance went to her net-curtained door to see who went in and out. It was a habit that she could not give up, even nowadays when her tenants were respectable settled people who would not do a moonlight flit.

She saw Louis Gray come home, late as usual. But tonight he had paused on the stairs, where he thought he was unobserved. She saw him take deep breaths like someone gasping for oxygen. Then, as if he were still unable to catch enough air, he sat down on the step and let his head drop down to his feet. He must be feeling faint, she thought. Her instinct was to go out to see what was wrong. Perhaps he had been taken ill.

But then she remembered the cold dead look in Lena's face earlier in the day. This was the end of the way for them, Ivy knew it now. Eventually Louis recovered himself and went on up the stairs. Ernest was happily looking at the television set.

"I'll get you a cup of tea," Ivy said. She was restless now, she couldn't concentrate.

"God, it's great to be spoiled," Ernest said.

It only seemed such a short time since Ivy had envied the young couple upstairs, the handsome young husband and wife who couldn't wait to get their hands on each other. She felt life had passed her by and she felt foolish and dull in the light of their passion and love. Now she ached to give Lena, who had been such a good friend, a share of the peace and security she had with the man she had always loved.

She sat at the table. He had guided her there with his arms on her shoulders. She fought the urge to hold on to him and plead, assure him that it didn't matter, he could have this other woman, whoever she was. Even if she was Irish and he had been looking at a hotel in Ireland with her. He could continue seeing her as much as he liked just as long as he didn't leave home, didn't leave Lena, his wife. Because she was his wife. He had said so over and over.

In everyone's eyes they were man and wife. So that is what they were. But the words didn't come. She sat and waited.

"I never wanted this to happen, Lena," he said.

She smiled at him a vague half smile, like the one she used when she was at work. All it involved was a small readjustment of the muscles. She wondered why people didn't teach it at school. It made you look such a good listener, alert, interested, receptive.

"We have always been utterly honest with each other." He reached for her hand. Her hand was cold, but so was his. It must be taking something from him too.

"Yes, of course," she said.

What did she mean by this? Been honest with each other, of course they hadn't. He had betrayed her with who knew how many women. He had told her lie after lie about his activities. She had lied to him about Kit and the lifeline she had established to her daughter and the life of Lough Glass. And yet they sat in a flat in West London and pretended that they had always been honest with each other.

"So, because of that I have to tell you . . . that I've found somebody else. Somebody I really love."

"But you really love me," she said in a small voice.

"I know, I know. Lena, what I have for you is something special that will never change."

"We've loved each other all our lives," she said. It was not argumentative, or defensive. She was just stating a fact.

"That's what I'm saying. Nobody could or indeed will replace what you and I had. It was strong and good and important."

She looked at him. These were mere lines he had learned for a play.

"But . . . ?" she said, helping him on to the next bit.

"But . . . I've met this girl . . ." The silence must have only been for a few seconds. But after what seemed a long time he said, "I didn't want it to happen, I wanted us to go on the way we were . . . but you don't know when these things happen, you don't invite them in, they just . . ." He was at a loss for words.

"Happen?" suggested Lena. She was not being ironic. She just wanted it to get to the bit where he said he was leaving. All the rest of it was unnecessary torture.

"Happen . . ." he repeated, unaware he had used the word so often himself. "And in the beginning it was just a bit of fun . . . you know, harmless . . . and then we knew . . . we knew that this was meant to be."

"Meant to be . . ." She repeated his words again, without any intonation except that of someone trying to realize their importance.

"Yes, she never really loved anyone before . . . and she took some time to realize what it was . . ."

"And you, Louis?"

"Well, I had and did, so it was both easier for me and more difficult, if you know what I mean . . ." She nodded dumbly.

"So?" said Lena.

"So, it developed and we got further into it and it got to the stage where it was too late to go back . . ."

"Too late?"

"Yes, we both know now that this is what we want . . . and what we must take. She had no one to tell but her parents . . . I have to tell you."

She looked at his face, sad to be causing such hurt to another. His handsome, loved face. And suddenly she knew why he was telling her, why he wasn't just rushing off and coming back to be forgiven when it didn't work out. The realization went right through her body causing her to shake.

"She's pregnant, isn't she?"

"Well, this was something . . . something that we are both very glad about now."

His chin was up, he was defiant. He was challenging her to say anything that might diminish his love.

"You're glad?" She was holding her throat.

"We're very proud and happy. I always wanted a child . . . Lena, you've had children. You know what it's like to have been there, seen a young person who is part of you . . . a new generation. I'm getting old, I want a son . . . or a daughter. I want to settle down, be someone in my own land instead of always on the run. You know that. You and I always felt that."

Her head felt very clear suddenly, like a fog lifting. She looked at him in disbelief. What was she meant to know, what were he and she meant to be agreeing? That she had left her husband and children for him, her children whom she loved and missed every day of those years. She had been pregnant with his child and lost it. She had wanted another child, Louis had said the time was wrong.

Now that her childbearing years were over he had discovered that he wanted to be a father. And he expected her to understand all this. Possibly even be glad for him. Louis Gray must be a man without any sensitivity at all. He must be lacking in any real brain as well. Perhaps he was a bit simple. Maybe that lopsided smile and those deep eyes were empty, meaningless things, not an indication of a loving soul.

Could it be true that he was only a shell and she hadn't seen it until now?

"Say something, please. Lena, say something."
His voice seemed very far away.

"What would you like me to say?"

"I suppose, impossible though it is, I'd like you to say that you understand."

"That I understand?"

"And that you forgive me even."

She still felt this strange clearness, and the very odd sensation that she was looking at him through the wrong end of a telescope, that he was miles away, and that his voice was far off.

"Very well," she said.

"What?"

"That's what I'll say."

"You'll say what?"

"What you'd like me to say, I understand what has happened, and I forgive you."

"But you don't mean that. You don't really, you're only saying what I asked you to."

"Come now, you can't have everything. How do we know what people mean? You said this morning as you were leaving, 'Love you.' You said that to me this morning. And you didn't mean it." She was quite calm.

"But I did in a way."

Yes, in a way he had meant it. "So maybe I mean this in a way."

"But Lena, you do realize it's over between us? I mean, I told Mary Paula, I told her I was telling you tonight. We're getting married in the New Year."

"Married?" she said.

"Yes, here in London. I've had to get a letter of freedom, would you believe, from a priest."

"A letter of freedom?"

"You know, to say that I haven't been married to anyone else."

"Imagine," she said.

"Are you all right, Lena?"

"Yes. What did you say her name was?"

"Mary Paula O'Connor. Her father's a hotelier. They're opening a new place in Ireland. I'm going to manage it."

"Mary Paula O'Connor? Daughter of Fingers O'Connor?"

"Yes, I didn't think you'd have heard of him."

"And will his family all be coming over for the wedding?"

"They're coming this New Year." He was at perfect ease telling her these facts of his new life. Was he mad, clinically mad? That he didn't realize that he was speaking of the ruined splinters of her life.

"And are you going tonight?"

"Once we've talked."

"We've talked, haven't we?" She was polite and distant.

"But I won't be back. You know sometimes in the past I went and came back . . . ?"

"Did you?"

"You know I did. I want it to be clear how sad I am to stand here and tell you this . . . you've been so good, so understanding, and in many ways you gave up so much for me . . ."

"We gave up things for each other, didn't we?" She was bright and helpful.

"Yes we did, that's true."

It was not true, Lena wanted to roar at him.

Louis Gray had given up nothing. He had come to her when he was penniless, alone in the world, and had run through all his other options. How dare he end what they had in this welter of invention.

"So I suppose you'd better pack."

"I don't think . . ."

"Or would you prefer to come back tomorrow and take things when I'm at work?"

"Wouldn't that be better . . . then you could sort of . . ."

"Sort of what?"

"Well, lay out what you want rid of and what you want to keep."

"Well, I would imagine you'll take your clothes and things. I mean I wouldn't want those."

"I'll leave all the things we got together, like pictures and books and bits of furniture."

"Yes, I don't imagine you'd want those."

"And of course I'll leave you the car."

"No, I gave you the car as a present, Louis."

"It's an office car."

"No, I bought it for you."

There were tears in his eyes. "You must keep it."

"No, truly. I walk to work."

There was a silence. "And I'll leave the key here," he said. "When I'm going."

"Or you could leave it with Ivy."

"No, that would mean explaining."

"Well, someone will have to explain to Ivy. She'd like to say good-bye, she's very fond of you."

"I think it would be best if I left it on the mantelpiece."

"Well, you must do what you think . . ."

"I can't just go like this."

"Why not?"

"We haven't talked anything out . . . explained."

"We have."

He was about to say more, she knew his face so well. He wanted to ask her to reassure him, tell him that she didn't think too badly of him, say that it had been great while it lasted, that she had found someone she loved too, that she was going to move to a new city, a new life . . . But he said nothing.

"I hope you'll be . . ." He stopped.

"I hope so too," she said, agreeing with him.

He walked out the door.

She stared in front of her for a long time. What she hoped was that she would be dead by the time Louis Gray married Mary Paula O'Connor, the girlfriend who was going to have his son.

Ivy saw Louis Gray leaving. His face was white and stained with tears.

She didn't sleep well thinking of the woman upstairs. No matter how many times she told herself that she should go up to Lena she always answered herself with the fact that Lena Gray had survived on being able to put a brave face on things. It was up to Lena, and only her, when she let that face drop.

There was a letter from Kit next day.

Ivy was pleased. This meant she had an excuse

to intercept Lena on the way out. The woman's face shocked her. It was as if someone had reached in and taken the life out of it.

"Thanks, Ivy." Lena put the letter in her handbag. Even her voice was dead.

"You know where I am," Ivy said.

"Indeed I do."

Ivy stood at the door and watched her go up the street. There was no lift in her step. She stopped at the traffic lights and leaned her head against the lamppost.

In the office there was the usual excitement on the day of the office party. People had brought in clothes to dress up in after work.

"I'm going to have a big lunch this time," Jennifer confided. "There was that year I got a bit tiddly and silly. This time I'm going to lay down a base for all that wine."

"Good idea." Lena nodded approvingly.

"A Mr. James Williams left a message asking you to ring him, Mrs. Gray."

"Thank you," said Lena.

"My mother sent you her love, I was there last night," Jessie said.

"That's very kind of her, is she keeping well?"

All the answers were adequate, but they were lifeless. By lunchtime everyone in the office had decided that Mrs. Gray was sickening for flu. There had been a lot of it going about.

"It would be a shame if she missed the party," Jennifer said.

Last year Louis Gray had turned up to collect her. He had only stayed five minutes, but long enough to make everyone feel they wished they knew him better.

She worked alone all morning, wanting no calls, no interruptions.

The receptionist came into her office. "Mr. Williams phoned again. I told him that I had given you the message. Was that right?"

"Absolutely. Thank you, dear." It was a pleasant remark, but dismissing her.

"They're wondering are you ill, Mrs. Gray," the girl said suddenly.

"I don't know. I hope not, thank you for asking." Her smile was strained.

Then there was a phone call from Ivy. There were some names that always got through to Mrs. Gray, this was one. "Lena, it's only Ivy. Sorry to interrupt, but just thought I'd tell you that Mr. Tyrone has been and gone, in case you wanted to rest your weary head or anything."

"Oh, thank you, Ivy. You must be psychic. I've got a load of stuff to finish up here, but I might well do that in the midafternoon."

"Give you a bit of energy for your office party."

"I think I'm coming down with a flu thing, I might have to cry off that."

"I'll put a hot-water bottle in your bed around four o'clock."

"Bless you, Ivy."

"And you, dear Lena."

She sent out for some Beechams Powders and asked for a mug of tea and a lemon drink.

"Anything to eat at all?" Jennifer was very sympathetic.

"No, but be a dear and try and keep people

738

away from me. I'm trying hard to get through all this in case I have to take a couple of days off with flu."

Jennifer seemed relieved that there was some physical explanation. She had looked at Lena several times that day and thought that her face was so drawn and abstracted that Mrs. Gray might be about to have some kind of mental breakdown. It was great to think it might only be flu.

She was very methodical. In her clear handwriting she attached a note to every one of the files that had to be dealt with. Here she suggested a letter offering a sizable reduction in consultancy fees to one client who was a good friend of the agency, there she suggested no allowances at all to another who was a late payer. She arranged that they cancel every one of her own public appearances and lectures for the next two months. There were reminders and notes from her own diary. Bills that should be paid, Christmas gifts that had been given in the past and would be expected now.

Then she dictated a long memo to Jessie incorporating a lot of what she had done.

About three o'clock she came and told them that she had been trying to fight it but she had to give in now to what seemed like a bad flu germ. "I'll keep away from you all in the hopes of not spreading it any further," she said.

They all tut-tutted and said she looked dreadful.

"Will I come round and see you'll be all right?" Jessie asked.

"No, no. I'll be well looked after."

They saw the elegant Mrs. Gray whose eyes were blurred and hollowed. None of them had ever remembered her taking a day off work in all their time there. It was such a pity that she would miss the party.

Lena was well known in the bank. "Sorry for leaving it toward closing time," she said to the young manager.

"Good customers like you are allowed all kinds of leniencies," he said.

"Right, I'd like to take up a little of your time. You see, I'm going away for a few weeks, I need to withdraw quite an amount of cash from my own account for myself."

"There's no problem there, Mrs. Gray."

"And I want to leave instructions that I won't be countersigning checks for the office for the next few weeks."

"Mr. and Mrs. Millar will be the only signatories needed."

"I have typed you a letter to that effect."

"Always efficient," he murmured admiringly.

"Yes, I hope so, but on this occasion I haven't yet informed Mr. and Mrs. Millar of my intention to take some time off because I don't know how much time it might take me . . . to get well . . ."

"Are you going to have an operation?"

"No, no. Just an illness I have to shake off. So I want everything to go smoothly in my absence."

"Certainly . . . I quite understand." He didn't understand anything at all, but he knew the woman who had been running that agency almost single-handed was giving him some kind of message. She was trying to tell him that she would be back at the helm sometime, and that he wasn't to give the Millars their head to run the agency into the ground.

A very complicated request for a banker.

But Mrs. Gray was a complex lady. He had always thought that. For one thing, she took hardly anything out of the business for herself. For another, she had bought her husband a car which she would have been perfectly entitled to have asked for as an office perk.

It was good to see women doing so well but they were, no matter what anyone said, hard to understand.

"I suppose you're not in a drinking mood." Ivy looked hopeful.

"Not a chance, Ivy. But come up and talk to me for a bit, will you?"

They went into the flat and Lena looked at the mantelpiece. There was the key in a little glass dish. The dish was new. It was good too, cut glass, probably one of the only presents he had ever bought for her. Beside it was a card. A plain white card with the words *Thank you* written on it.

She tore the card in two, and gave the dish to Ivy. "Would you like that?"

"I can't take that."

"It's you or the dustbin."

"Well, it's a nice thing, sure I'll have it. I'll leave it downstairs till you want it back."

"That'll be a time," Lena said. She opened the wardrobe and took out her two suitcases.

"Lena, no. Not you too," Ivy cried.

"Just for a while. I'll be back, Louis won't."

"Of course he will. He always comes back."

"No."

"Don't go. Where are you going anyway just before Christmas? You haven't any friends anywhere. Stay with me, stay here."

"I'll be back, I swear."

"I need you at Christmas. Ernest and I need you."

"No, you're just afraid I'll kill myself. I did think of it last night, but I'm through that now, I won't."

"One day you'll look back on this . . ." Ivy began.

"I know." She was folding her clothes neatly and putting her shoes into bags. Years of taking short trips to give talks and lectures had made packing second nature.

"Where are you going?"

"I don't know."

"You wouldn't let me walk out saying I didn't know where I was going. Come on, be fair, why should I let you?"

"I'll ring you."

"When? Tonight?"

"No, in a few days."

"I'm not letting you go."

"Ivy, you mean well, but . . ."

"Don't 'but Ivy' me . . . See how bloody good I am! I'm not asking you one question about your private life, I didn't come upstairs last night after he left even though I saw him go. You'll never have such a friend as me anywhere, don't throw it back in my face."

"I'll ring you tonight."

"And give me an answer about where you're staying?"

"I swear."

"All right, you can go then."

"Why aren't you begging me to stay?"

"You need to be out of these four walls . . . they still have Louis's memory written over them. If I knew when you were coming back I'd repaper the rooms."

Lena managed a weak smile. "No need to go that far."

"I would if I thought he really wasn't coming back. I don't want him to come and put his imprint on a whole new set of wallpaper."

"No. Truly, he's getting married."

Ivy didn't dare to meet Lena's eyes. She looked at the floor. "Right then," she sort of mumbled. "New wallpaper. A small print, do you think, or maybe Regency stripes?"

"Stripes," Lena said, remembering the huge sunflowers and birds of paradise on Ivy's own walls.

"Tonight before midnight. All right?"

"Yes, Mother," Lena said.

She went to Victoria Station. She couldn't think why. It was that or Euston.

Euston would take her to Ireland. She knew it would be dangerous to go, she must only go to Ireland when she was calm, prepared, ready for whatever might happen. She saw the destinations of the trains. In half an hour there was a train to Brighton, that's where she would go.

She would walk along that pier, and the beach and the promenade. She would feel the rain in her face and she would remember their plans and hopes when she was carrying his child. And maybe she might make some sense out of what had happened and plan what to do with the rest of her life.

For so many of the girls who had gone through Millar's she had been the crossroad, she had made them face decisions, take control of their lives, create a destiny for themselves. Now the legendary Mrs. Gray would take herself in hand.

She sat in a cafe and watched the pre-Christmas crowds swelling around. There were people on their way to and from office parties. There were shoppers up from the country for the day. There were businessmen going home after a day's work. Every one of them had a life to lead, a life with hopes and disappointments.

When she opened her handbag to get her purse and pay for the coffee she saw with a shock Kit's letter to her, unopened. Never before had her daughter written a letter which had not been enjoyed as soon as she could find the time. But today had been a day like no other. It would not have been possible to lose herself in Kit's world until she had escaped from her own. Here in the anonymity of this huge railway station, this was the right place to read it.

My dear Lena,

I didn't think I would be sad to read about Louis, that you think it's over and that he may

744

go away. Once this was the news I wanted to hear. I wanted you to be punished, and for him to leave you alone like you left us. But I don't feel that anymore. I would much much prefer to think that he was there and that you had a good life together.

Perhaps it's not true that he's thinking of going away. It's very hard to know what men are thinking. Not that I'm any kind of authority but I do know that hours and hours are spent in Frankie's flat, in cafes and after lectures, talking about men and what they are thinking and what they're planning . . . and it seems to turn out in the end that they're not thinking about anything or planning anything. I just tell you that in case it's some comfort.

Lena sat in the station cafe as the world moved about its business on either side of her . . . tears fell down her face, she didn't even wipe them away, she just read on.

Kit wrote of the dance, the endless difficulties put in their way by Dan and Mildred O'Brien, the fear that the guests would all spend so long in Paddles' before they arrived that there would be no bar business for the Central and that everyone would be drunk and disorderly.

And Kit wrote about Stevie Sullivan, about his childhood, what it had been like to have no shoes because his father had drunk the money that had been set aside to buy them. Stevie Sullivan wore the best of leather shoes now and always would. Stevie didn't drink alcohol, he didn't gamble, he worked hard, and of course as everyone knew had been a bit foolish in the past.

But one of the terrible things about a small Irish town was the way your past hung around forever. No one was allowed to make a fresh start. People still said he was old Billy Sullivan's boy, a drunkard's son. They said he was a wild boy who had been with all the girls in the parish. Wasn't it strange that they couldn't see how he had changed?

And as Lena read she heard the echo loud and clear. Kit thought of Stevie Sullivan in exactly the same protective and excusing way as she had thought of Louis Gray. She was blind to any criticism of him. She was her mother's daughter and she was about to follow exactly the same path.

Lena sat for a long time in the cafe and then with heavy limbs got up and took a train to the south coast of England.

"Ivy?"

"Where are you, Lena?"

"In a nice place in Brighton. Quiet, warm."

"What's its telephone number?"

"Now listen . . ."

"Just tell me. I won't ring you, just tell me for me, not for you."

She read it from the wall beside the phone.

"I had a Mr. James Williams around here looking for you."

"You didn't tell him?"

"What do you think? But he said most specially that if you were in touch to say he was very lonely for Christmas and he would love if you could . . ."

"Right Ivy . . . you're very good."

"Have you anyone to talk to?"

"I don't need anyone. I'm so tired."

"All right. When will you ring me again?" She fixed a day, three days ahead. "And this James Williams . . . ?"

"Will have to find someone else to play Santa Claus for him."

"He looked very nice," Ivy said.

"Good night, Ivy."

"Good night, pet. I wish you were upstairs."

"Louis, a minute."

Louis looked up from all his plans of the O'Connor visit. They were being a very troublesome group, constantly changing their plans. Firstly there were going to be five of them, then four and now two, and then five for Christmas and only three for New Year. It had played hell with the booking schedules, as if he weren't nervous enough meeting Mr. O'Connor.

He hadn't yet been filled in about the forthcoming event. He might not be overjoyed to meet his future son-in-law for the second time and hear such news. But Mary Paula had assured him that she lived her own life. She was very much her own person, and had been for years. She was twenty-eight years of age, a grown-up.

Louis wished that things were different, that he was nearer to her age than to her father's, that he had been able to prove himself at the new hotel before he proved himself able to father a child. Still, he would believe Mary Paula that it would sort itself out.

"Sorry, James," he said. "I seem to be pulled in a hundred ways today."

James Williams looked stern and unsmiling. "Lena's not at work today."

"I beg your pardon?"

"And she's not at home, I went round to ask the landlady."

"James, I don't understand . . ."

"Where is she, Louis?"

"I have no idea. I spoke to her last night, I told her everything, I went round this morning, took my things, left my key as we arranged."

"What did she say?"

"I don't think it's any of your business, actually."

"I think it is if my manager decides to take another job and move to another country, and then says ooops I forgot to tell her when I ask how his wife is taking it."

"She's not my wife, I told you yesterday."

"She bloody is your wife, if you lived with her for years and told everyone she was."

"You don't know the story, Lena wasn't free to marry."

"Wasn't she lucky the way things turned out."

"Look, I don't know what's brought all this on."

"I'll tell you what's brought it on, the behavior of a man who has acted like a selfish bastard. You've thought of nobody but yourself, Louis, all the time . . . self, self, self."

"I'm not going to stay here and listen to this."

"No, you're bloody right you're not. You can take your cards and leave today."

"On what grounds?"

"On the grounds that I couldn't look at your face while you worked out your notice."

"You can't be serious, James."

"Never more so."

"You'd let your personal feelings and the fact that you have always been attracted to Lena stand in the way of normal business behavior."

"You've had your reference, Louis, you've had the buildup that got you the new job, and made you an acceptable son-in-law for this Irish tycoon, now get out of here."

Louis's handsome face was very hard and cold. "It won't do you any good, all this posturing. Lena won't think any better of you. She thinks you're a cold, dull fish already, now she'll think you're just a petty one."

"By this afternoon, Louis." James Williams turned and left.

It took a lot of time and ingenuity but Louis Gray had many contacts and friends in the hotel business. He found a suite in another hotel, somewhere he could entertain the O'Connors in style. He would turn the whole business to his advantage, say that he had left the Dryden to concentrate on them properly.

Now of course he would have to organize a whole Christmas and New Year program for them. He must think what to do. For a wild moment he thought of asking Lena, she was always great about ideas and thinking up the right thing for the right occasion.

Wasn't it absurd that she had come to his mind just like that? But it was only natural, they had been together for so long it was obvious that they should still automatically think of consulting each other. He wondered whether James Williams was right about her having disappeared from work and from the flat in Earl's Court.

It was improbable; Lena had seemed so calm. As if she had known this was all inevitable. And the one sure and certain thing was that in any time of crisis you'd find Lena at her desk in that bloody agency. She was more married to Millar's than she ever would be to a man.

All the shops in Brighton were full of Christmas gifts. Lena looked in the windows at things she would like to have bought for her daughter. She had a handbag full of money. She could have bought the necklace and earrings set in a little musical box. She could have got her that smart coat which would have done so much for her coloring. The manicure set in the genuine leather case. The overnight case with the smart two-tone trim — it would be ideal for going up and down between Dublin and Lough Glass.

But why was she torturing herself? She would not send anything to her daughter.

This was a Christmas when she would give no presents and get none. When she would have to stay far from a church lest the sound of carols make her weep. She must not listen to the radio in case the programs of goodwill and celebration pointed out too clearly what she had lost.

The waves were high and crashing onto the big beach.

Was this the beach she had walked with Louis

when she was expecting his child? It seemed like a different age, and two different people. When she was here that time she had been waiting for the letter of abuse, and the torrent of rage and blame from Martin. She didn't know that they were dragging the lake in Lough Glass looking for her.

If she had the time all over again . . . ?

But it was an empty speculation. She wouldn't have the time all over again. It was useless to work out what she would have done. She must think what to do now. She walked, the spray and salt air in her face, her hair wet and curling in the damp. She didn't see anyone glance at her and wonder why a handsome woman should walk so ceaselessly, hands deep in pockets, unaware of the world around her, the weather, the season of the year.

Then she found a shelter and sat down to write to Kit. She wrote on pages of a notebook. Not her usual style of letter. And she didn't read it over as she normally would have done. Back at the guest house she got an envelope and stamp and went out to find a pillar box. She felt a little better, as if she had spoken to a good friend.

א א א

Kit's heart gave a jump when she saw the envelope with her mother's writing on it laid on the hall table upstairs. Surely her father had recognized it. That was the way Mother had always written. But apparently not.

751

It was the day before Christmas Eve. Kit and Philip had just come back from Dublin. Maura had decorated the house. It wasn't the same as Mother used to do, Mother would have had all leaves and ivy and holly. Maura had bought paper decorations and tinsel.

The house looked very festive. There were lots of Christmas cards on the mantelpiece and around the mirror. Maura sent and received many more than Helen McMahon had ever known.

Kit felt a rush of anxiety. Why had her mother been so rash as to write here? She was anxious to be alone to read the letter, but they were welcoming her home. Emmet had carried up her luggage including the dress box with the extravagant new dress bought on the compensation money. She had spent a fortune on it, and didn't want anyone to see it before the dance in case there might be a question of its being somewhat revealing.

She had told Clio that it was a bargain, marked down in a pre-Christmas sale.

"There are no pre-Christmas sales," Clio had said sagely. "You are turning into a mysterious and very sinister liar."

Maura was offering soup to take the chill off her, her father was eager to tell her all the news and how the Golf Club committee had thrown themselves behind the great New Year's Eve Dance. But Kit couldn't wait to be away from them. Eventually she decided that the bathroom was her only hope of peace and quiet. Sitting on the side of the bath she read

752

My dear Kit,

This is to wish you a very happy Christmas this year and every Christmas.

I was so pleased with the letter you wrote to me, I read in a railway station. All around there were people living their own lives, making journeys to see people or escape from people and I just sat there and read your letter over and over.

It's good to know that Stevie Sullivan was able to rise above his childhood and triumph over all the bad things that happened to him in his youth. It must have made him very strong. Of course the same goes for you. You had a lot happen to you in your youth that shouldn't have happened and you coped with it. You coped with the death of a mother and the rumors about that death. You thought your mother had committed suicide and was in hell. You met a ghost. You survived that.

In many ways I think you are well suited for each other. Of course, like every mother I worry for you. But perhaps I don't have the right to have those feelings. Maybe they were forfeited a long time ago.

It was kind of you to say that perhaps Louis was not thinking of going. But in fact he has gone. He is going to get married to someone else. Somebody much younger and they will have a child. So that part of my life is over now.

I just wanted to reassure you that I will make no more trouble for all the people I have hurt so much already. You may worry that since

Louis has left me I might become like a ship without a rudder. So I wanted you to set your heart at ease. I will disturb nothing that has been done.

I tell you this because I know it will cross your mind and also because I have an ache, a yearning to go back to Lough Glass and to see the dance that you have all been preparing. I had this feeling I could watch from the outside. So in a way I am writing this to tell myself that I must not go. May it be a great success for you all.

Peace, Kit. Peace and goodwill. Isn't that what we are all looking for when all is said and done?

Your loving mother,
Lena.

Kit sat in the bathroom looking at the letter in disbelief. This wasn't the kind of letter Lena wrote. The sentences were all wrong. Short jerky phrases, ramblings about sitting in railway stations. Lena had addressed this letter to the pharmacy, she had signed it *your loving mother.*

Louis had left her, he was getting married to another woman. Lena was not able to cope.

Kit behaved normally. She was sure that nobody knew there was a thing wrong. She wrapped gifts, she delivered Christmas cards by hand, she spent hours in the Central Hotel, she kept her voice and smile polite for Philip's parents, she made lists and timetables. She listened to Clio's

754

ramblings and complaints about Anna, about her parents, about Aunt Maura, about Michael not ringing to say good-bye before he left for London.

Her only hope was to work as hard as she could. When it was all over she would think what she could do to help Lena. But now there was nothing she could say or do or write that would help. She felt very much alone.

On Christmas Eve she lay awake for a long time and wondered about her mother lying in bed alone in that flat in London. She wished she could telephone her. But it would be easier to contact the planet Mars than to make a phone call from Lough Glass at Christmastime to someone in London.

And suppose Lena was so disturbed that she let everything be revealed. Suppose the phone call unhinged her and she told Maura and Father that she was alive . . . suppose Emmet were to hear.

Kit lay in her bed and wished she could tell someone. The only person she could tell was Stevie Sullivan.

But it wasn't her secret to tell.

The feeling of anxiety remained with her on Christmas Day and for no reason Kit found herself crying just at the wrong time. They were all getting ready to go up to Kellys' for a sherry and present giving.

Everyone wanted to go, Maura to see her sister, Father to see his friend Peter, Emmet to see the beloved Anna . . . only Kit didn't want to go.

But go she must. "I'll follow you up there," she called as she heard them getting ready to leave. She needed just a little time to compose herself, get herself ready for the Kellys.

She splashed cold water on her face and left the house. Her heart was like lead on this Christmas morning.

"Hey, wait for me." Stevie Sullivan had seen Kit leaving her house and he ran after her. She turned around to look at him. His smile was broad, his delight to see her was written all over his face. "You didn't call to say happy Christmas," he accused her.

"I thought I'd see you at Mass."

"Oh, I was at the back of the church, humble you know, not putting myself forward."

"Talking, doing deals I imagine," she mocked him.

He looked at her closely. "You've been crying," he said.

"Does it show? I couldn't bear the third degree from Clio."

"Only to me, I know every little bit of your face. Why were you crying, Kit?"

"I can't tell you."

"Is there anything I can do?"

"No thank you, Stevie. No."

"Will you ever tell me?"

"I might someday."

"You'll have forgotten."

"No, I'll never forget why I'm crying today." She sounded very serious.

"Michael and Kevin are having the time of Reilly over in London," Clio said. "He rang last night." Clio was pleased at this.

"What's she like, the sister?" Kit asked.

"I don't know, I only met her once."

"And the fellow she's marrying?"

"Oh, he's as old as the hills apparently. Michael says he could be her father."

"But nice?"

"Apparently."

"Is he a sugar daddy sort?"

"No, the total reverse, he hasn't a penny according to Michael."

"But he's going to be admitted to the ranks?"

"Yes, apparently he's a dynamo in the hotel industry over in London."

"Why isn't he rich then?" Kit wondered.

"Search me," Clio said. "But she's very stuck on him. Michael thinks that she might be pregnant."

"No!" Kit's eyes were round with excitement.

"Well, the marriage is very speedy apparently, speedier than one would have thought."

"What's his name?" Kit didn't care very much, but anything was better than answering Clio's questions.

"Louis. There, isn't that romantic? Louis Gray."

On the day after Christmas, Kit asked Stevie to drive her into the big town.

"Nothing will be open," he said, puzzled.

"That doesn't matter."

"Of course it matters. What's the point of going into Tombstone City in the rain? Why don't we stay here in the rain?"

"Please Stevie, I don't ask much."

757

He considered this. It was true, she didn't ask him favors. "Okay, fine," he said.

He didn't ask her why she wanted all the change to make a phone call from a hotel in the town. He sat and had a pint in the hotel bar and looked at her from a distance as she stood in the phone booth at the far end of the hall. Kit McMahon was running her hand through her hair and talking earnestly. Stevie realized the point of the journey through the rain was so that she could phone someone who would have been impossible to phone from home. She could have used the phone in the Central Hotel but it would still have meant going through Mona Fitz.

He wouldn't ask her. She would tell him when she was ready.

"Ivy Brown?"

"Yes, yes, who is this?"

"Mrs. Brown, I'm Kit McMahon. I met you once, do you know who I am?"

"Yes, yes of course I do." Ivy sounded worried. "Is anything wrong?"

"Could I talk to Lena do you think . . . ? I got the number from Directory Inquiries . . ."

"But love, she's not here . . ." Ivy said.

"Look, Ivy, I have to talk to her, I have to. I have some terrible news I want to give her."

"I think she's had all the bad news she can take."

"I know who he's marrying, he's marrying someone else, the bastard. The bastard out of hell."

"Kit, stop . . ."

"I won't stop. I've no money, Ivy. I can't leave

758

here, we have a huge thing I'm up to my neck in. I can't walk out on it, but I have to talk to Lena. You must tell me where she is."

"She was in Brighton, but she rang me from a coin box in London. She said she'd be away for a few days and she'd ring me on New Year's Day."

"Where?"

"She wouldn't say."

They had bookings for one hundred and fifty-eight people. The most the Golf Club had ever catered for was eighty-six. Philip O'Brien told Kit that he hadn't slept since Christmas Eve, not more than two hours at a time.

"It'll be great," Kit said.

"You're not sure, you're only encouraging me, you're only being nice."

"Jesus, Philip, you really piss me off at times. I'm saying what I mean, why do you accuse me of just being nice?"

"Because your mind is miles away," he said. "Since Christmas Day you've been thinking of something else entirely." Kit was silent. "Isn't that right?" Philip asked.

"I have a lot on my mind that's true, but I do think the dinner will be great."

"Will you tell me what's worrying you? I might be able to help," Philip said.

"I don't know," she said truthfully. "I don't know if I'll tell you." Why did she feel that she might be able to tell wild Stevie Sullivan all about her mother and the tragedies of her life, but that she wouldn't be able to explain them to good loyal Philip O'Brien?

"I'll always be here," he said.

"You're a great and good friend," she said truthfully.

"Tell me again it won't be a disaster," he said.

"Philip, it'll have them talking about it for a year. Now, back to business." She took out her clipboard and got back to the countdown.

They agreed that they would have big tables, set for anything from sixteen to twenty. And even though there would be guests from Dublin, the O'Connor brothers, Matthew (who was going to be watched by Kevin O'Connor all night in case anything untoward happened), Frankie, and more, the committee would all have to keep hawklike eyes out in case anything went wrong.

Kit was to be in charge of the food and training the group of girls from the convent in their waitress duties. Philip was responsible for the entire drink side of things, the opening and pouring of wine, the pulling of pints, the trays of alcohol being brought with speed to tables. Emmet was in charge of furniture. They had identified this as a possible problem, chairs and tables too close together, not leaving access for waiters, people wanting to join up with other tables. Emmet would appear miraculously when people started heaving and dragging things.

Anna was in charge of decoration. If bits of holly separated themselves from curtains, from the wine bottles holding candles, it was Anna who must replace them. She was to be forever vigilant and move around from table to table. Anna liked this. Stevie Sullivan was not going to be sitting at their table. This would give her a chance to mingle.

Patsy was to keep an eye on the ladies' room, make sure there were tissues and clean soaps. One of the downstairs rooms had been transformed with pink drapes and pink-and-white-striped Regency-style coverings on the furniture and artistic floral sprays. The two new lavatories that had been badly needed for the hotel were installed and functioning. The job had been done by Kevin Wall's brother, who had worked even on Christmas Eve to get everything finished.

Philip's parents had severe doubts about the expenditure, but they were so pleased by the attention the hotel was getting from Lough Glass and the entire surrounding countryside, they didn't protest too much. "It's about time that people took us seriously as a hotel," Mildred sniffed, when she heard more and more bookings coming in from landowners whose patronage they had never known before.

"I always said that this place would be recognized for what it was in the end," Dan O'Brien assured her, giving absolutely no credit to his son and his son's friends who had made the whole thing possible.

Clio had no specific responsibility, it was generally agreed that she should look after the guests from Dublin, keep everything going smoothly at the table, and cover over the fact that the others would be coming and going all night.

"We won't just dance with people at our own table, will we?" Anna asked.

Kit couldn't bear to see the look on Emmet's

face. "No, I think it should be open plan," Kit said. Of course it was going to be open plan. Stevie Sullivan had booked a table for some of his customers. There were going to be more men than women in the party.

In the afternoon Kit and Philip looked around. "We've done it," she said.

The tables were so festive, and the walls draped in greenery looked as if the whole place were out-of-doors. They would light the candles just before the people arrived. The convent school girls had come to show their uniform, every single one of them in white blouses and navy skirts and each wearing an embroidered badge with the letters CHL for Central Hotel Lough Glass. Kit had seen to it that those with hair flopping over their faces wore barrettes or ribbons.

She had rehearsed over and over what to do in the case of accidents. If somebody let a plate fall there was to be no giggling and no fussing, dustpans and brushes were stashed under some tables, hidden by the long tablecloths. She asked them all to repeat the names of the dishes and drummed it into them — hors d'oeuvres — say it after me, no, say it again, each one of you.

"What are these starters called?"

"Hors d'oeuvres."

"That's much better."

"Go home now," Philip said. "You all look terrific and be back here looking just like that at six-thirty."

They were giggling as they left.

Kit shouted at them suddenly. "What are

the starters called?"

"Hors d'oeuvres," the six girls chanted.

"And what are the main courses?"

"Chicken with tarragon, or beef in red wine."

"Great. What are the desserts?"

"Sherry trifle or apple tart and ice cream."

"Can people come back to the tables as often as they like?"

"Yes, as much as they want."

"Don't giggle as you say that," Kit said. "They want to feel welcome, they don't want to feel stupid." The girls looked at her respectfully. "Philip and I spend all our time at college learning this kind of thing." Kit wanted to take some of the harm out of her direction.

"You're getting it all for free," Philip added.

The girls smiled from one to the other. He would never be able to thank Kit for all her support over this.

"I got you a little corsage," he said. "It's in the fridge to keep it nice and fresh. Just to thank you, from one friend to another."

"You're a dear good friend," she said, and put her arms around his neck to hug him.

He felt her breasts against him and it was all he could do not to hold her to him tightly and kiss her on the lips. "So are you," he said in a voice that struggled to be casual.

The Dublin contingent came in three cars around six o'clock. The bar was bright and welcoming. Philip had the first round of mulled wine ready for them to sample. "If it lays you lot out then we'll know not to serve it to the real people," he said.

Kevin O'Connor looked at him with interest. This wasn't the mousy Philip he knew at college. This hotel was certainly not the dump Michael had said it was when he drove past it before. It was an elegant creeper-covered building, with a lot of attractive greenery in barrels around the entrance. The decorations for the New Year's Eve celebrations were stylish.

Their rooms were much more comfortable than he had been led to believe. Kevin was sharing a room with his friend Matthew. He had promised to watch Matthew's behavior. And anyway there was no point in sharing with his twin; Michael O'Connor would be entertaining Clio Kelly as the night went on. Kevin wondered how his brother had got so lucky with the Lough Glass girl he had chosen.

"Hell of a nice place this, Philip," Kevin said. The others agreed.

"Thank you." Philip seemed confident. He had kept his parents off the scene, saying that they should be there to greet guests in the bar at seven-thirty when it all began. But not before. He felt a surge of excitement like he had never known before. It was all going to happen. Tonight his career and his long-term plan of marrying Kit McMahon were all taking off.

Kit had asked her father and Maura to be among the early arrivals.

"I was hoping I might have a pint in Paddles' with Peter," Martin said.

"No, have it in the bar."

"It's a bit of a gloomy place . . . ." he began.

"Wait until you see it tonight," Kit promised.

Maura looked very well, she had on a black dress with black chiffon sleeves. "I hate wearing my coat over it but I suppose I'd freeze walking down without it . . ."

"It's only a few yards," Kit said. "You look so nice it's a pity to spoil it."

"Put on your coat, Maura, like a good woman, and don't be catching pneumonia."

"Lilian's wearing a stole, but I always look like a washerwoman in one." Maura's face seemed disappointed.

"Father, can I ask you something?" Martin looked a little surprised. "Do you remember the little fur stole that Mother had, it was like a little cape?"

"Yes, I think I do, why?"

"You probably don't remember because she hardly ever wore it. It's in my wardrobe in a box, in case I'd ever wear it. I don't think it suits me, why don't we give it to Maura to wear?" It was a risk, she knew this. They had never mentioned anything of Mother's before.

"That's very nice of you, Kit, but I really don't think . . ."

"Let me get it . . . I can, can't I, Father?"

"Child, it's yours and I'd be delighted if Maura would like it. Delighted."

Kit was back in a moment. It was in tissue paper in a box. There was a faint whiff of mothballs. The little cape had a fastener in the front. It was old-fashioned, dated almost, but it might look smart on Maura. Kit draped it around her stepmother's shoulders and stepped back to look at the effect. "It's *lovely* on you . . . come and look in a mirror."

It was indeed splendid. It could have been made for Maura around the shoulders but the fastener didn't meet. "This needs to be held together with some black ribbon," Kit said quick as a flash. "I have some in a drawer."

When she came back her father and Maura were holding hands, there were tears in Maura's eyes. She hoped nothing had gone wrong. "I was just saying that perhaps I shouldn't wear it. Someone might remember Helen wearing it on some other occasion . . ."

"I never saw Helen wear it, not in all my life."

"Did you buy it for her, Father?"

"I don't remember that I did. No, she must have had it already, but I can't ever recall seeing it on her anywhere. I'd love you to wear it, Maura dear."

"It might have been special to her." Maura was still doubtful.

"No, it couldn't have been or else she'd have . . ." Kit stopped, horrified. She nearly said she would have taken it with her to London.

"Or else . . . ?" Maura looked at her.

"Or else we'd have seen her wear it . . . Here, let me thread this ribbon in, you're the belle of the ball."

"When are you going to put on your dress?"

"I have it down at the hotel, I didn't want to put it on until I'm through in the kitchen."

"Does the chef not mind you taking over?"

"I don't think by any stretch of the imagination you could call Con Daly a chef . . . a cook is even stretching it a bit. He's so relieved that we're all there he's nearly licking our shoes with gratitude."

Emmet came in wanting his bow tie tied. "A girlfriend should be doing this for you," Maura said as she tied it expertly.

"Oh, I've no time to be interested in girls for a few years yet," Emmet said.

Kit caught his eye and smiled.

"Very sensible," Martin McMahon said. "The country would be in a better state if everyone thought the same."

"I'll see you down there." Kit ran off.

Stevie Sullivan knocked from an upstairs window. "Will you come on up here and help me dress?"

"Sadly no," she called back. "I'm on duty five minutes ago, and the battle orders are very strict. I made most of them myself."

"You're not exactly gussied up yourself," he said, disappointed.

She was wearing her duffel coat and her hair still in big loose rollers was under a headscarf. " 'Gussied up' . . . what a marvelous phrase . . . see you later."

He watched from the window as she ran into the hotel, the Central, which you wouldn't recognize with its smart barrels of greenery, its trimmed creeper, its glittering new sign perfectly illuminated by some fixture which also showed the old oak tree to its best.

Funny that Kit didn't see the naked longing in Philip O'Brien's face. She was not an unkind girl, she wouldn't play games with him. She simply didn't see that the young son of the hotel was head over heels in love with her.

Kit slipped into the kitchen, she didn't want to join the loud voices that were coming from the bar, she could hear Matthew booming away. She must remember to warn Kevin that very strict control should be exercised over Matthew.

The kitchen was too hot, she opened a window but the draft blew things from a shelf. "Hold the back door open with a chair," she ordered.

"I'll do it, that's the very thing," said Con Daly in his spotless whites. There had been a time when Con always looked as if somebody had spilled the contents of thirty-five dinner plates over him.

The young waitresses were standing in a little group, giggling with excitement. Kit frowned. How many times had she tried to tell them . . . but then when she and Clio were young they did nothing but laugh and giggle for about three years. Suppose they had been asked to help in O'Brien's.

"Listen," she said to the girls. "I know you think we're all quite old and probably mad, but I want to tell you what we're doing. We're trying to show that we can be as good as and better than the grown-ups. And the grown-ups think we're still children . . . so we need to look desperately polished. We need to be able to pronounce starters."

"Hors d'oeuvres."

"We need to know what tarragon is . . ."

"It's a herb in the sauce," they said.

"But most of all we want them to think you

are real waitresses, not schoolgirls. For some reason laughing and enjoying yourself make you look amateur. I don't know why, so I can't let you do it. We can all laugh our heads off when it's over. And Philip has said that if there's no laughing there's going to be an extra four shillings each for all of you." This was serious money. They looked at each other in disbelief. "But that's everyone. One giggler and nobody gets the four shillings extra. Okay?"

They nodded, faces solemn, afraid to meet each other's eyes.

"Great," Kit said. "Now, what else was I going to do?"

"Get dressed, I think," said one of the girls. The others reddened but managed not to laugh. Kit had them well frightened into earning their extra wage.

She took the scarlet dress from its hanger. Philip had told her she could change in his room. He had tidied it and left around it all kinds of things that would make her think better of him. Books he hadn't read, clean towels and a kind of soap that he had never used but it was expensive.

The dress fit perfectly, it was an off-the-shoulder model so there would be no bra. But again it was so perfectly molded that there would be no need. As she stood in her half slip and washed herself at Philip's handbasin Kit studied her face in the mirror. Her heart was not in tonight's festivities. If only she had been able to ring Lena and talk to her.

She was tired from all the work involved. She

looked pale, she thought. She must be sure not to waste tonight's opportunities. That's what it had all been about. She mustn't grant an inch to the poisonous little Anna Kelly who had bought a lime-colored dress in Brown Thomas. Reports were that it looked a knockout. Kit hadn't killed herself getting this hotel off the ground just so that Philip's parents could sit back and take all the credit. She had wanted an arena, a public place to allow Stevie Sullivan to be seen to fall for her.

She needed to wipe the two mean little eyes of Anna Kelly and make her flee sobbing back to poor innocent Emmet, who would of course take her. Kit had made a promise that she was going to deliver. But now it was much more than that, it was something she wanted so much and so badly that it nearly hurt.

There was a sizable crowd by the time that Kit made her entrance but Stevie and his clients had not arrived. Her eyes raked the room for them, but she couldn't see them. She went to where her father and Maura were standing with the Kellys. Maura was still wearing the little cape.

Lilian had admired it. "Very smart indeed," she had said, slightly enviously Maura thought.

"Yes, I think I'll leave it on for a bit, I can't imagine the O'Briens having the place warm enough," Maura whispered.

"I haven't seen you wearing it before."

"Not much cause really," Maura said. She had decided not to tell her sister that it had once belonged to Helen. And it was obvious that Lilian had never seen it before. What a strange woman

Helen McMahon must have been to have had a lovely thing like this and never worn it.

"I wouldn't have believed the place, Kit." Her father looked around him in amazement. "I'll have to let you into the pharmacy next."

"Fine, as long as you don't object to holes in the walls every two minutes like Mildred O'Brien did," Kit whispered. "Her bloody walls were falling down and great wedges of damp like lumps of penicillin and she says *Not too many nails in the wall.*"

Mildred was standing like royalty near the fireplace, accepting compliments from everyone. "Well, the old place *does* have its charm," she was saying modestly, as if it had looked like this all the time.

Then Kit joined Clio and the O'Connors. Clio wore a cream dress with a neckline of rosebud. It was attractive but it wasn't startling. You wouldn't pick Clio out in the crowd like you would Kit in her scarlet dress. Or Anna in her bright lime color. Clio seemed to sense it and the corners of her mouth turned down.

"Welcome to Lough Glass," Kit said to the group.

"You look terrific," Frankie Barry said.

"Thanks, it's very startling anyway. If I were in London you'd think I was a pillar box."

"Or a bus," Clio said. Everyone looked at her, surprised. "They're red too," Clio said lamely.

"Yes, of course," Kit said. "Tell me, how was your trip to London?" she asked the O'Connor twins.

"Fabulous . . ." Michael said.

"No one there to hold a candle to you, Kit," Kevin said.

Clio looked crosser than ever.

But Kit appeared not to notice. "Tell me about your sister's fiancé. Did he turn out to be okay?"

Clio wished she had thought to ask. Kit was winning everybody there. She didn't even remotely like Kevin O'Connor, and yet he was hanging on her every word.

"He was okay," Kevin said. "Like old and everything, but an all right fellow. You could see why she likes him. He drove us all round London in his car . . . down the docks, to Covent Garden . . . he was like a guide . . . in a way."

"Did he not have to go to work?" Kit asked.

"Well, it was Christmas."

"But isn't that the terrible thing about hotel work, we have to work at Christmas?"

Kevin looked at Michael. "That's true. I suppose he had time off."

"I think he's left his hotel, you know, already. And they're getting married very soon. Real soon, wink, wink," Michael said, nudging Clio.

Clio looked annoyed, but Kit was interested. "And will you all be going over for the wedding again?"

"No, they're coming over here. It'll be in Dublin."

Kit wanted to ask had they met his family, what had he been doing up to now. She wanted to get the two stupid boneheaded O'Connor boys up against a wall and beat the answers out of them. Then she wanted to tell them that Mary Paula had got herself hooked to a liar and deceiver in the international league. She wanted to say that she could tell them a story about their future brother-in-law and his deceptions that would make their pale greasy hair stand on end.

"Clio, is that a new watch?" she asked.

Clio had been displaying her wrist in a way that simply called out for attention. "Yes, Michael gave it to me." There was a little simper.

"It's lovely," Kit said, and they all admired it.

Next year it would be the engagement ring. That's the way the mating dance worked. The watch was a preliminary. Kit looked at Clio with new eyes as if she had never seen her before. Clio was going to marry Michael O'Connor. She would soon be a sister-in-law of Louis Gray's.

Mrs. Hanley was loud in her praise of how well the young people had done. "My Patsy was involved in it all," she told Mrs. Dillon from the news agency. "I'm surprised your Orla wasn't in on it from the start."

"Well, of course Orla has her own life to lead, what with being married and living so far out in the country."

"She won't be here tonight, will she?" Mrs. Hanley asked.

"One never knows," said Mrs. Dillon distantly and moved away.

She had told her daughter Orla that there was no question of her turning up alone at the Golf Club Dance. She either came with her husband and a family party or she didn't come at all. "That crowd wouldn't know what a dance was," Orla had said. "And I'll go on my own if I like, there'll be plenty who'll dance with me." Mrs. Dillon,

773

who feared greatly that Stevie Sullivan might dance only too much with her, had her mouth set in a grim line.

The buzz of conversation had become almost a roar when Philip and Kit decided that Bobby Boylan and his band should begin to play. They hadn't wanted them to start until the noise level was already high.

"Something gentle without too many rat-tat-tats to start," Philip had suggested.

"What does he mean rat-tat-tats?" Bobby Boylan asked indignantly.

"I think he means reverberating drum sounds," Kit said apologetically.

"He's got an odd way of putting things, your fellow."

"He's not my fellow." Kit didn't want even someone like Bobby Boylan, whom she might mercifully never see again, to go away with the wrong impression.

It was a five-piece band. They wore pale pink jackets, all of which must have been bought when the players were slimmer men, or else they had been borrowed from a skinnier band.

" 'Red Sails in the Sunset' gentle enough, do you think?" Billy Boylan asked. He hated hotel dinners. He would like to have been in a big dance hall on New Year's Eve, but times weren't what they used to be. These days it was listening to children in dinner jackets giving orders.

He sighed and waved his baton at the band that bore his name.

"How soon should we bring them in for the meal?" Philip asked Kit.

"They're all enjoying this bit, there's no one looking at their watches," Kit said.

"Did Clio show you her watch?"

"She did. I thought she might want Bobby Boylan to call for a roll of drums and have it carried round the room."

Philip laughed. "It's good to know you can be bitchy like everyone else."

"What, me? I'm hardly ever any other way. Let's wait another ten minutes anyway." She had noticed that Stevie Sullivan and his party hadn't turned up yet. She didn't want to begin until the main star was there.

Anna broke off in the middle of a conversation. "Excuse me, there's something I must do," she said.

Kit's eyes followed her. Surely the decorations hadn't fallen to bits yet. But no, Anna Kelly had seen Stevie Sullivan arrive. She wanted to be there to greet him.

Kit looked at Anna's perfect skin, her blond hair in curls down her back, little ribbons of precisely the same lime green as the dress threaded through her hair. She was like a vision.

Maybe Kit looked hard and tough by comparison. Perhaps scarlet had not been a good color. Too fast. Too showy for Lough Glass.

Stevie Sullivan and his friends had been in Paddles'. They were all in very good form.

"By God, I wouldn't know this place," said one of the car dealers. "Used to be a place you'd be afraid to talk to anyone in case they keeled over and died at your feet."

"And would you listen to the band, Stevie.

775

You've got great class getting us into a place like this."

They were red-faced men, bachelors maybe, people who had given big orders for tractors and vans and lorries over the years. They even bought a lot of their other farm machinery through young Stevie Sullivan, who acted as a broker but always got them a good deal and stood over whatever was delivered.

They were flattered that they should be invited to something with a name as fancy as the Lough Glass Golf Club Dinner Dance. It would not have been a place where they might normally have been invited.

Kit made a mental note to put extra warmed dinner rolls on their table. These were fellows who might eat the decorations if the food wasn't served quickly enough.

The names of the guests were in big writing on the tables. They didn't have to peer and fumble. Not a full seating plan, but just McMahon or Wall . . . the groups arranged their distribution with a maximum of fuss and confusion. Emmet stood about watchfully; he was in charge of chairs. He would run for extra ones if they were needed or ease people into corners.

The baskets of warmed rolls were on the tables, served by the solemn girls from the convent, each one looking earnest with eyes cast down. Kit had forgotten that if she ordered no giggling she also seemed to have bought no smiling. She would know another time.

They had rehearsed so many times how the line would begin. Kit would urge those sitting at tables farthest from the buffet to come up first. It worked like a dream. Soon the entire company had got the picture on how it would work out.

And also the huge reassurance that there was going to be enough food. "Please return as often as you like," the sepulchral-looking girls in their white blouses urged.

Con Daly, the cook who was normally never seen anywhere in polite society, stood beaming at the door of the kitchen in his white outfit and chef's hat, as if he had been responsible for everything rather than taking the most simple and basic directions from Kit and Philip.

Out of the corner of her eye Kit saw Orla Dillon — or whatever her married name was — arrive at the door. She looked small and shabby as if she had been in the rain for a while deciding whether or not to go in. Her dress looked limp, her hair lank. Years back they had all thought Orla a wild success, and had huge experience with men. Tonight she looked pathetic.

She was not at Mrs. Dillon's table, that was obvious. There were six people there who didn't look at all as if they might be welcoming the wild girl who had left her family home in the mountains for a night of fun.

Kit moved over to her.

"Hello, Kit." Her eyes looked dull.

"There you are, Orla. Are you with any particular group?"

"That's a gorgeous dress, did you get it in Dublin?"

"Yes." Kit looked anxious.

"I'd love to go to Dublin. To work even." She smelled of drink.

This was going to be awkward, Kit realized. She couldn't throw Orla out. But where was she going to seat her? She knew only too well of Orla's fling with Stevie Sullivan. That's probably why she was here. That was why she had come in from the back of beyond, to have a little New Year's Eve magic.

"Well now, Orla, where did you plan to sit for dinner?"

"I heard it was a table where you went and helped yourself."

"Well, yes of course it is."

"So what does it matter where I sit?"

"I wouldn't want you to be without a place to sit down."

"Don't get your knickers in a twist over it. I'll find somewhere."

This was all they needed, Kit thought. A drunk ex-girlfriend of Stevie's turning up. And for all they knew pursued by all her low-bred in-laws with hatchets.

Philip was at her side as Orla flounced off toward the food table. "What's the problem?"

"Plastered," Kit said succinctly.

"Jesus, what'll we do with her?"

"We could feed her more drink and she'd pass out and we could put her in a cupboard or something."

He looked at her in gratitude, she wasn't making a drama out of it. "Or we could give her to her mother, you know, that old saying 'to every cow its calf' . . ."

"It's not a saying Mrs. Dillon might feel any way enthusiastic about. No, I think the thing is to see where she weaves and sort of settle her there. Emmet will get her a chair."

They saw her weaving with a plate of food piled perilously high toward Stevie Sullivan's table. Emmet approached with an extra chair and hovered until he was waved forward.

"Well, at least she's sitting down," Kit said.

She was so cross that this bit of Stevie's past had come back to haunt him. Yet she was nothing to be jealous of, poor Orla with the pinched face and the slurred speech. Except of course Orla had known Stevie in a much different way. Orla hadn't been Miss Prissy like Kit was being, she had been all the way.

"It's not fair on poor Stevie to let her land in on top of all his party," Philip said. "He's so decent, look at the crowd he brought."

Kit felt a wave of guilt flood over her. If things went according to plan when the dancing began, she would be in Stevie's arms all night. Philip would not be referring to him as "poor Stevie."

She saw Stevie go over to the table where all their own gang sat. She saw him speak to his brother Michael and hand him some car keys. Michael was nodding earnestly and bursting with importance. Then Stevie was back at his own table. The band played numbers that wouldn't disturb the digestive juices, the heavier dance beat would come later. Bobby Boylan and his band would have a recess first and be fed in another room.

"Philip, it's all fine," Kit said. "It's even better

than we had hoped."

"The first of many."

"Isn't that what I said from the word go?"

They stood there proudly and watched. The unsmiling waitresses were beginning to clear the tables. As instructed, they did not scrape the plates there and then but piled them neatly and brought them to the kitchen. The desserts were being arranged on the long table. There would be no panic, everyone could see that bowl after bowl of trifle was lined up in readiness. Soon it would be time for the ladies to go and powder their noses, and the dancing to begin.

Kit told herself not to worry about Orla Dillon. Stevie Sullivan would cope with the sudden and unwelcome appearance of his past. He would know how to avoid a scene. Stevie Sullivan could cope with anything.

Michael Sullivan came up to Kit. "I know I'm meant to be helping clear the dance floor space, but something's come up."

"What exactly?"

"Stevie wants me to drive someone somewhere. Apparently she feels a bit sick."

"And will he not be driving her himself?"

"No, I'm to say he will but he won't, if you know what I mean."

"I know exactly what you mean," Kit said, pleased.

It was done very cleverly. Stevie guided a weaving Orla to the door and whispered something in her ear. She went like a lamb out to his car, where his brother Michael followed.

"Where'sh Stevie?" Orla slurred.

"I'm to drive you there, it's more discreet apparently, and he'll meet you there."

"Where'sh there?"

"We'll be off now, Orla," said Michael Sullivan, and drove through the moonlit night over the roads with their great view of the lake.

He drove eleven miles until he came to the Reillys' land and the house where Orla lived. There were sounds of a singsong in her kitchen.

"Hey, this isn't where I want to go," Orla said.

"This is what Stevie says is best. You're to say you went into town and bought a bottle of whiskey for the night that's in it."

"But I didn't. I haven't got one." Orla was frightened now.

"You did. Stevie's got one for you. I'm to wait, in case they think you were with Stevie or anything."

"But they'll know you're his brother."

"No they won't. I'm only a child in their eyes. I'm only a schoolboy, you wouldn't be with a schoolboy."

"I don't know." Orla looked at him. She got out of the car and walked unsteadily to the door. He prayed she wouldn't drop the bottle of whiskey.

One of the men opened the door. Michael could hear rough voices. "Who have you out in the car?" the man said pushing past her.

"A child," Orla said unsteadily.

The man came out to investigate.

"Good evening, Mr. Reilly," Michael said nervously. "The missus was getting you all a bottle of whiskey as a present and she had no lift back so Paddles asked me to drop her out this way."

"Why you?" the man said.

"I'm known to Mrs. Dillon, the lady's mother," said Michael.

"All right so, thanks." The man was gruff.

"Happy New Year," Michael called as he turned the car to get back on the road.

"And to you, young fellow," he said.

Michael drove back to the party. Things were great. He had told Stevie he would do him the favor if and only if Stevie got him a car of his own, even the cheapest of things. Stevie had been desperate.

By the time Michael got back the dancing was in full swing. "Did I miss anything?" he asked Emmet.

"Only lots of dragging tables and chairs out of the way. And the windows were opened to let out the smell of the people for a bit."

"Did it?" Michael asked with interest.

"I hope so because it blew out all the candles, which had to be lit again."

Bobby Boylan asked everyone to come in to the floor for "Carolina Moon."

"Will you dance, Kit?" Philip asked.

It was the least she could do. They had worked together so happily over the weeks, and now it was a triumph. Already she had heard people saying that it would never leave the Central. She had been told by Kevin Wall's father that there was going to be a big dinner in which he was involved; they had written to the Castle Hotel

782

for quotations but he could say categorically now that it would be held in the Central.

Dan O'Brien had shaken her hand and said that he felt she might have had some part in the organizing of it all and he would like it to be known that he was not ungrateful. Through the convoluted speech with all its double negatives Kit could see that he was so pleased he hardly trusted himself to speak.

Orla Dillon's mother had clutched her in the ladies' room and said that she was a girl of great worth, and that her tact over poor Orla's not feeling well would not be forgotten. "It will not be forgotten," Mrs. Dillon said several times. Kit was mystified. She felt she had handled Orla's arrival very poorly, but it did appear that the girl had been driven back to her mountainy men by Stevie's brother and that all was well.

Stevie. When would he speak to her?

As Bobby Boylan's band began to urge the Carolina moon to keep shining Kit and Philip took to the floor. They were the first out and as they began to dance their table stood up and cheered.

"Well done, Philip," they called. "Well done, Kit."

Everyone else clapped. The pretty girl in the scarlet dress and the son of the house. Kit was stricken. Suppose Stevie thought she was doing it on purpose, looking for attention, spelling it out that she was with Philip. But there was nothing she could do except smile and acknowledge the cheers.

Outside the windows the moon had come from behind the clouds. It was making a long, narrow silver triangle on the lake.

"Look at it, Philip. Isn't it like magic . . ."

In a way she pointed because it meant she could take her arms away from him. She knew Stevie was watching her. She didn't want to pull away from Philip too hurtfully. He looked. It was as they had hoped.

"Haven't you the most beautiful view in the world!" Kit exclaimed.

"We do," he said simply.

"I'm so proud of Lough Glass tonight," Kit said. "I could shout it from the roofs. Usually I have to get ready for people to say Where? when I say I'm from here."

"There's someone from the Castle Hotel . . . they came to report apparently."

"Well, they'll have a lot to tell." Kit managed to get them back to talking as the friends they were rather than being draped around each other.

"He was interested in the summerhouse, said it was a real feature. Apparently they just knocked one down over there . . . weren't we clever?" Philip said. They looked down from the big picture windows at the floodlit summerhouse and the lake stretching away beyond it. "You couldn't wish for a better setting to see in the New Year," Philip said.

Kit looked at the clock, it was a quarter to eleven. She had seventy-five minutes to get Stevie Sullivan out on the floor kissing her and wishing her Happy New Year in front of the town. She could barely wait.

Maura and Martin danced to the music of "On the Street Where You Live." "This must be the only place in the world where almost everybody does live on the same street," Martin said.

"Didn't they do a great job? It's much better than up at the Club, twenty times better."

"You look lovely tonight, Maura."

"And so do you, young and handsome."

"No no, that's going too far," he laughed at her.

"It's what I see." Maura was transparently honest.

He held her a little closer.

Nearby Peter and Lilian danced, stiffly and a little bit away from each other. It had all the hallmarks of a duty dance. Peter would go to the bar shortly.

Philip O'Brien was dancing with his mother.

He was a boy who knew how to do things right, Martin thought. Then he looked around for his beautiful daughter in her eye-catching scarlet dress. As he looked he saw her take the hand of Stevie Sullivan from the garage. Stevie looked like a film star, dark and brooding. As they began to dance Martin thought they looked very much as if they had been dancing together for a long time. Which was of course ridiculous, they hardly knew each other, those two.

"Not now, Emmet. I have to do the decorations," Anna Kelly snapped at him.

"Absolutely." He appeared not to see her rudeness. "I just wanted to make sure I danced with everyone at our table. Patsy," he raised his voice, "will you do me the honor?"

Patsy Hanley's face lit up. She had a very presentable taffeta dress with a big broad sash. Her mother beamed proudly from another table as she saw her daughter walk to the floor with handsome young Emmet McMahon from the pharmacy.

This was a night Lough Glass would remember forever. Kevin O'Connor was dancing with Frankie Barry. "This is a great place, isn't it," he said.

"Would you look at the view," Frankie said. "Philip O'Brien will be the biggest catch in Ireland with a hotel like this under his belt."

"Play your cards right then, Frankie," Kevin said, laughing.

"No, I think he only has eyes for Miss McMahon . . . like the rest of you."

"He'd want to be careful with Miss McMahon . . . she's the kind that could deal you a very sharp blow if you got out of order."

"Yeah, well, that guy she calls the boy next door isn't getting kicked too far away, is he?" asked Frankie.

And they looked at the tableau of Kit McMahon and Stevie Sullivan dancing as if there were no other people in the room, and no one had existed at any other time.

"You look great, Clio," Michael said.
"Why did you say that?"
"Because you do."
"And?"
"And because you're looking very glum."
"And?"
"Because I want you to come up to the room with me now."

"Now, in front of everyone? You must be mad!"

"This may come as a severe shock to you, Clio, my dream girl, but nobody in this room is looking at us, or thinking about us . . . they've all got their own concerns."

That was probably true. Clio looked at the dance floor. Kit must have gone quite mad, she was holding on to Stevie Sullivan as if she never wanted to let him go. Stevie Sullivan, who had been with everyone in the parish. She must have lost her mind.

"I'll go first as if I'm going to the ladies'. You wait for three mins. Okay?"

"Sure." Michael had thought it would be more difficult.

Anna Kelly came back to the table at that moment. "Would you like to dance?" she asked Michael.

"Later, okay?" he said. He saw her face flush a dark red.

"Not if you were the only man in the room with his own legs would I dance with you, Michael," she said. Michael watched her flounce over to a table where a lot of men sat. "I'm a great dancer," he heard her say.

She was also a great-looking girl in that lime-green color. He wasn't surprised that about five of the men rose unsteadily to their feet to compete for the honor. At least it had distracted her.

Michael slipped out of the room and upstairs.

"I've put on the electric fire," Clio said. She was already in the bed, her dress hanging carefully on the back of a chair. He was about to follow her with speed. "Lock the door, for God's sake," she whispered.

"You're very experienced at this sort of thing," Michael said in admiration.

Clio looked at him, alarmed. "You know I'm not. There's never been anyone but you."

"Aha, so you say."

"You know that's true, don't you?"

"Whatever you say, lady." He had his arms around her.

Clio's eyes were troubled. Suppose Michael really thought she might have been with other people, then that stopped her being special. "I love you, Michael," she said.

"Yes, and I love you too." He spoke automatically, as people respond to a greeting. Wasn't it impossible to know if people really meant what they said?

The man dancing with Anna Kelly was a Ford dealer. He covered a big area and Stevie Sullivan was one of his best customers. The boy had a genius for knowing where the business was. He was definitely going places. Joe Murphy was delighted to be invited to this do tonight. Stevie had asked him did he want to bring his wife . . . but Joe thought no, there was no point in complicating things. Now with this little angel in his arms he was even more pleased he hadn't. There would have been great trouble getting someone to mind the children, and anyway Carmel was shy. She wouldn't mix well.

"You're a terrific dancer," Anna said to him.

He held her tightly to him. This was a great place altogether. And to think that only this morning he had begun to think he was getting a bit old and fat, past the first excitement of youth. It had all been in his mind. "Let me dance you off your feet," he said to Anna as he did a tricky showy sidestep. It was true what they always said about large men being light on their feet. She seemed delighted with him.

"Don't move away from me," Stevie said.

"I think the music has stopped," Kit told him.

"Well, that's only temporary."

"I love you," she said.

"People can lip-read phrases like that."

"So you're afraid of what people may hear or read on your lips?"

"No, I'm not afraid. I love you, Kit McMahon. I love you until my heart aches. I can't bear any time without you. You're my woman . . . and I don't mean that in some awful possessive way . . . I mean I'm your man. That's what I mean." He smiled at her, a lovely crooked smile.

They were near a window. The music had begun again. There hadn't been a question of their separating.

"Look at that moon," Kit said. "It's as if we had arranged it with some electrician."

"The lake looks lovely. Maybe we might go and have a walk down there later . . . you know, run down by the summerhouse and onto the shore."

"I think it's probably the worst idea in the world."

"Yes," he agreed. "It is . . . I'd love to live down there, just beside the edge of the water . . ."

"Like Sister Madeleine used to."

"Yes, we might have a little cottage, you and I, one day."

"We'll not be together in a little cottage by the lake."

"Why do you go and say that?" He looked genuinely upset.

"Because we're only fooling ourselves. But listen, enough of that."

"A little cottage where the birds would come, where you could hear the water, like Sister Madeleine did."

"I miss her," Kit said.

"So do I."

They were the two people in Lough Glass who might have been expected to resent the hermit. She had harbored the man who had injured their families. But they both knew it had been from a good heart.

"I wonder where she is tonight."

"Oh, well tucked up in her bed in St. Brigid's," Stevie said.

"St. Brigid's? You know where she is?" Nobody else knew. Her departure and her destination had always been a mystery.

"Yes, I've seen her, met her there."

Kit could have fallen to the ground with astonishment. "I don't believe it."

"True. I was up there trying to persuade the Reverend Mother that if they bought a station wagon for the old gardener to drive instead of a truck he could take them in to the station and do a whole rake of things. And I saw her, just standing there, the eyes as blue and strange as ever."

"And did you speak to her?"

"Of course I did."

"Stevie, you amaze me."

"I'll take you out there to see her one day, she'd love that."

"Maybe she's hiding from people."

"She may be, but not from us."

She felt a shiver of pleasure the way he said "us."

And the dances went on and on. Bobby Boylan and his band fueling themselves with the pints that Philip thoughtfully provided at regular intervals.

The clearing-up had been a dream of efficiency. Kit and Philip had insisted that the kitchen be scrubbed, that utensils be seen to have been cleaned by being turned upside down to prove that even the bottoms had been scoured. Dishcloths and towels washed were hanging on a line. Food was either covered and put in the fridge or if it was for dogs or pigs it was in buckets out in a scullery, each one covered and labeled. Philip wanted to make sure that a few people were casually allowed to see the kitchen after the event, something that would never have been considered remotely likely up to now in the Central.

A certain level of democracy had been allowed. Con Daly and the rest of the staff had been allowed to join the revelers. An extra table had been added for them near the kitchen door. In between serving drinks and cleaning tables the solemn waitresses and the more gleeful waiters would come and sit, to enjoy the first and finest dance they had ever seen.

"Could I have the next dance?" Kevin O'Connor approached Anna Kelly. She was really a beautiful girl. He didn't know why his brother referred to her as some kind of monster or a savage dog.

"I beg your pardon," she said as if he had made the most incredibly obscene suggestion.

"I was just asking you to dance."

"And what made you think I might dance with you?" Anna asked. She was still seething with indignation about Michael having refused her. His twin brother was equally horrible.

"Well, we are at a dance." Kevin was uncertain of himself. Perhaps he was uncouth and forward. He remembered the solicitor's letter and shivered. "I meant no offense," he said humbly.

"I'm glad to hear it," Anna Kelly said sternly, and walked away.

Joe Murphy had been an unwise partner to have picked. He had let his hands roam around her in a very intimate way and even suggested that they go to his car, which was a brand-new model, he said, and there were only five of them in Ireland. She had found it necessary to lose him rather speedily.

But Stevie had seen her dance with him. She made sure Stevie saw her all the time. What was he doing with Kit, for heaven's sake? A duty dance was a duty dance, but this was ridiculous.

She looked around for her sister. Clio had been gone for ages. Then Anna's intelligent eyes noticed that Michael O'Connor wasn't there either. First she went to look for them in the summerhouse. They had all said during the preparations that it would be an ideal place for courting couples; only the outside was lit up. Nobody could see what was going on inside. There was a long bench there with a long cushion. It would have been cold of course . . .

But Anna tiptoed around to peer in. There was no sign of her sister and Michael O'Connor. She paused to look out at the lake. It had never been more beautiful. Why was Stevie Sullivan taking so long to recognize that she was there, all dressed up, grown up, and waiting for him. He could be standing out in the moonlight with her now. Or in the summerhouse.

She was just about to move onto the path when she saw a shape. There were so many shadows here that she thought it was part of the hedge, but she realized now it was somebody crouching there. The shape stood up, it was a woman. A woman in a long woolen skirt and a cloak, a cloak that she pulled up over her face and head when she saw Anna could see her. Then she ran away, down the path that went toward the lake.

Anna got such a fright that she couldn't even find a voice to scream with. Her breath was gone. This woman must have been just beside her for about five minutes, and would have said nothing, shown no presence until Anna had gone back to the path. Who was she, and what was she looking at?

Probably one of the travelers. They were always stealing things, no matter what her father said. They might have come to see could they get at people's valuables. Fur coats and the like. Anna had thought Kit and Clio were stupid to insist

that there be a proper cloakroom with someone to mind it. But now she realized they were
right. Tinkers, travelers, whatever you wanted to
call them, they weren't the same as other people.
Imagine crouching in a garden instead of getting
on with your life.

Her heart still pounding, Anna went back into
the hotel.

Stevie was right in her path as she joined the
dance. "Don't you look lovely," he said admiringly.

"Thank you, Stevie, and you look very handsome, I've never seen you dressed up before."

"Little Anna." He was full of admiration for
her.

"Not so little." She was cross. "And you
brought an interesting party with you," she said.

"Yeah, watch out for Joe Murphy though. He
has a wife and family." She was furious. Instead
of being jealous he was just giving her a friendly
warning, telling her that the man groping her was
a married man.

"I'm sure he has, God help them," Anna said
loftily.

"I'm going to the bar to rescue some of my
flock," Stevie said. "Otherwise I'd invite you to
dance, but I have to make sure they're not dis-
gracing me in there."

"I don't have a free dance as it happens," Anna
said.

"Well then, isn't it all for the best," Stevie said.

She wanted to pick up a nearby chair and hammer him to death with it.

In the bar Stevie found his cronies ordering

large brandies and regaling Peter Kelly and Martin McMahon with their life stories. Joe Murphy was telling them about the car he had, of which there were only five in Ireland. Harry Armstrong was telling them that he had been on a trip to Africa. It was the most interesting thing he had ever done in his life.

He kept stabbing Martin McMahon's chest. "Have you ever been to Africa?" he asked. And no matter how many times Martin said no, the farthest he had ever been was England and Belgium, Harry Armstrong didn't seem to have received this information.

"Africa is the place," he said over and over.

"What were you doing there?" Peter Kelly asked, hoping to lift the needle from the groove.

It was a complicated story, an opportunity that was meant to exist and hadn't turned out, a fellow who had a contact that hadn't materialized. Harry Armstrong hadn't given a fiddler's damn, he had enjoyed Africa, the whole fact of being there. And when he was down on his uppers he had gone and stayed with his uncle Jack, who was a priest out there, nay, more than a priest, a bishop, would you believe.

"That was a great thing, to be Bishop Armstrong in Africa."

"Arse Armstrong?" cried Peter Kelly and Martin McMahon in one voice. "You met Arse?"

"What? What?"

"You're a nephew of Arse?"

"I don't understand." Harry Armstrong did understand something, that these two men who weren't at all interested in him and his travels before, were now fascinated by him.

"Large brandy for the nephew of Arse Armstrong," Dr. Kelly shouted.

Stevie shook his head in confusion. This seemed to be going fine for some reason that nobody could fathom, except perhaps it might have had something to do with the strength of the drinks being served.

Clio and Michael were still not at the table. Anna had now looked everywhere, they were not in the bar where her father seemed to be getting progressively drunker with some of Stevie's friends, they were not in the lounge where some couples were sitting talking. Clio wasn't in the ladies' room, she wasn't in the gleaming kitchen.

Anna Kelly, who should have been the belle of the ball in the dress that had cost a fortune in Brown Thomas, felt very sorry for herself. Stevie Sullivan had no eyes for her at all. Nobody else at the table had been in any way gallant. Her only conquest had been a fat married man with groping fingers. She had been frightened to death by one of the tinkers.

She felt like having a good cry. But not in the newly refurbished ladies' room where everyone would see her. There was a sofa up on one of the landings. She would go up there and sit for a while in the dark. Nobody would see her.

Anna sat and sobbed over the unfairness of life, the fickleness of men, the hopelessness of living in a goldfish bowl like Lough Glass where everyone knew everything about you, the vulgarity and cheap common red dress that Kit McMahon was wearing and how much everyone seemed to like it.

Nearby she heard a door lock open and her heart jumped again. This place was full of strange sounds and shapes and noises. Then through the light she saw her sister start to creep out. Anna gave a gasp. Clio had been in Michael O'Connor's room. They really had been doing it. Making love. My God. Her gasp must have been audible, because Clio went straight back into the room again. Anna crept to the door.

"There's someone out there, I tell you," she was saying in a panic-stricken tone.

"Don't be ridiculous, who could it be?"

"I don't know. It could be anyone."

"Who's the worst person it could be?" Michael asked. His voice was shaky too.

"My mother, I suppose, or Mrs. O'Brien. Mrs. O'Brien, I think, because she'd tell my mother and she'd tell everybody and . . . Oh Jesus, Michael, what'll we do?"

Anna giggled to herself for a moment, then she rattled the door imperiously and called out at the top of her voice: "Open this door at once. This is Mildred O'Brien here, open this door or I'm sending for Sergeant O'Connor."

The door opened and they stood there. Anna had to put her hand in her mouth she laughed so much. She went into the room and threw herself on the bed with mirth. Eventually she blew her nose and wiped her eyes and looked to see if the others were laughing.

They were not. But they had relaxed a little.

Bad and all as it was being discovered by Anna there were worse things that could have happened.

"Very droll," Clio said eventually.

"Wonderful to meet someone with such a sense of humor." Michael had barely been able to recover his breath. "If the performance is over perhaps we could go downstairs."

"Oh, I've finished," Anna said, looking from one to the other. "Have you though?" Then she got another fit of uncontrollable mirth.

They eventually managed to walk down the stairs, the three of them. There was safety in numbers. And they needed it. Mrs. O'Brien was at the foot of the stairs. "And where have we all been, might I ask?"

"I was showing a few people the lovely view from the corridor upstairs," Anna said, cool as anything.

"It is a fine old place," Mrs. O'Brien said. "Not everyone appreciated it but still we've always known."

They were beginning to gather everyone together for the "Auld Lang Syne."

"Is it that time already?" Stevie said.

"I hope to God the place ran itself for the last few hours, I did nothing I was supposed to do," Kit said.

"You did everything you were supposed to do," Stevie said.

Bobby Boylan and the boys were giving little warning toots to tell people it was time to make the circle. The doors were opened so that they could hear the bells of the church ring out. Someone had the radio on to count down to twelve o'clock.

Stevie and Kit stood side by side as if they always had. Maura saw and her heart was heavy. Anna saw and knew she had lost the battle but maybe not the war. Clio saw and thought again that Kit needed her head examined. Frankie saw and decided that Kit had always fancied this guy since the world began and it had really taken off at that party in Dublin. Philip saw and knew it was all over.

And then they were all linking arms and crying out Happy New Year, the balloons were falling from the ceiling, the band was playing, the people were going out into the garden to call Happy New Year over the lake.

They could see the fires of the travelers over in the distance, across the lake. The place had never looked more beautiful.

Stevie Sullivan kissed Kit McMahon as if they were the only people on the earth. They stood in the garden of the Central Hotel with the lake in front of them and the path of moonlight which stretched out to the low hills and woods of the neighboring county. This was their place and their time only.

They didn't see anyone else in the garden. Everyone was inside where Bobby Boylan had started a conga line snaking in and out of all the downstairs rooms. It was headed by Con Daly, who was being hailed as a chef of the century.

And as Stevie and Kit clung to each other they might have heard the sound of the lake lapping below them but they didn't hear the tears fall from the figure that watched them. The figure in the darkness who had sat watching all night.

Anna saw the way they looked at each other. It was like a knife. That's what it was, as if someone had put a sharp knife in under her ribs where her dress was at its tightest and most uncomfortable. She looked very woebegone.

Emmet was watching. This might be his time. Everyone in the town had seen how Kit had taken Stevie Sullivan as her own. He knew that his father and Maura would be cluck-clucking about it. He would never be able to thank Kit enough. If he couldn't make Anna come back to him now he never would.

"Do you know what I'd like to do?" he asked Anna.

"No." She was ungracious, she was sure it would be to dance, to drink, to neck. She wanted none of these things, not with the broken heart.

"I'm tired of this, I'd love to go and sit in the summerhouse."

"And kiss and cuddle and take my dress off, I suppose."

"Certainly not." Emmet sounded shocked. "Hey, you and I made a bargain. You love someone else but that will never stop us from being friends."

"I don't think he loves me, I think your bloody sister managed to interfere there."

"Well, that had nothing to do with me, or with you," Emmet lied smoothly. "We're friends, you and I, and I wondered would we go and read some poetry in the summerhouse, like we used to do. Nobody reads poetry like you do, Anna."

"Would you like that?" She was suspicious.

"I would, very much."

"And when we get there it won't be all, now we're here we . . ."

"No, it's poetry, and I went and got a book in case." They stood and looked at each other.

"Yes, let's do that," Anna said. Anything would be better than witnessing the sickening failure of an evening that had gone so wrong.

Emmet had thought of everything. He had brought a rug so that they wouldn't be cold, he had a flask of drinking chocolate.

"Hey, this is nice," Anna said, feeling good for the first time for hours.

They had a poetry book but they didn't open it. They listened to the music thump out of the windows and across the lake.

"I just thought I'd say, speaking as a friend . . . that you look very beautiful," Emmet said.

"Thank you." Anna looked at him suspiciously.

"Not as a person about to make a lunge at you . . . just as an ordinary person . . . and the kind of thing a girl might say . . . the dress, it's just gorgeous. You look much better than a film star."

"Well, that's very nice of you, I must say."

"It would be a poor kind of friendship if I couldn't say what was in my mind," he said eagerly.

Anna looked at him, there were tears in her eyes.

"You know what I mean," Emmet said foolishly.

"Oh Emmet," Anna Kelly cried. "Emmet, I

love you. I'm so blind and stupid. Thank you for waiting for me, for understanding."

And they held each other and kissed in the summerhouse.

Watched a few yards away by a woman with a cloak over her head. A woman who cried too.

Kevin O'Connor and Frankie had discovered more about each other than they had ever known on this New Year night. They looked at each other with new eyes. They went walking together by the lakeshore, pausing for a bit of this and that. That's how they told it.

And when they were down near the boats they saw this woman, a woman with long hair and a white blouse, sitting with her head in her hands crying as if her heart would break. It had been nobody who was at the dance.

Neither of them had ever seen anyone so upset. A great dark cloak lay beside her on the ground. When they came near her and spoke she picked up the cloak and flung it around her and ran, leaping over the mooring ropes of the boats. She ran away into the dark.

They told this to the others when they were back at the hotel. The older people were leaving, the young had gathered in the lounge unwilling to end the night. Kevin and Frankie were obviously startled by the encounter; it had been eerie.

"I saw her earlier," Anna said. "It was one of the tinkers. She ran in that direction when she left. She was crouching in the garden looking at the hotel, spying, seeing what she could see." Emmet moved near her protectively as she shivered over the incident.

"No, it wasn't a traveler." Frankie was very definite.

"No, I saw her face," Kevin added. "She had a different face."

"And expensive clothes," Frankie said.

"Did she say anything?" Kit asked, a nervous knot beginning to form in her stomach.

"No, nothing at all."

"Would it be that ghost? Do you remember the woman years ago who was meant to have drowned herself in the lake and kept crying out . . ." Clio began. Then she saw the eyes fixed on her, Stevie's, Emmet's, Anna's, Kevin Wall's, Patsy Hanley's, all the children of Lough Glass who remembered who else had drowned in the lake. "I didn't mean . . ." Clio began.

But Kit had broken away. She had run out the door down the path toward the lake. "Lena," she was calling, "Lena, come back, Lena. Don't go again. Lena, come back, it's Kit."

The others stood at the door and watched in horror as Kit ran into the dark night, shouting through her tears. "Come back, Lena, come back."

CHAPTER TEN

They talked about the dance for ages.

There were so many things to tell. Of the bold strap Orla Dillon and how she had been sent back where she belonged. Of the amount of food there was on the table — a banquet was all it could be called. The marvelous spot prizes — crates of brandy, whiskey, and sherry seemed to have been donated, a turkey, legs of lamb, sides of beef, boxes of chocolates, tins of biscuits, fancy soaps, gents' scarves, ladies' blouses (can be changed if size is inappropriate). Nobody in the town had held back when asked to contribute.

"Do you remember the moment the balloons came down?" people said. "And Bobby Boylan's band playing like the Pied Piper as they all went through the kitchen. And wasn't the kitchen shining, it would put you to shame over your own place."

And the fur cape that Maura McMahon wore, she was like royalty. And the great crowd of hard men that were guests of the garage, who slept in their cars and started drinking all over again in Paddles' the following morning. And the moonlight on the lake.

And Stevie Sullivan and Kit. The way they danced all night. And how she ran out of there when someone told a silly story of seeing a ghost at the lake, and she thought it was her mother's ghost. Poor girl, and she went out calling don't leave me, or something. Nobody could hear. And how she had run out in the cold in her red dress and stood down by the lake until Stevie carried her home.

There were so many things to tell.

"You know, Maura, you can leave Stevie in the room. I swear we won't take off our clothes and get it started immediately."

"I didn't think you would." Maura was indignant.

She had brought chicken broth for two days to a shivering Kit, without a word of remonstration about the strange way the night had ended. She had cleaned the mud off the red dress, waiting until it dried so that she could brush it properly.

She had been uneasy when Stevie Sullivan called so often to see the patient. She had found excuse after excuse to come back into the room. Kit reached out and held her hand. "Maura, of course that's what you think. Hasn't Stevie been known for it with everyone in the county?"

"Well . . ." Maura reddened.

"But we've had plenty of places far more discreet and secluded than this, and if I didn't then I'm unlikely to succumb in my own house. Come on, isn't that true?"

"I don't want you to get hurt."

"I won't, I swear."

Maura put her hand on Kit's forehead. "I was given my orders by Peter to keep your temperature down. I think it's normal, but Stevie

805

Sullivan's not going to be much of a help in that department."

"I'd be worse without him, Maura." Kit spoke as an equal.

Maura felt touched by this. "I'll talk to your father."

"He wouldn't understand unless you said it properly. I mean, I couldn't say to Father that Stevie and I haven't done it yet, and won't start under this roof."

"I'll try to explain the situation a bit more diplomatically," Maura said.

Nobody had asked Kit about her strange upset. Even Dr. Kelly had said that it wasn't important. The story that the stupid girl from Dublin had told must have reminded Kit of the night her own mother disappeared. Nobody had told Dr. Kelly that it was his own daughter Clio who had brought the whole thing to a head, reminding them of the ghost of the girl who had died so long ago.

She lay there when there was nobody in with her, her hands gripping the sheets, her brain racing. It must have been Lena. Who else would have come and watched? She must have seen her son in the summerhouse with Anna Kelly. She must have seen her daughter locked in Stevie's arms as they stood on the grass in the moonlight. She may have seen Maura Hayes wearing her little fur cape.

She saw a town lit up with life and banners and balloons and flowers. A town which had been gray and oppressive when she lived here. She knew that among the revelers were the O'Connor boys, young brothers of the girl that Louis would marry. A crowd of nearly two hundred people having a wonderful time while her own heart was broken. Standing on the edge of a place that believed her dead.

Now Kit was a prisoner here. She had caught a chill and she was ordered to stay in bed. There was never a time when people would leave the house, a time when she could ring Ivy to know had Lena returned. Ivy would know. But how could she get to talk to her?

Emmet sat on her bed. "Are you all right, Kit? Tell me the truth."

"Yes, I am. Didn't the dance go so well?"

"But afterward?"

"Afterward I got upset, I got a fright. I was all nervous and tied up inside and I had nothing to eat with the fuss of it all."

"You were wonderful . . . it all worked so well."

"Yes."

"I'll never be able to thank you."

"I know a way," she said.

"What? I'll do anything."

She looked at him, his face eager to help, foolishly happy in love or what he thought of as the love of that dreadful Anna Kelly. In many ways he was still a child.

She just couldn't ask him to ring Ivy. She couldn't tell him everything. That his mother was alive, that she had come to look at them all, that she had run away again, run again toward the lake.

Clio came to visit. "I could have kicked myself.

I'm so thoughtless, why did I mention people in lakes, ghosts? I'm just so thick," she said.

"No, it doesn't matter. I was nervous, I'd had three drinks, no food . . ." This would be her excuse.

"Will you ever forgive me?"

"Of course."

"You must be very seriously sick if you say that. Normally you never forgive me."

"Oh, I forgive you this time." Kit smiled wanly.

"It was terrific, the dance, wasn't it?"

"You didn't get caught?" Kit asked.

"No, only by Anna. Who, by the way, asked me to come and spy out the lay of the land here . . . She wants me to find out all I can about you and Stevie Sullivan." Clio giggled as she spoke.

"And she asked you to do it diplomatically?"

"Yes, she said I was to be discreet."

"Oh, but you are," Kit agreed.

"I don't want to give that ghastly Anna one scrap of information. But this is for me . . . this is for myself . . . Kit, what in the name of God Almighty were you doing? Were you really drunk?"

"Yes, probably a bit."

"You never saw anything like it. You were wrapped around him. All night."

"I know," Kit remembered.

"Listen, it's not the end of the world. They'll forget it, eventually."

"Oh, I don't think so," Kit said.

"They will, they'll know it was just part of the madness of the night."

"Not when they see me glued to him for the

rest of my life they won't."

Clio's eyes and mouth were round. "Kit, you're crazy. Stevie Sullivan, of all the people in the world."

"Yes, of all the people in the world."

"No, Kit, he has a girl everywhere. He doesn't care who they are, married or single, fat or thin, you know what he's like."

"I do. I love him."

"You're still fevered, that's what it is."

"You asked me, you wanted to find out the lay of the land. Now you've found it out."

"Why did you tell me this . . . ? It can't be for real."

"Because you're my friend. You tell me you love Michael O'Connor and you've been to bed with him and that you love it. We're friends, we tell each other things." Her voice sounded a bit hysterical, Kit realized this as she spoke.

"But loving Michael is different, it's . . . well, it's what you'd expect. You can't love the fellow in the garage who's slept with every maid in the parish."

"His past isn't important," Kit said loftily.

"Ah, don't be ridiculous, it's not his past. Didn't you see Orla Dillon turn up at the dance looking like a madwoman just wanting more of it with Stevie?"

"Didn't you see him sending her home?"

"You're serious," Clio said in shock.

"You're the one who always said I was unnatural because I didn't love anyone. Now I do and that's wrong too . . ."

"Look, I'm going home . . . you're not well

809

enough for visitors."

"Okay, and tell Anna what I told you, that I'm crazy about him, and I won't rest until I get him."

"I'll tell her nothing of the sort, I'll say you were so pissed drunk you don't remember dancing with him."

"I'll tell her different and that'll get you into trouble for doing your job so badly."

"I'll ignore you, you're quite mad. I came down to ask was there anything I could do for you, post letters, get you messages . . . but now I think I should get you a psychiatrist."

"Thanks, Clio. You're a real pal."

Kit realized that though she had known Clio as long as she could remember, it was an odd friendship. If Clio was the last person on earth she wouldn't ask her to ring Ivy to give a simple message. She couldn't say, Clio please ring this woman in England and ask her is Lena all right. No questions, just do it. Clio would want every detail and the whole country would know every detail.

"Are you too tired? I won't stay long."

"No, Philip, it's fine. It's great to see you. Wasn't it the best dance in the world?"

"Oh yes. I'll never be able to thank you."

"For what, Philip? For making an eejit of myself . . . I just got upset when they started talking about ghosts."

"Oh, that," Philip said.

"Sure what did you think I meant?" Kit looked at him long and hard. "How are your parents?" she said eventually.

"Oh, throwing out a new wing here and a new wing there. They think it was all their idea, can't understand why I never saw the potential of the place."

"You're great, Philip," she said.

"But not great enough." His face was different. There was less doglike devotion there now. It was as if the dance had managed to convince him that there would be no future for them together.

She could trust him to the ends of the earth. But could she trust him to ring Ivy for her?

When Stevie arrived she was sitting up flushed and eager. "Leave the door open," she whispered.

"Why?"

"I want them to know we're not at it like knives on the bed."

"Why did you suggest that? I'm just about able to control myself, if I think it's out of the question. Don't even joke about it." His smile was broad.

"And I want to ask you something."

"Anything."

"I have it written down. I want you to do something, to make a call, but no one is to hear you."

"Where is it to?"

"To London."

"Sure."

"Would Mona listen in on the exchange, do you think?"

"Not to me, I have too many boring calls to Dagenham and Cowley and places like that."

"Not when Maura's there."

"Understood."

"It's the most important thing in my whole life. Could you do it now?"

"Straight away."

"I've written it down for you."

"Right."

"No, it's not just an ordinary message, wait till you go through it . . . Only Ivy, not her husband Ernest. Say you're my boyfriend, and that I've been sick and can't get to a phone . . . say I think I saw Lena here in Lough Glass on New Year's Eve. I want to know if Ivy's heard from her since then." Tears began to fall down Kit's cheeks.

Stevie took a handkerchief and wiped them away tenderly. "Will she tell me?"

"She might be worried, but you could say I trust you to ask the question but that you don't know anything else. You don't know the full story."

He nodded as if he understood. He was so dear to her, his long dark hair on the collar of his scarlet jersey. She knew he had washed and changed his shirt just to cross the road and visit her. That made her feel so touched she could have cried again.

"I'll be back soon," he said. "Drink your soup, it's going cold."

"Thanks, Stevie."

He had gone, he would do it, he had asked nothing. Kit closed her eyes. She was absolutely certain she had done the right thing.

א א א

"How did you get home?" Ivy asked, taking

the small bag from Lena's hand and removing the wet coat from her shoulders.

"Home?" Lena's face was blank.

"Well, back here to London?"

"I came by boat and train. It was easier. No talking to people, no booking . . . no giving your name. You just get on." The voice was flat and dead.

"You came by boat and train from Brighton?"

"I wasn't in Brighton."

"Yes you were, Lena. I rang you there."

"Oh, then? Yes, that's right."

"So where were you since?"

"Ireland."

"Ireland?"

"Lough Glass. I went to see them."

"I don't believe you."

"Yes."

"What did they say?"

"They didn't see me."

"They threw you out?"

"No, they didn't know I was there."

"Look, Lena, could I ask you have you had anything to eat . . . ?"

"I don't know."

"Suppose I were to make you something now . . . what would you like? I won't offer you turkey . . ."

"I don't mind, I haven't had any turkey this year." A very wan little smile, but it was better than nothing.

"Well, soup and a turkey sandwich?"

"A very small one, Ivy."

The phone rang. "Wouldn't you know," Ivy

said. "The operator said it was a call from Ireland."

"Kit!" Lena leaped up. "Give it to me."

"No, we don't know . . ." Ivy tried to take the phone back.

"Hello," a man's voice said. "Could I speak to Ivy please? This is Stevie Sullivan, I'm Kit McMahon's boyfriend."

"This is Ivy," Lena said.

"Well, it's about Lena. Kit wants to know is Lena all right? Has she phoned you?"

"Why isn't she phoning herself?" Lena wanted to know.

"She's sick and she's in bed."

"Is she bad, too bad to phone?"

"No, I think it's a kind of secret and she's not meant to be heard phoning from home."

"What do you mean, you think? You must know if you're phoning. You must know everything."

"Ivy," the man said. "I'm Kit's friend, she asked me to do this for her. She's distraught over someone called Lena. I don't know, truthfully I don't. But I want to go back across the street now and tell her if Lena's all right. Is she?"

"Yes," Lena said slowly. "Tell her she is."

"Excuse me, but could I give her just a bit more information than that? I don't want to know who Lena is, but Kit was very ill and distressed the other night and she kept calling for Lena. I don't know what it is, but it's important."

"Yes," Lena said in a flat voice. "It is important."

"So?" He waited.

"So if you could say that Lena got home fine, by boat and train and that . . . and that she's fine now and will write soon, a long long letter."

"She's very upset, is there anything you could say that would sort of prove I've spoken to you?" He was going to do this right, he wouldn't go back to Kit unless he had a message to convince her.

Lena paused for a moment.

"You could tell her . . . I suppose you could tell her that the hotel and the whole dance was a credit to her, that nobody could have believed the Central Hotel could look so well."

"And that would prove that I talked to you?"

"Yes, it would, I think."

There was another pause before Lena spoke. "You really don't know what it's about?" Lena asked.

"No."

"Thank you," she said.

"Thank you too, Ivy," he said, and hung up.

He ran across the road to tell Kit. He repeated the message word by word. When he told her about the praise for the Central Hotel she looked at him with two eyes as big as dinner plates.

"Say it again."

He did.

"You weren't talking to Ivy. You were talking to Lena."

She burst into tears.

Ivy helped Lena back to the table. "Well now . . . wasn't that timing? Suppose he had rung

815

half an hour ago, I wouldn't have had anything to tell him."

"Oh God," Lena said.

"What do you mean?"

"She's confiding in him. She'll tell him and then she'll be in his power forever."

"What do you mean?"

"Stevie Sullivan will know her secret. He'll have total power over her from now on. He'll make her do whatever he wants with her. And however badly he treats her she'll have to put up with it, because she can never escape. He knows her secret, he'll always be able to hold that over her."

"Why do you hate him so much?"

"I saw him, Ivy. I was as near to them as I am to you. I saw them kissing, I saw her eyes as she looked at him . . ."

"She's going to fall in love . . . you don't want her to be a nun?"

"No, but I saw him, Ivy."

"And what's wrong?"

"He was Louis all over again. He could have been Louis's son. Or his younger brother. She's going to do what I did. Look at the legacy I've given the child. To love someone who's going to break your heart."

"Jim, there's a letter from Lena," said Jessie.

"Oh, thank God. I thought she'd abandoned us totally. What does she say?"

"That's she's suffering from stress and her nerves, and that the doctor says it's overwork. And advised her to take some weeks off. She says she'll be back at the end of January."

"Well, that's a relief that she goes to a doctor anyway."

"And she does work too hard," Jessie said.

"We've tried to stop her, get her to take time off." Jim had, many times.

"She says she might go to Ireland for a while." Jessie was studying the letter.

"That would be good. It's more restful over there. That's where they're from so they probably have friends and family."

"She doesn't say anything about him."

"Well, he'll probably go too."

"She just says 'I' all the time . . . there's no 'We' mentioned at all."

Clio was having lunch with Michael O'Connor's family. They seemed to be very taken with her, accepting her into their number.

"You will come to Mary Paula's wedding?" Michael's mother asked Clio.

"Yes, I'd love to, Mrs. O'Connor." Things were going very well since New Year's Eve. Huge praise had been lavished on the festivities at the CHL, as it was now known among them all. The Central Hotel Lough Glass had done a great job.

Fingers O'Connor had been interested in every detail. "And how did your stepmother enjoy the dance? Maura Hayes?"

"She's my aunt, actually," Clio said.

"She's Kit's stepmother," Kevin O'Connor said.

"And Kit is . . . ?"

"Kit's the one I used to fancy," Kevin explained helpfully.

817

"Well, how is she?" Fingers was persistent.

"I think she's losing her marbles actually. She's involved with the local rake."

"Maura Hayes?" cried Fingers in disbelief.

"No, Kit," they all said.

Fingers was going to get no more information about that nice plump woman he had always had such hopes of having a dalliance with.

Kit was back in Dublin. By an unspoken agreement Stevie Sullivan was not mentioned when she met Clio.

"Tell me about Mary Paula's wedding. Is it going to be a big one?"

"No, dead quiet."

"That doesn't sound like the O'Connors."

"Apparently the lovely Louis hasn't any family . . . or any fit to field at a wedding."

Clio sounded so snobby Kit hated her for a moment. Then she remembered who she really hated. "So how are they going to do it then?"

"Not one of their own hotels. Marriage in University Church and sixteen people to lunch in a private room in the Russell. Just along Stephen's Green."

"The Russell! Lord, how posh."

"I know. I don't know what I'm going to wear. You wouldn't tell me where you keep getting these gorgeous outfits."

"You want to wear an off-the-shoulder scarlet evening dress to a lunch in the Russell?"

"Oh all right. I'll never know. There's so much I'll never know about you, Kit."

"And me about you. Aren't we women of mystery?"

"You look very pale. Are you better from whatever it was?"

"Yes, I'm just a bit tired." In fact she had been awake all night waiting for the letter that Lena had promised to send. A letter explaining everything. But which hadn't arrived yet.

"Aunt Maura, it's Clio. Do you remember that lovely little fur cape you wore at the dance?"

"Hello Clio. How nice to hear from you. All the way from Dublin."

"Yes. Yes, well, I can't talk long. But I was going to ask you a great favor."

"What's that?"

"I was wondering would you lend it to me for a wedding I'm going to. I really want to look terrific and I think it would be smashing over my cream-colored suit."

"You're very young for furs, Clio. They're really for older women like me."

"I know what you mean, but your one was particularly nice. It was really more suitable for a younger person altogether."

"Oh really," Maura said.

Clio tried to retrieve it. "What I meant was it looked so smart on you."

"Good, I'm glad you liked it."

"So I was wondering . . ." Maura let the pause rest between them. "I was wondering if you'd lend it to me. I'd be so careful of it . . ."

"No, I'm sorry." Maura's voice was cool. "I'd love to be able to help, but that's a very

819

special gift and I don't want to leave it out of my hands."

Stevie came to Dublin four nights a week, and on every one of those nights he and Kit went out together. They agreed that they meet out. The temptations of the bedroom, the quiet little bed-sit where no one would notice who came into the building and who left, had too many dangers.

Stevie wanted to be true to his promise. If staying with Kit meant staying out of bed with her he said that was the deal; he wanted to be with her.

They sat in chip shops and held hands. They took the bus to Dun Laoghaire and walked along the pier in the wind and rain. They went to the pictures in the big cinemas in O'Connell Street. They met no other people. They didn't need anyone.

And who would they meet? Philip, whose face would break both their hearts. Clio, who thought that Kit was throwing her life away. Frankie, who was so wrapped up in Kevin O'Connor that she had time for no one else.

But they never tired of talking and touching and laughing. If anyone had asked her what they talked about, Kit thought one night, she couldn't tell. The time had flown, but she didn't know what they had spoken of. They didn't talk about his past. Or his wish to love her in a different way. As they never mentioned the woman that he had spoken to that day on the phone. The woman who remained a secret that he never wanted to know. One day Kit would tell him it was her mother, but not yet.

My dearest Kit,

I have tried so many times. There's a waste-paper basket full of pages torn up, screwed into little balls. I think I had a sort of breakdown. That's all I can say. I hope it's over. But it won't be over really until Louis marries. It's on January 26th in Dublin. When it's all over and done with then I think I'll be back to normal again. Please believe me, Kit. Forgive me for this as you have in so many other things. Tell me you are well and strong. That you are back at work.

I talked to Stevie. He thought it was Ivy but you know it wasn't. He sounded very concerned about you. As if he loved you a lot. I'm saying this because I know you want to hear it. And also because I think it's true. This doesn't mean it's all for the best. I love you so much, Kit.

Whatever happens remember that.

> *Your loving mother,*
> *Lena.*

Kit was very worried. Lena had used the word "mother" again in a letter. Did she really have a breakdown? What was her warning about Stevie? And most of all why was she warning her to remember that Lena loved her whatever happened? What could happen that hadn't happened already?

"Do you know what I'd love you to do?"
"No, I dread to think," Kit said.

Clio's eyes were too bright. "Could you pinch Maura's cape for me to wear, she'll not notice it's gone. I'd pay your fare down to take it back after the wedding."

"Are you out of your mind?" Kit asked.

"That's my line to you. You're the one who's mad, not me. You're the one whose name is up with Stevie Sullivan all over the place. My mother was asking me what you were up to."

"I don't give a damn what your mother thinks, asks, or says."

"You've been saying that as long as I remember," Clio said.

"I must have had some reason. You always quote her as if she knows everything and the rest of us know nothing."

"Why are we fighting?" Clio asked.

"Because you were very rude and hurtful to me, as you almost always are."

"I'm sorry."

"No you're not, you just want Maura's cape."

"For a loan. Look at the way we lend each other everything, shoes, bags, lipsticks . . ."

"But those are ours, not someone else's."

"She won't know."

Kit paused. Imagine the irony that she was being asked to lend someone Lena's cape for Louis's wedding. Maybe Louis had given that cape to Mother. Years and years ago. Father didn't remember buying it. You'd remember buying a fur coat, for heaven's sake.

Should she let Clio wear it? Startle Louis at his wedding with the memory of the gift he had given to Lena. But men were so hopeless. They remembered nothing. Suppose he remembered it, he'd just think Clio had another one like it. This was such a dangerous area anyway. Kit had hardly been able to think about it. Each day she dreaded the discovery that the handsome Louis Gray had lived in London with a mysterious Irishwoman, and the further — unthinkable — discovery that the Irishwoman was in fact Helen McMahon. She had been trying to push this fear to the back of her mind. Clio watched her during the pause. It was as if Kit was deliberating. Deciding whether to give it or not.

"No," Kit said eventually. "Sorry for all the silly fighting and everything, but it's just not possible."

"I wish the bloody wedding was over," Clio said. "Everyone's very tense about it. Except the bridegroom apparently. He's invited four people, and he's as happy as Larry. He's a real smasher, by the way, for an old man."

"When did you meet him?"

"Oh, he's here. They were having drinks at Michael's father's the other night. He holds your hand in a way that you think if things were different he might fancy you. Oh, and she's definitely preggers. You'd know by the way she stands."

"Would we go to the North, you and I, next weekend?" Stevie asked her.

"No," Kit said. "I have to be in Dublin."

"What for? I thought you'd like a nice drive. I've got a business meeting that will take about twenty-five minutes and then we could go and see a banned movie . . ."

"To drive me mad with lust . . . ?"

"No, just for fun, and we might drive up the Antrim coast road. It's meant to be gorgeous, like Kerry."

"But we'd never do all that in a day."

"We could stay the night. In separate rooms. Hand on heart, I swear."

"No, I can't, Stevie, not this Saturday. I want to stay in Dublin really."

"Why?"

"Weren't you the one who said we should be free as the air, not asking each other questions?"

"Yes, you're right. I was. Sorry."

"I'll tell you," she said. "I want to go to the church and watch Michael O'Connor's sister getting married to this man, Louis Gray."

Stevie looked at her. "I was about to say What on earth for . . . but I remembered that we were to be free as the air, so I won't ask you."

"Thank you," she said.

"But I am going to volunteer that if you're not going to come with me to the North, I'll be back that evening and maybe we'll go out."

"I hope so." Her face was serious.

"So will we?"

"Could you call round to the flat, if I'm there I'm there."

"That's not much to drag a man a hundred and eighty miles back over long, dark roads from the North on a cold January night," he said.

"It's just that . . . well, it's just that I'm worried about something. I'm afraid something might go wrong."

"Would you like me to stay with you, be here just in case?"

She was tempted for a moment. But eventually she decided against it. This trip to the North might be the beginning of big business. And anyway she was probably mad. Lena couldn't really be thinking of coming to Louis's wedding.

Louis Gray felt his years. He had spent too many evenings with the young members of the O'Connor clan trying to prove himself a satisfactory brother-in-law. Their capacity for pints was endless. His turn to buy came up with startling speed. Mary Paula had severe morning sickness and was in no mood to console him. He had to be particularly consolatory to her.

Which was difficult since he was staying in one of the O'Connor hotels and she was in her father and mother's house. He spent a lot of his time familiarizing himself with the regimen of the business he was about to join.

The staff were extremely respectful but Louis knew that this was because he was the prospective son-in-law of the chairman, and the heir apparent. These were not waiters, porters, desk clerks, who would lavish such attention on the general public.

He found Fingers O'Connor, his future father-in-law, a difficult man, his wife a tiresome fusspot. There were many aspects of these crowded days which he found confusing. Like Mary Paula's brothers, two loutish lads; they seemed to be deeply involved in the affairs of Lough Glass, of all places. They had hurried home from London in order to attend some function there in the CHL.

On Louis's many previous secret visits to Lough Glass there had been no such hotel, only a run-down flyblown place that you would be afraid to go into. But the O'Connor boys were saying that its Georgian frontage and old-style charm might be the very thing that visitors to Ireland needed and looked for, rather than modern purpose-built blocks. It sounded utterly right to Louis, who couldn't of course agree with this notion since his future was tied up in a very plain functional modern hotel block, the management of which was going to be his wedding present from Fingers O'Connor.

Louis had looked up old acquaintances in Dublin. He was always able to parry questions about himself, usually he used a rueful laugh. "Ah, you don't want to be hearing all the mistakes I made, tell me about you now. Things going well?"

He had found a best man with no trouble. A man he had known in the retail business years ago. Presentable and unimaginative. Harry Nolan — a man who would think it reasonable that Louis Gray return to Ireland because he had managed to seduce the twenty-eight-year-old daughter of a wealthy hotelier and get a key management contract as a reward for making an honest woman of her.

Harry had many social skills, and like Louis was a better listener than talker. He was married but explained to Louis that his wife would not be a social addition to the scene so let the ceremony pass without involving her.

Ireland had changed, Harry assured his friend Louis. Business was business, people took chances where they could. Look at them both. They had been selling ladies' underwear once, now Louis was made, a hotelier of the future, Harry himself was the manager of a very important Grafton Street store and a man who moved in society.

Harry had been a perfect choice. The night before the wedding Louis and Harry had two drinks. Neither of them felt they could be confident of looking well after a batter, so the night was a moderate one.

Louis looked out over the Dublin roofs from his hotel room. He wished he could stop thinking about Lena, and where she was tonight. She had assured him she understood. Why was it so disturbing that she hadn't been seen at work or at home since?

He made one more call to Ivy. He disguised his voice and changed his name but he always felt she saw through him.

"I was wondering where Mrs. Gray is? I've made many attempts to contact her at work," he said.

"She's gone away," Ivy's sepulchral voice replied. "Nobody knows where or why. So I'm afraid I cannot help you."

It was cold but fine. There was a thin winter sunlight when Harry Nolan and Louis Gray arrived at University Church in St. Stephen's Green. The Saturday traffic passed by, people craning out of buses to see who was assembling at the smart church where wealthier people married.

"An hour from now the job will be done and we'll be in the Russell getting stuck into the gins and tonics," said Harry.

Louis peered into the distance. He was jittery today. Everything seemed to have a resonance of some kind. It turned out that Mary Paula's brother Michael had every intention of marrying that pretty Clio, the doctor's daughter from Lough Glass. Someone that Lena probably knew well. He reminded himself that they all thought Helen McMahon was dead. Nobody would ever believe him if it were brought up that he had lived with her for so many years.

Then, as he stood there in the sunlight, he saw a woman across the road, a woman in dark glasses who reminded him so much of Lena that it made him feel weak.

"I don't suppose you brought any kind of sustenance," he asked Harry.

"Yes, hip flask of brandy. Let's get inside the vestry before you attack it," Harry said.

Fingers O'Connor helped his daughter out of the large limousine. The others had gone into the church ahead. "You look lovely, Mary Paula," he said. "I hope he'll be good to you."

"He's what I want, Daddy," she said.

"Well then." He sounded not entirely convinced.

"I don't look fat, do I?"

"No of course you don't. Look at the people all admiring you." A small crowd of passersby had stopped to smile at the bride. Some of them even went into the back of the church to watch the ceremony from a discreet distance.

Kit had her head in her hands as if she were praying. She wore a belted raincoat and a checked head scarf. She was sure that none of the wedding party would see her. They were so far behind the action . . . those who had come to look on. But she wasn't praying, she was peering through her fingers. There were elderly people with their rosary beads talking silently but earnestly to God and his mother. There were a couple of students who were obviously killing time before lunch in Grafton Street. There were a couple of down-and-outs, a man in a sacking coat and a woman with five carrier bags.

She couldn't see Lena.

And then she saw a figure beside a confession box. A woman in a long, dark woolen skirt, and a very smart military-style jacket. She had been wearing a head scarf and dark glasses but she removed these and Kit saw her putting on a smart hat, a hat with a feather, a hat that had cost more than any headgear at this stylish but small wedding. The woman straightened herself up and prepared to join the body of the guests. She was going to sit on the groom's side.

Lena had done what Kit had hoped and prayed she would not do. She had come to Dublin and was going to break up Louis Gray's marriage day. She was going to lose anything she had left. Her dignity, her anonymity, and possibly her freedom. She might well be about to attack the groom or the bride. Lena's eyes were wild, Kit saw. She could not be held responsible for what she did. She might spend the night and a great deal of her life in prison.

The bride had gone up the church with her father and had been handed over to Louis, who stood there beaming.

Kit had only seen him once, but she remembered his smile. She even remembered how Clio had said that Louis Gray made you feel special. He made you feel that if things were different he might fancy you. She saw him there in front of everyone, like a handsome actor about to say his lines, and she realized that was all he had ever been and would ever be. Her wonderful mother could not, must not, lose anything over anyone as worthless as this.

Kit almost threw herself from one side of the church to the other. Nobody saw them, they were far too far behind the main action for anyone except the regular Rosary sayers or scattered minds to notice them. She caught Lena's arm before Lena had time to get more than a few steps up the aisle.

"What!" Lena wheeled on her.

"Take me with you," Kit hissed.

"Get out of here," Lena said.

"Whatever you do, Mother, I'm going with you," Kit whispered. "If you drag yourself down by this you'll drag me too."

"Kit, leave me, leave me. This has nothing to do with you." They struggled in the shadowy part of the church, unnoticed by the congregation near the altar rails who had their backs to them.

"I mean it," Kit said. "If you have a knife or

a gun I'm going with you, they can arrest me too."

"Don't be ridiculous, I haven't anything like that."

"Well, whatever trouble you're going to make I'll stand there too." By this stage the sacristan and two of the altar boys had noticed some fracas and strained to look, but none of the guests turned. "Believe me, I mean it," Kit said.

"What are you doing to your life?" Lena said, her eyes wild with panic.

"I'm doing nothing to it, you're the one destroying it," Kit said. It was a moment that went on forever. Kit felt the arm loosen, the resolve go. "Come out with me, come now." Lena stood there. "Mother, come with me."

"Don't call me that," Lena said.

Kit felt she was breathing normally. Things were back as they were. If Lena was prepared to retreat into the cover story again the crisis might be over.

Kit propelled her mother out into the open where it was crisp and cold. A wind blew along the street, raising little bits of litter from the gutters. Soon the bride and groom would come out and people would throw confetti. They must be long gone by then.

Lena said nothing. Not a word.

"Are you tired, Lena?" Kit asked her.

"So tired I could lie down here on the road and sleep."

"Come on, we'll go to the corner, there are taxis over there on a rank."

Lena didn't ask where the taxi would take

them. As they turned the corner a woman cried, "Kit." They both turned to see a smart woman in a swagger coat. It was Rita. Rita Moore who had worked with them in Lough Glass. Kit and Rita hugged each other. "This is a friend of mine, Lena Gray, from England."

"How do you do," Rita said.

"Hello, Rita."

Rita's head snapped up to look at her again as if she recognized the greeting.

"Lena's been a great friend of mine and given me lots of good advice. She runs an employment agency," Kit said desperately.

Rita was calm. "Of course, and what a good business to be in these days. Young people need all the advice they can get. You must get a lot of satisfaction in your work."

Lena said nothing.

"I've got to rush now," Kit said.

"Great to see you, Kit." Her eyes stayed long on Lena. "And you too, Mrs. . . . . Mrs. Gray," she said.

"She knew," Lena said when they were around the corner.

"Of course she didn't," said Kit. "But let's get you away really quickly in case we meet anyone else. It could be Mona Fitz's day for a shopping excursion."

The first taximan looked at them expectantly. "Where to, ladies?" he asked.

Lena looked blank. "Will we go first and collect your case?"

"Case?"

"Suitcase, luggage, wherever you left it." Kit

tried to sound casual.

"I have no luggage," Lena said.

Kit shivered. She might never know what her mother had intended to do at the wedding of Mary Paula O'Connor and Louis Gray. Lena had come to Dublin with no possessions, no plans of where she would stay at night. It was as if she had not expected to be a free agent by the time night fell.

"Will you come home and stay in my flat, rest now and stay the night?" Kit said. "I've always wanted to have you to stay. And there's a nightie for you and a hot-water bottle . . ."

"And will we fit in the bed?"

"I'll sleep on cushions on the floor." There was a pause. "I'd love you to come, Lena." Another pause. "I don't ask for much," Kit said.

"It's very true, you don't," Lena said.

Kit gave the taximan her address.

They climbed the stairs slowly. Lena said nothing when Kit opened the door. "Well, say you like it. Say it's nice . . . it's got character . . ." Kit was desperate. "Say it's got possibilities even."

Lena smiled at her. "I've dreamed so often what this place would be like. I thought the window was on the other side," she said.

"And what did you dream you might be offered for lunch when you came here?" Kit asked.

Lena saw on the little table beside the gas ring that there were four tomatoes and a loaf of bread.

"In my dreams I always had tomato sandwiches and tea," she said.

After that it was all right. They talked to

each other as friends.

And then finally, worn out, Lena went to sleep in the little single bed. It was only four o'clock in the afternoon. But Kit felt her mother might not have slept for many a night before now. Kit sat in a chair and looked out the window. She felt very empty. She wished that Stevie would come. The darkness came but she didn't put on a light.

About eight o'clock she saw Stevie's car. He paused to look up at her window. He had never been in this room. What a different way for him to see it from the way she had planned. With her mother lying in her bed.

She tiptoed to the door and beckoned him in. She pulled another chair to the window, a finger on her lips.

"She needs her sleep, don't wake her," she said. "It's Lena."

"I know."

They sat in silence. He had brought her a box of chocolate sweets that were only on sale north of the border. Things always seemed more exotic when you couldn't get them here. He stroked her hand.

"Was the trip okay?" she asked.

"Tiring," he said. "And the wedding?"

"Uneventful," she said.

"That's what you wanted, wasn't it?" He looked at her, she could see his face in the street light.

She nodded. "I'll tell you sometime. I swear."

"So do you want me to go now?" he asked.

Never had she seen such disappointment on

a face. He had driven in the cold and rain all the way back and she was going to ask him to leave because of Lena, an unexplained woman in the bed.

"No, I'll write her a note, tell her we've gone to the Chinese, if that suits you?"

"I was thinking about sweet-and-sour pork since Drogheda," he said.

"If she wakens up she might join us. But she'll know I'm coming back . . ."

"Can you see to write?" He stroked her hair as she bent over the table to write the note.

Lena, you were sleeping so peacefully I didn't want to wake you. It's eight-fifteen now, Stevie and I have gone to the Chinese restaurant. I've left its little card to show you where it is. Please come and join us there. If not, I'll be back by midnight and will sleep on the cushions . . . but I truly truly would love you to come and follow us there.

Love always, Kit.

Then they left the room on tiptoe, pulling the door behind them.

Lena sat up when they were gone. She read the note and stood at the window watching them walk along the road, arms draped around each other. She had learned that this boy did care for Kit, and cared a great deal. She agreed that he knew nothing of her circumstances, only that she was an unexplained friend, Lena from London.

And she also felt that he had every characteristic of Louis Gray. When he loved he would mean it at the time. But the time would not last very long in any given place. If only she could protect her girl from this.

Kit came back alone. She read the note.

> *I did wake up, but forgive me, I literally didn't have the energy to come out and join you. I had some biscuits here and now I'm going back to sleep. Bless you, dearest Kit, and see you in the morning.*

Kit lay on the cushion and rugs on the floor. She felt certain that her mother's breathing was too even somehow. It didn't sound like the breath of a woman getting her first deep sleep in weeks.

"Let me take you round Dublin," Kit offered.

"No, I'd better go back to London. The holiday is over."

Kit hated the way she grimaced when she said the word "holiday." She decided she would grasp it. "Not much of a holiday, Brighton on your own, two quick visits here."

"No, well. I'll organize it better another time."

"I wish you'd meet Stevie. I want you to."

"No."

"You think he's unreliable."

"He was only a child when I left, I rely on you for a definition of how he is."

"I've told you everything about him, every single thing . . . if you're going to get so buttoned up on me and purse-lipped I'll have to stop telling you things."

"I think you're just on the verge of stopping telling me things about him."

"You mean that we're going to be lovers?"

"Believe me, I'm not criticizing," Lena said.

"So why don't you approve?"

"I think he'll break your heart."

"So? It'll mend again."

"If they're badly broken they don't."

"Lena, I know you see . . . well, let's say some similarities . . ."

"If you see them then is it possible they might be there?"

"No, it's not." Kit's chin stuck out defensively.

Lena pleaded with her. "I know what's going through your head . . . you're going to say if only Lena had met Stevie a few months ago . . . suppose all this had happened when Louis was around . . . then she would have approved, understood, said you must follow your star."

"And so you would," Kit cried.

"I might not. I told you that it had been worth it. I mean, what would have been the point of anything if I hadn't believed I did the right thing. It would have meant I messed everyone's life up for nothing, which is what I did. Everyone, all because of me."

"No, that's not so." Kit was gentle.

"It is. I look around me and I see it."

"But Father's all right, and Maura. And Emmet is happy, and I'm in love. And you and Louis . . . well, what you had was very bright, you told me that once . . . that it was better to burn brightly . . . it was very good . . ."

Lena looked very lost. "In a way you're saying

837

I didn't mess up people's lives, that everyone survived fine, including Louis. Only my own. I destroyed my own as surely as if I had drowned that day."

"I certainly did not say that. Stop putting words in my mouth . . . I'm just saying don't feel so guilty. You've always been good for people, helping them, giving . . . not destructive."

"If you hadn't been there . . ."

Kit would not allow them down this road. "Tell me, what did you love most about Louis?"

"His face lighting up to see me, it was as if someone had turned on a switch . . ."

It was a funny phrase, Kit thought, especially when she had seen through Louis at his wedding ceremony, an actor reading lines. Of course he could turn on a switch. "And what was worst about him?"

"The way he thought I believed his lies. It made us both so stupid."

"And why do you think it didn't last? What you and he had?" She was gentle but probing, she felt Lena wanted to answer. To think it out.

"I don't know . . ." Lena said thoughtfully. "You tell me, what do you think it was?"

"Maybe it was about not having children. If you had ever been pregnant . . ."

"I was," Lena said. "I was more pregnant than Mary Paula O'Connor. That's why I left you and Emmet and Lough Glass and Ireland. Of course I was pregnant."

"And what happened?" Kit asked.

"I lost the baby. I lost it all over the train from Brighton and all over Victoria Station and in

Earl's Court. That's where our baby is. Louis's and my child."

Kit held her hand. "And could you not have . . . did you never try . . . ?"

"He didn't want a child. He didn't want a child until I was too old to have one, but by then he wanted one with someone else." Her mouth was in a hard white line.

Kit McMahon felt more troubled than she had ever been in her life.

They didn't speak of what had brought her to Dublin. Of what she might have done if Kit had not rescued her and taken her away in the nick of time. There would be another day when that could be talked about.

Lena was getting stronger by the hour. She was like a plant that needed water. Something was giving her back energy and hope and purpose. She was rapidly becoming the old Lena, full of plans and moving quickly. She had run to a phone box and found the times of planes. She had telephoned Ivy. To say she'd be back that night. And Jessie Millar to say she'd be at work next day.

"I'll come to the airport with you," Kit said.

"No, we could meet a dozen more people we know."

"I don't care. I'm coming."

"What about Stevie? Suppose he turns up here?"

"I'll leave a note on the door for him."

Lena looked at her thoughtfully. "He doesn't have a key?"

"You know he doesn't."

"Yes, I only meant maybe he should have."

"But I thought you said . . ."

"I know you love him." For Lena it was simple. Love was something that happened, you had no control of it. It took over.

Kit was bewildered. "But what about everything you told me of all that happened to you, and how you didn't want it to happen again?"

"It's too late." Lena was matter-of-fact. "The only thing you must learn from me is not to take the safe option. Not to run away and marry a good kind man just because he *is* good and kind. That's not the solution."

Kit thought of Philip. "I don't think I'd do that," she said slowly.

"You mightn't now, but if you were lonely you might. And it would be very wrong, well, you can see how much hurt and wrong came out of it."

Kit went back to what she had said earlier. "You think I should give Stevie a key to . . . here?"

"I think you should ask yourself why you are putting off something you want so much." They looked at each other in amazement. "The only mother in Ireland today taking this side in the age-old argument . . ." Lena said, and they collapsed in laughter. Whatever madness had taken Lena over seemed to have gone, or to have been replaced with a different one.

Stevie knocked at the door. "I'll only stay a moment," he said.

"Come in and meet Lena . . ." Kit opened the door.

"How do you do." She shook his hand firmly. "I'm very sorry for messing all your plans up this weekend. Kit has been very good to me."

"No, heavens no." His smile was warm. He was not awkward or ill at ease, which was remarkable, Lena thought, when he was in the middle of a situation he didn't even begin to understand.

"Anyway the good news is that I'm off to the airport now. I'm trying to persuade Kit not to come . . . so you're the ideal excuse. Perhaps we could all walk down to Busaras where I could catch the airport bus."

Before Kit could speak Stevie said: "I have a car at the door. It would be my pleasure to drive you out there and I'll sort of circle a bit while you say good-bye."

Lena accepted. Stevie looked around for her suitcase but didn't seem put out when he realized there wasn't one. Lena sat in the front of the car and Kit leaned on the back of the seat between them.

She pointed out landmarks. "I can't remember, was Liberty Hall there in your time?"

"Not in my time as such."

"Look, do you see this house on the corner? Frankie's grandfather lives there. He's as rich as anything and all the family keep calling on him and asking about his health. Imagine!"

"Does Frankie call on him?" Lena inquired.

"No, she's got more sense."

"He'll probably leave her everything just to spite them," Stevie said.

Lena looked at him with interest. Louis would have said that there was no harm in being nice to the old fellow, and you never knew the day

841

nor the hour. She would have thought that Stevie Sullivan would have gone that route also.

He talked about things that could cause no frisson. He asked her nothing about where she had come from or why she was here. Instead he told her about planes and how he'd love to fly one. It must be great to soar up there and swoop and have miles of sky at your disposal, not just a straight road.

He had never been on a plane, as it turned out. "Real country hick, Lena," he said with a grin. It was hard to believe that the son of dreary Kathleen Sullivan and her insane, drunken husband could turn out like this. Handsome and confident, but not pushy.

Her fingers tightened on her handbag. She knew that her daughter had lost her soul to this man. Nothing she could say in terms of warning would do any good. All she could do now was hope and pray.

He was as good as his word about circling around. He said his good-byes as he dropped her off. "Come back and see us sometime," he said, all warmth and invitation.

Lena responded in the same way. "Or you two come over and see me. At least it would get you on a plane."

Kit looked at her in delight. Stevie had been accepted. She could see that. Lena really did like him. She was overjoyed. As soon as he was out of hearing she clutched Lena's arm. "I knew you'd like him," she said excitedly.

"Of course I do. Who wouldn't like him?" Lena said.

She got out her wallet and paid for her ticket. She must have bought no return flight. What had she intended to do in Ireland, or had she not thought at all? She looked perfectly well now.

Kit walked to the departure gate with her.

"Soon, very soon, you'll come?" Lena's eyes looked deep into hers.

"Yes, as soon as you're settled in again. Of course I'll come."

"Thank you, Kit. Thank you for everything."

Kit didn't know what she was being thanked for. She had no idea what she had prevented. She was too choked to say good-bye so she just clung on to Lena for a long time and then ran back to the exit.

In the car she blew her nose loudly. "Now, that's better," Stevie said approvingly, as if he were talking to a toddler.

"It was very kind of you to drive her out."

"Nonsense."

"And thanks too for not asking and everything. Sometime I'll tell you, but it's too complicated."

"Sure. Would you like to go up the mountains?"

"Where?"

"You know, out in the Wicklow mountains. We could just go where you'd see no houses or people or anything, sort of empty your mind a bit."

"That would be lovely."

They sat companionably, saying nothing but feeling no need of chat until they were beyond Glendalough, up in the Wicklow Gap. Then they parked the car and walked in the cold clear air past the gorse bushes and over the springy turf and rocky crags.

Stevie was right, it was as if the whole population had left. There was nothing to look at except what had been there when the earth began, trees and mountains and a river.

Kit felt her mind emptying. She took deep, long breaths. They sat on a great big rock like a shelf and looked down at the valley below.

"It's a very long story," she began.

"She's your mother," Stevie said.

א א א

Ivy was overjoyed to see her.

"Come upstairs at once and see your new wallpaper," she said.

The room looked totally different. Pink and white stripes from ceiling down to floor. A little stool at the dressing table covered with matching material. The position of the bed had been changed slightly and there was a pink eiderdown with a trim of the striped fabric.

"It's beautiful, it's utterly gorgeous," Lena cried.

She could see the hours of time and work invested in this by Ivy. She could never thank her. But she knew that for Ivy to see her well again was reward enough.

"At least it's different," Ivy said gruffly.

"It's very different. It doesn't look like the same place."

"That's what I hoped." Ivy was grim.

"No, it's all right. I'm fine now, I promise."

"What were you doing in Ireland then?" Ivy wanted to know.

"I just went and saw it happen, saw with my own eyes that he married someone else. Now it's over."

"You went to the wedding?"

"Just in the church, not as a guest . . ." She laughed lightly.

"You amaze me," Ivy said. "And do you want to talk about it or about him, or is it better if we don't?"

"I think it's better not. That way I get on with my life."

Ivy seemed pleased. "I'm sure that's the right way," she said. "Now, I suppose this means you might be able to eat again. Because I've got some steaks for the three of us."

"A big rare steak . . . that's exactly what I was hoping you'd have," Lena said.

Ivy trotted happily downstairs to tell Ernest that Lena was cured.

"Ah, women get over these things," he said with the air of a man who understood the world.

Lena stood alone in the room where she had lived with Louis. She would speak of him no more, she would talk of him to nobody. But most of all she would think about him as little as was humanly possible.

She had seen him marry another woman. He had gone from her life. She was glad she had seen that, and been to the wedding. It finalized everything somehow.

It was a bit of a blur how she had got there and what she had intended to do. But that didn't matter, she had been and seen it. She had been so close to Kit and seen how she loved Stevie. Once this had frightened her. But now she felt there was no point in trying to fight it. It was just inevitable.

At work they were so pleased to see Mrs. Gray back. There had been a few problems, naturally they hadn't wanted to interrupt her on her sick leave, but it was great to see her back.

"The Christmas party wasn't the same without you," they said.

"The Christmas party!" How long ago that seemed now. She had forgotten she hadn't been there. "Oh, I'm sure you managed," she said.

"Not all that well. There was no spirit in it somehow . . . Did you have a nice Christmas or were you still poorly?"

"I was still poorly, but thank heavens I'm better now." Her smile was bright, her air was busy and let's-get-down-to-work. "I'll be having a meeting tomorrow, when I've caught up with everything. I am so sorry for leaving you all in the lurch but these things happen . . . so I'll want you to let me know by the end of today any areas in your control where you feel any anxiety."

Millar's gave a collective sigh of relief. Mrs. Gray was back, all was well.

"James?"

"Is that you, Lena?"

"Yes, I was wondering if you were free for lunch any day?"

"Any day is exactly when I'm free. Today, to-

846

morrow, every day in the year."

"Very gallant indeed, James. Could we say tomorrow, same place as last time, one o'clock?"

"I'm looking forward to it very much," he said.

Lena went through the papers, she saw where opportunities had been missed, contracts lost, unsuitable people given too much time. The normal monthly search through papers and publications trawling for possibilities had been poorly done. Even the office did not look quite as smart as usual. They were only small things but she noticed them.

There were wastepaper baskets not fully emptied, rings from cups left on desks, calendars not changed, flower water left to gather a little scum on it. She would have to be very diplomatic about all these things, make it appear that the staff had noticed them rather than she herself.

And also, she must smarten herself up as well as the office. She went to the salon after work. There were no questions from Grace West. But she was owed an explanation.

"He married a young girl who was pregnant. Her brothers are friends of my daughter. That's what Louis did next," she said.

"Married? He got a quick divorce, didn't he?" Grace said.

"No need, not an official marriage between us."

"I'm glad you have a daughter," Grace said simply.

James Williams was waiting at the table.

"You look so well," he said.

"I feel well now," she said.

"And I was so worried about you, I tried to get in touch."

"I know," she said.

"But why didn't you return any of my calls?"

"I wasn't well then, but I am now. So here we are." Her face was bright and cheerful.

"A glass of wine?" he suggested.

"Yes, I need it."

"I fired Louis," he said. "Did you know?"

"No, I didn't know that. I thought he stayed there until last week."

"No, I couldn't bear to look at him after what he did to you."

She was perfectly composed and calm. "I don't know what I should say, I suppose I should thank you because you did it on my behalf . . . but the reason I asked you to lunch was to tell you that Louis has gone now out of my life. I won't be talking about him, thinking about him, or referring back anymore . . ."

"Good," he said approvingly.

"Yes, I went four days ago . . . that's all it was, and watched him get married. It's all gone now."

"It won't last, you know. He'll cheat on her too."

"You mean very well, James. But it's no consolation or help to me to know how well rid of him I am. These things only come from within."

"I think you're perfectly right," he said. "His

name will not be spoken between us again, but . . ."

"Yes?"

"I hope we'll be able to speak of other things like perhaps your coming to the theatre with me, or to see an art exhibition or just to go out anywhere."

She looked at him thoughtfully. "From time to time I would love to go out with you as any friend, but that would be it. I don't want to anticipate anything on your part but I've learned that it's better to, should there be any misunderstandings . . ."

"Indeed," he murmured.

"I mean it, James. I've had two marriages as I call them, two long relationships. I haven't an intention in the world of getting involved again."

"I quite understand . . ."

"Not even a casual involvement. So if you'd like to be my friend we could buy each other the occasional lunch . . ."

"And dinner?" he said.

"And theatre ticket." She entered into the spirit of the thing.

"And one could always live in hope?" he said.

"But an intelligent man like you would know that to live in an unrealistic hope is a very foolish way to spend a life." She spoke with a steely edge to her voice. As if she knew that only too well.

He raised the glass to her. "To our friendship," he said.

Ivy watched her like a hawk.

Often she dropped in on her landlady. They had enlarged the room by knocking down a wall. Now Ernest sat looking at the television a distance away, shielded by a big screen.

It was a screen that Lena had found for them, in a secondhand shop, she said. In fact it was an antique. It was exactly right for the room. It also meant she could sit and talk to Ivy undisturbed.

Sometimes she had coffee, often Ivy persuaded her to take a sandwich. She was looking better, Ivy said approvingly. Her skin was firm and young again, she had put on those few pounds that made her look less anxious, less drawn. Kit's letters still came to Ivy even though there was no need. It was as if she sensed that Ivy liked being postman.

Sometimes Lena read her little extracts.

We went to see Sister Madeleine. She's exactly the same in many ways. She works in the kitchen and in the yard. She has a pigeon with a false leg that she made herself. She has a hare, a poor old hare that sleeps in a box all day and eats cornflakes. It got hit on the head running away from something apparently and doesn't know where it is.

She was so pleased to see me. She didn't ask about you by name of course and not in front of Stevie. But she did want to know if everything was fine over in London, and I told her it was. It's as if she were always there. If I tell her about people like Tommy, people she liked, she sort of looks vaguely away as if they were people she dreamed about once.

I wonder was she ever married. Remember I told you that tale she told Clio and myself years ago, and we kept it as such a secret? I asked Clio the other day what did she think. Clio said she'd forgotten it. I can't believe she's forgotten. It was the biggest secret we ever had when we were young. But then Clio has her own secrets and problems these days. This time she's almost definite that she's pregnant. And she's terrified to tell Michael.

"Isn't it wonderful that she can tell you all these things?" Ivy marveled.

Lena agreed. No mother could talk like this to a daughter. But there was something, she wasn't sure what it was, something about Stevie, that Kit wasn't telling. But she wasn't going to worry. She would tell one day . . . if it was important.

"I'm going to throw myself on your mercy," Clio said to Kit.

"Don't do that. You'll only regret it." They were in Kit's flat. Clio had called unexpectedly.

"I need help desperately."

"You're sure then, you've had a test?"

"Yes, I sent a sample of urine into Holles Street under a false name."

"And you still haven't told Michael?"

"I can't, Kit. It's too much for his father and mother. Two shotgun weddings in a few months."

"But they won't have to pay for your one, your

851

mother and father will."

"Jesus, I know. Why do you think I'm so afraid? I have to tell them too."

"Well, get it over with as quick as possible. Tell Michael today and I'll go home with you to Lough Glass and help you tell your parents. Now, will that do?" Kit looked at Clio, expecting to be thanked. She was being very generous. Clio had been nothing but dismissive and downright hostile about Stevie. Kit felt saintly to be returning such good for evil.

"No, that's not the favor I want."

"What else can I do?" Kit asked.

"I want to get an abortion."

"You're not serious?"

"It's the only way."

"You must be mad. Don't you want to marry him? Don't you keep saying that from morning to night? Now you have to. He has to."

"He mightn't."

"Of course he will. Anyway, you can't think of the other."

"Lots of people do. If we only knew where to go . . . I wanted you to ask around."

"Well, I'm asking nothing of the sort. Get ahold of yourself, Clio. This is the opportunity of a lifetime."

Clio was sobbing. "You don't understand. You don't know how awful it's going to be. You don't know what it's like."

Kit put her hand on Clio's shoulder. "Remember when we were younger we used to count the good points about things . . ."

"Did we?"

"Yes. Now let's see what are the plusses. He's respectable, your parents can't go berserk altogether as if it were someone like Stevie Sullivan."

"That's true," Clio said, sniffing.

"You love him and you think he loves you."

"I think he does, yes."

"His family can cope with shotgun weddings. They've been through it, they know the sky doesn't fall on you."

"Yes, yes."

"You can ask Maura to help you, intercede for you. She's terrific about heading off rows, I've watched her."

"Would she? I get the feeling she's gone off me."

"I'll ask her to," Kit said.

"But suppose, suppose . . ."

"And Maura could suggest you live in her flat, it's a great place. Michael could buy it from her, she was thinking of selling it. It's got a garden, it would be nice for a baby."

"Baby!" wailed Clio.

"That's what you're having," Kit explained.

"And will you be my bridesmaid?" Clio asked. "Suppose it all worked out?"

"Yes, yes, of course. Thank you," Kit said soothingly.

"And it needn't be big. Just a few of us . . . we could have it in the Central. Just Michael's family to come down, Mary Paula and Louis and . . ."

Kit's blood went cold. Louis Gray couldn't come to Lough Glass. She must think very fast. "I don't know if it's a good idea to have it at home. You know the way half the town will be offended if they're not asked."

"But if it's small . . ."

"They'll still be offended, the doctor's daughter and we weren't asked. You know how they are . . ."

"But where else?"

"Do you remember the place Maura got married? That was nice . . . and she'd be flattered if you asked her to try and set that up."

"Kit, you're very devious, you should have been an international spy," Clio said in admiration.

The Central Hotel Lough Glass got four more bookings as a direct result of the New Year's Eve Dinner Dance.

Philip began to panic. "We can't have Christmas candles all over the place."

"No, your parents are going to have to bite the bullet and get the place decorated. We can't disguise the walls forever. And suppose you had to have a lunch, something the light of day might shine on . . . then they'd see what it's really like."

"Will you help me tell them?" he pleaded.

"Why me?" She felt she was involved with too much on too many levels.

"Because you sound businesslike and calm, and you don't sound all up in a heap like the rest of us," he said.

"Okay."

"Can I ask you something else?"

"What? Will I organize them a bank loan?" Kit asked with a grin.

"No, I want to ask you are you serious about Stevie Sullivan?"

"Now, Philip, we agreed . . ."

"We agreed that I wouldn't discuss my feelings for you or show you any sign of them. I've kept to that, haven't I?"

"Yes, of course you have. Yes indeed."

"So could you tell me about Stevie?"

"Yes, I do love him a great deal. I didn't love anyone ever before but now I do. It's odd for someone to say it coldly out in the open, but you asked me and I'm telling you as a friend."

"But Stevie, Kit? You know, we know, everyone knows what he's like."

Her eyes narrowed. "I beg your pardon?"

"No, you're not going to be an ostrich about this. You and I used to make jokes about him and Orla Dillon and Deirdre Hanley and everything that moved."

"Yes, that was then and this is now. And I hope you won't be part of any jokes about him and Kit McMahon, that would not be the action of a friend."

"But I wouldn't be a friend if I didn't warn you and say maybe it's an infatuation or something. People are beginning to talk and they're very surprised."

"Thank you, Philip. I know you mean well, and truly I thank you for it. Now, can we go back to talking about the hotel and what kind of pressure I'm going to have to bring to bear on poor Dan and Mildred."

The huge refurbishment of the Central Hotel began almost at once.

Even if Dr. Kelly and his wife had wanted to hold the reception there they would not have been able. They were greatly helped over the whole distressing business by Maura.

"She's been so good to Clio," Lilian said over and over. "And I always thought that there was a bit of friction between them of late."

"Goes to show how wrong we are," Peter Kelly said. He was surprised at how strongly he felt about the news of his daughter's pregnancy. And at how casually it was being taken by Michael O'Connor, the young man responsible, and by Clio herself.

They all seemed to think that because Maura was selling them her flat that everything was falling into place. There was no mention of all the illicit sex that had led to this. Dr. Kelly came from the generation where there was no sexual activity until you married. How had everything changed in his own family without his being aware of it?

"I'm sure you knew, Daddy? You must have known I was pregnant," Clio asked him.

"No, no. I assure you it came as a very great shock to me."

"But doctors often know," she persisted.

"Not this one."

For no reason at all there came to his mind a memory, a memory of the night a long time ago when he had seen Helen McMahon and realized she was pregnant. And then she had thrown herself in the lake. At least the world had changed in some respects for the better, he thought to himself, and patted his daughter's arm.

"I'll tell you about what you'll wear as the bridesmaid," Clio said. "I'm going to talk to Mary Paula about it tonight, and we'll choose what everyone will wear."

"No, that's not the way round it at all. I'll tell you what I'm wearing as your bridesmaid," Kit said.

"What?"

"I'm wearing a cream silk dress with a jacket to match and depending on what you want I'll either wear a big picture hat or some concoction of flowers and ribbons in my hair. It's three-quarters length. I am not wearing an evening dress to parade up an icy cold church, and I'm not dressing up in fancy-dress outfits for whatever color scheme you and Mary Paula think up . . ."

"I — I don't believe you," Clio gasped.

"You'd better believe me, that's what you're going to get, or else change your bridesmaid."

"I might easily do that."

"It's your privilege, Clio. And please understand me that I don't mind at all if you do. There'll be no falling-out." In many ways it would be marvelous if they could fall out. Then she wouldn't have to go to a family gathering and meet Louis. Mother's Louis. But a serious falling-out would cloud the day for too many people.

Kit sighed.

"I don't know what you're sighing about," Clio said. "I'm the one putting up with all this. I'm the bride, for God's sake. People are meant to be nice to me."

"I am nice to you," Kit hissed at her. "I told you that clown would marry you, I told you about Maura as a middleman, about her flat, about the hotel in Dublin. Jesus, Mary, and Holy Saint Joseph how much bloody nicer could I have been?"

Her violent outburst made them both laugh.

"You win," said Clio. "I'll tell Mary Paula I've a mad bridesmaid. Just another cross to bear."

Would you and Stevie come over to London? There's a special Car and Motor Show, Lena wrote. *He'd love that and it would mean you and I could catch up on chat. Let me know if it's a good idea, and here's the fare anyway. I'm not paying for Stevie so that he'll have his pride, and he might use that as a real chance to see new cars and meet people.*

Let me know what you think.

Kit rang Lena.

"I opened it five minutes ago. We'd *love* to come to London. Now, how about that for being eager."

"And Stevie? He'd love it too?"

Lena's voice was light and happy that they were going to accept.

"He doesn't know yet but he's going to be thrilled. When I tell him."

"You sound very sure of him," Lena said.

"I'm very sure he'd like this," Kit said.

"Where are you? Let me imagine where you are now."

"I'm in the phone box outside my flat. You know, the one you made the calls from when you were booking the plane."

"I know it well, I can see you there now."

"Well, you should see the big smile on my face."

"I can imagine it. I can nearly see it," Lena said.

Philip was walking along the road.

"You look very cheerful," he said accusingly. It was so like something his mother would say.

She wondered did she have some of the same expressions as her mother. Perhaps everyone did. Take Clio — she said the same snobby things that Mrs. Kelly did, and Frankie Barry was shruggy and couldn't-care-less like her mother.

Perhaps I really am going to live the same kind of life as my mother, Kit thought with a shock. She looked at Philip as if she had never seen him before.

"Hey, Kit, take it easy . . . I mean it's good to look cheerful," he said.

"What?"

"Listen, are you awake yet? You're like someone sleepwalking," Philip grumbled.

She linked his arm on the way to college. They talked about things that they were not thinking about. Philip was wondering if Stevie Sullivan and Kit had gone all the way. Kit was wondering what Philip and all the O'Briens would say if she told them she was cheerful because her long dead mother had just invited her over to London.

I've booked you in a guest house near here.

Two single rooms. You're my guests, you can make your own arrangements about the beds, Lena wrote.

No need for any arrangements, I told you I'd tell you if there is any of that, Kit wrote.

"I've friends coming over . . . I'll put that plan we have on hold for a couple of weeks," Lena told the Millars at the Saturday lunch.

Their plan was to establish a branch of Millar's in Manchester. They had found the perfect woman to run it for them. Peggy Forbes was busy training with them in London. All that was needed was the right premises, the suitable staff, and a big launch. There were so many applications from the North of England that it made sense to have a presence there. Peggy was a Lancashire woman herself. If all went well, and they were sure it would, they would make her a partner soon.

"I can't bear that you've been on a plane before me," Stevie said as they checked in their bags in Dublin Airport.

"Oh, you've done a lot of things I've never done. Far too many in fact."

He hugged her there and then. "None of them were important," he said.

"I know that," Kit said loftily.

It wasn't a barrier between them, his wicked past and her virginity. It would sort itself out. Kit knew that Stevie had hopes it would sort itself out on this visit to London.

"Will you tell her I know?" he asked.

"Yes, I will. Though I think she probably guesses. We can read what isn't there when we write to each other. It's uncanny."

"I won't try to please her, to impress her and pretend I'm good enough for you." He spoke quite seriously.

"No, she'd see through you straight away," Kit said as they walked through the duty-free shop.

"I wonder what I'll get her." He stopped and looked at the shelves of drink and cigarettes. He paused in front of the champagne. "It doesn't matter whether she likes it or not. It's festive. It's celebration, that's what it is," he said.

From everything Lena had told her, this is exactly what Louis Gray would have said and done.

Lena was there to meet them. Stevie marveled at how well she looked. Her face had been gaunt two months ago, but now she was glowing with health and enthusiasm.

"I have a friend who insisted on driving me to meet you," she said. "I've got to meet him outside."

"I know you'll be tied up with cars but if you've any time at all I'd be very happy to show you my neck of the woods . . ." James said. "It's not that far out of town, and I'd love you all to come and stay in darkest Surrey."

Kit saw Lena frown. "Maybe on another visit, James," she said. "They don't have all that much time."

He was relaxed. "Certainly, but the offer's there. I'd love to show you. There are rolling green fields and parkland in England as well as Ireland."

"Probably much nicer here," Stevie said. "Not covered in broken farm machinery and falling-down cottages."

They had a meal in Earl's Court and then James said good-bye. He was driving home tonight.

"All that way?" Stevie asked.

"It's about as far from here to there as Lough Glass to Dublin," Lena said.

"Oh well, that's not too bad. I often drive that far four times a week, and back." His eyes rested fondly on Kit.

"Isn't it known that you're a canonized saint?" Kit said.

Stevie took their luggage and said he'd leave them to talk. "I'll put them in the right rooms, then I'll come back for you," he said.

They held hands, Kit and Lena, after he went. Kit looked with delight into her mother's eyes. Everything would be all right.

"Lena, he knows," she said. "I didn't tell him, he just knew."

"He's a bright boy, and he loves you very much. Of course he knows, we should have realized."

"It doesn't matter, nothing will change."

"I know."

"I mean it. Who knows? Ivy does, Stevie does, in a sort of a way Sister Madeleine knows. Anyone else?" Kit looked at her mother.

"No, James doesn't know."

"And none of these people are going to do anything that will upset us?"

"No, of course not. I'm glad Stevie knows.

862

Glad for you, because it's a strain having to keep a secret." Her face was thoughtful.

Kit realized that for years Lena had kept secrets. The letters first, and then the meeting. It must have been hard not to share that with someone you loved.

When he came back to collect them she stood up to kiss him. "It's great to have you here in London, Stevie. Now take us both to our homes, will you?"

The weekend was magical. They went to Trafalgar Square and were photographed with the pigeons. "Wouldn't Sister Madeleine go wild here?" Kit said. "She'd have to hire a transporter to get them all back with her, she'd be afraid they didn't like traffic or the petrol fumes."

They went to the National Gallery and wandered hand in hand around the pictures. "I'm going to have to learn about an artist a month as well as read a book a month," Stevie said. "I don't want you to be married to an ignoramus." It was the first time he had said "married." She looked at him sharply. "Someday," he said with his heartbreaking grin.

Stevie went and looked at cars a lot. He took Ernest with him one day and James another. Both of them said he was a knowledgeable fellow. There was nothing about the engine or chassis of a car he didn't understand.

Lena took Kit into her office. It was much larger and more splendid than Kit would have thought. And Lena was obviously the kingpin.

"A friend of mine from Ireland" was the introduction.

People seemed interested. Lena Gray brought so little of her private life into the office with her. Her handsome husband had not been seen or heard of for a long time. But nobody had asked straight out.

"And this is my own little broom cupboard," Lena laughed as she closed the door behind them.

Kit looked around her in amazement. The big carved desk, the pictures and certificates on the wall, the framed tributes and newspaper cuttings, the fresh flowers in a blue and gold vase.

Kit seemed at a loss for words.

"What are you thinking?" Lena asked gently.

"Well, oddly enough I was thinking that it's a great pity that people at home didn't know and will never know how well you did." There was a catch in her voice.

Lena spoke. "Sometimes I think that it's a great pity that nobody here will ever know how well I did in a different way . . . they'll never know that you are my daughter."

They were speaking seriously now. It was a different mood.

"Did you keep Louis very much apart from your work too?"

"Yes. Some kind of protection, I suppose. I had to have an area I could control. Not that it always worked. One of the best girls we ever had working here was one of Louis's lengthy list of lady friends, it turned out. Dawn, Dawn Jones. I still miss her."

"What happened to her?"

"I sacked her . . . I couldn't sit and look at

864

part of Louis's past every day," Lena said.

"Half the country is part of Stevie's past," Kit said ruefully. "I'm having to put up with that."

"Ah, but that's different," Lena said. "Past past is one thing, but when it's meant to be the present and these kinds of people turn up then that's not a good thing."

"No, that's true. I wouldn't like that," Kit said. She was biting her lip, Lena noticed.

"My mistake was that I looked the other way," Lena told her. "I think being utterly unquestioning and forgetful about the past as I was, that's right, but I should have let him know that I knew about the present . . . I think that was my mistake. I let him get away with everything just to keep him, or to keep some aspect of him."

Kit's mind was far away. It was with Clio saying that everyone knew Stevie was still running after girls. That if Kit wouldn't go to bed with him then he wasn't going to be short of people who would. It was a worrying thought.

The airport terminal was just down the road from them in the Cromwell Road. Lena came to see them off. "James would have driven us but you know . . ."

"You don't want to be too beholden to him," Kit suggested.

"Exactly. What a wonderful word."

"I have to keep a dictionary beside me to keep up with her," Stevie said.

"No you don't, Stevie. You don't fool me."

"I'm not trying to sell you a car either, but

why don't you have one? Kit said you had."

"She's right. I gave it to Louis. Actually I bought it for him so I let him take it, that's a more honest way of describing it." She spoke of Louis so casually to Stevie Kit was warmed by the sense of intimacy.

"You should have something, a little runaround that you could park easily. I'll think up what you should have and tell you when you come back."

"Not easy to come back to Lough Glass."

"I meant to Dublin."

"I don't know, it's funny. I got a really stupid feeling when I was flying away over the city after you drove me to the Dublin Airport. I felt that this was the last time I'd ever be there."

"That's a bit morbid," Stevie said.

"No, I didn't mean it like that. I knew I'd see you both again and go on seeing you . . . no, it wasn't to do with death or plane crashes or anything . . . it was just I felt that was a period of my life that was over now. Like next time you come you could come to Manchester and see the setup we have there . . ."

"But Ireland's your home." Kit's lip began to tremble.

"No, your home is your people, it's not a place. Believe me that's true. I'll always have you, won't I?"

"Are you not coming back to Dublin because Louis lives there?"

"He doesn't live there, not in any sense for me, I swear to you it's as if he was on the planet Mars. No it's just I thought you'd be coming here more and more . . . ."

"And you'll come to our wedding? In a few years time," Stevie said.

"Well, well, well. I didn't know about this," Lena said.

"Neither did I," Kit said.

"Is it possibly an all-time first for the West London Air Terminal, a proposal in the lounge?"

She was taking it lightly, so Kit decided to do the same. "Listen, Lena, don't mind him, by the time we get married, Stevie and I, you'll be so old you'll probably need a wheelchair. That's the kind of time scale we're working on."

Their flight was called.

Stevie kissed her on both cheeks.

"I'll never be able to thank you for all the good times you gave us, and introducing me to all your nice friends." Kit hugged her with tears in her eyes.

The crowd was filing out the exit and down to the buses. It was time to go.

Then suddenly Stevie turned and went back to hug her too. "I'll look after her, please believe me I'll be good to her. If I thought I wouldn't I'd go away now." She was so surprised it nearly took her breath away.

When they were on the bus she asked him: "Why did you do that?"

"I wanted to," he said. Then after a pause: "I got a funny feeling that I was never going to see her again."

"Well, thank you very much," Kit said in a fury. "Jesus, that's a great thing to say. Which of you am I meant to be losing? Am I going to lose my mother or the man I'm going to marry?"

"Got you," said Stevie happily. "You've promised to marry me. Did you hear that?" He turned to an American tourist. "Mary Katherine McMahon has agreed to marry me."

"Think of the alimony," said the man who looked as if he had had to think about a fair amount of it in his life.

ℵ ℵ ℵ

Clio's wedding was going to be more difficult than Kit would have believed. And every detail of it apparently had to be discussed with her bridesmaid.

"I'll ask Stevie if you insist," Clio said, "but that means one more on Michael's side and he says he has it down to a bare minimum already and that if he has one more it will open the floodgates."

"Stevie's busy anyway," Kit said. He wasn't busy and she was deeply annoyed that he had not been invited. He would also have been such a helpful person there if only stupid Clio realized.

But then two days later there was an aunt of Michael's from Belfast who would be visiting Dublin. She would be included so Stevie could now come.

Clio grumbled about the hotel. It wasn't smart enough.

"You wanted it small," Kit said.

"No, you wanted it small," Clio said.

"Is Michael happy about the baby?"

"Please don't talk about the baby," Clio hushed her.

"Look, I'm not going to get up at the wedding breakfast and make a speech about it, but I was just asking you if your future husband is pleased about fatherhood."

"Well, he's not like Louis, if that's what you mean. Louis never has his hand off Mary Paula's stomach. He's so boring about it, he thinks it's kicking or twitching or something."

"Yours is smaller, younger, it's not doing that."

"Oh, shut up about mine," Clio said. "It's the honeymoon that's the problem now. Mr. O'Connor thinks that Michael should do this kind of intensive course in bookkeeping so that he can put him into one of the hotels."

"Yes, well, that makes sense. He's not trained as a hotelier, he'll need some job."

"We wanted to go to the South of France," Clio complained. She looked like a four-year-old whose dolly had been taken away.

"Will you wear that fur cape that looked so well on you? It would be a nice thing for Clio's wedding," Martin asked.

"No love, if you don't mind. I have a different outfit planned."

"It really did look smart on you," Martin said.

"I'll keep it and wear it at Kit's wedding," Maura said.

"Don't tell me that's going to be imminent." Martin McMahon looked alarmed.

"No, of course not," Maura laughed. "But she will marry one day and with luck you and I will be here for it."

"She's very taken with Stevie." He sounded worried.

"I know. I was alarmed in the beginning but he's a reformed boy. None of the lassies ringing him up. The only one he rushes out of the office to see is Kit."

"I suppose there are men who can be reformed by a woman." Martin McMahon was doubtful.

"Well, it's part of history certainly." Maura was reassuring, hoping he wouldn't ask her what part of history. All she could think of was Helen of Troy or Cleopatra or Kittie O'Shea, who had brought Parnell down, all of them troublemakers. She couldn't think of a single woman apart from in a Wild West movie who had reformed a man.

It was a curiously dispiriting day, Clio Kelly's wedding day.

Any appearance of jollity and papering over pregnancy problems that the O'Connors had been able to muster had been used up. Fingers O'Connor had grasped Maura McMahon by the arm as soon as he saw her. "Bad business this, bad business," he said.

Maura removed his hand very deliberately. "Perhaps if you had shown your sons some better example in the way to behave it might not have happened," she said primly.

Lilian Kelly certainly never expected her first daughter's wedding to take place under such a cloud. Many times in her mind she had planned it. Always seeing it taking place in her own home-town, with the reception in the Castle Hotel. This anonymous Dublin church and the same hotel as poor Maura had chosen all seemed very second rate.

Clio wore a white dress but Kit looked extremely casual in that outfit. The girl was pretty, there was no gainsaying that, and her big soft white hat with the long ribbons was elegant.

It was some scant consolation to Lilian Kelly to know that Kit's disgrace was even greater than Clio's. All right, so everyone might suspect that Clio's wedding had been somewhat rushed, but at least she was marrying into the O'Connor family. Kit was hanging around with that teddy boy, the boy with the terrible reputation, son of poor old Kathleen and her mad drunken husband. That was a seriously unacceptable thing to do.

Stevie was a great addition to the wedding party, as Kit had known he would be. He talked to Michael's aunt about Belfast, told her of his visits there on motor-related business, promised to look out for a good secondhand Morris Minor the next time he was up there. He asked Mr. O'Connor educated questions about the hotel business, promised Father Baily about the possibility of getting a car for a raffle. He spoke to Maura in such clear terms about the visit to London that she was reassured that there had been different rooms in the guesthouse.

"How did you find it?" she asked innocently.

"Oh, in this business you're always finding fellows who know places," he said.

He spoke to Kevin about the great night on New Year's Eve.

He told Martin McMahon about his plans to expand the garage. "I don't want to be ruining life for all my good neighbors if I do get more business . . . I'll move down the town to more open space," he said, allaying a worry Martin had been keeping to himself for some time.

And then he approached Mary Paula and Louis. Louis was so warm and easygoing Stevie felt a lump in his throat. It was for this man that Kit's mother left home, allowed a drowning to be believed. She had lived with him and with his betrayals for so long until it had almost cost her her mind.

Louis spoke of his own car, a Triumph Herald he had got in London. He had had it awhile now but it still looked good and was no trouble. No, he had bought it new.

The bile rose in Stevie's throat as he heard the story unfold. How Mary Paula had first met him when he was driving it to a seminar. She had admired the man in the white Triumph. "I said to him, 'That's a nice car,' he said to me, 'Let's take it on a test drive then,' " and neither of them had gone to the seminar at all.

"Don't tell that to my father-in-law though," Louis whispered. "He might think I was unreliable." Mary Paula giggled.

"And you're not?" Stevie said stonily.

"No." Louis looked alarmed. The boy was looking at him oddly.

Stevie moved away very quickly. Kit had been watching. "Please," she whispered in his ear. "Please, for her sake, we must say nothing. For Father, for Maura."

She looked across at Louis, her eyes full of hate. Was he a moron that he didn't know who they

872

all were? He knew that Lena was married to Martin McMahon, pharmacist from Lough Glass. He knew that Clio was from Lough Glass. Did he just not care? Was his life with Lena so much in the past that it didn't matter that her husband and daughter turned up at a festivity where he was with his pregnant wife?

Of course, he thought that they all thought Helen McMahon was dead, drowned in the lake and buried in the churchyard. But surely it must have cost him something to face these people.

Lena had never mentioned his name to Father. That much Kit knew. She had always said that she had loved another man. She had never pronounced his name because it made it too real. She had written it, of course, in the letter. But that was the letter Martin had never got.

There would be no singsong, no extended drinking in the bar of this quiet hotel. The proceedings would end earlier than most enthusiastic Irish wedding guests would have expected. Clio went to change.

"That was wonderful," Kit lied as she helped her friend out of the dress.

"It was diabolical," said Clio.

"You're wrong, wait till you see the pictures."

"Wait till I forget the look in everyone's eyes, that's more like. Jesus, isn't Mrs. O'Connor a pill? Her own daughter's pregnant and there's not a word about it. But I'm the one who led her son astray, it's written all over her face."

"Stop now. It was great," Kit soothed her.

"Stevie certainly behaved himself."

"Good," said Kit in a clipped tone.

"He sort of moved around and talked to people as if he's used to it."

"He probably is, in the car business." Kit kept herself in control with dignity.

"No, I meant used to people like who were here."

There would be no throwing the bouquet. Just a few more minutes showing off her going-away costume and then Clio and Michael would leave. The rest would follow soon after.

Louis Gray looked around him. The wedding had not been a huge social success. Even his practiced charm had seemed not to work. He was very uneasy about the whole connection with Lough Glass — of all the villages in Ireland, it was surely bad luck to get involved with this one. Still, he reassured himself, nobody there would have any suspicions; and he would have to face the place sometime. Probably sooner than later. And he would have to talk to Lena's daughter as well. Might as well be now.

Louis came over to join Kit as she knew he would. He knew she was the daughter of Lena but he had no idea that she knew of any connection at all.

She wanted to be as far as possible from him, but it would be rude not to return his warm smile. "Great day, isn't it?"

"Yes indeed."

"But nothing between you and the best man? This won't be the making of another wedding, I'm not going to get another lovely sister-in-law?"

"No, no. Kevin's going out with my friend

874

Frankie." The words came out slowly, she felt very uneasy. She moved away.

Slightly at a loss, Louis turned to talk to someone else. Young women didn't normally walk away from him like that. Stevie had been watching, he saw the way Louis had laid his hand on Kit's arm with his easy familiar charm. It had made Stevie rage inside.

The crowd were gathering near the door to wave good-bye to the bride and groom. Louis and Stevie were on the edge of the crowd. "You're from Lough Glass too, Clio tells me. It sounds a good place, we must go there sometime," he said.

Stevie put his face very near him. In a slow and deliberate voice he said: "You've been to Lough Glass." There was a pause. And then with a heavy menace he said: "And if you know what's good for you you won't go again." Then he moved away.

Louis had gone white. What did the fellow mean? He saw Stevie put his arm around Kit's shoulder and she held his hand tightly. Kit McMahon, Lena's daughter. And her boyfriend. But they didn't *know*, for God's sake.

None of them *knew*.

א א א

Lena was in Manchester, she wrote. The people were so friendly and they seemed to have more time for each other than in London, they weren't always rushing off. And if you met someone you were likely to meet them again. More like Dublin really, though of course one met too many people in Dublin. Lena only vaguely remembered meeting Rita, but she knew Kit must have handled it. She wondered had she had a blackout or had she gone mad for a time.

It didn't matter now. All that mattered was that she be there for her daughter as much as Kit needed her.

Lena realized that she had to give up on Emmet. She had lost too much of his life to see him now. She had left when he was a child, a real child. Now he was old enough to hold a girl in his arms and tell her he loved her. There was no way she could come back into his life, and she was finished with fantasy . . . there would be none of that anymore.

She was even going to get herself a small flat in Manchester. Peggy Forbes lived with her mother and anyway it would not be a good idea to share a flat with someone from work. Peggy was divorced, fortyish, wonderful with people. When next Stevie and Kit came to England they should come to Manchester. Peggy would show them all what life in the North was like.

Sometimes Kit showed parts of the letters to Stevie.

"I don't like reading what she's written to you, it's meant to be private."

"I only show you bits, I keep the private bits."

"Are they about me?"

"Sometimes."

"Warnings, like don't follow her down the primrose path?" He looked at her anxiously. He really wanted to know.

"They used to be. Not now."

"When did she change?"

"When she met you."

Clio and Michael moved into Maura's flat almost immediately after the wedding. The price had been arranged very quickly. Fingers had written the check without haggling.

"But Pa, I'm sure that's just the asking price," Michael said. "She'd probably come down a couple of hundred if you start to bargain."

"I'll pay what's asked." Fingers had had enough reproofs from Maura Hayes and her stepdaughter Kit to do him for a long time. There would be no haggling and drawing their wrath on him.

"You must come round and see it," Clio said. "You can even bring Stevie if you want to."

"No thanks. I'll come round some evening he's not in Dublin."

"Are there many of those?" Clio asked.

"Well, he does live and work in a place two hours journey away from here." She knew she sounded defensive and sarcastic. Only Clio brought this out in her.

Clio was in very grumpy form the evening she did go around to the flat. "Have you had your tea?" she asked ungraciously.

"Well, no. But I'm not hungry," said Kit.

"I didn't think . . ."

"It doesn't matter." Kit wondered how you

wouldn't think, if you asked someone to visit you at six o'clock. Most people had something to eat in the evening.

Kit admired the place and the wedding presents. Some of them still unpacked stood around in boxes.

"I think I'm getting *pre*natal depression," Clio said. "Did you ever hear of that?"

"No," said Kit truthfully. "I heard you were meant to be excited and thrilled and knitting things and getting dinner for your husband and your friends."

Clio burst into tears.

"Tell me, tell me," Kit said. She knew she was going to hear some story of woes. Should Clio be shaken until her teeth rattled? Should this have been done years ago? Dr. Kelly and his wife had always let her get away with murder.

"Everything's absolutely terrible. Michael was out all night on Wednesday, there was a party up in the hotel where he's working and none of them got home. Louis didn't even go back to the house that he lives in beside the hotel. And Mary Paula's absolutely furious even though Louis gives her flowers every day. Michael's given me no flowers, he just says I'm a nag. Already! I'm only a few weeks married and I'm a nag."

"Shush, shush. He doesn't mean it," Kit said.

"And Daddy's no help, nor Mummy. I said I'd like to go down and stay a few days there and they said no. All this about making my bed and having to lie in it. And I hate this place, it has Aunt Maura written all over it . . . Everyone's

878

in such bad tempers, Kit."

"I'm not."

"That's because you're being screwed silly by Stevie Sullivan and you can't think of anything else."

"I'm not, as it happens."

"Well, maybe you should be."

"Clio, you're the one who's upset. Talk to me. Let's look at the good points. Michael only stayed out one night and he was with . . . your brother-in-law, so you don't think he was up to no good."

"I don't know," Clio said darkly. "Mary Paula told me there were other girls there, fast girls."

Kit wondered wildly whether Mary Paula and Clio, who had both been pregnant brides in recent months, were actually in a position to be calling other girls fast. But she let it pass.

"What other good points are there?" Kit continued doggedly. "You have a lovely home, Michael's got a job. You're going to have a baby."

"Which means I can't have a job," Clio complained.

"You didn't *want* a job. You said you were going to college to get a husband. Now you've got one."

"Nothing's the same as it was," Clio wept.

"No, it's different, but we've got to change too. I suppose that's it."

"I wish we were young again, going to Sister Madeleine, coming home for tea."

"Well, we're the ones who have to make tea nowadays. Will I go out and get some things?"

"Would you? I feel so awful and waddly, I can't move."

"You're as bad as Mary Paula. When's her baby due?"

"This week, that's why it's all so awful about Louis and everything. And Michael's father has had a row with Louis about money. Apparently he just pockets his salary every month and didn't know he was meant to pay bills with it. There was an awful scene up there the other night."

"Talking of money I don't have much, if I'm to buy things for supper . . ." said Kit.

"Oh, there's a fiver under the clock." Clio waved at it. The phone rang. "Will you answer it, Kit, please?"

It was Louis.

"That's not Clio," he said.

"No, it's Kit McMahon. What can I do for you?"

"My wife's been taken into hospital and she's gone into labor."

"Congratulations," Kit said in a dull voice.

"No wait. I was hoping Clio could ring her father-in-law and tell him."

"Why don't you ring him yourself?"

"Well, to be perfectly frank I've had some words with him. I think he'd prefer to be told by another member of his family. I can't find Michael, and Kevin's nowhere either."

"Yes, I heard there was a problem with your father-in-law all right." Kit didn't know why she had said this. It was just the thought of the free-loader Louis sponging off everyone that made her feel sick.

His voice had changed. "What do you mean you heard? Where did you hear this?"

"From Clio, who heard it from your wife." She was brazen now.

"And is it any of your business?"

"No, none at all," she agreed.

"So can you put me on to Clio?"

"She's not here."

"Well, all right then."

"Do you want me to ring Fingers?"

"What?"

"Fingers O'Connor. That's his name, isn't it?"

"That's an offensive nickname certainly. His name is Mr. O'Connor."

"Do you want me to ring him and tell him Mary Paula's in the labor ward? That you didn't want to tell him yourself?"

Louis hung up.

"What was that about?" Clio's mouth was open in astonishment.

"That creep Louis Gray, afraid to talk to your father-in-law."

"Why were you so rude to him?"

"I hate him."

"Why on earth do you hate him?"

"I don't know, irrational. Sometimes you get an irrational dislike."

"Well, they're my bloody in-laws, Kit. Don't work out your own hatreds on them just because things aren't going well with Stevie."

"Who said things weren't going well with Stevie?"

"They can't be or else he wouldn't have been at that party up in the hotel where Louis and Michael were. The one on Wednesday night."

Kit looked at her in disbelief. "Stevie was there?"

"Yes, didn't he tell you?"

"You know he didn't tell me."

Wednesday last . . . he had told her that he had to go to a function in Athlone. God damn him and all other conniving handsome men to the pit of hell. Kit put on her jacket and went to the door.

"Kit, the fiver," Clio pointed to the mantelpiece.

"Get your own tea, Clio," Kit said, and banged the door behind her.

She longed to write to Lena to tell her that Louis's marriage was in trouble only five months after it had taken place. She ached to put her arms around her mother and cry. To ask her should she tackle Stevie, ask him straight out had he been there? Should she check if the function in Athlone had existed?

Wasn't this the road her mother had gone down and lived to regret, the constant checking and then deciding to ignore it? She walked along looking at the other people, whose lives were not in ruins, going about their business. Men coming home from work, wives opening doors, children playing in gardens in the June evening sunshine.

She must not tell Lena the news of Louis's fall from grace. Lena said her only peace was to know nothing of him. There was always the danger even at this late stage that Lena would take him back. Forget, forgive so much. After all, what was a wife and baby to forgive when she had put up with so much?

Lena and Peggy Forbes were having supper in an Indian restaurant in Manchester after the official opening. Peggy was forty-three, blond, well groomed. She had married very young and very foolishly, she said. A man who should have married a bookie. She had met him at the races, which should have given her some inkling but it hadn't. She had been divorced at the age of twenty-seven, after six years of a very unsatisfactory marriage.

She began to work then, very hard. She got a great deal of pleasure from it, she said. Not the money itself, she didn't regard wealth as a goal. She liked the people she met and enjoyed urging them on. She also liked the fact that she had some security and didn't need to fear that some man was going to sell the dining table and chairs, as had happened to her on her twenty-fifth birthday.

Peggy said she didn't usually tell her whole life story to someone but since Lena was putting such faith in her she wanted her to know the background.

"I have a very confused background myself," Lena said. "I was married to two men, but neither marriage worked. I don't say anything at work about either marriage, in fact most people at work know nothing about my first marriage and think my second one is still in existence."

Peggy nodded. "It's better that way," she said.

"The only reason I'm telling you," explained

Lena, "is that I don't want to respond to your frankness with a blank brick wall."

"I wouldn't have been upset."

"That's because you're a practical woman, and you realize I'm the boss, but I would also like to be your friend."

"I'm sure we'll be that."

"And it would be very nice if we could go out sometimes here in Manchester, to the pictures or for a meal. Maybe I could visit your mother? But I'm not one for clubs or that kind of evening out."

"Nor am I," Peggy said. "The younger girls I work with pity me, and they're always trying to get me out for what they call a good time."

"I have that too," Lena sympathized.

"The only thing I'm sorry about is that I didn't have children. I'd have liked a daughter, wouldn't you?"

Lena hesitated. "I have a daughter, as it happens. But that's not known."

"Don't worry, I won't talk about it," Peggy said, and smiled a broad friendly smile.

"We're going to make this agency as big as the one in London," Lena promised.

"We'll be calling you our Junior Branch in five years time," said Peggy.

"I really think we made a great choice." Lena was talking to Jim and Jessie Millar back in the London office. They were amused to hear they would soon be the Junior Branch.

"That's the spirit we need," said Jim.

Lena smiled to herself, thinking about how

cautious he had always been at the start, and how every change no matter how minor had to be negotiated past him with care.

The receptionist came in. "I'm so sorry Mrs. Gray, but you know what you said about using your initiative?"

"Yes, Karen. Who is it?"

"It's Mr. Gray. He says it's an emergency and he has to talk to you."

"Use this room," Jim Millar said, and he and Jessie got up to leave.

But Lena wouldn't hear of it. "Take his number, Karen, and tell him I'll ring back in five minutes."

She went to her office and looked at herself in the mirror. She was alive and well. She was sane. He would not upset her. There was no emergency in his life that could touch her.

She telephoned the Dublin number and they answered with the name of a hotel. Louis was ringing her from work. What else was new?

"It's Lena," she said.

"Thanks for ringing back. I should have known you would, you were always so reliable."

"That's true. What can I do for you?" Her voice was calm.

"Are you alone?"

"As alone as any of us are on these kinds of lines. Why?"

"I'm in great trouble and so are you."

"Why am I in trouble?"

"They know."

"Who knows?"

"Everyone in Lough Glass knows."

"What do they know, Louis?"

"They know about you."

"I doubt that. Unless you told them."

"I swear to God I haven't opened my mouth. Not to anyone. Up to now I haven't said a word."

It was there, the threat. The blackmail in his tone. Up to now. "And who in particular seems to know things?" she asked.

"A fellow called Sullivan. Do you know him?"

"I remember him. His people own a garage."

"And Kit . . . Kit knows. She was so rude to me just yesterday. She bit the head off me."

"I doubt that."

"She did. She said she heard rumors of my having a fight with my father-in-law."

"I'm sorry to hear you've fallen out with your relations." Her voice was so hard she could hardly recognize it herself.

"Lena, cut this out. I'm in trouble too." She waited. "They expect me to have more cash than I have."

"Yes?"

"And I was reading in the papers how you've opened a new office in Manchester . . . reading about the agency in the financial pages no less."

"Yes. Aren't the Millars doing well."

"I looked it up, Lena."

"What?"

"I got someone to go to Companies House. You're a director."

"So, Louis?"

"So you're a part of it. You're in a position

to help me. I never begged in my life, I'm begging you now."

"No indeed, that's not what you're doing, you're trying to blackmail me."

"I thought you were saying this might be an open line."

"It's probably not at my end, who knows about yours."

There was a silence. "We parted friends, Lena, can we not remain friends?"

"We didn't part friends."

"Yes we did. I remember the night."

"We parted without a fight or a scene. I certainly wasn't your friend then, nor am I now." There was a silence.

Lena spoke again. "So if that's all may I wish you well. And hope you get over this problem with your father-in-law. I'm sure you will, you're a man of great charm."

"One payment, Lena. You'll never hear me asking again."

"No, I hope you won't telephone me again. If you do, I shall ask the staff not to put your call through."

"You're not going to get away with this high-and-mighty attitude. You don't know who you're dealing with," he cried.

"A man who owes his father-in-law money, it would appear."

"Not in any sense like borrowing or stealing. It's just he expects me to have private means."

"Or to put your hand in your pocket sometimes."

That was exactly the phrase Fingers had used.

887

Louis had lied to him, he had said he was saving for the birth of his baby.

"I have a son," he said.

"That's wonderful," Lena said.

"No, I need some money to start a savings account for him. That's what I *said* I was doing, saving toward an account."

"Good-bye, Louis."

"You'll be sorry."

"What can you do to me?"

"I can bring you down. Tell these country plodders, Martin and Maura and Peter and all, that you're *not* dead. You're living the high life of a director of companies over in England. By God, that'll get the fur flying down there in Lough Glass. Bigamous marriage, Maura a woman of easy virtue . . . Kit and her brother abandoned by their feckless mother."

He didn't even know Emmet's name, Lena realized. "Do that, Louis, and you go down further than you ever thought you could go down."

"Easy threats," he laughed.

"No, not at all. You made a great great mistake by telephoning me today with this news. If you had sold your blood pint by pint to the blood bank, or done a smash-and-grab raid at a jeweler's in Grafton Street, you'd have got your money quicker."

"Lena . . ." he said.

But the line was dead.

She dialed Sullivan's garage. Maura McMahon answered the phone. Lena considered hanging up but time was of the essence. She disguised

888

her voice into a poor imitation of a Cockney accent. She asked to speak to Stevie.

"I'm afraid he's not available at the moment. Can you tell me who's calling?"

She had forgotten Maura's accent. The courteous tones, the soft voice. She felt even more determined than ever that this woman should not be disturbed in the even tenor of her life. Her happiness with Martin McMahon must not be overturned.

"It's really quite urgent. This is a guesthouse in London where he was staying."

"Oh yes?" Maura sounded anxious now, alert . . .

"And you're sure he can't come to the phone?"

"Was there a problem with the bill or anything?"

"No, no. Nothing like that," Lena knew her accent was all over the place but it was the best she could do.

"Well, can he return your call when he comes back?"

"When will that be?"

"Tomorrow. He's in Dublin."

"Is there any way of contacting him there?"

"I'm afraid not. But if I could have your name and number . . ."

She gave Maura Ivy's name and telephone number. And then she put her head in her hands.

Stevie was her only hope.

Kit rang home that night and spoke to Maura. "I hear Clio's an auntie-in-law," Maura said. "Oh, is that right?" Kit said.

889

"Yes, a little boy, so Lilian was telling me."

"Super," Kit said.

"So you've had another row with Clio?"

"This is the last one."

"Glad to hear that."

"No, I mean the friendship's over."

"Kit, you're too old to think that. Friendships are never over."

"If they weren't ever real they could be," said Kit.

"Let's get on to happier subjects," Maura said. "Are you seeing Stevie tonight?"

"I don't know," Kit said truthfully. The arrangement had been that if he was able to he would call to the flat at eight. She didn't know whether she wanted to see him or not.

"Well, if you do, will you give him a message?"

"Hold on." Kit got out a notebook. "Fire ahead, Maura."

"He's to ring this guesthouse in London . . ."

"What?"

"No, it's not about a bill, I asked. But the woman was tight as anything, she wouldn't tell me. She wants him to ring her at this number . . ."

"I think I have the number," Kit said.

"Let me give it to you anyway. It's Ivy Brown, and this is the London number."

Ivy. Kit leaned against the side of the phone box. There must be something wrong with Lena. And it must be very bad if they asked Stevie to ring. Kit felt very weak indeed. What could have happened?

Wouldn't it be great to have enough money

to make a call to London from a phone box just like that. Instead of keeping the coins aside for a couple of days to ring Lough Glass. She couldn't wait until eight o'clock, it was only six-fifteen now. She would go and borrow the money from someone.

As she left the phone box she saw Stevie's car pull up. He opened the boot and took out his good jacket. He often drove in his old one, he said, for comfort. Imagine, he still wanted to look good for her.

"Vain peacock," she said, remembering the stories of Louis Gray's jackets hanging in Lena's cupboard. But she needed him now. She went over to him before he had put his old jacket away.

"You caught me," he said.

"That's not something you'd mind being caught at, surely?"

"What's wrong?"

"What do you mean?"

"You sound as if there was a list of other crimes I would mind being caught at," he said.

"Aren't there?" she asked.

"No there aren't, as it happens. What's wrong? You're white as a sheet."

She told him about the call. "It must be a message, a code."

"I'll ring," he said. "Do you want to come into the box."

"No." She drew away from him. She didn't want the intimacy of the phone box, both of them pressed up together.

"All right so."

She saw him talking on the phone for a while

then hanging up and being phoned back. Whatever it was it must be serious. She walked around by the box, but his face didn't look shocked or distressed as it would if it was the news of an illness or an accident. He seemed very angry.

She opened the door of the phone box tentatively. She heard him say ". . . no, no. I won't tell her until it's sorted out. I quite understand. Yes, you can trust me. I'll ring you tomorrow. Good-bye."

Then he came out.

"What is it?" she asked.

"Your mother's fine. I was talking to her, she's in perfect health and sounds very calm. She had something she wants me to sort out for her and I'm going to do it. But it's not something she wants you involved in."

"I don't believe you."

"Well that's odd. If you told me something like that I'd believe you."

"I can't trust you an inch," she shouted at him. "This is some other devious thing. You've used my mother in some way to give yourself a cover story."

"Kit, you're going mad," he said in a matter-of-fact way. "You gave me the message, I rang the number, this is the way it's turned out. I don't know what you're talking about."

"Yes you do, it's about last Wednesday. You want her to cover for you."

"Wednesday?" He seemed genuinely bewildered.

"Wednesday. Someone's told you the story was blown so you're hatching some deal with her because you think she likes you."

"She does like me, I hope. And she certainly trusts me."

"Stevie, you're a liar."

"No," he said quite simply, "I'm not." They stood for a long time looking at each other. "Now, I'm not going to walk off on you over some misunderstanding. But I think you're too angry to explain it to me . . . so what will we do, where would you like us to go?"

"I'd like you to go to hell," Kit said.

"Why, why do you say that?"

"Because I'm my mother's daughter, certainly, but I'm not going to put up with all she put up with in her life. And it's better you understand this now, than years down the line."

"I have to go and do something now. Do something for your mother. I'd like to come back and talk to you."

"You'll come back to a locked door," Kit said.

"She particularly asked me to keep you out of it, but if you want to check up on me and add further grief and problems to her you can always telephone her yourself and check I'm telling you the truth. But then, what's the point?"

"What indeed?" Kit asked.

"I mean, if you don't believe me and have to check up on me you probably won't believe her, so save your money." He got into his car and drove off very fast indeed.

She was awake for a very long time but he didn't come to the flat. He left no note, no message.

She was red-eyed when the morning came at last.

She met Philip in the college. "Have you a cold, Kit? How are you?"

"A bit of a one, how are you?"

"Fine. Overworked. We have six tours booked in this summer. Kit, you wouldn't come and work in the hotel, would you? Have you a placement yet?"

"I don't know, Philip. This isn't a good day to ask."

"I'll have to know someday soon," he said.

"End of the week," she promised.

"Oh, and Kit, Clio was looking for you."

"When?"

"Just before I left my flat. She said if I saw you to ask you to ring her. It was very urgent."

"It always is with her," Kit said. "She probably wants someone to pass her a handkerchief."

At noon Kit came out of a lecture room and saw Clio sitting in the hall. "Aren't you afraid you'll get germs, coming so far from your part of fashionable Dublin?" Kit said.

Clio was snow white. "It was all my fault, Kit. I just said that to get even with you."

"Said what?"

"About Stevie being at the party. He wasn't. I just made it up because you looked so smug."

"So all right. Thanks for telling me now anyway."

Kit's eyes were dancing, her heart was high. She should have known all the time that it was Clio's mean spirit. That Stevie wasn't telling her lies. Then she thought of last night's conversation at the phone box and shivered.

Clio was still looking at her.

"You needn't have come the whole way just to tell me," Kit said.

"But I had to. After what happened."

"What happened?"

"Stevie. He went up to the hotel and beat the living daylights out of Louis, he's lost three teeth and he has a broken jaw."

"What?"

"He's in hospital. Mary Paula is nearly out of her mind. The christening is next week and Louis looks like something you'd pick up on the docks after closing time."

"But why did Stevie do that?"

"I suppose he thought it was Louis that told you he was at the party."

"I never mentioned the party to Stevie."

"Well, someone else must have told him that Louis said it. Why else would he have gone to beat him up? Jesus, I'm so sorry, Kit. What things are happening these days."

Lena had a lot to sort out. There was a message from Manchester. They hadn't known that there was an escort agency upstairs. People were getting the two agencies confused. It needed someone with huge diplomacy and even the cash to resettle the escort agency somewhere else and take over its premises. She would come up and see to it herself.

In the afternoon Louis rang. "I see you haven't put my name on the blacklist yet. I got straight through."

"What's happened to your voice, Louis? You sound different."

"As if you didn't know. You sent a thug to beat me up."

"No I didn't. I sent a friend to reason with you."

"He broke my jaw, I have a black eye and three teeth knocked out. I'm going to look a sight at the christening."

"That's hard luck."

"No, it's not hard luck, it's bad news for you. I'm going to sue him, and I'm going to explain in an open court why I'm doing it. The fellow has plenty of money, and of course you'll cough up if the award is bigger than we think."

Lena laughed. "You'd never do that. Throw away all you've got? A cushy job, a young wife and baby . . . You won't let them know you've been shacked up with someone who ran away from her husband and children. No, I know you well enough to know you're bluffing."

"I might have been until you sent the prize-fighter in. Now everything's gone already. I've nothing to lose. Any credibility I have is gone. I am going down, but I'm taking you with me. I just wanted you to know that, in case you're having the luxury of sleeping well."

"I don't believe you, and from now on you *are* on the blacklist. You'll never make a call to me again."

"No, but you'll sure hear about me and what I've done to you, Helen McMahon."

"Don't go tonight," Jessie said. "You've had a long day."

896

"No, the sooner I'm there the better it'll be."

"Take the train then, you can sleep on it."

"I'll need the car when I'm there." Lena had bought a Volkswagen Beetle on Stevie's advice. It had never let her down and she found it invaluable. "I quite like being wrapped up in the car on my own, it's a little world that's different. I can think things out."

"Don't think too hard," Jessie said, "and do pull in if you're tired. Manchester's a long way."

"Oh, go in the morning," Ivy said.

"Nonsense. Lovely long nights. It'll be daylight most of the way," Lena said.

"Take a flask of coffee. I'll make it in two minutes while you're packing your overnight bag."

"Right. Wait'll I get a little flat of my own there, and I won't have to pack a bag."

"Talk about the jet set," said Ivy.

She was well out on the A6 when she got that feeling, the one she had that time after New Year's Eve, when nothing felt real, and the floor seemed very far away and sounds were distorted. It went with a tightness in the chest, a fear she was going to faint or fall.

But this was idiotic. Here she was in her car, going at a perfectly normal speed. Should she pull in? She saw a place that was suitable and drew in to the side of the road. She sipped her coffee and then got out to stretch her legs. But that odd sensation returned of the ground being at a peculiar angle. She held the car to steady herself. Louis's face was everywhere around her,

897

and his voice. "I've got nothing to lose. I'll bring you down with me, Helen McMahon."

She couldn't drive like this. But she couldn't stay here either. She should get back into the car. The seat and steering wheel would support her and it was just her mind playing tricks on her. After a while she moved out into the stream of cars heading north. She forced herself to think about the premises in Manchester. How had they not checked the other offices? Perhaps it was called something so respectable that no one would ever have known until the situation became apparent.

People had their lights on now. The road was shiny, it must have been wet, must have been raining here. Louis's face was coming back again. She couldn't imagine it as it was now, bruised, injured, teeth missing. She had asked Stevie to threaten him. Not to hit him. Perhaps she had not explained properly. But there it was again. His face, handsome, petulant, impatient, the way he was when he didn't get what he wanted.

"Get out of here, Louis," she said aloud.

"I've nothing to lose now," Louis said. "I'll bring you down with me, you'll be sorry you didn't listen to me. I've nothing to lose."

There was a huge truck. The lights of a truck and a terrible shattering of glass and . . .

Then there was nothing.

Peggy Forbes expected a call as soon as Lena checked into the hotel. It would be eleven P.M. at the latest. By midnight she was worried.

The hotel was also annoyed. "We could have

given her room away several times," they said.

"I think the main thing is to find out whether Mrs. Gray has had an accident rather than concentrating on room occupancy," Peggy Forbes said.

They were very apologetic.

It was Ivy who heard at two A.M.

A young policeman came to her door. "I wonder if I could come in," he said.

"Ernest," she called. "Ernest, come quickly. Lena's dead."

It was instantaneous, they told Ivy. She had crossed the road, into the oncoming traffic. She may have fallen asleep or lost concentration. The driver of the truck was not to be consoled. He was crying like a baby on the side of the road, said he'd never forget it to his dying day. He would like to tell her family how he couldn't have avoided it in a million years. Her car was out of control. But that was probably no consolation to her family, he said then.

"She has no family," Ivy told the policeman. "Her work and me, that's all she has. We're her family and I'll tell her work in the morning."

"These are the only addresses given in her diary and wallet apparently," the policeman said. "Our people on the spot said that only you and Millars were there as contacts, so I suppose that's in order then."

"That's in order then," Ivy said. "Thank you, Officer, that's in order."

Ivy went to Millar's at nine A.M. She dressed

carefully in black. She had a list of things she would discuss with Jessie Millar. The police formalities and what they would involve, the undertakers, the funeral, the announcement in the papers.

Jessie Millar was grief-stricken in a way that Ivy would never have believed possible. This wasn't a colleague, this was a true friend. When the weeping was over they settled everything.

"The question of Mr. Gray is a delicate one, perhaps I could handle that," Ivy suggested.

"Please, please. Come in and sit at her desk. Make whatever calls you like. Use the place as your own."

Ivy had never sat in a posh office like this. She would have loved to talk to Lena about it, but instead she was sitting there arranging Lena's funeral with the undertaker. She would deal with Mr. Gray next. She remembered the name of the hotel where he worked. She was unprepared for the violence of his response.

"This is some cheap, dirty trick, Ivy," he said.

"Would to God that it were." Ivy's voice was shaking.

"If she thinks she can get out of it by saying this, she has another think coming."

"The funeral's next Thursday, Louis. It would be best if you were here."

"Funeral! Don't make me laugh," he said.

She gave him the name and phone number of the undertaker's. She said she would confirm it in writing to him and mark the envelope personal. Again she said in a level voice, "It would be best if you were there."

Then she rang Stevie Sullivan. She spoke to the woman who must be Martin McMahon's second wife. "This is Ivy," she said.

"Oh, we spoke before, you're from the guest-house." Maura was pleasant.

Ivy remembered the ruse. Imagine, it was only a couple of days ago and Lena had been alive and well. "Can I speak to him?" she asked.

"Certainly." Maura was puzzled. This woman Ivy sounded totally different this time around.

"I have to go to Dublin, Maura," Stevie said, throwing some papers into a briefcase and taking the keys of a car. "It's sudden and important and I'll be gone a few days."

"You have appointments, people to meet . . ."

"Cancel them if you would."

"Any excuse?"

"No, not one I can give now. But you make one."

"Can you tell me any more? Please, Stevie. I'm a little anxious, these calls from London . . ."

Stevie looked at her. "Yes, I'm going to London actually. I'm stopping to pick up Kit. A friend of ours died."

"But what friend . . . ?"

"Please, Maura . . . I know you're worried but please. This is a bad time."

"Her father will want to know what she's doing dashing off . . ."

"No, it's not dashing off. Now, I know you don't think I'm the most reliable man in the world but I'd die rather than let any harm happen to Kit. I think you know that. I haven't seduced her, I won't try . . . eventually in years and years

901

from now I hope she'll marry me, but she may not. I can't tell you straighter than this."

"Go and pack your things, Stevie," she said. "I'll sort it out."

He took Kit from class. He held out both his hands to her. "This is the second time someone has had to tell you this news, Kit," he said. And she put her head on his shoulder and cried her eyes out.

Standing in the distance, Philip O'Brien saw them.

The body was released from the hospital and came to a funeral parlor in London. Stevie held Kit's hand as they went in. They stood together beside the casket. Lena looked as if she were asleep. Whatever discoloring and wounding there was in her forehead was hidden by her hair. She looked completely at peace. Neither of them cried. They just stood there and looked for a long time.

Ivy asked them to stay in Lena's flat. "That's where she'd want you to be," she said. "I've left it ready for you." They went upstairs, limbs moving slowly as if in a dream.

"You've changed the wallpaper, she told me," Kit said.

"After he left, to get the memory of him out of the place. I think it worked for a bit."

"It sure did," Stevie said.

"She had all her living ahead of her," Ivy said, her face puckering. She turned away. "I'll leave you here and come down if you need anything."

"It's only got one bed," said Stevie.

"We can survive that," Kit said. She took off her dress and laid it on a chair, and her open-toed shoes. She stood in her slip at the handbasin where Mother must have stood so often and washed her face and arms and neck. Then she lay down on one side of the bed. Stevie lay on the other side, their hands held. And eventually he realized that she had gone to sleep.

He got up and sat by the window. Had he done what he was asked to do, or was he somehow to blame for Lena's death? Louis had shouted that they'd all be sorry for this as he left. Could he possibly have done the wrong thing and not what she'd asked?

"He won't come to the funeral," Ivy said.

"Yes, he will," Kit said. She was pale but calm.

"Maybe we're better without him. He caused all that upset," Ernest said.

"I won't have her laid to rest without that bastard standing there watching," Kit said. "She deserves that much. She deserves him standing there with a black tie at her funeral."

"But if he won't come?"

"I'll make him come to her funeral," Kit said.

Louis Gray would not take a call from London from Kit McMahon. A secretary said she had instructions not to put Miss McMahon through. "Give him a message from me please."

"Certainly."

"There's a certain gathering that he is expected at here in London, and I will need to know whether or not he plans to attend."

"Hold on and I'll inquire." She came back. "I'm sorry the answer is regretfully no."

"Then could you tell him that regretfully I shall have to come and collect him." Kit hung up.

At the office she borrowed a hundred pounds from Jessie. She said it was for funeral arrangements. It was given willingly. Then she left a note for Stevie and went straight to the airport. The flight took an hour, the taxi to Louis's hotel another hour. She was calm when she asked to see him. He was in a meeting, they said, with Mr. O'Connor, Senior, and some of the board members.

"I have a taxi waiting," Kit said, "so I'd better go in and speak to him." Before the receptionist could stop her Kit was in the boardroom. "I do beg your pardon for this but it's an emergency," she said.

Fingers recognized his daughter-in-law's friend, the girl who could and did cause so much trouble.

"Leave this minute," Louis said.

"Louis, listen to her," Fingers ordered.

Louis's hand was at his throat.

"I'm afraid that a great friend of ours in London has died and we all need you at the funeral. I wouldn't make such a drama out of it, but your presence is very much needed."

"Who was this friend?" Fingers O'Connor asked, since Louis seemed to have lost his voice.

Very clearly Kit said: "His name was Leonard Williams, a brother of James Williams, your previous employer. The family are most insistent that you come." She looked directly at Louis as she spoke. She was telling him that she'd keep the secret, she would drop him in a flash if he came.

"That James Williams we met at the Dryden the first time?" Fingers asked.

"Yes, that Mr. Williams. Can I say you'll be with me? I have a taxi outside."

"They can't expect me to come now," Louis gasped.

"It's a matter of being there as soon as possible." Their eyes were still locked.

Louis knew that Kit would go the distance. That he had no option. "I have to be back for the christening," he said.

"In the midst of life we are in death," Kit said. "Christenings mercifully can be delayed but sudden death and funerals can't."

"I'll go later tonight," he said.

"You know where to go, to the house in West London. All the details are there."

"Yes, yes. I know."

"What's your involvement in this?" Fingers looked suspicious.

"The deceased was very, very good to me, and good to all of us. That's why the people who were important in the deceased's life must be at the funeral," she said.

The others in the room who didn't know what was happening looked at each other in mystification. First, Louis Gray the new hotshot manager was beaten up like someone after a barroom brawl, now there were all these heavily loaded signals from some youngster to whom Fingers was listening with an uncharacteristic respect.

Louis Gray and his father-in-law left the room together and watched Kit getting back into her taxi. "Better go, Louis," Fingers said. "If she has you by the balls like the rest of us, then we're all sunk."

The day was too sunny for a funeral. London looked too well to be hosting something sad like this. Kit wore a plain black cotton dress and one of Lena's own hats. She carried a small black bag she had found in Lena's dressing table drawer.

Ivy, Jessie, Grace West, old Mrs. Park in her wheelchair, Peggy Forbes heartbroken from Manchester, came. The entire staff of Millar's, James Williams, all the tenants in the house, clients of the agency, waiters from the local restaurants, clerks from the bank. There was a very large crowd in the Catholic church that Kit had found for the funeral Mass.

As the priest read out the prayer about this night being in heaven and may the angels come to meet her, Kit held Stevie's hand very tight. They had both been in the parish church in Lough Glass when Father Baily had read this prayer for Lena before. But in those days the angels were being asked to meet Helen McMahon.

The priest had asked earlier if there was any particular hymn they would like. Kit couldn't think of any hymn. Not one. Something she might have sung at school, the priest prompted.

"Hail Queen of Heaven," Kit had said.

It had not been a good choice. The organist

began twice but the congregation, most of them Church of England, did not know this hymn to the Blessed Virgin Mary. Kit was not going to let it falter. She would sing it if nobody else did.

Hail Queen of Heaven, she began, and Stevie
    joined in.
The ocean star,
Guide of the wanderer here below.
Thrown on life's surge, we claim thy care
Save us from peril and from woe.

And then another voice joined in and they saw it was Louis Gray in his dark coat with his black tie, his face bruised and at an angle, his eye blackened. Most people thought he had been in the accident with her. He had a good strong voice and he helped Stevie and Kit along.

Mother of Christ, star of the sea,
Pray for the wanderer, pray for me.

The organist, pleased that someone had sung, struck up a second verse. They sang what had been sung already, all three of them. By the time it came to *Pray for the wanderer, pray for me,* everyone in the church had joined in. Kit and Stevie looked at each other. They had done Lena proud in London.

Only a few people went to the crematorium, that's what Ivy and Kit suggested.

Louis looked pathetically at Kit. "Am I to go?"

"Yes," she said.

It was so alien to anything that Kit had ever known; no coffin going into the earth, no sounds of spades and clay falling, just curtains parting and closing. It seemed totally unreal.

They stood outside the little chapel in the crematorium. "When did you find out?" he asked Kit.

"I always knew," she said.

"That's rubbish. The first Christmas she nearly died of grief because she couldn't ring you."

"She rang me soon after," Kit said.

"I don't believe you."

"Suit yourself. I was the secret you didn't know about, you had many many that she didn't know about. Let's call it quits."

"All right," Louis said.

He looked old and tired. That was Kit's revenge.

They had to talk to a solicitor. Lena's entire estate had been left to Mary Katherine McMahon of Lough Glass. Apart from bequests to Ivy and Grace West, her quarter share of Millar's Agency now belonged to Kit. In a codicil she had left the car in which she had been killed to Steven Sullivan, also of Lough Glass. His eyes were brimming with tears when he heard it.

"How will I arrange for it to be transferred to you after probate? We're talking about forty or fifty thousand pounds," the solicitor said.

"I'll write to you about it later," said Kit.

They hired a car, drove home through England. Through fields and woods and small towns, and then up through Wales. They would come back, they said, back to London to see friends like Ivy and Ernest and Grace and Jessie.

But now they wanted to go home.

"What'll I do with the money? I can't say I've been given fifty thousand pounds."

"No." Stevie was thoughtful.

"So what will I do? She wants me to have it . . . but I have to do it right. It would be terrible to blow the whole story at this stage."

"You could give it to me," Stevie said.

"What?"

"You could invest it in my business."

"Are you mad?"

"No, I could transform the whole place, and when you marry me it'll all be yours anyway. Meanwhile I'll just look after it for you."

"Why should I trust you?"

"Lena did."

"That's true. But this would be sheer madness."

"No it wouldn't. We could get a lawyer and do it legally. You could be a sleeping partner. Well, in that sense anyway."

"I don't know, Stevie."

"Think of a better idea," he said, and they drove along the roads of Wales.

They stayed the night in Anglesey.

It was a lovely little guesthouse with a woman who had a singsong accent. "I have a beautiful room for you," she said. "A four-poster bed and you can nearly see Ireland from there."

They were too tired to talk to her about the situation, or they each thought the other would.

And anyway, they had slept blamelessly side by side in Lena's bed in London. They went upstairs and lay down. He looked so beautiful in the moonlight, with his long, dark hair on the pillow. Kit reached out to him. "If I'm going to be a sleeping partner," she said, "I suppose I'd better practice it properly."

They stayed three days in Anglesey. And three nights.

And then they went home.

There were a lot of explanations but they didn't care. Kit agreed to work in the Central Hotel for the summer. Stevie told Maura that he might have an injection of money for the garage.

"I know where you got that money," Maura said suddenly.

"Jesus, do you?" said Stevie.

"Yes, it was the greyhounds," Maura said triumphantly. "Was it? Tell me."

"It was something like that," Stevie said, looking shamefaced.

"And you think I should regard you as reliable?"

"But you do, don't you?"

"Yes. Oddly, that day before you went off on your jaunt I knew you were telling me the truth about not seducing Kit," Maura said.

Stevie hoped she wouldn't ask him again.

It was the shortest night of the year. They rowed out on the lake, Stevie and Kit.

Everyone was used to seeing them together now, wandering hand in hand by the lake. People didn't bother to gossip anymore. Like Anna Kelly and Emmet, they had been together for as long as people could remember. And Philip O'Brien and the marvelous bossy girl who had come to work as a pharmacy student in McMahon's. Her name was Barbara and she was exactly the kind of girl Philip O'Brien was looking for all his life, people said, and hadn't known it. People had forgotten Sister Madeleine, and Orla Dillon rarely came to town. Paddles' was full at night. Mona Fitz was in the sanatorium.

Life went on. And it was very usual to see young people taking a boat out over the quiet water of the lake in Lough Glass at night.

Stevie and Kit took the little box of ashes and sprinkled them in the lake. The moon was high in the sky and they didn't feel sad. It wasn't really a funeral. All that was over, in London and years ago . . . the first time. This wasn't a sad thing, it was just the right thing to do.

As having a honeymoon in Wales had seemed the right thing to do. In years to come when people would look back on the history of the place and talk about the people who lived here they might mention Helen McMahon who died in the lake. This way it would be true, her body was in the lake now, like so many who had gone before, but it had gone there peacefully.

It was strange this shorthand which meant that you didn't have to say things like that to each other. Stevie knew and Kit knew it. As they knew they would live on the lakeshore someday.

Someday when they were old enough to settle down.

The employees of G.K. HALL hope you have enjoyed this Large Print book. All our Large Print titles are designed for easy reading, and all our books are made to last. Other G.K. Hall Large Print books are available at your library, through selected bookstores, or directly from us. For more information about current and up-coming titles, please call or mail your name and address to:

G.K. HALL
PO Box 159
Thorndike, Maine 04986
800/223-6121
207/948-2962